Texas
Short Stories 2

Edited by
Billy Bob Hill
and Laurie Champion

Texas
Short Stories 2

BB
BROWDER SPRINGS BOOKS • DALLAS, TEXAS

ISBN: 0-9651359-6-9 paper

Library of Congress Catalog Card Number: 99-067755

This publication is the fourth of the American Regional Book Series from Browder Springs Books. The first is Paul Ruffin's *Circling*, the second *Texas Short Stories* (first edition), and the third, *A Cowtown Chronicle: William D. Barney Poetry*

For website information about Browder Springs: http:/Browdersprings.com or Texasshortstories.com   Mailing address: P.O. Box 823521, Dallas TX 75382; Fax: 214.739.9149

Cover illustration: Filberto Chapa
Jacket/Book design: Margie Adkins Graphic Design

ACKNOWLEDGMENTS

For their interest, help, and general patience, Laurie and I would like to thank the authors in this edition as well as those Texans who sent in stories for the contest. We would also like to thank the following people, who in some way, contributed to the book: Filberto Chapa, Sara Ellis Cardona, Martha Duran, Margie Adkins West, Jack West, Judy Greene, Glenn Clayton, Theresa Sternet, Sally Hogue, Tom and Prissy Brawner, Charles Daniel, Lee Veal, Julia Hill, Paul Oswalt, Jimmy Clarke, Stan Phillips, Greg Smith, Toy Thomas, Jack Myers, Thea Temple, Janet McIntosh, Dave Gallman, and Elana Abernathy. ✪

Contents

PREFACE

Whether one collects scholarly or creative works, editing an anthology always has its challenges. Among these, editors define what type of works are to be collected. The defined parameters, usually denoted in the titles of anthologies, can raise complicated questions:

What genre(s) will be included?

Will only specific themes or subjects be chosen?

Are selected works limited to geographical definitions?

Are biographical facts about the authors a factor?

How many selections will be included?

How to balance geographic, ethnic, and gender diversity of the stories and authors?

As the title *Texas Short Stories 2* suggests, Billy Bob and I intended to collect Texas short stories; however, having received many submissions that might be short stories but could also be poems or essays, we soon found ourselves answering the age-old question that defines genre. Unfortunately, neither of us is able to articulate a precise definition for a short story, so we opted for the easy answer by assuming that you know what we mean by "short story." Of course, added to this complexity is the issue of novel excerpts—if a chapter is excerpted and published in an anthology of short stories, does it by virtue of editorial definition become a short story? We're not quite sure we're able to answer this question, but we did include some novel excerpts and labeled them short stories.

We didn't limit our selections to specific themes or subjects, but if, for example, we received twenty submissions that reveal left-handed children whose blind dogs died while in route from Hawaii to Tennessee, we decided that including one was probably enough. Likewise, had we received twenty remarkably well written stories (and even a couple of novel excerpts and an essay or two) told from the point of view of entrapped rattlesnakes during the annual rattlesnake round-up in Sweetwater, we might have edited a separate sub-anthology with a title that defined these parameters and published all twenty.

As the title *Texas Short Stories 2* suggests, we limited the works to include Texas stories by Texas authors. Does a Texas story only involve cowboys, multi-billionaire ranchers, and women who wear holsters and smile really big? Do Texans include those who recently moved to Texas or only those who were born here and whose folks have resided here for at least five generations? One definition of a Texan that we considered involved anyone residing in Texas or the area around Texas who once in his or her life posted a sign on the homestead to warn potential trespassers. There were those who spent their youth here, yet have long resided in other states. We didn't want to exclude a potential Katherine Ann Porter. We also concluded that most of us know a Texas author when we see one, or at least, when we hear one read.

After resolving these problems, all sorts of paper shuffling had to be done. I placed in deep stacks the thousand or so stories across my large desk, all arranged in alphabetical order, and created computer-generated grids that listed authors and submissions, but that system quickly became impossible. Aside from performing administrative tasks, we read every story. Near the end, as the choices narrowed down, it became far more challenging to make selections. At this stage, subject and theme were key factors. When only one story at the expense of another could make the final cut, Billy Bob and I considered which story might better enrich the collection as a whole. In the end, we chose stories that would represent Texas and might entertain readers. ❀

Laurie Champion and Billy Bob Hill, editors

INTRODUCTION

The late Robert Penn Warren once said that—with the exception of Eudora Welty—he didn't think there was a "natural" short story writer in America and, further, he thought it an art that cannot be taught. He was rarely satisfied with his own short stories, Warren said, because he simply "had not been born to write them."

I can identify with such sentiments: of the perhaps 200 short stories I have started in a forty year writing career, I only *finished* about twenty of them, and I (as well as a number of editors) only thought four of them fit to be published. I persist in reading the short story, however, because it is a fascinating fictional form and I occasionally still sneak-write one—or start it, anyway. When a short story I am reading really hits me where I live, by making a connection with my heart or my head, the sense of enjoyment is almost as sharp as my pangs of envy.

Some of the stories in this collection from Texas writers are, by my arbitrary standards, too long to be "short." Anything over 3,000 words bothers me, but to show that a foolish consistency really *is* the hobgoblin of little minds, as Emerson claimed, what I think may be *my* best short story runs almost 7,000 words. So sue me

Ideally, a good zinging short story contains both a plot and at least one strong character we care about whether that character is narrator or protagonist. I, for one, grow impatient with "stream of consciousness" spewings or yarns with no resolution: give me a *result* that indicates *why* what happened happened or I don't care how poetic or sensitive your effort is I toss it on the trash heap. This, of course, is again the arbitrary judgement of an old codger long set in his ways, and it could be that my standard is not yours. Happily for me, most of the short stories in the worthy anthology seem to follow or try ot follow my basic dictates. Only a couple of times did I find myself thinking *Jesus! What is this all about?* But I am far too clever to here name names.

This, as the book's title indicates, is the second anthology of short stories published by Browder Springs Books (Dallas); it is more diverse than the first volume that appeared in 1997 because there seems to be more of minorities—African-Americans, Latin-Americans, Asian-Americans, and, yes, Women-Americans—represented than in an earlier time. Twenty-odd years ago a banquet speaker railed at the Texas Institute of Letters for not having more minority members and at Texas editors for not seeking to include first-hand minority experiences in their reports of the Texas culture. Good strides in that direction have been made within the last decade, and the open-to-all writers policy of Editors Billy Bob Hill and Laurie Champion in *Texas Short Stories 2* has been helpful in the cause of showing our state's diversities. We get stories, here, from city and small town, from the Big Bend to the Big Thicket, from men and women, from black and white and brown, from familiar names of veteran Texas writers as well as from younger writers just beginning to blossom, and we get points of view from all over the big map. We get comedy and drama and irony and answers and even a few touches of mystery.

I will not list the writers here: the table of contents does that, and detailed author's sketches will tell you more about the individual writers than I have space or time to tell. I have my favorite writers and stories in this collection, but I'll never confess them. You, the reader, should be left free of bias to make your own choices.

Enjoy. I certainly did. ✹

Larry L. King

TEXAS SHORT STORIES 2

FAT DOG

by Michael Adams

We called him Fat Dog. His real name was Harvey. No one outside the family knew his real name. Uncle Wallace had named him after one of his army buddies, but, according to Uncle Wallace, he started calling him Fat Dog after he observed the effects of Fat Dog's first meal.

Uncle Wallace claimed Fat Dog was a Golden Retriever, but everyone who saw him said there was something else in him. Something else that made him so big and fat. He had the head and body shape of a Golden Retriever, and his long fur was golden all right, but Fat Dog was the size of a St. Bernard and he had this softness about him. There wasn't a lean muscle in his body. His mouth was always open as if smiling and when he walked he sashayed his butt back and forth. This sashaying, as Uncle Wallace called it, got worse if he were excited to see someone, which was everyone, if someone had brought him food, which he always presumed, or if he were about to engage in his favorite thing—rearing up on his hind legs and with all the force of his weight channeled to his huge front paws, knocking a human being to the ground. Fat Dog was a bully. Bullying was Fat Dog's game.

There wasn't anyone in our rather large family that Fat Dog hadn't "floored," as Uncle Wallace used to chortle. "Uh, oh," Uncle Wallace would say. "You've been floored." Only the unsuspecting thought that that happy, smiling face and that sashaying hip coming at him were just the demeanor of a sweet dog. After they had been floored once, they realized that all that swaggering and sashaying was just Fat Dog loading up. Loading up his weight.

Fat Dog came into my life the day of Uncle Wallace's funeral. It was actually the funeral for Uncle Wallace and his only son James, my cousin, both killed in a car wreck on the way to Corpus Christi to fish. He'd asked me to dog sit. It was the first time I had stayed away from home. I was twelve and three-quarters. Fat Dog was almost seven.

In some ways, Uncle Wallace was an embarrassment to the family. Living in a small farming community, everybody knew everything, and everybody knew about Fat Dog. Even those who had never been inside Uncle Wallace's house had an idea what it looked like. You see, the rumor was that Fat Dog ran things at Uncle Wallace's.

This was true to some extent. Fat Dog went where he wanted to go and when he wanted to go, and he slept where he wanted to, usually in the middle of Uncle Wallace's bed or on the couch, especially during the early afternoon, or on the back porch where he liked to cool his fat belly on the cement. For the most part, Uncle Wallace had given up keeping Fat Dog's coat brushed, so one could always find a few burrs or twigs, or spots of goo here and there. Every now and then Fat Dog would hop into the river to bathe, but Fat Dog wasn't a great swimmer, and his tendency to sink was about the only fearful moment in his life.

For a few hours after Uncle Wallace's death, the immediate family, pondered over who would get what of Uncle Wallace's, especially since his only child and logical heir was dead as well, but there was one thing everyone hoped that Uncle Wallace hadn't left them—Fat Dog. "That Dog," as Mom called him. It was, in fact, a question more alarming than anything that might be contained within the will. Who will have to take care of Fat Dog? Everyone in the family, my mother, who was Uncle Wallace's youngest of three sisters, and my uncles, George and Ed, her brothers, had all made it clear that Fat Dog was not their responsibility. At that point I was not in the picture.

And then Fat Dog did something that shaped my life forever. James, Uncle Wallace's son, was, to me, the guardian spirit of an elder brother. Although he was nine years older and lived two farms away, we saw each other weekly, fishing, hunting, swinging on grapevines, running trotlines, digging up worms, throwing rocks at snakes and spiders, even birds, and most of all, just walking the river. James had given me my first pocket knife, a two-blader with imitation ivory handle. He taught me how to lie still in the eastern meadow, trying to get the vultures to begin their ritualistic circling.

James had been married only a few weeks before his death. He had promised that he wouldn't let marriage "change his life," which meant I would remain in it. His bride, with the wonderfully suggestive name of Sylvia Rose, was beautiful and exotic—exotic because she came from a farm way north in the county and she was the only female I had ever seen with truly black hair. Blueblack and long, and, bangs right above her black eyebrows and alert black eyes. The family wondered why she would go for someone like James. It couldn't have been his money since he didn't yet have any land of his own, and he wasn't the best-looking available young man, surely. Mother, I remember, pointed out that it could have been love, something so simple, but for some reason the rest of the family thought that unlikely. One thing for certain, she brought changes in James' life. James built a wooden privacy fence to enclose them a backyard, and it wasn't long before, especially on Sunday afternoons, they began riding their matching Harley-Davidsons around the country roads.

Sylvia Rose, Evenin' Rose James called her, was always kind to me. She had only been around the family for two weeks, but she tried real hard to fit in, washing the dishes after a family gathering, the first to volunteer, the last to stay behind and clean up. She willingly and dutifully remained in the kitchen after dinner while all the men took their places in the den, there among the deer heads and family photographs. She was even planning to help Mom make cakes for the upcoming church social. But then the wreck.

It was while everyone else was at the grave side that it happened. Sylvia had told everyone that she just couldn't make it to the grave. She had always had an aversion to graveyards. Mom told me to stay home to take care of her. I knew she meant to keep an eye of Fat Dog. Keep an eye on "That" she emphasized.

I don't remember exactly how we got back into the bedroom, but there we were. It smelled of James and fresh boot wax. Sylvia had taken down her black hair and was dressed only in black slip and stockings. Her eyes were red and wet from crying. After all these years I can still feel the presence of carnality inside me. It was intense. It was my first.

She asked me to lie down beside her. And I did. Then she wanted me to hug her. From behind. She pushed herself way into me and took my hand and pulled it onto her stomach. She rubbed it very gently. I became intoxicated, totally in her power.

It wasn't long before she pulled my hand up to her breasts and massaged herself with my hand. And then she brushed her blue-black hair out of the way, and turned, and began kissing me softly, here and there. The scent, the slight taste of salt, the flesh, I had been entranced. I was hers. There was nothing I could do. Sudden and heavy thoughts of James came and went, beyond my will. I knew I was in the midst of sin. And in heaven.

And then, just as we were about to slip into evil, sending me forever into internal and psychological hell, the door burst open. There was Fat Dog. From his point of view, there were two human beings on his bed. And they looked like they were ready to play. They were just asking to be floored.

He hit us so hard that my head whiplashed into Slyvia's before she flipped backwards and off the bed. Her thigh slapped into the corner of the night stand. She limped around the rest of the day. Only I knew that the inside of her lip was busted. She told Mom that she had walked into the back of the kitchen table. Mother asked me if Fat Dog had behaved, and I told her he most certainly had. And there it was. Fat Dog was in my life.

Sylvia Rose went back to her family that very evening. Her abrupt departure startled everyone. Some thought it rude.

That meant that someone would have to watch Uncle Wallace's house and his dog. I volunteered. Mom thought it was thoughtful of me. I volunteered, I would understand years later, because I had no choice. Many, many years from then, I would realize, as we all realize, that there were events in our lives that had they gone differently, we would have become a different person. I didn't realize it then, but a very fat dog had become part of who I was to become.

"Absolutely not," Mom said. Dad agreed. "He's just too unruly, Son. He would have our entire house torn up in a minute. You've seen Uncle Wallace's. It's just the price Fat Dog has to pay for his owner not getting him under control. The pound will find a good home for him."

"You know that's not true, Dad. You know they will have to kill him."

"Now, Son," Mom reached out and touched me. She always did this when I was distressed. "Don't be so dramatic. No one's going to kill Fat Dog. It's. . . ."

"But if no one will take him, they *will* kill him, and no one will take him and. . . ." And then. And then I did it. I told my first unforgivable, shameful lie ". . . besides, I promised Uncle Wallace I'd take care of Fat Dog in case anything happened to him. I PROMISED! I PROMISED ON THE BIBLE!"

It was an elaborate story. I made it all up as I went along. Uncle Wallace and I were out running the trotlines one night. Fat Dog was on the side of the bank sniffing the air. Uncle Wallace turned to me and told me that he had something very important to ask me, one of the most important things he had ever discussed with anyone, and he wouldn't be discussing it with me except for the fact that I was now old enough to be trusted with such adult matters and do such manly things like swear on the Bible that I would take care of his dog if something happened to him.

I don't know to this day if my mother and father suspected I was lying. They certainly didn't let on. Mom's only response was "Well, you're just a boy and Wallace shouldn't have been asking you such things." Dad said "It might be a lesson in life, Son. Some promises you just can't keep."

Since lying didn't work, I went into, quite instinctively, my next gear—temper tantrum. I can't remember exactly what I did and said. It was all dramatic. I do remember that amidst all the throwing things and yelling and stomping and waving, I said something about God, Jesus, the Bible, and family loyalty, and violation of a promise somehow entangled with the survival of my very soul. I slammed the door and walked out into the south pasture where I was determined to stay the night. I had taken Fat Dog with me, but he wasn't accustomed to staying outdoors, so he found his way back to Uncle Wallace's front porch. Mom had pinned a note on the screen door. "We'll talk more tomorrow. Love, Mom."

Perhaps it was Mom's weakness for sentimental displays like mine, perhaps it was out of respect for her brother, but the next morning I got the agreement. Fat Dog would get a week's tryout. If he were not perfectly behaved, perfectly obedient, perfectly controllable and, most important, if he had not learned to stop flooring people, then he would have to go. It was her one and only offer. I took it with great glee. And then she added the unreachable condition—Fat Dog had to live outside.

Fat Dog failed the test only thirty minutes after sunset. He stood at the door to the front porch and howled. A huge, forlorn howl that sent shivers over my sister's skin—or so she claimed. Dad whipped him with a belt and came back in, but soon Fat Dog was back at it. Then Dad took him to the barn and tied him up. It wasn't long before the barn became a huge megaphone out of which came the most forlorn of howls, "like the voice of some underground god" my sister said. She had been studying Greek mythology. And like an angry god, Fat Dog would not let up. And Dad would not let me go to him. He had to "howl himself out," Dad said. I knew Dad had underestimated Fat Dog. Hour after hour he kept at it. It was somewhere after midnight that Dad told me to go shut him up or he was taking him away first thing in the morning. That night I slept in the barn with Fat Dog. Every few minutes I bribed him with pieces from Mom's coffee cake I had stolen from the kitchen counter.

After three days and nights of training and sleeping in the barn with Fat Dog, my eyes became dark and encircled. I was losing weight and sleep. Good thing it was summer, Mom had said. Fat Dog had learned only one thing. How to offer his paw to shake. Of course, he expected an immediate treat, a piece of the beef jerky I kept stashed high in the hayloft.

It was about day four that Mother said we'd have a one-night experiment. Fat Dog could stay on the front porch, but he could not get on the old couch that she kept covered with Mexican blankets. "This is absolutely the last chance."

Fat Dog did well until about an hour into his sleep. And then it began. Something he had not done in the barn, perhaps because outside he remained alert for sounds all night. He began to snore. It began as a kind of guttural groan, but then it rose—and rose—and rose. And then it transformed into the most discordant explosion of snorting and wheezing, sequenceless and rambunctious. And then a sudden crescendo that would literally make you jump. My sister, Anna was her real name but we called her Sister, shouted "Shut that dog up!" Mom came out and warned me that it was "barn time" if he kept it up. A little later it was barn time for me and Fat Dog.

The next day Dad issued the last ultimatum—one more day. That night I laid out blankets and pillows and several of Fat Dog's favorite toys—deflated inner tube, gnawed soft ball, what remained of one of Uncle Wallace's boots. Fat Dog had been given several balls, but he didn't go for them. He didn't go for anything. Fetch was something humans were supposed to do for him

I lectured Fat Dog that night. I had decided I would sleep by him and the moment he began snoring I'd slap him awake. It would be hard on me, but small sacrifice for someone who had sworn on the Holy Bible that he would take care of this misunderstood creature.

I don't know if Fat Dog snored that night. I was so exhausted that I fell into a deep sleep—only to be awakened by an explosion. My heart beating, I shot up from the couch. The evidence was before me. The entire screen door was missing. It had been floored. Fat Dog was wandering out in the yard, taking a pee.

The mistake I had made was putting the latch on the door. Otherwise Fat Dog could have pushed himself on outside. But Fat Dog didn't have any patience for latches. Dad stood within the hollow space and stared into the yard. "That's it," he said.

I spent the rest of the night trying to figure out how I could change their minds. Other lies came to me. For some reason the one that kept returning was that Uncle Wallace and I had actually cut our wrists and become blood brothers the night we swore on the Holy Bible.

Years later I would see that Fat Dog lived under the guidance of

Sirius, the dog star, who must have helped him in his life. To think that he needed help from something so mortal as I.

Fat Dog, Dad said, had no one to blame but himself. He had created his own destiny. Life was not always easy. Some stranger was due to arrive in a few days to pick up Fat Dog. I was to prepare myself. And then Mom's two spinster sisters, Aunt Patty and Aunt Patsy, arrived. Dad called them Cow Patty and Cow Pie. He referred to them both as the Cow Pies. He had long hated them both. And he and Uncle Wallace were both grateful the Cow Pies spent a lot of time in Houston where they had bought a get-away home.

Mother always defended them in her polite kind of way, but she didn't care much for them either. Uncle Wallace had stopped seeing them years ago. Dad said that it was a good thing they were out of the country when it happened because Wallace would have been furious if they actually insulted him by attending his funeral.

Uncle Wallace's problem with them was the same as Dad's. They had inherited, from an eccentric and doting aunt, a large farm around Taylor. Very black, rich soil. They had become very prosperous. And in Uncle Wallace's words "too damn good for the real world."

Dad knew very well that they thought their young sister had married poor and unwisely. They were not very subtle women. Before Mom and Dad's marriage, they offered Mom some river-bottom land if only she would reconsider and think seriously about an alternative, like the Gilberts' son who had been Dad's rival.

The worst insult came years later when the Cow Patties offered Dad the same river-bottom land, if he and Mom would move to it, leaving behind the "shackiness." It came with a large, white house. Uncle Wallace told me that Dad was so angry that he rewired a quarter mile of fence that day. He worked late into the night.

They weren't twins, but they looked alike. And they each wore glasses framed with pointed wings. They were tall and skinny, and they sat on the couch like two Siamese cats. Their knees were always firmly pressed together. They wore new black dresses, all the way from New York, and their hair was neatly shaped and fixed—by a male beautician in Houston. After, at Mom's instruction, Sister and I shook their hands, we stood behind Mom's rocker. Dad was under the house working on the plumbing. He yelled hello up at them.

The day the Cow Patties arrived, I had pretty much resigned myself to Fat Dog's departure. I had considered running away with him, but I exercised a rare moment of common sense—a common sense that put me in a fatiguing sadness. Now I know I was fretting over nothing. Sirius wouldn't let Fat Dog down.

The sisters were sorry they couldn't make the funeral, but they were away on a cruise in Greece. They brought Mom a cluster of purple glass gapes with a real wooden stem. Nothing for Dad.

Sister didn't know how they got onto the conversation, but somehow it got onto Fat Dog. Aunt Patty said that that dog should be taken out and shot—he wasn't good for anything except eating up money. Only a fool would keep such a dog. And most certainly he couldn't stay with us. What a laughing stock that would make us.

That was it. Fat Dog was now safe for the rest of his life. Mom's sisters had thrown down the gauntlet and Dad had picked it up. Fat Dog now became a matter of principle, a symbol of some kind. Through Fat Dog he would defy them. And perhaps they would never return to visit as long as Fat Dog was there. And just in case Dad had any second-thoughts, Fat Dog went right to work.

It was during a small break in the conversation. The two sisters had set their eye-glasses on the coffee table so that they could read the guest names at Uncle Wallace and James's funeral. Then they moved into the kitchen for a moment so that Mom could show them the photo album that Uncle Wallace had kept—old pictures of their parents. While they were gone, Fat Dog struck.

We're not sure how he got into the house. Most likely, the front door didn't close all the way. It didn't matter. When the Cow Patties returned, they found their purses ripped, their glasses and frames gnawed into bits and scraps.

That was the last straw. That just proved their point. Mom apologized. She said we were just keeping the dog until we could find a good home. Patty said they would never find a good home for such a beast. Best of all, they couldn't stay into the night. They would have to immediately drive back to Taylor. All that remained to help them see was a pair of wrong-prescription sun glasses Patty kept in the car. They would need to get back home before the sun set. And Patsy made it clear. They would never return to our house as long as that ghastly monstrosity was there. Dad's deepest wish had been granted. Fat Dog had found himself a home.

Dad was still firm with me and he had his conditions and he made it clear I would have to work on getting Fat Dog under control. He would talk to the vet about his snoring. But Fat Dog was mine. Mom said the first order of business was a sure-fire diet.

Fat Dog came into Uncle Wallace's life on a Sunday evening, just after sunset. Uncle Wallace was on his tractor, plowing up the summer stubble, when he saw a car stop along the side of the old farm-to-market road 272, just past the Maxdale bridge. It was rarely used these days. The car slowed down. A back door opened up. Someone pitched something out, the door shut, and the car sped away. That something was Fat Dog.

Uncle Wallace finished the last six rows and then went over to see what they had thrown out. And there he was. A stout puppy, only a few months old. He was whining, Uncle Wallace told us, and sniffing the air as if searching.

Uncle Wallace named him after a man called Harvey he knew in the war. Harvey's family bred and sold dogs. Harvey was crazy about dogs. He and Uncle Wallace went through "ever-loving, bloody hell" in France. Harvey didn't die in the war. He caught some virus on the ship on the way back and died. But all he talked about was his dogs. How much he was looking forward to getting back and seeing them. Uncle Wallace had always been a bit sentimental, even more so than Mom. Perhaps the abandoned dog triggered the memory of his dying friend and led him to christen him and keep him.

The first story we ever heard about Fat Dog, and heard repeated many times afterwards, began the very night Uncle Wallace took Fat Dog home. It always made Sister cry. For the next month, every single night, after his evening meal, Fat Dog, or Harvey as he was called in those days, walked out of Uncle Wallace's yard and across the field and under the fence and he lay down in the exact spot where he had been tossed. And there he slept all night. A couple of times Uncle Wallace stayed with him a while and tried to coax him back with food, but there Harvey needed to stay and there he would stay. His hard head showing even in those puppy days. He repeated his odyssey night after night, without exception. It would be several months before Fat Dog gave up.

I told Sylvia that story. She said something like "Oh, that's so touching," and she reached out and touched me. We were sitting on the couch together. The house was silent except for the ticking of Uncle Wallace's grandfather clock. She took my hand and held it. Then she placed both her hands around mine and held it on her knees. I could feel the stockings against my skin. As she spoke softly she rubbed my hand back and forth over her knees and ever so slightly up her thigh, in a kind of sorrowful rhythm. "I don't know how I can live," she said. At one point her knees opened slightly and she kept rocking. Streaks of black mascara dropped down from the outside corner of each eye.

When Fat Dog died, four years later, I got a card from Sylvia. She had written "I know how special he was to you. Be strong. Love you, Sylvia." It was a mystery how she found out. The envelope was marked Boulder, Colorado. I know she must think of us from time to time. I'm sure I'm as much a part of her memory as she is of mine.

To Mom's delight and Dad's relief, Fat Dog finally realized that compromise of a small sort was required if he were to find any peace from the shouts and slaps. In a very general sense, he was under control. He no longer took food off the dinner table, ate shoes, stuck his head up Mom's skirts, dragged her panties out into the living room floor for desert. I kept him clean and brushed and beside me always. For some reason even his snoring got better. Or else we all became accustomed to it. We knew we were a poor family. Dad's pride became our own.

But the one thing Fat Dog couldn't seem to get the hang of was why human beings didn't like to be floored. He wouldn't mind if they tried it with him. It was just part of what it meant to be alive. To floor people was his insatiable desire. When anyone came to our house and approached the door, whoever was closest headed for the leash.

During that fall, Fat Dog and I made the headlines of *The Florence Gazette*. I had taken him to the junior high football game. It was a lovely fall day. There were only one hundred students in our junior high, so there were barely enough for a football team. Eighteen, counting the coach's son who was below the minimum weight requirement. Kempner's junior high was not much larger. They had only fourteen players. There had even been talk about returning to 6-man football.

The game had barely started, and I knew right away that Fat Dog knew that this was his kind of game. He stood at the fence, near the gate. His eyes surveillant and eager.

I had agreed to meet Tracy Lowry, one of the three cheerleaders. We had talked about dogs at school and she wanted to meet Fat Dog. She had seen him from a distance, but she wanted to pet him. Her parents would not let her have a dog. Fat Dog, I learned, was proving more valuable as the months went by. Tracy was beautiful, frail, almost waif like. With her skinny legs, it was a wonder that she could jump at all. But she had spring and pep and an eagerness about her that lured me. She was taking a break from her cheering to talk with me and Fat Dog. Her hair was wild with the wind. Her face was flush with the six cartwheels she had just performed. I was watching her brush off some grass from her knees when the leash went out of my hand. Fat Dog was off.

He knocked down several people on his way to the open gate, and, suddenly, like an apparition, there he was—on the playing field of life.

The first boy he pushed over was the offensive end. Then he went for the quarterback. A guard and tackle tried to shoo him away, but both ended up flat on their backs. One was knocked out of breath so badly, he lay there as if dead. One of the officials waved a flag at Fat Dog, for what earthly reason to this day I do not know, but Fat Dog thought it was part of the sport, and off the official went running, but when Fat Dog was playing his game, nobody got away. Down went the official, face down. For a moment Fat Dog stood with front paws on top of him, his eyes full of spirit, searching for his next victim.

I eventually got to Fat Dog. I pretended to hit him hard, and I shouted "bad boy" several times, but he knew that that was part of *my* game.

As I led him away, I looked back. There they lay scattered, like dead and wounded soldiers on a battlefield, and there we went, off the field and into infamy and onto the front page of *The Florence Gazette*: Fat Dog Defeats Entire Team. Fat Dog and I posed outside the stadium for the photograph. Fat Dog seemed to be smiling, slobbering actually, his eyes were shut as if laughing. I, skinny, in sleeveless muscle shirt, stood smiling proudly. "Goofy" my sister called it.

It's funny now, but I only remember in my later days how Mom reacted. Dad said that he had warned me about something like that and that I could never take him to a public place again. Mom chuckled. Then Sister. Then Dad. Then I joined in. It was as if Mom's giggle and laugh negated what Dad had just said. The very next weekend we were all at a county picnic and Dad said not a word. Mom had whispered to me to make sure I held the leash tight.

Mom was on her death bed about ten years later. Fat Dog was long gone. Sister was on one side of the bed, I was on the other. Dad was over in the corner, slunk in, with his legs straight out. He was taking it all very hard. All day he had been going to his room and shutting the door.

Mom smiled up at us that night. And out of the blue she said. "Remember that crazy Fat Dog? Remember what he did on that football field?"

It was Sister's time to chuckle first, then mine. It took a while, but Dad joined in. I've always wondered if the memory just appeared to Mom or whether she deliberately recalled it in order to cheer us up. "We've had some good times," she said. "Don't be so sad. Jesus is waiting for me. I'm not scared." She asked Sister to read her a psalm from the Bible. I cannot remember which one.

Fat Dog died four years after he first came into our house. He'd been suffering from cancer for about three months. It had been a rainy night. Stormy, with fierce winds and hard rain. Fat Dog had spent most of the evening by the front door, as he had been doing lately.

He now had his own way to get out the back door—a huge dog door I had built. Mom said I might as well just leave the door open all the time. We don't know what time during the night he went out. Mom thought she heard him stirring and walking through the house in the blue of morning.

I can still remember the smell of the frying bacon. Mom was wiggling my toes. "Fat Dog's gone out and hadn't come back," she said.

Sister and Dad were already up. Dad was reading the paper. Sister was in her pink curlers.

I went outside and called for him. I felt a silence coming back. I put on my goulashes and walked down to the river. Mother said she had already checked the barn. When I got back, Dad suggested it—that we all get in the pickup and go looking for him. I noted at the time that it was an unusual suggestion coming from Dad, but I didn't know why.

The pickup smelled of wet hay and grease. There in the bed was a rusted seat from a long-ago abandoned tractor and some old, grease-spotted rope. Sister and I stood in the back with our arms pressed into the top of the cab. We stood side by side, our eyes searching up ahead. When Dad turned onto the old dirt road, I think I knew it. I knew where he was. Fat Dog had gone back to the very spot where he had been abandoned years ago—in order to die.

Dad made us wait in the truck. Mom stood on the ground with her door open, her chin resting on the bottom of the window. There was Fat Dog ahead of us—a lump along the side of the road. Dad waved his hand over the body. Then he shouted at me—to pull out the old blanket he kept behind the seat and bring it to him. I remember very little, except squinting so hard that I could barely see. I knew that it was important that I didn't display too much emotion. I was not like my sister. Dad wrapped up Fat Dog so we couldn't see him. He didn't ask me to help him lift Fat Dog, but I could see he was straining. Rigor mortis had already set in. He was stiff. And heavy. All his alive fatness had seemed to settle. One on each side, we carried him back to the pickup. At one point, Dad stumbled and I had to pull the body closer. I felt his stiff neck bend toward the ground.

Dad scooted Fat Dog's body up below the cab window. Sister was now sitting inside the cab with Mom. Her crying was lightly rocking the truck. I chose, the now man I was, to ride in the back with Fat Dog. As Dad started the engine, a quick memory of Sylvia of the black hair darted in and out and vanished. Inwardly. I let the wind soothe me. I kept my boot toe just at the edge of the blanket. ✿

MIDNIGHT BLUE

by Keddy Ann Outlaw

Whenever I walked Zeely to school, I was keenly aware of the thrill it gave me when the school crossing guard stopped traffic so we could cross 19th Street. I hadn't always had the privilege of walking a child to school, as I was mother by chance. Zeely's biological mother died when she was a toddler. Her father passed her around to various caretakers for the next seven years. A few years ago she started living here in Houston with me. But it was still an honor whenever the welcome mat to the Family of Man was laid down for us.

Having a child equaled belonging. If Zeely's father (my ex-husband) hadn't left her with me when having a child got inconvenient, I would still be a dreamy singleton with no semblance of family life. Years ago, on one of my temporary jobs, I had photographed classrooms of children in the Houston Independent School District. Then I thought of those children as one big multi-limbed, squiggly mass that wouldn't sit still. The pay was lousy. None of the little darlings pulled at my heartstrings.

When Zeely appeared, I underwent a chemical change. There is a hormone I'm convinced will be discovered someday—I call it Mother-Tonin. (Maybe men feel it too. In that case, a name change may be needed.) The MotherTonin flowed through me like warm milk spiked with brandy. Made me mellow. Made me hypersensitive too, protective of my young. Best of all, in caring for her, I forgot myself. Became less neurotic, more down to earth. When the MotherTonin first kicked in, I thought it was a fluke. You know, like romantic love—a passing exuberance. But the flow never stopped. Three years with Zeely flew right by. She was twelve now.

Once I had a child by my side, I was welcomed into the sorority-to-end-all-sororities of Motherhood. I have never been a person who "belonged." I was a bashful photographer and artist. I finished my college degree by correspondence from the University of Texas at Austin even though I lived in Austin at the time.

I hardly ever went to parties or nightclubs. I took easily to solitude. Yet I loved cities. They were magical to me, compared to my place of origin— the back woods of Maine. Cities were high energy places where you could commune with people indirectly and imbibe from many cultures, yet draw a circle around your own distinct territory. Not that I was a complete loner.

I did have a weakness for artistic, introverted men, and if I really liked one, that was when I came out of my shell and became the extrovert to their introvert.

One of those old boyfriends had made his way back into my life recently. Dale Lennon moved to Houston from Austin last year. We were "seeing each other," at least that's the way I thought of it. We'd had coffee together twice, dinner once, and talked on the phone for hours. Good hugs. No kissing.

I was two blocks from home, thinking it was one of those days I'd be late for work. I hated my secretarial job at the insurance agency, but, at least, they had a flexible attitude towards work start times. Big boss Ron "Rebate" Ronell allowed me to be as late as 10 a.m. most days, as long as I worked eight hours. He allowed me to take a working lunch so that I could leave the office at 6 p.m.

Full of spring fever, I took a detour down Nelldora Street to walk past the Community Garden. As I got closer, I wished I had my camera. Right next door to the garden lot, an old Heights warehouse was being torn down. I don't believe I had ever seen a wrecking ball in action before. The guy driving the crane waved to me from behind his glass cab. The loopy swing of the wrecking ball as it crashed into the masonry had me mesmerized. Its action was powerful, even sensual. Yet cartoonish. Loud, too— wham, wham, whirly, bang! I wished Zeely were with me so she could see it. She was into saying "Wow" a lot lately, and this was worth wowing.

The juxtaposition of the wrecking-in-progress and the garden scene behind it would make a great photo. I stepped back from the curb to get a longer view, cursing myself for not having a camera in hand. The belly of the ball continued its heaving dance. In the lush, green garden, a man wearing a big straw hat bent down over a jungle of tomato plants, seemingly blind and deaf to the action thirty yards away.

Apparently I was not using all my senses either. Something big, metallic and mint green whizzed by behind me. I felt the heat of it before I got a look at what it was: a Lincoln Continental which glided to a stop farther down the street. Though the sensation was quick, my lower back had been scraped. For a split second, I wondered if the wrecking ball had thrown a whirligig, coming at me. But it must have been the Lincoln's rear view mirror. I sunk down to the curb, mortified There I was, daydreaming as usual, and nearly killed by a luxury car one block from home.

"Are you all right?" the driver shouted, a worried looking old gal with big hair made worse by a bad tangerine dye job.

"Oh, I think so. Just a little shook up." I patted around under my sweat shirt awkwardly, feeling for blood or lumps. Everything seemed okay back there, just a little tender.

The Caterpillar driver swung down from his machine and ambled toward us.

"I saw you walking backwards, honey," Missus Tangerine said, "and I thought, well, surely she's just stepping into the gutter. But you kept coming! I swerved but it was too late. Do you think we should call someone?"

"No, no, I'm fine. I'll just go on home now."

"Your husband, perhaps or the family doctor?"

The wrecking ball man offered his assistance. "I'll take you to the emergency room, if you need to." He spoke in a slow Southern drawl. "I got me a truck, right over there." He pointed to a black pickup parked under a shade tree. He wore a skull and crossbones ring on his pinky finger. "My name's Ray. I feel partly responsible, seeing as how you were watching me when you got bumped."

"No, really, I'll walk. It's not far. I don't think there's any major damage."

Tangerine looked nervous. "Well, if you're sure." She patted her bombshell hair. I could see the sweat on her upper lip. The rusty-looking lipstick she wore was sliding off her mouth. With a fleshy bounce, she turned and hightailed it towards her car.

"But you didn't even get her license or phone number!" Ray protested. "Quick, memorize her plates. You might want to sue her later on! You could end up crippled for life."

I backed away. Then I remembered that ambulating backward had gotten me into this fix. I stopped in my tracks. "Listen, how much longer are you going to be here today, Ray? I'd like to come back with my camera and take some pictures."

"Lady, and I do mean lady—for I can see that you are one—if I had a dollar for every time someone took a picture of me doing demolitions, why I'd be a rich son-of-a-gun. People love to watch things getting wrecked. Sure, I'll be here. Got another job in Oakforest, but that's not till this afternoon."

I walked home quickly. I decided to call in sick. It was not every day that I almost got killed.

How was I fixed for film?

Looking at anything through a camera lens was more interesting than ordinary sight. I learned that the first time someone (my favorite aunt) put me behind a camera. I was a restless child, the kind that adults were always telling to sit still. Maybe I had some kind of undiagnosed attention deficit disorder. I didn't realize it at the time, but there was medicine in photography.

The eye of the camera became my favorite eye, a third eye; it calmed my vision at the same time that it enriched it immeasurably. It was all about frames, boundaries, limiting and focusing. I photographed everything in my small world. My mother's arm, her hand pinching a clothespin to a dish towel blowing in the wind. Tractor wheels. Daddy's scuffed Red Wing steel-toed boots, my sister's dolls posed on her bed: these were the first things my third eye found. Photography made life on a rundown farm ten miles from town much more bearable.

Two rolls of wrecking ball pictures were in the can. I didn't know if I'd like them or not, and that didn't matter. What mattered was making the effort, not dreaming about it, which was one of the problems I had lately (that and running out of money for film). What money I'd made from photography I was proud of, but it had never been enough to support me. I did greeting cards mostly, thematic scenes suitable for Valentines, Christmas, Easter or Halloween. The wrecking ball pictures were probably not destined for commercial use, but you never knew. If divorce cards ever came into favor, I might be able to work them in....

Lately I'd had luck with Day of the Dead cards. I posed small skeleton figurines with beer cans, artificial flowers, buried in a box of broken necklaces, even inside the refrigerator leering out of the vegetable bin. In Houston, Day of the Dead had become popular, seeping north from Mexico, an exotic add-on to Halloween. Honoring the dead had become politically correct, especially in the mystical yet fun-loving way the Mexicans celebrated.

I had the rest of the day to myself, which was unusual. I tried not to blow all my time on practical things like laundry and house cleaning. My back began to ache but I belly danced the pain away. There hadn't been much time for dancing lately. It was a new hobby of mine, taken up because I bought a box of instructional videotapes for two dollars at a garage sale. Once I got the basic motions down, I was hooked. Because Zeely always wanted to do whatever I did (photography, bicycling, baking, on and on), I had to be careful what I shared with her. The womanly art of belly dancing would be fine later on when she was older, but I didn't think she needed to grow up any faster than she already was.

Tomorrow night, I was meeting Dale for dinner. Zeely was going to spend the night at a friend's house, which was a big first for her. Regular parties, you couldn't keep her away—but whenever she was invited to sleep overs, she backed out of them at the last moment. Even one where all the girls were going to give each other manicures, something she loved, at the last minute she had changed her mind and stayed home.

"I couldn't sleep if I wasn't in my own bed," she would tell me. Or "I'd get the creeps. I'd rather stay home with you, Sharon." Up to now, I always thought she displayed a normal amount of insecurity for a child who has been through several shifts of make-do mothers. Now she seemed more confident and ready for independence. If she really went this time, how would *I* feel, being home overnight without her for the first time?

I had an alluring thought: perhaps Dale would spend the night with me. But he seemed timid about physical contact since we met again. I sensed he was avoiding the whole subject. Well, I had been in sexual retirement myself. That's right—no major sexual relationships to speak of since Zeely came into my life, not that I'm sure she's the reason. We moved to the Houston Heights seven months ago, to a funky neighborhood I've always loved. In between fixing up the old house I bought, working full-time, and trying to do my photography, there never seemed to be time for man-hunting.

That's why it was so wonderful to have Dale drop into my life again. He was recently divorced, obviously a little charred around the edges, but very much a candidate for romance. I could live without a significant other, but what single woman didn't have hopes of finding a soul mate somewhere? Even though I had been married and divorced twice, I still believed in Love. I thought Love might come any minute, or even twenty years from now when I'm fifty-three. Sometime it would find me, zap me good. Oh, Dale was probably not the One, but concentrating on him made me feel I was opening doors long slammed shut.

"Oh, Sharon, do you think I should take my camera?"

"If you want, Zeely."

"But what if someone like, steps on it? We'll be sleeping on the floor, that's what I heard. In our sleeping bags, you know. And I'm not sure about pillows. Do you think I need to bring one?" Pacing the floor, packing an already stuffed bag, Zeely was a study in preteen anxiety.

"Sure, but go get a clean pillowcase. Clean pillows smell so good, it will be like a little bit of home."

Zeely's frown turned to a smile. "That's a good idea. I *would* like to have my own home-sweet-home pillow along. And I think I will bring my camera. Maybe there will be a pillow fight and I can take some action shots! Do you believe it—April Smith said she was bringing a camcorder! Maybe we'll make music videos! Or do makeovers!"

I drove Zeely three blocks to the party, glad she wouldn't be too far from home on her first night away from me. I remembered the first pajama party I went to in fifth grade, where a bunch of town girls talked me into drinking Coke with Excedrins, which made me dizzy. Plus there were boys in the house for the first part of the party, and I was too shy to talk to a single one. How relieved I had been when they left. That's all I remembered about the party, nothing I wanted to tell Zeely.

She said good-bye and ran from the car without a backwards glance. I was on my own, licentious with a sense of rare freedom. Perhaps I had been taking motherhood a bit too seriously.

Dale called an hour later. "I've got a fever, plus I'm coughing. Whatever it is, Sharon, I don't want you to get it. I'm afraid I can't see you tonight."

"Gosh, I'm sorry you're sick." Dale had always been something of a hypochondriac when I knew him in Austin, so I couldn't help but be the tiniest bit skeptical. "What's your temperature?"

"Only ninety-nine point two, but it feels much hotter. And I'm short of breath after I cough. It could be pneumonia. I should never have moved to Houston. It's too damp here."

"Yes, but all that moisture is good for your complexion," I joked. "Well, do you need anything? Aspirins, cough drops?"

"No, I have all that."

He would, wouldn't he? "Well, then, I guess I'll let you go. Take care of yourself." What would I do with myself? I felt intensely restless.

"Don't hang up yet," Dale pleaded. "I'm sorry I let you down at the last moment. Talk to me a little longer. It's going to be a long night lying here wondering if I'll live. I think I overdid things today. I spent the whole day digging in the garden. I went to Teas Nursery and bought a bunch of rose bushes. Yellow roses. When they bloom I'll bring you a whole blooming bunch, Sharon."

"Very Texan of you, Dale."

"Yeah, I must admit, that's one of the reasons I like yellow roses. Pink and red are too predictable. I do like the Peace rose, though. Have you seen it? It's pale yellow with pink edges, beautiful."

His voice sounded perfectly normal now, and he hadn't coughed once. Was he avoiding me for some reason? I still didn't know much about why his marriage broke up. I felt my romantic daydreams about Dale slipping away. But I didn't want to lose his friendship.

"When you feel better, do you still want to go garage sale-ing with me?"

"Absolutely," he said. "You've got the magic touch, Sharon, and maybe I'll catch it. That roll of velvet you found—I still can't believe it."

"Only in River Oaks! Saturday comes around again real soon. Are we on?"

"If I'm better, sure, count me in. We'll get started nice and early."

I thought we might have hung up about then, if he was so sick, but he kept talking. I listened with half a mind, trying to think of what I wanted to do with the rest of the evening.

Dale had good color sense. We talked about how I might use the emerald green velvet I found last month at some rich people's garage sale, practically begging to be saved.

"Green was always Margaret's favorite color," Dale sighed. (Now he did sound a little sick.)

Margaret was his ex-wife. I wasn't sure yet who broke up with whom. "Did you two decorate with green?"

"No, not particularly, though she had a collection of photographs we hung that were mostly green, you know, nature photos, very relaxing and primeval. She was really into nature. She only wore natural colors, browns and greens, mostly."

"I like green, but I can't wear it. I do have one 50s vintage party dress with a black top and green skirt I can get away with." I rattled away to Dale about clothes all the time. He had a degree in art, had even thought about becoming a fashion designer before he got into advertising. He was easy to talk to, almost like a girlfriend in that way.

"Parties, don't mention them."

"Why?"

"I went to one, two nights ago, a very international crowd, and. . . ."

"What?"

"Oh, nothing, just some dumb thing that got to be the main topic of conversation right before I left. It made me depressed the rest of the night." His voice dropped. "Made me think of Margaret, the one thing I'm trying not to do."

"Tell me."

"Do I have to? All right. This was the question posed, and everyone had a different response to it: If you were in a room at a party comprised solely of all the people you ever loved, I mean, who had been your lovers, or even that you had wanted to be lovers with—well, who would you leave with? Like kind of a final choice, a one-time-only offer."

"Wow."

"Yeah, right. Of course, most of the married people that were there said they would leave with each other. Liars! Well, maybe a few of them, *would* really want to leave together, but other couples—boy, you could see the raw nerves, and it made you wonder what would be said between them on the way home in the car. That damn question made the atmosphere of the party positively libidinous. People were pouring out their souls to each other. I don't know, the whole thing made me nervous."

"Hmm hmmm."

"Made me think of Margaret. Maybe I shouldn't tell you this, Sharon, but if I had to choose such a person, it would still be her. Margaret. She was the love of my life."

What was I supposed to say? Sorry? Great?

But Dale covered the pause with a long, flat sigh. He rushed on with his confidences. "We could have gotten past our problems, if we had just tried a little harder. We had already picked out our children's names and everything. I wanted a girl first. Margaret, too. We liked the name Kyrie. Like in 'Kyrie eleision'—have you ever heard that sung in church? 'Kyrie', it sounds so lyrical. But then we found out it meant 'Lord', and that 'Kyrie eleision' means Lord have mercy in Greek. Well, we couldn't call her Lord, could we, so we decided on Mercy. Now that name haunts me. When I thought about leaving that party with the one I loved most, well, Mercy was there along with Margaret. Mercy was a little ghost shadow, I couldn't quite make out her face, but I felt her presence. She had this aura about her, of happy golden light, and it spread to me and Margaret."

"There's time yet, Dale," I said softly. "You'll meet someone else, fall in love again. Men are lucky—they can have children at almost any age."

"Listen, Sharon, I'm sorry. I didn't mean to go on and on like this," he sniffed. "But it's done me good. I feel better just talking to you."

Before he hung up, we chatted for a few more minutes. By the tone of his voice, I could tell he felt better. "I almost forgot I was sick for a minute," he admitted.

I didn't get around to telling him about the Tangerine lady, the wrecking ball, and the pear-shaped purple bruise on my back. Curiously, I was not angry or depressed after such a sorry phone call. True, it looked like Dale was not going to be my Prince Charming of the day, week, evening or year, but maybe I'd already known that all along.

I found myself wondering who *I* would leave with from that final party if I had a choice. Zeely's father, Jeff, came to mind, probably because I was guilty of an impossible fantasy where Zeely got her father back, and we remade ourselves into a happy little family. But no, he was not my dream lover, my ultimate Prince. He was too immature and had always been too much a ladies' man. But I didn't want to leave that theoretical party alone.

I ran through my heart files, gathered the suspects together. I included everyone, even the most unrequited lovers: my college photography teacher, the too-good-looking medical student who lived upstairs from me years ago on Gray Street, and Mr. Saharanian, a (married) insurance agent whose dark Egyptian eyes seemed to tease me from across the room at work. And all the boyfriends I ever had, and my two ex-husbands, I crowded them into the tableau. Their images came to me in black and white, like an old movie, like *Casablanca* or the finest photographic portraits by Avedon. Every man was frozen in his finest moment, as if the camera found their soul. Their many qualities merged together. They were gallant, kind, spiritual, sexy, handsome, or kind. And they all wanted me.

I threw back my head and laughed, a rib-tickling laugh from the gut. No, I would not pick a single one of them. Let them all trail after me, I thought. Let them stumble and claw at each other. Send me the one who wants me the most. Send me one true man. But don't make me pick.

Did I race out of the house, try to fill my Saturday night with what the big city of Houston had to offer? Tempt fate to send me that lover in a crowded coffeehouse or bar? No. I stayed home. Let the house fill with Mideastern music. Loud Mideastern music. Lit candles. Pulled out some gauzy scarfs, my midnight blue gypsy skirt and matching silken top, and my brass ankle bells. Danced in front of the mirror, danced with the shadows on the wall. Danced like the women painted on ancient Egyptian urns, women whose custom it was to entertain the dead as they had been entertained in life.

If there was a sadness to my solitary dance, it was a familiar, eternal sadness, one that I recognized, even welcomed. Dale's sadness over his unborn child, my lost chance of a future with him, my lack of a soul mate, made my dance all the more poignant, fueled its desperate rhythms. In our earthly world there was always loss, sadness and death. The trick was to go on. I held out my skirt to its full circle of midnight blue, a blue that was worthy of sadness, capable of absorbing it, yet refusing to turn a nihilistic black. I carried stars within my darkness, stars bursting from the jangling bells on my ankles, stars that danced on and on, past all reason.

This was the best way I knew to put the past behind me, to get up from the card game and spill the deck again. Movement laced with ritual and innovation, a kind of dance I shared with no one. It always cleared the way, and took me where I needed to go. If I wanted for anything in midst of my dance, it was for tribe. Not for a lover. Not just then. I had no need to be a courtesan enticing some prince. But I wouldn't have minded a crowd of dancing women to come down off their urn and surround me until we were one in our dance. If men were to be our audience, let them be tribe, too, connected to us in the most pure and honoring way. If they were worthy, let them join us in the dance. As if sex were a sacrament, and our dance the language of its initiation.

The scratchy *Turkish Ottoman Quartet* record played on. Just when I knew I had nearly exhausted my energy, I moved in slow motion past the three windows facing the front of the house. In the middle of the windows, in a tiny gap where the curtains were not quite drawn shut, I saw someone crouch down in the shrubbery. My God, a peeping Tom, I thought.

There was a crowbar on the floor near the front door, the nearest thing to a weapon I owned. Hardly stopping to think, I grabbed it and ran outside. A familiar giggle emanated from the azaleas. Zeely.

She rose from the ground, flinching at the sight of me. I must have looked like a mad cavewoman advancing with club in hand. "I didn't mean to do anything wrong," she blubbered. "I just thought I'd come see how you were doing, maybe say hello to Dale."

"You left the party? Zeely, you walked here alone in the middle of the night? What happened, did something go wrong?"

"No, they were all playing some dumb hide and seek game in the backyard. There were floodlights going on and off. I didn't like them—they were so bright, and there was one of those bug zappers where I was hiding. The fried bug noises made me want to puke. I slipped away. I thought I could get home and back before anyone missed me. They probably haven't even noticed I'm gone. I'm sorry, Sharon. I guess it was a stupid thing to do. But I like your dancing, Sharon. How come I never saw you dance like that before? I love your blue skirt. How come I've never seen it before either? Where's Dale? Is he around?"

"No, he got sick. Come on inside." I dropped the crowbar gently on the entrance mat. "God, you scared me, Zeely. I thought you were a burglar."

"Really?"

"Yes, really. We better call Annie's mom and tell her you're over here. Now, do you want to go back, or are you home for good?"

She looked around the room as if in search of more of my secrets. I shed my ankle bells as quietly as possible and turned off the stereo.

"I'll go back. But please don't call them, Shar. Please? They'll think I was some kind of baby running home like this. Just walk me there?"

"All right. First let me change into my jeans."

"No—please don't change. I like the way you look in those things. Like a snake charmtress or something."

"Hmmm. Okay, but, listen, Zeely—no more peeking in windows like that, understand? Not even in your own house. You should have come right to the door and knocked, so I knew you were here."

Zeely nodded. "Yes, Sharon. I'm sorry." She always wanted to please me. There was not a trace of sarcasm in her tone.

"Sorry I peeped," she added. Her balefulness transited into unabashed silliness. She giggled. We both giggled. She was a good kid, and I was lucky to have her.

We walked back because she didn't want her friends to see my car pull up at the curb. We had a small chat about belly dancing, sensuality, private rituals, black eyeliner, and bicycle shorts.

It wasn't until Zeely had disappeared back into the party that I had second thoughts about the way I was dressed. Walking with Zeely, the MotherTonin switched on, pumping its font of love and wisdom, I hadn't felt self conscious dressed like "a snake charmtress." Now I was conscious of how provocative my costume was. I felt like an actress who had lost her way off stage. I felt vulnerable.

At least I had taken off my bells, I thought, tiptoeing along, hoping no one would see me. I imagined carloads of drunken men looking for Saturday night excitement. But the street was quiet. I relaxed and strolled along nonchalantly, though I felt tension in—of all places—my stomach. Mideastern dancing had done wonders for that region of my body. I flexed my stomach muscles back and forth, undulating as I walked. Almost dancing, but not.

I liked the way the world looked at night, the ways colors changed, almost disappeared. I liked to imagine the way the world looked before electricity when night was truly, truly dark. How magical firelight must have been, surely more sacred than today's taken for granted electricity.

I thought of Maine, of our old farm, and of what the soil concealed when the potatoes grew—especially the red potatoes—how their thin skin of color separated white potato flesh from the dark dirt in exotic contrast. I had always begged my father to grow the red ones, red being my favorite color whether in jelly beans, crayons or potatoes. Now the world was not so simple. I had no favorite color, and steeped myself in all of them. In a way I found hard to explain, colors were always with me, like tones washing over my brain. Or perhaps it was my soul.

I made it home, feeling lucky no one had seen me. I was suddenly lonesome now that the excitement of my three block dash was over. Midnight on a Saturday night, and I had no one to come home to. I walked around back to the yard. It was a mess of overgrown weeds and Saint Augustine grass badly in need of mowing. But in one corner we had begun to landscape in our own silly way: with a silver gazing ball set on a pedestal. A gazing ball, like they had in Victorian gardens to reflect the loveliness of lavish flowers and greenery. I thought of it as a promise to myself, that someday we would create a pretty garden for the ball to reflect. Mostly we just made funny faces in front of it. Anything reflected there fascinated me, the world warped into its roundness.

I stared at the gaudy thing now. I loved the way it blazed in the dark like some dime store moon. I leaned in close for a look at my distorted self, and waved my skirt at its roundness. Its silver moon turned blue. I held my head closer for more freakish results. There I was with just one large all-knowing eye, like a cyclops looking for the ocean, lost in a Houston back-yard. This grotesque oracle seemed to have something to tell me. The house stretched out in wings behind its large head. Two lit windows became mysterious flares in the iridescent reflection of the globe.

The creature in the ball was not at all beautiful, yet she was undoubtedly feminine. I stared at her, wondering if she was happy in her own freakish way. I saw a compassionate gleam in her eye that gave me her answer. For a long, still moment we were one. Enough—she told me, oh yes, this is enough. With a solemn intensity, I nodded back. In some elemental, primitive way, I was rich, so very rich.

Seconds later, I stirred toward the house, stepping high over the shaggy grass which tickled the calves of my legs. The thick, tropical air seemed to resist movement, but I pushed on. My hands swished the gypsy flounces of my skirt through the familiar dampness. I walked tall toward the horizon of home. ✿

By-Pass

by Violette Newton

Gran'mere Robichaux, she come to us at Port Arthur for by-pass, stay here awhile, or maybe forever. We give her front bedroom, best furniture. Nurse and Nurse Aide, they come from Home Health, and we want them see how nice we got it. Gran'mere little old lady, seventy-nine, and ain't goin live long, maybe.

Nurse Aide come every day, wait on her, listen heart and lung, give her good wash, change sheet on bed. One day she say, "Mis' Evangeline, where you get that name? Off hot pepper-sauce bottle?"

Gran, she give her the serious eye. "Where your mind been all these year, girl? Ain't you know long-time story? Ain't you been St. Martin' and see big tree where lover find each other?"

"Never been," Nurse Aide say.

"Well," Gran say, "them lover is parted long time, she look all round country for him, find him under big tree, town of St. Martinville."

"Yeah?"

"Yeah, but he already marry."

Nurse Aide pulling sheet tight and smooth, say, "Man can't wait long, you know."

"She wait!"

"Yeah, well, too bad for her, huh?"

"Now you know sad story."

Nurse Aide get out bottle brown stuff, paint Gran'mere long wound. "I tell you something," she says. "Port Arthur is capitol Louisiana!"

"Why you say crazy thing like that?"

"Cause most everybody here is from there!"

"Still plenty left over there," Gran say.

"I don't know. Everybody but me from there, must not be many left."

"Oh, they making more all the time!"

Nurse Aide slap in air at Gran, laugh. "Now you get that leg up, let me put on 'lastic stocking." Gran stiffen up leg, hold it out, look at it. Scar is all way up from ankle to way yonder, all the way up that skinny old leg.

"Ain't that pretty sight!" Gran say. "Me, I ain't wearing no bikini this year!"

"You ain't wearing no bikini no time. That old scar ain't goin away." She get the foot part of stocking on, begin tugging at ankle.

"Why they do that to me, cut my leg?"

"It for your heart by-pass."

"My heart ain't in my leg."

Nurse Aide stop a minute, look at her. "Where your heart, Mis' Evangeline?"

"Right cheer where everybody heart be. Only, the saw me open here, too. How come they mean to me?"

"You eat too much shrimp gumbo is why. Your artery clog up with it and blood can't get through."

"That right?"

"That right."

"So how come they cut open my leg?"

"Get the vein out, make the by-pass."

"They cut me open and I don't know it?"

"They knock you out first."

Gran'mere sigh. "God know what else they do me while I knock out."

"Mis' Evangeline, they save your life!"

"They ain't save the gumbo though?"

Nurse Aide look serious. "They can't get it out. It stop up and gotta stay there."

Gran think about that. "It's goin' spoil without no 'frigeration!"

Nurse Aide roll eyes, put hand on hip, and shake head. She done got one stocking on and start other. She say, "Mis' Evangeline, you know what is by-pass?"

"Is what they do me."

"They take piece vein out of leg, sew it on artery, two places round clog, let blood go through."

"They got they nerve, cutting me open. All them clasps in chest hurt."

"They going stay there, too."

"All my life?"

"Think so."

"Oh, well, I ain't goin live long anyway. I bet, if they take x-ray, I look like junkyard in there." She think a minute. "How come they cut my leg so far for little bitty old piece vein?"

"They need lots. You got five by-pass, Mis' Evangeline."

Fran stare out in space like she somewhere else, look up and say, "Lots gumbo, huh?"

"Lots."

Then she smile. "How about crawfish etouffee? That clog up, too?"

"I bet"

Gran purse up lip. "Don't pay eat good no more. My state goin have to close down."

"Oh, no. Everybody learn to eat healthy. Lots vegetable, salad."

"You call that eating? Girl, we catch fish, fry him. We catch pullet, fry her."

"No more frying, Mis' Robichaux!"

Gran rest head back on prop-up pillow, say, "Ain't no use living no more."

Nurse Aide tug and pull on 'lastic stocking. "This keep veins good," she say. "Keep from swelling."

"What vein? They done took it out."

"Oh, you got some left."

"How I goin dance some more? Leg feel like they got on corset."

"They to get you well."

Gran got frown on face. "Look like" she say, "they let old lady about to die in peace."

"You not dying! They save your life!" She pull up sheet, smooth bed off. "And let me tell you something, you my favorite patient."

Fran look at her, say, "Yeah? You tell that all them."

"No. It's true."

"How come?"

"You the only lady I got what knows something."

"What you mean, girl?"

"Them others, they don't know straight up."

"What you say?"

"They done lost it, they minds."

"And you ain't find it on the floor nearby?"

I ain't find it nowhere." She brush and fluff up Gran's hair. "You kinda cute, too. I bet you got lotsa boyfriend back home."

Gran'mere lie still, close eyes. "Me, I'm gonna die and you talk about boyfriend!"

"Mis' Evangeline, you years ahead! Them doctors fix you up good, so you got years to live. You sit up and get your mind straight." Gran lie still. "You sit up! You got to do your breathing exercise. You got to breathe in this blue thing, make your lungs strong." She pull Gran up, give her the little machine. "Blow now!" And Gran blow. "Harder. That good." Gran lie down some more, tired. "Now, you never answer me my last question. You got boyfriend?"

Gran think and look coy. "I got one," she say.

Nurse Aide stop like she surprise. "One boyfriend! Hot diggity! He cute?"

"He old man."

"No!"

"Yeah."

"He rich, live on plantation, like in story?"

"Live in retirement home."

"Ah ha! I bet you go there, see him some?"

"Some."

"And what happen, now you gone away, all them other lady hanging on him."

Gran'mere huff up a bit. "That happen, I don't care."

"You do too! I bet he like you, too."

Gran'mere look dreamy-like, little smile play on face. "Yeah, he do."

She grin. He keep saying, 'Evangeleen, you slip in here sometime, spend night with me.'"

"Why, that old fox! He still got the devil in him, huh?"

"Ain't they all?" Gran sit up, laugh.

Nurse Aide eyes roll. "Mis' Evangeline, you do that, you find yourself expecting."

"I kill myself then," Gran say.

"Aw, no! Think how cute you look, push baby buggy down sidewalk, baby crying, 'Granma-Mama!'

"You plumb silly, girl."

"Could happen! They do all kind miracle. They got test-tube baby now, funny sheep without papa."

Gran'mere roll around eyes, giggle. "That ain't no fun," she say.

"They do all kind miracle! Those men went to moon."

"Ain't nobody home up there. Who they go see?"

"They finding out stuff, Mis' Evangeline."

"Me, I rather go New Orleans."

Nurse Aide putting her things away. She say, "I'm goin come here on my day off, cut your hair and give you home permanent, so when you go home, you look cute and young, for him."

"You hush your mouth!"

Nurse Aide make like to slap her, then hand mirror out. "Here," she say, "Look how you look! I'm goin' make you look better. He goin' be glad you made this pass by Texas, you be looking so good."

Gran look at her and look in mirror. "Give me home permanent, yes?"

"Miss' Robichaux, you need hair all fluffy, fuzzy, make you look young."

"Young, you say?"

"Yes. When you look good, you happy. When you happy, you look young."

"How come nobody not tell me that before?"

"Maybe you never need it before."

Gran be thinking awhile, then say, "How long you think leg be done heal up before it do 'Cottonmouth Joe'?"

"That 'Cotton-Eye Joe,' Mis Evangeline."

"I like them boot and big hat," Gran say.

"You ever do that dance at home?"

"Do Cajun dance."

"Well, it ain't hard to do."

"How long you think?"

"That depend on how much you wanta do it."

Gran out down mirror. "I'm ready now!" she say.

Nurse Aide shake her head. "You rarin to see that old man, dance with him."

"What man?" Gran'mere ask.

"Old fellow you left behind, if he ain't married yet."

Gran give wicked grin to Nurse Aide. "I leave him to old lady."

"Just when I'm getting you all fixed up!"

"Yeah," Gran say.

"Well, what's the use of fixing up if there ain't no man in the picture?"

Gran laugh. "I told you I like them big hat and boot and big belt buckle. Me, I'm goin stay in this place and catch me a Texas fellow! We goin shake a leg like you never see before!"

Nurse Aide close up bag with zipper. "You ain't fixin to die no more?"

"What you talking about, girl!" Gran'mere say and take up mirror again and look and look at herself. And grin. 🏵

LOPSIDED LOVE

By Patrick Bennett

A man with only one eye fell under the spell of a woman with only one ear. The situation possessed a certain symmetry. Yet the ancient Romans had a proverb: There is a threeness to all things perfect.

The name of the man with only one eye was Rudy Beck, and he thought of himself as an artist, but he worked as a shoe repairman to support himself. He was stocky and wide-chested, which gave the impression he was shorter than his five feet eleven inches. He filled his face's empty right socket with a glass eye, and at work he added an eye-patch to shield it from leather dust around the finisher.

The woman, whom he initially knew only as Lulu, was a waitress at a Lone Star Cafe around the corner from the shoe shop where Rudy worked. Lulu was a stringy, rangy gal, the kind fashion magazines might call "gamine," with big brown eyes, a wide mouth, long dishwater blonde hair. She looked like a person who would have a gold front tooth, only she didn't.

In the past, Rudy had been attracted to plump women, the type who wore 44 DD brassieres, females who would not look out of place strolling unclad across a canvas painted by Peter Paul Rubens or Auguste Renoir. Being a painter in oils, Rudy was especially sensitive to a woman's appearance. Looks and plumpness had led him astray six years back in choosing a mate for his brief, combative marriage.

As a fellow human being, Rudy found Lulu amiable enough. They joked politely, she kept his coffee cup brim-full, he left a tip. Friendly. That was about it.

Then one day, cleaning up the table next to his, Lulu stooped to retrieve a spoon from the floor and her long hair tumbled in such a way as to reveal an ugly scar where her left ear should have been.

Rudy barely kept "You're missing an ear!" from falling out of his mouth.

When Lulu straightened up again, their eyes met and she smiled, and he returned her smile. As he walked back to the shop, he thought about the place under her hair where the ear ought to have been; he pondered her earlessness while he sewed on a particularly difficult patch on a cowboy boot.

The last Sunday in August, in a converted downtown building, the West Texas Art League held a retrospective show for a defunct local painter. Rudy Beck attended, slicked up in a necktie and sports coat. His glass eye filled his socket; his eyepatch slept back home in his drawer.

There were several display rooms, in the first of which was a refreshments table. Rudy claimed a plastic cup of punch and loaded a dainty plastic dish with a few petite treats. He chatted a few minutes with the widow of the artist, he viewed a room or two of the paintings (which he privately considered sixtyish and rather dated).

Finally, he stood idly in the large room listening to the string quartet's effort. That's when he spotted Lulu, seated with the other three musicians, a bonafide member of the string quartet. Dressed in a long black gown, she caressed sound from a cello. She and the other three musicians were finishing off the composition, galloping across Mozart's coda.

Rudy had taken only one bite from a diminutive, two-bite pimento cheese sandwich when he became aware of her. The second half remained suspended in his hand, halfway to his open mouth, forgotten, while Rudy watched the musicians bowing off the final bars of music. Lulu closed her sheet music on the stand before she looked up and recognized Rudy. She flashed him the shy smile he had first seen after she picked up the fallen spoon. This time her hair covered her loss of an ear, but he was acutely conscious of its hidden absence.

While she laid aside her cello and stood—her stringy body seemed worthy of a Neiman-Marcus ad model in the formal black sheath—he made his way to her through the scattered listeners.

"I didn't know you were a musician."

"I try."

She explained that a death in his family had called the quartet's regular cellist out of town, that she had reluctantly agreed to fill in with only two rehearsals.

"You sound like you belong."

"Thank you."

"You look like you belong. I would like to paint you, in that outfit, playing the cello...."

Instead of painting her, he took her to dinner the following Thursday. She was off Monday and Thursday nights weekly, but the symphony orchestra rehearsed Mondays. He discovered her full name: Louise Planchet. They did not talk about his ex-wife or her ex-husband. They talked about painting and music and movies and theater; they got along swimmingly.

One chill, rainy Thursday night in November he phoned just before six to ask if she was in the mood for pizza.

"Why not, but only if I can eat it in blue jeans."

"Who ever heard of pizza in an evening gown."

In the warmth of a pizza joint booth, both of them dressed in jeans and sweatshirts, they talked and washed their meal down with a carafe of wine. The icy weather penetrated their coats on the way back to her apartment, so she asked him up for a cup of hot cocoa.

Her apartment was small, and the furniture was crammed in. Her half bath was so small that her clothes hamper inside prevented the door it stood behind from opening completely. Her bed, with its old fashioned quilt, was only two good steps from her breakfast table.

Instead of drinking hot cocoa at the table, they utilized the bed to make love for the first time. The weather being what it was, they kept their socks on.

In the course of this development, Rudy observed that Lulu was indeed a skinny girl. Not only did she not need a 44 DD brassiere; she hardly needed a brassiere at all. He found he did not mind.

She asked him about his missing eye. After relating how he had lost it as a teenager in a motorcycle accident, he asked if she could hear on her earless side.

"Oh yes. I probably don't have the sound gathering capacity for sounds coming from in front. But inside, the machinery is still A-one."

"I certainly can't see out of this damned glass peeper." And he thought: These things are never one for one. Nature, really and truly, never makes its matches one for one.

He asked how she lost the ear.

"That's a long story," Lulu said. "It concerns my ex-husband. I can't discuss it." She got up and began putting her clothes back on.

Thursdays came, Thursdays went, and they became more and more emotionally wrapped up in one another. The virus of romantic attachment works mysteriously; he dimly understood that the hiatus on the side of Lulu's head had brought on the displacement of the soft, chubby woman as his abstract ideal of womanhood, had displaced her with the skinny woman so that he now turned his head when a stringy, tough specimen passed him on the street.

A month or so after the crucial pizza supper, on his break at a time when few others were in the diner, he asked her to pose for him. She agreed with one proviso:

"Not nude."

"If you will wear that slinky black thing you played Mozart in."

"Want me to bring my cello?"

"That's a great idea."

So she began coming over to his place after they dined out on Thursday evenings. His studio, so-called, was really a large upstairs room in a former office building.

In one end of his single big room, he had arranged a table, bed (almost always unmade), steamer trunk, and a laundry cart with an overhead rod on which hung his rather limited wardrobe. The other half of the room housed his easel, palette, paints, brushes, lay figures, all the rigmarole of the artist. The first time that she climbed the stairs and looked into the place, she half expected to discover a copy of *La Vie Boheme* lying around.

Trudging up the stairs each Thursday, she would carry the cased cello in her right hand, a clothing bag containing the black gown in her left. She would modestly go into his half bath to put on the gown for her sitting. Even his little half bath seemed much larger than hers, perhaps because it had no clothes hamper behind the door.

Finding happiness is rather like the metropolitan sport of shooting at someone out of a speeding automobile. The aimer is actually moving in an unrelated direction, his target is headed toward somewhere else, there are bumps in the road, other persons are on the street, the bang event bobs past quickly and is gone. Rudy Beck and Lulu Planchet hit a happiness bullseye while she sat in her silky black gown with her cello, and he labored on canvas with brush and palette knife.

At the end of the sitting, she would carefully remove the gown. Then before she redonned her street clothes, they would enjoy an interlude of passion. Contentment is too thin and sickly a word for their feelings as they lay exhausted on his tumbled bed afterward.

The sittings also gave them a chance to talk, to thoroughly know one another.

"I love music," she said on one occasion, "and sometimes I wish I had been a country musician."

"Can you play the guitar?"

"I can strum around a little, but I'm no Chet Atkins."

"Why on earth would you want to get up and yodel like Jimmy Rodgers?"

"The audiences. When you do something good, they hoot and holler and stamp their feet. Concert hall audiences are so terribly polite."

"Is that why you work as a waitress in a little diner? Because you want something a bit earthy?"

"Really it is. I worked awhile as a secretary in the symphony office. Lots of politics and back stabbing, but everybody was always terribly polite."

After a short silence, she asked, "You're not the control kind, are you?"

"I believe in five-oh, five-oh. I don't believe in lopsided love."

They were not fifty-fifty about revealing pasts. He hinted a couple of times that he was curious about the missing ear, but was confronted with a stone wall of silence on one occasion and actual tears on the second. After that, he swallowed his curiosity.

Between two sittings, he put leather taps on her dress shoes and shined them. When he gave them to her at their next artistic tryst, she asked him about his day job. How did he get into it?

"Genetically, I am a shoe repairman. It took a lot of hard work and study to make myself an artist."

"That's no explanation."

My great-grandfather, on my mother's side, was a harness worker. But horses went out, and horsepower came in, so three of his sons became shoe repairmen instead. My grandfather, who grew up in a family of honest tillers of the soil, married one of the cobbler's daughters and apprenticed with his father-in-law. Grandfather then moved to another town and opened his own shoe shop, and his son, my father, added a shoe store."

"That's where you work?"

"My two older brothers inherited the repair shop and store. I inherited only a BA in fine art."

"And the family cat."

"Just the brushes and paints, I'm afraid. No Puss in Boots cats."

"And you can't make a living at painting."

"Not real art. I worked for an ad agency as a commercial artist for a while. 'Commercial art' is an oxymoron. I'd rather half sole shoes."

"There's no money in real music either. Mama told me that, but I didn't believe her."

Then one Thursday in late October, Lulu showed up in a queer mood at the cafeteria where she was to dine with Rudy. She didn't have much to say, and she only gave him a one-and-a-half second smile. He selected a chicken-fried steak with gravy, corn, and English peas. She asked for a small serving of the vegetable-casserole alone, and at their table only picked at that.

"What's wrong?"

"Don't ask, Rudy."

To fill the void, he launched into a long anecdote about a cowboy who wanted his boot heels heightened. She smiled occasionally, but her mind was obviously looking out the window while trying to stroll along with his tale.

At his apartment-studio, he began to paint her slender ankles and long, serviceable feet but his brushstrokes seemed to cover no living flesh and bone that evening. He put down his palette and brushes and walked over to her.

"Lulu, I love you, and I want to help you with whatever is troubling you. Please, if you care for me, tell me."

"Of course, I care for you.

"Well?"

"My ex-husband has been paroled from Huntsville."

"Ah, he has." Rudy hadn't known her ex was in prison.

Like pus from a lanced abscess, Lulu's story tumbled out. Gordon Sewell—she had divorced both person and surname—was a not very successful writer who aspired to write horror stories while he supported himself as a used car salesman. In public always smooth and courteous, at home he sometimes exhibited a Neanderthal attitude toward his mate. When she crossed him, he beat her; when he lost a big car sale, he came home in a rage that found an outlet in abusing her.

"We married much too young, in the foetal stage of our personalities. When we had finished developing, I had become this . . . "

"Which I like very much," he interjected.

" . . . and he had become one of the monsters he wrote about."

Gordon Sewell had grown more violent and overbearing, until about five years into their life together, he had come home drinking and in a rage one evening and cursed her about the quality of supper.

"He just got worked up worse and worse. I had a rehearsal that evening, and he hated the idea. I tried to get out and he blocked the door. I ran to the back door in the kitchen, and he caught me just as I opened it. He said, 'I'll give you a reason for staying home,' and he grabbed a kitchen knife and cut off my ear."

"Good Lord!"

"After I jammed a dishtowel against my head to staunch the bleeding, I ran in to call 911 for the police. He thought I was calling the hospital.

He said, '"They're not going to sew it right back on either.' And he ate my ear."

"Ate your ear!"

"Chewed it up. Choked it down."

She was weeping now. Beck had the zany sense of the comic that relishes John Cleese, the Marx Brothers, and *America's Funniest Home Videos*. Beck was appalled and yet felt something akin to laughter gurgling up inside him. He thought of Freud; he thought of La Rochefoucauld. But Lulu was weeping, so he jammed the traitorous smile down into his boots and took her in his arms.

"Now they've let him out again."

She sobbed so hard he could hardly understand. Slowly Lulu told Beck. The police had come, taken her to the hospital, Sewell to jail. Once they had her spouse jugged, they discovered his description matched that of a robber who had hit two convenience stores—Gordon Sewell had felt the world owed a writer a living. The court packed him off to prison for a substantial swatch of time, but word had reached Lulu that afternoon of his release on parole only three years later.

"Now I'm afraid to go to my apartment."

"I'll go with you, make sure everything's okay."

Weakly she protested, too weakly for him to take her seriously.

Driving her own car, Lulu arrived at the rundown apartment complex a minute or two ahead of Beck in his car. She waited behind the wheel, doors locked, windows up. She only unlocked and got out when Rudy arrived to park beside her.

After they climbed the stairway, she noticed faint light escaping under the door.

"Oh, you've left a light turned on." He said it to reassure her.

The table lamp was burning beside where her neatly made bed crowded into her sleeping corner. They stopped momentarily to survey the small, furniture-crammed chamber but saw no one else in the room. He closed the door behind them and took her in his arms for a passionate, tongue-searching kiss.

While their lips were sealed together, the bathroom door opened and out stepped a stringy, blackhaired man with thick glasses.

"Well, Louise, I see you've kept up an active social life."

As he came apart from Lulu, Rudy saw the man held a double barreled shotgun in his hand.

"Hello, Gordie." Beneath Lulu's words, Rudy could hear the under-tone of fright.

The stringy man was no taller than Lulu, but he exuded menace. Irrationally, Rudy thought: But it is illegal for a person on parole to possess a firearm.

"You've been cheating on me, Louise."

"We're divorced, Gordie."

"You're cheating on me. Looks like I'll have to take that other ear."

"Gordie, it's such a shock seeing you. I have to go to the bathroom."

"You stay right where you are, dear one."

Disregarding him, she swept by him into the jammed half bath and shut the door.

"As for you, Romeo, I ought to just put one barrel of buckshot between your ribs now."

One part of Rudy wanted to fall on his knees and beg for his life. Another part was annoyed at the appearance of this monster from Lulu's past, and the annoyance swelled to anger and prevailed.

"Gordon, haven't you caused Lulu enough trouble?"

"Mr. Sewell to you, Romeo. She's my wife!"

Rudy just managed to hold his tongue.

The two faced one another across the room for what seemed years of time. Rudy considered a lunge at Sewell, but a dinette chair and dresser stool were between them in the crowded room.

While continuing to hold the shotgun pointed at Rudy's chest, Sewell looked closer at the other man, studying the eyepatch and then Rudy's good eye.

"I haven't ever eaten an eye," Sewell grinned wickedly.

Rudy considered the chair and stool between them more seriously. Sewell noted his glance.

"Go ahead and try."

They stood immobilized still. Rudy could hear the toothed gear in Lulu's cheap battery clock leaping second to second. Sewell impatiently banged on the bathroom door.

"Come out of there, dearest one."

When there was no answer, he grasped the handle and flung the door back inside so hard it bounced against the hamper. The room appeared empty.

"Louise!"

Forgetting Rudy in his surprise, Sewell turned and went into the room. Lulu, who had climbed on top of the hamper behind the door, leaped onto his back, pinning his arms to his waist. Rudy kicked the stool sprawling as he rushed to help her.

During the struggle the gun, pointing down at Sewell himself, fired. Lulu phoned 911, the police came, the ambulance came. When the physician in the emergency room examined Lulu's ex-husband, he found the twin barrels had completely blasted off Gordon Sewell's right foot, reducing its remnants to shattered bone and ground flesh.

Back in prison, Sewell was fitted with an artificial foot, but it will be a many years before he tests it outside state property. After Sewell's new trial and additional sentencing, Rudy Beck and Lulu Planchet were wed. Just to be on the safe side, Rudy and Lulu moved to another city and assumed the name of . . . well, maybe we shouldn't say exactly what, the parole system being what it is. 🌸

Blood on the Moon

by Phyllis W. Allen

"Edgar Lee don't see the leavin' in that gal's eyes," Mama Minnie said for the fourth morning in a row as she stood staring out toward the rise where Uncle Edgar and Aunt Cyrisse lived.

"Miz Minnie, you probably just feeling uneasy 'cause Edgar fixin to leave again to go work at the refinery. Cyrisse seemed fine yesterday when I saw her," Mama answered trying unsuccessfully to convince Mama Minnie that her "second sight" was simply all in her mind. More than anything I wanted to ask Mama Minnie what she meant by "leavin' in her eyes," but I had learned a long time ago that conversations between "grown" folks had no space for children. Usually what happened was if I waited long enough something would happen and straighten out Mama Minnie's meaning for me.

Like the time that she predicted that Charlie Gooden's young wife Cylla was coming to no good end for making Charlie the fool. "Charlie Gooden ain't never been one to forgive easily. I seen blood on the moon the other night over by the Gooden place. Somethin' bad gonna happen for sure," Mama Minnie had said.

I went out and looked. There wasn't a drop of blood on the moon that I could see. But it wasn't but a week or so later that Cylla and young Kenny Smith lay dead from Charlie Gooden's shotgun blasts. I was never really sure why he shot them, but it had something to do with them being at his house while he wasn't home. For weeks after that Mama Minnie walked around saying, "That moon was dripping blood. I knew it wouldn't be long."

I figured it probably had more to do with the fact that Cylla was the second wife that had met the business end of Mr. Gooden's shotgun, than a bloody moon, that gave Mama Minnie advance warning of her untimely end.

Anyway here was another prediction that solid, quiet and good as gold Aunt Cyrisse was thinking of leaving Uncle Edgar. It was true that they didn't have children on their place and Uncle Edgar didn't talk much, but then neither did Aunt Cyrisse. What they did was help out with the farm and help my Mama raise me since my daddy wasn't there.

Aunt Cyrisse was nut brown with the sweetest smile and she made the best oatmeal raisin cookies in all of the county, even better than Mama Minnie. Which may have been one of her faults in Mama Minnie's eyes because there were all sorts of things that she did better than anybody in the county, including Mama Minnie. She was considered the best housekeeper, made the best pineapple coconut cake, raised the most beautiful roses and her handmade quilts won prizes at the county fair every year. Last year she beat out Mama's Minnie's "flying geese" quilt with her "six little girls." It was a quilt that commemorated the Birminingham bombing. Mama Minnie didn't say so, but you could see that she didn't like it.

Aunt Cyrisse was also the schoolteacher at our school, the Frederick Douglass Negro School. That's how Uncle Edgar met her. Back then the schoolteacher didn't come from Ferrin County, but was hired from outside. Usually the teacher boarded with one of the Ferrin County families. When Cyrisse Turner, who came from New York City, took the teaching position, it was our house that she called home. Uncle Edgar started coming every night to our house for dinner without even being asked. One night he invited Miz Turner out for a walk. After that they saw a lot of each other and it wasn't but about six months later that he and Miz Turner came into Mama Minnie's parlor one night holding hands tight like they had a secret clutched there.

A month later they were married and Miz Turner became Aunt Cyrisse.

Aunt Cyrisse taught all eight grades in one big room with the youngest up front and the rest of the ages grouped together based on their age and ability to do the demanding work that she assigned. I tried to stay away from Aunt Cyrisse while at school cause the last thing that I needed was the kids calling me teacher's pet. It was bad enough that they all knew that she was my aunt. In spite of the teasing that I sometimes took for Aunt Cyrisse's strict teaching methods or stern discipline, I liked her. Now Mama Minnie was saying that she had leavin' in her eyes.

The walk to school was cold and the roads were still muddy in patches from the rains that had come last week. Trudging along I couldn't get Mama Minnie's words out of my mind and as soon as I got to school and hung my heavy scratchy wool coat in the cloakroom, I looked in Aunt Cyrisse's eyes for any signs of leavin'. All I saw was the same butterscotch brown with little flecks of green as always, but her mouth, normally full and on the verge of a smile was tight and drawn into a thin line.

"Everybody stand for the pledge of allegiance. Darnell get the flag out and lead us in prayer," Aunt Cyrisse said just like every morning, but this morning she seemed to be thinking of something else.

Maybe Mama Minnie was wrong, the leavin' didn't seem to be in her eyes, looked more like it was gripping her around the mouth making it hard to squeeze out words so familiar they were a part of her.

All day I watched. During math I watched as Aunt Cyrisse kept shaking her head slightly and saying, "Just a minute class let me find my place again." I watched during recess as Aunt Cyrisse stood with her back to us on the makeshift playground and looked toward Griffin's Woods as if she were watching for something. She kept watching even as Jimmy Mitchell and all the twelve-year-old boys got the girls up in the air on the seesaw and then jumped off. I watched that afternoon as I wrapped my head in the Mama Minnie mandatory headscarf and Aunt Cyrisse sat, head bowed low on her desk, the soft snuffling sounds not covered by the north wind howling against the window.

It took only that day to convince me that Mama Minnie was right, Aunt Cyrisse had *something* in her eyes.

That evening at dinner Mama Minnie and Mama talked about the weather, "Miz Minnie I don't think I've ever seen it so cold this time of year."

"Sho' right. It ain't even hardly November and the road out front been frozen solid for over a week. Looks like we in for a long winter."

"Yes Ma'am, good thing that we got plenty of canned goods put up."

They went on like that until Mama went into the kitchen to bring out the apple cobbler that she'd made for dessert. As soon as Mama Minnie's spoon scooped up the buttery, flaky crust and tartly sweet apples she said, "Sure is good pie Mary, mighty good. You enter a pie like this in the County Fair pie contest you sure to win. Specially since seems like ain't gon' be many bakers left here in Ferrin County. Edgar Lee was over here this evenin' and it's like I told you."

"Miz Minnie can we talk about this later? Azja, start clearing the table and get ready to help me get the kitchen cleaned," Mama said looking at Mama Minnie as if she couldn't be sure what her next words would be.

Knowing better than to argue with Mama, I took my plate and Mama Minnie's and headed for the kitchen. Once there I started to fill the sink with hot water and moved close to the swinging door with a glass in my hand. My best friend, Mae Alice Pearsons, taught me how to listen at doors with a glass, works just like a microphone.

Mama Minnie was talking again, "Edgar Lee come this mornin' say that he don't want to go up to Bay City to work at the refinery 'cause something wrong with Cyrisse. Said the other night he woke up and she was sitting in the living room lookin' out the window and cryin'. Wasn't no moon or nothin', so he knowed that she couldn't be lookin' at nothin'. Just sittin' there cryin' and carryin' on. Edgar Lee beside hisself with worry and talkin' bout not goin' to work this year, knowin' how bad he need the money. Mary, I'm tellin' you that girl got leavin' in her eyes."

Backing away from the door I couldn't hear Mama's response because I had put the glass in the sink to be washed. When I went back into the dining room Mama was saying, "Well, could just be that time of month, you know Cyrisse always suffers so during her monthlies."

Rising from the table Mama filled her hands and arms with dishes, half filled bowls of uneaten food and headed to kitchen carrying them like a shield in front of her. Mama Minnie kept talking as if to herself, "Even so just wish there was somethin' that I could do to stop what I feel in every one of my bones is comin'. That's the one thing wrong with bein' a mama , the bigger the babies get the less you can protect them."

Scooping up the last of the dishes from the smooth oilcloth, that covered the dining table every day of the year except for Thanksgiving and Christmas and any Sunday that the preacher chose to have dinner with us, I tried not to look at Mama Minnie. She had that look in her eyes that she sometimes got when she talked about my daddy being gone. A look that crossed between fear and pain, like you get when you step on a nail walking barefoot after your mama told you not to.

Days passed. Uncle Edgar loaded up the truck and left for Bay City looking back and waving long past the point that he usually did. Mama, Mama Minnie, and I stood in the road waving back until we could no longer hear the rumble of the truck.

"Well, I've still got dinner to get on the table and Azja, I bet you still haven't started on your homework," is what Mama said.

We turned and started back toward the house and still Mama Minnie stood in the road as little swirls of wind tossed leaves blew up around her feet like tiny tornadoes. Finally, she turned toward Mama and me and started into the house. She walked right up the steps, into the house, and down the hall into her room without acknowledging either Mama or me. The thud her door made when she closed it seemed to say, "Do Not Enter."

The next week everything seemed fine. Aunt Cyrisse was teaching as usual with her same pleasant smile and quiet voice. The distracted haunted look left her eyes. She looked happy like Christmas morning or something. During recess she stood in the playground, "Jimmy Mitchell if I see you tormenting those girls again, it'll be no recess for you for the rest of this month. Stanley Turner put those chains right back like you found them on that swing." That was the old Aunt Cyrisse. Nothing missed her.

On Saturday Mama Minnie called me in from the backyard where Mae Alice and I were busy building a raft to use in the summer on Catfish Gap pond. "Azja, come here baby and take these fresh caramel rolls down to your Aunt Cyrisse. Now you watch it, they are hot and don't you and Mae Alice be dawdling cause I want Cyrisse to have 'em while they still warm. She's over there alone and she does love my caramel rolls"

Mae Alice and I started down through the stand of pine trees that separated our house from Uncle Edgar and Aunt Cyrisse's house. As we climbed the soft hill to the house we saw a lady standing on the side porch. Dressed in flowing gold colored pants and blouse with a scarf tied backwards on her head and huge gold hoops in ears, she looked like a butter toffee pirate, only instead of a saber she was holding a paintbrush. She would look out toward the meadow where the wildflowers bloomed in the spring, squint, and then make strokes on the easel in front of her.

Something, like an unseen hand, stopped me on the top of the hill and for a moment Mae Alice and I just stood there looking at this woman, unlike any either of us had seen in Ferrin County. The screen door opened and Aunt Cyrisse came out. From where we were standing you could see that she was smiling at the unknown lady on her porch. Then she walked up to the pirate lady and they kissed, right there on the front porch. On the mouth.

For just a moment everything seemed to stand totally still and then the sound of Mae Alice's voice, almost a shout, "Did you see that?" filled my ears.

It must have filled Aunt Cyrisse's ears too because she looked up toward the hill where we were standing and then ran into the house. The pirate lady just stood with her paintbrush extended as if uncertain where to make the next stroke. After what seemed like hours, but must have only been minutes, she laid down the paintbrush and headed toward us.

An icy breeze kicked up around my ankles and then I realized that the plate was no longer warm against my fingers. Mae Alice wasn't saying anthing now, in fact, I couldn't even hear Mae Alice's breath even though I felt its warmth against my ear. My feet seemed unable to move, but it was the sound of the lady's voice that uprooted me.

"So you must be Azja. Your Aunt Cyrisse had to go, well, uh I guess you saw that she went back into the house. Are these for her?" she asked.

Releasing the cold china plate into her slim smooth hand, being careful not to touch, I stumbled past Mae Alice and headed back toward my house. Entering through the warm buttery scented kitchen, I headed to my room ignoring the questioning looks passing between Mama Minnie and Mama.

It was a long time before I could bring myself to form a mental image of what I had seen. I'd never heard of two women kissing on the mouth. Sure, I'd seen women kiss all my life. Mama Minnie kissed the ladies in her Ruth Circle at church. Mama always kissed Aunt Betty Ann and Aunt Bobbie Jean when they came down from Dallas. I'd even seen women kiss on television, the times when I'd been allowed to visit Janet Harris, the only person in our area with a television, but never on the mouth.

It was disturbing.

Mama stood outside my door knocking lightly, "Azja, honey, what's wrong? Mae Alice said that you fell on the way back from Cyrisse's. You all right?"

"Uh huh."

Did you skin your knee? You need some iodine or monkey's blood or something? Well, dinner's going to be ready soon. You get washed up. You hear?"

I laid there on my bed, staring out into the pitch black backyard. Ever since Mama Minnie and I had stopped sharing a bedroom, I felt grownup. Sleeping by yourself tended to do that. But also I missed her, there was no one to snuggle under when the house grew cold on winter nights and no one's back to hide your face in when strange sounds filtered out of the closet or from underneath the bed.

That's what I wanted now, somewhere to hide my face. I had seen something strange and upsetting and there was no refuge.

It struck me odd that Aunt Cyrisse should seem so comfortable with the strange woman. Why would she kiss her like that and then run in the house when she saw Mae Alice and me?

There were too many questions. I closed my eyes.

On Monday at school, Mae Alice came to me and said, "I promise on my little brother, Alfred, that I won't tell nobody what we saw. Anyway, the more I think about it the more I'm sure we didn't really see nothing. Just some kissing and my mama's always kissing somebody."

I didn't answer. Couldn't.

Aunt Cyrisse came in looking worse than she had before Uncle Edgar left. Her eyes sank deep into her beautiful face and dark circles ringed them like a full moon. Her hair was carelessly pulled back and pinned down. She kept looking away from the corner where Mae Alice and I shared a work-table. Her voice was low and could barely be heard over the twelve-year-olds' chatter and laughter, something she never tolerated.

The day drug as Aunt Cyrisse went through the motions of teaching us math, reading, and history. It was almost three o'clock, the hour of free-dom, when the door opened and in walked the toffee colored pirate woman. Instead of the loose flowing pants and top she was draped in gauzy layers of jewel-toned turquoise, gold, and wine. The pirate scarf was gone revealing a smooth cap of close-cropped curls that were toast brown. Huge gold hoops in her ears completed the outfit.

Aunt Cyrisse's hand went to her throat in a gesture that looked like she was trying to protect the softness there. The room seemed too small to contain the pirate woman. Aunt Cyrisse stopped talking and started to move back until the chalk covered blackboard blocked her exit.

"Rissa, we must talk," the woman said.

"I'm in the middle of my class now, maybe later," was all that Aunt Cyrisse could say and even that was choked and muffled.

It was then that everything spun out of control because at that moment Mae Alice said in a loud whisper, "That's the woman that was kissing your Auntie."

Just before the hush descended on the room a loud and collective gasp filled the air and all of the class, even the little ones, moved forward in their seats as if waiting for the next shoe to drop.

The pirate woman turned to look at Mae Alice, eyes shooting daggers, "Don't say that!"

It was too late!

Aunt Cyrisse stood behind the desk with the same look in her eyes that I've seen in rabbits caught in one of Uncle Edgar's snares. Her mouth made a perfect "O" and her hand went to her head as if trying to hold it on. Then recovering, "Class dismissed," was all Aunt Cyrisse was able to say before her shoulders started to shake.

We quickly rose from our seats, like felons fleeing the scene of a crime and made our way into the cloak-room. The little ones, that Aunt Cyrisse usually had to help on with rubbers or winter coats, buttoned their heavy woolen coats with abnormally dexterous fingers and hurried out of the tiny schoolhouse. Everyone seemed to want to be somewhere else, especially Mae Alice who stood by the hook that held my plaid wool coat with her mouth opening and closing liked a hooked catfish.

"I didn't mean to say it," she kept repeating.

I dressed in my coat, gloves and headscarf without ever looking up. When I was done I made a big show of sidestepping Mae Alice and headed out of the suddenly choking hot cloakroom.

As I glanced back into the classroom Aunt Cyrisse stood with her back to the open door and the woman was seated in one of the tiny desks at the front. Aunt Cyrisse's face wasn't visible but the sag of her shoulders and the way her body was swaying filled the room. I stood at the door looking as if by watching I could get answers to all the questions that were swirling in my head.

There was nothing.

As I pushed open the heavy door to the outside the older kids stood in clumps out in the schoolyard watching me as I walked by. When I reached each group, instead of calling out or making some wisecrack like usual, they would look away and pretend to be deep in some conversation. Up by the oak tree, where we always met, stood Mae Alice, hands rammed deep in the pockets of her worn woolen coat. She was watching me like she thought that today was any other day and we would walk home together laughing at what happened at school.

Balling my hands into tight fists and pushing them as far down in my coat pockets as possible I tried to walk by and pretend that I didn't see Mae Alice.

"Azja, hey! Wait up! I want to talk to you," Mae Alice said trying to fall into a comfortable rhythm beside me.

"Look I know you mad at me. Heck, I would be too. I don't why I said it. I was just surprised to see that woman come in the school like that"

I kept right on walking with my head down trying to keep that cold "pneumonia" wind out of my face. That's what Mama Minnie called any winter wind with a trace of moisture. She would say, "Child it ain't the cold that gets a body it's that "pneumonia" wind blowing that ice right down in your lungs until they freeze up and turn all green."

Mae Alice continued to match my steps without saying anything. Suddenly she stopped and threw her books on the frozen ground.

"You think you the only one that feels bad about this. How you think I feel or Miz Thomas? What about your Mama Minnie? How she gonna feel when this get out. You know right now every kid in our class old enough to talk is going home and tell their Mama and Daddy that "something" happened at school today. When they folks start to question and find out it got to do with the teacher kissing another woman, what you think gon' happen to Miz Thomas? So Miz Azja Thomasina Thomas this ain't just about you!"

I stopped and watched as Mae Alice's body sagged.

Anyway guess I do know why I said what I said today. Just once I wanted someone else's family to be the one that folks talk about. Just once I wanted to be the one that everybody come running up to, to talk. Wanted them to ask me questions about what happened. It made me feel important. You got any idea how it feel to be the daughter of the town drunk and his whore? Folks think I don't know what they mean when they point at my little brother Alfred cause he so light skinned with that curly red hair. And Lonnie, my daddy or mama neither one don't have no green eyes. What about "Bay Bro"? You think I can't see that he's black and smooth with long legs and arms just like "Uncle" Johnny, my daddy's best friend? I done heard these stories all my life and I done felt people looking down on me. I heard the arguments where my daddy sayin, 'You an evil woman what will lay down with any man.' I heard my mama tell him, 'It's a damn good thing that someone in this family got something that someone will pay for since every penny you get you drink up!' Try going to sleep at night after that. Folks in Ferrin County look up to your family. I'm ashamed but I think that just once I wanted people to look at your family like they look at mine.

Mae Alice stopped in the road and stood with her head down.

For a minute I forgot that Aunt Cyrisse had "leavin'" in her eyes. I forgot that Mama Minnie was going to be upset and Mama was going to get those tight lines around her mouth. I even forgot how sad Uncle Edgar, my favorite uncle, looked as he left for Bay City. All I could think of was the things that I had heard about the Pearsons all my life. Mama Minnie saying, "There ain't two folks in this county that belongs together more than Lucinda and Jocko Pearsons. She lay down with anything drawin' breath and him too drunk, most times, to do anything about it. Got a houseful of "Heinz 57" kids and neither one of them tryin to change."

At the time I hadn't understood what she meant. Miz Lucinda was fun. When I slipped off and went to Mae Alice's house, Miz Lucinda would be walking around in her slip with her gold hair kinda ruffled all over her her head sayin, "Child I swear you the spittin' image of your daddy. Heard you was as smart as him too. Ooh Lord, that man was fine!" she would say in a dream voice.

She always offered me cookies and told me that as soon as I filled out I was going to be "right pretty." That's why I liked to go to Mae Alice's house, even if Mama and Mama Minnie swore they would skin me alive if they found out I was there. Miz Lucinda was a nice lady. Now here was Mae Alice, her own daughter saying awful things about her. All of a sudden I wasn't mad at Mae Alice anymore, 'cause I couldn't imagine ever saying anything like that about my mama, even thinking them.

Mae Alice still stood with her head dropped low and her books were strewn on the frozen frost tipped dirt. I stopped to pick up the books and through the trees I saw Aunt Cyrisse and the pirate lady standing in the playground. Aunt Cyrisse seemed to be crying but the pirate lady just stood there looking like she was ready to take on the world.

As I handed Mae Alice her books a wet icy wind caused me to shiver. As it blew by it seemed to say, "That gal's got leavin' in her eyes." ✿

THE BRICKLAYER

by Marshall Terry

We children were natural prey to the prejudices and concerns of our father. He held them strongly.

Except for the fact that, after the Second World War, Hiroshima, and the rise of the Bear as Godless Communism, Russia would with dreadful certainty get the Bomb and use it on us, my father's strongest conviction was that F.D.R. had sold out America to socialism, and we were heading inevitably toward a second deep Depression. He had earned this conviction through the turns of his life.

Dad rambled his way through Ohio State and Kenyon without much concern for learning, cherishing college as a place to play tennis. He was pretty good at it, once, the story goes, beating Don Budge. His innate enthusiasm and sense of the glory of American free enterprise led him naturally down the path to advertising. A dashing figure at the age of twenty-five, he married the Homecoming Queen of Miami U. and started his own advertising agency in his native Cleveland. At twenty-seven, in the depth of the Depression, he lost it.

His father also lost what he had. My father sold copper pots and pans from door to door. He began his cursing of Roosevelt, who desperately created the socialistic support network that would surely rob Americans of their initiative and freedom. I was born premature and could not be kept in hospital and barely made it. 'Twas parlous times.

Dad pulled out of it all right, going on to a productive, enthusiastic career in selling and marketing, which somehow transmuted, to his dismay, in my brother and me both becoming teachers. But along the way we had constant lectures on the absolute necessity of learning to do something useful with your hands so that when the other fellow was out of work and destitute, people would still need you, and pay you, to do some basic thing.

For, sure as the guy named Franklin D. Shit had gone to court to change his name and when the judge asked him how, said he wanted to change it to Joe Shit, if we were not obliterated first, we would have another Depression and lose in it whatever fancy jobs and titles we had, and our earthly means.

My brother was to be an electrician. I was to learn bricklaying.

These were basic, useful skills and were, my father thought, geared to our respective levels of intelligence.

At any rate, last spring, as I was going to say, I was invited to represent my university at the inauguration of a younger friend of mine as president of a college up in Michigan. I was pleased to do so. I was myself at the time an administrator, a provost, as well as professor and looked forward to joining the other delegates from colleges across the land to the ringing of bells in the historic domed chapel on the hill.

As I emerged from the small airport building looking for a taxi, a fellow hailed me. He was standing, smiling with pride, by a gleaming long Cadillac in high style a decade and a half ago with BOBBY'S TRANSPORT SERVICE painted on the slightly dented door.

Seeing no other vehicle in sight, I allowed Bobby to set me deep within the blue leather backseat and glide me along to my hotel downtown. He had a crossed eye, a few teeth and en route I noticed in the rearview mirror, a long scar on his left cheek. Bobby loved to talk, all on the subject of transportation by his fleet composed of this car, a Dodge van, and an old Lincoln Towncar even as we spoke being beaten back into shape to be the premier limo in the stable. He would take me to Detroit for a hundred fifty or to Grand Rapids for just sixty. He seemed rather crestfallen that I was not in need of going either place.

"It's ten dollars to the college. Flat rate. Might cost you more or less in a taxi, but there's no taxis. So what's happening at the college?"

"They are inaugurating the new president there."

"Oh yeah? Bunch of you guys coming in for it?"

"Yes. Probably mostly coming from this and adjoining states. Probably in their own cars."

"Oh." Bobby made a face like what does a guy have to do? "So how do you do that?" he said. "Inaugurate him?"

"Oh, we get on our robes, and they ring the bells and we have a procession."

"Yeah?" His uncocked eye lit up. "So maybe I could drive you in the procession? You see what a shined-up, smooth rider this Caddy is? I could shine her up even more, and all the brass can see her."

"Not that kind of procession. I mean, not a parade. We just march, I think from the library to the chapel, and have the ceremony."

"Oh." Bobby's face went blank.

From the hotel that afternoon I walked along the desultory street, "two miels" as the woman at the desk told me in that Michigander's hard, sharp accent I had forgotten, to the college. I walked its grounds, beheld its hills, viewed its domes and spires and visited with my friend in his booked and wood-burnished office.

Walking back it began to rain. It grew cold and began to pour. Foolishly I had not worn my Burberry, had on a tweed jacket getting soggy and the cap with my university's logo on it that had made my friend laugh at my own boyish wearing of it, and had a good "miel" and more to go. I stood at the intersection hoping desperately not to take pneumonia. The day had been bright, and I had been happy in it, so foolishly trusting myself to the weather of an unfamiliar place.

I spied a miraculous something, a yellow taxi, coming down the street. It slowed, and u-turned and pulled up to the curb. The window cranked down.

"Use a ride?" the fellow said.

I got in and squeezed some water from my sleeves. It fell into some sort of sandy grit on the floor. The cab was disreputable, the seats ripped, the inside all scarred and dirty. The driver, not looking to see just where he was going in the rain, turned to say his name was Freeman. Asked where I was from. When I told him he said, "Well, howdy! Welcome to Michigan. And congratulations. You have found the one honest taxicab driver in this town. Oh, bingo! These shocks are shot. Well, they should be, this old car has let's see just about two-hunnert fifty thousand miels on it."

He might have been handsome, blue eyes, silver hair, about my age, full set of teeth or a plate, as he kept turning his head around to talk to me, except that his head did not seem to be set quite right on his neck and shoulders. Turning, his head made an odd angle to his body.

"Not many flowers out yet," I said to him. "Of course, there would not be, here, yet."

"No," Freeman said, smiling at the subject. "I was never a flower child, I'll tell you, in fact, I was a hawk, was in the service and all, well, back then, you know, Korea. Anyhow, I always was a flower boy! Yes, sir! I dig a great wide plot for flowers in the spring. You ever been to Holland, seen the tulips? Well, you should go and see 'em. I grow flowers even in winter, you see, little tiny ones that they come up through the snow. Called snowdrops. They are pretty, coming up like that in winter."

A pause, then he said, "I didn't drive this old heap 'til four years ago. I was a bricklayer. Broke my back. That's how I come to be doing this. Driving."

"Fell," he said, pulling in the hotel driveway, taking me right to the door. "Yes, sir," he said. "Broke my back. Anyways, where you from?"

I reminded him. The rain was slackening. "My favorite team," he said. "Go Cowboys."

"How about picking me up at nine tomorrow morning?" I said, thinking I did not want to walk however many miles it was carrying my robe in God knew what weather. "And," I said, in a flush of feeling for Freeman, "then I will need a ride to the airport Sunday morning."

Somehow he managed to get his head turned around on his neck and shoulders so he could beam at me as I opened the car door and edged out.

"I'll be here!" he said. I got out before he could manage to offer to shake hands, wet, cold, my shoes gritty from the compound of sand and soil on his passenger floor. "I'll call now and tell that son of a bitch dispatcher I have a pickup for tomorrow morning and the next morning, too. S.O.B. never gives me the good runs. Nine sharp tomorrow. Yes, sir, I will be here."

I came down carrying my gown and hood and cap carefully on a hanger to the immense interest of the young bellman at the hotel door. I asked whether they had a van that could take me to the airport the next morning.

He said they did and I made the arrangement. Outside Freeman was there, standing by his battered hunk of yellow, five minutes early. He smiled and brought his strangely angled body around and opened the door, with a pop and a shriek, for me and tried to take my cap and gown from me. We clunked off, Freeman trying to turn his head on his trunk to talk to me so that a delivery truck almost hit us as we twisted by it into the left lane without looking.

"Yes, sir," Freeman said. "Go Cowboys."

Several minutes later I realized we were going a different route. I looked at my watch. Robing was at 9:15 and we were to march at 9:45.

"Thought I'd go a little different way today," said my friend. "Look there, coming up the street to the right, there? See that? I laid those bricks. Nice little brick house, in with all those wood frames."

"I see," I said.

He turned left and showed me another example of his work. Then we drove by a high redbrick wall and I guessed it, the place where he had fallen and broken his back. A good straight solid wall. "I didn't fall all that far," he confessed, "but I fell wrong. Got a little clumsy in my old age. Surprised the poppyseed out of me, as my granma used to say—"

I nodded sympathetically, as we turned on yet another small street in a direction I sensed was going away from the college. The nonexistent shock absorbers bumped and thumped as we stopped by a small wall, a zigzagged, curving wall intricately made with craft and precision, if you looked at it in detail.

"This here is my masterpiece," Freeman said, pointing at it. But the hand seemed soft and white, not rough and strong as I imagined a bricklayer's hand. It was the hand of a man who planted flowers soon as he could in the spring up here and brought tiny flowers—snowdrops—out of the snow. I adjusted up my robe and rubbed at its hem, which had slid into the grime of the floor of the cab.

As we pulled away I looked at my watch again. It was 9:25.

"Well—it must be a good feeling to be able to go by and see things you did—that you made," I said.

"Yes," he said. "It is. These brick walls, why, they will be here—"

He veered sharply onto another street heading the heap at a strain in another direction. "Don't worry," he said, "we are heading straight for it now. I wanted to show you some of what I built. I didn't do anything at the college, you know—Ha! I guess not, it was all done more'n a hunnert years ago. Nice brick tho'. A kind of darker brick than I ever had to work, I'm trying to think what they call it. . . . It's three dollars, flat fee," he said, stopping his car at the base of the long hill on which sat the domed chapel. "Just the same as yesterday. I sure won't charge you for the tour. And what time do you need me for in the morning?"

I handed him a five. "Keep the change," I said.

"Oh, well—"

"And I guess I won't need you in the morning," I said, elevating my cap and gown and hood and whisking them out of the filthy car. "I'm being taken to the airport."

"Oh," he said. "Well, sir, thank you and thank you for the tip, then."

I nodded to him, peering through the side window, which he had heaved himself over to roll down.

"All right, then. Have a good one. Inauguration? Say, maybe whenever you come back, I'll be working again. Laying brick. Some days I think I might. Anyways, good luck to you."

"Yes. Good luck to you," I said.

He clanked off, with a limp wave of his hand, and I turned to walk up the hill crowned by the chapel. ✿

THE GEORGE WEST MESQUITE AT BATSON, TEXAS

by Bill Brett

The first time I run across the story about the mesquite must have been 1938 or maybe '39. The Depression was on and I was pickin' up a day or two's work whenever and at whatever I could, and at seventeen glad to git the dollar a day that day labor paid.

I stayed pretty busy durin' the summer at cow work and at this particular time I was ridin' for Mr. Dave Neal up above Moss Hill. He was runnin' a good many cattle, and we was several days workin' all of them and got through a little after dinner the last day, and he said he needed me another day and paid ever'body else off.

What he needed me for was this country was all free range then—didn't have a stock law until 1956—and mostly unfenced, and eight or ten head of cattle had strayed off and wound up over in the Batson Oilfield about eight miles east of his place, and me and him was goin' to go and bring them back to their home range.

Mr. Dave's place was maybe a mile north of Moss Hill on the old Liberty to Nacogdoches stage road and the next mornin' before good daylight we rode out. Should have went about a mile back to Moss Hill and had a good country dirt road clear into Batson, but instead we went about a half north and then turned east on a woods road goin' to Whaley Cove. It was good ridin' on the road and through the cove, but we hit some bad haw thickets at the east edge of the cove and then had to bog across Gum Gully and tear through heavy briars for a good ways. Light'nin' Struck Slough was pretty wide and deep in mud where we crossed it, but after that it was open woods and good travelin' until we got to Butterbean Island and hit the Moss Hill-Batson road. I guess comin' the way we did saved us a good bit better'n a mile.

It was a little after six I guess when we got to maybe within a mile of

Batson and we angled off a little left of the road through the woods and toward the oilfield. It wasn't far 'til we rode out onto the big prairie where it's at and right there close was a man tendin' to a well. Mr. Dave had had a general store at Batson once and knowed him—Mr. Jesse James McCreight was who it was I found out later—and we rode over and they shook hands and visited a minute. Before we left he told us he'd seen a little bunch of D-branded cattle day before over close to that George West Mesquite.

That's the first time I'd ever heard of the George West Mesquite and wouldn't have knowed a mesquite tree if I'd met it in the road, but Mr. Dave knew where it was and we rode maybe a mile over to it. I thought maybe I'd know it by some other name, but one look and I knew it was a stranger to me by any name.

We rode on by it and d'reckly seen cattle grazin' over toward Pine Island Bayou and made a little circle and got between them and the wood, and it was the ones we's lookin' for and we rode in and started them back toward home.

They was good handlin' cattle and all grown and it wasn't long after we hit the Moss Hill Road 'bout where we'd left it that they acted like they knowed where they was goin', got in that long steady walk them old range cows use't to travel in, all we had to do was keep up.

We quit the road at Butterbean Island and went back 'bout the way we'd come through earlier and dropped the cattle in the Cove, and we was back at Mr. Dave's by dinner.

On the way, I'd asked him why that mesquite was the George West and he told me the story and told it like he knowed it for shore.

Said that 'bout 1900 there was a bad drought down in South Texas and a rancher named George West went to shippin' his cattle to Felicia, the town is gone now, but it was on the Southern Pacific Railroad about twenty miles west of Beaumont.

I've found out since then that George West was from Live Oak County and there's a town there named after him.

Anyways, the railroad had stock pens at Felicia and West's hands would unload the cattle and start drivin' them, mosty pretty well north and after a day or two or three drivin', they'd drop the bunch and head back for more, and there's been one crew that'd camped one night where the tree had later growed up. Mr. Dave said there was a pretty good spring there at the time was why they'd done it.

I run into the same story a year or two later from Pete Rogers, a friend of mine that lived up at Batson. We use't to ride together a good bit and once he showed up with the first silk manila rope I ever seen, and it was way better handlin' than the old grass ropes, and I asked him to git me one when he could.

I was livin' with an aunt between Hull and Hardin and a few days later I was off workin', and he come by the house and left the rope thirty-four foot of it and told Aunt Sudie I owed him a dollar.

It wasn't but about eight miles up to Batson and I wasn't workin' the next day, and I left home about the usual leavin' time to take Pete his money. I had a brown horse I'd traded from Birchey Taylor and he had a runnin' walk that'd cover eight miles nearly before you noticed and so smooth you'd git down with your hind a laughin'. I got there before six and caught Pete saddin' up and just leavin' and he said come on, we had a calf to catch.

Best I remember it took us two or three hours to find the pair and maybe five minutes to rope the calf and Pete git down and earmark it. They'd missed it the last time they'd gathered.

We rode by the George West Tree on the way back and I asked Pete if he knowed anythin' about it. He told me practically the same thing Mr. Dave had 'cept he said that he'd heard it from some of the old-timers.

I didn't hear the tree story anymore, but I was told a time or two that some local cattleman would drive West's cattle further on, off their range, and some of them wound up clear over in Louisiana. One fellar told me about some of them short brush hands gittin' lost in the woods and havin' to be hunted for, but this was all second or third-hand and come from people that lived further up in the Big Thicket. I never did hear anythin' about any of the cattle being moved back to South Texas or sold up here and that don't seem right, does it?

About fifty years after I'd went through the above, I got up one mornin' with that mesquite on my mind and got some coffee and went to Batson. It's still jist eight miles up there and started askin' people if they knowed of such a tree in the Batson Oilfield. Don't know how many said "no," but finally, finally one said he did and told me where, and it was jist above town on the road goin' to the oilfield. I knew he was wrong. I'd been up that road hundreds of times, but I drove up there anyway and it damn shore is there, nearly in the road and about even with the granite monument markin' the '03 Discovery Well. It's forked right at the top of the ground and each trunk is about thirty-eight inches around and it's a good twenty-five feet tall or better, and a nine-pound tree book I borrowed said it was a Honey Mesquite and could well be ninety years old.

After I looked up all that, I knew I'd found the George West Mesquite but it seemed to me it was in the wrong location. I drove back up there and it damned shore wasn't where it'd been pointed out to me by Mr. Dave and Pete, and I went on three or four hundred yard further to the Ada Belle Oil Company lease and asked Doodlebug Payne, he's the Superintendent, if he knew of another mesquite anywhere up there. He's been in that oil field nearly since we got out of school and he said he didn't. Said there was a big huisache maybe a hundred yard back of the office but he didn't know of a mesquite. I thought I'd walk back there and look at it and did and knew quick as I seen it, it was my George West Mesquite. My George West Mesquite was a damn scrubby huisache. I guess I was so sure of it because the Ada Belle was in the same place it'd been at in the 1930's and I finally remembered it.

Just to be sure I measured the five trunks jist above the ground and went back to that nine-pound book under "huisache" and it sent me to "acacia" and there it said it could be old enough to have sprouted in 1900, and I said to hell with it and ain't bothered it since.

I guess maybe a bird or something had seeded that tree by the road, or it could have been them South Texas hands. There ain't no way of knowin' now. ❁

My Baby, the Chupacabra

by Guadalupe Flores

David put his beer down and started laughing.

I scowled. "It wasn't meant to be funny."

Still laughing, he coughed out, "I know. That's why I'm laughing."

He picked up his beer and held the sweaty glass to his forehead, rolling it along his eyebrow. He smiled and sighed. "She sucks goats."

I turned and walked to the kitchen of his apartment. I shouted over my shoulder, "She sucks goats' blood, asshole." I reached in to grab one of the dwindling number of bocks, shutting the door with my knee as I twisted the cap off. I flicked the cap at David over the counter dividing the two areas, causing him to cringe in mock terror. "You're making it sound like some sort of sexual deviance."

He reached around the arm of the overstuffed chair he sat in, grabbing, then flinging the bottle cap back at me in one fluid move. "So is this like some sort of family curse or something? A Mexican version of *The Howling*, maybe?"

The whirling disc caught me in the corner of the eye. "Fucker," I muttered. Rubbing my eye, tears welling under my kneading finger, I explained it in a distracted manner, mildly relieved that he was willing to listen.

"It's some sort of virus. Her family owns a whole bunch of land down there, farming and ranching kind of thing." I took a swig of my beer. "She was out there for a week while on break from school. She says her dad wants her to have hands-on experience with the dirty part of the business, so she spent time camping out with two of her brothers."

Kicking out with my left leg, I knocked his left one off of his knee. It swung out, catching the soft spot between foot and ankle on the edge of the coffee table. He grunted, then grimaced, reaching down to grasp the injured extremity.

"Okay, man, quits. You won that one." He held his hand up in surrender. "So where does sucking goats' blood come in?"

"Well, while they were out there, they slaughtered a goat for fresh meat. They don't have H•E•B.'s down there, I guess." I sat down and put my feet up on the coffee table, cradling my beer on my sternum. "This virus was in the goat they ate. Her brothers get a couple of boils flaring up now and then, but Mercy gets the whole trip. Once a month, she gets transmogrified."

I leaned my head back and closed my eyes. "I've never seen it happen. Saw the final result." My eyes opened to stare at the tiny shadows cast by the pebbly surface of the ceiling. "It's pretty damn ugly."

David leaned forward, resting his hands on his knees, hanging his head between them. His head came up again, a grin splitting his face.

"And you still want to marry her. Damn, it must be love!"

As a rule, I hate chuckling. Always seemed like a coward's laugh, afraid to commit to the real thing. David was the only person who could make me do it.

"Yeah, she was surprised that I still wanted to get married after I saw her that way." I sat up a bit, locking my knees, tapping glass against teeth as I swallowed more beer. "You're the first person I've told."

"No shit?" He actually paused to think. It's not often that I surprise him. "Oh man. What the hell is your mom and the Sarge going to say?"

"Dunno. Neither of them like Nationals that much. They always feel like they're being looked down on 'cause they're Tex-Mex," I grinned. "This oughta help relieve that inferiority complex."

David drained his beer and stood. His brow furrowed in exaggerated seriousness. "Well, I can hear your mom now. 'Mi'jo, are you using a condom?'" His voice started to shake with renewed laughter. "And what about the children, Esteban? Will they be chupacabras also?" He moved his hand to his breast, eyes widening, perfectly mimicking my mother. "She won't try to suck the blood of my cats, will she? Not Granny and Jethro?"

I played along, maybe practicing for the real thing. "No, Mom, she won't bother the cats. She sucks the blood of goats. If there aren't any goats around, she just goes thirty." I rolled my eyes and sighed. "And yes, I'm using a condom, and no, the kids won't be chupacabras, okay?"

David was David again. "And the Sarge?"

I looked at him straight on, the way brothers and best friends do.

"Man, I haven't the slightest."

He nodded. "Yeah. Crazy old man, your dad."

We both fell silent. I did not notice his leg draw back, then kick the side of the coffee table, sliding free under my feet. The heel of my right foot slammed into the floor, jarring muscle and bone with the impact. He turned and moved to the kitchen at the unintelligible shout that flew from me, his hand and shoulders moving up in a shrug.

"So I lied. No quits."

Bastard.

I like working Sunday mornings. The video store is always quiet, giving me time to sort out the store as well as my head. The few customers I get in are either losers or video geeks, neither of which require much attention. She was the anomaly, beautiful and unschooled in popular American culture. Pure-bred.

I was putting together the latest Disney cardboard display when the door chime rang. Her eyes seemed to move several feet in front of the rest of her, pulling me along with them. I think she asked me a question several times before I realized I should listen to what she was saying, far too late to keep from making a fool of myself because she was laughing before I finally managed to answer her intelligibly.

"I'm sorry, uh, what?"

"Do you have *The Age of Innocence* by Scorcese?"

"Uh, yeah. Yes, we do."

She held a smile tightly, trying to keep from bursting into a grin.

"Well, where is it?"

I started, eyes widening. "Oh shit, I'm sorry. It's right over here."

I began moving toward the proper section, then stopped short, grimacing.

"Fuck, sorry, I didn't mean to say 'shit.' I mean, I usually don't curse a lot. Damn it."

I winced as I became aware of my clumsiness.

She laughed and touched my forearm, making me jump. "It's okay. I'm trying to learn English slang, so the curse words help me along."

"It's not English slang."

Her face opened, surprise spreading her eyes. "What?"

Finally. Something I could control here. "It's American slang. I'll give you an example. Someone from England would say that I was a 'stupid wanker.' An American would say that I was a 'stupid dumbass.' Same thing, but big difference, in the feel of it."

She smiled again. Christ, I really liked that smile.

"Should I refer to you as dumbass then, or do you have a name?"

I felt able to smile back without feeling like a complete idiot. "My name's Esteban. Most everybody calls me Steve."

"I am not everybody, Esteban. My name is Mercedes. Will you now show me where this movie is?"

"I was able to talk her into renting *Mean Streets* instead of her first choice. I suppose I convinced her that she would get more from the working-class language in Scorcese's earlier film. I also convinced her when she returned the video a couple of days later to go out with me.

Maybe I should have been leery when she explained to me on our first time out that she was a Mexican National, and a very wealthy one at that. Considering my parents' attitudes, I should have foreseen possible trouble. I guess that's what they mean by a blinding lust. I definitely should have heard alarms when she told me she was going to the law school at St. Mary's.

Knowing she was studying to be a lawyer, I shouldn't have been too surprised when she revealed to me, soon after we slept together for the first time, that once a month she changed into a hideous, blood-sucking monstrosity. By then, it was too late.

I was in love with her.

❀ ❀ ❀

We call my dad Sarge. Not just my brother, sister, and I, but everybody who comes into contact with him. Even my mom does it. I suppose she may call him by his name in bed when they are alone, but that's not something you want of think of your parents doing.

He had been an Airborne Ranger, served in 'Nam, medals and wounds, the real deal. Nobody had better screw with him 'cause he was the original badass. Fucking-A-Tweety. Which is probably why I mess with him every chance I get. I have a feeling this latest news I was going to give him would be the ultimate mindscrew.

My mom had been cool about it. At least once, I explained that this virus that Mercy has couldn't be passed on by sex. Whatever children Mercy may have would be unaffected. Seems that the ingestion of infected flesh was required to be a chupacabra. She cried a little bit, mostly because I was getting married, so I hugged her and told her we were going to stay in San Antonio, which made her feel better. Mercy's dad wants her near a major trade center involving NAFTA matters, making my hometown the perfect base for his company's American branch.

I stood at the sliding doors of the kitchen, watching my dad working on some battered appliance that someone else had thrown away. He was always finding objects that others considered junk, fixing them up and selling them at flea markets. My sister thought he did this because of his migrant worker background. I though he did it because he was crazy.

"Mi'jo, are you sure you don't want something to eat?"

"I rolled my eyes and shook my head, "No, Mom, I'm not hungry." Under my breath I muttered, "for the hundredth damn time."

Louder. "I need to go tell Dad, anyway." I put my hand on the latch. "Do you know if he's doing the flea market thing today?"

"He's staying home. 'Course, he's always changing his mind. You know your father."

"Yeah. Well . . . better get it over with."

This was kind of weird. I should have been anticipating how much this might mess with him. Instead, I actually wanted him to be happy for me.

I stepped out into the backyard, closing the doors behind me gently.

Though he always complained about his bad hearing, he always knows when someone is trying to be quiet or sneaky around him, even if he can't directly observe them. Maybe an instinct developed in the war. His head came up and turned, and when he saw me, he gave me one of his rare smiles. Damn it. It was almost as if he was deliberately trying to make this hard on me.

"What's up?"

"Hiya, Dad. Whatcha working on now?"

He held up the battered square of metal. "Toaster oven. The stupid-ass that threw it away. Coulda just replaced one of the heating elements. I figure I can get fifteen bucks for it."

I tried something I rarely attempt. I agreed with him. "Oh yeah, easily. Definitely a stupid-ass, who threw that away."

Mistake. I saw the look of suspicion wiggle onto his face, then burrow back down as he returned to working on the adopted appliance.

"So, you've talked to your mom already?"

"Yep." Shit. This was harder than I expected.

I sat on the edge of the concrete slab my parents call a porch. It is really more of a heat sink, soaking up the sun year round, always radiating heat, even during winter months. I made a show of retying my shoes, trying to think of a way of broaching the subject. How do you tell your father, a man who may be the biggest asshole in the world, that the woman you want to marry is a bloodthirsty, goat-rending creature of legend?

Screw it. Go in head first.

"Dad, I got. . . ."

He almost shouted, "So how's the rich girlfriend doing?"

Damn. It's like he knows. "She's cool. About Mercedes. . . ."

He laughed. "That name. Upper-class Mexicans."

I bristled. He saw me struggling to find an insult to defend her and surprised me for the second time of the day.

"I like her, though. She's a nice girl." He looked down, almost shyly, embarrassed for showing sensitivity.

"Yeah, all right. I like her too."

"You know, you two should get married."

Fucker! Psychic bastard, he does know.

I had to laugh. After all these years of conflict, me thinking my old man didn't have a clue, couldn't understand me. He knew. I realized then that despite all the crap that he had given me growing up, all the aggravation piled on top of hassle, I loved him. Now how the hell was I going to tell him about the bloodsucking part?

He solved the problem for me, effortless in his crude diplomacy.

"You know how you and Mercy are always trying to get me and your mom out to the ranch in Bulverde?"

"Yeah. . . ."

"Well, your sister and Benny want a weekend away to themselves. They want us to watch Jake. I was thinking this might be a good time to go. We could take the boy with us, let him run around, chase the chickens."

My sister and her husband have a little boy, Jacob. A three-year-old fireball, he'd definitely love the ranch. Only problem was, this weekend was scheduled for the Transformation. My baby, the Chupacabra, in all her glory.

Okay, work with this. If they came up to the ranch, they could relax, observe Mercedes in her other aspect, her more unsightly form. One thing about her transformation, it was ninety percent physical, mostly a severe case of the ugliness and the remaining percent a thirst for goats' blood. The only thing in danger were the goats around her.

"You know, Dad, that's a good idea. Let's do it." I stood, making a show of brushing off the seat of my jeans. "Tell little sister she's free for a weekend. Jake's all ours."

And the old man did it again, surprising and delighting me more than once in the same day. He smiled and used a word he often attributed to the language of hippies, enemies nearly as evil as the Viet Cong he had hunted in distant, sweaty jungles. "Cool."

I woke up confused. The light was different, brighter than what I was used to.

I remembered. We were at the ranch. Mom, Dad, Jacob, and I,

spending the weekend. I sat up in bed, turning to see an empty space beside me. She was gone, out into the woods.

I dressed, going to the kitchen in search of family and coffee. I found my mother swallowing caffeine and newsprint, looking fresh in the hill country air.

"Morning, Mom." I poured a cup and slumped in an empty chair, holding my head in my free hand. Mercy was always very horny before her transformation, leaving me to recover slowly the morning after, sore and exhausted.

"Esteban." Subdued, I suspected we might have been a little too noisy last night.

"Where are the guys?"

"They went for a walk. They knocked on your door, but they couldn't wake you up." Her eyebrows went up while her eyes studiously examined the paper in front of her. "Stay up late last night?"

"Uh, yeah." Uncomfortable silence.

I put my cup down. "Maybe I'll go catch up with them."

"I think they would like that." The paper in front of her must have been intensely interesting, considering she had not removed her eyes from it.

"Okay, see you in a while." I practically ran from the house.

The ranch covers forty acres, small in Texas terms. It is covered in enough tress and brush to hide a small army of medium-sized chupacabras, which was all that is needed. The only livestock on hand is a small herd of goats, for obvious reasons. These animals are kept penned to make them available to Mercedes as well as preventing them from defoliating the ranch land. It was to this containment area that I headed for, guessing that Jake would want to see animals that he couldn't see in his suburban environment.

Making my way across the ground separating the house from the goat pen, I noticed a rustling on my right, a shiver of brush and soil. I figured it was Mercy, shadowing me as she often did during these periods, protecting what she considered hers in the blur of her temporary savagery. I ignored it, trying to spot my father and nephew ahead in the brightening landscape.

"Uncle Steve!"

Jake sat on my father's shoulders, a grin splitting his face. Like most children, he delighted in being hoisted to a great height, to be taller than the adults he loved. I grinned back and picked up my pace. It was then that I saw the dog.

We found out later that one of the property owners bordering Mercy's ranch bred fighting dogs, abusing pit bulls to the point of their insanity. I personally don't care much for dogs. What happened next did not encourage a change of heart.

It appeared on the edge of the hard-pack, surrounding the goatpen, obviously drawn by the smell of herd animals. Spotting my father and nephew, it decided on a closer prey and began an attacking charge, hackles up, teeth bared. My father saw the dog at the same time I did. He quickly brought Jacob down, placing himself between the boy and the advancing animal, baring his teeth in a mirror image of the snarling canine. I broke into a run, hoping to intercept the animal before it reached them, not quite sure what I would do if I did.

It was only seconds into my dash when I realized that I would not make it in time. I pushed harder, the strain nightmarish. Then it was all taken out of my hands.

The dog began a leap, jaws wide to crush whatever flesh it fell upon. My eyes focused on bright, white teeth, nearly missing the blur flying from the brush bordering the coral. As the dog reached the apogee of its leap, black talons flew up from beneath a shadow, sinking deep into the dog's chest. The only way I can describe it is that it's as if a ballplayer slid into home plate while catching the ball as it sped toward him. The dog yelped, snagged in mid-air, flipped end over end to land in the pile of its own intestines. The blur that had just saved the lives of my father and nephew sped past me, still managing to touch me lightly in a familiar way, making me ache even in the rush of terror.

I ran over to Dad and Jake. They were holding tightly to each other, their eyes in a contest to see which could grow wider. When Jake began to whimper, my father pulled him closer, murmuring wordless comforts. I slowed and came to a stop at their shoulders, realizing I was close to tears, unsure if they sprang from fear or relief.

"Are you guys okay?" I heard my voice shake.

Dad nodded. He stroked Jacob's hair, then gestured with his index finger for me to come close. And he surprised me again, the cagey old bastard.

"Exactly what the hell do you get a chupacabra for a wedding present, anyway?" ❀

THE LIFEGUARDS' NUDE SWIM

by Jay Brandon

It was only in the water that he didn't feel awkward.

The summer he was fourteen, Louis Sommers—Lou—reinvented himself, developed his first full-blown crush, and wriggled in the hard grip of puberty. On dry ground he was likely to trip over nothing even when standing still, he was afraid of what sound might emerge from his mouth even when he could think of something to say, and at any moment he might have to worry about what angle his newly-independent penis was assuming. Fourteen was hard work. Its burden only floated off his shoulders when he slid underwater and went shimmering across the pool.

Under the water of the large public pool on the north side of San Antonio, Lou was as smooth as water himself, formless, a being of pure energy pulsing through its own element. He would go under at the side, consciously kick only once, and find himself across the pool. His legs, so awkward on land, carried him effortlessly through the water. He could turn almost at right angles and dart away anew, but because he couldn't judge his strength very well, he occasionally bumped someone treading through the four-foot water. Summer afternoons, that fellow bather was likely to be a woman or a child. When Lou's head broke water, if it was a woman's abdomen or thigh he'd contacted, Lou would be transformed into another pure element, fire. His face and possibly his swim trunks ablaze, he would mutter apology and quickly submerge again.

When he got tired of swimming there was nothing else to do. At the beginning of the summer Lou's best friend had moved away, to Kansas. "No one moves *to* Kansas," Lou had said incredulously, but his friend had only shrugged and disappeared. His absence left Lou lonely, but it also gave him the opportunity, Lou soon realized, to turn himself into a different person. He would be one of those guys who hung out at the pool, growing tanned and muscular and ogling girls openly rather than furtively, uttering carelessly clever come-ons in a bass voice.

He started by renaming himself. His parents had named him Louis, which had been okay when he was in third grade, but which, since he'd been a teenager, he'd realized was a completely unworkable moniker. Louis. Louisss. It was sissy at best, overly formal, dumb. That summer he named himself Lou instead. Now there was a man's name. Tough, competent. *Hey, Lou, hand me that wrench, willya?* "Lou," Louis would say to himself, in a chair beside the pool or looking into a mirror, fancying a cigarette dangling from the corner of his mouth.

But he had no one on whom to try the new name, no one to talk to about what was happening to his body (not that he would have, agh!), and his new personality remained a caustic shadow no one else could see or hear. He grew darker and stronger, said "hey" to a few people from school, and at suppertime trudged home alone.

The summertime pool was a manless world. Women from young to old lounged in the shade reading and chatting or went into the water with their young children. Occupants of those age groups weren't individually visible to Lou and his peers. Only other teenagers fully emerged from the background. There were more girls than boys who hung around the pool, and the girls seemed more confident in their skin. Seldom in the water, they would promenade the length of the pool, shoulders back and strides long, as if wearing expensive new dresses. Some of them already had attention-grabbing breasts and some had slimmer waists than others, but they all sported taut, uplifted bodies. Gravity hadn't touched these kids, and in spite of the evidence all around them, they had no inkling it ever would.

One afternoon as Lou ooched across the hot pavement in that awkward transition from the shade to the water, a black bathing suit and a slender arm brushed by him. "Sorry," the lifeguard said, and then as Lou stood literally open-mouthed and she rose into the air above him, taking long steps to climb into the tall lifeguard's chair. Sitting in the white wooden chair, she adjusted her baby blue cap, crossed her golden legs, and settled back, her shoulders spreading like wings.

Lou continued to stare until she glanced down at him and smiled so that he had to leap into the water and zoom to the far side of the pool. Even under water he could still feel the touch of her arm. He held onto that tactile memory as long as he could, late into that night.

Her name was Darla. As the summer progressed her long legs grew impossibly more golden. Her cap and sunblock kept her face several shades lighter. She had blue, blue eyes and a nose that when she grew older might be called "patrician"; it needed the balance of her smile, which appeared often, displaying teeth that dazzled like looking into the sun, and cheeks of perfect near-plumpness. Her long hair was blond, sometimes pulled back into a ponytail so that the sun stole its color unevenly, in swimmer's streaks a grown woman would have spent two hundred dollars to acquire in a salon.

She was perfect, yes, but what Lou loved about her was that she didn't seem to know it. Darla took her job very seriously, scanning the pool and tweeting her whistle kindly, but firmly, at rambunctious kids who banged into each other or hung on the ropes that separated the swim lanes. When the kids didn't respond swiftly enough Lou's whole body went stiff with the desire to smash their heads together.

He learned her schedule and was always there when Darla was on duty. He stared at her unselfconsciously until her gaze crossing him made Lou feel like an ugly voyeur. Then he would swim, trying to merge again into the mindlessness of the cool, clear water. On land, he thought about contriving to brush against her again, but decided against it, a decision reached by a committee of his squeamishness and his legs, which refused to carry him close to Darla.

He did occasionally sit on the edge of the pool beside her tall chair, both enjoying and mortified by the illusion of companionableness between them.

During her breaks Darla sat in the shade and read, sometimes paperback novels, sometimes thick textbook-looking tomes as if she were studying for a summer course. Technically, she wasn't unapproachable at such times, because occasionally one of her fellow lifeguards would saunter by and call to her, even stop to laugh, and when that happened Darla would answer pleasantly enough, but she held her place in her book all the while so that Lou was disgusted by the insensitivity of these clods who could interrupt her.

Gradually Lou's infatuation with her began to fade a little, crushed by its hopelessness, when one day in early August, school only two weeks away, he dove into one end of the big pool, scooted smoothly past a gang of kids, circled a middle-aged lady like a dolphin playing around a shrimp boat, rose up, submerged, and shot half the length of the pool like a missile. Surfacing, he more leisurely stroked to the side of the pool and out. As he sat and shook water out of his eyes, he heard a voice from above say, "You swim very well."

For a moment Lou feared fantasy had gotten the better of him, but when he looked up Darla was leaning over, looking down from her stilt chair at him, smiling.

"Really? Thanks." Lou scrambled to his feet, cleared his throat, and leaned one elbow against the long leg of her chair. "I've been practicing a lot," he said.

"I can tell."

He was thrilled not just by her reply that indicated she'd noticed him, but by the fact that he'd said two phrases to her. Desperately casting around for conversation, he thought of the month and said, "Almost school time again. You going to be a senior this year?"

"I just was," she said gently.

Which made her four years older than Lou, a different generation, an impossibility. Nevertheless Lou stood there for another fifteen minutes, and though he and Darla didn't exchange another word he felt they shared some attitude that set them apart from everyone else at the pool.

That evening he hurried home for dinner, ate it fast enough to choke, then put back on his still-damp suit, making his skin shrivel and pucker, and in his thongs nearly ran back to the pool. Lou was in that difficult transportation period—too young to drive, too old to be driven, too mature for a bicycle—that left him afoot a lot. Tonight he didn't mind. Needing a ride was part of his strategy. His plan was to stay at the pool until closing, maybe help Darla clean up, then let her offer him a lift home. Or if she wanted to stop somewhere for a Coke, well, he could spare the time.

Twilight was slow to come, then fast to depart. When Lou returned the crowd was thinning out. At closing time there were only a dozen or so adults and twice that many children. When the lifeguards blew their last whistle chorus at eight o'clock these slow-finishing customers leisurely gathered up their equipment while Lou silently urged them all to vanish. Darla climbed down from her perch. Across the pool another lifeguard, one of the girls, called to her about division of closing-up duties and Darla nodded. Then one of the boy lifeguards, one with huge shoulders and already-hairy legs stopped to tell Darla about some incident in the diving pool. Darla listened politely but seemed distracted. Lou was glad to see her get the pool-skimmer on its long pole and begin working, as if she were anxious to be off. When she saw him watching her she said, "Sorry, pool's closed."

"Oh, yeah, I know. I just thought—Do you need? No, guess—well, I've just got to wait for somebody, so I'll be, uh—" He nodded toward the parking lot, hoping she got the chain of associations. She watched him kindly but with slight puzzlement.

Lou went out through the men's changing room and put on dry short pants and t-shirt. By 8:15 he was sitting on a planter box outside the door of the pool, his wet bathing suit wrapped in a towel at his feet, watching dusk turn into night, deleting the nearby houses and turning up the volume of bird cries and squirrel rustlings. Night seemed to transport the pool into the country. The air didn't cool but the sun was no longer baking his skin. Lou sat and breathed deeply and listened for the sound of the pool's doors unlocking to admit her.

Insects joined the noise. Listening intently as he was, Lou could hear everything, except some sign that Darla was emerging. He stood and walked. All around the pool was a ten-foot brick wall that offered no handholds, peepholes, or good listening posts. When Lou came near the end of the wall that enclosed the twelve-foot deep diving pool he heard one rising laugh, then a splash, and he remembered the rumor.

It couldn't really be called a rumor—no one claimed personal knowledge—the story was more of a speculation. What did the lifeguards do after they were the only ones at the pool and night had fallen? There were closing-up chores and an adult supervising them, but the chores were light and the adult pool manager was always the first to leave, sometimes even before closing time. How did those half-dozen athletic teenage girls and boys use that magic hour when they alone owned the pool? Denied the water most of the day by duty, imprisoning them in their tall chairs, wouldn't they take a last dip after closing time? While relaxing, wouldn't they start talking, laughing together, wouldn't a boy's arm naturally go around a girl's shoulder? And there in the dark, deep water, only half-visible to each other, wouldn't they—

Lou remembered hearing a boy say it to another boy, staring at a girl lifeguard and fantasizing about closing time: "They strip down, all of them, and they swim naked. They swim around each other and through each other's legs, and breathe bubbles—"

"Even the girls?"

"They have to, it's part of the deal, like an initiation into the life-guards' club," the boy had answered knowledgeably. His friend wasn't quite convinced.

"How do you know? Have you seen 'em?"

"Wouldn't you?"

The smirking boy's last answer lingered in Lou's mind as he stood in the dark outside the wall. Wouldn't you, given the chance? Hell yes. But not Darla, studious Darla.

Lou listened and thought he heard low voices. It must be 8:30 by now, the chairs around the pool's edge would all be straightened, the water skimmed of leaves, the chemicals added to the dark water. The chores were done, but Darla remained inside with the others. What did he know about Darla? She was eighteen, bound for college in a few weeks; almost an adult, almost on her own. Who knew what experience she had, or wanted? He knew little more about her than he did about the other lifeguards, a brawny, easygoing group. Darla stayed in the pool with them, part of the gang.

He could picture her on the edge of the diving pool, making them wait for her. She was so easy in her body. He imagined calm, serious Darla seriously shedding her suit: reaching up to hook her thumbs in the shoulder straps of the one-piece black suit, pulling the straps out and down, over her shoulders, freeing her breasts, removing one arm at a time then peeling the suit down over her abdomen, over her hips, revealing whiter flesh at chest and hips that would display her nipples and hair as she pulled the suit down over her ankles and then stood, hands on hips, before diving into the pool, arcing out over the water in a monochrome rainbow of flesh.

Now Lou could hear nothing but the ripple of the water, night-tinged, oily, the pool's surface dancing high from the undulations within it. He turned suddenly and trudged home in his squishy thongs, droplets of water evaporating off his skin and being replaced by sweat. His towel made a damp stripe atop his shoulder.

That fall he took Basic Lifesaving and CPR at the YMCA.

The next summer when Lou took his place for the first time on the high seat, he didn't think that he was sitting where Darla's bottom had nestled. He didn't think about Darla any more. She had gone away to college and so except in the most technical sense no longer existed. Lou had a year of high school behind him now. He was no longer the panicked freshman. He had learned a little algebra, a dab of world history, and that it was possible to get from a class on the south end of the second floor of the main building, down to his locker on the first floor, and out to the annex in the six minutes alotted between classes.

He hadn't started dating, but he had contemplated the idea. He had been to half a dozen boy-and-girl parties. He had made the decision to try to dance rather than sit on someone's patio with forlorn superiority watching other people looking silly and having fun at it. He had stood at a girl's locker and talked to her for five minutes without shifting from foot to foot. Even the penis situation was under better control; Lou had learned the uses of a desktop, that straining with his arms or legs against an immovable object tended to deflate other body parts, and the disguises of pants folds.

What he thought about that first day as he climbed in his baggy trunks and white t-shirt to the high lifeguard's seat was the awful responsibility. He looked at all those children and few old people in the water, seeing them individually for the first time, and was struck cold by the dreadful possibility of making a fool of himself.

Because they all looked like they were about to drown. Eight-year-old boys pushed each other's heads under water. You could snap a skinny neck that way. Smaller kids swimming underwater for the first time banged their heads into the concrete side of the pool. And that old man floating on his back in the swim lane had obviously fallen asleep—or had he stopped breathing? Lou could have blown his whistle five times in his first minute on the job, and he was just about to leap into the water to begin CPR on a three-year-old girl doing a dead man's float when a hand encircled his ankle, holding him in place. Lou gasped but managed not to fall out of the chair.

He looked down and saw Susan looking up at him with mild, cheerful concern. She wore a sort of inverted white sailor's cap over her dark hair. But the sun had stolen under that cap some time: he could see a few freckles across her nose.

Shading her eyes with her hand, Susan asked, "You okay?"

"Sure, sure."

"It's easy, Lou. Just don't drift off and don't let your legs fall asleep."

"Thanks."

Susan gave him not much of a smile and walked away. Just doing her job. Susan was great. She not only had a year's more experience than Lou, but also an undemonstrative authority that had led the manager to name her head lifeguard over no dissents. Knowing Lou was new, Susan had taken him in hand in such a companionable, unforceful way that every instruction she gave him seemed to be followed by an unspoken, "But you knew that, didn't you?" She'd raise her eyebrows and Lou would nod.

He knew he'd seen Susan around school during the year, but she hadn't made an impression. One of those girls walking in straight lines, pressing books against her chest, probably spent her free time making pep squad spirit posters. But at the pool she seemed the center of all order. He could always find her, in her bright blue bathing suit. He watched her walking away in her careful stride, one foot in front of the other, no roll to her hips. Lou's eye caught on the thong of her whistle at the back of Susan's neck. He would have liked to adjust it for her.

When Lou scanned the pool again it seemed less disorderly and life-threatening. But his shoulders went tense again as a whistle blast shredded the serenity. All the swimmers stood silent, looking across the pool. Julia sat in the lifeguard's chair on the other side, knees apart, her wild red hair unfettered by cap or comb. She still had the whistle in her mouth, but it was hard to see what had driven her to shrill it. After a moment Julia waved a finger toward a clump of boys, who goggled at her and stood in the water afraid to resume any activity. People relaxed, among them Julia, who sat back and grinned across the pool at Lou. He knew why she'd whistled. Things had just been too quiet: the whistle was only crazy Julia shaking things up.

The day burned on. Children reddened, mothers took them home, others took their place. Later in the afternoon more high school kids appeared. A couple stopped to chat with Lou. He kept his eye on the water as he talked. He stayed alert, but he had relaxed on the job. Thinking about it, Lou couldn't remember, in all the hours he'd spent at this pool, ever seeing a lifeguard jump into the water to make a rescue. The big main pool was only four feet deep at its deepest. Children who couldn't swim were closely attended by a parent, and even if they weren't, the pool was usually crowded; any sputtering child could find an arm to grab within a few feet.

Lou had never heard of a drowning at the pool. The rumors were from an earlier epoch when there'd been a ten-meter platform at the diving pool. Stories persisted of a boy or boys who had run off the platform and splatted into legend on the twenty feet of concrete sidewalk separating the main and diving pools.

But no drownings. The pool rumors were of other matters.

Lou had started working at noon. He took his dinner break early, sitting at a plastic table in the shade and eating a hamburger from the snack bar. His eyes kept flicking from person to person around him in the snack area and his ears kept snapping up at the sound of squeals from the pool.

Soon Julia appeared on her own break. She had swum across the pool. When she leaned over Lou from behind, suddenly kneading his shoulders, water dripped from her suit onto his hair, down his neck.

"How's it going, Champ?" He could hear the grin in her voice. "Take it easy, we haven't lost a lifeguard yet."

"Ha ha," Lou said, more than the old joke deserved. Julia laughed at his reaction, threw herself down into a chair beside him, and began eating the remainder of Lou's french fries. She fluttered her eyelashes in a mockery of coyness or seductiveness as she fed a particularly long, rippled fry into her still-laughing mouth. Lou shook his head in appreciation. Julia was lanky, one might almost say gangly; her legs tended to sprawl. The regulation one-piece blue lifeguard's suit (the pool manager had decided last year's black was too mournful) fit her tightly across the bust and loosely in the waist. She had a wide mouth, usually open, and freckles here and there, everywhere Lou could see. She wasn't, objectively speaking, an attractive girl, but you could have fooled Julia on that score; she flirted as easily as she swam, and she swam like a demon.

Looking over Lou's head, Julia said, "We gonna break the kid in tonight?"

Susan was standing over him, her face showing no sign that Julia had spoken to her. Susan had a clipboard.

"Lou, you take the diving pool when your break's over, okay?"

"Okay, sure."

After a day in the sun, Susan was still pale-skinned in the shade. She was careful to use sunblock and a loose white jacket. Susan wouldn't lose a day's work to too much sun. But where her suit slipped down a bare half inch at its top you could see that in fact her chest had tanned a bit. It was two or three shades darker than her natural white color could be glimpsed at the tops of her breasts.

"What about me, boss?"

Susan watched her clipboard, not glancing at Julia. "You see if you can take Lou's place and do as good a job, okay?"

Julia widened her mouth at Lou. "Ooh, if you'd known, you could have left me a love note hidden in the umbrella. Or did you?"

Susan tapped Julia lightly on the top of her flaming head with the clipboard and left. Turning back from watching her walk away, Lou said, "What was that you said about breaking in the new kid?"

Julia grabbed the last french fry and wiggled her eyebrows, Groucho-like, at him.

At Lou's approach Brent stood atop the lifeguard stand at the diving pool and stretched. "Oh, man, thanks. I'm sweating." This was akin to a mud wrestler announcing she'd gotten a trifle dishevelled on the job, but Brent said it as if his sweat had a particularly urgent quality. Brent was smooth and hairless, like an Olympic swimmer, muscles countable along his ribcage. His tightly curled blond hair was cut short, almost invisible in the sun. Brent looked like a boy stripped down to essentials for the last sprint into manhood. He wore the small tight Speedo version of the male lifeguard's official swimsuit. Lou looked away from him, into the pool.

"You know, you close up the diving pool about half an hour early, when it starts getting shady at this end so you can't see the bottom any more," Brent explained.

"Yeah, thanks."

"Whenever you think it's time," Brent added. "Well, see you."

Brent looked carefully around, then dived from his high perch, arcing upward then down, entering the water with almost no splash. Lou watched. Yes, he could still see to the deep bottom of the diving pool. He saw Brent touch it, push off, and swim easily the twenty-five meters across to the other side.

Lou took his place, barely hearing the cries and shouts of the children any more. He tweeted his whistle once to tell a five-year-old to stop running on the wet concrete, and settled into lifeguard's isolation on his tall chair.

He gazed around the pool. Brent had walked to the other pool, where Susan had stopped him. She pointed at something on her clipboard, then they both looked up at Lou. They were too far away, he couldn't hear what they said. He couldn't even tell whether Susan smiled as she turned away.

It was true, even while the air was still bright enough to see a hundred yards across to the clock over the pool's main doors, a dark shadow grew in the depth of the diving pool. At 7:30 Lou hastily blew his whistle to close the diving pool. After he'd made sure the last complaining kid had climbed out and was trudging back to the main pool, Lou dived in, penetrating that darkness at the bottom of the pool, spreading his arms and legs wide, stretching for any contact of flesh. The water enfolded and extended him. But except for him, the diving pool was empty.

He had it skimmed and was standing there absent-mindedly when the chorus of closing-time whistles from the other pool revived him. Lou realized he was tired, with the weird electric tiredness of youth: tired of sitting, tired of being alert. He wanted to swim the length of the pool and back.

The main pool emptied out. Lou jumped into it and fetched out a few left-behind toys, then began turning the pool chairs around so dew wouldn't collect on their seats. The manager watched him approvingly. "Somebody's been teaching you," he said. That was a signal for Susan to come up beside Lou, smiling. "We can handle it, Coach."

The pool manager coached track and soccer at the high school during the school year. A compact man who never went in the water, at the end of the day his shoulders slumped. "Thanks, Susan," he said, and trudged away. Coach was the only one of them who had to get home to a family. Watching him walk away filled Lou with energy. He stretched his arms sideways and up. Susan drifted away.

When he looked for her she was down at the side of the diving pool with the rest of the lifeguard crew: Julia, Brent, and big galumphing Shad, who had nearly dislocated Lou's shoulder giving him a welcoming slap on the back during the training session. They were gathered around Susan and her clipboard, obviously getting the next day's assignment. In the twilight, fingers of night stealing through the air, they looked like an intense business group, or a huddle of athletes.

Lou joined them. Susan turned her back on the diving pool and he did the same, looking over her shoulder. Unaccountably Susan said, "Don't worry, Lou, it"—then Julia interrupted the reassurance by standing close in front of Lou. She smiled wickedly at him and lifted his arms over her shoulders, as if drawing him in for a kiss. But she was just trapping his arms, so that when his trunks slid down his legs, he couldn't grab to stop them.

"Hey!" Lou shouted, with Julia still standing in front of him, still holding his arms, but now Lou's swim trunks were on the concrete apron at his feet. He tried to bend to retrieve them, lost his balance and stepped back, out of the trunks because Julia had her foot on them. So then he was naked, completely, on the edge of the diving pool, the boy lifeguards on either side of him, Julia still in front, grinning widely, Susan turning toward him with a slight smile as if apologizing for the horseplay, but that didn't appease Lou at all. His face was radiating heat as if he would burn them all. He was just about to scream, or leap, or turn and swing his fist into a grinning face, when big Shad gave him a remarkably gentle push and Lou, still off-balance, went flailing back into the pool.

That was a relief in a strange way. He was clothed in water. Lou sank into the familiar element, bubbles rising, the water cooling his embarrassment. But even before he started rising again, he knew what he would find above: the others waving his swim suit mockingly, then running away with it and the rest of his clothes so Lou would have to dig up an old towel or an umbrella cover or call his parents and have to explain the lifeguards' stupid initiation or in some other horribly embarrassing way get home.

But when his head broke the surface they were all still there. Julia was holding Lou's swim trunks all right, smiling and waving at him, but the others weren't laughing. They watched Lou rather studiously, like a group of doctors conferring over a difficult case. Lou felt his insides liquefy. They were going to do something even worse to him.

When the other lifeguards saw that he had come up safely, the group broke apart. The boys walked along the edge of the diving pool to Lou's left. Julia stayed where she was. Susan walked the other direction along the edge of the pool, tossing her clipboard back toward the main pool. It hit the ground with an enormously loud clap, like the clop of a Clydesdale's hoof on concrete. Lou stared at her, finding it hard to believe that kindly, serious Susan was part of this. She must be the organizer, in fact. Lou trod water, wanting to break for safety but seeing no opening. They were surrounding him.

Then Susan, nearly in profile to him, crossed her arms over her breasts, caught the straps of her swimsuit, and pulled them down her arms. Lou stared. The suit peeled down easily over Susan's damp, thin body. Freed of the restraint of the suit, her breasts were bigger than he'd imagined, uptilted from her chest.

Susan didn't pose. She pulled her suit to the ground, stepped out of it, put her hands on her hips for a moment, and dove into the pool twenty feet from Lou.

Now he was terrified. He heard a splash from the other direction, saw that Brent had disappeared, saw Brent's tiny puddle of Spandex suit lying on that side of the diving pool, and almost panicked. Lou swam forward, aiming for the side of the pool and out, but Julia still stood there in front of him. "Watch this," she said, and for once she wasn't talking about herself. She pointed, and Lou turned and looked at the low diving board, where Shad stood, naked, hairy, massive. Shad took two long strides, bounced on the end of the board, and went impossibly high, so it seemed he might come down anywhere in the diving pool, or beyond it. At the top of his arc he pulled his legs in to his chest and entered the water in a cannonball. Lou's fear subsided long enough for him to wonder, Didn't that hurt?

Shad's splash pattered down on the whole pool like a cloudburst. Using it like a curtain rising, Julia took her turn. Of course, she made more of a production of it than the others had. She pulled the strap down over her left arm, let that breast pop out, then cocked her hips and shoulders, combed back her curly mane with her fingers, and stood there like an Amazon.

It was Brent who came up five feet from Lou, said, "Knock it off, Julia," and sent a splash toward her. Julia dropped her pose and her swimsuit, winked at Lou from the edge of the pool and then dived over him. For an instant her whole pale, freckled, muscled body was displayed above him, but it was too fast for Lou to take it in. When Julia splashed behind him he swam away, waiting for her to come up next to him or grab his leg underwater.

He was free then. His suit lay on the concrete. He could swim out, grab it, and be dressed again in a flash. He could grab all the others' suits too, if he wanted. It was this inexplicable freedom that stopped him at the edge of the pool, treading water and staring.

For that moment he seemed alone in the diving pool. All the others had submerged. Just as that aloneness sent prickles of suspense up his back again, Shad surfaced on the far side of the pool, coming up half out of the water like a whale breaching, then dived back into the water, displaying for a moment his strapping white buttocks and thick legs as he went under again.

Nearby Susan's head emerged from the water less spectacularly. Her dark hair flattened on her head and neck and her face looked more bare as she shook water from it. Then her eyes opened and her face was no longer featureless. Susan had brown eyes, warm and sincere, but in this near-darkness their color disappeared, leaving dark spots in her pale face. She didn't look familiar until she spoke.

"Sorry, Lou," she said, continuing the apology that had been so bizarrely interrupted. "It's just a little—thing we do. I would have warned you, but. . . ." Lou heard the unspoken, *You understand, don't you?*

Susan turned and swam, out toward the center of the pool. She almost met Brent there, as he swam eel-like across the pool from side to side, arms at his sides, but before their paths met Susan went underwater and they made a giant X without touching. Shad went floating by on his back, idling, raising one long arm at a time like a steamboat's paddlewheels. Julia swam circles around him without Shad's seeming to notice.

Lou let himself drift away from the edge, back into the pool. With trepidation he ducked his head under the water, then with long sideways strokes swam downward toward the center and the bottom. The water flowed sensuously around him. His eyes were open but he couldn't see anything around him. It was like swimming through night, a lonely comet.

There was a disturbance in the water near him. Somehow he knew it was Julia, but they didn't touch. She angled by, changed direction to slip by him again, then broke for the far side of the pool.

When he came up Brent was talking to Susan across the pool. Lou stared unhappily, thinking this was where it began: the kissing, the sex play, and it was Susan and Brent who were together. But they just chatted for a moment, then Brent swam away and Susan pulled herself up and sat unselfconsciously on the side of the pool. She saw Lou staring at her and smiled at him.

His staring was somehow ineffective. There she was in front of him, the first naked girl he'd ever seen, but the effect wasn't what Lou would have expected. There was nothing pornographic about it, barely even erotic. Standing close to Susan in order to peek down her swimsuit at the cleft between her breasts would have made him breathe faster and have to jump into the water, but seeing her whole unclothed body removed any taint of nastiness. It was just Susan, all over. Her whole body looked like Susan. Lou swam toward her. Susan slipped back into the water and swam to meet him. She put her hand on his shoulder for just a second, said, "Okay?" and he nodded. She swam and he turned to swim with her.

For half an hour they played like dolphins. The lifeguards dived, floated, stroked elegantly through the water. Occasionally they touched, but that was incidental. Water connected them. They turned in unison, slid across nearly the same space of water at nearly the same moment, glided like torpedoes fired from parallel tubes. The most nearly erotic moment was when Julia climbed out the ladder on the far side of the pool from the diving boards and urgently waved Lou out. He climbed out and stood in front of her with his back to the water. Julia made him clasp his hands together, put her hands on his shoulders, to make him stoop a little, said, "Ready?" then stepped into the hammock of Lou's hands and shot upward, straightening her legs and her body as Lou straightened too, so that he threw her up and over his head. Julia bent forward and smoothly guided her downward course into a dive, as Lou turned and thought he saw her smile as she disappeared into the water, her long legs seeming to hang in the air for a long moment. It was only then he felt how her whole body had gone sliding up next to his, so close the hairs on his arms were still standing from the electric current her passage had raised. But when it happened he wasn't thinking about that. He was concentrating on keeping his hands together, on being strong enough for Julia, rising in concert with her and heaving hard enough that she wouldn't hurt herself by falling back to the concrete. He was concentrating on the elegance of her dive.

When Julia came up Susan frowned at her. "Okay, Mom," Julia laughed.

Except for the splashing they were quiet, mindful of the houses within two hundred yards of them. But the darkness was isolating. Lou felt the black diving pool lifting slowly into the sky, becoming one with the night. They were the only five people alive.

It wasn't even late when Susan said, "Well. . . ." and they all knew what she meant. There were no objections, no cries for one last dive. They weren't children, and it was the end of a working day for all of them. Susan picked up her swim suit and walked toward the ladies' changing room, her cute little behind looking sexy as hell as her white jacket fell over it.

It was a night of images Lou wanted to hold tight forever, but as pictures they were elusive. He lay in bed that night remembering, but the images flattened out. It had been his first sight of breasts, but the body parts weren't primary in his memory as they should have been. What he remembered were Julia and Susan talking as they sat on the side of the pool, Julia's chin resting on one raised knee, her other foot trailing into the water, an unaccustomed seriousness on her face, as if Susan had infected her. He remembered Susan racing Shad across the pool. Shad was at least a foot taller and bore those heavy shoulders and arms, but Lou noticed for the first time how much of Susan's height was legs, and how the muscles in her thighs bunched large as she stooped to dive, how her legs tapered to almost nothing. At Brent's soft starter's call Susan and Shad seemed to elevate out over the water. Susan entered it farther and shallower than Shad, she was swimming while he was still fighting back to the surface, and Susan of course had much less meat to propel through the water. Lou realized it wasn't just quiet authority that had earned Susan the head lifeguard's spot, as she touched the opposite wall a good five feet ahead of Shad.

Not the next night. Not every night. Lou didn't spend the days quivering with anticipation. The lifeguard crew understood wordlessly whether it was a good night for an after-hours swim. They'd glance at each other and shrug or shake their heads. "Got a date," Julia said once, making Lou understand definitively that she wasn't interested in him that way; flirting was just the way she was. Another night when Shad bowed out for the same reason, Lou thought, But how could you pass up this for an ordinary date with an ordinary girl?

There were other lifeguards, but no one else in the after-hours group, which made Lou proud but also made him wonder at the selection standards. Brent was a smart guy, near the top of his class, soon to go off to college to major in pre-med, but his intelligence was so school-focused that he could say things like, "Nice night, huh?" and think he was making multi-layered conversation. Lou had taken Shad for a big clod because he was that, big. But it was Shad who came up beside him that first night in the diving pool and said, "It was my idea to yank your trunks off like that. Sorry. My first time, they just told me to take mine off and when they tried to make me, people got hurt. And I've seen where everybody else takes off their suits first and then the new kid stands there just shaking, not wanting to be, like, in a spotlight, you know?, still thinking it's some kind of prank. It's—I don't know—harder if you make the person do it themselves. You know?"

"Yeah, thanks," Lou had said, touched by the odd brutish sensitivity.

Julia only grew more herself when naked. She was what she was, not faking and not hiding anything. Her winks and grins at Lou across the daytime pool grew no sexier than they'd been the first time she'd met him.

And Susan. He loved Susan. When he'd first met her she'd seemed such an ordinary girl. Maybe she was. Lou had a glimmer of near-insight. Maybe all ordinary girls were so extraordinary. On duty he noticed that Susan not only whistled, she clapped. When a three-year-old boy willingly put his face underwater for the first time, when an eight-year-old swam the length of the pool, Susan noticed and applauded softly, but somehow aiming her applause so that the kid noticed and blushed and acknowledged the praise. Susan spoke to everyone by name, passing among them as gently and as unthanked as a drift of cool breeze in July.

A year ago Lou imagined that naked people were fundamentally different. That summer taught him otherwise. Susan remained herself when she took off her suit. Even her black pubic hair was serious. It lay disciplined and naturally combed, parted down the middle like the hair of a 1920's clerk. Julia's was like Julia, a wild red bush, even when wet.

They were easy and unselfconscious with each other in the water, but still blushed or chuckled when the subject of dating came up. Lou began to suspect, without dwelling on it, that they were all virgins. Certainly they were with each other. But when the time came that they wanted to share their bodies with someone else, they would be a little more knowledgeable, a little less frantic, a shade less awkward than other first-time lovers. They had given each other that.

One night as they sat on the edge of the dark diving pool Lou turned to Susan, surprised to find that it took all his courage to do so, and said, "So, uh, did—Would you like to go get a Coke or something?"

She sounded slightly puzzled as she answered, "I guess. Why, is there—?" then she turned and looked into his face and saw what he meant and her expression turned stricken. "Oh, Lou," she said. "I'm sorry."

He was sorry, too. Sorry that he had risked spoiling things by asking her. He suddenly realized that amid all the fantastic rumors, there was one hard fact. He had never heard of lifeguards' dating each other. They were the most intimate of working crews, they pulled together like slave-sailors chained to the same oar, but by the same token they had to go elsewhere to find the mystery of romance. In the instant of Susan's looking remorsefully at him, he realized all that, and that that was what Susan was begging him to understand. That was why she apologized, afraid she had held out to him something that didn't exist.

He smiled at her. "It's okay," he said. And it was. Understanding made him feel closer to her than if she'd accepted his invitation.

Susan must have understood, too. She pulled him to his feet, smiled ruefully, and hugged him. It was Lou's only full-body contact of the summer. The part of the touch that meant most to him was her cheek on his shoulder, soft as the touch of night. After a moment Susan's nipples crinkled against his chest. He didn't even know what that meant until long afterwards, but he knew something more significant as he stood holding her. Susan would never be more, or less, than a great friend. A friend with crinkled nipples. To her he was a friend with, once, a little pressure against her thigh.

Summer ended without a big splash. The management held a pool-closing party for the lifeguards, during which Coach Hansen collected their keys and handed out praise and they all watched the pool drain, down to a foot or so in the big pool, a few dark feet in the diving pool, that would grow murkier and more leaf-strewn during the fallow months.

It wasn't a big parting. Brent went away to Baylor, but the rest of them were in the same high school. Shad was a captain and star of the football team. On the few occasions when Lou saw him, Shad would give him a big unsecretive grin and another slap on the back. Julia ran with a popular senior crowd. The smiles she flashed at Lou were no more intimate than the ones she gave everyone.

Susan was a year older than Lou, they didn't share any classes, and the halls were too busy for chats. The first time Lou saw her walking away from school with a boy's arm around her shoulders he felt a sharp pang, partly of jealousy but also akin to the loss a man feels when his daughter starts dating. He wanted to have a talk with the boy.

In December, there was a dance, for which the gym was decorated with cut-out moons and stars illustrating the theme "Magic in the Night." The decorations didn't do it. Lou knew magic. Magic was a friend of his. This was no magic. But the occasion was special, because it was his first date. Her name was Patty. Lou had first been attracted to her when he'd seen her during a math quiz pause, chewing her pencil, then laughing silently as she started working the problem. She should have someone to share her laughs with, he'd thought.

The night of the dance, in her first formal, Patty's exposed collarbones looked both timid and hopeful. They were dancing the first dance when

Lou caught sight of Susan. She saw him too, over her own date's shoulder. Glancing at his date, Susan shot at Lou a smile that seemed to carry a question, as if she asked, *Is she more like Julia? Or like me?* Or maybe just wishing him luck, in a secret-sisterly way. It was a mix, and Lou understood everything blended into Susan's smile.

"Who are you smiling at?" Patty asked.

Shifting his gaze a fraction, which changed his focus, Lou said, "At you."

Shyly, but meeting his eyes, she smiled back. ❀

WORKING SATURDAY

by Camilla Carr

I shouldn't have done it. I just never should have told Lydelle Witt that I would work for her on Saturday. But she had been good to me. Since I started losing my eyesight last November, Lydelle had agreed not only to drive me to work when I had to give up driving my car, but for three dollars an hour, she had agreed to stay at my office and do the work I could no longer see to do. Which was simply all of the bookkeeping for Haggard Funeral Home. Needless to say, I was not especially eager to let Lester Haggard know that I could no longer *really* see because I was afraid he might replace me. I would have! But since Lester was only here when we had a funeral (he and his wife Organ, named after a pedal-organ, not a body-one! had their main funeral home in Odell, a few miles away) and when they were here, they were both so distracted by changing body fluids and whatnot, such as comforting the bereaved family, that they had hardly a moment to devote to what I was doing or how I was doing it or even *if* I was doing it. So they really didn't know Lydelle was working for me. They just thought she was here, paying her respects, and whenever she sat for a body, they just thought she was doing me a favor. Which she was!

But this Saturday morning, Lydelle couldn't stay. Her oldest daughter was in from Austin, and Lydelle said she would pick me up and drive me, but that she was unable to sit with the body that had just come in last night from Rosevine, Texas.

So she helped me out of the car and into the funeral home, and we turned on the lights to my office, and we filled up and started the coffee pot, and then she was on her way.

I walked on in to where the body was to tell old Mr. Hack Penn that he could go on home. He had been there all night. He always sat overnight with the bodies, as neither me or Lydelle would.

Hack had fallen asleep in a chair. (I knew this because he was snoring). But when I walked in, he woke up. "Oh, hi there, Precious," he said. (I can't help it! That is my name and will always be my name, and although I have gone through life just begging people to call me Helen or Dorothy or Evelyn or some adult kind of a name, none will! I am eighty and Precious and blind at a bat and can't help any of it!)

"You can go on home now, Hack," I said. And after a cup of coffee, he did. But not before filling me in on what he knew about the body in the coffin, which was very little. She had been born here fifty-three years ago, a Pauline Smith, but had moved off to Fort Worth after she got married, eventually settling in Rosevine, (wherever that is!) Her parents were a Mr. Wilson Smith and a Mrs. Beulah Smith but of course there were so many Smiths buried out in our cemetery, it was hard to remember one from the other and how they were all related, especially if you hadn't really known them! Anyway, Pauline Smith (who had married and become a Jones) wanted to be buried close to her parents. Right here in the Chillicothe cemetery.

So here she was.

Hack went on home, and I went back to my office and had put the sugar in my coffee and was stirring in the cream when the first visitor arrived.

"Good morning," I said. "Are you here to see Mrs. Jones?"

"She is here, then?" a man's voice asked.

"As far as I know," I said. "That's what I was told. Are you a family member?"

"Not exactly," he said. "Have any of them been here?"

"I just got here a minute ago, so I don't know. Would you like a cup of coffee?"

"No, ma'am."

"Would you like to view the body?" I asked. "Pay your respects?"

"What I would like is to sit right here in your office and watch the visitors come in. Can we turn this light off?" he asked. "And pull the door closed a bit?"

I'm sure I must have looked very puzzled. Anyway, the next thing I knew, the room grew dark when he shut the light off.

"You're sure you won't take any coffee?" I asked.

"No," he said. "And I'd appreciate it if you'd turn the coffee pot off. I need it to look like nobody's here. I want you to go back in the restroom," he said. "And stay there."

"I can't do that," I protested. "I'm paid to watch this place. What's going on?"

"I'm the FBI," he said. "And I'm looking for a couple of folks."

I'm sure my mouth formed a great big O and my two blind eyes just rolled back in my head! I would have left right then, but the front door opened and here came some people in. There was considerable commotion and crying, so I figured it must be the family.

"Go out and get them to sign the guest book," he said. "If anyone of them is named Driskell or Reese Jones, come back and tell me."

I went out there, my insides shaking, and did as he told me, except I introduced myself, since I couldn't see the guest book. "Hello," I said. "I'm Mrs. Precious Connally. I'm blind and can't see you—are you the family of Mrs. Pauline Jones?"

Someone spoke. A woman. "I'm her oldest daughter, Virginia," she said, fighting grief and tears. "And this is my baby brother, Reese, our middle brother, Driskell, our oldest brother Howard and his wife, Roberta, and our baby sister, Willeen. . . ."

I hadn't even welcomed them good before that FBI man was behind me, saying something like, "Hands up, FBI."

I found out later they had been looking for Reese and Driskell Jones for over five years. If their mama hadn't died, the FBI probably never would have found them! Of course, they had to arrest those brothers on the Saturday morning I was working! I can't describe the uproar right then and there, with family members being hauled off, and bereavement turning from astonishment to outrage and all! What chaos! The funeral had to be postponed! It was several days later when Mrs. Pauline Jones finally got her service, since the whole family had left for Dallas to try to get attorneys!

The news spread through town like fire. Lydelle and her daughter from Austin couldn't get there fast enough. When I told her what happened,

Lydelle was so jealous, she asked for a raise! But that was *it*, for me. I told Lydelle she could have the job. I was just too old and blind for any more funeral home shenanigans. But if she got in a jam and couldn't do it, I just might consider working Saturdays. ❀

CROSSINGS

by Jan Epton Seale

They say that astronauts' hands float when they sleep. The hands of Carlos float, touching lightly the underside of his grave, beautifully manicured hands with rings. He's finished clapping. He'd have slapped his knees if he could, bent over double, red-faced from laughter. It was a story that good, what happened when his memory crossed the Rio Grande.

One saved such stories for *Tripa* club meetings, held under the stars and the mesquites on somebody's ranch, the tangled *tripas* sizzling on the grill and plenty of cold Carta Blanca.

All who knew him agree: Carlos would need a story like that to keep him entertained in eternity. For Carlos had a throttle that was wide open all the time. He was good at many things and excessive at most. *¡Impresionante! ¡Asombroso!* Bigger than life, he left it, moving off all at once, laughing and singing, in his prime.

Some deplore the circumstances, a boating accident, while others secretly admire the timing (a double-lived life, a hundred years packed into fifty). Without decline. Without forgetfulness, arthritis, or a clogged heart when the years of feasting played out their chemistry in his veins. "God deliver me from old age," he'd roar privately when one of his elderly patients hung on to life past season.

As many meals as could be a party, Carlos made them so. As many nights as could be reveled in, Carlos planned and executed. Flying in from a bank or a medical or an alumni or a philanthropic gathering, he would call home from 35,000 feet. "Go get some meat," he'd tell his wife Judy, "I want a cookout. Get fifteen pounds of fajitas and a dozen T-bones. And get a video. And call the Peñas and the Karams."

For his wife's birthday party, he had his representative claim the flag that had flown over the capitol in Austin that day and deliver it personally to her.

Once Carlos bought a ranch in the next county and *then* informed his family. Another time, he remembered a marimba band he'd heard deep in Mexico, traced them down and imported them, crossed them, for a *pachanga* in his McAllen backyard. Of course, first he had to cross a trio of workers to build a *palapa* for their stage.

Carlos loved crossings. He was one himself, born a South Texan and sent back to school in Guadalajara to learn proper Spanish. He never recognized el río as anything but a piece of geography. Meeting a cousin in Sonora, a crony in Mazatlán, friends for supper in Reynosa, these were as natural to him as daylight.

In his casket, open at the back of Our Lady of Sorrows, he lay smiling, filling the whole space, full-chested, his hair still black and beautiful, his mustache commanding, his lingering presence oddly comforting (acting as both cause and effect). But for little things like breath and pulse, he would have thundered to the mourners, "Come in! Come in! So nice to see you!" folding each shaky tearful admirer in a double *abrazo*, his potpourri of cumin and garlic and beer and shaving lotion and disinfectant blending as all the incense they would ever need.

So for these and a thousand other reasons, his wife, his five children, and the general South Texas population were loath to grant Carlos his longstanding wish for a *short* happy life. Notwithstanding, she and the children determined he must have the most beautiful, the grandest monument ever to grace Roselawn.

Still, a year passes, then two. His followers, many of them his patients, continue their pilgrimage to his grave. Coordinated offerings of aqua and fuchsia, ribbons and plastic chrysanthemums, stuffed animals, notes ("Thank you, Dr. G., for saving my precious Julio," *"Gracias a Dios a Ti "*). One or two mourners confront Judy, ask where's the gravestone. "It's on order," she tells them.

Finally Judy wakes one morning with her grief intact, contained: she can act. She calls a designer. Then Mr. Gonzalez, the local monument dealer, seeing that Judy wants to order something bigger than the United

States, suggests they go to Mexico, to a stone cutter up the river. They'll cross at Roma and head west. After all, death is done large and well in Mexico.

"Don't get it in Mexico," one son upstate says with an authority she is accustomed to. "You'll have too hard a time crossing it."

"Your dad never had any trouble crossing things." She has grown her own authority. And he knows to leave well enough alone.

It's a headstone but it's shaped like a sarcophagus. Carlos isn't inside but he might be, to the stranger's eye. The structure is ten feet long with a giant bivalve seashell carved in the middle like the one Botticelli's naked, wild-haired Venus steps from. In South Texas yard art, *La Virgen*, blue-clad, demure, steps from the shell. Judy smiles, wondering which woman Carlos would prefer. Neither will be on this one. Just the shell imprint on three tons of cantera mounted on a concrete base.

Men will haul the stone out of the Sierra Madres, God only knows how, maybe from a quarry near Horsetail Falls where Carlos went many times in his fifty packed years. He loved the mountains.

It's going to be too plain. Judy chooses blue and yellow tiles for a border.

Three months pass and Mr. Gonzalez calls. *El monumento* is ready. They must go and get it. Bring *pesos*. She meets him at the Roma crossing, parking her car and riding over with him in his pickup pulling a flatbed trailer. Outside Miguel Aleman, they pull into the stone yard.

Judy goes inside to settle up. First there's small talk, condolences, a bit of sympathetic sighing, then a deliberately complicated writing of the receipt, to justify the cost. All this takes awhile and when she comes out and walks back through the broken brick and dogs and children to where Mr. Gonzalez is, the stones are already loaded. A couple of dusty workers are tying ropes over six huge mounds wrapped in, of all things, old cardboard boxes. There's lettering of orange juice and green beans and toilet paper and starch covering her husband's memory. She can't see the *cantera* but Mr. Gonzalez seems satisfied, explaining how the sections will be fitted together.

Three tons of rock wrapped in cardboard and balanced on a flatbed trailer. It is a unique sight. They wind slowly back through Miguel Aleman and cross the small bridge, lowering to the U.S. side to idle in the line of cars. "Thank goodness the line's not long," Judy says.

"¡Sí!" Mr. Gonzalez replies. He's a man of few words. They sit, each thinking how, if it were evening or morning, they'd be there in the middle of the bridge, the murky Rio Grande far below, doing a little math in their heads to answer whether their own weight added to the loaded trucks also in line constituted a significant architectural stress to this old pre-NAFTA structure.

When they drive into the crossing lane on the U.S. side, they are unlucky, drawing the red light that signals random inspection. The situation brings out Mr. Gonzalez. "Aiiee, I don't know how this is going to happen," he says mildly. An agent steps out, signaling them over. They pull into the bay, taking up two stations.

The agent leans into the window. "U.S. citizens?" They nod. "What are you carrying?"

"Rock," Mr. Gonzalez says, "for this lady's husband's monument."

"Yeah?" The agent looks back at the cardboard-covered lumps. "Well, our policy is to ask you to unload."

"Maybe I could tear one of the cardboards a little?" Mr. Gonzalez offers. "I've crossed stones before. Not this big, of course."

Judy and Mr. Gonzalez get out of the truck and stand respectfully before the United States Immigration Service. Judy is five-feet-two inches tall. Mr. Gonzalez is sixty-five years old; he received a pacemaker last year.

"That won't give us the whole picture," the agent says, hands on hips, one lightly on his gun.

They all stand in silence, the agent looking at the lumps, Mr. Gonzalez wiping his brow, Judy concentrating on not smiling.

Then the agent has a bright idea. "We'll bring in the dogs," he says.

It's a threat they gladly accept, to be sure, an indignity, this being sniffed by animals, but an enlightened alternative.

The agent signals the trainer and Sparkie and Tab are brought forth, happy to be released from their wire enclosures, straining toward their work.

On signal they leap to the flatbed, joyfully begin their job sniffing at the cardboard behemoths. They're confident. They check out the Joya and Pampers boxes. The trainer moves with them, calling out encouragements. They go on to Niagra and Del Monte. Once, one of the dogs returns to Pennzoil, rechecks, is satisfied. Perhaps it was only a mouse nest from the previous use of the box.

Do they find drugs, contraband? It is obvious these stones have Just Said No. Humans! What will they think up next?

But just as Carlos was irresistibly charming, so his tombstone lures and, when the dogs are called, Sparkie takes a quick break, wetting the closest lump. The trainer reddens, looks contritely at the widow Judy. "Sorry, ma'am. They're not supposed to do that."

Somewhere Carlos roars out laughing. *El que ríe al último, se ríe mejor.* Laughing best and last, his mouthful of white teeth flashing, clapping with hands that never sleep, enjoying this joke of a little mortal drama.

And Mr. Gonzalez and the widow are excused to go their way, crossing three tons of mountain from Mexico into Texas. For a mountain of a man who crossed over muy vigoroso from this life into the next. ✿

CLAYTON AND BUNGALO

by Jas. Mardis

The Bungalo Dairy House of Grisolm, Texas, sat idle only nine hours of every day. Each of those hours found Clayton Porchia resting wearily beneath a worn, postage stamp patterned quilt, stretched over the soiled, clumped mattress of a jail house bunk. A makeshift addition of three sturdy crates supported the thirteen additional inches that completed Clayton Porchia. He learned to negotiate the creaking, wooden ottomans by ignoring the pain and wishing for sleep. Two months of aching calves, ankles, and feet. Then, his body and the worn nerves of his legs yielded. Now, all this time later, with the necessity of the short resting time before it was all to begin again, he had learned to rest quickly. The occassional pinch of splinters, damp concrete walls and the beastial, vomiting drunks were among the many pains that Clayton Porchia could never allow to master his attentions. In time, they all faded into a necessary twist deep within him.

Clayton's incarceration for public drunkenness was bartered out to the Bungalo Dairy. He had not been in public when the Sheriff arrested him. They spotted him behind the home of his brother-in-law, Robert Jackson, down at the creek, setting a trot line. The mason jar gripped in his hand. It was the creek that made it public. Clayton was known across the County as, *"the hardest working buck any man could get his hands on!"* But, he preferred his farm and family, and for sustenance the Porchia's bartered among black farmers. They owned their land and handed it down, generation to generation. Clayton was nearly untouchable, until that day and that drinking jar. When news of his arrest made the rounds every White man with a need came by the jail to catch a view. Before leaving, each of them scribbled a number on a slip of paper and placed it in the jar on Sheriff Haley Wimms' desk.

At the trial, Sheriff Haley recommended ninety days, but Judge Harland was swayed by a case of Two Fingers Whiskey and the promise of morning fresh dairy, and two hand-made quilts left with a note at his chamber's door. Later, the Judge would take one of those quilts by the jail for Clayton, but first he prepared a sentence of one hundred and eighty days at the Prison Camp. In court, Claude Bungalo stood up on cue and bid for Clayton's time at the Dairy. To balance out the easy dairy work against the prison's hard labor, Judge Harland tacked on twenty more days. Clayton would sleep at the Grisolm Jail and work at the Dairy. He also got two Sunday visitations a month. "*Son, that Dairy is good time,*" the Judge said rising to his feet and exiting the bench, "*You can mess it up, but there's hard time with your name on it at the Camp . . . an' won't be no visits from that ol' black sis of yours!*"

Clayton accepted.

Clayton remembered that day as pain amid his rest. It shot up from his calves, through his thighs and straight into his lower back. It made him coil inside, but he swallowed it. He wrapped his mind around the coming end of it all. He rested the thought of his predicament around the discomforted muscles and he slept.

Then, timed and alarmed, the dark hand of Clayton Porchia was suddenly turning loose the familiar motion of things. By routines that were done in half sleeps; half dead walks through the world of tight, small Southern streets and byways; half remembered; half taught to the muscles; half danced from the soul; half forced through veins with tired blood seeping into a waking head, he began the dairy's ritualized ascent into servitude. Knobs and dials and grinding, pivoting heads and switches with thick, heavily insulated cables of wires collapsed under Clayton's lone command. Here, in the yield of early morning hours, he manned over the world. Here, there would not be challenges to his order or his will. If a cow turned surly, Clayton could bend it back into a proper will, back into its place, he decided, but only in these hours. Here was a place for his ideas of manhood, despite that this place had been forced upon him and hundreds of days beyond his control. He wanted to control this place, if only for a moment. Here in his longest day, control begged his command. Suddenly, he slammed a lever into the "closed" position and heard the gears, chains, and suction devices pulse and screech to a halt. He savored the draining hymn of power and electricity through the lever in his hand. But Clayton's satisfaction collapsed within moments as some of the cows were startled by the sudden absence of suction. Clayton reversed the lever and listened for the returning sound of smooth motion. His command.

Claude Bungalo had risen in the same hour. Disturbed and confused by the awkwardness of that awakening he lay on his side and imagined the wallpaper ahead of him in the dark. After a moment he rewarded himself with an idea, swirls and flower petals: pink, red, and daisy-yellow with strips of blue. He laughed a slight chuckle that made the bed shake, but did not wake his wife. He wanted her to stir and ask him the matter. He wanted her attention so that he would not be alone in the awkwardness and ideas of that early hour. He stirred again, this time ricocheting the headpost of the bed off the wall. When her hand laced his thigh he became aroused and mounted his sleep-weary wife trying to bring her into his awakeness. But she was not with him. Her body was a damp cavity, folded in his direction, open and vacant at all hours. It was an act to his satisfaction, but as he left her, a worry began within him. Not of his command.

Bungalo had long ago confided to a handful of men close to him how *"that old, black sum'bitch made his shop run good."* He also knew that Clayton Porchia would never work another day in his life at the Dairy once his time was done. Bungalo cursed himself for talking the Judge into tacking on another hundred days for the spooked cow incident. It wasn't the first time that a new cow had gone spooked by the pump and suction of the machines "Hell," he thought now, "it wasn't even the most damage that a cow had done to the place," but Clayton didn't know that. *"Hell,"* Bungalo thought again, remembering how Jr. Cobb had found Clayton pinned under the scared animal. *"He was about done for with that cow across his chest, cutting his breath in half."* But, Clayton Porchia was a big man. Strong as any two regular men at the Dairy, he'd managed to lift that cow to one side of him before falling out. *"Hell,"* Bungalo returned to himself, gathering his pillow and blanket to him, *"To Hell with that too good, too strong Porchia Nigga."* Bungalo tried again to sleep.

Before any other face had known the warmth of coffeed breath bouncing off of roughly rubbed palms, the dairy was moving fast and heavy with its own dance. Outside, large metal vats of still warm milk had been loaded onto Bungalo Dairy delivery trucks with cold, unstarted engines. Clayton was full on awake as blasts of morning wind found its way between his undershirt and sweating back. Soon, the others would be arriving, full of rest and horseplay, but Clayton would be ready for them. Their trucks and wagons were stocked for delivery; the loading docks were full of crates and bottles to be cleaned and made ready. Even the Dairy floors would be clear of debris, baling wire, hay, and feed sacks. Clayton looked above the sliding doors and saw that it was time for the delivery men to arrive. He threw aside his apron, freed the ring of spare keys from his back pocket and jumped into one of the waiting trucks. He leapt from truck to truck until the rattling purr of six engines echoed off the wooden fence of the Bungalo Dairy. Clayton hung the ring of keys on a nail and tightened his apron.

By the time that "Black Earl" and Jr. Cobb arrived, knocking their lunch tins against the heavy, wooden doors, Clayton had readied their deliveries and steadied the young cows for a second time. "Three hun'ded an' twelve days, there Clay!", Black Earl growled and lifted his lunch pail onto a wooden rack just inside the door. Jr. Cobb shook the thought of that grief from his head before looking up to catch Clayton's reaction. Then, he spit a brown chip of tobacco off his tongue and joined in with a grinning, "*Boy. Boy. Boy.*" Clayton pulled at the loose strap of his overalls and allowed the thought to pass him by. He would not become anxious, he promised himself. He did not want a repeat of the cow incident. He also did not want another hundred days under Bungalo's thumb.

"Ain't got time for that now, Earl, Jr. Cobb. Y'all's trucks is ready to move it on. Now, get in 'em and get 'em movin,'" Clayton's command shocked the two men. They did as he spoke. As did the three White men who arrived through the door with a stunned look as the two black men departed. Another pair of men got the word as they entered the gate. Figuring that it was from old man Bungalo, they never stopped to deposit their lunch pails. Instead, they were in the trucks and out the gate in three minutes flat. Clayton readied six more truck loads on the dock. Four more men, dock workers, took his lead and the morning was a symphony of action.

Clayton could not ignore the sweet, wheezing significance of his final day's work in Bungalo's servitude. His command. None of it but this moment, he reminded himself as the hours passed pitifully about him, falling away in fits and squirts, as though mimicking the cadence of a nervous udder. Time was a reluctant heifer, and she served him droplets of seconds, minutes and finally hours that came and went away like the moaning bay of a lost calf. Clayton studied every errant act and motion of the cows. He looked only twice at his watch for confirmation of the time, and calmed himself by passing out early farewells to the cows with a sturdy caress of each quivering, fly swatting, thinly haired rump.

Claude Bungalo was awake again when the second round of trucks exited the Dairy, but could not get his mind around what still disturbed him so. For a moment he turned that confusion again onto his wife; her sex; the need to turn his awkwardness into her. When she did not stir, when she could not raise her worn flesh into his prodding, he lay back and took stock of himself. It was a moral stock, rather, more of a man's tally: strength, forcefulness, a strong will, a powerful voice, and a good business sense. He was not a man easy to worry or careful in action, but there was something on the morning that bothered him to a caution. What it was, was a sound carried on the winds of Grisolm. It was stale on the early breeze that slipped through a cracked window sill; he tasted it. Once on his tongue it made him sorely awake and caused Claude Bungalo to rise and ponder a solution to Clayton Porchia's last day under his command.

Bungalo laughed at the idea that, in the smallest town of the largest state, one man's leaving could bring falter to the slumber of another. But, Bungalo could not stomach that this faltering between he and Clayton Porchia had been long in coming and was now upon him. Claude Bungalo let the stirring in him build toward a desire and turned it onto his wife. He did not bother to wake her and her body did not bother to refuse him although she was waking as he entered her. He was violent now and his wife stirred, turning her hips, sliding away from his thrusts. But she was no match for the rage that was pulsing through him, and he did not hear her calling out to him. He pushed her onto her stomach, her head into the pillow, and his full weight into her. Within a few minutes Bungalo relieved a small portion of the rage within her, but it was such a pitifully, small part of it. His wife, hurt and startled, touched the tender skin at the back of her neck where the welts had begun and held down her sobbing until she heard the water running heavily into the tub.

Before the rooster could ready himself for the crow, Claude Bungalo was washed, dressed and passing one of his delivery trucks on the fork at Bridge-Road 64, a quarter mile beyond the Dairy's gate. He wanted to continue savoring the taking of his wife, but the truck startled him. It was too early for that route and Bungalo damned the "*black sonofabitch*" for "getting it sideways!"

Now, the whole day would be screwed. Deliveries had a schedule. People depended on that schedule. The damn college could wait until the grade and high schools were delivered. The State Prison could wait until the church was delivered, and he just didn't give a damn about the little store down at the end of the edition that sold to the coloreds.

Bungalo signaled for the truck to pull to the side of the road and then he fidgeted himself up to the driver's window. "*What t'Hell 'R'yu' doing headin' to t'damn college . . . y'stupid sonofabitch?*" Bungalo fumed. Jr. Cobb stuttered, "*MmmmmMista BUNG'lo, Clayton don' . . . ,*" but Bungalo didn't let him finish the statement. "*Boy, if yu want t'keep dis'here employment . . . yu best git dis'here truck back t'the Dairy . . . an' I means right fast! Dat Nigger Clay ain't writing yo check on t'day, nor any other!*" He slammed the driver's door and charged back to his truck.

Bungalo, in fact, Mr. Claude Heath Bungalo, since that was the mindset that had now taken over his demeanor, conjuring the fervor and determination of his father, his namesake, crossed through the bridge canopy and skidded to a stop on the gravel drive. He entered the double sliding doors of his dairy with a hard, swift kick that parted the doors like the curious fingers of a wide, wooden hand, causing them to dislodge from the spring-loaded hinge. Bungalo rejoiced at his display and took quick note of the number of startled workers standing around the make-ready floor. He glanced back at the huge clock above the now unhinged door and read the time: eight-twenty-two! Fuming, he ratcheted out a series of unintelligible cuss before managing, "*What t'Hell is goin'on here! I swear t'GodAlmighty dat I'll fire t'furst wage stealing Nigger dat don't git bac't'wurk . . . an' I mean right now!*" Bungalo's face and torso shook as the last of his words fell in spits from his mouth across the motionless work floor.

The men, some of them immediately compliant with fear, acted out the motion of their jobs. A handful of White workers turned to their power dead machinery with the stupid motion of punching on the whining electricity. Their faces were flush with what Claude Bungalo could do to their lives. The Dairy was good work, despite the constant threat of Bungalo's vengeance: his interpretation of your worth to his bottom line. The silent cacophony of a few wooden palates being put back into their place was suddenly made into a noisy music of unnecessary work on the floor.

Claude Bungalo sniffed his disgust at the men on the floor and wanted to fire somebody to make his example, but was suddenly interrupted by a strong voice coming from the loading dock, "*Missta Bungalo?*" As he turned his attention to his left, a dark figure ascended the long ramp of shadow from the belly of the dock, speaking in a direct, but conciliatory tone, "*Sar, de wurk has been don, Missta Bungalo. Yessar. We wuz jus' az surprised as yu is now. . . . Seems dat Clayton. . . .*" Bungalo ignored the rest and made out the voice to be one of the black workmen. His form was all shoulders and a bulked torso: strong. Good, he thought, that's the one!

He pointed a finger at the man and called out for him. "*C'mere, boy,*" the sneer in his voice was wrong. Taking a few steps into the Dairy's lighted floor, the black workman became Buddy Cobb, Jr. Cobb's brother. Bungalo sneered and glanced over the floor for an audience. Nearly every man's eye was stayed on him in anticipation. Buddy Cobb leapt from the delivery platform and was nearing Bungalo when. . . .

"*Nigga, is dat whut I assed yu?*" Bungalo turned against him.

"*Well, Nigga?*" his words became bits of spittle that rocketed from his mouth and landed on his chin.

Bungalo laughed at Buddy Cobb's surprised look and stumble over apologetic words. *"Missta Bungalo, sir, I ain't meant no disrespect, No Sar, Missta Bungalo."* Silence circled the room and crawled along, mingling with the worker's anticipation. Every man wanted to speak, but realized the risk. Bungalo was not a sensible man in anger. He preferred fear and example.

Clayton's voice broke the circling anticipation and Bungalo's building wrath, *"It wus me Mr. Bungalo, not that boy you's cuttin' into. . . ."*

Bungalo recognized the voice and the disrespect for his command coming from behind him, through the dislodged doors. In his limbs, his arms, shoulders, back, and finally, in the highest division of the neck, Claude Bungalo recognized the awkward frenzy that had awaken and stirred him so early that morning. His turn toward Clayton was slow and in a manner that he imagined would appear threatening and terse: tightened fists, thrusted chest, a militaristic kicking out of the foot-turned quickly into an instrument of pivot. In his mouth was a sudden bitter tongue, the dried enamel of his teeth; a tastelessness and the growing sensitivity of his palate. His breath came in and from his nostrils, which were flared and recessed back into the folds of flushed cheeks. Bungalo turned and did not give quarter to the fearful faces of his workers. He wrapped his mind's cruel focus on the voice and *"dat Porchia nigga's smirk."*

Clayton Porchia did not wait on Bungalo's wrath. He did not want to live it over and again on all the days that would come after this moment. He did not want to leave the memory of a full-boared Claude Bungalo on the minds and deeds of these men who had done nothing to wrong the Dairy. So, Clayton Porchia advanced toward Claude Bungalo and spoke clearly and directly and without shame or fear of his impassioned wrath.

"It's me what don dis here, Sar!" His voice did not tarry or waste the length of distance that was shrinking between he and Bungalo.

"I've don sent out th'day's milk, Mr. Bungalo. By the time dese here boys made it in the trucks wus loaded and dey got'em movin', Sar." The sound of his words and his low, barrel-toned voice, bounced off the still turning Claude Bungalo and chiseled myriad paths through the fog-thick anticipation on the Dairy house floor.

"We's don with all but what's in the yard and de one yu stopped over at the bridge, Sar," Clayton waited until Bungalo had turned and was facing him to say the rest of what was coming. He wanted to make certain that he was seen, so he waited until he could see his reflection in the irritated eyes of the man under whose thumb he had been pressed for nearly a year.

It surprised Bungalo that Clayton was standing so close. He had assumed fifteen or so feet away, at least ten. It would be a distance worthy of the shout building in him; the cursing disregard, the pissant staring down of him in front of the others. Instead, Clayton was within touching distance. Touching. Reaching out and grasping distance. It was a sudden recognition and it stirred Claude Heath Bungalo. It stirred him, and he took a half step backward before he could reason the whole thing out and stop himself, before the consideration of such a step could be taken.

A ring of gasps showered the room when Bungalo faltered. It rolled up to the rafters and over the dull gleam of the ironworks, then out into the world, passing around Clayton Porchia before wafting through the unhinged doors. Now, something truly new and disturbing was on the morning breeze traveling through the town of Grisolm, Texas. It was growing, even as it gleaned the mist heavy waters beneath the 64 Bridge Road canopy at the end of the Dairy property. Throughout the town people were suddenly stirring and bothered for reasons unknown, but pulsing through them just the same.

"Bungalo, my time wit'chu is done. I paid my sentence and got all the work outta here 'fo de sun hit the sky. Now, I'm goin' home to my family. I'm done here!" Clayton's words rang and clattered throughout the room. Every man was in his attention and grateful for the light work day of scrubbing down the floors and machinery. They'd all be home by noon instead of three o'clock. Without thinking fully, a few of the men applauded Clayton Porchia's freedom. They said his name and held it with a regard worthy of something needing to be recognized. And, Clayton finished his selected, long pondered words to Bungalo by untying his apron and tossing it over a dead machine. The black worker's gasped and held back hoots and howls that the action deserved. Claude Heath Bungalo went flush.

Clayton turned and started the eight steps that would take him out of the Dairy. It was a move that suddenly had him remembering the touch of his wife, her smile, and the comfort of his bed. He smiled, then lurched two steps nearer the broken door. He brushed off the hiss of growing voices behind him and consumed another step. Now, four steps into and away from freedom he heard the rising scrap of Bungalo's brogans.

"*Look outthere Clay!*" Buddy Cobb shouted as the other men, White and black, chorused, "*Clayton!*" alerting him to Bungalo's advance.

"*Lookahere, NIGGA!, Yu's done when Isays yu's done!*" Bungalo's words rolled out like the verse of an personal spiritual. "*I'mmo show yu who'sthe BOSS!*" another stanza caught Clayton as he lurched through the door space and onto the gravel walk. He turned to catch Bungalo's pace and a glimpse of his twisted visage.

"*Nawsur, I'm done!*"

Clayton turned and found his bearings: the bridge canopy, the Dairy exit. As he turned away from the dairy door, Clayton counted the three quick steps of Bungalo's advance, then made three quicker ones of his own. His only thought was distance. Keep him out of range. Bungalo was heavy and Clayton counted on him tiring, soon.

Instead, Bungalo emerged from the dairy with a two-by-four in hand and a quicker step. He was flushed crimson and a pasty spittle formed at his mouth.

"*Nigga, Isaid Iain't don wit'chu!*" Bungalo's verse was sewn together with his weight shifting, quick advance. "*Nigga, yu sass me again an' I'll knock yu down an' beat t'Hell outtaya!*" The plank jostled clumsily in his hand and fell to the ground catching Clayton's quick attention. Bungalo bent to pick it up, but stumbled as he missed the single, controlled motion that he had hoped for. When he noticed that Clayton had stopped and turned to face him, Bungalo straightened and took an averting step.

"*If yu hitme wit' dat two-by-fo', I'm goin' t'Hell an' takin' yu wit'me!*" Clayton spoke these words clearly and stood firmly in the gravel, digging his heels between the stone particles.

Bungalo looked back across the yard at the growing number of workers, silent and curious in the event of Clayton's challenge. He could manage only a pitiful, sinister, "*Nigga!*" that trailed away beneath his breath as he looked around for some other weapon. Clayton turned and stepped toward the bridge canopy exit and noticed a car was rolling to a stop. Clayton wondered about a ride back to the Jail. He hoped. He hoped.

Bungalo watched Clayton then remembered the pop-knife inside his jacket pocket. He fidgeted after the knife and grinned out a call to Clayton, *"Hey boy. Nigga! I tol' yu dat Iwan't don witchu, didn't I?"* the sinisterly sewn cadence in his verse had returned. *"Yeah! that's what I said an'that's what I meant, boy."*

He moved so awkwardly that he slipped on the gravel in his advance. It caught Clayton's attention, which made him stop and consider Claude Bungalo, anew. He watched Bungalo wrestling within his pocket and figured it for a knife or box cutter. He measured the distances from him to Bungalo and him to the bridge house, turning his head back and forth between the them. Bungalo was nearer him than Clayton was to the bridge canopy and the road. So, to slow him Clayton threw out his chest and yelled . . . *"If I wus yu, Mr. Bungalo, I wouldn't do that."*

Clayton was surprised that his words were so gentle in their warning. He had hoped to sound more harsh and threatening, more tightened and feverish.

Suddenly, Bungalo was upon him and Clayton felt foolish and scared, realizing the dissolving space between him and Bungalo. Clayton jumped backward just as Bungalo swiped at him with a half-closed switchblade from his pocket. Both of his feet slipped as he threw all of his weight backward, and Clayton landed at the wooden bridge railing ten feet from the canopy. He struggled to rise, but slipped again and caught glimpses of Claude Bungalo fumbling to unfold the knife.

Bungalo cursed the rust-stuck blade and took two steps toward the fallen Clayton, then stopped and hit the instrument in his hand. *"Dam'mit". "Dam'mit!"* his cuss focused Clayton's effort to rise.

"Yu bes' stop right there, ol' man!" Clayton did not press caution into these words. He let them stumble into the heavy breath falling in excited bursts from his mouth. *"Yu bes'. . . ."*

Claude Bungalo slapped the knife into his palm and watched it slip from him and fall to the ground. His first thought was to leave it where it landed and charge the frightened "nigga," but he heard the blade chisel open on the ground. He picked up the now-opened knife. He did not bother with the necessity of Clayton at all. He'd still be there, against the fence . . . "stupid nigga," but first, pick up the blade, he instincted . . . and did.

For both men, it was a series of moments so quick that the mind's eye honored it with abbreviated movement.

Bungalo saw the rusted blade opening at his feet, circled by gravel stones of many hues and shapes lit in the early light of morning. He saw the tip of his shoe digging and holding his weight steady. He saw his hand slice the cooled space between him and the graveled drive and pick up the ready blade. He felt the anger for Clayton Porchia rise in him with the blade. He had not considered this moment, really, but now it was upon him. He had not prepared himself for cutting a man. The knife was a consequence of his youth. The quick response of the blade to the button. The excitement of seeing the bland metal turned suddenly into a weapon. It was not a nail picker. Not a whittler. As a boy, everyone he knew carried a "pop-knife." His was merely a hold over, until this moment. Now, it was going into "that sassing, Porchia nigga!" It was going into him all right! Claude Bungalo sprang to his feet and made a single motion of lunging at the black man positioned against the railing.

Clayton Porchia also saw the rusted blade opening at Bungalo's feet, but was not surprised by it. *Rusty blade*, the idea of being stuck with a rusty blade enflamed him. The coil loosened and pulsed through him. It made him calmer, this recognition of his feelings for Bungalo. He lifted his weight from the fence and stood firmly on his feet, planting the hard sole of his shoes beneath the shifting stones. Clayton saw clearly the movement of Claude Bungalo: ripping the open knife from the rocks, grinning, ready to take more of his life. Three hundred days of labor had not been enough. Clayton wrestled for a short moment with being away from home any longer with Bungalo's death tacked onto his sentence. He reckoned the Prison Camp. He thought again of the rusted blade coming after him and the certainty of lockjaw, the slow wane of muscles dirtied and made useless by such a cut. Then, Clayton Porchia stood and made a focus on Bungalo's knife.

But, Claude Heath Bungalo stumbled. He had lifted his heavy, angered, sweat-laced body into the air, lunging and screaming the death of Clayton Porchia for all to hear and witness. He had raised within himself the very awkwardness that had awaken him so early on that day. He had, and was again now, tasting it on the air rushing past his clinched teeth, into his swollen, anger wreaked lungs. Claude Heath Bungalo had the intention of death within him. He had the lesson of lessons for the "niggas" who watched and wooed and readied themselves for this final hour of Clayton Porchia. Claude Bungalo grinned as he rose and lunged at the nigga. He pushed all of himself into the tightest fist of a body and launched all of that fist forward with a shrill fit of consumption. His arm outstretched, his hand holding firm the gritty handle of that pop-knife, his knife, a stiff, reddish-brown death flag. Then, in the midst of that launch and anger, Claude Heath Bungalo stumbled. The toe of his brogans, the left foot in particular, getting caught in an eddy of disrupted stones and seizing his advance.

Clayton Porchia caught the surprise sweeping over Bungalo's reddened face as his feet failed him. He watched the sudden halt of Bungalo's fleshy launch ripple and reverse then tumble awkwardly to earth. Clayton saw it all and wished for a larger role in it. Clayton saw the extended arm, shorter, even in this act, rubber band back to the body of Claude Bungalo. He marveled at the efficiency of that weapon arm made suddenly a vile rejoinder of what should be: the lesson returning to the teacher. The golden rule in effect, Clayton mused as the heavily angered Bungalo fell onto his recoiling, knife filled fist, his scream turning abruptly to a gurgled screech. Clayton watched and did not bother himself with the body's jerk and jostle against the embedded knife in Bungalo's throat. He did not bother himself with the remembrance of this death at one's own hand. He did not caution his heart or offer prayer to his tormented tormentor. As well, Clayton Porchia did not passion any further a desire to revenge his year of servitude.

The men at the unhinged, wooden doors stood, then suddenly advanced on the jerking Bungalo. Among them there was no attempt at revival or ceasing the knife's damage. Instead, they stood around him in wonder. Clayton turned away from it all and headed into the bridge canopy and toward home. Turning, he pondered the price of his confrontation with the behind him, dying Claude Bungalo. There would be prison regardless of Bungalo's assault and falter. Clayton could not count on the broken men standing and awed behind him. These were not his people, his friends, his neighbors. Clayton put out a hand and walked it along the painted planks of the canopy to steady himself against his own faltering. He stepped and felt the horrible fear of fire and beatings that was surely to be his now. He wretched the empty bile from his stomach and followed that with dry heaving that bricked his entire body, head to weakened legs,. Then Clayton collapsed to his knees and wept.

He sobbed there, amid the paint and wood aroma of the bridge canopy, not for Bungalo, but for himself and his challenge of what could not be beaten by a black hand. As he did, he could hear footsteps spinning around him, not a mass of stepping, but a pair. The steps were measured and certain. Clayton rose from his knee in the direction of that stepping and found the long, full figured silhouette of Judge Harland coming toward him. Beyond the canopy, the car purred and sputtered in the growing morning light. In one hand, Judge Harland gripped the honey colored handle of a revolver, carrying it like a loose memory. He stared at Clayton, rising from the canopy floor, the front of his pants damp with urine and tears. Judge Harland's long, thin arms swung awkwardly as he strode through the canopy. His stride, a mixed bag of nerves, cautions and disbelief over what he had been witness to. His jaw was suddenly slack. His eyes sank deeper beneath his brow with each step. Clayton studied the shifting figure of Judge Harland making its way into the dim canopy light. Through the Judge's arm, between errant swings and short, shuffle-steps, Clayton could see the door of the automobile swug open, swaying free in the fractured morning light. ✿

ATTENTION SINGLE LADY

by Cynthia Stroman

On the wide, south porch, coffee cup in hand, Helen Reeves anxiously scanned the Thursday morning *Abilene Reporter*, checking the market report. She'd been planning to send Abe to the sale with a load of dry cows, but if dairy cattle still flooded the market, she would have to wait. When she located the farm section and verified her suspicions, she decided to see if San Angelo's auction projected better prices. She could just as easily go south with her cattle. She picked up the *Livestock Weekly*, a San Angelo paper, and flipped to their agricultural forecast.

"Well, forget that," she sighed, as the prices again failed to meet her expectations. As she casually glanced through the ad section, a headline caught her eye. "Attention Single Lady." She had to read on.

Laugh if you like, but I am a single sincere rancher in my late forties wishing to meet that special one in my life. I know she is out there somewhere, but where? I have not the time to chase around in night clubs or single bars, or play around like a clown just for the hell of it. My health is excellent. I am a non-tobacco user. I like to laugh and be around happy people. My physical size is average; I have no family; I believe in God and am a Christian.

If you are a single lady with an alcohol problem, diabetes, lung problem, drug habit, mental deficiency, no morals, obesity, a severe handicap, or just looking for a free ride, do not write me; just laugh at this public ad. My name is not Box Holder, but if you think you might hear the same drum cadence that I march to, give me your confidential reply. I will reply and your letter will never be seen or known of by anyone but me. I have taken step one by presenting this ad in person to this publishing office. Write me at:

BOX HOLDER
Box 1169
San Angelo, TX 76902

Helen read it all, and then she reread it in disbelief. Her first reaction was to laugh, and then she wished desperately for someone to laugh with.

Widowed for only two years, Helen missed her husband. Life with John Allen, a grizzly bear of a man with a sharp wit and an equally sharp tongue, had never been boring. He'd convinced her to abandon her career plans at Texas Women's University twenty years ago and had brought her to the Rocking A ranch. He had worked hard, played hard, loved hard, and died early of a heart attack at forty-four, leaving Helen to run the ranch alone. She missed the laughter, noise, heat, and joy of John Allen. For twenty years he had filled her life with boisterous love. His death created a void.

She knew John Allen would have loved this ad. She could visualize how he would have laughed deep, mouth open, and eyes squinting until he puffed for breath, barrel chest heaving. How she missed him. How long had it been? Only two years, yet it seemed an eternity. Her John Allen, her man . . . as if every woman needed a man's love before she had any identity of her own.

Helen read the ad for the third time, mesmerized. How odd. Advertising for a wife like any breeding stock in a livestock publication, and yet there was a poignancy about it. Helen tried to imagine what kind of man would open himself to ridicule in such a way. He must be desperate. Frowning, she tried to picture him, but could only project on the screen of her mind an inadequate version of John Allen.

Abe interrupted her, greasy hat in hand, early morning sweat beaded on his swarthy cheek. "Miz Reeves, whatcha 'spect me ta do 'bout them yearlin's ya lost outta the south pasture?" His frown indicated his displeasure as he swished tobacco juice from one side of his jaw to the other.

"Well, Abe, I suppose we must find them." Helen bit back a sharper response. John Allen had earned Abe's worship by cussing and storming, and Helen realized that, to the elderly hand, she must seem a weak substitute. "Let me finish my coffee and I will go with you."

"Yeah, lotta good that's gonna do," Abe snorted as he stomped off the porch, his rusty spurs raking the steps, and headed for the used-up Ford pickup.

Helen clenched her small fist against trembling lips to prevent an angry retort. She reminded herself for the thousandth time that this onerous old man who had worked for the Rocking A for twenty-five years could never get a job anywhere else at his age. As frustrating as he was, she felt responsible for him. Sighing, she set her coffee cup down with studied calm, squared her shoulders, and rose to follow him.

"Do you see anything yet, Abe?" As they bounced through the rocky pasture in third gear, Helen choked on the dust which boiled over the fenders and clutched frantically for the door handle.

"Nope. They ain't gonna be here, I tell ya. Any dern fool knows not ta turn new-boughten yearlin's out the first day. Ya gotta feed 'em fer a coupla days in the lot, till they gets their bearin's, ya know." The derision in his voice was not lost on Helen.

"But, Abe, last year I turned out the yearlings I bought the first day, and they did just fine," Helen countered, wondering why she was defending herself to the hired hand. She looked down to see herself twisting her gold wedding band around nervously on her slender finger, as if to conjure up John Allen. He had always known what to do in any situation.

"Humph," grunted Abe, as he slammed on the brake, nearly throwing her through the windshield. He heaved himself out of the pickup and limped toward the south fence which leaned precariously north in places. When she had composed herself, small oval face set in determined good humor, Helen followed.

"Miz Reeves, look here." Abe spat tobacco juice in the cinnamon dust as Helen climbed the ridge where he stood. Her short brown hair, streaked with gray in spots, blew back from her forehead as she topped the hill and the breeze could reach her. "Here's where them yearlin's went through the fence. Why, I figure they could be in Sterling City by now!" His lip curled up with disgust. "Whatcha' wanna do now?"

"Well, Abe, I guess we keep following their tracks, don't we?" She wanted to sound confident, give commands like John Allen would have, but she wasn't really sure what to do—wanted someone to tell her.

He hawked and spat precariously near her boot. "Why that could take days!"

Helen became obstinate, dark eyes snapping. "Then we'll spend days! Come on!" She marched back to the pickup, catching her boot heel in a clump of grass and feeling ridiculous.

As they drove slowly down one county road after another looking for tracks with Abe sullenly hanging his head out the window and mumbling to himself, Helen remembered the newspaper ad. For a fleeting moment she felt an urge to answer it, just to be able to put life back into a man's hands again, just to feel safe, protected. "Ridiculous. You're losing your grip," she breathed and concentrated on looking out her window for tracks in the chalky dust.

Two crawling miles later, Abe spotted the prints of several calves in the road and grudgingly admitted they might be onto something. "But they're movin' on," he cautioned grumpily.

"Then let's move also," said Helen, her usually full lips in a straight line.

"But we're already outta Mitchell County," Abe retorted.

"Well, just because cattle cross county lines doesn't mean that we can't follow, Abe." Helen seldom lost control, but now her voice was stiff. "Let's go."

The two antagonists drove a few more miles without speaking, but they lost the tracks finally at an intersection and couldn't tell which way to go. "Anyway," said Abe bitterly, "it's nearly noon and I ain't fed at the barn yet, and I'm gonna miss *Days of our Lives*."

Helen gave up with an impatient snarl. "Okay, let's go home." That was the problem. She had no one to see things through, the way John Allen had always done.

That night, as Helen watched the 10:00 news in her bedroom, a commentary on the plight of single-parent families reminded her of the *Livestock Weekly* ad. Her hairbrush poised in midair, she wondered if the "single, sincere rancher" had received any replies from slender, sober women. Then her mind followed a tangent as she imagined what the "hard working, laughter loving" rancher would do about sixteen missing yearlings. She didn't think he sounded like the type who would let the hired hand call the shots. He was direct. He went after whatever it was he wanted and didn't care what people thought.

She studied herself in the mirror. Face it, Helen, she thought, you have tiptoed around for two years, afraid to make decisions because some "real" rancher might laugh at you—doing only what you saw John Allen do and not always knowing why he did it that way. For heavens sake, do something for once the way you would do it! With an emphatic nod at herself in the mirror, Helen gave herself a mental pat on the back. Then her face slumped as she wondered how she would do it. She didn't even know what she really wanted to do. She frowned at the forty-year-old petite brunette in the mirror, still pretty enough, but beginning to wrinkle around the eyes and mouth.

"Well," now she was talking out loud in the empty bedroom, "I know I want those sixteen yearlings back. I can't afford to lose them. But I also really want someone else to take the responsibility of running the ranch. And I . . . I want . . . to finish my college degree, maybe even teach school somewhere." Surprised at herself, Helen stopped. She wondered why she hadn't finished school. It had not been a matter of money. John Allen had always provided well for them. Nor had it been a lack of time. She had never had to work outside the home. No children. No real responsibilities. John Allen had always felt women belonged in the home, that's all. And she had never questioned John Allen.

"Then why did you have to go and die and suddenly force me to run things?" Helen was surprised at her bitterness. Embarrassed by her outburst, she felt guilt flood her, leaving bile in her throat. With a half sob, she turned out the lights and crawled between cold sheets.

Morning brought fresh resolution. Tears had no place in the sunlight. Helen marched into the bright kitchen neatly dressed in cotton blouse and denim skirt, poured a cup of strong coffee, seated herself at the kitchen desk computer before her, and printed out two notices. The first read:

> Lost: Sixteen 350 lb. black baldy steer yearlings near Mitchell-Sterling County line. Contact Rocking A Ranch, Box 677, Colorado City, Texas 79512.

The second read:

> Wanted: Responsible rancher to manage 10 section ranch near Colorado City. Contact Rocking A Ranch, Box 677, Colorado City, Texas 79512.

Then taking pen in hand, Helen began a personal letter.

Dear Box Holder,

> I hope you find the woman you seek. I am writing this letter to thank you for helping me to realize that I was unhappy with my own life and that I can do something to change it. I have taken steps to do that. Your letter might seem funny to some people, but to me it showed courage and a willingness to express your need, even though it exposed you to others. I can do no less.

With sincere appreciation,

New Woman
Box 677
Colorado City, TX 79512

With the barest smile on her lips, Helen Reeves pasted a stamp on the letter, stacked the ads neatly and got in the car to drive to San Angelo. She had two stops to make—the *Livestock Weekly* office and the registrar's office at Angelo State University. ❀

Lyin'-Stealin'-Cheatin'

by Chuck Taylor

It was April 1988. Cruel April, in the rottenest year of my life. I was forty-four and still unwilling to face the body's advancing years, working the graveyard shift in Austin at the Texas School for the Deaf.

I was sleeping three, maybe four hours after riding the bus home from work. During the long numb hours awake at home and work, I'd down over a dozen cups of coffee and developed a rash all over my body. My memory grew so dim I had to write down the number to remember which bus I caught home from work.

Why was I working with twenty-five teenage boys in a residence cottage at the State Deaf School on South Congress Avenue? Money, of course—and a vague desire to do something useful. I loved learning sign language and hanging with those teenagers, who were just like any other teenagers. But I got to be with them just two hours each night.

My main task was to be a kind of Peeping Tom, to steal a peak through a crack in the door of every boy's room each half hour through the night, thus to guarantee no one had slipped out a window into a neighboring girl's cottage. The state lived in deathly fear of being sued—if one of the young ladies got in a family way.

I had hoped to do writing through the night between checking on the boys, but my brain was fried. I sat instead in front of the TV and switched from cable station to cable station. If the supervisor caught anyone sleeping while making the rounds, it was grounds for dismissal. A few times I nodded off, but heard the key turning in the door and got my eyes open just in time. The supervisor was a woman who liked to come by and talk for hours. I wondered if she liked me, but was too beat to do more than fantasize.

Six months earlier, my wife Laura and I had been living like Henry David Thoreau at Walden Pond, sleeping in tents amongst cedar woods high on a bluff along the greenbelt overlooking Barton Creek, about five miles out from downtown Austin. I loved the rustic life. It required just one day of work a week to meet necessities. The rest of the week was mine. I was keeping a journal, going to poetry readings, planting a garden, and hiking in the woods along the creek, studying plant life.

But Laura hated it. She packed her belongings and hiked back to the city to stay with her grown son, and our love slid into a crisis. To get back in Laura's good graces, I swore no more damp tents. We'd get decent digs in the sylvan center of town. Austin rents, of course, were insane compared to the rest of the state. I needed to find at least a semi-professional gig that'd cover expenses and provide womanly comforts.

I tried working at a small independent bookstore in Barton Creek Mall, but with poor management the place had no chance against the big bookstore chains. It was at that point, after I had quit the mall job (which Laura also disapproved of, for environmental reasons), that the Deaf School called for an interview. I'd forgotten turning in the application ten months earlier.

Our new cozy two bedroom house, tucked in the backyard of another small two bedroom near the Elizabeth Ney Museum, was just what Laura desired, but the graveyard shift at the Deaf School meant little time to spend with each other. Laura, an extrovert, had to keep mouse quiet while I tried to sleep. She got mad because I did not wipe the honey jar before putting it back in the cabinet; I got mad because she never locked the door when she went to work.

I found myself fantasizing more and more about other women, just as she, I learned from peeks in her journal, was thinking of other men. I opened a PO box at a nearby post office and started reading the "Women Want Men" personals in the *Austin Chronicle*.

I was bringing in about seven hundred a month, a modest sum to be sure, but after living on forty dollars a week in a tent, it seemed substantial. I bought a new bathrobe at Penney's in hopes of improving the love life. I had my station wagon towed out of a friend's driveway and paid for a new generator and battery. Yet, I did not feel flush enough to buy insurance.

My wife scoffed at my lack of funds—she was making less working for minimum wage part-time—and I suppose she was right. I might have managed insurance payments broken down month by month, but I had been living on little money for so long I'd developed a poverty consciousness, a pride in my ability to cut corners, to survive on wits and beat the system.

For many years I had driven without auto insurance in violation of state law. I had gotten away with it by being an exemplary driver who never exceeded the speed limit, never slid through stop signs, and never failed to signal right or left when changing lanes or turning. I was the law abiding citizen who makes other drivers furious and endangers public safety.

Ah, poverty consciousness. I saw myself as inordinately clever. I could outwit materialistic America and outsmart the bureaucrats' regulations. No man owned me; my life was my own. A cocky attitude makes being poor more tolerable. Living poor in the United States, as Hemingway once observed, is seen as a crime against humanity and God, deserving severe punishment.

So I needed a sticker to put on the rear license plate of my 1976 Oldsmobile wagon. Without a sticker, the cops would pull me over—no matter how well I drove—and ask for insurance. No insurance meant a large fine I'd have to work off in the city jail and that meant I'd lose my Deaf School job.

Laura deplored deviousness, and so to avoid her critical gaze—and to see if she would notice my absence in the middle of the night for future imagined dalliances—I planned to get up around two and stalk the streets of the central city for a sticker. I'd do it on a night when not working the graveyard shift. When off, I tried to catch up on sleep and be with Laura by going to bed at her normal time, around eleven.

It was not difficult getting up at two in the morning, since I was sleeping badly anyway. I slipped on my clothes and slipped out into the warm April night. Did I have any guilt about stealing a sticker? A little. The person wouldn't notice and would certainly get stopped. He or she would need to get up in front of a judge with a piece of paper proving they'd purchased a sticker previously—if they wished the ticket waived.

In those days, stickers were being ripped off cars all over Texas, since the state required proof of insurance during inspections or when paying tax and title. Up until the mid-1970's—in deference to Mexican Nationals driving in Texas—no insurance had been required. Texas had been a free place, a wild and woolly frontier. My unlucky year—1988—Ralph Nader paid a visit to Texas and declared that the state insurance board should receive its salary from the insurance companies, since it represented only their interests.

I saw cop cars with stickers ripped off the license plates. The situation got so bad that in the 1990's the state developed a new system that put the sticker inside the front window, driver's side, next to the inspection decal. But yes—back then—I felt guilty inconveniencing some poor soul by ripping off a sticker. Still, I had my excuses.

I was poor and had to find ways to beat the system. I had worked out various tricks, most of them legal, to live on little money. I had no credit cards and never borrowed money. I had no checking account where you paid a fee each month. We ate mostly vegetarian, and for a long time Laura and I lived in the basement of a downtown bookstore we operated. To supplement our income, I sometimes performed magic at children's birthday parties or did home weddings as a minister in the Universal Life Church, which I'd joined twenty years earlier to avoid getting sent to Vietnam.

If people are paranoid about car wrecks, I reasoned, they are free to buy a special insurance to protect themselves against uninsured motorists. No one should be required to buy insurance in a free society, I explained to friends who were also poor. They, of course, agreed.

I considered myself, basically, an honest person. I did not like to steal and I did not like telling lies. In this case, however, a higher law applied. Freedom from oppression by the state. Many who steal rationalize a higher law—and they're not always wrong. If a man steals a loaf of bread to eat, we recognize a higher law—the right to life over the right to property.

In Texas, with its poor public transportation, surviving without a car is a daunting challenge. Some do indeed steal license plate stickers out of a need to survive—or not to be terribly inconvenienced. Be honest. What would you do? Drive an illegal car or ride a bus four hours a day back and forth to a minimum wage job?

So that spring night—a Tuesday night—I sauntered the streets of central Austin searching for a sticker to peal off some innocent citizen's back license plate. It all seems hilarious now, a much ado about nothing, because I live differently, actually own mutual funds, a house, and a duplex, but back then it was exciting to stroll the streets in the middle of the night, a thrill to look at these scruffy but lovely old Hyde Park homes. Yes, what fun—to be skulking about when the vast body of humanity was prone asleep. America—the rational land of the Protestant day—yet we all yearn for the mysterious and seductive ways of night.

I avoided the main thoroughfares and saw no moving cars and no people. The dead of night is the dead of night. Would Laura wake up and realize I was gone? Would some owner see me bent over the back bumper of his automobile, then rummage a closet to brandish a shotgun?

Stealing a sticker may seem a small act of disobedience, but remember the Republic of Austin is in Texas, a place where frontier justice does indeed still apply. I was glad to be walking the streets. Even if someone did summon the police, I could slip down an alley or into a backyard. I was much less vulnerable on foot than in a car, which must stay on roads. Everyone in Austin knows of the policeman who used to hate college boys, and would take them to the top level of the Dobie Mall parking garage to beat them up undetected.

I searched for the perfect vehicle to steal a sticker from. I wanted a car parked in the street—not in a driveway. I wanted a car with cars around it front and back, a car parked next to a big bush, a car away from a street lamp, a car out of view of windows in a house, perhaps, parked in front of a vacant lot. I also wanted the sticker to be on top of a couple of older stickers—not to have the sticker bonded tight to the metal of the license plate. A sticker with a bunch under it would be easier to slide off undamaged.

I walked a lot of back streets that cruel April night. I walked from 45th Street on down to 15th, looking for the perfect sticker on the perfect car which rested at the curb under the most ideal conditions to do the dastardly deed. I walked and walked and walked in my dim, sleep deprived state, just like the homeless walk the streets after they've been discharged from the state mental hospital. The fear grew in my body. As I walked, I constructed alibis to explain why I was out wandering so late.

And then it happened—around 4 a.m. Two young UT students came tumbling down stairs of a bungalow set up under trees on a side street. In a matter of seconds they were in front of me. At first they didn't notice my presence—they were busy laughing at sophomoric witticisms. But then one asked, "What are you doing? Looking to rob a house?"

"No way," I laughed. "I drank too much. Fought with my old lady. I'm out clearing my head."

"Yeah, sure you are," the other guy sneered.

"So what are you doing?" The best defense was offense. "What's on your mind that you accuse the first guy you see?"

"What you saying, old man? You say I'm a thief?" One of the collegiates crowded my face.

"Come on, Shea. Back off. He ain't worth it." The other guy pushed between us. "Leave the guy alone."

And then they were gone—down the street walking fast, still laughing.

Was I so obvious? How had the college boy been so perceptive—to guess my bad intentions? Fear began to dig deeper inside—yet I did not head back home. I picked up the pace, putting blocks between myself and the two young men, and then resumed checking for the perfect sticker to pull off the perfect car.

I slowed down when I saw a police car pass up on Duval cruising leisurely south. Had the cops spotted me? Would they circle back to question—or pick me up as suspicious and offer a ride home? I looked for bushes to duck inside. I was a half mile now from my house, a block from the Elizabeth Ney museum. I hurried behind the museum, across an old cement bridge that spanned a creek, and ducked into a patch of woods. No way they'd find me now.

Believe it or not, in my fear I crawled inside a large bush not far from the creek. Elizabeth Ney, the woman sculptor who had built the studio that now houses the museum in her name, had been one of my heroes back in the 1970's. A feminist who refused to take her husband's name, she had been one of the first women to study sculpture. Back in the nineteenth century, when work was done with mallet and chisel, it had been considered too muscular for a frail female. Ney had sculpted philosopher Schopenhaur and caused him to alter his opinion of women.

Back in the 1970's, when researching Ney's letters, I had made love to a fiery feminist poet with long blonde hair in the basement of the museum. Now I was crouching in a bush. Where had those righteous days gone?

I had a wife who recoiled when I touched her. Laura refused the label of feminist, yet complained all the time of male ways and power. When we got together, I believed we'd help each other make great art to transform the world. The man who lived in the house in front of us—a Ph.D. candidate in botany, a small, bald guy whose wife had moved out a month earlier while he was on a field trip in Big Bend—was often in our living room. He'd pick flowers off shrubs in neighbors' front lawns and give them to Laura. She loved it, never complaining about his lack of morals.

At last it felt safe to crawl out of the bushes, to cross 38th Street and head back into the Avenues neighborhood. It was five in the morning and I felt beater than any beatnik. Laura would be getting up at seven to get ready for work at the telephone sales office. I could sleep after she left, before going to the Deaf School at midnight.

I finally settled on a target a half block from my house. It was an old tan Volkswagen parked under a street lamp in front of this tiny one room place. From the bumper stickers I surmised the person inside was a woman hippie student. I was about to rob from one of my kind. Yet even if she saw me, she would be unlikely to blast away with a shotgun—or telephone the police.

I got a pen knife out of my pocket, opened the small blade, and worked the sticker off in less than a minute. Into the pocket and seven minutes later I was inside the door of our backyard house. Quickly, I removed my clothes and eased into bed. Laura did not move. Had she noticed me absent? Probably not. I'd been an insomniac for a decade and often escaped to the living room to work on stories or poems.

Laura said nothing the next morning. I super-glued the sticker on the license plate after she left for work. She continued to cruise around with me in the illegal Oldsmobile, never once asking how I'd gotten the plates up to date.

By the end of that unlucky year I was living by myself in south Austin, working a computer job more financially rewarding, but still driving the illegal station wagon. I'd worked some extra volunteer days at the Deaf School because of a budget shortfall, and then been laid off for falling asleep a couple of times and failing to show up for work.

By 1991, I was living with a new lady and Laura and I had divorced. In the divorce settlement, Laura got the big library we'd accumulated over the years; I got the Olds wagon. I was happy. If you own a station wagon, you never have to worry about a place to stay.

The next sticker I stole from a recently totaled vehicle I spotted in a junk yard. A friend drove me out South Congress and we walked around the lot. Junkyards have always inspired me to reverence like in a church or at a museum in front of Brontosaurus bones. Whitman would have loved strolling in junk yards. I pretended that day I was looking for a rear view mirror.

Now it is 1998 and I am fifty-four. My beloved Olds wagon died in my driveway in 1993 after a trip down from Dallas. I sold what parts I could and then sold the remaining by the pound as scrap steel to be melted down, so she got a proper, recycled burial. Dust to dust, car to car.

I now own a 1981 Chevy van, a 1977 Nissan 280Z, a 1991 Izuzu Stylus, a 1986 Mustang, and a 1976 Winnebago Chieftain. I spend a lot of enjoyable time wandering junkyards on the edges of cities searching for parts. The combined cost of my golden oldies is less than what you'd pay for a single family vehicle. I now also have a retirement fund, in recognition of the body's fading powers.

So many years living poor, I know, has made me a tad obsessive. A family must have wheels. You never know who might be at your front door when you need to flee out the back and drive away into the night. I subscribe to the white trash dictum: a lot of old wrecks in the yard and one is bound to work. Whichever we're driving at the time, I make sure they're inspected, licensed, registered, and insured.

I have not talked to Laura in five years. She's back in the woods, somewhere in the lost pines of Bastrop country east of Austin, living on ten acres in a trailer with no electricity or water. She's got a no trespassing sign nailed to the front gate and wrote me once that the Law would be fetched if I showed my face on her property.

It has taken a long time to clear my system of poverty consciousness. I like to think that once being poor means I'll always be crafty. My family still lives without credit cards. For Christmas I mail to friends and relatives homemade chapbooks of poetry. My wife and daughter, we eat out maybe four times a year.

I have a wise aunt who refuses to even ride in a pickup because her family lost everything during the depression and ended up scratching on an uncle's farm. I have a "new" mother-in-law, from my six-year marriage, who saves string and cannot throw out paper boxes. She's got two rooms in her four bedroom house stuffed with string in boxes. In the paper I read about a Vietnamese woman who has been in the U.S. for ten years. She began by crushing aluminum cans picked up off the street, but she's a millionaire now. She drives an old Ford wagon, and lives in a small apartment with a roommate. ✿

THE SHAPE OF THE WORLD

by Carolyn Osborn

Marshall was quiet, so quiet he hardly said a word all the way back to the place. Not wanting to leave him in the back all alone, Carter put the boy in the front seat between him and Sarah. He was used to bridling and saddling, to working with cinches and bits, but he'd fumbled at first with the door after Sarah, in her quick way, reminded him with a silent glance, how the boy's parents had died. Carter knew he would remember the day they went to pick up their nephew long after Marsh was a grown man with children of his own.

When they learned they couldn't have a child, he and Sarah comforted themselves by telling each other there were enough children in the world, certainly enough in their families. They would enjoy their nieces and nephews. The horses they raised would be useful for riding lessons. Maybe they would have gone on believing other people's children were enough, maybe they would have gone on making do and it would have been all right. But they got Marshall, and everything was different. The world grew rounder, Carter decided. He was given to amplitude, to ease and patience. Sarah . . . well, Sarah was different. He'd realized early he was drawn to her because she was. She had piercing eyes, soothsaying eyes, though too often she foresaw darkness. He often teased her out of gloom. Not that day though.

"He may still be in shock," she warned when they left home to drive over to Henry's.

It was early in the summer, June. Rains were good that year. They had just planted the second crop of coastal. The field was a dark brown patch outlined in green. Indian blankets and coreopsis turned the ditches by the highway into a red and yellow blur. With enough rain the hill country looked rich, grass and wildflowers almost covered the limestone ridges. By

August the land would begin to show its bones again.

"Surely he'll still be grieving," she said. They had already waited for a week after his parents' funeral before meeting with the rest of the family to decide who would raise ten-year-old Marshall. Marshall's father, Carl McNeil, had two brothers and a sister, and his mother Liz had one brother and five sisters. As large as both families were, they had all agreed Carter and Sarah should take the boy. A sister on each side had never married. The rest either had all the children they could look after and men gone off to serve, or were too old or unsuited one way or another. Carl hadn't said in his will who should raise his son, neither had Liz. They had trusted the family to work it out. In forty-two with a war on nobody knew what might happen anyway.

When he and Sarah arrived at Henry's, Carter still had to ask him, "Are you sure?" With two boys of his own, Henry was the only other real candidate. Everyone agreed a boy needed a father, and both of them had agricultural exemptions from the draft. Henry was running the home place. Carter who'd sworn there must be other ways of making a living beside raising cotton, had taken up breaking horses and chasing cows for the double W, the nearest ranch of any size. Slowly he and Sarah were buying their own ranch.

"You and Sarah will be good for him. He'll get all the attention this way. We'll all help, Carter."

He'd told him they would probably need all the help they could get. Except for having the nieces and nephews out to spend weekends, he and Sarah had no experience with children. Just then Marsh started downstairs in a pair of faded green shorts, a white tee shirt and tennis shoes already looking too small for him. He was carrying a big old brown striped suitcase, one of his father's probably, that bumped against one leg. And, looking up at him, at his eyes intent on his steps, his hair still showing the thrust of a wet comb through it, his mouth set in a line, Carter reached for the suitcase. "Let me help you," he said. Sarah eyes were full of tears as she spread her arms wide to welcome the boy.

At first they were uncomfortable, mainly they were all unsure, but there was time for them to get used to living with each other before school started. Marshall had never been talkative. Accustomed to being the only child, he could amuse himself for hours reading alone. Sarah didn't want that. She coaxed him into the kitchen, let him read at the round oak table while she made cookies, got him to talk while he ate. Every night they sat in the living room listening to some anonymous droning voice or Winchell's frenzied report of the war news. Marshall, filled with a child's outrage, announced, "I hate Hitler!" Carter started to laugh and held it. In a way he too hated Hitler although he'd never profoundly hated anyone or anything except perhaps cancer and a long drought.

Slowly the boy began to join their lives, to go with him to the barn, to look after a puppy somebody had dumped at the farm's front gate, to watch when he gave the young horses their first lessons. Marsh gave him back his boyhood. He took him catfishing in the creek and taught him the patience required to train a two-year-old to allow a saddle to touch his back. Often he was startled to hear his father's sayings coming out of his mouth, to listen to himself telling Marsh, "Every horse has its own personality." The boy's questions led him to speak of things he'd hadn't spoken of often. Raised mainly in town, a visitor in the country, he wanted to know every-thing—who had owned the land before any of the McNeils did, why stallions were inclined to be more nervous than geldings, what led quail to nest on the ground and lose their hatch to a heavy rain, exactly how wet roads could make cars skid.

Of course, they told him it was a car wreck. It was a rainy night and the car skidded. Who was going to tell him any different? Some of them on Liz's side didn't know or didn't want to know. The McNeils kept quiet. Probably no one knew the whole story but Henry and him. And they couldn't really know more than about half, Carter decided. That was all right. Carl and Liz could have mended the quarrel everybody knew they'd been having, an old fight about money, saving or spending. Every young couple had the same one then. There was so little of it, and Carl had just lost his land to the government's new airfield. They'd paid him, called it that, but not enough to buy the same acreage. There was something more. Always was. Carl had a terrible temper and Liz equaled him. They shouted at each other when they were mad, and sometimes they hit each other,

Carl had confessed to Henry. Maybe they had made up by the time their car went off the road into the river. Carter, thinking about that moment, always hoped that they died from the fall down the cliff, not from drowning in the car. He couldn't drive that road without wondering about them.

A lot of country was marked for him . . . a rose bush in a pasture was all that was left of the log cabin where Mama and Daddy spent their first year, the spring where he found arrowheads after rains, the Spanish oak he'd come upon half-covered with a silvery collapsed weather balloon, the fence post with a hole hiding a wren's nest. Some he'd marked himself like the graveyard for favorite horses—Keeper, Dan, Samson—all buried under tall crosses made of metal poles. Between them laid the dogs, their names on wooden crosses . . . easier to carve those than to scratch the horses' names in. His fences followed property lines made before he was born. Probably the house and barn would last longer. In the end the country could easily claim it all again just as the river claimed Carl and Liz . . . never had shown Marsh that spot . . . better for him not to know. At the time he'd been safe at Henry's spending the night with his cousins.

Twelve years later when Marsh came home for Thanksgiving bringing Marianne, Carter thought of the small boy coming down the stairs holding onto the too big suitcase like it was part of his life. That was the way he held onto Marianne's hand. Like it or not, he and Sarah watched him switch loyalties. Strange at first . . . Marsh going off so far to school and wanting to marry somebody from up in Tennessee. What did that matter? After all the McNeils had come from there. Outgrowing the ground his father held, his own father shifted his way west right after the Civil War. Sarah's people started out in Virginia and got to Texas a generation earlier. Marianne talked different, Sarah said, forgetting her own people had. Why shouldn't Marianne? A city girl from the South. Marsh wanted a wife. It was going to be someone. He was prepared to get along with her. Sarah was a harder case. Women, he thought without rancor, always believed there was more at stake.

After Marsh and Marianne had left they sat on the porch and talked while the dark settled in.

Sarah's voice was hesitant when she began. "Her family sounds . . . I don't know . . . peculiar. She laughs about them a lot, but I wonder— Sounds to me like they've gone to drink and decline."

"Maybe we sound the same to them," he teased. " An old cowboy and his wife who wears her boots in the kitchen from a family still hanging onto land so drought-bitten nobody can raise anything but rocks."

"Still...."

"It doesn't matter how they sound, Sarah. He's going back up there and he'll marry her. And it doesn't matter she wasn't raised in the country and isn't a Baptist. She's a good rider."

"Horses!" Sarah accused him. He could almost see her eyes glinting in the dusk. "That's all you think about! That girl doesn't go to church even."

"Oh well," Carter said mildly. He wasn't heavy on church himself. Religion took all kinds of shapes. There were plenty that showed up every Sunday that weren't particularly good folks. Sarah would like Marianne well enough given some time.

It took longer than he'd thought. Most women he'd known became friends in their kitchens, but Marianne would hardly come near Sarah's. Of course, like the rest of them, she did walk in the house through the kitchen door . . . carrying a pie sometimes. She was good with pies, even Sarah admitted. Otherwise she stayed close to Marsh, went out to the stables with him, rode with him, sat in the living room with both of them like she didn't know she should be in the kitchen. It got so he had to get in the kitchen himself, lay the table, pour the iced tea. If he didn't Sarah worked up such a head of steam, he feared she'd let it boil out on the girl.

Washing up after they left, Sarah snapped, "She's used to servants, I guess. Well, I won't be hers! Miss Hoity-Toity!"

"Oh, Sarah—"

"Whether they had help or not, she should know it's only common decency—Nevermind!" She reversed herself as she was liable to when she got mad. "I can do them. I'm used to doing dishes."

"You could ask her—"

"I don't want to."

Stubbornness starched her back so, it aggravated him. Her shoulders bent, her hands clutching the side of the sink, she looked like a cat about to hiss. He started toward her, came as near as he ever had to shaking her before he caught himself. Ashamed at his anger over such a small thing, he edged away to stack the plates he'd just dried in a clattering heap on the cabinet's shelf.

He didn't understand why she wouldn't let go a little, but what was the use of quarreling with his own wife over kitchen chores. Sarah wasn't altogether uncharitable. She'd forgiven him many a time for snubbing a horse too close. Those first years when they were trying to make a little extra by breaking other people's horses at home, she'd been the one on back of her own gelding with the reins of the horse he was breaking wrapped around her saddle horn. Close, sometimes so close they were leg to leg and he feared breaking hers, but she kept his horse from throwing his head up and bucking. They worked together like they had one mind. She wasn't of the same mind now. She wasn't unkind, not outright, but she continued to be a fault-finder.

After a while Marianne started helping more. She was the one who laid the table. Marsh must have caught on. Probably he told her she needed to do something beside pies. He began putting up the dishes, said he remembered where everything went, so Marianne took over the washing. It was like they had agreed on this between themselves before they drove out to the country.

Then it was clothes. Sarah thought she either dressed up too much or not enough. She came out to the house wearing high heels the first time. Later she took to wearing bluejeans every visit, and that didn't suit Sarah any better.

He argued, "If she goes to the barn with us, she needs to wear britches."

"She could wear some that don't need mending," Sarah snapped. Marianne displeased her by being herself. Eventually he saw jealousy was part of it. Sarah hadn't wanted to let go of Marsh. They were late getting him. Maybe she hadn't got through mothering by the time he married. When he faced her with this, she said they had only raised him to let him go like she knew she was supposed to say it. Her hardness wore on him.

As a boy Marsh didn't inherit much of Carl's temper, but when he sensed any sort of unfairness he was quick to talk back. About the time he was fourteen he began to get in fights often, generally with bigger boys. Maybe it wasn't all because of bullying; high spirits led to fighting sometimes like it did with young horses. Marsh was light, so he lost a lot. One of his teachers suggested they get him to run track. He was too light for football, running would be good for him. Accustomed to training young horses to a long walk and a fox-trot for men who needed a good traveling horse to ride all day, running for the sport of it seemed a strange notion at first. When Marsh began running he walked beside him on a horse, then at the boy's insistence, let him go alone. Probably it was too discouraging to run against a horse. The world grew again, stretched out to the oval of a race course where Marsh ran against other boys, ran against time. Sarah and he went to all the meets, talked to the rest of the parents.

"We should adopt him," Sarah said.

But hadn't they already? And hadn't he adopted them?

Sarah seemed to agree until he married. Not until the babies were born did she soften up. At first she thought Marianne ought to quit her job and stay home with the children. He told her not to say so. She didn't need to say anything directly. Instead, she asked Marianne a lot of sharp questions about the woman she'd hired to help, talked about the shortness of childhood, carried on about the girls. They came to visit whenever Marianne would let them. Sarah complained it wasn't often enough. Gradually Kate and Sally did what Marianne couldn't do alone. They played with measuring spoons and old tin bowls and dough till Sarah taught them both how to make biscuits even though Kate was the only one really old enough to learn.

They were messing around with that about the time he retired . . . too soon. No help for it, and no use to feel sorry for himself either. He wasn't needed. That was all. He kept telling Sarah he wasn't unhappy. Well, maybe he was a little. People quit buying horses for a while; or they weren't interested in the kind he trained, or in the eighties, less of them could afford horses. He kept three of his own, two geldings he loosed to run in the small pasture in front of the house and a stallion he put to stud. The stallion brought him a little company, brought people who liked to talk horses. Easy to stand around a corral or down at the feed store jawing, too easy. He turned to improving his small herd of cattle, to trying different breeds of bulls then began restoring an unused horse trap behind the bard. He planted native grasses mixed with wildflowers—big bluestem, Indian grass, little blue, side oats, and switch grass, combined with Engehlman daisies, Maxmillian sunflowers, bluebonnets, coreopsis, paintbrush gay feather. Many of the wildflowers like pucoon and purple dalea he'd never heard of before. Blistering his hands harvesting, he re-sowed, repeating the names to Sarah until she knew them, the same way they had taught the name of heroes and dates of battles to Marsh. Gave him history, he said when he went off to college to study more of it. Carter filled in the hours with other tasks. In wet times he mended water gaps, checked on fence staples, kept after the weeds in his vegetable garden, and in dry months he shored up the small dam he'd built on the creek, reset fence posts, cleaned out the tank, repaired gates. The country busied him enough. Sarah, when they were younger and poorer, kept chickens, but he wouldn't raise hogs. He'd take up serious fishing before he'd take up hogs.

Every afternoon late he leaned against one of the peeled cedar posts on the front porch and watched his horses running in the pasture. There was never one by himself; they stuck together. Two with the stallion was all he could afford, all he could manage without help, without somebody to feed, muck out, groom, exercise. Of course, there was Marsh living in Austin with Marianne and the children, three counting the new baby, the first boy.

"Young daddies don't have as much time as they used to," Sarah said. "They help out with babies more now."

How would she know a thing like that? Read the paper, watched. Kept those dark eyes trained on young couples with children at church.

Soon after Martin was born, Marsh bought the old Clayton place down the road and said he wanted to go into horse breeding and training. They joked about trying to buy both the places in between so the land would be adjoining. The money it took to run a horse farm was no joking matter though. Carter said he'd do what he could to help him, but what made Marsh think he could make enough to live on?

"I don't really have to, Uncle Carter. With what we've both inherited and Marianne's job, we can manage . . .barely."

They brought all three children along with them while he and Marsh worked on the barn. When Marianne decided to help, she left the little girls with Sarah.

"Won't you let me keep the baby, too?" she begged.

Carter had warned her that Marianne might not leave Martin. He didn't think she was vindictive. She only wanted to keep the new one close, the way some mares were more protective of their colts than others. Of course, he didn't say so. Long ago Sarah had broken him of comparing women to horses . . .out loud.

Gradually Marianne began to share the baby. Another boy for Sarah. A way of doing it again. She could talk to Marianne about raising boys. Her world shrank to the size of a bassinet. She was that crazy about the baby. Carter worried a little about Kate and Sally noticing. Instead they acted as if it were normal. And maybe it was. Some women were partial to babies.

Everything seemed normal for a while. Carter, caught by the current of his life, enjoyed an older man's pleasures, found himself considering the right size of horse for Martin's first lessons, the spots he and Marsh would take him fishing, then Martin died all alone in the night in his baby bed for no reason. He didn't like to say it, not even to himself. Crib death. Ugly sounding. Unnatural. That was what happened though. In a rare spell of misery, Carter held onto the iron of reality. Early in November when all the earth had turned dry brown and gray they had a little private funeral at the graveyard, put him next to Carl and Liz, his grandparents who had given up a son to him and Sarah and had never lived to see their grandson. After the service they went home all numb and knowing nothing.

Marianne would have nothing to do with any of them. Did she turn on Marsh, too?

"She won't let me help" Sarah cried.

"I expect she's not feeling too . . .too. . . ." What was it he wanted to say? "Generous." Was that it? Or was Marianne numb as he was? Carter didn't think so. Maybe she just seemed to be. Sometimes grief was like being in a bad dream that wouldn't end when you woke up. It went on and on so you wished you could sleep forever. Was that the way it took Marianne?

Sarah had tried. They had gone to the house, taken food. Sarah took charge of the kitchen, looked after all the flowers people insisted on sending though Marsh and Marianne had asked them not to. Kate and Sally had been sent away to a friend who had children their age. Best for them, Marianne said. They were too young, five and three, to come to a funeral, she and Marsh said. Children that age couldn't understand death.

"They know he's gone. They slept in the same room with him. That's enough for now."

Who would speak against them? Carter couldn't, nor could Sarah.

Marianne's cousin Fergus was the only one from her family to come down from Tennessee. He wasn't there long, and Sarah vowed he drank the whole time. "All of the Moores do."

"Hush," Carter said knowing she might be quiet, but she'd go on thinking it. Maybe they would have another baby, maybe not. His and Sarah's world became the shape of the small country cemetery and it seemed to be ruled by accident.

Sarah tried to comfort him, to comfort both of them by talking about all the other McNeils. She reeled off the names of the next generation, fourteen of them. The only time he ever saw some of those children was Christmas at Henry's house. He didn't like to say so, but he forgot the names of two or three. Kate and Sally and Martin were his and Sarah's.

Marsh seemed as quiet about the loss of his son as he'd been about losing his parents. Grief was strangely private and public. Some people it diminished; some it made larger. Marsh and Marianne were lean in their grief. Sarah kept on cooking for them as if she might stuff them both so full there wouldn't be any room for hurt. He could tell they weren't eating much. Sorrow already filled them up. They rocked on that way awhile, he and Sarah alone at the place, Marsh and Marianne staying in town with the girls.

When Marianne called, Sarah couldn't tell him what she said right away.

"What is it?" He kept asking.

"She wants me to keep Kate and Sally awhile, a week maybe. She asked me to, Carter." She sat down on the sofa letting herself go slack against the pillows, looking like she'd had the wind knocked out of her.

"You going to?"

"What do you think?"

He could have pointed out Marianne and Marsh had a lot of friends. There were plenty of others they could have called on. Hard as she'd been for years, she was the one fortunate enough to be chosen.

"She needs some time by herself she says."

Again he nodded. He could already see the world widening again as her arms opened to encircle Marianne and the two girls. ✿

FRIENDLY FIGHT

by Jerry Craven

"Can you do the two-step?" Angela asked.

Jason sat beside Angela in Hyram's extended-cab pickup. He had been on Hyram's ranch only a few days, but he already knew that if he admitted to ignorance of anything, he would draw a look of bemused tolerance from the ranch hand, a laugh from Hyram, or a sneer from Angela. He shrugged. "I don't know."

"That answer's dimwitted as a possum. You know how or you don't."

"It ain't likely he can," Hyram put in. "I'd risk all my egg money on the proposition that them folks over in Malaysia don't exactly make a habit of the two-step on a given Saturday night."

Jason stared at Hyram. "You have such a colorful way of talking that I often don't understand."

"Hang on to your buttons and it'll all come to you in time." Hyram looked pleased.

"So do you, or what?"

"He don't, and that's a natural fact. But Angela, honey, it ain't because he's stupid, which he ain't. It's just ignorance born of privation. A body is stuck with stupidity for life. Ignorance is curable, which is how come you're gonna teach him the Texas two-step."

"Can't judge a man by dance steps," Odom said from the back seat. Jason glanced at him. Like my grandfather, Jason thought: Odom looks like a Texas version of my grandfather who wouldn't know the two-step from a broad jump, but the old ranch hand managed to tell me that the two-step is a kind of dance. At least now Jason knew the subject of the conversation. And he knew that the place they said they were going, the Crystal Pistol, had to be a dance hall. When he first heard the name, he thought it sounded like a bordello in a western movie.

Jason considered telling them that he had once taken ballroom dance lessons then decided that would draw laughter. But isn't a waltz something they would understand? He remembered reading about frontier people dancing to waltz music. "I can dance to some kinds of music," he offered.

"That's a start, I guess. Tonight, you learn the two-step from an expert. Me."

"She's right there," Hyram said. "The two-step is her trump suit."

"He'll have ever cowgirl in the place hot to trot for him soon as they look at the proper way we dressed him. Them that don't fall in love with him right off will do so just as soon as he learns the two-step." Angela laughed.

With a nod Jason accepted the compliment, though he felt less certain about his costume. In Malaysia where he had lived for the previous decade, anyone seeing him would assume he was going to a masquerade ball, dressed as a Hollywood cowboy.

Hyram and Angela had taken Jason shopping for the weird western clothing, then, when he was suited up, they informed him that they were going to The Crystal Pistol in Amarillo. Hyram said it was time to introduce Jason to proper night life. When Jason asked what The Crystal Pistol was, Hyram had laughed and quoted a dirty limerick about a cowboy named Chuck who spent Saturday nights doing things that rhymed with his name.

The limerick made The Crystal Pistol seem even more like a bordello. But Jason dismissed the possibility since it seemed unlikely Angela would go to such a place. He decided they were going to a western bar, and he had not risked further ridicule by asking more questions about the place.

Hyram waved a hand at the street. "This is Amarillo Boulevard, once known as North-East Eighth. Part of the old Route Sixty-Six. Keep an eye out and you'll see some of the local gals. There's two now."

The women he pointed out wore sequined, low-cut blouses, tight shorts, nylon stockings, and high heels. They waved at men in trucks, motioning for them to pull over to the curb.

"Them's busy bodies," Odom said.

"Yep," Hyram said. "You can see them infesting the Boulevard from

St. Anthony's Hospital to the old air force base. Cops crack down from time to time and run the hustling indoors, but them pavement princesses keep coming back, working the truckers and cowboys."

"Hyram, you gonna let on you never had an eye for a fallen angel?" Angela asked.

"Never underestimate them gals," Hyram said. "I done one up in a poem once":

A flatbacker floozie from Amarillo
hung by her heels from a willow.
She said 'I'd prefer,' to her John
an oak tree or a pecan,
but a willow is better'n a pillow.

Hyram looked pleased with himself.

"So you do have an eye for some of them rental models?"

"An eye, yes—at one time. Back when my teeth weren't wore down much and I was too young to have the sense God gave a goose. But an eye, that's all I had for them. Them painted ladies was interested in other parts of a man's anatomy than his eyeballs, so I weren't too popular with them."

When they drove into the parking lot of The Crystal Pistol, Jason thought it looked like a converted barn, an impression reinforced by the appearance of the interior.

"Ain't but a few folks dancing," Hyram said. "But that'll change as the night gets on. What do you say we take that table over there? It's got the dance floor on one side for us dancers and the bar on the other for Odom."

"Y'all take the table," Odom said. "I aim to sit on a bar stool and paint my tonsils with some Wild Turkey whiskey. Dance while I gab with the beer wrangler standing over there on the sober side of the bar."

Hyram pulled out a chair for Angela. Jason sat beside her at a tiny table. A waitress placed a bowl of pretzels and three glasses of ice water on the table. "Draws all around," Hyram told her. "No. Make that two draws, and you ask this cowboy what he wants."

The waitress turned to Jason. "Bottle beer? A mixed drink, maybe?"

"Bring me a cola."

The waitress nodded and left. "Bring me a cola," Angela mocked.

"Jason, you gotta do better than that."

Hyram chuckled. "Me, I'm heading for the throne room. You two get out there and work on teaching him the two-step." Hyram went to the men's room.

"Not yet, Angela. I want to watch first and have you describe what I'm supposed to do."

The band played "Jose Cuervo, You're a Friend of Mine," and two couples danced, moving around the floor with speed and energy. Angela leaned close and described the two-step. While she talked, Jason noticed a tall man sitting at the bar next to Odom seemed to be staring at them. He clutched a beer mug and slit his eyes in a mean way.

During the next song, the man came over to them, set his beer on the table, and announced, "Pretty woman, you're going to dance this one with me."

Angela glanced at him, then returned her attention to Jason. "No I ain't."

"Come on, sweetpea." The man took her wrist. She struggled to pull back, and he held tight. The man laughed.

"Let go of her." Jason started to stand, but the man's fist caught him just below his left eye before he was on his feet. The blow threw him back into the chair, and the chair fell over backward.

"Now. About that dance."

"I don't dance with drunks." Angela jerked away from him.

Jason, stunned, began getting to his feet as Odom tapped the man on the shoulder. He turned and looked down at Odom. "What do you want, pops?"

"Just to learn you some manners." Odom's fist shot out, catching the man in the stomach. Jason heard him expel his breath just before Odom's other fist connected with the man's ribs. Odom hit him twice more as he fell. "You all right, Angela?" Odom asked.

She nodded. Jason picked up his chair as Hyram returned. Odom looked with contempt at the man on the floor, picked up a beer and poured it on the man's crotch, then returned to his bar stool. Jason looked around. A few people glanced at the man as he rolled to one side, clutching his stomach, but other than that, people ignored them. Jason sat down.

"People act as if that attack was normal."

"It ain't normal. But it also ain't none of their business." Hyram nudged the man with the toe of a boot. "Seems to be awake." He sat across from Jason. "I told the bouncer to lug that sack of pig bones out of here. A man that would cross Odom has the IQ of a cantaloupe. He might look like a skinny little runt, but Odom would fight a buzz saw and give it three turns head start. You doing all right, honey?"

"I'm fine. It was nothing, Hyram. I could have handled the drunk. Odom didn't have to step in like that, fists swinging."

Jason poured ice water on a napkin and daubed his cheek.

"He tagged you a good one, there," Hyram observed. "That eye will get black as the inside of a coffin. Come tomorrow, me and Odom will show you a few Texas tricks with your feet and fists so next time you can avoid getting pounded like that. But tonight, you learn to two-step."

Angela and Hyram leaned toward one another so they could make a show of talking rather than watch Jason holding a wet napkin to his eye.

Jason looked at the man on the floor. Somebody ought to do something for him, Jason thought. But not me. I'm too angry at him.

The bouncer picked the man up by his belt and dragged him toward a side door. "What will he do with the fellow?" Jason asked.

"Dunno. Maybe put him in his pickup. Maybe just toss him out in the alley. Forget him. You ready to have Angela teach you a proper Texas dance?"

Sunday afternoon Jason heard the rattle of Odom's pickup and looked out the window. Odom got out, squatted beside the tack shed and began rolling a smoke. Jason, sitting in Hyram's formal living room, heard Hyram enter. "You got to be the only person ever to use this room, except for when I throw a party."

Hyram looked normal to Jason, which was something of a surprise, considering how much beer the man had drunk the previous evening. It had been necessary for Jason to drive home. Angela went to sleep after climbing into the back seat of the extended cab pickup. Odom and Hyram rode up front, laughing and singing dirty songs.

"Why did Odom just arrive? I thought he didn't come out to the ranch on Sundays."

"Mostly he don't, except when he needs to do something. Today some of what he needs to do involves you, so how about putting your boots on and joining us out back? By the tack shed." Hyram left without waiting for a response.

Jason eyed his boots with distaste. They had put a blister on one toe and chaffed his feet in a few places. He would have preferred tennis shoes, but Hyram had specified boots. I guess that means he and Odom are going to teach me to ride a horse, Jason thought with resignation. Hadn't Angela said something about needing boot heels in order to ride?

Before putting the boots on, Jason wrapped his blistered toe in a band-aid. When he got outside, he found Hyram holding out a can of tobacco for Odom. Both men were stuffing brown wads into their mouths. "Wanna dip?" Hyram offered.

"Thanks. I'll pass for now."

Hyram laughed. "Dipping ain't a prerequisite to be a real cowboy, but it don't hurt a man's image." He put a lid on the can and slipped it into his hip pocket.

"Your eye ain't half bad," Odom said.

"What he means is, that cowboy that knocked you one last night was either dog-shit stupid, thinking he could get by with a friendly punch, or he didn't know nothing about a barroom fight. Odom wants to show you what to do next time somebody takes a notion to hit you like that."

"There won't be a next time."

Odom and Hyram laughed as if Jason had told a good joke. Hyram slapped him on the back. "Odom is a man of few words, but he's a crack-erjack with his fists, as you saw last night. He'll show you how to bring a man down in a variety of ways, and I'll tell you when to go about choosing the right way."

"You're going to teach me to brawl?" Jason felt repulsed by the offer, but he tried not to show it.

"Basic rule in a bar," Odom said, "is never let a man get close like that cowboy done when I come up to him." Odom moved within inches of Jason. "Like this. Never let a man in like this."

"Jason, right now, Odom is showing you how to lay it on a man, so he won't get up for a long spell. Never hit a friend the way he's about to show you."

"If you aim to clean a man's plough, you get in close like this. Say something to him, maybe something that could get took as social, maybe even nice—just to distract him. Hold your arms loose, like this, with your hitting arm up a little high, but don't make a fist. Look him in the eye and hit him while you're talking. Hit him here." Odom set his fist against Jason's ribs. "Hook him hard with your knuckles, then follow up with the other fist, here."

Jason looked in amazement at Odom. Hyram laughed. "A blow like that might well crack a fellow's ribs. Like as not that cowboy Odom laid out at the Crystal Pistol is nursing busted ribs today. Like I said, hitting like that is something you reserve for somebody you don't mind hurting."

"Two is usually enough, if you go about it right. You might want to stick one or two more on him while he's going down, if he done something bad enough to deserve it." Odom stepped back. "Now come up to me, talking in a casual kind of way, and show me where you would hit me."

"Make like he just walloped Angela, but you let on that you took no notice of it, Jason. You don't want to warn a man of your intentions, or he won't let you get close."

"What do I say? Odom said threatening things last night as he went up to that man."

"But he said them in a nice voice. Besides, most cowboys look at Odom and size him up as harmless, him being skinny and old and not overly tall. But you ain't none of them things, so you gotta talk nice when you move in close. The tone is more important than the words, cause usually the man you aim to bring down is a tad drunk and slow to think on words. Say anything. Say, 'gosh, feller, would you mind if . . .' and then lay it to him like Odom showed you."

"Come on, now," Odom said.

Jason had no idea that there was an entire etiquette associated with violence. Certainly he had never come across such an idea while living in Malaysia. Maybe only Texans had rules about talk before beatings. But what the heck, he told himself, it'll do no harm to humor these men. "Gosh, mister, would you mind if I. . . ." He stepped close to Odom. "Then I would hit you here and then here."

"Good. But don't swing with your shoulder, or you might be in for a real fight. You want to avoid a real fight by ending it right off. Swing with your arm only. Jerk your fist up, keeping your shoulder still. Like this."

Odom had Jason go through the motions several more times, complete with speaking his lines. Jason felt as if he were rehearsing for a play.

"I do believe you got it." Odom looked pleased.

"Remember, Jason, to reserve rib cracking punches for them that needs pain. But if you get into a fight with a friend, you go about it different. Show him, Odom."

"A friend?" Jason felt confused.

"Start off more than arm's length. And you start with words." Odom stood in front of Jason. "Say stuff like this. You dumb sumbitch. You don't got the sense to pour piss out of a boot. Maybe you say some other choice things, and you go to lifting your dukes, only don't ball your fists just yet, cause you gotta let him say some things before you hit him."

"Fight a friend?"

"Odom's right. You go about it different. You might get pissed enough to put on your raking spurs, but you gotta keep everything in perspective. You don't want to break ribs or even lay out a fellow in a fight like that. You both might need to blow off a little steam, so you punch the shoulders and maybe the face. Odom'll show you. Remember the words are important. In a friendly fight, a man who can't cuss is useless as tits on a boar hog."

"But what do I say?" The whole affair seemed so absurd to Jason that he decided he might as well go along with it. He knew he would never use any of the skills Hyram and Odom seemed so bent on imparting, so it wouldn't hurt to learn them.

"The word *sumbitch* is a good one," Hyram said. "Use it when you can't think of nothing else. You might say something like 'you dumb sumbitch, your breath would knock a buzzard off a shit wagon.' I'll tell you later more about the fine art of swearing."

"When you're done with words, you want a fellow to feel pain, maybe even bleed some. But you don't put a buddy in the hospital, unless he done something that's gonna make him not ever your buddy again. You swing with your shoulder, like this." Odom took an exaggerated swing at Jason. "Swing hard, though, cause if you do connect, the other fellow will be moving back. Chances are you won't hurt him permanent. Now. Show me what you know."

Jason faced Odom. "You half pint of pig livers. Beside a son of a bitch like you, a goat's turd would look both tall and handsome."

Odom flushed and lifted his fists. "You dumb sumbitch," Odom growled. Jason stepped back, startled by the edge in Odom's voice and by the way his eyes hardened, as if the intelligence went out of them, replaced by cold fury. He swung a roundhouse that Jason saw coming from the way Odom moved his shoulders. Jason ducked under it.

Stepping between them, Hyram caught Odom's arm as it launched into another swing. "Don't go to getting snakes in your boots, Odom. The boy's just doing what you taught him." He held Odom's arm a moment.

"I guess." Odom ceased struggling.

Hyram looked at Jason. "Easy on the words during practice, boy. We don't want this to turn into a real fight of any sort. Odom, the boy's good with words, wouldn't you say?"

Odom struggled to work up a smile. "Fair to middling. But you gotta say *sumbitch* proper. Say it."

"Sumbitch. Did I do it right that time?" Jason tried to sound contrite.

"Accent ain't right. But it'll have to do for now." Odom sounded placated.

"Odom, you done good by the boy. We'll call it a day. Later, you can show him what to do if he can't get in close for busting the ribs of a genuine sumbitch, and he finds himself in real fight that means going to it buck tooth and hangnail."

"Thanks, Odom." Jason felt relief that the lesson was over.

Odom nodded. Hyram pointed toward the house. "Come on, Odom. I want your advice on where to put a barbecue pit when it comes time for my birthday party."

That afternoon, after Odom had left the ranch, Hyram asked Jason: "You ever buy a rubber?"

"Rubber?"

"A condom. Used to buy them myself, when I was about a hundred years younger. Somebody told me the best ones was made from sheepskin and not rubber at all. So I went into Walgreens and found the rubber displays and picked up a package of sheeskins marked 'size large,' me being young and having a notion that I was something of a stud. But come Saturday night, I couldn't get the thing on. It was too small, and being made out of sheepskin instead of rubber, it didn't stretch none. Dang near ruint my whole night. Next day I went back to Walgreens and discovered what I missed before. There was two other sizes of sheepskins other than large: extra large and extra extra large. The folks that made them condoms figured with some accuracy that no man would buy a size small, so they just jacked up the terminology some, calling *small* a *large* and the other sizes degrees of large. Men are sure enough funny when it comes to pecker size."

"That's a good story, Hyram."

"It ain't just a story. It's the unvarnished truth. And there's a lesson in it, for them that looks, especially for anybody wanting to learn to get along with Texas men. In Texas, you don't mention a man's height if he's a tad short. You can call a big man *tiny*, if you take a notion, and no harm could come of it. But you got to take care about talking to men who wear pockets low to the ground. Even when you're spoofing with a friend, you take care about naming words that have to do with size. Odom near busted a blood vessel when you called him a half pint and let on as he was smaller than a goat's turd." Hyram laughed. "I got to admit I admired your feel for swearing even if it didn't show good judgment."

"I meant no offense. Is Odom still angry with me?"

"Shoot no. He understood you was just cussing him cause he told you to. It's just that he popped a cork when he heard you imply he might have to jump some to be eye-level with your belly button. He must of figured you knew better, even joshing, but on reflection, he got over being so pissed. Him and me, we discussed the matter some, and he now believes that you learned your lesson about them short words. If you use one again around him, you better count on fighting your first friendly fight." ✿

El Soñador

by René Saldaña, Jr.

"Come here!" screamed my mother from the top of the hill behind our house. "¡Ven pronto, Armando!"

I dropped my shovel where I was digging our new trash dump and ran to be by her side. On the way I was slapped on the sides of my face and body by the branches of the shrubs that served as walls for the zigzagging labyrinth leading up to the hill's peak.

Even the mesquite trees seemed to have it out for me, knowing that I had a place where to be. I remember the week before having heard the cries of coyotes from somewhere close. I needed to get to my mother as quickly as my feet could carry me. "¡Mi'jo!" she screamed out again. "¡Apurate!"

I did. I tried to hurry. My legs, that were used to running up and down the mazes of the hill, had become weak. I could barely keep up this pace. I could see the top of the hill now and still hear my mother yelling out. My lungs had taken in too much oxygen it felt. My chest was burning. I could hardly take another breath.

The lashing of the branches didn't matter now. I was so close. So close that the whippings were nothing to me now. My only thought was to reach my mother. She needed my help.

"¿Mama, que te pasa? What's wrong?" I looked around frantically, to my left and my right, behind me, into the trees. Her back still to me. I tried making out what it could be that was made invisible by the black and brown brush, whatever it was that was causing my mother to scream like she was. But there was nothing. I looked all around and in the meantime tried to get the strength back in my legs and catch my breath. Here and there I could find nothing. A snake? A coyote that came close and left at her shrieking?

Then I looked at my mother, having walked up beside her. I had been more worried about protecting her from a would-be attacker that I had failed to notice her. I felt her presence there beside me, and I could hear her whimpering and whispering, so I knew she was alive and well. Scared, if anything. But alive.

I heard her talking again—but not to me. She was directing her words at her arms. I turned to her and said, "What's the matter, Mama? Why did you yell out for me? What do you have in your arms?" She looked up at me and smiled like I remembered her doing when for the first time she had shown me my baby sister. Her eyes back then were armfuls of moon, oceans of light. Her forehead was still wet from the delivery, drenched was she. Her hair slick from the sweat.

But she held Elisabet to me, wrapped in a cloth my grandmother had finished knitting in pink yarn. There was no doubt in her mind that I would be having a baby sister when she began her sabana, which told the story of a pink bird flying to a pink moon and laughing pink songs of children playing. She told me later, "Most people, they think it was a lucky guess. But I had a vision, mi'jito. La vi yo, and when I saw her, only she was already a woman with her own children in my dream, I knew you would have a sister."

My mother had already decided a week or two earlier that if it was a girl, she would name her Elisabet, and if it was a boy, Pedro. My grandmother, mi abuelita with black eyes that it appears she has no pupils, had also sewn in my sister's name.

My mother, right now, stood before me, with that same look in her eyes and smiling. I looked into her arms and chest, and I saw a naked baby boy. His hair, already growing out, was a light brown , almost yellow, and he had green eyes. "Andava buscando chiles, and look what I found instead. He was lying on his stomach by the coma bushes over there. He was playing in the dirt, writing baby letters. He looked up at me and laughed." She held his little naked body out to me, and I was hesitant at first to take him. Who is he? To whom did he belong? How did he get up this hill?

He reached out for me with his little piggy fingers and I took him. He laughed like church bells and then peed on me. My mother and he laughed and laughed like the world was coming to a hilarious end, or as though they had just heard a joke. At that instant I experienced my first vision, similar, I thought, to my grandmother's. I saw him sitting on the fence of rocks my father began building long before I was born and didn't get to finish, having died shortly after Elisabet's first birthday. But this boy, with brown hair and skin, with green eyes, was drinking water out of the bucket using the ladle. And my mother and Elisabet were there too. And we had just finished eating. A vision? Or my imagination?

I said to my mother and answered my first question, "His name will be Juan Antonio. And he will be my brother and your son. And Elisabet will love him also." He belonged with us. The answer to the last question: God would have let us know if it were important enough.

My mother took him from me and looked deep into his eyes and whispered to him: "Juan Antonio. It's a good strong name." She turned to me and said, "Juan Antonio, like your father." She wrapped him up in her apron and handed him to me.

I carried my baby brother in my crib-like arms wrapped snugly in my mother's apron dirty from cooking all her life. The baby seemed to be smelling in the wrap all that would be his future. He appeared to know that he would never be hungry. And I knew that he would grow up to be my brother. I whispered in his ear, low enough so that my mother could not hear me, "Siempre seras mi hermanito. What do you think about that? You will always be my little brother." And he only gurgled and spit up at me, but I knew he understood.

This time, going down the hill, I was careful not to let the branches touch any part of me so that Juan Antonio would not be hurt. And as though the mesquites knew this was a joyous occasion, instead of looking menacing, they danced in the wind. Their branches reaching to the skies in praise. These trees also were my brothers and sisters. My grandmother had taught me that long ago.

I did not know which to tell my grandmother first when she looked up from tending her rosales, whose flowers were a dark red, she told me, because of the blood she soaks the dirt in as a result of the thorns on the stems. That I could not believe because those thorns kissed the palms of her hands rather than prick them. They loved her like she did them.

Shoulders bent, she took the boy from me, made the sign of the cross on his forehead, and kneeled before the rosebushes. She took the finger from his right hand, punctured it with one of the thorns, and spilled a few drops of blood into the ground. Juan Antonio tried yanking his hand from her grasp, all the while yelling, cursing my grandmother for catching him off guard. She kissed his finger, put him on the ground, and he laughed again when he mixed his blood in with the wet earth.

"What's his name?" she asked. "And how are you, mi'jo?"

She held out her hand and elbow to me so that I could help her up. "Juan Antonio. We are calling him Juan Antonio."

"Anything else you want to tell me?" She was up already and walking to the rocking chair close by. "We'll talk later."

Mama had picked up Juan Antonio and sat next to Abuelita. "What shall we do, Mama?" she asked my grandmother. "He was up there all by himself, and no clothes on. Shall we report this to the sheriff? Someone must be missing him by now? But who would be so uncaring to leave a poor baby up in a hill? And you know he was left there on purpose because there was no other way he could have climbed all the way up there by himself. So. . . ."

"What does Armando have to say about it?" she asked my mother.

"He said he was my son, his brother and Elisabet's. But. . . ."

"No buts then. He is my grandson. No need to call the sheriff." After a few minutes she said, "I imagine Juan Antonio is hungry, and Elisabet will be home from school soon." My mother stood and took the boy into the house and fed him tamales heated up on the black comal. He also finished the bowl of beans a la charra my grandmother had left over from lunch time. Then he got his bath and slept.

Outside, my abuelita rubbed her eyes and yawned. "Is it time I start teaching you about the visions, Armando?"

"What?"

"You told your mother about how you decided on Juan Antonio?"

"No." I shook my head.

"Good. You shouldn't. Not yet anyway. Mira, people always come to me wanting to know what I see. They believe I can see. They have no problem with that. But when I tell them I see nothing, or I tell them what I see and it's not what they want to hear, they call me una vieja senil, inutil." My grandmother was holding my hand, both resting on her armrest. "A crazy witch, they say. And I can hear them even if they think I am deaf besides being useless. People are funny that way. That's my first lesson for you."

"Pero, you're telling me this why?" I asked her. "I could just have made up all those pictures in my head."

"Do you really think that? No, mi'jo. You have the sight. And for it you will be feared and cast out. Oh, the people will tell you hello when you go into town to buy groceries, but they will never look you in the eye. Tienen miedo. Afraid of the truth."

"So what if it is what you say?"

"It is, and you know it. I've been waiting for it to start."

I shook my head slightly, confused still about how she knew all this already. "Okay, assuming it is true—"

"It is."

"Okay, it is. Why would I want to be feared and cast out and be called names just because I see my brother drinking from that bucket there some twelve years in the future? I could just not tell anyone. And if I ask you not to tell, I know you won't."

"You're right. I wouldn't tell. Your question leads to lesson number two: weigh the options in your heart. I won't lie to you. You will be made the fool when you bump into a pole because you are staring out into the distance. But that same stare from you will cause people to faint also when you turn it on them." She sighed. "So, you have to decide. Share your vision, or hide it. Either way, you will still see life as it will happen. But the outcomes will be so different depending on your choice. It will be difficult. Because along with visions, you have the power of healing. And that is a good thing. So you give up parts of yourself, certainly, but have the privilege of so much more. Tonight, pray about it, and we'll talk more tomorrow."

I prayed. I prayed all the night long, my candles burning out before sunrise. All my Saints and the Virgin were shadows. I was sweating all the while. The smoke from the wax mingled with the smell of cilantro from just outside my window caused me to become more tired.

I dreamed while I was talking to God. I was talking to my father and to Juan Antonio out on the river. We were all wading, chest high in the rushing, cold water of the Rio Grande. The smell of the mud and cows and cactus on the banks was heavy in my lungs. My father and Juan Antonio were already in the middle of the river when I got there. I had heard their laughter wafting in the air. We gave one another an abrazo, and Juan Antonio was already old, and I could see his green eyes in the light of the moon. And my dad was biting down on a fruit of the mesquite like he used to do in the summers.

They stopped what they were talking about and looked at me. "What's your question? You will also have the power to heal. I don't see what the problem is," they both said. "You cannot turn your back on your people, think what they will. You have seen your brother sitting on the fence. And you and he finish building it."

"But what happens when I see him dying?" I asked.

"Your duty then is to help them deal with the pain. Trust me, mi'jo, it was no less difficult for me when your grandmother didn't share with me the time and circumstances of my death. I still cry because I cannot hold your mother as we sleep. Or help Elisabet blow out the candles on her cake. Or know my new son. Or teach you how to find answers in the earth. But Abuela was strong, no? She told you all those stories about me you thought you had forgotten, and it helped."

"You're right. But I am scared."

"Mi hermano is afraid! How can that be? You were ready to fight off a pack of coyotes if your mother was in danger the day you found me. Remember how scared you were then? But you knew you would do it. You knew you *could* do it."

"Tienes razón, Juan Antonio." And then we were on the bank of the river again rolling up our pants legs and began fishing. And while I fished I prayed and that's when I noticed my candles had burned out. The smoke from them was slithering around the heads of the saints.

I went to the makeshift crib my mother had made out of two tomato crates and the swabs of cloth leftover from my grandmother's quilting. The baby was wrapped in my mother's apron still, a habit he would never grow out of. As he became older, though, he asked our grandmother to sew it into a quilt of his own. That way he would not be embarrassed that he was covering himself with an old apron. The apron always covered his chest held tight by his chin right under his nose, even when it was made into the quilt. This morning he grabbed hold of my finger in his and smiled in his sleep. I could see him dreaming of the mole and the arroz my mother was expert at preparing every Sunday.

I checked in on Elisabet, who slept in the living room. She was sound asleep, her books scattered on the floor, the pencil still in her hand. I kissed her on the forehead.

My mother was out in the garden picking two good tomatoes for breakfast. "I'll start the coffee," I told her through the screened window.

She looked in my direction, and I imagined that all she saw was my silhouette because of the light of the kitchen behind me. She raised her hand and said, "Pero fuerte. Strong, like your grandmother and I like it."

My grandmother was out watering the rosales already. As I walked up behind her, she said, "In the hot months, it's better to get the earth nice and wet early so that the sun will not have a chance to dry up my babies. How went your praying?"

"My father sends his greetings. He told me to hug you and to kiss you."

"He's such a good son." The water from the hose was splattering the morning dirt, clouds of dust rising. "Was he able to help?"

"Yes, Abuela. He told me you would make a good teacher. So how could I say no?"

"Que bien," she said. "Now, take this hose and water my roses.

Knowing the earth is the third lesson for us dreamers."

I took the hose from her and saw how the ground was drinking in the water, getting ready to be friends with the sun instead of enemies. They would sit around a table like old friends and talk about how beautiful my grandmother's rosales are.

SET PIECE

by Carol Cullar

—— Alice, how long you been sitting on this porch?——
—— Hump! Nigh on to fifteen years, girl. And you? —— Their litany ran like a fanfare before the wire walker glides out onto the high wire. Rehearsed a thousand times, neither missed a cue as they began their opening routine. They played to the long-departed crowd, not bothering to listen to one another more than half the time.

—— What you think about that new day-girl? ——
—— Which one? Baggy Pants or Leg Weights? —— Alice's clouded eye followed the thrump-thrump of a chrome-loaded Chevy down the block. She watched its blur turn onto Pecan Street and heard the screech as it headed out of Cut and Shoot. Her good eye slid to Maureen on her left, who fiddled with her chin whiskers. Maureen captured one offending hair between horned nails and gave a sharp pluck. —— Leg Weights. ——

—— Hump. You're not letting her run get Cokes for you, are you? —
—— Huh. Johnson-in-twelve sat for four hours the other day with a soda straw in his mouth like some fool anteater, and she never brought his coin purse back. You gonna tell the Doc when she comes around? ——

—— Maybe, maybe not. Are you? —— Alice watched a blue Volvo roll west. Her grandchildren's car was blue like that, but not that shiny.

—— Could be, could be. —— Maureen savored the balancing act between action and inaction, played out both scenes behind the curtains of her flesh before continuing, —— Say, how's that Johnson-in-twelve strike you? ——

—— Not bad, when he's not drooling. —— Alice tucked a stray lock under her chiffon head scarf. Today it was hot pink, and her gnarled hand hovered over a mother of pearl button on her flat chest.

—— Huh. Had his pecker out the other morning in the dayroom, he did. Half hour before Baggy Pants came by and zipped him up. I saw you eyeing him. ——

—— Hump. That's what you say. —— Alice contemplated an interruption to the performance, decided it was probably worth it as a dirty Nissan skittered by. No one she knew. The plates looked to be Louisiana, anyway.

When she failed to move on to the next gentleman resident of Bluebonnet Manor, the vanished audience gasped. There was a pregnant pause. —— I did more than that, girl.—— The performer fell into the waiting net.

—— You never. —— Maureen had much experience with these little trips and slips Alice occasionally threw her way, but she was too much a veteran to let a small side step divert the routine, besides if she admitted it, a little impromptu added freshness to the performance, so she covered her partner's diversion by adjusting her glasses and wiping the corners of her lips free of straying lipstick. Today it was palest orange.

—— What do you think? —— Alice's cheeks wrinkled all the way up to her ears.

Maureen leaned over the arm of her chair, her full attention on the shriveled face of the woman she had lived beside for more years than she cared to count—ever since her hip broke and Doyle moved his family to Dallas. The smirk on her friend's face caught the weak sun, trapping its brief bounty in a thousand crevices and wrinkles. Circus balloons were not more bright.

—— Time's too short for lies, Alice Ann. You tell me now what you did with Johnson-in-twelve.—

—— And have you tell that preacher son of yours? Ha. Not likely, Maureen Potts. I've heard enough sermons in this lifetime. You just put your teeth back in your mouth and get that wrinkle out of your drawers. I'm every day of eighty-six years old, and if I want to die with a smile on my face, I just will—without you sermonizing, or some tom-fool, pompous ass praying over me. Is that the Doc's car turning the corner there? ——

—— Don't change the subject. You've already upset everything. And we were gonna enjoy a nice, long visit in the sun. ——— By now the audience would have lost interest and departed for the next sideshow. There'd be no applause at all now. She contemplated that bitter prospect.

——— Hump. ———

——— Are you my lifelong friend or not? ———

——— Hump. ———

——— Don't I read to you—Ann Landers and Dear Abby—every day? ———

Hump. Is that Doc's car turning in the drive? You going to mention Leg Weights? ———

——— No. That's not her car. You're just putting me off. After all these years I thought I meant more to you. ——— Maureen began to collect her pocketbook, kleenex, sweater. There were tears in her eyes.

———Where are you going? ——— Maybe she would share some of the details. She hadn't heard what Dear Abby had to say today. It wasn't as if Johnson-in-twelve had sworn her to silence—he hadn't uttered six words, just beamed his gratitude, hugged her close. She did wish he hadn't called her Sarah! Sarah! But Sarah was long gone, and it wasn't as if she were stealing anything from him, not like Leg Weights on the morning shift.

——— All right. But not one word to that tom-fool son of yours, you hear me? ——— She'd always hated clowns. ✸

Pink Mess With Lettuce

by Harold Knight

Sure looked to me back then like Grady O'Malley screwed things up for himself by bulldozing J.L. Smith with his stump. Grady walked up to J.L. and hauled his stump straight out and let his books fall to the ground. Without so much as a pause in the swing, he cranked his stump right into J.L.'s face.

J.L. flopped back and hollered and blood shot out of his nose. Blood covered his face and ran down inside his half-buttoned shirt and slopped onto his black-haired chest. J.L.'s nose began to swell up till it looked ready to explode. I, for one, never knew so much blood could run out of a guy's nose without him dying on the spot.

Grady should've known nobody could bulldoze J.L. and get away with it, specially if they broke his nose. Grady picked up his books and walked off with them in the crook of his stump in front of him like a girl instead of grabbing them in the one good hand God gave him and holding them against his hip like any other guy would—which is what had started the ruckus in the first place. J.L. called him a sissy and made fun of the way Grady held his books.

And Grady picking up his books and walking away, leaving J.L. stretched out on the ground in a pool of blood and growling from the pain didn't end it. The worst thing was that J.L. passed out cold. Imagine that, the toughest guy in school, muscle-bound and hairy—only a junior, and already center, both offensive and defensive, on our Class B football team. They beat the big school across the river last fall because the Double-A team didn't have anyone as mean as him. And he was bulldozed by a stump.

Grady crossed the quadrangle right where the sign said Keep off the Grass and went direct to the principal's office. He told me later all he said to Miller was he was sorry to cause trouble, that he got mad and hit J.L., but that he didn't mean to hurt him so bad. And wouldn't you know J.L. got in trouble because Grady told the truth. Miller liked that.

A long time later us guys got so we could laugh about it. We told each other Grady back-stumped J.L.—like back-handed. Get it? Guess you had to be there. J.L. doesn't laugh about it, though. Ever. Even now. I think he looks sexy with the crook in his nose and his black hair grown out like James Dean's since he got back from the army, but he doesn't think so. I guess J.L. would be proud of his crooked nose if he'd gotten it in a real fight with some guy he respected instead of some guy he still calls pussy and bitch and cunt and any other sissy-word he can think of, a guy that doesn't even have two fists but a useless half stump with five little bubbles on the end for fingers.

J.L.'s had his crooked nose ten years now. It happened that long ago and I for one remember it like it was yesterday. In a funny way it was the biggest day of my life, and the way J.L. still carries on about it, you'd guess it was the biggest thing ever happened to him, too.

Grady didn't have much of a chance from the day he showed up here a week before the big game—the first guy we'd ever had from an orphanage. And from some place up north—like Nebraska. No, he didn't have a chance. None at all, but not because of that useless stump. The guys actually thought the stump was kind of cool at first.

But he started getting the best grades and stuff like that, and the teachers liked him. So, of course, the guys got to thinking he was plain weird. Skinny as a rail. He wore work boots laced halfway up and sort of dangling at the end of his legs because he was tall and gawky and didn't fill them up, baggy jeans held up by a skinny belt with the end dangling down in front of his button fly, and a pink western shirt buttoned up to the top, one sleeve folded up—buttoned over that stump. He had blue eyes—I mean a strange kind of blue—like shiny metal. And that red hair of his. Long like a mop up front, not a normal crew-cut, and too smelly with Brylcreem.

Us guys laughed at everything else about Grady, but we knew better than to make fun of his stump because the teachers were strict about us being nice to handicaps. I guess you could say some of the guys hated Grady because he didn't get it about being weird. You could get away with something as weird as a stump if you made everything else about yourself real normal.

I should have told you that J.L. and Grady and me are the only ones from our gang who never moved away—still live around here. Not that Grady was actually part of the gang. But you wouldn't think it would have turned out like that. The gang broke up after graduation. Most of the guys left town and went other places and ended up in the same sort of grunt jobs they'd have had here if there'd been any. Make a half decent salary working in feed stores, driving trucks, teaching school—just average normal stuff.

A couple guys have made it big. Danny's cleaned up in real estate in Denver, and Billy the quarterback went into baseball and is up in the big leagues pitching for—I forget—the Reds maybe. Gary is in charge of building and grounds at some stuck-up college in Iowa, and Howard's got a dirty magazine store in Dallas.

But here J.L. and Grady and me are, stuck in the old home town but making a pretty good go of it. J.L. unloads insurance. I'm not sure how honest he is. You can bet he's not my agent. He still doesn't get it that Grady and me are close. Grady's got a bookstore. Sign says The Dig it UP Shop. Fancy place where people from all over the county come and order special books. Out of print, hard to get, or expensive gift-type books— books like I never read. And I've got my dirt moving business. I make out OK. A couple of dump trucks, a grader, a wheel loader, a dozer—and four good-looking Community College jocks to work for me.

Anyway, you might guess us guys couldn't believe Grady was strong enough to dump J.L. to the ground. J.L. came to and we stood around him with Danny bent over trying to clean up the blood, and he said someone should take J.L. up to the emergency room or make a call for the police ambulance. Miller came back with Grady, and he'd already called the ambulance. He asked J.L. if he wanted to go to Methodist Hospital or the

Charity Sisters.

J.L. said, "I ain't one of Father Flannigan's wimps."

And Miller said, "You want to tell me what happened?"

And J.L. said, "I get my hands on that one-armed Irish pussy, and he'll wish he hadn't messed with me."

Miller said, "Who started it?"

"Fucker can't take a joke," J.L. said. Must have been out of his mind with pain to say that word to Miller. He was just piling his problems up and making Grady look better and better in Miller's eyes.

The ambulance pulled up, and the emergency guys picked J.L. up real careful. They held him on one of those wheely stretcher things and loaded him in the back, his head raised up at a pretty good grade so he could see over his swollen nose—I guess to make sure he didn't drown in his own blood—and they headed to Methodist Hospital across the river. Grady stood there with his books tucked up under his stump in front of him. He had this kind of not mean but hard look in his eyes like the blue really had turned to some kind of metal. The other guys headed off to class. I felt like I had to say something to Grady.

"He had it coming," I said.

"It's useless fighting," Grady said and walked up the steps without even looking at me. He didn't walk awkward like you might think just to look at him. He was too sure of himself, I guess, and it didn't matter he was so skinny. Maybe that was another reason the guys didn't like him.

I sure wanted the whole business to be over, but I knew that was dumb because I knew J.L. I didn't know if I should care what happened to Grady anyway. I didn't know if the time we spent together made me weird, too—or made us friends, or made me a pussy, or made me Miller's pet, or backed me into the same corner with Grady—or what.

Like I said, I wanted it to be over, but I knew it wasn't.

J.L. showed up at school about noon with this humongous bandage over the bridge of his nose. Made him look even meaner than usual. And now he was the hero. Funny how he turned things around—made sure everyone knew he got the shaft because Miller was on Grady's side and would punish J.L. A broken nose and punished, too.

Of course J.L. meant to get even with Grady, and he went over to Grady's table in the cafeteria and sat down across from him. Didn't say a word, just sat down—Danny on one side of him and Billy on the other. Me and Gary and Howard sat across the table from J.L. like we always did. I was real nervous because that put Grady beside me.

Grady didn't look up from the dishes spread out on the table in front of him. They were serving those greasy sloppy joes, even greasier French fries you could smell clear up in the chemistry lab, and Lima beans. Wouldn't you know Grady had a salad with Thousand Island dressing in one of those heavy white cafeteria bowls. I knew whatever happened that pink dressing glopped on lettuce was going to make matters worse.

"So," J.L. said to Grady, "think that stump's pretty strong, don't you?"

Grady didn't say anything.

"Hey, you fuckin' freak, I'm talking to you." J.L. was getting hot under the collar, and everyone at the table was making like nothing was going on even though we could see the jig was up for Grady. J.L. was quiet for awhile and finished his sloppy joe. He squinted and stared at Grady the whole time, elbows on the table. J.L. never let up on the pressure.

Grady finished his sloppy joe, too, and stared somewhere that it was hard to tell. But it wasn't at J.L. Grady picked up his fork to eat his salad. He stabbed at it, and J.L. slid his hand across the table and back-handed the bowl so it flipped up and smacked Grady in the jaw, and about half the dressing stuck to his chin. The bowl turned over a couple of times and landed right in his crotch.

Nothing happened for a minute except Grady turned to stare at J.L. with those metally eyes of his. You gotta understand about that look in Grady's eye. He still has it and it still takes people by surprise. It's like he knows something—knows what's up. Like after being born deformed and being an orphan and living at the orphanage, he knows stuff the rest of us don't. And it's scary when he's mad, but it's real sexy. Sexier by far than J.L.'s crooked nose. And I don't ever want Grady to let his cold eyes, metally and blue, zero in on me if he's mad.

Grady stood up and let the bowl fall to the floor. It broke into about a hundred pieces, and he walked off and didn't even brush the pink glop off his face or the lettuce off his button fly, and he didn't bus his tray.

He headed upstairs, and you'd think everyone would laugh at a guy walking around with glop on his chin and his fly, but Grady acted like nothing was up. That look—those metally eyes—somehow made it not funny. J.L. got madder than ever, sort of like that bull we caged in the corner of a fence that afternoon J.L. took us out to his uncle's ranch.

Grady showed up at afternoon classes with Thousand Island caked onto his chin and that pink mess with lettuce turned brown and limp stuck to his fly, and no one said a thing or even snickered. We all smelled Thousand Island and waited—just waited—to see what happened next.

All afternoon J.L. looked meaner than when he was on the field waiting to snap the football. He told Billy and me that he was making up a plan, and he made us promise to help him. I wanted to tell him to lay off Grady, but I figured J.L. would say I was a one-armed-Irish-pussy-lover, and I sure as hell didn't want to give him a chance to find out how much time I spent with Grady.

You have to understand that just about every guy in the school was out for spring football training—even the guys who hadn't made the team last fall—because we all wanted a chance to be on the second team in a row that could bulldoze the Double A team from across the river. Except guys like Grady and the sullen Indian who didn't want to play white boys' games, and the useless fat kid and the music teacher's son who played the violin.

The game was everything to us, and we showed up to practice right after school and Coach Backhoff's sign was on the door of the Stink Hole:

"Suit up. Running gear. Laps & stretches. J.L. Lead warm ups till I get there."

I began to worry. Backhoff lived for football—couldn't teach anything but remedial math—and for him to be late was weird.

I hated the Stink Hole. Oh, it deserved its name all right. Six periods of boys' P.E. every day, plus football, and nowhere to hang the towel they issued you at the first of the week. Stuff it in your locker with your gear. Everyone's sweaty clothes washed once a week—you had to take your gear home on Friday because they emptied the wire lockers on Saturday and hosed them down. If you forgot, on Monday you had to hold your nose and dig to the bottom of the "strays" barrel—this big old packing barrel that'd been around forever—and hope to find your own gear. Wearing some other guy's forgotten jockstrap—or maybe left on purpose because it was so disgusting—that'd been left in the strays barrel soaking up sweat so long it smelled like vinegar made you feel—well, I wasn't sure how it would make me feel. Thought about it a lot, though. I tell you all of that because today was Friday, and the place had the five-day stink of mildewy towels, funky jockstraps, sweaty socks and running shoes, and stinky blue-and-gold warm-up jerseys. We were all getting changed as quick as we could so we could get out into the fresh air.

I looked around at the guys, watched them strip, but I had to be careful—be real shifty and quick with my eyes. I specially wanted to see about J.L., see if the hospital had cleaned all the blood out of his hairy chest. Besides his muscles, his chest hair is the best thing about him. Certainly not his personality. He stripped, but I couldn't see his chest for sure without being too obvious. Funny thing was, he just stood there naked with his clothes piled on a bench, like he wasn't in a hurry, waiting like, and I knew something was up.

I tossed my clothes on the bench by my locker. I ducked around behind Backhoff's cage, where the strays barrel was, to put on my jock and running shorts. I was nervous and wanted to hide. But I knew Howard would be right behind me, headed for the strays barrel. He was too cheap to buy himself a jock, and, besides, I think he got some kind of kick out of hauling one of the smelly old things out of the barrel to wear every day. He was so weird.

I heard Howard behind me. He sort of whistled through his teeth—like he always did just before he did some weird thing. He whispered right close to my ear, "Jeezus. Would you look at that?" Then he shouted.

We'd seen Grady at the same time, dropped down into the strays barrel, arms tied behind him with stinky jockstraps collected for weeks on end, naked except for a mildewy towel wrapped around his head like one of those Arab turbans. It'd taken somebody some doing to tie his arms together, him so skinny and with only one wrist and all.

Poor guy. He was so skinny his bones showed in his rib-cage. No body-hair except under his arms and around his dick. He was too tall for the barrel to cover that up. And anybody could see he had the reddest crotch in the school. Hey, everybody knew from showers together for years what everybody else looked like. And now everyone else knew about Grady, too. His pubes were kind of pinkish, not quite as dark as on his head. But you want to see a red-haired Irishman? Well it's Grady.

All the guys crowded around behind coach's cage to see. J.L. stood there naked in front of the barrel with this snarly smile on his face that actually scared me. I finally knew what the Double-A football line had seen that scared them into getting beaten. I couldn't imagine what J.L. was going to do but I knew making Grady look stupid wasn't all he had in mind. I knew he wouldn't actually hurt Grady—get himself in deeper shit with Miller than he already was. If things got out of hand, I hoped I might even have the guts to try to stop him. And where was Backhoff, anyway, I wondered.

We all tried to crowd around the barrel. For the first time I saw Grady looking beat. His eyes went sort of blank, lost the metal look. Well, wouldn't you be beat? The poor guy looked like he wanted to die, and I wanted to crawl under the floor. How do you help a guy out who's your friend—or something—and no one even knows it, and it makes you feel chickenshit that you don't want them to know.

And all of a sudden J.L. says, "Jeezus. Look at that thing. It's as long as his stump."

It was so weird—like J.L. was so anxious to get even with Grady that he hadn't even noticed what I'd known for weeks. No one else in the school was anywhere near Grady's size. And the minute J.L. noticed, Grady had them all again. His eyes came back to life, and he stood there like he was in charge or maybe like we weren't even there. Like none of it—stump, good grades, orphanage, Thousand Island, J.L.—especially poor old bandaged-up J.L.—made any difference. Grady knew something no one else in that locker room knew.

And what he knew was making J.L. madder by the minute.

J.L. growled, "Hey, assholes, we got to teach the son-of-a-bitch a lesson."

Everyone said yeah, sure, OK, but we couldn't figure out what J.L. wanted us to do, and the guys couldn't stop staring at what we later called Grady's second stump.

And J.L. hauled this pair of scissors from his locker. Yeah, sure, like they just happened to be there.

"I get the first cut," he said. He pulled up a twist of Grady's pubes. J.L. snipped the twist of hair off and dropped it in the barrel.

"Next?" he said. No one moved. It was too much.

"Bunch of pussies?" J.L. made a wild move with the scissors.

Howard couldn't pass up anything that weird, and he grabbed the scissors from J.L. and took a snip, but he didn't drop the hair. He looked at it and rubbed it between his fingers and turned it around in the light and said, "Shit's red like he uses Clairol."

A couple more guys moved up and took their turns—snipped, cautious, embarrassed—like they were just doing J.L. a favor.

Grady didn't move. He stared. Didn't even look down at what they were doing, but stared face to face at any of the guys who dared look his way. He kept his chin up and sort of looked down his nose at them, and they all got embarrassed and looked away.

J.L. said, "We got to go all the way."

It wouldn't have been so weird if it wasn't obvious that someone would have to take ahold of Grady—well, you know how—to finish the job. Someone would have to get real close to Grady to trim him clean. It was just crazy.

"You all wimps? Irish pussies?" J.L. was getting mad at us now.

No one moved. No one wanted to get any closer. J.L. should have known he couldn't ask us to do this and get away with it. And it sure looked like J.L. had screwed things up for himself.

So J.L. did it himself. Got down on his knees in front of Grady. Imagine him in that position. He was that determined. And he took ahold of Grady, stretched him down to keep him still—the guys couldn't believe it and they just looked at the floor. J.L. hauled the scissors right up close to Grady's crotch, and he squinted over his bandaged nose, and he clipped.

Grady didn't flinch. Didn't move. Didn't make a sound. He stood there with his stump and arm tied behind his back and stared at us, and no part of his body moved. I sure would have watched to see what was going on if someone had ahold of me like that and was whacking away at my pubes close enough to cut. But not Grady. He just held his head up and stared over the crook of his nose like the king of Ireland or something.

And you know what happened? J.L began to get a boner—like holding Grady that way turned him on. And Grady's stump wasn't weird any more.

Cause J.L. was crooked. The harder he got, the more his boner stuck out to the side, so crooked it looked useless—right angle crooked—and weirder than weird. And his face turned red, and he looked desperate, 'cause he knew he was screwed.

No one said a thing or even snickered, or hardly even watched. And poor old J.L. knew he wasn't going to get one bit of help, so he just finished the job himself, slow and careful. ✸

GUNFIGHT AT STUDY BUTTE STORE

by Kate K. Davis

To say it is hot is to not only state the obvious but to also violate the unwritten code of the porch. Regardless of how hot it is at any other time of the year, the heat is a taboo subject in months with no R. Like eating oysters out of season and not letting the little critters have time to reproduce, talking about the blast furnace heat and lack of rain ensures more of the same.

The porch is the social center of town. Downtown Study Butte, the major suburb of Terlingua, is merely a collection of adobe and rock buildings, trailers, and shanties spread thinly along two miles of warped asphalt. The Study Butte Store sells canned goods, frozen pork chops, soft apples, half-melted ice-cream bars, and the real necessities of the desert—gasoline and beer. Locals buy six packs and put them in the ice-vending machine outside. They pop one, drink a little, then slide the can into a colorful thermo-insulator—a koozie. Every Texan has a koozie issued at birth. Most are neoprene rubber tubes emblazoned with slogans such as: "I Used To Have A Drinking Problem . . . Now I Can Afford It!" or "Sexy Senior Citizen," or "If You're Rich, I'm Single." Locals are identified by their koozies, by what they drive, and by their dog. So when you drive into the lot, you know immediately who is there before you even step foot on the porch. If the owner of a beer leaves for the outhouse, you figure where he was sitting by the koozie, and you start talking about him before he gets back.

So it was on a hot—typical July day, mercury to the top and no breeze, that George and Morris drove south to party. Few heads stirred when they drove in. Some tipped their beers as the boys entered the store.

George's dirty shirt hung out of his shorts. His brown hair sought freedom from beneath his cap, and his abalone-shell toenails poked through orange Converse All-Stars. Despite the unshaven, skip tooth, bandito first impression, George was somewhat the self-styled dandy. He'd bow or kiss the hands of ladies and always offer to carry anything heavy. Somewhere in George's past, or past life, he had money and education. But no one knew or asked or even cared. You're judged at face value in Study Butte. And some faces are mug shots for sure.

Like Morris's. Morris never even tried to be pleasant. He figured if he was prickly from the start people wouldn't get upset at him later if he had a bad hair day, which was most days. He was dark, born with a five o'clock shadow and wild blue eyes, and he always wore long pants. People figured he was Mexican, because no one had ever seen a Mexican man wear shorts. Only Morris was Italian, from Houston, via Odessa, with supposed mob connections to an Uncle Morris, or Mauricio, from the old country, New Jersey. Morris grunted "Howdy" at Randy and young Charlie.

The boys purchased a case of Miller Genuine Draft and handed a beer to the regulars, the porch dogs. Faces brightened, positively beamed. Free beer. It was a good day all around. Morris and George maneuvered into story-telling position and proceeded.

Seems they'd heard, from more than one source, that there was gold in the hills and soil around Nine Point Mesa. At the mention of gold, shoulders tensed, legs uncrossed, eyes narrowed. Gold is about the only thing can make a man stir in that hea . . . temperature. They feigned disinterest. No one wanted to seem overly anxious or eager at the prospects of gold, easy money.

"It's in the soil and yuccas and daggers and stuff take it up into their roots."

"Like fertilizer, supposed to be good for them," Morris added.

"So how come we ain't dug up all the yuccas in some vegetation-inspired gold rush?" young Charlie ventured. "If it's that close to the surface, how come we ain't heard about it before?"

"Well, it ain't the plants, Charlie. They got too little in them to make them economically viable to exploit," George's past life shone through, slightly. "It's in what eats them you find it."

This was just too fantastic for Dr. Doug. He stood up, stepped over a sleeping dog, and grumbled something under his breath about not having fallen off a turnip truck yesterday and needing a cold one. Dr. Doug Blackmon, locally appointed porch psychotherapist and token Scotsman, knew a shaggy dog coming a mile away. He'd heard them all.

"No, it's true," insisted Morris. "Them that eats the dagger and yucca roots gets it on their teeth and in their livers. We got proof." Morris caught George's eye.

"Think we ought to show them?" George goaded.

"Nope," Morris said flatly and strode off to take a leak against a truck out back. All eyes followed him, then looked at George. George sat back and guzzled his beer, opened another with no hurry and no intention of saying more. No, he'd wait until asked. Wait until the nibble gnawed a hole in the silence big enough for a man to step through. Let them wait. He liked a little suspense. Timing is everything.

A green, two-tone 1968 bus careened into the parking lot and rested next to the propane tank. Instantly, everyone sat up. Tourists. But not just regular sight-seeing, RV-driving, old-fart grandmas and grandpas, this was the Green Tortoise Bus full of Europeans. Unshaven women and olive-drab men smelling of patchouli, who all slept together on benches instead of bus seats. Germans, French, Dutch even an occasional Swede or Swiss crossing the States together, two weeks for $300 dollars everything included. Boston to San Francisco via the Big Bend. Or San Francisco to Boston via Study Butte. They'd spend the night at La Kiva campground, shower for the first time in a week, eat steaks all around, dance with anyone, and drink lots of Shiner and Bohemia. And some lucky local would get some, for sure, or, at least, one always did, according to local lore. A story handed down fourth or fifth-hand of uninhibited erotic one-night stands at the hands of unmerciful French nymphets or a German-lisping dominatrix. Black-widow women who'd leave their lovers spent in the sand of Terlingua Creek and blithely board the bus unscathed.

This was reason to sit up, get an instrument, and play. So Randy fired up his accordion and started the "Terlingua Blues." George held the door as the patchouli streamed in. He bowed to the ladies and saluted the guys.

He pointed to the outhouses, through the back door, up the path, women's on the right. Bewildered faces smiled as eyes adjusted to the dark of the cavernous store. Cigarettes, T-shirts, fudgesicles, granola bars, juice, tampons, and beer, all foraged and purchased.

The bus driver and owner knew the routine. Neither was in any rush. He got a free six-pack for bringing them in, and she made the light bill. Slowly the store disgorged its contents onto the porch. Discarded clothing was pushed off the bench so everyone could sit. Extra chairs surfaced from under tables, and Charlie gave up his seat.

George scoped out his prey—a tall German girl with buzz-cut side-walls, green-dyed forelock, sixteen or seventeen earrings, angular shoulders, no bra, long waist, tank top, exposed navel, big butt collected into oversized cut-off jeans shorts cinched in by the ugliest black belt he had ever seen. She'd do.

"Hilda, right?" he asked. Had to be.

"No, Greta," she replied. She crossed her hairy legs.

"Of course," George smiled. She'd do. He sang falsetto, his best Pavarotti, to the porch standard: "My Dog Has Fleas, But she never screwed my buddies, She's a damned sight easier than you to please." Everyone laughed. Everyone always laughs. It was an international hit, top of the charts, and Greta smiled at George. He was going to get some, for sure!

Morris had settled discontentedly on a folding metal chair perched just on the edge of the shade. His back was in the sun and it was ho—seasonal. He glared at George. George, who couldn't even wipe his hairy butt unless he asked first. George, a two-bit, two-timing cactus rustler with an over-bite. George, who never bought the beers, getting some ass. No way was Morris going to let that happen.

"Y'all want to see what I found?" Eyes turned to Morris as he unsteadily rose from the chair and stood plum, smack dab in the middle of the jam session, hand out-stretched. "That there, little lady, that there is a gold javelina tooth."

Necks craned to see. Gold. The Tower of Babel crumbled and went silent.

"I found this tusk in the jaw of the big ole granddaddy javelina we shot this morning." Morris continued, "We was out on the flats when we found two of them sleeping in a cave—"

"Weren't even a cave, just a hole in the dirt," interjected George. Morris shot him a death ray.

"So, we popped them, right there. And this was in the big ole boar's mouth." Morris grinned. "He's been eating yucca so long he's got gold-plated tusks!"

A chorus of "Wows" and "Ahs" burbled porch-wide.

"Yeah, they was just sleeping there. So we shot them and got his teeth," George elaborated. "Easy. There's got to be more out there!"

Greta looked at George. Her bushy brows became one. Rose bud lips contorted, tried several shapes before emitting, "You just go take gun and shoot for teeth? You not eat meat?"

"Uh, oh," thought George. He had an environmentalist on his hands. And, what was worse, the whole bench leaned inward, closed ranks around her. He circled his wagons, thought fast. The night's rapture gone if this turned ugly.

"I didn't shoot them. Morris did," and he pointed to Morris, who was showing the tooth to Dr. Doug.

"Why you sorry sonofabitch, George. You know you shot Grandpa and Grandma Wart Hog point blank as they slept! Cold blooded. Didn't even have a chance." Morris stepped back. The line had been crossed—no one ever accuses anyone of anything in Study Butte, at least, not to their face. They just hint around long enough until suggestion becomes fact.

Greta squeaked something in German to the tune of "Savage American Brute," but not so polite. George panicked. She was slipping away. His Eurydice into oblivion, lost forever, unless....

"Morris, I've had it with your lying bullshit! I am tired of always taking the blame for your sorry ass." He strode up to Morris and elephant seal slammed his chest against him. Morris clenched his teeth and snarled, stepped back, and turned to leave. George knew this was just too easy. Morris would never let such an insult go unpunished. It was contrary to his Italian nature. His people chopped fingers off for less.

Morris hadn't capitulated, just rearmed, went ballistic. His rifle. The truck. George ran out the porch front, crossed to the other side of the pickup, and grabbed his shotgun the same time Morris's hand reached through the open window to his. They glared at each other, two closed doors and a seat apart. Morris raised the barrel to his eye.

He's serious, thought George, the fucker's gone postal. And he realized his gun *was* empty. He *had* spent all his shells on the pigs.

George did what any man in his position would have done. He leapt around the hood, grasped his rifle by the barrel, and commenced to swatting at Morris. And Morris met the challenge, swung his shotgun, caught George in the side.

"Stop! Stop!" cried Greta.

"Dey are killing!" shouted a male voice, "just like movies!" Tourists surged onto the asphalt alternately cheering and screaming. Not one local moved.

Morris and George stepped back, then lunged, swung more viciously. A crack resounded against Morris's ear as red spurted from George's nose. Both fell flat. A draw.

"My Got! My Got! Are dey dead?" The crowd stood motionless, catching flies. Greta kneeled and lifted George's bloody face onto her lap. Another Rhine maiden hoisted Morris to her bosom. His eyes opened to her concerned face. He smiled, and then winked at George, nose dabbed dry, hair all smoothed.

And that, friends, is the true story, straight from the horse's mouth. Heard from more than one source. Reliable sources. From somebody who was married to a man, who knew a guy, whose cousin went to school with a girl, who knew George and Morris, and was on the porch the day of the Gun Fight at Study Butte Store. 🏵

THE FAMILY

by Betsy Berry

As boundary lines establish beginnings and endings or frames surround paintings that speak of a moment or time, floods were the markers of twenty-five years of the family. A fourth of a century to sand the tight corners of the family, the triangular paper points that pinned their pictures, the progression of their lives, onto heavy pages in a book.

Few photographs—and not a painting or a book—survived the water the second time, though people who have not known floods, the rise and roil, think a flood is a matter of fixing, a drying-out period. The sun to soothe and heal, a fresh breeze to assuage. As if nature was in the business of making reparations. This the family had learned.

In the very beginning, for the daughter, and for the husband and wife who would one day be a family of four, was an island setting. A tropical paradise, American soil, where the husband, an air force officer, was sent for service. Stationed, they called it, a good term because the husband, the father, was often away. They had a little boy, born in a midwest "Yankee" state—the mother had no truck with the midwest and linked its inhabitants with easterners—and they were glad that here on the island, in the heat of a southern sun was born to them a little girl. The father, a pilot and somewhere above Cuba when his daughter arrived, raced toward home through the blue of skyscapes and time zones.

Flying in low, right over the pale pink house where now a family of four would live, his plane carried aromatic cigars and bottles of thick rum and painted wooden animals for his wife and the new baby. Most of the pilots brought in the occasional contraband. These were days when parties were happy ones, full of laughter and wonder of the exotic—the lovely mixture of tastes that a cocktail could be.

Their lives were uncluttered; a dream they seemed to live in this protected little cove of paradise, plucking fresh mangoes off the trees in their yard. This was a family who was to make mistakes, to know heartache, to grow older along with the earth. But in the beginning there was the four of them together, surrounded by the beauty of an island.

And one day the father came home from the beach with two sheets of printed music and the song to this day he swore was written for his little girl. A group of men, native to the island, gathered on the beach to play alongside the rhythm of the sea and the flap of palm tree fronds in the wind. They knew the daughter, the tiny girl whose parents carried like a fragile sea creature to the beach and plopped gingerly down at the edge of the warm ocean. And this was the song they had written with her in mind:

All day all night, Miss Betsy Anne
Down by the seaside sifting sand
Todos pocos niños join the band
They're all in love with Miss Betsy Anne

Betsy Anne, Betsy Anne, will you marry me?
We'll love in a bamboo hut
With coffee in our tea

Sweet Betsy Anne,
Miss Betsy Anne,
Beside the deep blue sea.

When she was able to understand the words, the daughter took them to heart and, like many other little girls, vowed to marry her father, the man she already loved more than any other. When she was almost six, the family moved, leaving behind their tropical island in a wake of jet fuel from a plane the father flew in as a passenger. Following them was a transport plane in which the mother had smuggled a dozen tiny banana trees to graft in her new garden, wherever that garden might be. She had left her mark on paradise, coaxing the flora and fauna to grow in chosen shapes and in chosen places as if they were trained pets. The son left behind a group of playmates and a large iguana. The iguana he had kept in an open air cage in the corner of the yard, but when he took him out to walk him on a short rope he tied around the lizard's neck and then later roped him to a palm tree, it made the boy's sister sad. In the eyes of the creature, there or missing from them, was something she took with her when she left the island of her birth. The last she saw of that island was from the plane, the soft foam lapping the west shore and, beyond the sunlit stucco houses that dotted the new air force base there, the shiny green density of the jungle.

When the father retired from his service, the family lived in a house they designed and had built on a small, man-made island on a small lake, created from a dam off the Guadalupe river. The place looked less like Texas than it did Florida, where weekend fishermen had to contend with the whine of jet skis and wide wakes from passing speedboats. The three of them lived there, the father and mother and daughter, who attended high school in the city thirty miles away. The son had finished college and was starting a new life in another city a few hours drive east.

Early in the first hours of a morning which had been preceded by almost a month of soft but steady rain, the daughter was awakened by the phone, by what she sensed was the final two rings of a long attempt to waken the family. She thought of her brother first, and that an insistent call so late must mean trouble. But the lull of the long rain was like a sleeping tablet, and even when she heard the pounding on the door from her bedroom at the front of the house it took her a moment to thread her hands through the sleeves of her robe and stumble into the hall. Outside the door, in long, wet slickers and various hats, stood three men. One stepped close to her, his foot partially inside the door.

"Get your parents up and dressed, little girl! There's a thirty foot wall of water coming down from Placid!"

Placid was a lake just north, and the notion of how fast such a sheet of water, like a tidal wave, could reach the island terrified her. She ran back to her parents' bedroom, shouting.

"Mim! Dad! Get up! Get up now! Don't stop to get anything—we have to leave at once!" The men had told her this before they left for the next house on the street.

As the father scrambled into pants and reached in the back of his closet for his metal lockbox of records and documents, the mother switched on the television. When no station came on, she mistook the noise of the static for the water.

"Is that it?" the mother cried. "Has the water come?"

In the frenzied moments of what they later remembered as happening in slow, sharp detail, they got in the car and—water coming through the bottom of the door and over the floorboard—they made it across the only bridge to the island.

That was in 1973. They called it a hundred year flood plain, here where the parents had chosen to live out their lives, although they had not heard or talked much about floods. Four years ago, when they had first come there, to the lake, to visit friends, the sky had opened up and a sonnel and their families, the sun had been suddenly eclipsed by dark clouds and a cool, stiff wind frothed the calm water into white peaks. A young couple with their three year old son and infant daughter were in a rowboat between the shore and the island, not half a mile in distance. Just three of them, the mother and father and son, soaked to the bone and in shock, returned to the land, where the other picnickers had then become a rescue party. The rowboat had overturned and the mother held on to the little boy. The baby girl, someone in the crowd said, had "sunk like a rock." The daughter of the family, who would later live in the middle of this body of water, covered her ears to stop the voices of the frantic searchers. Her brother was one of the divers, but not in the group that hours later found the baby on the lake bed and still covered in her blanket, "laying there like she was asleep." When the numbing shroud of the mother's shock had been melted by a blanket and the offer of a cup of hot tea, she began to sob. A keening it was really, an animal wail, thought the daughter of the family. She remembered the sound years later in dreams.

"It's such a beautiful place here," someone had said that day. "But with water, you never know. You just never know."

❀　❀　❀

The National Guard had taken their station after the waters of the family's first flood flowed back to their place once again, and when it was declared safe to open the island its residents were allowed to see what the fury had done to their homes. The water that had come hadn't been in the form of a wall but a great swell, a bursting upwards and outwards that crested to five feet inside those homes, like the family's, nearest the lake's edge. A sponge cake the mother had baked and left on the stove at the back of the house had floated up front to greet them in the entrance hall. Helicopters flew in pairs overhead, their blades beating time with each new discovery of what had been ruined. In the family's driveway people gathered, comparing their fates.

"Didn't get the mud they did on the other side," said one neighbor who lived across the street. "Hell of a lucky thing." But the fury which had been unleashed left its mark.

The brother came in from out of town and with a bad sense of timing had brought a new girlfriend with him. "I've been dying to meet ya'll," she chirped to the mother. "Not under such conditions, of course."

The mother looked at her blankly, holding her husband's ruined portrait by a corner of the busted frame.

"The way I'd look at it," the girlfriend said, "is that you're okay. And you still have some stuff."

"Yes, well," said the mother after a moment. "Wet stuff." And she turned to go back into her ruined home.

"What a time to bring her here, really," said the sister privately to her brother.

"What do *you* know, Miss Priss? It may be a good time, actually. Something like this, families should stick together."

Together, with the help of good friends and neighbors and workers and a hard summer sun, the family rebuilt their house, slowly replacing their possessions. Twenty-five years later, two failed marriages between the son and daughter and two new ones begun, the family would still point out to visitors the spot where the water had crested and then just as quickly flowed back out of their lives.

"We've loved it here, living by the water," the mother would tell people. "But nature will have its moments."

The daughter remembered something from a book she'd read, a line she didn't share with the family. "Nothing brings violence and death closer than an abundance of life and beauty."

In October of the year when the mother and father turned seventy-five a serious rain began. This time a week's worth fell in a day's time, a dense blanket of rain. The heavy drops sounded like hail as they hammered the roof and sluiced down the outside walls of the house. The river rushed so fast into the lake that it rose inches at a time. So quick was the rise it was hard to remember where the lake's level had been a half hour before.

The daughter, in the city where she now lived, an hour's drive north of the lake, was on the phone with her mother. From her kitchen window she watched the rain fall. She had slept the night without dreams, the sleep of the dead. That morning she woke groggy and slow, to putter away a dark, rainy day with small chores that would restore some order to her home. She and her husband had planned to leave early for the drive to her parents' house, where they would spend a night.

But this delicious late morning and its soaking, cleansing rain, she imagined the baby tomato plants they'd planted two days before swelling outwards, embracing the rain. She was happy to be where she was. They could go later in the afternoon and still have the night to visit with her mother and father, watch a movie, play a game of Trivial Pursuit or read.

In the cocoon of her floodlit kitchen she sipped from a mid-morning cup of coffee and phoned her mother to let her know when they could be expected to arrive. In the lake house bathed by rain her mother had finished her daily cup and resented the intrusion as the telephone jangled. Since the rain had begun the late afternoon before the mother had twice stopped her husband from turning on the television for a weather report. "That TV's on too much as it is. Think of how long it's been since you heard that beautiful sound on the roof!"

And outside the rain came down, making up for its absence. As the mother passed the large living room window to answer the phone, she noticed how close the level of the water was to the dock. There had been other times since the last time the water flowed into the house that flooding threatened. Her children had dismissed her fears so many times that now it was like crying wolf.

"Yes?" she answered.

"Mim?"

"Pete!" she said, the daughter's childhood nickname.

"How's the weather there? It's raining so hard here we'd like to wait 'til later this afternoon to come."

"We've had it all last evening and through the night," her mother told her. "I can hardly see the other side of the lake. I just don't know. . . ."

A quarter of a century since the daughter had opened the front door of the family's home to the men in wet slickers. "Don't start now, Mim. I'll call you when we're leaving."

It wasn't a duty for her, or for her husband, visiting the family. In a John Updike novel she liked, "Rabbit" Angstrom describes a childhood memory of a little girl in school, "so full of life her nose would start bleeding for no reason." The daughter imagined her mother and father like that, the sights and sounds, pleasures and pains, the run-off from a full life lived. Her father was still the funniest man she had ever known, would ever know, and she had had boyfriends she was sure hung around her to hear her mother sing and dance, telling the oldest jokes in the world as if you were hearing them for the first time. Age had grayed but not tarnished them, the dropping off of a few feathers. They were still, magically, in love.

After an hour or two more and no let-up of rain, she dialed her mother again.

"Yes, still coming down here," her mother said. "A bit ago we heard a loudspeaker announcement from off the island, somewhere across the lake, I think over near the old campground." Where the baby girl had drowned.

And again the daughter reassured her mother. She didn't believe it anyway, that the water might rise again to drive the family from their home. After they had recovered from the last flood, her father had said to them, the daughter and the son, "Well, the next time it will be up to the two of you to deal with it if you keep the house after we're gone." They had smiled as he said it.

Not now. Not for a hundred years.

The small TV in the kitchen was on, sound muted, and as she hung up from the call to her mother a report from the weather channel inched its way across the bottom of the picture. *Cold front stalled over central Texas, inches fallen presently exceeds prediction by 8 to 10, local rivers and creeks rising, expecting to crest above flood level in the following counties. . . .*

No, not this time. The county where her mother and father lived hadn't appeared in the alphabetical list. She began putting a day and night's worth of clothes in a bag for her and her husband, books, vitamins, and coffee—better than the kind her parents made—she threw in a paper sack.

It was when she made the final call, to say they would soon be on the road, that she began to waver from her hundred-year conviction. There was the authority of the written word, which right or wrong the daughter generally trusted, there it was again at the bottom of the TV screen—not in a looping scroll this time, but fixed in place.

EVACUATIONS UNDERWAY. Stay tuned for details regarding your area.

She grabbed the remote control and jabbed it furiously, turning up the volume and switching to a local channel. It was showing a remote from above the banks of an overflowing creek in her city. The reporter was wearing a rain hood and a slicker.

"A special thanks to our weather watchers who've called in," he said into the camera. "Took us all a little by surprise, but as you can see behind me, it has made its presence known. Back to you, Troy."

Meteorologist Troy, seated behind his desk at the TV station, read from the latest bulletins. This time it named Guadalupe County, the same name as the river that for twenty-five springs and summers and falls of the family's life had remained obediently in its place. Setting the bulletins down on his desk, the weatherman removed his glasses for a moment and looked straight into the camera.

"For those of you who have just tuned in, let me repeat. We have a dangerous, potentially deadly situation and will continue to review safety procedures. Crests on some waterways may reach up to thirty feet. That is a level higher, I repeat, higher than the Guadalupe County Flood of 1973."

The daughter stood frozen to her spot as he put his glasses back on and began reading emergency and safety procedures.

People in the following areas should immediately seek higher ground. Do not attempt to cross low water areas by any means. Park well away from rising water and, if feasible, remain in the safety of your automobile until water has receded. The force of cresting water presents hazards for the heaviest cars and the strongest swimmers. Floods threaten families.

The last warning came from an audiotape played in her head, ironic in its monotone, a newsflash happening close by and still a world away.

This time when she telephoned her mother she didn't tell her not to say it, not to think about it, a rising tide that would not touch them. Nor did she tell her, at first, of the report she had seen. But while her mother was warning her not to set out just now, the truck with the loudspeaker that the mother thought she'd heard passed slowly down the road the family lived on. "Well, here we go, I guess. It's here," said the mother calmly. "Evacuate the island immediately, they're saying. I guess we'll get some things together." She was speaking quietly, slowly, sounding almost calm.

"Where will you go? What will you do?" said the daughter, her thoughts gathering together in a panic that traveled from her head to her stomach and down into her legs. Now, the three local stations were solely on emergency weather watch, their warnings blurring together as she flipped through the channels.

"We're leaving the island, Pete. We'll drive to higher ground nearby—wait it out in the car, if we can, 'til they let us back on."

"We're on our way!" the daughter pleaded.

"No, no! You can't. When we talked to your brother twenty minutes ago he told us parts of the highway have already been closed down."

"Promise me," said the daughter. "Promise you'll call us the very second you're safe. The minute you can get to a phone."

Helpless, she waited. Fifteen minutes seemed like an hour, and she dialed them again. This time it was her father who answered, her father sounding exactly as her mother had sounded twenty-five years ago when her daughter awakened her with the news.

Is that it? Has the water come?

The water was now rising, halfway up the backyard toward the house, her father shouting into the phone that they had loaded some things in the car and that now they must go. The truck warning people to leave their homes was no longer on the island.

And the rain fell inside the daughter's city, the threatening rain that brought the island closer and now bound them together. When the electricity went out, the daughter lit candles and sat at the kitchen table with her husband, where they waited. Her brother had called from his city, where it rained and he waited.

A dozen times she picked up the phone just to hear the hum of the dial tone, a connection. Not until early evening did it ring again. Her mother and father, some of the last off the island and with less than an hour before the water would rise over the bridge. They had driven to a gas station-convenience store five miles away and had planned to camp there until the water crested. But a store employee, leaving after her shift, had checked on them in their car and insisted they follow her to her home on higher ground. Still, her house was near enough to the river feeding the lake that there was talk in the middle of the night of an escape, if need be, in a rowboat tethered to a wall in the garage. The father had not slept a minute, not thinking as much about the lake swallowing his house as wondering how he, a seventy-five year old man who used a cane to walk, could get himself and his wife into a tiny boat.

As with the other flood they would later be asked what it was like to imagine their home actually in the lake, the island a lake bed, its houses a suburban Atlantis. Again, all the many things they had collected, accumulated in their long lives, drowned in a putrid gray-brown foam. One of course did not imagine, could not imagine. It was something that happened outside of experience or knowledge, apart from prediction or certainty. It was science fiction, an ending of a place and time.

In the middle of the night the phone line to the house where the mother and father were staying the night went out. Now there was nothing to do but listen to endless weather bulletins and warnings—and wait. By early morning the rain had stopped, and still they waited. The daughter was finally able to again get through by phone to the house that had sheltered her parents, and she was told by the woman there that her parents had gone. Once, about five in the morning, as the water retreated, she was told, her parents had tried to drive back toward the island, but a deep stream of water over the road had forced them to turn back. Now, mid-morning, they had told their hosts that they intended to set out in another direction, this time the drive north to their daughter's home.

When her doorbell rang, she opened the door to the mother and father, mud-streaked and in shock. This day they wore the full uniform of their advanced age, a watermark of its own kind. The mother and daughter hugged, both weeping, while the father told his son-in-law the silly things he had grabbed to put in the car—a blank notebook, the wrong pillow, some frozen lobster tails they had bought to cook for the daughter's visit. Medicine, documents and records, and other items that would be impossible to replace, these had been left behind to fend with the water.

The four together held out hope. There were no news reports of how much the lake had overflowed its banks, nor was there confirmation that it had flooded period. They would see, would have to see for themselves what had happened, and until they saw it was easier to believe that they had been spared. That nature had considered them, had withdrawn its claim at the last moment.

Later in the day, her parents in their soiled clothes, the only ones they had, went with the daughter and her husband to a Mexican restaurant. They laughed and talked, ate and drank, and only every once in a while would the mother grow quiet, shaking her head from side to side. "We have lived too long," she would say. And the daughter would look at her mother's eyes and almost believe her.

They spent the night, and initially thought they would stay another day, and the four of them would drive to the island Saturday morning. But by early morning Friday much of the natural self-defense, the cloak of shock, had fallen away. Her mother's mood swung wildly from one extreme to the other, her need to witness the tearing down of so many years they had built as a family. From that to the declaration that she would leave it as it was, and never go back at all.

"I've told your father," she said. "I say this time we just walk away from that house and everything in it. I don't care if I never see any of it."

"That's your home, Mim—our home," the son-in-law said quietly.

She looked at him a moment, uncomprehendingly. "That's the home of that goddamn lake, that goddamn Guadalupe," she said. And they all laughed as if at one of her ancient jokes. "The temptation that's irresistible to me now is never to have to move again from this spot right here," she said. This from the woman who had loved to travel—when she had somewhere to come home to.

They were on the highway, a fine mist falling, a weak sun showing itself from time to time. The daughter drove her car, her mother with her, and her husband drove his father-in-law in the parents' car. The mother would wring her hands at times; at others she would sit frozen, unblinking. There was much traffic and the wet highway to negotiate, so that the hour long trip took much longer, worsening as they neared Guadalupe county. A mile from the island police were directing long single lanes of traffic and National Guard trucks were parked in muddy ditches on the sides of the road. The family knew the worst, that there hadn't *not* been a flood. That they had paid for their human intrusion, land-dwellers flirting on the edge, and a price had been exacted. As soon as they exited the highway, still a few miles from the house, flooded fields far from the river spread out on both sides of the road.

Finally on the island, they made their way slowly to the white house down the road covered with debris washed in from the lake and out of the houses. When they drove into the driveway they saw the thin, tell-tale line of dirt marking the height of the water inches below the gray slate roof. The mist had turned to a soft rain; the quiet around them was the thick silence that follows a deep snow. They didn't need to use a key; warped and bowed the door pushed open against the slime that coated the entrance hallway, such slippery footing that the father had to go back to wait in the car. Which was just as well.

The devastation of the house's interior could not be described to those not able to see the fullness of it for themselves. Water's force is mightier than any circus strongman, than any amount of prestige money and ambition can purchase. The idea that water simply rises, steadily and by degrees until it has soaked carpets and walls and furniture and then retreats to let things dry is more comforting than the reality of a flood, the slime and smell, the gray green of plants that had collapsed under the weight of that which they needed to grow.

Lifeless silver minnows lined the floors and cabinets and pieces of furniture by the hundreds. The sheet rock of the walls and ceilings had given way, spilling out thick chunks of sodden gray insulation over everything around, so that the interior of the house lacked color of any kind. The son-in-law was reminded of a trip he had taken with his wife, an elevator's ride a mile below ground, in the caverns beneath Carlsbad, New Mexico. The inverted, upside down world of a nature possibly meant to remain hidden, a planet's inner depths submerged in the grayish tones of the womb, the texture of nightmare.

Furniture from one room was now in another, or missing entirely, carried out a backdoor and into the lake. The basin in what had been the daughter's bathroom had been ripped from the cabinet and was overturned in the mud on the floor. The island stove in the kitchen was also upside down. The beautiful stacks of leather-bound literature that was one day to have gone to the daughter were ravaged, even on the highest shelf in the built in bookcase, nine feet tall. One length of books had been macabrely rearranged, spines up, neatly stuck together in a row, their bottoms an inch from the top and bottom of a lower shelf.

And all around were constant reminders that nature made its own choices. A pencil had risen with the water to rest impossibly balanced in the shallow mortar between bricks near the top of the wall behind the fireplace, a magic trick that remained to be seen, defying every physical law of the force and pull of water retreating. Mattresses were no longer on their bed frames but across the room; the boat in back of the house was upside down, its bow stuck in the mud in the shallow slime under the boathouse. A Queen Ann silver chest, long a favorite of the mother's, rested upright in the backyard. When they used a screwdriver to pry open drawers locked shut by the water, plump minnows shimmered alongside stacks of gleaming cutlery. A few were still alive, gasping for breath in impossibly small puddles of water droplets. Too much water it had been and now not enough. Even for them it took away.

When the daughter knew the true extent of the damage was when the mother and father began visiting "assisted care" facilities as they looked for a small apartment. "A bunker" her father called it—when he was in a mood to say anything, not so often now. The mother's hearing failed decisively, swiftly; she perceived everything as an attack. There was much talk, in a rush, of what little had dried and warped and still held its place and how it would be distributed. "We haven't much time left," said the mother, whose photographic record of great legs and a smile like a lamp was forever gone. She said this, or a variation, often enough, not as if there was work left to be done, places yet to be experienced, but hopefully, as if the final fraction was a test of will, to be endured.

"They weren't hurt, though, your parents?" asked a younger friend of the daughter's. Her mother had died the past year of cancer at fifty-three. "The rest of it, all of that, it's just stuff."

But that was what the daughter called "see-through" talk, sounding pat and tidy but hollow, a transparent, emotionless box with nothing inside of it. What their daily lives had been made from, and now it was gone, records of their existence to faint sworls of memory by nature's handprint. In the moldy, murky aftermath of disbelief and the gray other-world of depression and inertia, something positive grew.

The son was older than his sister, so that when she was still a young girl just entering her teens, he was a young man beginning a new career in a new city, creating a life apart from the family. He talked infrequently with his sister, and when he did it was about the weather or a good restaurant he'd found, a golf tournament he'd played in or how the Oilers' season looked that year. When she learned that he would be marrying the woman she had met and knew as the wife of his neighbor, the news came from their mother. Her father told her when the son's business went bust. When he spoke to her of their parents, to whom he remained as close or closer than most young men. his age and station, he would refer to them as "your mother" and "your father." He was very social, popular with his friends, someone who told a joke well and enjoyed a good party or a night out on the town. His sister felt that she knew him, on the surface of what it was to know someone.

A few days after the flood he had piled his Suburban full of the silver his mother had collected during her marriage. His sister watched him drive away, sunlight catching the glint of bowls and soup tureens and trays and wine goblets like jewels through the windows.

"This is hard to say to you," she told him later, long-distance. "All of that so dear to Mim and Dad, what we were to have later in our homes." And, inescapably, there was the financial value to be considered—money, the gouge, the prying apart of families, of relationships.

"I brought it to my house so our girl could polish it," he said. By "our girl" he meant the maid, and it seemed terrible to talk about when it had been their father who had polished before holidays or parties in their home, when they had had a home in which to celebrate holidays and give parties.

He knew that his sister was angry, assuming it was because she thought he had taken the silver to keep. But why she was angry was because of the wasted years, documented by photos in high school yearbooks and photo albums now gone, during which they had lived separate lives even when they were together. And the next time they talked, when he was in her city for a day and night to visit a college friend, she told him so. She thought she would have to make him hear her, but instead he did so on his own. And this was the positive thing that grew from the flood, that at last she had talked to her brother, and at last he had heard her.

By the summer of that year, the last year before the century would turn, the news stories at decade's end were of murders and suicides, accidents and tragedies, massacres and bombings. So that when you heard about a natural disaster—the hailstorm that took away a farmer's life savings, the tornado that roaring through "like a freight train" took lives and homes with it—you saw in its stark horror something which stood alone, outside human knowledge, human purpose.

Not that the flood hadn't come as close as anything could to breaking the father. One terrible night during an argument that erupted during a routine talk the daughter was delivering about bucking up and rebuilding their lives, he had uttered unutterable words, words he failed to grab back before they escaped and so were said forever. "I could kill you," he shouted in fear and helplessness to his wife. "And you too," he said to the daughter. "I swear I could!" But this was the nadir of flood despair, and from this point he began to move back, toward the life he had lived, they all had lived, without reflection.

For they were still a family. And it became easier for them to form themselves so anew, for the son to comfort his wife after she lost her job, for the daughter to write her poems, her husband to plant a garden. For the mother and father to decide to live, for a second time, in the home they created for whatever time remained. To build again the house by the water that had born witness to so many years in their lives.

For as surely as the storm is the soft breeze, the shadow and light, the caterpillar that breaks its bonds with the earth, that carries life along, toward an end. Still the same year of the flood, before May had become June and the Texas summer sucked away the breath of everything living under it, the family met at a beach house they rented on the gulf coast. They watched their skin change to colors of copper and bronze; they boiled shrimp and crawfish over a fire they made from sticks in the sand. They laughed and walked on the sand, where the warm gulf water rushed in to bathe their ankles and wash their footprints away. Water rushing into the shallow indentations made by six pairs of feet standing together. And then back to the line of the horizon, where the sun dipped by degrees into the ocean. 🏵

SINS OF THE FATHERS

by Greg Garrett

I do not hate my father. We made our peace when he was lying in a Lubbock hospital bed dying of prostate cancer. It was a death that made a cruel kind of sense: my father was constitutionally incapable of the vulnerability it would have required to allow a doctor to examine him. He died wretchedly, alone and in pain, in a semi-private green hospital room at St. Mary's whose other occupant, beyond the curtain, seemed to be expiring slowly of some respiratory disease, hacking himself to death. I took my second wife, Glenette, out to West Texas to meet him—she and I had been married at that point for seventeen years—and after the introductions, after I told him I was still coaching high school baseball, after I said that my team had gone all the way to state that year, the three of us sat in silence, and I could hear the siren from an ambulance or a police car drawing closer and closer.

"You turned out good, Anthony," my father said, finally, without raising his eyes from the fingers interlaced on his chest, from his huge wrinkled blue-veined hands. "You turned out good. But not because of anything I did. I was a lousy father."

Glenette shifted uncomfortably in her chair, looked away, studied the striped wallpaper. Behind his curtain, the cougher coughed. Out at the nurses' station I heard the angry chirping of an unanswered telephone.

"Yes," I said, without anger, as simple agreement. "You were a lousy father."

He inclined his head gravely, a gesture of surprising dignity, and just looked at me. He had the same cool gray eyes I see in the mirror every morning; I could almost have been looking at myself twenty years down the road.

"A dying man, Tony," Glenette later said on the drive to the airport.

"Couldn't you have been a little kinder?"

"No," I said. I focused on the highway ahead of me, slick with spring snow. I am a Catholic, and I believe in accountability, responsibility, reciprocity.

I also believe in the truth. I am older now than he was when I left home and he ceased to be my father, certainly too old to lie to myself or to stand by while others lie.

The truth can be harsh, but it can also heal. Our other conversations at St. Mary's were kinder with that cruel acknowledgment out of the way. One afternoon we even watched a baseball game together, Royals at Detroit, and when his hand fumbled for the water at his bedside table, I picked it up, leaned over him, and held it to his lips. His eyes, still cool and unblinking, flicked to my face as he sipped, and I like to think they expressed the thanks he could not give.

I felt closer to him after that, and after he died, I took his hands—those same huge hands that once beat me until I coughed up blood—in mine. They felt cold, and artificial, like a vinyl shower curtain, and I knew he was gone.

I do not hate my father, but this is not to say that I condone his actions. I have struggled my whole life not to follow his example. When I feel anger at my wife or at my girls or at my players, when my fists clench and my breath catches in my chest and my stomach jumps like I've swallowed live trout, I turn around. I walk away.

When I was growing up, I took out my frustrations through sports; now I vent my anger on weeds, pulling them up by the handful, delighting in the contest of muscle and flesh with fast-growing plant, the totally self-induced pain in shoulders and back and hands after a summer morning spent on my knees tugging Johnson grass, Texas dandelion, crabgrass out of my lush close-cropped Bermuda.

Long ago I decided to master my anger, not allow it to control me as his had him. My father was a cruel and violent man. I saw him hit my mother many times, even when she was sick and getting sicker. He would land short compact jabs in places where they would hurt the most, kidneys, stomach, breasts. He never hit either of us anywhere it would show. He was only a high-school dropout, but when it came to dealing pain, he could have given seminars for police states.

When my mother couldn't hold her food down anymore, my granddad, an Oklahoma farmer who moved with great deliberation, stepped out on the back porch of our little house on 25th Street and motioned for my father to follow with the barest tilt of the head. They meant to get away from me, but I could still hear them. I had plenty of practice in that house listening for trouble, and I hovered breathless at the upstairs bathroom window as they talked beneath me.

"We got to take her to the hospital," Grampa Roy said. "This is the real thing."

"I've seen her worse than this," my father said. "She's just all worked up. That's all. Hysterical. She thinks it's cancer or something."

There was silence. My father stayed out on the porch and lit up a Winston. My granddad came in, bundled up my mother, and took her to the hospital.

My mother was right. It was cancer.

And the funny thing is that despite all of that, I couldn't help but love him. He was my father. He was handsome, and funny, and quick to volunteer help when a friend was in need. I never knew anyone with more friends.

He could confound you.

Take this, for example: when I was growing up, every Sunday after mass, no matter what might have happened at home the night before, we went out to eat at Stubbs Barbecue, the three of us in our Sunday clothes sitting at a table underneath a signed picture of Jimmy Dean, them on one side, me on the other. After we finished the brisket, beans, and potato salad, we had cobbler and ice cream. Then we'd go home, and if there was baseball on TV we'd sit, the three of us, on the couch, my mother doing needlework but looking up occasionally when the crowd cheered.

"Watch this guy," my father would say of Juan Marichal or Steve Carlton or Jim Palmer. "Just look at that ball break." And he would take my hand in his and show me where to put my fingers on the ball to throw the pitch myself, show me the exact twisting of the wrist that would send the ball arcing in. "But don't go throwing those until you're a few years older," he'd say, snapping a few experimentally himself. "Hard on your arm."

And he might smile and flip me the ball before settling back to watch the next inning.

My life would have been so much easier if I could just have painted a stage mustache on him, dressed him in black, remembered him only as the monster who came out at night. In the day he was a very different creature; I would have died for him.

Sometimes I think maybe I did.

I do not hate my father, although I feared him for many years, that fear a cold hard part of me buried in my deepest center like the chunks of gravel we used to build slushballs around in winter. When he drank, he hurt people; it was as simple as that. If he didn't hurt someone at a bar and get it out of his system before he came home, it would be my mother; it would be me.

When he came home from the plant late, the house itself seemed to hold its breath, the air inside settled, sluggish and heavy. My mother rarely spoke, and if she did, it was in the shortest and least complicated of sentences: "Finish your supper" or "sit up straight." For many years, I wondered why she allowed me to stay up later on the nights my father was gone. Now I know that she did not want to wait alone, the clock's tick swimming through that stagnant air, the hours passing like days as she waited for the storm door to fly open, for the jingle of my father fumbling with his keys in the darkness, for his fist pounding on the door in frustration and his voice, harsh and strained like someone who had gargled Drano: "Delores! Delores! Open the door!" I can understand now how waiting alone night after night might have felt, how her heart must have started crawling up her throat, how the turgid air would have become impossible to draw into her lungs.

I always tried to blame the drinking, not my father. Sober he was, everyone said, a prince of a fellow, and hearing this, I made the mistake of assuming that alcohol conferred absolution, that if my father could use it as an excuse, maybe I could, too.

Not even Glenette knows the truth about why my first marriage ended, and even now it is hard for me to relate: when I was a nineteen year old college pitcher in College Station, married only four months and with a child already on the way, I lost a close game in the final inning on my shortstop's wild throw. After the game, I spent three hours angrily tossing back cold ones with some of the guys, staggered back to my apartment in married student housing, and beat my wife because my dinner was cold.

She did not press charges, although I did not deserve such generosity. I never found out why, because her parents checked her out of the hospital a week later while I was at school and took her back to Houston. Seven months later she gave birth to a baby—my son—and put him up for adoption. I have not seen either of them since.

It was a hard lesson, but God is a just God, and the lesson truly changed my life: I learned that I no longer needed to carry around the fear of my father's cruelty; I learned that the same blood truly flowed in our veins, that what was cold and hard at the core of my being was not something he caused but a cold, hard, and violent part of myself; I learned that if you aren't careful, you can become the very thing you hate the most.

I do not hate my father, or my father's father, or any of those in the long line that began as dairy farmers and cheese makers in the Emilia-Romagna Province in northern Italy and culminates, improbably, with me, a high school baseball coach in Lorena, Texas. I am the end of the line, the last of the Mohicans, and to be honest, it doesn't feel so bad. Maybe it was time for an end.

I guess baseball was the only thing my father and I ever could share. We were not much good at talking to each other, and when my mother died and my grandparents asked me to come live with them, my father didn't stand in my way. I went to a tiny high school in northwest

Oklahoma, married my high school sweetheart, entered Texas A&M on a baseball scholarship, and when we went all the way to the College World Series my senior year, my father drove all the way to Omaha, Nebraska to watch me play.

When I got out on the mound, he called to me from his seat behind our dugout, and through the first inning I pitched, no matter how hard I tried to tune everything out, at the very edge of my awareness was my father bellowing chatter like a little league shortstop.

He didn't make it to the second inning. When a guy asked him if he could hold it down just a little, my father took offense, knocked him cold, and got dragged out of the stadium by security.

After the game, Glenette, who I'd met in an English lit class a year after my first marriage was annulled, told me about the noisy drunk sitting down in front of her. "It took four of them to carry him out," she said, "and when they went past, I could pick up the stink. I'm so glad you don't drink." She took my arm, lay her beautiful head on my sweaty shoulder.

"Yes," I said. "I am too."

"It sounded like he was yelling at you." She turned her face up to mine. "Who was he?"

"Nobody," I said.

On my run this morning, the trees overhanging the lane were still gray and gaunt, but I think spring is finally on its way. Saturday morning and then again yesterday afternoon after mass the girls and I worked on the ballfield at the high school, raking the infield, carrying shovels full of sand to the depressions that have formed over the winter, pulling weeds. Last night I sat out on the back porch with Glenette, a citronella candle keeping new-hatched mosquitoes at bay while out in the ravine behind our house the first crickets chirped their serenades. Today I will teach one class of College Preparatory English, two classes of sophomore world lit, head over to the field house to grade my papers. Then sixth hour I will go out and meet my team, watch the new boys throw, pick out a few to work with. My assistant coach can handle batting practice—you never have to twist a kid's arm to hit—but pitchers require care and patience.

When I take them out to the mound, the four or five boys looking on,

I will do for each of them what my father once did for me. I will show them the grips—rising fastball held across the seams, cut fastball held with the seams, curveball with the fingers to one side, slider, screwball, circle change—and then I will hand the ball to the first of them, and with my fingers, nudge his closer together, farther apart, shift the ball slightly in his grasp so that it's exactly right.

When I do this, I will see my father's hands, his big knuckles and callused palms, the grease caught black beneath his fingernails like a fossil preserved in amber, and I will remember how on an April day in our backyard in Lubbock he positioned the ball just so in my hands and then walked back fifty feet and crouched in front of me, how he held up his old padded catcher's mitt and said, "Okay, Tony, let's see your best pitch," how I wound up and let it fly. ❁

WORK

by Teresa Palomo Acosta

The thing is that all my *primas* all have a favorite story about *Tía* working all the time. So anytime I want to mention, as a joke, her carrying on like a regular woman, or wanting to be a *floja* on occasion, they give me the hardest time and one of those *miradas* meant to silence–the kind that only my blood sisters are allowed when I've bugged them for the fifth time in an hour.

"You're not going to start with that again, are you? Not with *Tía's novios.*"

"What *novios?*" I practically snarl. "I was going to enlighten you once again about her underground activities with the *Raza Unida* Party, all carried on in a family that had been kidnapped by Republican Party slogans and promises of a BMW in every garage."

"Now *Tía* never did all that *Raza Unida* stuff," they retort, twisting their Republican *elefante* key chains around red fingernails. "That's just an ugly rumor."

"Oh, but she did. She made plenty of banners and placards for the school walkouts, and she helped me with my Ramsey Muñiz for Governor posters and. . . ."

Parale ya is the likely response they'll give me before they start off another story about all the dimes she made sweeping community centers and looking after babies for her church's nursery.

Such a sweet Southern lady.

She even converted and was born again, they claim, preferring to lay their Southern Baptist roots on her head instead of theirs.

But I have had it up to here with all that. *Puro pedo.* I know what Liliana was up to when the family wasn't paying attention, so trusting that she was always at work somewhere, paying attention to the rich folks' kids while hers waited at home for her. Waited and waited for her. Sort of like all the children of the Central American nannies of failed white female Supreme Court justice nominees or white men trying to become Secretaries of this or that for the President.

Liliana, *tía de pura hierba buena*, was not about to let watching the rich people's children for a few *centavos* get in the way of trying to "liberate," as she put it, her own children's generation.

"Ya eso de andar de rodillas se acabo."

"Yes, the Bible tells me so," she liked to add, invoking her favorite born again phrase. It was a refrain she had picked up in Bible studies and used for her own purposes.

So once all those children were settled down for naps, out came the markers for the reams of posters; out came the letters to the school boards, announcing demands for *español* and *mujeres* studies—the latter the underground of the underground revolutionary demands. Out came the staple, the paper clips, the stacks of envelopes. Out came the pens she used to compose her own placards that we would carry at the next march, at least one hundred miles from her town, from the church nursery where she read both the Bible and the RUP *mujeres' noticias y libritos.*

She would hug me and whisper *"dale gas, mujer"* as she handed me the neat piles she'd put together after she had finished her three times a week 3–11 p.m. shift at the nursing home.

When she died tewnty years after the *movimiento*, after a whole lot of radical Chicanas had gone on to either help their people or hurt them, her son UPS'd me five thick and neatly packed boxes with everything she'd ever made for *la causa*. The papers inside were frayed from use. Brittle, yellow tape barely held some together. Family photographs lay in between layers of them.

I put all of the papers in a pile and lit a match to them, just as her will had ordered.

It's not only the words that must always be saved. She had written on the scrap of paper that made them mine.

But I don't tell that to my *primas*, who are still trying to get the BMW, and move into a big house, and receive invitiations to George and Barbara Bush's summer home. They call me a *tonta*.

Instead, at night I dream that eventually, I'll find a real job, too. 🏵

REVENGE OF THE LOVEBUG

by Charlcie Hopkins

Lovebugs fly in tandem during mating season;
many pairs remain bound in this fashion until the
female has laid her eggs and the male succumbs.

from Encyclopedia Of Entomology

Malvina contemplates the complications of her existence. Claude Ray hasn't made love in six years. Says he's too old and anyway nothing works right any more. So I says hell's bells, there's more than one way to skin a cat, use your imagination. But resourcefulness is not one of Claude Ray's strong points.

I know he can't help it. It's that damned diabetes, he says. So we just stumble along, acting like everything's fine, and so it is. I'm telling you that man used to be a firecracker. Now we pretend it isn't nothing.

And Bud! That Bud's hanging around with one rough crowd. Darlene found trashy magazines tucked up under the slats on his bed. Just what was Darlene looking up through the slats on Buddy's bed for? Honey, who knows? Haven't I asked myself that same question umpteen times? I know it wasn't any of her business or anything but hell, maybe she had a reason. Both of 'em aren't nothing but a handful.

Well, the fact of the matter is that Darlene found the nasty stuff and so comes straight to me about it. What could I do? I couldn't ignore it. Claude Ray, he could ignore it. Claude Ray ignores everything. He can't see daylight for sunshine.

And did I tell you about Ivo? You know, my brother Ivo, one of the twins. Both Ivo and Arlo married women named Ruby. Ruby Bell and Ruby Dewhurst. They married in the same year, in the fall. Well, Ivo calls the other night and tells me him and Ruby should be celebrating their wedding anniversary but instead they're getting divorced. Just like that! And I can guaran-damn-tee you what'll be happening next. Arlo and his Ruby will be doing the same thing. Everything Ivo does, Arlo does. Everything Arlo does, Ivo does. That's the way it is, always has been, always will be. And dammit, those Rubies are the mainstays of this family. Always doing things up for holidays. One year Ruby Bell has Thanksgiving and Ruby Dew does Christmas. Next year they switch around. So now what will happen? I'll tell you what will happen. It'll all fall on me. Thanksgiving and Christmas both, the whole squabbling bunch, and Claude Ray'll have a fit. He can't stand family all around. But to me that's what's important in life.

*Hey, wait a minute here! Where is this
going? Who are all these people, this
Claude Ray, this Malvina and all these
Rubies? And where's the quotation marks?*

Scooter come over the other day, his face all hangdog. Says to me, Aunt Mal, Mama and Daddy are over there yelling again and I can't stand it. I says, honey, come on in and set down. Have a Coca-Cola. What are they carrying on about?

He says, Aunt Malvina, they're fussing about Mama's cats.

Her cats, you say?

Yes ma'am. Daddy says that the whole house smells like a cat box. Says it's either him or them cats.

Him or the cats, huh?

That's what he says.

And that's something to yell about?

You can hear'em clear down the road.

Is that what they're gettin' this damn divorce over? Those fool cats?

That's part of it.

Cats, huh?

Yes, ma'am.

Lord have mercy, what a feeble excuse to tear up a family. They need some good ideas for a divorce, let'em come over thisaway and poke around. Let'em see what some folks put up with.

Mama says them cats love her better than Daddy does.

I can believe that.

Says they smell better, too.

My own brother—

She says—

Ruby hired a maid name of Silvia. Last name Kuppia. It was her real name. We called her Silver Cup. She was slow-witted but had a heart of pure gold. Ruby said there was never a woman in the world could cook frito pie better than Silver Cup. It had a secret ingredient and no one ever figured out what it was. She was a very affectionate woman and the children thought she hung the stars. But even so, there was problems.

That was when we all had that place over at Bolivar, spent every summer there, and it was Silver's job to look after the kids. But every time Silver Cup got near the water she had a hissy fit. Fear controlled that woman like the moon does the tide. She'd been raised to believe monsters lived in the sea and they'd rise right up and suck her down if she got too close to the water's edge. Ruby Dew claimed she'd been scared by a Godzilla picture show when she was young. I say it was those superstitious people of hers. Family has a powerful influence, I tell you.

Well, the fact is we loved going to the Gulf and we loved Silver Cup, too. So Ivo took a notion to tie a rope around Silver's waist and that way the sea monsters couldn't pull her out to sea. Ivo would be walking along the shoreline with Silver tied to the rope and then finally she'd be able to relax and enjoy herself some. But folks wouldn't know what to make of it. They'd stare and scowl. What was a man walking a woman along the beach just like a dog for? Especially tourists from up north, they'd get the most suspicious looks on their faces. You could tell they were thinking it was some terrible method of control. One of 'em even called the police. And Ivo got sick and tired of having to explain.

But Silver Cup wouldn't go near the water 'less she had her tether on. Is this for real?

Barth says truth slides into shade,
shade into fancy, all become one:
this funhouse—

It's just absurd. . . . Here, honey, sit on the porch and let me tell you what's happening this evening.

Claude Ray hasn't—well, you know—soon to be seven years. Used to be he was fit to be tied but now he just gives up and shrugs. Lord, how he hates me telling. Well, I can't help it. It's the way things are and I tell it like it is. He claims I don't know the difference between what's real and what's not. I still love the man, I surely do.

Life's peculiar, isn't it? We learn to live with whatever occurs, no matter what. Just exist and keep on. Like Silver and her monsters, she felt safe only as long as she was tied to a leash.

Nothing and nobody's perfect. Not even Bud. He might think he's perfect now, but he'll soon learn. He's young yet. Life'll slap him down sure as I been slapping these pesky bugs.

We all try to do the best we can with what we got. It's all we have to work with. Folks grab hold of each other in the most unusual ways, then won't let go no matter what. Like those lovebugs there.

Love's a mighty, mighty force. Always yearning, always reaching, always trying to connect. And it all comes down to the same old thing. We wake up in the morning, we go to bed at night and in between . . . well . . . love and death.

Watch out for that lovebug, sugar. Grammaw used to call 'em the devil's pets, said they'd drift right into a person's mouth and six days later that person would die. They're so in a swoon they can't tell whichaway's what. This time of year they're out swarming and mating; floating in the air like cottonwood seeds.

Hand me that newspaper, will you, and I'll soon put an end—

Claude Ray says it's just that they're so stupid and blind. Get stuck together like that and can't figure it out, even with two heads. Hold still, you little—

Oh, damn! Did I get 'em? Swat one and here comes two more to take its place. It's never ending. Love is what it's all about. That's all.

Love and death. 🏵️

SIDE STEP

by Ivanov Reyez

The Valley was swarming with "snowbirds," winter tourists from the North. From Padre Island to the public library and the downtown streets, they flurried about in couples or groups with their silver hair and pale skins and blue veins radiant in the December sun. Perhaps they had celebrated Christmas with their families back home, building snowmen with their grandkids, before rushing to our subtropical climate in South Texas.

"I'm glad they come every year," I told Pete, one of my high-school friends. We were walking to his house to get his books. "They really do help the economy, here and across, except they probably return home with bad images and stories of the poor people here. Now that's not good."

"Tomorrow is the thirtieth, Rita's birthday," he said. "I don't know what to buy her. You got any suggestions? She thinks I'm crazy sometimes, but I'm very serious about her."

"Wouldn't it be nice to go up North, to see snow?"

"I'm thinking of a cross and chain, nothing too too expensive. I got her a watch for Christmas."

"Now that was expensive. I hope she takes good care of it."

After Pete had found his books, we headed for the library. We were on Levee Street, singing loudly and crazily, when suddenly out of a black Volkswagen driving by a blonde woman smiled and waved. Mrs. Heinz! I thought. Bunnie in the back seat! My chest was instantly warm and excited. "Mrs. Heinz!" I told Pete. "Mrs. Heinz! Man, I'm sure that was her!" But what was she doing back in Texas? Perhaps she was visiting friends for the Christmas holidays. Perhaps she had come for some of her furniture, which her landlady had stored for her in June 1963.

Although we had barely corresponded since then, I had never forgotten

Georgeanne. She was Mrs. Heinz's oldest daughter. In September 1962, at the start of my junior year of high school, I created an illusion with this blue-eyed blonde who sauntered into study hall. Eventually, I met her. We walked home in the sunlit rain, and I was in love. Despite meeting her mother and her siblings, despite all of us cramming into the VW beetle and going to the Charro Drive-In where Georgeanne and I sat alone, despite our frolic at dusk in the October waves of the Gulf, despite more, our relationship remained superficial. The school year had months when we did not see each other anywhere. Not once did I kiss her. She dated others and we drifted apart. I wrote poems about her and she returned to Ohio and my illusion deepened.

I spent my senior year aching to run after her. I neglected my studies. A homosexual vice principal was harassing me. I became irresponsible. Georgeanne valued scholarship and one course, geometry, kept me from graduating. The geometry teacher, who resembled a T-Rex (but without the ferocity), could not explain mathematics; and the rowdy students continually thwarted his feeble attempts to do so. Above all, I was too disinterested and self-conscious to play with a cheap compass and a protractor. And then came the greatest hurt: Cosima, the girl who had haunted me since childhood, came to spend the summer with us. She chastised me for not graduating and my family liked her. I had no money to run to Ohio. I started to suffer Cosima's presence, to fall in love with her again. How innocent and shocked I was when I learned that she was involved in a lesbian affair with an older woman. We argued; we wept. By the end of summer Cosima was gone. I returned to school for geometry and stability.

In the library, I was still excited by the image of the waving blonde woman. I moved among the shelves with Pete, quietly empowered by presentiment. A blonde girl stared at me. Her eyes were blue. She was with a little girl, perhaps her sister. Georgeanne! my heart thudded. I was flattered and hid in a philosophy book. When Pete and I went home, we separated in front of my house. He could tell I was not interested in chatting. I could not stop thinking of Mrs. Heinz (Lillian, as she had always insisted I should call her). I told my brother that I had seen her and Bunnie in the

Volkswagen. I also gushed about the girl in the library. "Any girl who looks at you and smiles, you think right away it's Georgeanne," he said. I left for the library again and sat at one of the long tables to read.

All of a sudden a girl was reading over my left shoulder, her long blonde hair dangling and bright. I looked up: Georgeanne! Mrs. Heinz! I stood up, excited and shaky, and Georgeanne took my hand. Heads rose around us. Looking into Georgeanne's eyes was like probing into a diamond. She was unbelievably fresh and pink, radiant and gold. I had secretly called her "Flavia" because of her yellow hair. She was the young Venus that my hitchhiking buddies and I had always dreamed of meeting on Padre Island. And she was holding my hand.

"How in the world are you?" said Georgeanne. "You look good, yummy good."

"I—I'm fine, thank—"

"We've missed you," said Mrs. Heinz. "It's been so long, over a year."

I felt she expected a hug, an emotion beyond my nervousness.

"We knew we'd find you here," said Georgeanne, looking around.

"Hey, we can't talk here. Let's go somewhere else."

"George, he's reading. We can't just fly in here and take him away."

"Yes, we can. Right, Casimiro?"

"We can go somewhere. I don't mind."

"Let him check his book out," said Mrs. Heinz. "We're not in a hurry. It's just getting dark."

"Yes, we are." She turned to me, her eyes determined. "Do you need to check out the book?"

"No. We can go."

It was chilly outside. I was nervous and quivering. I followed the women through the shadows. Where was their darkness taking me?

"I feel so strange," I said. "All this seems so unreal."

"Why did you write asking for your letters?" asked Georgeanne. "Are you planning to compile them into a book?"

"No, I just—"

"I hope Karl and Richard are not worrying about us," said Mrs. Heinz. "You know they've been talking of seeing Málaga tonight."

"Mother, we'll get there. Stop worrying. Just walk faster."

How naive of Georgeanne, I thought, to suggest that people would be interested in reading the collected letters of Casimiro Sefardí. Casimiro, the nobody. I wanted my letters so she would not own anything of mine.

We reached a dirty black Cadillac. It was parked several feet from the other cars. I had expected the black Volkswagen. I asked the women if they had been driving the VW that afternoon.

"Sorry, not us," said Georgeanne. "We came—"

"The VW is back in Ohio. We came in Karl's car, this one. It's roomier. And I've been having a load of problems with my bug. We've been all over the country with it."

I sat between Georgeanne and Mrs. Heinz. Georgeanne was driving. I was uncomfortable, out of context, used to being alone.

"I like Karl's car, especially when I get to drive. You can take naps in the back seat. You can—"

"Do a lot more," said Mrs. Heinz.

"Mother! Be quiet."

Georgeanne's long blonde hair was shiny, beautiful when we passed the light posts. It smelled clean against my face, an ice-cream smell I had always loved. I imagined her brushing it vigorously.

"Karl's also a vegetarian, said Georgeanne, "and he's got boxes of pecans and walnuts back there. You can eat and nap and enjoy all that space."

A strange emotion blazed within me: it was as though I had been holding my breath for over a year and now the joy of breathing was overwhelming me. One question from them about my life and I started talking. I spoke about the change that I had undergone in the last few months. No longer was I interested in poetry, novels, and drama. I was mainly focused on philosophy and political science. I wanted to elaborate on my transformation, on how these disciplines strengthened me, but I felt that the women were not paying attention. Perhaps the night was for entertainment, not intellectual conversation.

"Where did you get your high ideals?" asked Mrs. Heinz.

Her tone surprised me. Didn't she know me? Did she think that living in a Texas border town was incongruous with higher knowledge and ambition? How could she, a rather crude woman without wealth or education, ask that question?

"Ma'am, are you suggesting that—"

"This traffic!" said Georgeanne, slapping the steering wheel. "I have to get used to these narrow streets again."

"Call me Lillian. Don't call me 'ma'am.'"

"We're going to gas up for tomorrow, Mother. Cass, if you're wondering where we're going, we're taking you straight to Ohio, okay?"

"I'm ready. Let's go. Maybe I'll find the books I've been wanting to read for a long time, like Sartre's *Nausea*."

"I wish we could," said Mrs. Heinz, "but tonight we'll have to settle for the apartment house. You remember where we lived last year. We're staying with the landlady. Really, Casimiro, I'd love it if you made it up to Akron next summer."

Georgeanne stopped at a gas station. She rushed out to pump the gas. I felt useless, frozen in the silvery light. Mrs. Heinz smelled like warm milk. Her thigh was huge against mine.

"We've missed you a lot. We made so many memories here. Bunnie and the kids stayed home crying because they couldn't come on this trip." We looked at Georgeanne and the gas attendant. "She likes to pump her own gas. Don't you think she's beautiful? I'm very proud of her. She's grown so much in the last year."

"Very beautiful, yes."

The landlady greeted us at the door of the apartment. She was smoking. I remembered her as always smoking. She was stocky and manly. I had always been curious and slightly jealous about the way she looked at Mrs. Heinz, the way she kissed her on the cheek close to her mouth, and the way she circled her thick arm around her waist as they walked. Tonight was no different, except that now I was disturbed. I imagined Mrs. Heinz in the landlady's bed, prostituting herself for room and board, even moaning her pleasure. I was introduced and the landlady looked at me curiously. "I think I remember you, one of Georgeanne's boyfriends. Come on in. That cold air is my death."

In the living room I met Karl and Richard. Karl was slender and soft-spoken, probably in his thirties like Mrs. Heinz. Richard was about twenty-one, sandy-haired and chubby. He reminded me of one of my hitchhiking friends. Was he Georgeanne's lover? Suddenly I wanted to go home. He had been traveling with them. He knew their intimacies. What was I doing here? He was drafting something on the coffee table. "You're going to Málaga with us," said Georgeanne to me. "You know that, right?" I smiled. She and Mrs. Heinz disappeared into a bedroom to change clothes. The men were ready to go, but they showed the patience and silence of chess players.

Georgeanne emerged in a white dress and tennis shoes. She had worn army-green tights and a white long-sleeved blouse. Now in her tight dress she was beautiful and feminine. The tennis shoes struck me as odd, but she and her mother had never allowed the lack of money and proper clothes to thwart their desires. Mrs. Heinz's eccentricity had always been their freedom. Buying old bread at the bakery, stuffing all her family and me into the VW and sneaking us into the Charro for a dollar, wearing thongs most of the year, and doing much more, this bohemian woman surprised and entertained the Valley with her simple aggression and thick hairy calves.

"Do you speak Spanish?" asked the landlady, looking at me.

"He speaks beautiful Spanish," said Georgeanne.

The landlady set a red candle on one of the end tables.

"Enough to order a taco," I smiled, "but if I had to discuss philosophy I wouldn't have the vocabulary."

"Mother, let's go! We're just standing here!"

"Now, George, let Lillian be," said Richard. "You had your time."

"Shut up, Richard. Play by yourself."

The landlady had lit the candle and the flame looked stiff as a golden icicle. It struck me that her apartment was crowded, Victorian, a thick, faded carpet. Oscar Wilde would have been comfortable here.

"I've been here all my adult life and I still can't survive in Spanish," said the landlady. "It seems the border has never entered me."

Mrs. Heinz emerged in a long flowery dress and tennis shoes. Like Georgeanne's, her shoes were smudgy. She was carrying a brown paper bag.

"Hon, you look wonderful, simply darling," said the landlady, reaching for Mrs. Heinz's waist.

It had been decided that we would walk to Málaga. I did not question why, although I understood they were not going to drive in chaotic Málaga nor call a taxi. The night was starry, moonless, awfully silent. I was chilly and still nervous. We stopped at a phone booth. Georgeanne wanted to call her grandmother in Ohio. Mrs. Heinz and the men walked on, and I started to follow. "Cass, where are you going? Stay with me." I stayed and she asked her grandmother for Bunnie and the kids. And then she was screaming. I moved away. "Damn! That woman can't hear!" I had seen Georgeanne's temper before, but this was excessive. She was fuming, cursing, demanding information. "Shit! Get yourself a spoon and scoop out that fucking wax from your fucking ears!" She slammed the phone and I was stunned.

"Forgive my French, Cass, but that old woman drives me nuts. You see, I've been trying to buy this old Hudson from a guy I was dating. He said before I left that he would drop off the car and the keys at Grandma's, so I could drive it when I got back. But my grandmother barely knows who I am. If you come to Ohio next summer, and you'd better, maybe we can drive the Hudson to the New York World's Fair."

She was not the Georgeanne that I had romanticized in my thoughts for two years. I had no desire to travel anywhere with her. We were on the black road leading toward the old bridge, trying to catch up with Mrs. Heinz and the men. I was quiet, numb, reluctant. I seemed glued, obligated to this scenario, without the sense or strength to just walk away.

"You're not going to say anything?" she asked.

"About what?"

"About anything."

"I don't know what to say."

"You always have something to say. Why not now? Say there are a bunch of cars tonight, a lot of lights."

We were like refugees in the dark, lit by the passing cars. I refused to look at her. We were almost at the bridge, and we could see Mrs. Heinz and the men waiting for us near the customs office. Mrs. Heinz was slightly taller than the men. She moved in the silvery light like a restless moth while the men moved in and out of the shadows like spiders.

"You know, Cass, we didn't ask you if you needed to go to your house for anything. We just dragged you with us."

"It's all right."

"Now that I'm a senior, I'm starting to check on the different colleges. I'm thinking of traveling and being free. We used to talk about this, remember?"

"Yes, I remember."

"You still want to travel all over, don't you? I want to see Miami, Greece, Alaska, and Germany, just to mention a few."

"I would like to see Germany because of German philosophy. I would especially like to spend time in Munich and walk the streets that Hitler used to walk. In other words, learn more of its history."

We reached the bridge and joined the others. During the holidays, both bridges were loaded with cars. Despite the distance, sometimes it was wiser and safer to walk all the way to downtown Málaga. Before crossing the bridge, while Mrs. Heinz was competing with the drivers to pay the man in the tollbooth, I looked back toward the woods and the railroad tracks leading to nearby La Muralla. Cosima and I had grown up in that section of town. My family had moved out in 1962 to our present house on Adams Street. In that year, I had met Georgeanne. Last August, from that house I had brought Cosima to these woods. A few days later she left the house and me.

"All those cars and just one toll collector," said Mrs. Heinz. "What is the government doing with all that money?"

"They usually have one man working both sides of the booth, but tonight they should have two because of the holidays," I said. "Maybe the other man stepped out for a moment."

Karl and Richard walked ahead of us on the bridge, as if they knew where they were going. Mrs. Heinz asked me to carry her paper bag. She started asking Georgeanne about the phone call. I walked behind them on the narrow, slatted passageway. Through the boards, one could see the quiet river below. It was scary in the daytime because one saw the poor condition of the boards—some old and loose, others broken—and the long drop to the river. I watched the lights of Resurrection, the pale El Jardín Hotel, and heard the cars inching beside me across the bridge. I heard voices and yelling, a radio blaring "As Tears Go By," and a locomotive working somewhere in the distance. We were entering Málaga: I was eighteen and this was the only Paris I could afford.

"Well, you shouldn't be ugly to her," Mrs. Heinz was saying. "Take care of your business when you get home. You can't do anything from here."

"Okay, Mother, I will. I promise."

They turned around and urged me to join them. Mexican customs officers were busy inspecting cars, getting trunks opened, and looking important. People on foot were usually given a nod or a slow motion of the finger to go on through. We descended the hilly street and gradually sank into the smells and people of Málaga. Alone in this city, I usually roamed the drizzly streets and sat in a café and listened to the wind. Now I was following these people. Now I was immune to Málaga's reticent beauty, to her foreignness, her exoticism, her dark *verijas*. I could not see Málaga with them, only through them, and I was critical. How poor and resigned she was.

Mrs. Heinz wanted to go to the Mercado Juárez. We were warm and tired of walking. The venders at the market were very aggressive and annoying. They seemed angry when we ignored them. They found it incongruous that blonde hair should walk by without buying. But when they noticed the women's tennis shoes and a clear lack of refinement, they understood these were not rich Americans. Their anger turned to disparagement. I expected them to spit at our heels. The male venders did not miss Georgeanne's tight dress and healthy haunches. Their focus was brazen, their remarks crude: "*Qué caballona, qué culito,*" and "*Se la mamo toda la noche.*"

We reached the fruit and vegetable venders after going around in circles. "This market is like a maze," I said. Mrs. Heinz and Georgeanne were quickly fascinated by the variety of the produce. They were feeling the mangoes and the papayas. The fruit vender rushed to explain the origin of the fruits. Karl and Richard were more interested in the bags of peeled pecans. "Who wants to share this avocado with me?" asked Georgeanne. A vender from the adjacent stall had brought her the avocado. His voice sounded like a meow. Then the fruit vender gave Mrs. Heinz a tangerine, and her blue eyes beamed with surprise and gratitude. I was repelled.

"You're giving me a tangerine? Well, thank you very very much." She was smiling and smelling the tangerine. "Isn't he an angel?"

"Don't say thank you, ma'am," I said. "Thank you is a bad word."

She looked at me strangely. I could not stand extremely nice people. On the one hand, they softened my heart and weakened me. They made me realize pain and suffering, the vulnerability I was too impotent to alleviate. On the other hand, I felt they were hypocritical and could hurt me. Since my experience with Cosima, I had become more withdrawn and distrustful of people.

"My life is like a lame horse," I told Georgeanne. We were on the busy streets again. Mrs. Heinz had bought some bananas, and Georgeanne had given me two avocado seeds to pocket for her. I was telling Georgeanne about my failure to graduate, about being in school again to pass geometry. I had no job and no prospects for the future. I was addicted to reading, to the library and my room, to the night wind and classical music. I read until my father threatened to steal my light bulb at three or four in the morning.

"How much deeper can I go into myself? I could never be worthy of you. I'm not worthy of you at all."

"Yes, you are," said Georgeanne.

The cars were moist and shiny. A truck had a sign on the radiator grille: *DIOS POR DELANTE*. The aroma of tacos, onions and cabrito, floated everywhere. On these streets I had held on to my father's thumb. He was taking me to the barbershop.

"Are you growing a beard?" she asked, cupping my chin. It felt peculiar being touched, especially by her. She was so beautiful.

"No, I just haven't shaved."

"Finish school so we can go to the University of Houston together," she said.

"Together. It's been a long time."

"You're going to like it."

"All this is so unreal," I said, looking up at the gray-purplish sky. "You know that in Paris the wind blows without me."

Mrs. Heinz joined us and asked me if I knew the Paradise nightclub. I said yes, remembering that last summer a friend and I had walked in to look.

"Karl and I want to go there, see if we can dance a little. Do you know where it is?"

"It's only about two blocks from here. I'll take you there."

"Oh, you're a sweet," she said, glancing at Georgeanne and rushing off to rejoin the men.

"You're good," said Georgeanne, reaching for my hand.

"I'm a failure. I'm a bum."

"You're not a failure. You're not a bum either. You're good!"

Mrs. Heinz returned to us. Georgeanne said her eyes were burning and went to ask Richard a question. The men were in front of us, but I was giving directions. While Mrs. Heinz discoursed on psychoanalysis, the law of karma, and her I AM religion, Georgeanne's words kept echoing in my head. I cursed myself for not trying to graduate. What was wrong with me? Did I want her to hate me? What was I going to do? What was I doing to myself? What was I doing in the world? Nothing. I was shit.

I told everyone the Paradise was half a block away. Mrs. Heinz suddenly stopped and asked for the paper bag I was carrying. I gave it to her and she took out a pair of shiny blue-green shoes. "They're new," she said. "They're my social shoes. I could not afford it if they got lost or ruined." She took off her tennis shoes and put on the new shoes. I had never seen anyone do this in the streets. She was bending over, her haunches wide, her calves thick. People walked around her barely looking, stepping off the narrow sidewalk and avoiding mud and puddles. She now felt well-dressed.

Mrs. Heinz returned the paper bag with the tennis shoes in it. I told her to watch out for speeding cars splashing her. "I'm also watching out for holes in the pavement," she said. "Richard almost stepped in one." I watched Georgeanne and suddenly felt I loved her. I wanted to embrace her, to kiss her smooth pink lips. I imagined us sitting in a tide pool, the water clean and clear in the sunlight, our legs pale. Then I despaired: she was too beautiful and would certainly reject me. She knew something grave was troubling me, but she was not going to help me. Her face was now a cautious stare.

Outside the nightclub, we stared at the black-and-white photographs of the floor-show performers. Pictured were young women with small waists and full thighs in attractive costumes. There were also two *charros* with caterpillar moustaches. We were going to enter the dark mysterious place. I was nervous: what was expected of me? A fat watchman stood near the entrance. For a few pesos he would guard any car against theft or damage. Dressed in khaki, with a saucer cap and red-brown ankle boots, he resembled a policeman. His face was brown, pock-marked, and fat as a bulldog's. He had the thick neck of a wrestler, and his eyes were cold and shrewd.

Karl appeared decently dressed with his white shirt, bow tie, and blazer. Mrs. Heinz said that Richard and I should have worn black ties. Had she forgotten that I had been taken from the library? Besides, I did not have any ties. Richard at least wore a white shirt, although it was unclean and somewhat wrinkled. But why was she fussing so much? Money spoke here too, not clothes. In the dim light, with the fine band and sensual Latin music and mixed drinks, who cared?

We sat down and the waiter swooped down upon us. No one drank liquor, so orange juice and pineapple juice were ordered. The waiter probably thought we were crazy. I felt uneasy and useless, mainly because I was broke. "We don't even drink Cokes," said Mrs. Heinz. Richard and Karl wanted to dance. The women eagerly joined them. It did not bother me that Richard held Georgeanne tightly, even affectionately. I just wanted to go home. Nightclubs and aggressive waiters intimidated me. The whole scene bored me. I was wasting my time.

Mrs. Heinz and Karl returned to the table. Richard wanted to continue dancing. Karl went to the restroom and Mrs. Heinz started to discuss her I AM religion. I was not interested in purple auras and whatnot, so I nicely told her of my predilection for Judaism. She immediately went silent. Then she leaned toward me, her lips at my right ear, and whispered: "You should ask George for a dance. Don't let Richard monopolize her. It's an excuse to get close to her."

"But I can't dance. I've never learned how. I can't feel the music in my legs, only in my brain."

"She will feel hurt," said Mrs. Heinz, her hand on my forearm.

"But I feel nothing."

"Think about her feelings," she said, gripping me.

She probably thought that I was the farthest thing from a Lothario. Karl returned and she told him to watch the table. She grabbed my hand and dragged me onto the dance floor. I kept telling her that I could not dance. Besides, I felt awkward and excited holding her warm body near mine. Her waist was small and youthful, alarmingly pliant in my right hand. The music was slow and romantic. I carefully moved my feet among the fragrant dancers. I tried to use steps I remembered from movies. I looked around self-consciously: I could not see Georgeanne and Richard anywhere. Perhaps they had gone to the restroom. At our table, Karl nursed his pineapple juice and watched the musicians and the smartly dressed people with their sophisticated mixed drinks.

"You're doing fine," said Mrs. Heinz. "You see, you're doing fine. Just stay close to me. I'll take good care of you."

"I really don't know what I'm doing. I'm just moving my feet. My brother and sisters—boy, they can dance."

Suddenly someone's buttocks were tightly against mine. Then I was bumped. I turned around and Georgeanne was smiling. Her face was very red. Somehow her excitement disgusted me.

"Mother, how in the world did you manage? You know Cass hates to dance. I'm simply floored!"

"He's not as bad as he says. Honey, let me dance a little more with him, then he's all yours."

"Mother, you'd better return him in one piece," she said, smiling and winking.

Georgeanne and Richard returned to the table. The music stopped and I realized we had been yelling. Mrs. Heinz was not ready to quit. Like Georgeanne and Richard, she wanted to milk the night club experience to the fullest. When the music started again, she hid me among the couples in the dark. We held each other: it was like dancing. I felt her hipbones and her strong thighs against mine. It struck me that I had always spent more time with her than with Georgeanne. While Georgeanne and Bunnie had been splashing in the Gulf, Mrs. Heinz and I had been chatting on the shore. When I visited, she and I spent hours together after the girls had gone to bed. I was comfortable with her, very secure.

"Whew! It's hot in here. I'm sweating and my face is burning. Mrs. Heinz, maybe we should—"

"Lillian. Call me Lillian."

"But I feel funny."

"You used to call me Lillian," she said, her mouth almost on mine.

"Ma'am, I—"

"You're side-stepping me. If you come to Ohio, and you must, I'll take good care of you, okay?"

"Okay," I said, trembling.

"Call me Lillian. Say it before we go."

"Okay. Lillian."

"Okay. You're smiling."

We headed for the table. How delicious and dangerous Mrs. Heinz had been. Mothers had always treated me fondly.

"Mother, you're wet," said Georgeanne, smiling.

"It's pretty hot in there—all those people, so much energy. Where's Richard?"

"He left, said he wasn't feeling well. I think he's getting the bug."

"Well, that's too bad. He was really enjoying himself."

"He'll be all right. I told him to go down the street we came."

"Calle 6," I said, "straight to the bridge."

Georgeanne had her legs crossed: her calves were full and lovely. Mrs. Heinz and I sat down and the waiter appeared. They wanted to stay for the floor show, so Karl ordered another round of juices. I looked at Georgeanne while Mrs. Heinz talked with Karl. The band started playing an old love song. Someone started singing. The lyrics intensified my desperation. Georgeanne stared at me.

"What now?" I asked.

"I don't know," she said. "Let me brace myself."

"Cass, be a dear, and translate the song for us," said Mrs. Heinz. "It sounds beautiful."

"Ma'am, the song—"

"Lillian, Lillian," she said.

"Mother, Lillian? Lillian, Mother?"

"Hush up."

"Mother, I thought you had returned him to me."

"The song is called 'El Reloj,' which means 'The Clock.' I've known it since I was a kid. The singer is asking the clock to quit measuring the time because otherwise he'll go mad. The woman he loves is leaving forever at dawn."

"Where are the drinks?" asked Karl, obviously bored, his narrow face in his bony hands.

"He says we only have this night to live our love. He's suffering. Make tonight eternal, he says, so she won't leave me. Prevent the dawn. Quit ticking."

"That is beautiful, Cass," said Mrs. Heinz. "Wish we had danced to that one."

"Without her love he is nothing."

"You're a romantic," said Georgeanne.

"Pain is real. It can cause real things like suicide."

"As much as I like you, Cass, sometimes you irritate me."

The waiter brought the juices and asked if we were staying for the floor show. Karl and Mrs. Heinz said yes. He said there was a cover charge of five dollars. Everyone was shocked. Karl refused to pay and Mrs. Heinz argued that we had had no knowledge. It was embarrassing to sit there rushing through our drinks and looking at each other. We could not afford the table, and the waiter needed high-spending customers. We walked out as the drums were rolling for the floor show.

Everyone was fuming. The cool, moist air and the cold stars did nothing to alleviate the heat. Our mouths were smoking. I was glad to be out of the nightclub. We walked around even though an argument was brewing between Mrs. Heinz and Georgeanne. I could smell tacos and shrimp, onions, vanilla, and cinnamon. We passed by the plaza. The lampposts and the dusty palm trees looked somber. Some men started howling. I occasionally caught bits of the spat between the women. They had slept on the beach last night. Mrs. Heinz rebuked Georgeanne for having done nothing but "screw" with Richard. I was sure I had heard correctly. I wished I had not seen them. They sickened me.

I was glad when we crossed the bridge. I looked down at the shiny grasses on the banks of the river, at the city lights reflected on the water. I was carrying Mrs. Heinz's bag of bananas. She was walking beside me because she had gotten tired of arguing. Georgeanne and Karl were ahead of us. From the tollbooth I looked toward the woods again. I felt the moist breeze and thought of the thirty-year-old woman whom I had recently brought to those woods. I had sought to relive my walk with Cosima.

The customs officer told Georgeanne and Mrs. Heinz that they could not take the orange across. I thought of the avocado seeds in my pockets and wondered if the officer would get suspicious and search me. He only asked me what I had in the bag. I answered bananas. "Well, can we eat the orange here?" asked Georgeanne. The officer wrinkled his face and said okay. Another officer nearby smiled and shook his blond head. I was embarrassed and yet delighted. The women exuded their usual freedom and strength. Even one orange to them was sacred and loaded with vitamins. So they asked the officers for permission to eat it inside their office. They agreed and we went inside. It was very quiet.

Georgeanne sat on a folding chair and crossed her lovely legs. She began to peel the orange slowly, carefully, and gently, as though she had all night. Karl, Mrs. Heinz, and I stood in front of her. The officers across the room observed us. Georgeanne their major focus. They said something to themselves and smiled. "No sense in wasting the nutritious orange by throwing it away," said Mrs. Heinz. Karl appeared bored, tired, and anxious to leave. I was smiling and mostly admiring Georgeanne. She had such beautiful legs and blue eyes. Her hair and skin were healthy, very luminous. For an instant I felt calm. I looked at her soft stomach. I could not believe her beauty. When she smiled and winked at me like old times, I felt it was all a dream and that I could never get near her. The more I hungered for her, to kiss her and fondle her, the more unreal and divine she became. She knew she was ripe and sensual. Karl and Mrs. Heinz watched me as we each ate a piece of orange. They could see the desire on my face.

Karl walked down the long black road ahead of us. He had not said a word. We saw him far off very small in the night. His blazer looked blue. We were going home and nothing had happened. I felt despair. I felt lost. Nothing seemed real or sensible. It was all like a dream, a biblical tale. The breeze was cold, cutting through the grasses. The silence and the emptiness kept me tense and delirious and restless. I was on the verge of crying out and running like an idiot. I stared at Georgeanne's blonde hair so dazzling, almost like platinum, and neither Georgeanne nor Mrs. Heinz truly understood what I was undergoing. Sometimes the way they looked at me revealed a hidden preoccupation or anticipation of something dreadful. They probably cared for me, but I could not feel it. I could not clear my head and believe I was worth anything.

"I'm a bum!" I started shouting. "I'm a bum!" They stared at me in calm horror. "Oh, ma'am, why did you have to come? You brought heaven with you and now you're going to leave me in hell. I won't be able to sleep tonight—nor ever!"

Georgeanne walked about six feet in front of us. Her arms were crossed. Again I began to shout.

"Oh, George, why did I have to see you? Why!"

Mrs. Heinz stared at me as if truly seeing me for the first time. I raised my arms toward the black sky when I shouted. About me was the silence of the railroad tracks and the dusty bushes. I felt myself rebellious in the middle of a calm, orderly world. Georgeanne turned around and tried to form a smile. Her bewilderment was obvious. The fragile smile dissolved and her eyes were squinting gravely.

"You're not a bum," said Mrs. Heinz. "Don't say that. Don't call yourself that. We care for you. You have literature to—"

"Literature! Nothing but accumulated emotions! The collected passions of a fool! Of what value is literature?"

"Casimiro, what has happened to you since we left in '63? You were so gentle and calm then. Now you are forceful and appear to be struggling to achieve something by escaping something else. Did you meet some girl?"

"No, ma'am. I haven't met any girl. I can't explain why I act this way."

Her words did not dilute my despair. I felt I deserved to die. Georgeanne looked disturbed. She said she was tired of walking and needed to get home to rest. My hot chest was about to explode. I wanted to disappear into the night like Karl.

When we arrived at the apartments, I started to thank them for the outing. "Oh, you're not saying good night just yet," said Mrs. Heinz, reaching for the bag of bananas. She led us to the porch of the landlady's apartment. We sat on the steps and started talking about their trip back to Ohio. Then I focused on myself. I wanted to confess all that had happened to me with Cosima: how she was no longer pristine, how she had left me, and how she haunted me mercilessly. But I focused on myself alone.

"Even when you met me I was a loner. This is a fact, not a complaint. But since last summer I have become a stranger to everything. I walk around fatigued. The slightest effort tires me, enrages me. I don't want to see anybody, do anything, hear anything."

They sat silently and the night wind was getting colder and we shivered a little. Mrs. Heinz looked at the paper bag sitting beside her. I looked at the plants stirring and heard a dog barking. An occasional car sped by, as if running late.

"I have virtually destroyed all my relationships, the few I had. Even with my family there's friction. In my room I walk back and forth every night, discoursing to an imaginary audience. I'm like a madman angry at the world. Sometime ago I started going to the Presbyterian chapel with some guys. Maybe I was hoping to find answers in religion. Anyway, I ended up quarreling with the guys over mysterious reasons and meeting a woman who was more interested in me than in my problems."

Mrs. Heinz opened the bag of bananas. She pulled out a banana and held it in both hands.

"Honey, Cass, do you want a banana? I feel like having one. They smell so delicious."

"Hmm, they sure do, Mother, but I'll pass."

"No, ma'am, I'm fine."

"Well, then I'll circumcise it for myself," she smiled, slowly peeling the banana.

"Actually, I wasn't quarreling with the guys," I continued. "They simply were envious because the girls understood me as poet and the preacher called me 'Socrates.'"

Mrs. Heinz was eating her banana, her mouth rounded as it descended for the next bite. She looked up at Georgeanne before she bit, obviously trying to communicate something. Georgeanne returned her look. I kept on talking.

"I did argue with one of the women there, one of the big honchos. She didn't like it when I disagreed with her religious views. Anyway, all this is unimportant. What's important is that since you left I have been trying, mostly dreaming, of getting to Ohio. My dreams of San Francisco and Greenwich Village meant nothing compared to being with you. And now I'm in school and I'm supposed to wait till next summer to be free. You're here and I can't go with you."

"If you have enough interest in me you can wait," said Georgeanne.

"Oh, I've been waiting. That's why I'm braying on this still night. You have been everywhere, in everything I have experienced. Even in Chinese music late at night on the radio. I have had too many chances to cry, to feel abandoned."

"Cass, concentrate on—"

"Honey, let me talk to you for a bit," said Mrs. Heinz. "Cass, will you excuse us for a sec?"

"Yeah, sure. I'll just go over here."

The women started whispering like conspirators. I approached some plants and they immediately rustled with the breeze. I thought of walking home, of screaming, of going mute.

"Cass," said Mrs. Heinz.

"Yes, ma'am," I said, walking over.

The women started to get up from the steps. I reached out to help Mrs. Heinz and her legs spread, but her dress was over her knees.

"Cass, I'm sorry, but I'm so sleepy. I need to call it a night. I've been going since early morning." She stretched her arms and yawned. "It's been wonderful seeing you, and I pray you visit us next summer. And, Cass, no more sad talk, okay?"

"Okay, Mother, get your bananas and go inside," said Georgeanne.

Mrs. Heinz hugged me and said, "I really enjoyed dancing with you. Don't ever say you can't dance."

"Mother, let go," said Georgeanne.

Mrs. Heinz kissed me on the cheek, her lips moist, and whispered, "You know I wanted more." I quivered and she stepped back. "Well, good night to both of you. And, honey, don't stay up too late."

We said good night and she got her bananas and went up the steps. She stood on the porch, looked across the street, then entered the house. To sleep on the cold floor with Karl? To sleep in a warm bed with the landlady?

"I need to get something from the car for tomorrow," said Georgeanne. "Let me run inside for the keys. Don't go anywhere."

I felt lonely and trapped on the sidewalk. Again I heard the breeze rustle the plants. I wanted to go home. Suddenly I remembered the sea breeze across the deserted beach in October. While Georgeanne frolicked in the cold water like a dolphin, I occasionally sat on the sand with Mrs. Heinz and the seagulls. She was lying on a cot, reading to me from either a vegetarian book or one of her religious pamphlets. She was wearing dark blue shorts, slightly loose despite her thick legs. From a close-up her thighs were enormous. Her golden hairs were glinting in the late afternoon sun.

Georgeanne came out and we went to their car right in front on the curb. I held the door open while she knelt in the front seat, her buttocks beautiful and bouncy to the dashboard. She reached into the back seat and started opening some cardboard boxes. "I'm looking for two blouses," she said. "One for me and one for Mother." I looked down at her full calves:

how strong, how symmetrical. Each jerky movement of hers caused her buttocks to quiver sensually, and the light shooting at her loose hair made it dazzle like yellow-white ribbons. "Your beauty is so real it's unreal," I said.

She was complaining about not finding the blouses. Although I wondered if it was a pretext, stuck my head into the car and looked into the back seat. Her lovely hands were searching, digging into the packed boxes, and she looked so beautiful and big. I was excited in the shadows created by her dangling hair. I got out of the car and stared at the night. I felt like a lost child and wondered what tomorrow would bring. All night long I had struggled to understand the night and the emotions it provoked in me. I was urged by a cryptic something to flee and kill myself because after all I was a damn failure. Then it struck me that Georgeanne was deliberately taking her time so I would wise up and climb in and shut the door. But she was probably too smart and too cold to wriggle herself into such a situation purposely, unless her mother had asked her to seduce me for Christmas. What a present.

Finally, she found the blouses and a pair of shabby tennis shoes, dark brown with dirt, stuffed with socks. She turned around and sat down and placed the shoes on the floor between her feet. She folded the blouses and set them on the driver's seat, just under the steering wheel. The keys she kept on her lap between her thighs. I wondered how she smelled. "Get in and close the door," she said calmly. It's like in the movies, I thought. I climbed in and squeezed myself next to her and swung shut the heavy door. Her thigh was soft and powerful against mine. "Let me turn off the light," she said. "I don't know about this door." She leaned back against the seat, her breasts high and pointing upward, and stretched her right arm to the ceiling to click off the light. I felt she wanted me to touch her, but I had my confused hands on my lap like a fool. I studied the darkness and the houses like a film director composing a scene. I sensed that Mrs. Heinz was watching us from a window. Perhaps she was just making love with Karl in a soft bed or else on the cold floor.

Again it was late October or early November on the beach, two years ago, and Mrs. Heinz lay on her cot reading. I sat on the sand beside her, awed by her long legs, politely listening to her explications. Occasionally, she sat up to make a point and her pale blue eyes scanned the roughwaves before lying down again. The brim of her shorts had curled like pouting lips, like angry waves, and I froze before the sight of her white cotton underwear and the mighty glimpse of a few hairs. How powerful, how empowering the tiny white pillow, serenely strong between her massive thighs. I dug my fingers into the moist sand and felt as beautiful as the seagulls gliding. Suddenly reborn, suddenly I wanted to rush into the Gulf where Georgeanne was splashing alone.

Georgeanne was unrolling and shaking her white socks to put them on. I placed my left arm around her shoulders and watched her. Never had I seen her so beautiful; never had we been so intimately alone. She slipped off her tennis shoes and crossed her left leg to put on a sock. She wiped her foot and her dress tightened and still rubbed up. I focused on her knees and the ball of her calf and the lower part of her thighs. They were lovely and I shivered and began to play with her hair. I held it in my hands and smelled it and tasted it. The saliva in my mouth accumulated. She was putting on her other sock and again her soft legs overwhelmed me. I jerked like a lobster out of water.

"Are you all right?" she asked.

"Yeah, yeah, I'm fine. It's just that you're such a prize, George. Man, you're something—a beautiful prize. It would be very hard for me to win you."

She smiled and her eyes shone seriously. It struck me that her smile resembled Cosima's. She appeared uneasy, perhaps exasperated.

"You're a prize," I repeated, my eyes glued to her legs.

I felt like sliding my hand under her dress, along her thigh, and touching her cunny. I imagined it spongy-warm with gold-brown hairs and deliciously smelling and tasting between the lips. I wondered if she would let me fondle her. She put on her old tennis shoes while I licked her hair and rubbed her flesh from the nape to her moving hands. Was she going to sleep with her shoes on? I pictured her travelling in the car with them on and the sun hot on her lap and she complaining silently. Actually, I considered her a stoic. I also pictured her hitchhiking on the highway like a beatnik, the soles of her tennis shoes black with tar and her hair smelling of wild wind and her flesh dusty and free.

She finished tying her shoes and settled back peacefully, although I detected a slight tension. She sat still, not talking but waiting, her eyes fixed on some object straight ahead. I had not stopped playing with her hair.

"I like your profile," I said. "There's something classical about it."

"Hmm. Probably my broken nose."

"You used to say that. You're still saying it."

"I still mean it," she said, obviously bored.

I was caressing her neck and her throat, smelling her hair, enjoying her. Still, I felt that this was expected of me.

"Hmmm. Hmm. I like how your hair smells, like vanilla ice cream. Hmm."

"It's not clean," she said. "I haven't washed it yet."

"I don't care. I like it the way it is. I don't like clean hair that smells of stupid soap. Some soaps nauseate me and I get headaches."

"It smells of the sea," she said, knowing that her remark would please me.

"Hmmm, Georgeanne, Georgeanne. I like your hair long and smooth. Oh, yes, your mother said you slept on the beach last night."

Immediately, I wondered if Richard had walked with Georgeanne all night. Had he made love to her by the tide under the fine drizzle? Had he enjoyed her young breasts, wet and frothy, almost silvery at twilight? Had Georgeanne thought of me and that night in June, our last trip to the beach? Perhaps not. She was not the sentimental type. Had my younger brother kissed her as he claimed?

"It was so cold and beautiful out there," she said. "It was fun and the water was icy and I loved the dawn. My hair was blowing."

"I wish I had been there with you. That would've been great."

She smiled faintly. I felt I was forcing her to talk, to say what I wanted to hear. With all my fondling, her flesh was warm and sensual, emanating a hot odor. It was the smell of naked flesh in a sultry room: the smell of fish and saliva, of cunt and weeds and water. It was the smell of a girl I had often visited when her mother was away. I held Georgeanne's right hand in my right hand. Sometimes I put her fingers in my mouth, bit them gently, then kissed them sweetly. I felt her nails and she tasted good and I swallowed my teeming saliva carefully. I did not want the sound to betray my arousal, although I noticed that she too was swallowing often. I assumed she was excited. And yet why was her hand limp and lifeless in mine?

She was unresponsive. Her lovely fingers did not circle mine as I kissed them and fondled them. But they occasionally quivered and I was thrilled. I interpreted their warmth as sensual heat. But how long could I fondle her hands and her neck? Till she was raw and bled? Could I tell her that Cosima haunted me like a curse? I had little else to do. Perhaps Mrs. Heinz was enjoying Karl. "I think I really loved Mrs. Heinz," I once told my brother. "I believe you," he quickly said. He had always thought it was peculiar, downright ludicrous, that mothers attracted me more than daughters. I imagined Mrs. Heinz's thick hips against mine, her thick legs scissoring Karl.

"You like to delve into many subjects," said Georgeanne suddenly. "You love to analyze. But tell me what causes your unhappiness. I'm here and it doesn't matter."

"It does matter," I said, squirming. "It has always mattered. Since you left, little else has mattered except—"

"What? What?" she urged.

I pictured my oldest sister cleaning my room, working to help me. "If you do not graduate Mom won't give you a nickel to go away."

"Except finishing school and going away."

"Well, finish and next fall we can go to the University of Houston together."

"I don't know. It seems like only math can shut my mouth, and geometry keeps doing it. It is life right now. Failing it is death. I don't like to blame teachers, but my geometry teacher can't seem to explain the material. Part of the problem is the disruptive students who throw chalk at him and laugh. The poor man freezes with rage. Actually, I can't see myself playing with a protractor and a compass. I can't see myself—"

"Can you see this?" she asked, kissing my cheek.

I was surprised, confused, numb. I assumed that now I had to respond. She was facing me. I was supposed to unleash a hurricane of passion. I kissed her lightly on the lips. This was enough fact for me, enough history.

"Now was that bad?" she asked. "Do you want to do it again?"

"I don't even know what I'm doing."

"Yes, you do. Do you want to kiss me again?"

I kissed her. The kiss was soft, wet. Her arm went around me, seriously holding me. I imagined Mrs. Heinz's loose shorts, her white underwear, her eyes watching me watching her. I felt uneasy, trapped. Georgeanne would not release me. Mrs. Heinz was strolling on the beach with me, dancing with me, her body making me cry. Georgeanne kissed my ear, then my lips.

"This is just a moment," I said. "I'm afraid of tomorrow."

"Cass, what happened to you? Who hurt you?"

"I've always been this way. You know it."

"Who hurt you? What happened?"

"A girl was living with us this past summer, a girl from my childhood, someone very significant. She became more significant. Then I found out she was doing something wrong. It destroyed me. I was trapped in the house with her, in the summer with her. I had no money to run away. One night I confronted her about what she was doing. She wept and packed and left. After that, I was no longer the same. Or maybe I was just worse."

Georgeanne started to release me. The left arm that had swept to my right shoulder was melting. It slid to her lap. She was looking straight ahead. "Many times I tried to organize the events of last summer, to understand the pain and loneliness. The girl and I could never communicate. She kept on defying me and the world, indulging, indulging in her darkness. Sometimes I felt I was going mad. Soon I cared nothing for no one."

"Let's get the hell out of here!" said Georgeanne. "Come on." She slapped my knee twice. "Come on. Open the damn door!"

We scrambled out and she slammed the door. We stood on the cold sidewalk. I heard the breeze stirring the plants. We looked at each other.

Was Mrs. Heinz watching us?

"I told you this was just a moment, a side step," I said. "I'm sorry for withdrawing into the flower in my heart. Now I'm afraid to return to the dance alone."

"No, you have nothing to be sorry about. I probably have more to be sorry about, much more." She held my hand and squeezed it. The corner street lamp made her blonde hair platinum. Her blue eyes glittered. For a moment I saw her as I had first seen her two years before. "I'll return to Texas in the summer. Is that all right?"

"I can't wait until August," I said.

"Concentrate on something—on school."

"Uuuu, that's a bad word," I said, conscious of her hand still holding mine.

"Well, you've got something to concentrate on—your poetry."

"The minute I get home I'll write you a letter."

"That's no way to say goodbye," she smiled. "In case, just in case, I can't make the trip down here I want you to for sure go up there. You can spend the summer with me. The library is very good. You'll be in her—in it—all the time."

She squeezed my hand and kissed me lightly on the cheek. We said goodbye and she went up the steps. I started walking off before she opened the door to go inside. I did not want to look at her white dress, at her haunches and her calves. The breeze was hissing through the plants and the leaves of the trees. It was starting to drizzle.

Georgeanne and the entire night seemed like a dream, an illusion. Nonetheless, I felt I had accomplished something. It was about three in the morning, and I missed my room. This was my darkness, my rain, my streets. I was finally going home. Suddenly, I sensed something following me, creeping alongside me. I turned and it was a black car in the dark. A blonde head popped out.

"Get in," said Mrs. Heinz. 🏵

Borges's Dagger

by Rolando Hinojosa-Smith

In Norman Thomas de Giovanni's fine translation of Borges's poem regarding a dagger in his desk, a dagger given Borges by his good friend and fellow-Argentinian writer, Evaristo Carriego, Borges muses about the dagger's lack of violent use. Instead of opening bodies through violence (a tiger is mentioned in the poem), the dagger serves as a letter opener; an ignoble use, in Borges's estimation.

Much like Hemingway's frozen leopard in the Kilimanjaro mountain top where the American midwesterner tells us no one knows what the leopard was doing at that altitude, Borges's dagger was once in the possession of Rigo Contreras, a native of Belken County down in the Lower Rio Grande Valley. What was it doing there? How did it come to be there in the first place?

Since I own it now, perhaps the story is best explained this way:

The last time I visited Contreras I asked him how and when Borges's dagger wound up in his possession so many years ago.

Nothing to it. I wrote the poet, expressed curiosity in the dagger, complimented him on the poem—in which he, Borges, said he collaborated with de Giovanni—and then, on a lark—and what did I have to lose,—and then, as I said, just like that, I asked him for it.

"I wasn't about to offer to pay for the postage since I thought this would be an imposition if not an insult. I then mailed the letter and waited for Borges's answer.

"It came, to my surprise," continued Contreras. "It came, and along with it, the offer for the dagger. Was I, the letter read, was I still interested in the dagger? Would it be put to other uses, other than the opening of letters, say?"

Contreras took a long pull from his iced-down beer, looked at me, and shook his head.

"I know, I know, you're sitting there wondering when the young men in their white coats are showing up one more time to cart me away to San Antonio or wherever the Lone Star State now keeps the criminally insane. Am I right in this?"

I waited for a moment. "Was the cell comfortable, Rigo?"

"For a county jail? Yes."

I told him that after some ten years, I'd just reread the *Klail City Enterprise News* again. That I had followed the story of his stabbing young Calixto Cepeda back then, and now, although I'd come on business, I'd also come to visit him as an old friend.

"As a curious old friend, right?"

I shrugged. "Why did you stab him? You hardly knew him. As far as I know, there'd been no bad blood between you and the Cepeda family. It was the violence, Rigo, that's what I found unsettling. And unprovoked, from what the papers and everyone there said. Unprovoked."

Without meaning to, I shook my head, and Contreras must have taken this as disapproval. "I had to."

Philosophers tell us that simple, cryptic answers are clear and unclear and thus illuminate and hide at the same time.

"So, you wrote to Borges, he mails the dagger, and then years later, and exactly one year after his peaceful death, you walk into the Aquí me quedo and then, without a word, grab Cepeda by the back of the head, pull his hair downward, thus exposing. . . ."

"His neck, go on, say it. His neck and all its veins and then I cut it open. That's it, nothing to it."

I offered him a cigarette which was followed by a nod of thanks and a smile.

"It was the knife, can't you see that? Look, I'd laid it on my right hand drawer, much like Borges, and I'd take it out, admire it, and polish that gleaming bluish-steel till it shone like a crescent moon. But it was doing nothing sitting there, crouched there, lifeless. Nothing, I tell you.

"Now, I wasn't about to demean it and use it to open the utility or the phone bill, can you understand that? It was a tiger, used to violence, and it was just there, caged. In that desk of mine. Ten long years of nothing but boring frustrating inactivity. Why had I bothered to ask for it in the first place, if I weren't going to use it? What's a knife for anyway?"

Before I could say anything, Rigo Contreras raised his hand.

"It talked to me." There was smugness in that smile.

"So, your attorney pleads insanity, three years go by, and here you are, free again."

"It talked to me, and it's calling me now. I don't know where the county keeps it, but it's my property. Mine. A gift from one of the best poets of this century, and I want it back."

"And then? What if it talks to you again?"

"¿Quíen sabe? old friend."

"Not good enough, Rigo. Not near well good enough."

I stood by the door and looked at him for the last time.

"I don't get many visitors. And then, you, of all people. What did you want from me? What did you expect me to say? What brought you here? It couldn't've been friendship. What, then?"

"This." I extended my hand and showed him a U.S. Army Colt .45.

"Well, since I can't have the knife, the gun'll have to do."

"This is goodbye, Rigo."

"Goodbye?"

"Yes, goodbye." ❀

SCISSORS STONE PAPER

by Kay Merkel Boruff

The supreme pleasure consists in capturing the taste of reality,
In successfully rendering the atmosphere of being.

Boris Pasternak

I'VE ALWAYS HAD AFFAIRS. It may be the stars. Libras are supposed to be sex-crazed. It may be the incestuous experience with my brother. That's supposed to mark young girls. Or it may be my first piano recital. I forgot the entire piece. My mother stood behind me on stage, I was too shy at five to be out there alone. I sat on the padded bench, my black patent Mary Janes not touching the pedals. I sat for an eternity, not playing a single note, not even beginning and then forgetting. Mother whispered in my ear, Get up and curtsey, and then leave the stage. She never said, You retarded child, no daughter of mine, how could you embarrass me, but rather intoned, Be a lady. My father lead the applause as I walked to the edge of the stage, performed a perfect curtsey, my taffeta-ruffled dress soft in my small hands, my hands spread like angel wings, my right foot sweeping in a half circle, behind my left leg, dipping low to the floor, dipping for a long time and finally lowering my head because my mother instructed me this was the thing that ladies did. I curtsied slowly, in control.

Sixteen years was my longest affair, longer then either one of my marriages. The first marriage ended before the third anniversary. We lived in Viêt-Nam, and he was killed flying helicopters in Laos. The second marriage ended after ten years. He left when I brought home an infant to adopt. Either the baby goes or I do, he told me. I chose my three-hour-old daughter. The sixteen years was preceded by an affair that lasted four years, the last four years of my marriage. It's not the sex. It's the intimacy without the sock-folding. I don't fold socks I told the man with whom I'm currently having an affair.

I miss the stolen conversations. A friend from high school who is more or less happily married calls me from phone booths when he is away from home giving speeches. Motivational speeches. How to love America and stay married and increase your productivity and be a terrific grandfather. He says he can't pass by a phone booth without getting a hard-on. He calls to cheer me up, to be sure I haven't slit my wrists or maxed out my Neiman's account. My best friend did both, figuratively speaking. She was gravely ill and felt like she was a burden, draining her estate to pay her doctor bills. She put a plastic bag over her head and suffocated. She read *Final Exit* to get the medication correct, not to end up a vegetable. That was a pact we had. If either of us ended up on life support, the other one would pull the plug. Now if I'm a vegetable, I'll just drool myself into oblivion.

My divorce attorney, the sixteen-year affair, had a photograph of his three-month-old daughter on his desk. I don't know who was the first to suggest the affair. Maybe it was mutual. The daughter became the glue that held his marriage and our relationship together. Since I teach young children, I would never break up a marriage. Marriage-maker. Heartbreaker is closer to the truth. Living in a war zone, you develop a taste for excitement. I threw away my black and white television when it grew fuzzy. I don't want to be connected to the world. Opposites in my life seem to balance, the very earthiness of twelve-year-olds, doing homework, not doing homework, reading Mark Twain, writing poetry about a teacher with carrots in her ears, the presentness and the war-zone living, I grew another self.

I had affairs before I went to Southeast Asia. A four-year affair in high school. One in college, the one I pulled the telephone from the wall over, the three-week-in-lock-up one. A brief one when I was newly wed to my first husband. He was in one state, and I was in another. If a man leaves my bed for too long, he's out of my existence. It must connect to the piano recital. I couldn't recall a single note. The piece didn't exist. The next move must be motion in any direction.

The panic comes easily. It starts with my heart. It beats irregularly like an arrhythmia. My hands become icy. My throat tightens. My eyes dilate. S. Eliot for my masters in the field of hermeneutics. In Eliot's dissertation he wrote that humans learn to think abstractly by making connections, relating one object to another until they have a catharsis. Fifty years later when Harvard wanted to publish his paper, he said he didn't remember what he meant. I can't remember all my affairs, but I think that's what I'm doing, connecting those affairs that I do remember, remembering those objects, connecting them like a loose, woven necklace, bead after polished bead, waiting for a catharsis, or for Godot, or for a room with a view.

My attorney knew before the wedding that his wife was not the woman he should marry. After the wedding, she immediately became pregnant. She had two children from previous marriages. And then, of course, he loved his daughter. My second husband wouldn't sleep with me. He slept wrapped up in a blue blanket like the Ice King in a cocoon. One night I tried to wrap myself inside the blue blanket with him. He was Catholic and was afraid I would get pregnant. I tried to get pregnant by someone else. My friend who committed suicide found a suitable partner. The man and I had sex in her son's twin bed when she took her son to a movie. I had a hysterectomy at thirty-four. I never got pregnant.

My mother never said, Why didn't you practice more? She never said, Why did you divorce? She said nothing when I told her I was having an affair with my attorney. The affair was my link to reality. If I connected to this man, I wouldn't pull the telephone from the wall. Those nouns I remember. Telephone. Door facing. Splinters. Lockup. It wasn't because my boyfriend wasn't attractive to me. He was. One day he told me he was going to throw me on the ground and rape me if we didn't have sex. I wanted him to do just that. It's about control. In marriage, you're controlled. In an affair, you control. It's my body. I'll fuck whom I choose.

I can control the attorney. Or at least most of the time. He is younger and trapped. Even though he lives in a house with a pool and has a country club membership, I'm free, and he isn't. You'll never be closer to anyone than you were to me. That's what he told me the last time we broke up, his voice, soft, melodious, Missourian. I can picture his blue eyes and aquiline nose, his head lying on my pillow in the middle of the day.

I can picture the sky when we were driving back from his friend's ranch in East Texas, the darkness broken only by a few stars. I kept thinking the stars ought to be more brilliant, so far from the city. The night before, we lay in the bed of a pickup and wrapped a blanket around us to keep out the cold and traded secrets. He wanted to take me to Pattaya Beach and see the Emerald Buddha. I wanted to be married or have a best seller, one or the other, but not both. Too much happiness wrecks my karma. My feet were in his lap, my toes wiggling in time to the reggae music coming from the CD.

You're giving me more to think about than the oncoming traffic, he says.

Those are my intentions, I say.

After several miles and two more tracks on the CD, he slowed down and turned into a dark country road going God knows where. He slowly drives the length of the narrow lane, turns in to the entrance of a pasture, the gate padlocked, cattle-guarded for strays. He backs up, parks, and turns off the headlights.

Now, put your tush where your feet were.

I raise my skirt, and we make love in the front seat of his family car.

We have a new head at the school where I teach. He wears round glasses and shirts without any logos on them. He is slightly balding, and he has a three-year-old named Dedalus, as in James Joyce. He teaches English, and his attorney wife advised him not to use the computer-enhanced signature on his report card as all the other teachers do. He prefers to write his own signature rather than have the computer do it. One day, I am standing behind him and pat him on the back of his right shoulder, as I often do fellow co-workers, and ask him, How's Dedalus? I jerk my hand off—an electric response. Oh God. I guess I can't do that now. Sexual Harassment Brady Bill 666 Screwloose. He turns, slowly, faces me, his round glasses level to my eyes, my reading glasses perched on my head. That's an acceptable area to touch without permission, he says. Baby boomers have no fucking sense of humor. He would never have an affair. He's got no balls.

I once catheterized my friend, the one who put a bag over her head. She lay on the Persian carpet in her bathroom, a room the size of my bedroom, mirrors on three sides up to the high ceiling, the catheter the size for a child. She weighted eighty pounds. Her eyes were yellow. She had RTA, a rare kidney disease. I knew her longer than my attorney. Twenty-two years. Longer than anyone except a friend from grade school. My grade school friend and I would run from opposite directions to the river bank, two scant tumbleweeds blowing through mesquite trees, through chinaberry bushes clustered along murky water, spindly branches filled with poisonous shriveled pale orange berries. We hugged each other and told secrets. Our world was complete. Then my friend moved away.

In *Women in Love*, Birkin wants an eternal union with both a man and a woman to achieve a sheer intimacy. His wife Gudrin says that's perverse, that he can't have two kinds of love. Jung writes that the true soul is born knowing itself.

A man in my neighborhood was left for dead on Mt. Everest. Like Lazarus, he walked into camp, his arms clinking like frozen glass. As his hands were being amputated, I thought about folding argyle socks with my friend. The man's face has black patches of skin that aren't suppose to scar. The scar from my hysterectomy is now brown. No socks necessary in Nassau. Affairs aren't necessary in Nassau. I move my limbs diagonally, across the bed, the shaft of light from the window falls on the white bedspread. I write in my dream journal.

Affairs start nowhere and go somewhere. Affairs start somewhere and go everywhere. Like Everyman. Affairs make me feel like I'm still alive, like I live in a foreign country. Affairs are my secret obsession, now you know all about my affairs.

The CD plays Rachmaninoff's *Concerto in C# Minor*, my last piano recital piece. I run my fingers down the inside of your arm. I trace the time and the music. Like Judas, I kiss your lips, I kiss your nose, your cheeks, your voice, the stars. I kiss the tears the day your mother died. ❀

SEX ON THE BEACH

by Clay Reynolds

The Poet sat on a bar stool in the club of the cut-rate motel in the small eastern Tennessee city and listened to the music while he contemplated his surroundings. Cheapo-depot, he thought to himself. They let him park the camper in the lot for ten bucks, but not without an argument.

"Rooms are only twenty-two-fifty," the pimply little desk clerk smacked in a wide-mouthed drawl. She must have be working on twelve sticks of gum at once, he thought.

"We ain't s'posed to 'llow nobody to park an' sleep in the lot," she chewed on. "People sell them drugs out of outfits like yours." Her chipped metal name tag identified her as Denise, Assistant Night Manager. At maybe nineteen years old, she was, perhaps, the most unattractive woman he had directly spoken to in years.

He told her he was there at the invitation of the college. He didn't want to be robbed, he didn't believe in drugs. "Just say no," he smiled, turned on the charm. He assured her he would love to pay for a room, but he truly lacked the funds. "I'm a writer," he explained, "A poet. Poetry just doesn't provide a great income."

"Poet?" She cocked a crusty eyebrow. Dandruff or psoriasis, he couldn't tell.

"I am."

"Never had no poet stayin' here. Now, we're overrun with 'em. What kind of stuff you write?"

"Oh, traditional verse. You'd like it. Maybe you could come to the reading."

"Couldn't 'ford that," she said and offered him a well rehearsed speech, "Can't even 'ford to go the the show. They want six dollars just to see a show. You beat that?" She looked out the window. The streets were dusty and dry. It was hard to believe there was anything like a college within a hundred miles. "They charge us townies like shit to come to stuff over to the college, too. Think we're bunch of white trash hicks. Don't know nothin'. It's our *tax* dollars pays for that college outfit."

He knew better than to think there would be any charge for his reading. "I'll get you a free ticket," he promised. "C'mon, let me park out there. Around back."

She studied him and chewed a fingernail. Her teeth were stained, and she had a slight mustache. "Well, okay. But it's ten bucks. Cash. No credit cards."

He peeled a ten-spot off his small roll. She stuffed it into her blouse. Just like in the movies, he thought.

"'Way 'round back, hear? You can forget that ticket, I guess. I really don't know nothin' 'bout poetry if it don't rhyme or nothin'. Like in a song? I never was good in English."

"Can I get a receipt?"

She smiled. "Don't push it."

He finally received an Guggenheim. It took over two decades and a small fortune in photocopying and postage to convince him that there was no way the committee ever gave such things out to addresses west of the Mississippi. Finally, he bribed his old editor with a five-hundred-dollar promise to let him use his Manhattan address. And it worked. He kicked himself for not using the New York return address before. He should have figured that out. He had figured out almost everything else.

But the money was there. It came in right on time, and by the time he paid the taxes on it, paid off Felix, and put a down payment on a used pickup with a camper, he barely had enough left to send out the mailers to try and get another tour. This time on his own. It wasn't much, he told himself when he started out, but it was a start. A way back. It was the only chance he had left to keep from cracking up.

"Crashed and burned," he sometimes repeated to himself. It was an expression he recalled from high school. It had to do with failing to find a date, being turned down after weeks of anxious build-up. The irony of using it in a different context appealed to him. But he was no stranger to prolonged anxiety. The prospect of crashing, burning, finally losing what little pride he had left was tangible.

He had no new poems. Nothing worked anymore. The ideas and visions he had sometimes seen flickering on the horizons of his imagination vanished completely when he sat down and tried to form them into verse. Like mirages on the highway, they evaporated when he approached them, reached to touch them. As he drove from school to school, he scoured garage sales, used book stores, junk shops, hunting for old paperback anthologies to re-read, searching for the inspiration he once had relied on utterly. But it wouldn't come. The verse in the books lay on the page, flaccid, dead. It wouldn't sing.

He hadn't had a real lover in years. That, he told himself over and over, was the cause of the whole thing, the complete blank-page impotence that came over him. He needed to get laid, and well laid. There never had been inspiration in the printed page. He had always found it in moist, tangled sheets in late night cheap motels. Reading poetry was never a substitute for that.

He tried hookers, but that didn't work. He tried older women, the worn-out hags who hung around the fleabag rooming house-hotel in Austin where he set up headquarters. Those who would have him made him gag. Half of them were senile, others were junkies, diseased. Those who were the least bit attractive looked at him as if he were a leper. He couldn't score with anyone who might inspire him. No way. He had lost it. He was old, gross, worn out. Desirable women were apparently a figment of his memory. So, apparently, were the poems.

But he still had his old stuff. All of it was out of print, forgotten anyway, and a new generation of young poets and would-be poets were teaching the creative writing classes. They had only heard of him, most of them, remembered reading his work a decade ago when he was hot, and they were thrilled when they read in the self-printed flyers he sent out that he was available.

Available, he thought. He was fucking desperate.

"I remember you!" they said when they called him on the pay phone at the rooming house. He usually had to kick aside two or three winos and crack heads to get to it when it was ringing, fight them off while he was talking. "I heard you read when I was in college. That was a long time ago. You were hot stuff a few years back."

He had been. He still was, he assured them. He had been out of circulation for a while, but he was now working on a new book, a major departure from his old stuff: a comeback. It was still all closed form, but different forms, new ideas in new new poems. He wooed them with his old argument: Strong stuff. Good stuff. True verse.

"I'm better than ever," he quipped. There was hope that X. J. Kennedy or maybe D. Snodgrass would do the introduction, he blatantly lied. The professors croaked back in their teenage-sounding voices that they would *definitely* get him a reading. It would be an honor, they said. He lined up twenty-four schools for a twelve-week, four-state tour across the South, gassed up the pickup, and set out.

And he worked cheap: a hundred for a reading, fifty for a workshop, fifty more to judge a student contest. Lectures he threw in for free. He covered his own expenses: slept in the camper, ate cold soup right out of the can, drank cheap beer, and smoked generic cigarettes, kept the old vehicle rolling on retreads. Retreads, he thought when he sat on the spares in the bed and ate his supper: That's exactly how he felt. But he was confident. It would take time, but it would work. It had to. He was building something new. He could make it back. One school at a time. One reading at a time. If he could only find the poems. If they would only return to him.

It was ladies' night at the bar. He lit a cigarette and ordered another shot and a draught. A country band grunted and groaned in the corner, and a few rednecks polished their belt-buckles on their newfound sweethearts' bellies while they shuffled around on the floor. Two or three single women eyed him, decided he was too old, too fat, too bald, too whatever, then returned their bored stares out to the multi-colored lights that flickered on the dance floor. It didn't matter. He had other plans, reluctant as he was to implement them. But every sip of beer moved him closer to a decision.

This small city was just like his old hometown, he reminded himself while he watched the imitation Southern cowboys push their short, pudgy partners around on the floor. How in God's name did a poet of his caliber ever emerge from such a West Texas backwater? It was laughable, ludicrous. This was Tennessee, but it didn't matter. Small town America was small town America, he reminded himself: Skoal, Budweiser, Resistols, Tony Llamas, and C&W music. It was a fucking national cult that defied geography.

There were three other poets at the same motel: Jack Something, Ray Something, and a Packistani-American named Afgar. He'd seen none of them, knew none of them, not even by reputation. All were more than twenty years younger than he, but tomorrow he would headline the session. They would follow. He'd pull out his best stuff, poetry he knew had worked before. Start with lots of comedy, then hit them with that long sad one about the kid who kills himself right in front of his father. It always left an audience worn out, wrung completely of emotion, and if he followed with the narrative he finished two years before, the long one set on the Kansas plains that turned its phrasings with such compressed wit, such controlled chagrin.

He would exhaust them, leave nothing for any reader who followed him, no matter how young, energetic, and potentially successful any of them were. It was the only unpublished poem he had. But it built his confidence to know it was in his arsenal.

He *was* back, he told himself: Fucking-A.

The kid at the college—Associate Professor Steven P. Randolph, if you please—who ran the creative writing program had set this up on his own, with little help from a hostile administration, showed up and invited him into the motel cafe to eat. The other poets weren't there yet, and he was relieved. He and Randolph had drinks, then more drinks, and then dinner with wine, and he'd told the kid about his experience with cretinous colleagues of his past.

"You were right to get out," Randolph agreed. "I get *no* credit for publishing creative work. I mean, I've got a collection of stories and twenty poems published, but they don't care. They gave *full* merit credit to Rita Johnson—the new *assistant* prof—for a *quarter* page in *Notes and Queries*.

A *quarter* page! Can you beat *that?*"

He liked Randolph: he talked in italics. He nodded in sympathy. "Is she black or just a she?" he asked.

"Gay," Randolph whispered. "But only our chair*person* knows for sure, if you get my drift."

He nodded. "It's a cold, cruel, politically correct world."

"If you're white *and* male, it is," Randolph shook his head. "If I were a woman or a minority, I'd have a *decent* job. I've got *my* Ph.D., published *my* dissertation. Or I will. But *here* I am, at the corner of Dust and Kudzu, my thumb in the air."

"Better than up your ass," he said and emptied the wine bottle into their glasses. Like mine, he added, silently.

"Anyway," Randolph said and signaled casually for a new bottle, "I'm getting the money for this whole gig out of Student Services. The director's a friend of mine, but *she* doesn't know what it's going for. Thinks it's a job fair. When she finds out, she'll have a fit. But *I* don't give a damn. I've got tenure. What can they do? *Fire* me?"

"Believe me," he said, "they can do a hell of a lot more than that."

It was mostly an tech-ag college in the southwest end of the state where the Cumberland Gap gave up trying to be pretty and descended into Arkansas ugly. The land around here was flat and dusty, more like West Texas than anywhere in the South, he thought. The college itself was small, totally overshadowed by U-Tennessee and Memphis State, Ol' Miss and Auburn. But they had a good enrollment, and they were making money, more than any other college their size in the region. Still, it was an underdog, and Randolph moaned when he turned the conversation to a complaint about his pay, his course load, the general lack of support anyone who did anything received.

"Anyway," Randolph concluded with slurring speech. The second bottle of wine was gone. He ordered brandy. Randolph was getting sloppy, holding onto the side of the table for support. "That's why the *goddamn* honorarium is so low. We just didn't have enough to go around. And I didn't dare give it all to just *one* reader. But these guys who're on the program with you are unknown: nobodies, kids, really, hot-shot shitheads, for the most part. Part of that Southern Poetry Circuit that thinks so god-damn much of itself. You're a *big* name. They'll have to take notice when they see how much the students like you."

"You think they will?"

"Hell, yes. They're hungry for *good* stuff. They'll eat it up." He lowered his voice. "Listen," he whispered, "*I've* got friends. I'm connected with a whole fucking network across the South. Alabama, Georgia, Florida. I can get *you* a reading a week, if you like. You're *good*, and your stuff should get a *lot* of play. I can do you a *lot* of good."

"And what do I have to do?" He was interested, excited in spite of himself. Randolph might be a kid, but he was serious. This could be the key to the whole thing. If he didn't blow it. He made up his mind not to blow it. He ordered another round of brandies, drank both of them.

They staggered out into the lobby, him supporting Randolph as if he were walking wounded. He wouldn't let Randolph drive. His girl-friend, Millie, had to come get him. He got her number from the young professor and made the call from the motel's lobby while Randolph slumped on a sofa and fought unconsciousness. When she arrived, she was a surprise: Short, pretty, and unbelievably cute with perky little tits under a snap-button yolk shirt, high heeled boots, and jeans so tight they looked painted on her firm, tubular thighs and a firm ass.

Years fell away from him like so many unnecessary clothes. Nostalgia swept through him for a self he believed had abandoned him long before. Her bright brown eyes stirred old fires, made him feel the tight across the chest when she smiled at him and took his hand in introduction: She held it too long, he thought, flashed her big eyes too much when she said his name, smiled too genuinely.

It was like they had known each other forever. In a way, he thought, they had. She made him deliciously uncomfortable.

But he turned away and concentrated on an ugly painting of a pioneer woodsman on the wall. He fought to put his mind on other things. There was a glimmer of a poem, and he shook his head quickly, tried to clear the dust away from it. It disappeared.

"Do you need a ride, too?" she asked. "I can only carry one at a time.

I got a new car. One of those little bitty ones. A Miata. Just two seats."

"No," he said firmly. "I'm here. Staying here." He pulled Randolph to his feet and steered him uncertainly toward her.

Randolph swayed and leaned over on her. "He's *staying* here," he repeated. "Right *here*. He's a real poet! *All* the poets stay here!"

"He's a little drunk," she said, smiled again, this time with apology.

"Yeah," he said. "The wine seemed to hit him all at once." Her smile warmed him, gave him an uncomfortable feeling once more.

"Wine! You drank *wine*," she scolded Randolph. "You know you can't drink wine." She looked up to explain, "He has no tolerance for wine. Two glasses is his limit. And that's with food."

"I fear we split two bottles." I fear, he thought. Sound like an English fop. Why he hadn't added a "my dear" or two he couldn't imagine. He was old enough to be her father. "We seem to have had a few cocktails as well."

"No wonder in the world!" she cried. "He'll be in fine shape tomorrow. I'd better get him home." She looked up, blushed. "To *his* home."

"I'm sorry. I didn't know about the wine," he said. "I would have stopped him."

His home, he repeated to himself, searching her eyes once more. Did he mistake the inflection, or did she speak in italics, too?

"Oh, that's all right. *He* knows. He ought to." She shouldered his weight. "I like wine, too. But I can handle it."

Would you like to have a glass? he mentally asked her, a bottle? Then he bit off the thoughts with a helpless grin. "Do you need some help?" Randolph was dangerously tottering, now singing lightly.

"No, that's okay." She sighed deeply. "I've done this before. I guess I'll do it again. He's just a big baby. Bet y'all were talking politics."

"School."

"Yep. I knew it. His favorite subject, especially when he gets like this. C'mon, Stevie, let's get you home." They staggered off, Randolph towering a good foot over her, leaning heavily on her. "Say," she turned. "You need anything? A ride anywhere? I can come back. He only lives a few blocks from here."

He looked at her, at her eyes, her legs encased in the tight jeans, the empty circle between the tops of her thighs. Her voice was moonlight. He shook his head.

"Might have a drink, later," he offered, hating himself for it. *Don't blow it*, he pleaded with himself. *Don't.* He bit the inside of his cheek and relished the pain.

"Maybe. I'd really like to talk to you about your poetry. I have a degree in English, you know. Teach high school. Don't let this cowgirl outfit fool you. We had 'Western Day' at school. Why don't you call me after while? You've got my number, right?"

"Right," he said. "Goodnight, Professor Randolph. See you tomorrow."

"I just hope he can see *you* is all," she said, and she and Associate Professor Stephen P. Randolph limped out into the parking lot. While he watched her hips move beneath the tight denim, he tried to decide if she gave him one more knowing—or was it telling?—look before they left.

He was burning inside. He hadn't felt that way for a long time. It almost hurt, made his breath short. He knew it as well as he knew anything: She was the one.

He went into the bar, nursed four shots and beers, smoked half a pack of cigarettes, and watched the dancers, sought for a dizzying buzz, wished time would pass more quickly. He vowed he wouldn't call her. It gave him a terrible sense of pending loss, of missed opportunity. Randolph was a good boy—a good man—and he was a real fan of his work and, not incidentally, he could do him a lot of good. Of all the regions besides California, the South was the hardest to penetrate. Even when he was at his best, when his books were selling well and he was a name, he couldn't get more than a half-dozen readings at a time anywhere below the Mason-Dixon. They took care of their own first, and they were notoriously hostile to outsiders.

This tour was only possible because he would work cheap, as cheap as the relatively unknown youngsters who were billed with him. But Randolph promised that his connections could put him into the circuit. He liked him well enough to do that. He deserved better than to have his girlfriend boffed in the back of a broken-down old poet's pickup.

He would *not* call her, he told himself.

But the old yearning was there, like a hunger that worsened with every sip of beer or whiskey he put inside him, and none of the girls in the bar—pros or not—seemed at all interested in him. The poems would come back if he called her. He knew it. He also knew that unless something or someone else turned up—and fast—he *would* call her. He couldn't help himself. The more he drank, the less important his vow not to seemed.

He felt the need of a woman more now than he had in years, not since the grant came through. It wasn't just for the poem—or poems—he thought she might summon, either. He just wanted to be with someone. Not with some impersonal whore, but with her. He shook his head and knocked back another shot. No, he said. With another woman: any other woman.

He scanned the room, but the girls alone at the bar were younger even than Millie. They returned his gaze with flat, disinterested eyes, sized him up for the fat old coot he was and ignored him. He imagined giving them a line, inviting them to his camper to hear some poetry. It used to work, he thought, there was a time when it couldn't miss. Here, he observed with a look at the rednecks, who had begun to take narrow, sideways notice of him now that the crowd was thinning, he could get his butt whipped. That, too, had happened before.

But it would work with Millie. He knew that as certainly as he knew anything. And he also knew that sometime before it became ridiculously late—vow or no vow—he was going to call her.

"I find that I can't sleep," he would say.

"Let me come over and keep you company," she would say.

"It's too much trouble, sorry I bothered you," he would say.

"It's okay," she would say. "I wanted you to talk to me about your poetry anyway. I'll be right over. Shall I bring some wine?"

That's the way it would go, he knew. That's the way it always went.

He groped for the poem he had sensed when he was speaking with her. He could almost feel it, see it. But it eluded him as the band swung into their fourth bad rendition of "Cotton-Eyed Joe" of the night. He was still searching as they finished and tried out a rock and roll medley.

"Something about a steel guitar just fucks up rock and roll," he said to the bartender. The squat man frowned and pointed a stubby finger at a sign over the bar. NO PROFANITY, it said.

He finished the beer, left a dollar tip on the bar, and got up to leave, knowing exactly where he was going. The vision of the pay phone in the lobby beckoned to him. Then a grossly fat woman barreled into him and almost knocked him over.

"My name is Tina Louise, an' you're goin' to dance with me!" she announced, and she swung him out onto the floor.

She was grotesque, huge, and she whirled him about like he was a sack of grain. He felt he was being pushed around by a truck. The musicians watched the show, laughed, and segued into a high-gear country melody and gave momentum to their mad cavort.

He was no dancer, had never been a dancer, particularly a country dancer. He hated country music. His feet flew from under him as she whipped him around on the floor and banged him against the other dancers. His breath came in gasps. The lights swam around him, and the alcohol in his system began to make him sick.

"I gotta get out of here," he yelled over the electric fiddle that squawked a cajun polka in his ear. "I'm fixin' to throw up."

Tina Louise laughed and swung him around one more time. Her palms were wet, and he slipped loose, thudding into a knot of high-hatted, heavy-booted men who had spent the evening blocking the bar's entrance. They stepped back slightly and let him fall onto the floor.

"Say, you better watch where you're going," one said in a low voice.

"Sorry," he said.

"You're a clumsy son-of-a-bitch. Ruint my shine," another said, holding up a bright boot toe for his inspection. "I ought to whip your ass."

"I apologize." He got himself together and stood. "I really didn't have control."

"Control this, Asshole," the first cowboy said, raising a middle finger in front of his face.

"Hey, where you goin'?" Tina Louise barked at him when she rushed up, breathless. She led him away from the belligerent would-be cowboys.

"I don't feel well," he said. "I need some air." He peeled her fat fingers from his wrist. His eyes sought the exit.

"Well, you come right on back," she warned. "Else, I'll come lookin' for you. There ain't a *real* man in the joint." She reached out and squeezed his groin painfully, then gave the rednecks a mean look. They shuffled out of his way as he plunged toward the men's room.

He couldn't vomit. He tried. He stuck a finger down his throat, tried to force it. But nothing worked. He washed his face, used a dirty Rollo-wipe to dry it, then lit a cigarette and studied himself in the mirror. His reflection looked alarmed. What was left of his hair was white. When had that happened? He couldn't remember it turning gray all around the ring that raced backwards from his forehead. But there it was. And he needed a shave. Salt and pepper bristles stuck out all over. His teeth were gray from neglect, and wrinkles covered his forehead. He felt greasy, dirty, tired.

"When did you get so fucking old?" he wondered aloud.

"'The longest journey/ Is the journey inwards of him who has chosen his destiny,'" his reflection commented dryly back.

Then he thought of Millie. Had he imagined the look in her eyes, that familiar, "I'm willing" look? How could anyone in her right mind be interested in a worn out old man like him or in ten-to-twenty-year-old poetry? Hell, she couldn't have been out of high school when his last reprint was remaindered. The poem he sensed when he looked at her flitted again across his mind, but when he reached for it, it moved away, out of sight. He wanted to cry.

"You're done," he said. "Washed up. Kidding yourself." He envisioned himself taking a swan dive into an empty swimming pool. Crash and burn, he thought: Do the world a favor. Lean into the pitch, take one on the bean, for the team, for the rest of humanity. He looked at his watch: 1:30. He had a workshop at ten. Then the full-scale reading with the other three at noon. Then a long drive down into northern Mississippi for the next gig. Then Biloxi, Mobile, Marion, then back up to Birmingham—or was it Chatanooga? He couldn't remember. He didn't know or care. There wasn't a real college in the bunch, not one first-tier university. But it was his last chance, and success in most if not all of them could herald a real comeback.

The poem he sensed before was gone. He wondered if it had ever been there, if it was the last one he would ever have so much as a glimpse of. He knew that if he called Millie, if he took her back to his truck, talked a little poetry, undressed those thin thighs and crawled between them, filled that wonderful space between her legs with pure lust that it might come back, that it *would* come back. But at what price? he asked himself.

Poems were whores, he told himself, they gave something, sure, but they charged for it. They charged too much. They had always wanted his pride, his self-respect, his health, his life. Now, they wanted his soul.

"Road back," he said aloud. "Road to hell."

A pair of rednecks came into the room just as he spoke, stopped and stared at him peering into the mirror, talking to himself. He immediately turned on the tap, washed his face once more. They went into a stall, and in a moment he heard a lighter strike, smelled the drug, broke out of the door in a panic. This is all I need, he silently screamed at himself. Who would think that out here in the middle of Redneckville, Tennessee . . . Probably not a pickup in a hundred miles without a loaded gunrack and a series of right-wing bumper stickers plastered on it . . . It was worse than a nightmare, he thought, and then he spotted the pay phone at the far end of the lobby. No, he warned himself and rubbed the heels of his hands into this eyes, it is a nightmare. It won't let me go.

Music still thudded out from the bar, but he took a breath, composed himself, turned left, and went into the lobby. One good poem, he thought in a half-promise. Just one really good one to prove that I still can. He stopped and pondered the promise. Did he really mean it? he asked himself. Could he stop with just one? Would Millie be the end of some-thing or only a new beginning? Was there anything wrong with a new beginning, with fucking Randolph's girl in exchange for what might or might not be a different road back? Or would she just accelerate his fall? The debate froze him, and he realized he had become the object of observation from the lobby.

Three young men sat around in the threadbare, overstuffed chairs. A bottle of bourbon was on the table, and they poured from it into plastic motel-room cups and continued talking when he looked over toward them, noticed them staring at his rumpled, tortured form.

"Say," he stepped toward them, stopped, hesitated. They were all well-dressed, casual, but carefully studied style: not businessmen, not redneck salesmen. L.L. Bean, a little Land's End and Eddy Bauer to soften the effect: The other poets. A small clutter of chapbooks on the table next to the bottle confirmed it. "Could you spare a shot of that?"

They looked at each other, a little embarrassed, and one, a tall youngster with glasses, nodded. "What the hell? It's late. Have a seat."

He fell into a chair, took a cup half full of whiskey from the one who had spoken, and held it in both hands as he sipped it. The tall one was Jack Something, he thought, trying to remember the flyer and pictures Associate Professor Stephen P. Randolph had sent him.

"Well, I thought he was dead," Jack said. He ignored the newcomer and sat back with a refreshed drink.

"Everyone thought Penn Warren was dead, too," another, who he identified as Ray, said. "Spender, as well, and Auden."

"Spender's not dead, Ray," the first one said.

"How can you tell?" the darkest member of the trio—the Pakistani-American, Afgar—asked. There was laughter.

"Old poets never die," Jack said, "They just drink themselves away."

"I hear they get AIDS," Ray replied and laughed.

"Not this old boy. He's a lech, not a queer."

"I don't believe half of it," Jack said. "Nobody gets that lucky all the time. Besides, he's an old fart." He poured their glasses full. They were drunk, or nearly, paying no attention to him at all. He heard his name again.

"Well, I think it's true." Afgar insisted. He had no trace of an accent. He was considerably more American than Pakistani. "I've got a friend who was at U-Iowa when he came through. He hit on half the women in the workshop, scored with three, I hear. Hell, he was only there two days."

"I heard he did the same thing at Cincinnati," Ray offered. "Only it was four days, five women, including the department head's daughter." He shook his hand as if something was stuck to his fingers. "She was something, too: stone fox, professional model. Did a spread in *Playboy* two years later: Miss May. But that son of a bitch got there first. Took all the fun out of it."

"You're just jealous," Jack accused. "Both of you."

"Maybe." Afgar leaned forward and refilled his glass. "But I'm telling you: Greg, my friend, he says he was like a one-man fucking machine. He was over forty then. Wonder what he was like when he was young."

He thought back for a moment, remembered, reflected. Iowa: he barely could recall it. Diana, that was one of them. And she was. Diaphanous: clear and light. That's what he had told her anyway. She was the only one who took him up on it, though. The others chickened out. But she was worth it: sophomore sensuous. He had no recollection of Cincinnati. He had been there, but it was too foggy to recall. *Playboy?* he asked himself, Miss May? Had he ever done that well? He shook his head and accepted another drink from Jack, who was waving the bottle around.

"Well, I've got a buddy from South Carolina," Jack said. "I tell you, he says he's nothing but a drunk and a braggart. Hell, when he was there, he passed out during the reading." He pointed a finger at his friends. "Fact: You cannot *fuck* when you're too drunk to *read*. He was too drunk to see, let alone read. Or fuck."

That's not true, he remembered. He had been drunk. Awfully drunk. He leaned on the podium, struggled to stay awake between poems, but he got through it, and he didn't pass out. Shit, that wasn't that long ago. What? Five years. Seven? It was hard to remember. In a sudden flash he recalled buying dinner for—how many was it?—seventeen, eighteen people. Insisted on paying. Got angry about it, made a show. He made the waitress put it all on one ticket, sent them all away, then used an expired credit card, the only thing he had on him. Damned embarrassing, he guessed, but he remembered laughing about it later, with a sweet little strawberry blonde named Mary St. Something. He had teased her about that, called her "Saint Mary." She wore a bra that hooked in front, and had tiny but perfectly formed breasts, firm, red little nipples, and almost no pubic hair, just a gossamer covering, soft as down. He remembered her well, had two poems come to him because of her. The rest of the experience was a haze. But it was clear that he was not too drunk to fuck.

But he had met her later, at the party after the reading. Maybe he had sobered up, by then.

Who was he trying to impress at the restaurant? he wondered. What could her name have been? What had she looked like? When he thought back on his life, it was nothing but a steady parade of young girls—like Mary, like Randolph's Millie—like all of them. And the more of them there were, the more he wrote. That was true, too. That was where his energy went. That was where his poetry came from. But that was where he had gone, as well.

"Well, I've got the story to end all stories," Ray spoke up. "I had a reading at Chicago, oh, about two, three years ago. Right after I got runner-up for Yale Younger Poet." He smiled quickly, waited for comment, got none, continued. "They put me up in the dean's guest house. Nice place, sort of a converted garage apartment, but real nice. There was a liquor cabinet, but it was locked up. And there was this odd hole in the wall by the bed. It had all these loose wires hanging out of it, looked like it something had been ripped out. I wondered about that, because, you know, the place was so well kept, so nice, otherwise.

"Well, he was there the month before. He got drunk—hell, from what I hear, he *came* drunk. He went through that liquor cabinet like a fox through an arbor, drank it dry the first night. Then, he showed up at breakfast still sloshed and wondered if there wasn't more around. And the dean's wife went out, bought more, and restocked it."

"So, he drinks," Jack said, refilling his glass again. "So what? I drink, you drink. We *all* drink. Everybody but Davis Collins drinks, and he's a Baptist. 'The Christy-yan Poet,'" he concluded in a bad imitation of a television evangelist.

"Wait. He comes in that night, after his reading, and uses this room-to-room intercom to call up the dean's daughter. She's, oh, maybe seventeen, eighteen. Real airhead, you know. Showed him some poems of hers over dinner, I hear, and he offered to counsel her, said he could get her published. Papa and Mama Dean were thrilled to death. He said he'd talk to her that very night."

"Over the intercom?" Jack guessed. "That was the hole in the wall, right?"

"Direct link to her room." Ray shook his head in amazement. "Anyway, when he doesn't show up at breakfast the next morning, Mrs. Dean calls him up on the horn, but the "transmit" button's on, so the whole family is treated to their sweet young daughter going at it hot and heavy in the guest house with you know who."

"Man, that's radio." Afgar said.

"Yeah, well it sure as hell screwed me. They locked up the liquor and women when I showed up. I was lucky to get a beer. Never did see the daughter or anything else in a skirt."

"Well," Jack said. "It don't matter, boys. He's here tomorrow, and he's got top billing. He's also got a Gugge. But keep one hand on your women and the other on your poetry."

"He doesn't steal poems, does he?"

"Well, it's been said . . ."

"*And* it's a goddamn lie!" He bellowed and stood. He felt the hair on his neck sticking up. He was guilty of a lot of things, of everything they said—and worse—but not that. Never that. "I've never stolen a poem in my goddamned life! Not a single line, not a single word! Whoever said that is a goddamned liar!"

The four young men sat backwards in their chairs and gaped at him. He could see it in their eyes: madman.

"How *dare* you?" he yelled. "You know who I am, and you've heard all about me. But you don't know a goddamned thing! Not a thing. I could write circles around you. I had books in *print* before you were born. I've got fucking *shirts* older than you. *This* shirt, he tugged at the faded blue denim he wore, is older than any two of you put together!"

He was ranting, and the pimply desk clerk yelled something over at him, but he waved her off. "Steal poems? Damn it! I've never read a fucking poem by anybody I thought enough of to steal from. Who can write poetry anyway?" The echo of his voice came back to him from the lobby walls, smashed against his ears. He felt himself deflate like an old basketball.

"It's two o'clock in the morning," he croaked, moving his face to look at each of the young men who squirmed as he scanned them. "I'm tired,

279

sick, lonely. But I've been there, you bastards. I've fucking *been* there. Where you *want* to go, where you *think* you want to go. Oh, 'Success is counted sweetest/ By those who ne'er succeed' all right. But I can tell you, boys, it's not what you think. It's not that sweet at all. You don't know the first fucking thing about it. And you don't know the first fucking thing about poetry, either."

Spent, he flopped back down into the chair. The three men sat motionless, stunned. "Give me another drink, Jack," he said, "And I'll tell you all about it. I won't name names because I can't remember them. But I'll tell you what was good, what was bad, and what gets worse and worse until you can't stand it anymore. I'll tell you what it's like to look up and see nothing but your own asshole."

They exchanged careful, uncomfortable glances, then Jack poured a dollop of whiskey into his cup. He sipped it, held it up to the light.

"You know how much I've had to drink tonight?" They stared and slowly shook their heads, like freshmen presented with a thorny philosophical question. "I had the best part of a bottle of tequila as soon as I got here. Then I went to dinner. Two, three strong scotches—doubles. Split two bottles of wine with ol' Associate Professor Randolph. You know Randolph?"

"The guy at the college," Jack guessed obligingly. "I know him."

"Right! Associate Goddamn Fucking Professor Stephen P-for-piss-cutter-Randolph. The guy who put this little shoot-out together. Put my name right at the top of the fucking program, way up at the top. Way ahead of yours, drunk or sober. Top billing and bigger print. That's no accident, boys. Hell, he knows who can get his dick hard around here, he knows who's a poet and who's not. Well, he and me split a bottle of pretty damned good burgandy. Then we split another one. And right in the middle of our second brandy after our overcooked steaks, right there in the old motel eatery, he went to shit. But did I go to shit? Did I?"

"No?" Jack ventured.

"Goddamn right I didn't. I can hold *my* liquor. I can drink wine, whiskey, tequila, and I can still get it up. I stayed right where I was and finished my brandy, then his, then I called us his current piece of ass—little

Dale-Evans-cowgirl twist named Millie—to take him home, sober him up for tomorrow's festivities. And then I went into the bar where I drank a shot and a beer, and another, and another. Four, all told. Buck for the shot. Buck for the beer: Eight bucks. Buck for a tip: Nine. That's damn near ten percent of what I'm getting for tomorrow's little run at poetry. What'd'ya thank of that?"

"We're all getting the same thing," Afgar said.

"Oh no," he said. "Oh no. We're *all* getting the hundred. You bet. And we'll all get free lunch. But you'll sell a few books, and that'll put you up a bit. And you'll make buddies with old Associate Professor Stephen P. Randolph, and you'll be asked back. But I won't. You know why?"

They said nothing. He was rising to a new peak, a higher and more dangerous one, and they each put hands on the arms of their chairs as if expecting a lift-off.

"I'll tell you why. Because, in about two minutes, I'm going to go over to that phone over there and call ol' Millie-Dale up. And she's going to come out to my camper, and we're going to climb onto that narrow little single-mattress cot I've got in there, lay right down on the peter tracks and fart stains, and we're going to test out that old truck's dual suspension system. And there's not one goddamn thing that Associate Fucking Professor Randolph—or you—or *anybody* can do about it. Not even God 'will say a word.' Because that's what I do. I write poetry, read poetry, and when I get drunk enough, I fuck women. Beautiful women. Anybody's women. And then, I write more poetry. It's all connected. What do you think of that?"

"I think it's late," Jack said, rising.

"And you think I'm drunk."

"Yes," he replied quietly. "I think you're drunk, and disgusting, and not a little pathetic."

"Well, I wish you were right," he said. "And you are, mostly. I'm gross, and old, and fat, and I'm as pathetic as any road-kill you've ever seen, and twice as disgusting as any wino on any street corner. But I'm not drunk. I wish to God in heaven I were, but it doesn't work anymore. I drink and drink, but it just doesn't fucking work anymore. Nothing works anymore, nothing but that dark empty feeling inside, that goddamned tight, dark, hollow feeling inside whenever I see somebody as warm and wet and willing as young Millie. But you wouldn't know about that, would you, Jack? None of you would. You're so fucking afraid of failure, so fucking afraid of life that you're too scared to beat off. Isn't that right, Jack? Isn't that just the blue-balled shits?"

"Well, where in the name of the cream-colored Jesus have you been?" A shrill soprano voice cut through the tension of the room, sent it scattering for dark corners. The quartet settled like so many dust bugs. Tina Louise flounced in and filled the area. She moved quickly up behind Jack, slapped him on the back, and pushed him back down into this chair. "I been waitin' on you!"

The three poets shifted uncomfortably. She tried to sit on the arm of Jack's chair, but her heft was too great, and she could only lean on him, one massive hip pushing him over to one side. She draped a huge paw across his shoulders and squeezed him with her left arm, then pointed across the room toward where he sat.

"He's my dancin' partner!" she announced loudly. "I been in there waitin' on him, an' he's out here bullshittin' with y'all. What is this, anyway? A queer's convention? Don't y'all like girls? I come out here to get him. Time to dance!"

"Well, you can have him," Ray said. "We're about to retire."

"Whoo," she said, and winked at him. "You're too young 'to retire.' Too cute, too. It's the shank of the evenin'!"

Under the lobby's blistering lights, he could see that she was even more grotesque than she had appeared in the muted, colored bulbs inside the bar. Her cheeks were small red islands swimming in fat and rising to encircle her watery blue eyes. Stringy, badly dyed blond hair frayed up in a dozen directions. She was squeezed into a pair of corduroy jeans no less than two sizes too small, and her enormous belly bulged out and expanded the flap of the fly to expose the extent of the zipper's strain. Everything about her was obese. Even her fingers seemed two or three times too big for her hands which were wrapped double around an oversized cocktail glass full of dull orange liquid. But the biggest thing about her was her smile. It dimmed the light in the room, forced each of the men to look away from its brilliance.

Ray failed to read her remark correctly and took offense. A fault of the young, he thought.

"I expect I'm older than you," he said huffily.

"Well, ain't *you* somethin'," she hollered. "Hey, Denise," she yelled at the desk clerk who made a motion to quiet her. "This little peckerwood thinks he's older'n me." She formed a sly grin and winked at Ray, "I tell you what, Sweetmeat, let's head off to your room, an' we can tell each other lies all night." She made a sucking sound with her lips.

The young poet shifted. "God," he muttered.

"Oh, heck, don't pay me no mind," she said, squeezing Jack's shoulder once more and shifting even more of her weight onto him. "I'm drunk! I've had me two Cocksuckers tonight."

"What?" Ray asked.

He wondered why Ray didn't just shut up. This was her turf, and she was going to win.

"Course, they ain't as good as a Motherfucker," she said with a dour frown. "Not as sweet." She shifted more weight even more onto Jack who squirmed away from her mass. "I don't 'spect you'd like them," she continued into the silence that had fallen over the group. "You look more like you'd like Sex on the Beach. I had me that twice tonight."

"What?" Ray, who was the youngest of the group, was genuinely shocked. He hadn't learned a thing from the previous exchange.

"Sex on the Beach," she squealed. "Don't you know nothin'? Don't tell me you've never had Sex on the Beach."

"There's not a beach in five hundred miles of here," Ray insisted.

"It's a drink, you asshole," Jack said. He rose and pushed Tina Louise off of him. "They're *all* drinks. 'Sex on the Beach' is a *drink*. Jesus!" He worked his way out from under her bulk and stood.

"Well sure!" Tina Louise settled into his chair and crooked a fat leg over it. Her pants wouldn't quite bend. A booted foot floated out almost straight. "What'd'y'all think?" Her eyes were platters of innocence. "Boy, this is a warm seat," she giggled. "You got a tiny li'l ol' butt, but you're a pistol where it counts, I'll bet."

"I'm going to bed," Jack said. The others rose as well.

He stayed put. "Leave the bottle," he said to Jack when the young man leaned over to pick it up. It was but a quarter full, yet it looked good. "For old times."

Jack stiffened, then stood up. "Look," he said. "I'm sorry. We were just talking. The booze was talking. We didn't know you were . . . it shouldn't matter. Whether you were here or not. We shouldn't have said all that stuff. I'm sorry."

"Apology accepted. And you were right. Mostly. But I never stole a poem. Leave the fucking bottle."

"You were kind of a legend, once. I read your stuff. Still do. You were good. Really good. I never heard you read, but I've heard about you. You set standards, took no shit from anybody. What happened?"

"Hell, I don't know," he said. "I guess I just kind of forgot why I wrote. I just lost it somewhere. Or maybe I lost the courage to go looking for it."

Jack glanced at the bottle. "It was in one of those, right?"

"Nope," he said with a quick glance at Tina Louise who was about to cop a feel on Afgar's behind. "In one of those."

"Look what I can do," she shouted suddenly and sat up straight. All eyes turned. She flicked out her tongue and ran it over her left cheek and then her right. Then she snaked it out and ran it across the bottom of her triple chin.

"It's kind of a family thing," she said, laughing at their looks of shock and disgust. "I got a brother who can lick his eyebrows. Just like a cat. I think it's 'cause our folks is second cousins."

"God, I'm going to bed," Ray said, and he stalked off. Afgar followed.

Jack looked down at him once more. "See you tomorrow," he said. "I'm looking forward to it. And I am sorry."

He lifted his plastic cup and pretended to examine the liquid inside.

"'It should do good to heart and head
When your soul's in my soul's stead;
And I will friend you if I may,
In the dark and cloudy day.'

No harm done," he said.

"Yeah, well, good night."

"Goodnight, Sugar," Tina Louise called as Jack followed his companions out of the lobby and across the parking lot. "Don't get any on you."

He put aside the cup and sipped directly from the bottle, thought again of Millie. He looked at his watch: 2:15.

"Well, what 'bout it? We goin' to dance, or what?" Tina Louise demanded after a moment's silence.

As if in answer to her question, the lead guitar and bass man passed through the lobby with their instruments. It was after two. The bar was closed.

"Looks like we're out of music," he said. He took another hit off the bottle. He really wanted to be drunk. But he didn't think he could stand to be alone. He looked at her smiling, fat face for a moment, let his eyes scan her from her frowsy greenish-blond wisps of hair all the way down to her fat thighs and thick corduroy covered calves as they descended to cover the stressed vamps of low-top purple boots. He shook his head, but not in denial, finished off the bottle at a gulp, and smiled back at her.

"They got radios on the TV sets in the rooms," she said with a wink.

He tried to imagine it. He couldn't. Just looking at her made his stomach churn, his throat close. He couldn't go that low. He wouldn't. Then his eyes drifted over to the pay phone, and Millie's light brown eyes and suggestive smile crossed his mind. He felt as if he were standing on the brink of two gaping holes. He had to choose one to dive into, and neither would save him.

"I don't have a room. All I have is a camper shell with a cot."

"Camper shell!"

He nodded. "On the back of a broken-down pickup." And a half-full bottle of tequila, he added, silently clenching his teeth. "Do not go gently into that good night," he thought.

"Why, hell, ol' son, I can do better than that," she cried, winked broadly, came to her feet, grabbed his hand and pulled him up. "C'mon! I got me a fuckin' Winnebago!" 🌑

Bad Luck Creek

by H. Palmer Hall

That morning, the water in the little creek flowed sluggishly. It was hot and even the always humid thicket had grown dry with little wind. Upstream, where Billy Hicks sat on the bank fishing, only the deepest holes retained much water at all. Billy thought maybe he could boil an egg in the creek. If I had an egg, he thought.

But there was other heat, also. All that summer, the men who lived back in the thicket had been moving deeper and deeper into its wildest, least accessible parts. Captain Charles Bullock, who, before the war had often hunted with them, and his company in their gray uniforms tried to flush them out and make them either join the Confederate Army or stand trial for treason. Most of the men who lived back in the thicket, though, agreed with General Sam Houston that Texas didn't have any business abandoning the Union or thought, at the very least, that the whole mess wasn't any business of theirs. They'd left Georgia and the Carolinas back in the 40's, some in the late 50's to avoid what they had seen as an inevitable war. They had not moved into the southeast Texas thicket just to pick up an old fight that would not, could not, matter to them. They had not owned slaves. Most had never even owned their own land until they got to Texas.

During the drought in that October back in 1865, at the very tail end of the war, hunted by the Confederate Army as traitors to the South, they gathered from time to time at a place they had started to call Union Wells. Located down in a hollow about a hundred yards from the head of the small, unnamed creek, the two clear wells filled with cool water that was free of the tannin that turned all the creeks in the thicket a deep brown color and made the water, though fresh enough and good enough in an emergency, bitter to drink, was a logical meeting place. Whenever they heard the noise made by Bullock's cavalry, the men melted back into the undergrowth and hid all traces of their passage. Stace and Warren Collins, Uncle Big Bill Hicks, Buck Hooks, Oliver Overstreet, and the other men, knowing that the mostly town-raised soldiers would not stay out in the thicket at night, often walked home to see their wives and children and to have breakfast before hightailing it back into the woods and gathering at what they had begun to call Union Wells.

The previous night, Billy Hicks had walked down the trail on the bank of the creek to find holes deep enough to contain the crappie and catfish he most enjoyed eating. As with most of the people who lived back in the thicket, when he went on such expeditions Billy packed his gun, an old cap and ball muzzle loader that had belonged to his grandfather and then his father. He carried the rifle not so much because he wanted to hunt, but because in 1863 the thicket still teemed with wildlife, and he had, on more than one occasion, spooked both black bears and panthers coming down to the creek for water.

Little Billy was called "Little" Billy to distinguish him from his uncle on his father's side, Big Bill Hicks, but he was already fifteen and stood five feet eleven inches tall, three inchers taller than his uncle. He preferred to be called Bill, but in his family no one would do it. When one of his aunts made a visit to the shotgun house he had been brought up in, she would inevitably comment on "how much Little Billy has grown and how he's gonna be even taller than Big Billy when he's got his full height." On this day, as he walked along the creek, he had seen neither bear nor panther, only a few grey squirrels and he had not even needed to get the ball, cloth, and powder out of his pack. Though the thicket had been cooler than normal that October morning, he was tired after fishing all night.

He stopped off at the home of Stace Collins. He figured Mrs. Collins would have biscuits and bacon and just maybe some fresh eggs ready to cook in exchange for one or two of the crappie he had caught earlier. He thought, too, that Gaylynne Collins might have a few minutes to take a short walk up the creek for a more private conversation. People grew up fast back in the thicket, and he and Gaylynne had been courting for almost a full year. No place better than an almost dry creek to hold hands and maybe steal a kiss or two. Maybe even hold each other real close for a few minutes.

When he turned in at the Collins place, he saw the buckboard and oxen that belonged to old man Runyon. A fresh-dressed deer was laid out in the back, and the blooding the night before had stained the weathered boards a sticky dark brown. Billy jumped up on the wooden porch and kicked the dirt off his shoes, then knocked on the door. Mrs. Collins answered and invited him in with a light hug—her "Why it's Little Billy!" turned his face red as he saw Gaylynne choking back a laugh. He took off his hat and held it as he stepped into the kitchen. "Good mornin', Mrs. Collins, Mr. Runyon, Gaylynne," he mumbled. "Just passin' by and thought I'd stop in for a few minutes. Got a mess of crappie and a couple of bass from up the creek last night."

"Sit down, Little Billy, have some breakfast. Just biscuits with honey and some fried squirrel legs, I'm afraid. Since that Charles Bullock started hunting Stace and Warren, we haven't had a whole lot more. Last night, a new man came by, some Captain Kaiser from Galveston. His men took all the chickens and eggs."

"You're welcome to some of the deer meat, Mrs. Collins," Runyon said. "That old buck walked right up to my team last night. Wasn't really hunting and don't need all the meat."

"I got lots of fish," Billy said. "Plenty to spare."

"Don't worry, honey. We'll do okay. Sit down now."

Billy sat on one of the straight back chairs and propped his elbows on the table. He broke open one of the biscuits and poured fresh honey over it. "Creek sure is drying up. Everything's turning brown, even the cypress trees. Pretty soon, we'll have to walk all the way on down to Cypress Creek just to fish." He looked around, his eyes resting on Gaylynne. "Y'all seen very much of Mr. Stace lately?"

"He was here for a few minutes last night," Gaylynne said. "He's got a lot more on his mind than just where he's goin' to find a spot to fish."

Billy flushed deep red. "They'll be after me next year. Then I'll be joining your daddy and live in the woods." He didn't think very often about the war. Back in what they were already calling the Big Thicket, the war had had hardly any effect except to move men out of Texas and kill them on battlefields throughout the South. No fighting had actually happened anywhere near the thicket and, to most of the men in the woods, the war wasn't really any of their business. They'd follow Sam Houston from up around Conroe—he was one of them, but old Sam had already risked his career and reputation trying to keep Texas in the Union and out of the war.

When he finished his breakfast, Billy had just about gotten up his nerve to ask Gaylynne to walk down to the creek for a brief chat, when he heard horses galloping down the trail and into the front yard. Old Man Runyon peeked out through the window. "Soldiers," he said. "At least twenty-five, all wearin' gray, with young Bullock on that brown horse he always rides."

"You folks stay inside here," Mrs. Collins said and walked out onto the front porch. Billy heard her shout at the men in the yard. "Whatcha want here, Charles Bullock? We ain't got nothing that's yours and your friend from Galveston stole most of what's ours."

"And good morning to you, too, Mrs. Collins. Stace around? I'd like to have a little chat with him." Billy could hear the sarcasm in Bullock's voice.

"He's got sense enough to stay away when a bunch of thieves and kidnappers shows up. Now you men get out of my yard! This is private property."

Peeking through the window, Billy saw Bullock smile down at Mrs. Collins. "We'll go when we want to, Mrs. Collins. We're on official business." But he turned his horse and waved his men back down the trail.

Mrs. Collins came back in the house and sat down at the table. "Someone's going to get killed before this is all over," she said. She wiped her hands on her apron and rubbed off the table. "Billy, you run on out to the Wells and tell Stace and Warren to stay put today."

Before Billy could pick up his rifle and fishing pole, old man Runyon stopped him. "Look, boy. I ain't a part of any of this. If they see you runnin', though, they're gonna think I am. So you wait right here 'til I can get out of the way."

Billy picked up his things. "I'll give you five minutes, Mr. Runyon. But then I need to get out of here to warn Mr. Stace and Mr. Warren."

Just then, the back door of the house swung open and Stace Collins walked in. "Warn me of what, Little Billy? I got Bill Overstreet and a few of the other boys here, so you can tell me now."

Before Billy could say anything, Stace's wife raced across the floor and grabbed his arm. "You got to get out of here right now! Bullock's just out of sight and he's got a whole company of horsemen with him just looking for a fight."

Stace pulled his wife into his arms and gave her a big kiss right there in front of everybody. "If they want a fight, Carol Ann, we can give it to them."

"Not here, Stace Collins. Not with Gaylynne and Little Billy here. You get on out of here before it's too late."

Billy watched Stace hesitate for a minute. "You go on and warn Warren," he said to Billy. Then the big man kissed his wife again and left through the back door.

Runyon picked up his rifle and headed out the front door to his wagon. He looked back at the house for a minute and saw Mrs. Collins standing on the front porch. "Sorry to eat and run, ma'am, but this just ain't my fight."

Billy, right behind him, came to a quick stop and darted back into the house when he heard the sound of horses. Bullock's troops had hidden in a small stand of Magnolia trees across the dry creek bed. When they saw Stace's men leave the hummock of tall grass, they scrambled their horses across the creek bed and opened fire. Bullock rode right into the yard and fired point-blank at Runyon, his ball piercing his gut and cutting the blue and black gussels that held up his baggy pants. Billy saw his pants hit the ground before the rest of him. "Shot him!" Bullock shouted. "Cut his gussels right off! The one with the ripped off gussels is mine, boys. Get the rest!"

Stace yelled back at the house, "Let Warren know what's happening!" then disappeared into the underbrush with the rest of the men.

When the shooting began to taper off, then finally stopped altogether, Billy walked out into the front yard. Old Man Runyon lay hunched over on the ground next to his wagon, stone-cold dead. Charles Bullock, still sitting his big brown horse, just above him, looked toward the bushes where Stace Collins and his men had disappeared.

Billy leaned over the old man and checked his heart. "You killed him," he said. His eyes bored into Bullock's. "He wasn't a part of this, just an old man. You didn't have to kill him."

"Wake up, boy. There ain't a person in this country who ain't a part of this. The old man down there. Yeah. He was part of it, too. You got to choose a side or get chosen." Bullock turned his horse and rode away.

Billy sat down on the grass next to the old man. This is war, he thought. This is what it's all about. It ain't about slaves. It ain't about freedom. This is it. All Billy had ever wanted was his own piece of land in the thicket, a place he could hunt and fish. That's all the Collinses and the other men and women in the thicket had wanted. He wanted to raise a family, too, when he was a little older. When he looked around, everything was peaceful. The creek bed needed water, the thicket was parched, but that would pass. He closed Runyon's eyes.

Gaylynn walked slowly over to him. "You'd better get going, Bill. Uncle Warren needs to know." She leaned over and kissed him lightly on the lips.

"I'm taking him back to his house first. It's almost on the way." He wrapped his arms around the old man and dragged him up into the wagon letting him fall on top of the deer. "I'll be back." He climbed up onto the wagon seat and clucked at the oxen. When he looked back, Gaylynne was no longer there and he guided the wagon along the old ruts.

The path to Runyon's log and clay house ran along the creek for half a mile, then turned and went back along the edge of a now dried up slough. The ferns and cattails had been parched brown and flies buzzed over the few holes with any brackish water still standing. When he got to the house, he hoisted Runyon out of the wagon and carried him inside. No one was there, but he laid him out on the dog trot between the kitchen and the bedroom. After unhitching the oxen and swatting them on the rear to get them moving, he set out cross country for Union Wells.

Billy had been playing and hunting in the thicket since his father had died eight years earlier. He didn't know all of it, no one could, but he knew this area and what he didn't know he could find if someone gave him an idea of where it might be. He walked off the path, dodging between two sweet gum trees and jogged through a large stand of loblolly pines so thick and tall, the bed of pine needles mulched into a thick carpet, that not enough light could get through to pull the grasses and blackberries and weeds above the ground.

He loped slowly along the deer path, looking ahead of him for any sign of Confederate troops, but the only things he saw for the first few miles were a couple of deer that ran away and the claw marks of a black bear. He stopped for a moment, but when he saw that those were not fresh, he turned back down the trail.

When the path turned left to skirt the edge of a drying slough, the air felt heavy with the odor of rotted, drying swamp weeds and lilies. Dead and dying fish lay on their sides, flies and gnats buzzed everywhere. He slowed down to a walk and breathed softly, pulling his bandana over his nose and mouth. He watched, waiting, as a four foot long cottonmouth water mocassin, looking for other marshy areas, slithered across the trail. When the snake had moved all the way across, Billy walked on, carefully, not wanting to make a noise in case Kaiser's or Bullock's men might be close.

Billy knew he was too young to be drafted, but he also knew Bullock or Kaiser would not consider his age if they found out he was helping the Collinses and the other men. When he heard horses' hooves, he hid behind a small cluster of titi trees until they had passed. As he peeked through the scrub trees, the green moldy striations baked away from the bark, he saw the guidon and knew that these were Kaiser's men and not Bullock's. He watched as the Captain divided the horsemen into two files. One group rode to the west and the other continued straight ahead, moving toward the east side of the Wells.

When they had all passed, he ran across the small clearing and made his way carefully through thick fields of palmettoes. He could feel himself bleeding, his ankles torn by the rough trunks of the plants. He kept his eyes down on the ground. Rattlesnakes often nested in such places.

What happened, he told himself later, was that he wasn't thinking right. His mind wandered, and he thought mostly about Gaylynne's kissing him and calling him "Bill" instead of "Billy" or "Little Billy" or maybe he was concentrating too hard on snakes. Whatever the reason, when he had gotten through the palmettoes and over a small hill covered with mayhaws, he walked straight out onto a dirt road without looking right or left and almost bumped into the nose of a horse carrying a man in a dirty gray uniform. Fortunately, the horse jumped and when the man yelled at him to stop, Billy had time to race across the road. Just as he was about to push between some blackberries and behind a sycamore tree, he heard a rifle shot and then felt a giant kick in his left leg and fell, tumbling into a bunch of blackberry bushes.

"I said stop, boy," the man screamed at him. Billy held his leg and felt, rather than saw, the warmth of his blood soaking his fingers. His eyes were fixed on the man as he slipped off his horse and let the reins trail down to the ground. Billy pushed back into the bushes and reached down into his pocket to get his powder, cloth and ball. While the Confederate soldier walked toward him, not able to see him in the bushes, he poured the powder into the barrel, then slipped the cloth over the muzzle and dropped a small lead ball onto it. He cut the cloth with his knife, then rammed the ball and cloth down the barrel and tamped it in.

He backed up in the brush and groaned as he felt the calf of his left leg, pain shooting from it. When the soldier heard him, he turned and ran toward the blackberry bush. Billy got his musket pointed up and, just as the soldier pushed into the brush, squeezed the trigger.

The soldier fell backward and lay still. Billy crawled out of the bush and pulled himself over to where the man, unmoving, his blood spilling onto the dry dirt. "Ah, Jesus," Billy said. "I didn't want to kill no one." He stared at the man's face, pale, eyes wide open staring up at the hot sun. When he reached out to close the soldier's eyes, Billy felt the skin, still warm with the heat of the day, but cool to his touch.

He crawled back into the blackberries before looking at his own wound. He squeezed it, making it bleed again, then wrapped his bandana around it, pulling it into a tight compress. He left the dead man behind him and hobbled into the thicket.

When he reached the wells, Warren Collins, his uncle Big Bill and the other men weren't there. He limped over to the closer of the two wells and dropped the bucket in. When he pulled it up, he emptied it over his head, drenching himself, the water pouring over his head and chest. He shivered in the hot breeze as he felt it drip down into his pants. He unwrapped the bandana and soaked it with a second bucket of water before tying it back over the bullet wound and sitting down to wait.

He rested for close to an hour before he heard, not yet seeing them, the sounds of men in the woods around him. As he sat up, he saw Warren Collins come out of the brush first. He was a big man, with a full beard, not fat, heavily muscled, and tall. His clothes were torn and he looked like he hadn't had any sleep for a while, but when he saw Billy by the well, he ran forward, panting a little from the exertion, then stopped, staring down at him. "What the hell are you doing here, boy?" He was joined by Big Bill Hicks and three or four other men before Billy could answer. Warren saw the bandana, its red stained brown by the drying blood. "You been shot."

"Yes, sir," Billy said. "But Mrs. Carol Ann said I should come warn you."

"Warn us? Hell, Little Billy, we heard the soldiers a long time ago. Heard the shots, too, but thought maybe they'd snuck up on some old bear. You hurt bad?" his uncle asked.

"No, sir, Uncle Billy. He just grazed my left leg a little. That's probably the shots you heard. But it hurt pretty bad at first." Billy turned his head to look at Warren Collins again. "Mrs. Collins said to tell you there are two groups of them. That Captain Bullock rode up to your house earlier today, but she hadn't seen Captain Kaiser since the day before." Billy added, more quietly, "Bullock killed old man Runyon. Mrs. Collins is afraid they got something bad planned."

Big Bill Hicks, who stood about five feet eight inches tall, knelt down next to his taller nephew. "Let me take a look at that, Billy," he said and untied the bandana. When he saw the scab, he asked Warren to bring him a bucket of water. "We need to wash this out real good, son. It don't look bad, but you got to be careful." He dipped the bandana in the cold water and scrubbed both the entrance and the exit wounds. Billy held his breath, but didn't make any noises. When he'd finished, Big Bill tied the bandana back on. "It's going to be okay, just stay off it as much as possible for a few days."

"We got some jerky left, Little Billy . . . if you're hungry," Warren said. "Not a whole lot, but we can always get more."

Billy nodded his head, then looked around him. "Do you smell something?"

Warren Collins made an elaborate sniffing noise, then shook his head. "Probably just Big Bill. He hasn't had a bath in weeks."

"No. It's smoke," Billy said. "Something's burning."

"I smell it, too, Warren," Big Bill said. "Kaiser and Bullock are up to something."

Warren sniffed again and then turned to Buck Hooks. "You shinny up that tree, Buck, and can see can you spot anything."

Buck moved over to a tall magnolia tree, its limbs spread almost like a ladder, and climbed up. "Damn, they're burning the whole thicket!" he screamed down at them. "Over to the east, about a half mile, it's all ablaze!"

When he got back down, he took a big drink from the bucket. "We gotta get out of here. I saw smoke to north and south, too. They're trying to burn us all."

Already the other men could see clouds of black smoke rising in the east. Big Bill picked his nephew up. "I can walk," Billy said. "Put me down."

"Best thing to do is try to get over to Cypress Creek. We ought to be able to float down to Village Creek and get away from it. You come with me, Little Billy. Carol Ann and Gaylynne would have my hide if anything happened to you." All of the men raced back to the west.

Warren and Billy cut through the woods, walking slowly at first, both knowing the way across to Bad Luck Creek. As they pushed through a cane brake and started up a low hill, they could see the smoke rising in front of them. Billy's foot hurt, but he managed to keep up and followed Warren as he turned back to the right and ducked into heavy undergrowth, the leaves of low scrub trees brushing against their shirts.

The thicket had been dry, though, for months and, as they walked on a small rise between two dried out ponds, the smoke began to burn their eyes. "No one but a fool would start a fire in here when it's like this," Warren told Billy. "It could just as easily turn back on them."

"Not with the wind blowing like this, Mr. Collins," Billy said. "It's coming this way."

The fire made the wind rush even faster past them, the tall pine trees flared up and sparks blew ahead of the fire, starting new fires, flames leaping from tree to tree and, only then, burning down the trunks to reach the undergrowth. The small dry creek beds couldn't stop it and Billy and Warren began to cough as they ran.

"We need to reach Cypress Creek, Billy. That one might be big enough." Warren pulled his own bandana out and tied it over his nose and mouth. "It'll slow down when we're out of the pines. Nothing burns as fast as these big old pine trees. Just a little farther and we'll be into the feeder creek."

It wasn't just the smoke and heat now that were bothering Little Billy Hicks. The noise was deafening, like a hundred steam engines all racing together through the thicket. His skin was pinpricked with the hot sparks that raced ahead of the fire and he ran faster. "Jeez, Mr. Collins," he panted, "look at that." He pointed to his left where a black bear, easily 700 pounds, paralleled them through the woods.

"He ain't interested in us, son. Save your breath!" Collins had to shout to make himself heard. "Just a little more. It's right in front of us."

Billy settled into an automatic run. He kept looking to his left. The big bear raced through the thicket, saliva dripping from the sides of its mouth. The sparks that landed on the thick black fur began to stick and the bear screamed in rage. Directly above the bear, a tall hickory flared up, the dry leaves combusting in a flash. The bear rose onto its hind feet, almost as if dogs had cornered it, its eyes blazed red, reflecting the flames behind them. Billy gasped as he saw the bear's coat begin to smoke in the heat, popping and sparking. The last he saw of the bear it was rolling over and over, pushing down small bushes, screaming.

"Over here, Billy!" Warren turned to his right and disappeared over the bank of the small creek. When Billy jumped over, he saw that it was dry, but that Warren was heading in what would have been a downstream direction had there been water in the creek. He was tired. Not just from the run, but from the whole day. He couldn't get the bear out of his mind. He knew Warren and Stace and even his uncle had hunted the big bears up in the hurricane clearing, but this had been different. He could not understand how a man like Bullock, a man who had grown up in the thicket, who knew Buck and the Colllinses and the Hickses, who had hunted with them and fished, had married an Overstreet woman, could deliberately start a fire that would kill his own kin and destroy such a large section of the thicket.

He stumbled on a tree root and fell face down in the dried out mud. Warren raced back and lifted him to his feet. "Hang in there, Billy. There's a hole up ahead a ways."

When they reached the stagnant pond in the middle of the creek, both of them fell more than jumped into it. "Coat yourself with mud," Warren shouted. "And get wet all over. We need to get out of here. There'll be more along the way now."

All Billy wanted to do was sit in the pool, his baked skin now cool, his muscles relaxing, but he could see the birds flying away, hear the roar of the fire. He pulled himself up and staggered out of the water. "Okay, Mr. Collins. I'm ready." He followed Warren back onto the bank of the creek and forced his legs to break into a run. "Not too far, Mr. Collins. Cypress Creek's right around the next bend." He could feel the heat, feel the air being sucked out of him, the mud beginning to cake on his skin. One last effort and he pitched head first into the warm water of the larger creek. Turning he saw Warren, his shirt on fire leap out over the water and thought he could hear the shirt sizzle as the water quenched the small flame.

He swam over to the big man. "We still need to get out of here, Mr.

Collins. I don't fancy getting boiled when the trees go up. Oh, Jesus, Mr. Collins, are you all right?"

"Just tired, Billy. Let's go." Billy followed him as he kicked his legs and went downstream with the current of the larger creek. Floating on his back, he saw the fire jump across the creek, coughed as the smoke filled his throat, but they had broken through. The fire raged on, traveling a full mile beyond Cypress Creek before it reached Village Creek. Maybe the wind changed, there was no rain, but the fire burned itself out.

Three days later, Billy and Warren met with the rest of the men who had been holed up near what was now called Kaiser's Burn-Out along a creek that had earned the name of Bad Luck. It had been bad luck for Big Bill Hicks, for Dumas Overstreet, for old man Runyon, for a half dozen men who had had no desire to fight on the side of the Confederacy.

Thousands of acres of the thicket had been burned down by Kaiser and his men and Warren Collins still couldn't put a shirt on, the cloth hurt his burned skin too much. The reason the men all gathered was to hear Warren Collins read a letter that had arrived from Galveston. "On June 2, 1865, we received word here in Galveston that General Robert E. Lee has surrendered at Appomatox. The war is over."

Billy was quiet as the men around him began to shout. He turned away and walked back into the woods. He sat down next to Bad Luck Creek and dipped his feet into the water. "It was already over," he said out loud. "There never was a need for Kaiser to burn the thicket."

When the other men went back home to their families, Little Billy, now simply Bill, sat alone by the creek. The sun went down, but he continued to sit quietly. Nothing seemed really worth it. His father had been killed earlier in the war up in Tennessee and his mom had died much earlier. Now his Uncle Big Bill was gone. But if his uncle's death was useless because it happened after the war was over, how much more useful had been the death of his father? None of it mattered, only the thicket and that would grow back, maybe not in his lifetime, at least not that part that everyone had already started calling

Kaiser's Burn-Out.

He looked up and, through the hickory branches and the sweetgum, he saw the stars, bright and flickering, not a cloud in sight. ❀

TAKE ME TO THE WATER

by Bernestine Singley

Elfin McEachern cut his eyes to the right when he heard one of the boys sitting halfway down the pew behind him raise a howl, but he knew better than to turn his head. He didn't want to get in trouble with Grandma Annie. Neither did he want to see anyone doing anything that he really felt like doing or he just might do it too and then he'd really get in trouble.

Elfin and four other seven-year olds were lined up on the front pew waiting to be baptized at the evening service. The twins were holding hands and staring straight ahead. Dinky Cato was weeping quietly. Every now and then, he would close his mouth, sniff real hard and drag snot back up his nose. But as soon as he dropped his bottom lip and started breathing again, his little trail of slime began its slow descent.

Elise Mitchell leaned forward to get a better view of the howling boy sitting a few spaces down from her in the middle of the nine-year olds. She glared her disapproval and reached up, tugging a huge pink-flowered bouffant-style shower cap down over her ears and letting it snap into place.

Suddenly, the howling stopped. Elise smiled. Her smallest finger crept beneath the plastic cap's lace-lined elastic edge and scratched daintily along her temple. The howling boy cranked up again, a spasm of hiccups occasionally interrupting his braying. Elise turned a deaf ear as both her hands methodically worked their way around her head, scratching furiously. It was all unsettling to Elfin. Plus, now he had to pee.

If Lolly Redfern, Elfin's best friend, had been sitting next to him, he would have felt a lot better.

As it was, Lolly was already up there, firmly in Rev. Clemmon's grip, raising Cain, thrashing and flailing trying desperately to get loose. She was soaking wet and so was he even though she was the first Candidate for Baptism and he hadn't even taken her down yet. Lolly's body glistened, looking for all the world as though it had been put together from someone else's spare parts. Her sun-browned face and arms stood in stark contrast to the creamy whiteness that stretched from her puny chest down to the tops of her thighs.

Nobody was surprised that Lolly was raising hell. Or that she showed up to be baptized in a chartreuse double-knit bikini. Everybody had a Lolly story and a Lolly story couldn't end until somebody said, "Jes' lak her momma." Then somebody else had to say, "Unh-huh."

The men made their points, always directed towards Elfin, a different way.

"She gone be hard to handle, li'l man. Yes, indeedy!" Or "You thank you gone be able to keep her in line when y'all get married?"

Whenever someone teased him like that, Elfin just smiled sweetly. He sensed that he was being complimented on his choice, but he was not at all certain about whatever else they meant.

Now in the gloom of the Sunday evening service with all of the windows raised and the fans whirring overhead, one long tremor came out of nowhere and slipped through the soles of his feet. It snaked up his skinny little body and spread out, icy, across the top of his head. He sat there shivering on the pew feeling naked as a jay bird in the middle of winter.

Grandma Annie's alto harmonized somewhere behind him, picking him up and carrying him back to the previous night's conversation on the back stoop. It floated up and hung, suspended and heavy, over his head.

"Coloreds ain't safe nowhere," Deacon Beaty volunteered. *"Them crackers ovah theah in Jasper hitched that boy to they pickup and dragged him around 'til they pulled his head and arms clean off."*

"Lak he wurn't no mo' than a June bug or sumpin'," Brother Bohannen agreed.

"And they ain't gone do no time either. We already know that." He straddled his chair, balancing on its two back legs and leaning against the brick wall separating the two apartments sharing a stoop.

"Y'all, hush," Grandma Annie hissed, rolling her eyes first towards the child in her lap and then towards the one at her feet.

"Don't talk like that in front of these children." She wrapped her arms tighter around the small boy sitting in her lap with his back to her chest. Her knees brushed gently from side to side against the little girl whose bent back had stiffened and whose fingers had suddenly stopped twirling the grass at her feet.

"Why not?" Brother Bohannen asked, indignation raising his voice. "Sooner they know, the better."

"Know what?" Grandma Annie shot back. "That black folks scared and white folks crazy? They born knowing that lesson. You can't add nothin' to somethin' that's already full without causin' it tuh spill over."

"Agreed, agreed," Brother Bohannen nodded slowly.

"Tha's perzackly whut ah'm talkin' 'bout. You gotta teach 'em the rest of the lesson, how to protect they'sef when the spillovah spill ovah. They know 'bout the bein' scared part. Now they need to know 'bout protection."

"If God don't protect us, we doomed anyway," Grandma Annie cautioned.

Brother Bohannen brought the kitchen chair down hard on its front legs. Lolly jumped at the sound of metal scraping concrete, then rose to stand between him and Grandma Annie. She leaned into the old woman's muscled rose-scented firmness.

"God! God?!!" Brother Bohannen shouted. "See, there you go agin. First off, you ain't nevah seent yo' God walking nayah street in dis neighborhood. Second, he sent his son down here umpteen years ago and let the crackers kill 'im. "Man cain't take care ah his own flesh and blood, I sho' hell ain' trustin' him tuh take care ah me an' whut's mine." Scuse me fuh the cussin', chil'ren," Brother Bohannen said, his huge paw falling in gentle thuds against Lolly's back. A cloud of black cherry smoke rose from the embers in his pipe and momentarily wrapped itself around them before wafting lazily away.

Deacon Beaty swatted at fireflies with a rolled up copy of "The Blue Street News." He shifted his weight from his foot on the ground to the one on the stoop and waited.

"You ol' fool!" Grandma Annie sputtered. "You ol' infidel!"

"These two young'uns gonna be fine. They done give they life to Christ and tomorrow night, they gone be washed in the blood, gone be white as snow. Caint *nuthin' harm 'em now.*

"You, on the other hand, is a diff'rent story. You already knee deep in Purgatory, but yo' neck so stiff, the devil won't let you see it.

"If you had one eye and half sense, you'd brang yo' heathen ass up in the church and try to git right wif God before it's too late."

A knot grew in Elfin's stomach just beneath Grandma Annie's clasped hands. This was the first he'd heard about being washed in blood and turning white.

He glanced sideways at Lolly. She had climbed into Brother Bohannen's lap and had her head thrown back trying to blow his smoke in different directions. She didn't seem to be bothered one bit by what was, at least for Elfin, this new and startling piece of information.

"C'mon now, y'all," Deacon Beaty pleaded softly.

Brother Bohannen laughed and leaned towards Grandma Annie. "I oughta come jes' to see you sittin' up somewhere in some church. What is it anyhoo? Second time maybe since that boy was born that you even set foot in a church? Now you tryin' to sound lak you da bride of Christ or something. Yup, that right theah all by itse'f would be wor'f a trip to church!"

"A little child shall lead them!" someone screamed a few pews behind Elfin, snatching him back to the matter at hand.

Lolly's whimpering had changed pitch. She looked completely spent and sagged against the preacher.

Rev. Clemmons beamed out at the congregation, nearly smug at having finally wrestled his wriggling charge into submission. His right temple throbbed, his blood percolating along the big vein that ran from the side of his head, down his neck, and disappeared underneath his starched white collar.

For the fourth time that night, Rev. Clemmons released his grip on Lolly and raised his right hand to God. He started his prayer again.

"Door by whom to God we come, the light, the truth, the way. The stony, rocky path we trod; Lord, teach us how to pray."

The children on the bench bowed their heads and knotted their fingers, limp from relief, grateful that they had just been bestowed, at the very least, a fifteen-minute reprieve.

"Yes, Lord." "Praise God." "Sweet Jesus. Do, Jesus. Do, Sweet Jesus." Lolly hiccuped.

Even though his head was bowed, Elfin watched Lolly through eyes so squinted they fluttered from the strain. He waited, confident that he would not watch her suffer and fail to render aid.

Rev. Clemmons droned on.

"This evening, our Heavenly Father, once more and again, we. . . ."

Suddenly, Lolly folded from the waist, pulling Rev. Clemmons forward and off-balance. He caught her just in time to keep her from falling face first into the water. For a moment, she hung over his left arm like a pair of worn trousers.

Suddenly Elfin's eyes flew wide open and Lolly, upside down, locked in on him with laser precision.

"Faaaaatherrrrr!" Rev. Clemmons, face suffused with victory, crowed his praises even louder. Grandma Annie began softly singing the hymn for the occasion.

"Take me to the water, take me to the water, take me to the waaaaaterrrrr to be baptized. None but the righteous, none but the riiiiighteous, none but the riiiigtheous shall see God. . . ."

Lolly straightened up so fast you could hear the air move. She smashed the back of her head into Rev. Clemmons' chest, bounced off him, and dived into the water.

"Umph. . .!" Rev. Clemmons' breath left him in a whoosh as he crashed backwards into the pool. His white robe fanned out around him, keeping him afloat and giving them all a notion for the very first time of what a black angel might look like.

Lolly surfaced, coughing and sputtering, just out his reach at the other end of the pool and scrambled over the side. When she hit the floor, her toe caught on the carpet that had been rolled back from over the pulpit. She kicked herself free, rolled over three times and came to a stop on her feet directly in front of Elfin.

Elfin's hand closed over hers and the two of them bolted down the aisle.

Grandma Annie's eyes were sealed against the events unfolding around her. Bent on securing the protection of the Almighty for Elfin and Lolly, she threw herself into the second verse again for good measure.

"None but the righteous, none but the righteous, none but the righteous shall see God."

The children burst into the hot summer night and stopped at the church steps. Lolly peeled off her bikini top and dropped it at her feet. She sat down, patting a place next to her on the steps. Elfin lowered himself beside her.

They sat for a moment in silence, surveying the scene. As the strains of the hymn died down to a wordless hum, Eflin stood and pulled his white choir robe over his head, and folded it neatly. When he sat back down, he placed it in his lap and rested his elbows on his knees, his chin in his cupped hands.

"You scared of the water," he said sympathetically, not looking at Lolly.

"No, boy!" she said indignantly. "You know I can swim."

"Why then?" Elfin persisted.

Lolly shook her head. Her wet hair whipped the sides of her face and flung water in every direction. Elfin wiped dry his ear nearest her.

"'Cause I didn't wanna get my hair wet."

"Oh."

"Here," Lolly fumbled along the waist band of her bikini and pulled out a stick of Juicy Fruit chewing gum which she tore into two equal pieces. She popped her piece in her mouth.

Elfin carefully scraped off the bits of silver foil and yellow paper that clung to the dampened gum. When he was satisfied with his work, he rolled the gum between his fingers and then stuck it in his mouth. He curled his tongue around the sweetness.

Brother Bohannen stepped out of the shadows of the weeping willow branches that kissed the ground in some places even as the tree trunk leaned away from the church. For a moment, it seemed as though he were laughing at them above his pipe. Then with a kind but stern voice, he turned to Elfin.

"Son," he said, "I think we better have a talk." Lolly stuck her fingers in her ears. Brother Bohannen leaned over and, taking each of her hands in his, removed them from her ears.

"Miss Lolly," he whispered, "go git yo' clothes on and we'll walk you home. Go on, now."

Then he planted her fingers back in her ears and started up the stairs towards the door. When she recovered enough to take aim with her most deadly eye daggers, he winked.

The church door shut behind them, leaving Elfin and Brother Bohannen standing face to face alone in the dimly lit vestibule.

Finally the old man broke the silence.

"Looks lak it's time for you to gone back inside and face the music, son," Brother Bohannen advised, his lips opening and closing around his pipe stem

Elfin pulled his robe over his head and smoothed out the front. He reached for the door, then paused. He could feel the old man standing close behind him, could smell black cherry and Old Spice mingling a few feet in the air directly above him.

Elfin cocked his head back and a little to the side and opened the door to the sanctuary. When he headed down the aisle, Brother Bohannen followed a few steps behind. ✿

A HEAVY HAND

by Charlie McMurtry

By the time I was twenty-four years old, I was a young rancher in a business dominated by old-timers, like Dad. Oh, there were a few young cowboys around, but not any young ranchers. Most of the sons of area ranchers found better ways of making a living.

Dad was a small, slim man with a booming voice and a giant reputation as an honest, dependable, hard-working manager. He demanded a lot of himself and every bit that much from me. Dad enjoyed good health, other than the usual broken bones from cowboy mishaps over the years, right up until he had a stroke, the summer when he was seventy-three. I was left pretty much alone running the ranch, though he made me come by the house twice a day, every day, to report on things. By calf-shipping time in late September, he was getting around good using a walker and had begun to drive himself places again. The afternoon before I was to weigh and ship the calves, Dad said he'd be there the next morning in plenty of time to witness everything. I said we'd be looking for him.

Long before daylight the next morning, I was stuffing Rolaids in my mouth three at a time. My baby had the colic and cried most of every night, and between her, my wife, Dad, and the ranch, I wasn't getting a whole lot of rest.

By sunup, we had penned the cows and calves and were separating them in preparation for weighing the calves. I was sitting on my horse, watching the work and thinking about what needed to be done next when Dad drove up. He stopped near the livestock scale house, and I watched him drag his walker and a cane out of the back of his pickup. He ambled over to the shade of the scale house and watched us.

We had to separate the steer and heifer calves then, since ranch custom dictated that steers and heifers are weighed separately. Steers customarily sold for three dollars per hundred pounds more than heifers, so since they were worth more money, they were weighed first; it was that simple.

Everything was going according to plan when I noticed Dad standing next to the corral fence, waving his cane at me. I stopped the work, as I was right in the middle of it then, and rode over to see what he wanted. I got off of my horse and looked through the fence at him.

"What do you want, Dad?" I asked.

"What are you doing?" he replied.

I took off my hat and wiped the dust from my forehead, puzzled. He could see what we were doing, and he knew that I knew how to do it.

"Dad, we're separating the steers and heifers right now," I said, "and then we'll be ready to weigh." I got back on my horse and as I turned back to the work, I noticed the tense set of his jaw. I'd seen that look a thousand times, but I rode on off while he made his way back to the shade of the scale house. I looked back once and he was talking to our neighbor, G. C., and the calf buyer, Doug Brown. G. C. would do the weighing as a neutral party, even though he was Dad's good friend.

We finished separating the steers and heifers, and Wayne and I got ready to run a bunch of steers onto the scales. Wayne worked for a neighboring ranch and had been close friends with Dad and me for years. We were talking, waiting on G. C., when Dad made his way to the fence again.

"What are you about to do?" he asked, looking straight at me.

I simply couldn't understand why he'd ask a question like that twice within an hour when he knew damn well what I was about to do.

"Dad, we're going to weigh the steers and then we'll weigh the heifers," I said, "like we always do." Wayne edged a little closer to hear what was going on.

Dad stood there, looking back and forth between me and the steers for a minute, thinking.

"Was there something you wanted me to do first, Dad?" I asked.

Dad looked right at me. "Yes, by God there is," he said. "I want you to weigh the heifers first."

I honestly didn't believe it. The morning was going so well. I was sure

I'd heard him wrong, so I leaned over the top rail, closer to him.

"You want me to do what?" I asked again.

"I said, I want you to weigh the heifers first," Dad repeated, and he began pointing his cane in various directions, indicating how he wanted me to move the stock around.

"Take these steers out of this pen and put the heifers in to be weighed first," he commanded.

I looked to Wayne for help, but he just shook his head. There wasn't any explaining this move. Before we could make a move, G. C. and Mr. Brown walked up.

"Okay, we're ready," G. C. said, "what's the holdup?"

Dad looked annoyed but turned to address G. C.

"I told John that I want to weigh the heifers first," Dad said. "They're going to have to move the cattle around, so it'll be a few more minutes." There were several minutes of awkward silence as Dad's order soaked in. No one knew what to say. No rancher ever weighed heifers first. Mr. Brown looked embarrassed, but didn't say a word. The longer the steers milled around in the pens, losing weight, the less they would cost him. G. C. was stunned but didn't say anything.

I made a mighty effort to control my temper. I didn't understand why Dad was insisting on this, but I thought that I was old enough to deserve an answer.

"Dad, do you mind if I ask why you want to weigh the heifers first?" I asked. "We've always done it the other way."

Dad drew himself up as close to me as he could get. He had all of our attention.

"By God, because I said to weigh the heifers first," he said, "and that's all the reason you need."

I just looked at him but didn't know what else to say. Directly Wayne motioned for me to get on with the work, and we did exactly what Dad said to do.

"Why did Dad do that?" I asked Wayne sometime later as we sat waiting to weigh another pen of heifers.

"I don't know," Wayne replied. "It sure didn't make any sense to me."

"It didn't make any sense to anybody," I said. "He was wrong."

"Yeah, he was," Wayne said, "but that doesn't change anything."

My heart was pounding in anger and defeat.

"Everybody here knew it was wrong," I said, to no one in particular. "Goddamn right he was wrong. I know he was wrong, and I'm damned tired of it."

"He's an old man, John," Wayne said, trying to make another excuse for Dad.

"So what?" I nearly screamed. "That's all the more reason he has to be glad that I know how to do this ranching shit."

We put another bunch of calves on the scales, and I looked over at Dad. He was laughing and talking about something with Mr. Brown, oblivious to me, my anger, my feelings.

"Look at him, Goddamit!" I cursed. "Would you just look? It's like nothing has happened."

"Goddamn him!" I said one more time, nearly screaming. "There's not one son-of-a-bitching thing I can do." I felt that my chest would burst.

Wayne had not said a word, letting me work off steam. We'd been through this sort of thing many times.

"Why don't you quit this life, John?" Wayne asked. He'd not suggested that possibility before, not in all the times that things like this had happened.

"Hell," Wayne went on, "you got a college degree. Do something else. Quit this shit!"

I thought about that a minute. "Wayne, I quit football one time because I thought that Dad needed me to help him. I couldn't figure any other reason why he didn't encourage me to play. You know what he said?"

"No, but I can guess," he replied.

"Dad said that he didn't plan on raising any Goddamn quitters," I said. "That's what he told me."

We let it go for a few minutes, giving our attention to the work. I calmed down, but something had happened.

"John, I don't think that anybody would call it quitting," Wayne said. "Just think about it."

"Yeah, I'll think about it," I said.

Nothing else happened that morning. Nothing else could have happened. We finished the weighing, loaded the trucks with the calves, and the neighbors went home. Dad left while I was closing the gates and seeing that things were put in order. I couldn't get my mind off what Wayne said about doing something else for a living. I couldn't believe that I'd never thought of it, but I hadn't.

Then again, maybe that was easy for Wayne to say. He didn't come from a family that had produced nine ranchers, Dad being the last until I came along. I was good at what I did, real good, and sometimes even I believed that. I unsaddled my horse and put my saddle in the old barn. I was just going through the motions, not really seeing the ground, and things were sort of blurred, as I grabbed the handle of the heavy barn door and slammed it shut one more time. ❁

THE PARSON'S TALE

by Paul Christensen

Beauregard Parson was the last of the Parsons and lived in the old family mansion on the east side of town. He was elderly and frail and had a big Mexican woman look after him on the week days. Cooking was little trouble for her, since he had reduced his diet to a grapefruit in the morning, and shirred eggs for dinner. He hardly touched his food, even at that, and slept most of the time. But he was particular about his clothing and kept up old family traditions by dressing for morning coffee, changing for afternoon tea on the porch, and getting into a dark suit and tie for supper. It taxed the energies of Maria Sanchez, the maid, who regretted ever taking employment at the Parson house. She would have preferred working at the Crestview Nursing Home, where her sister was a night nurse. It would have been less trouble.

Mr. Parson, though elderly and fragile as a wren's egg, was vigilant and perversely detailed, and insisted on the uniformity of his ways. He caught her every evasion and delinquent act and would make her crawl from the vexations of his tongue. He was a powerful talker and knew what rasping, hissing phrase would wither her with shame and revulsion. They needed each other, for the one was half the human body, and the other completed it to make an individual.

Beauregard Thrustle Parson was not always that way. When he started out at the Parson Lumber Company as a young college graduate, a powerfully knit man with a wide brow and penetrating eyes, the town was younger and brighter, and business was good. It was war time, and the government was building an airfield up the road, requiring lots of lumber and hardware, which Parson Lumber was only too eager to provide. His older brother and his two elderly uncles stood behind the wrought iron windows of the main office, dressed alike in striped shirts and black sleeve garters, green visors slung down raffishly over their foreheads, with a glass-sided hand-cranked Burroughs adding machine to compute their customer accounts.

The girls would make up any excuse to buy thumbtacks and a six-inch rule just so Beauregard would count out the change in their palms and touch their hands with his finger-ends. Beauregard was busy, but he took the time to wait on each of Bryan's fair daughters, and they came at least once or twice a week to giggle, blush, and stammer their requests.

Beauregard was a Parson, and the Parson men were known for their solidity, long life, and good manners. They were also known to be covert in their evening and week-end hours and reluctant to socialize. The Parson house windows were closely draped after sundown, and lights blazed only in the foyer and on the porches as the sign of their civic obligation. But the world could intrude no further on Parson intimacy.

Old man Parson, Eusebius Hoyle Parson, started the company during the Civil War, when Texas became the safe keeper of Confederate cotton, cattle, and slaves to be returned after victory. Alas, those goods never went east again, but stayed in the hands of certain ranchers along the major river valleys, and their new owners acquired such wealth and prestige as to create the aristocracy of present-day Texas.

The maintenance of the newly elite Texans during Reconstruction involved considerable building and expansion of humble abodes, which fell to the class below, which included the Parsons of Brazos County. Their claim to the piney woods of the Big Thicket made certain Parson Lumber would never run out of Number 2 yellow pine and Ponderosa long-grain for the making of Victorian mansions and the floors of second and third stories, where oak was unnecessary.

The Parsons thrived in the 1870's, expanded in the 1880's, and came to be the lumber kings of the Gilded Age and the first decades of the American century. Mr. Eusebius Hoyle Parson drove the first automobile to stir the dust of Bryan's Main Street, to the accompaniment of the Agricultural College marching band, and the megaphone-aided voice of the mayor, Thad Clemner, Jr., Eusebius, and his son, Clayton, a youth tending to obesity, were pillars of Bryan society, and when Beauregard

Thrustle joined their ranks a generation later, the house of Parson supplied enough pillars to hold up the Parthenon.

It would have been a great family had the Parsons understood women better. But the unhappy relations of Parson men and their wives allowed the town to get its ear between the cracks of the Parson front door, and to glimpse the flaws, the hair-line cracks riddling the otherwise stout supports of town principles.

It all began with Eusebius, who married a Shackley of Madisonville, a dynasty of cattle breeders known for their Scottish bulls. The flower of Shackley husbandry, Elvira Mason, brought to the Parson blood line a love of horses and fine food and elegant social life. She insisted on these amenities as the essentials of her survival.

In time, after many slights and misunderstandings, the once vibrant and flushed Elvira grew hollow and thorny. Her duty to the Parsons was fulfilled in her first boy, Clayton Winston, whom she foaled at the end of her seventeeth year, hardly nine months into the marriage. The boy's pudgy yellow flesh never lost its pallor. Some thirty years later, she was made to yield a second son, Beauregard, and died in childbirth. Missus Elvie was buried quietly, and no other woman graced the halls while Eusebius was patriarch.

But the town knew more than it let on. It had information that would have piqued the curiosity of Charles Dickens, had he come through town on his national lecture tour. It seems Eusebius had a roving eye for the shop girls and would take one out to his little country house over the river, to spend a few riotous hours over brandy and the gramophone, high-stepping with his young Mazie or Lovie-Sue, and come home pink-eyed and short-tempered. Elvira suffered her humiliation in private.

Clayton knew of his father's nocturnal romps and had crept up one evening to observe first hand the wild gyrations of his father as he swung round the front room of his rustic cabin, clutching the fingers of his pig-tailed mistress, her skirts flying above her knees, her Mexican boots scattering glitter. The old man's mouth was cracked with smiles, the wattles of his throat red as a rooster's. Clayton watched and wished dearly his old tormentor would meet his end in such degrading acts. But in truth, these capers on the rag rug invigorated him.

It taught Clayton the virtue of indifference, and the art of living peacefully between the lord and the devil. On Sundays, no one prayed with more pious fervor than Eusebius or sung more emphatically over the drones of his townsmen. Or concealed his whiskey breath with a lozenge of slippery elm and a jigger of mint water.

Clayton would never be the same man his father was. He was unattractive to women, and his manners were those of a man who could not restrain his lust for food or drink. After Eusebius passed away in his sleep one night at the age of ninety-three, Clayton was heir and successor of the family seat at fifty-three. Business was not as good under his direction, and there were rivals getting footholds in the building trades. He looked for new markets and invested for a time in a Japanese company that made prefabricated cottages. But Texans are slow to adapt to changes in the local architecture, and the thought of building a domicile from the contents of a truck, and of unwrapping rooms and roof from paper cartons caused many a chin to be rubbed and eyes to crinkle. Clayton's experiment came to be known as "Jap cabins," and "dog palaces." A man bought up the unsold kits and established a nudist colony in the woods.

Clayton aged and became a dull old man in a few years. He seldom went out, but began answering the door to a stout woman who passed herself off as a family relation. She came from Dallas, and wore large topaz rings and old-fashioned necklaces. She drove a big Dodge sedan with a sun visor over the windshield and smelled of patchouli. She would stand on the porch wearing a flouncy dress and straw hat and enter the house looking over her shoulder. Finally, Clayton moved her in, and she parked the car in the big triple garage at the back. The shades remained pulled day and night, and no one saw much of Mrs. Zeba Canterbury after that.

When Clayton ate his last fritter this side of the Jordan, Mrs. Canterbury wept loudly in the First Baptist Church. She became uncontrollable upon discovering Clayton bequeathed to her not one nail, screw, or scrap of yellow pine to compensate her for unstinting affection. She went away as she had come, with a yellow valise and the big gray Dodge.

Whereupon Beauregard Thrustle Parson raised his scepter over a shrinking kingdom of pine and bins of galvanized brads. The world was growing complicated, and merchants had matured to the point of monopolizing markets through chain stores and discount hardware outlets. The men of Parson Lumber stood vigil at their grilled windows, awaiting orders from an empty foyer.

Beauregard was young, a man with vision. He bid cheap on supplying the university's construction projects. He began to win some bids, to elbow out rivals from Houston and Fort Worth, who would take a loss to get a foot in the door. He bid to the bone, and gave himself profit margins of 2% or less. He hired more men to cut wood and bought a flat-bed hauler for bringing wood up from his yards in Cut-and-Shoot. He hired young men from the college to stand at the windows, and he discovered being behind the times appealed to the community. People liked ordering screws by the ounce, watching a young man dig a metal scoop into a bin, weigh the screws on an old Fairbanks scale, and ring up the charge on a noisy brass-bound register. Bells rang, and handles cranked, scoops crunched up nails by the half pound, and little bags came through the grills bearing hinges, dowels, molly bolts, and picture wire. The old carpenters came in overalls caked with sawdust and chewed plug waiting to purchase several hundred running feet of white pine. The town lost its past, but here stood a final oasis of nostalgia and good feeling, and older white men came for the privilege of being served in the old way.

The money trickled back into the coffers of the Parson bank accounts. The old mansion received new gingerbread on eaves and dormers and fresh paint on the orioles and sleeping porch. Painters worked all summer on the trimwork in and out of the house; the floor sander spent a month sanding away the grit and dullness of two generations. A dark blue porch graced the front, and white trim deepened the expensive luster of gray shingle on the exterior walls. The tall windows were reglazed, and cracked panes replaced. The front door was painted blood red, and louvered green shutters enclosed the elegant entry. A new wrought iron fence surrounded the spacious grounds.

Beauregard accepted the patriarchal mantle with grace and dignity and lived alone as the town's most eligible bachelor.

The girls who had come to be served by him when young were the women who eyed him now from their pews at the front of church. He came and went, noticed by a dozen females who chose to wait rather than accept more common clay for husbands. A Parson was a sliver of nobility, a piece of the Old South, something to elevate the common names of the town. And the common names pursued him as far as they dared. Someone got the novel idea of sending him flowers for his birthday, and received a note of thanks with breathless interest. Another called him for his advice and lured him out to the country club for tennis. But he was a poor player and went away ashamed of all the balls he had pitched into the woods.

Others would drift by his house and hope to glimpse him on his mower, tearing around the apple trees in the side yard. He made a dashing figure in his white shorts and blue tee shirt, an old cowboy hat slung back from his forehead, shocks of blond hair tufting from the rim. His teeth were white and straight and his smile made a few hearts jump. There he was, slyly observing the pace of certain automobiles driven by familiar women. He watched them go out of sight.

When a good housekeeper was needed at the Parson house, the news drifted through the shady streets and girls wondered how best to put the matter of their interest. Clearly a housekeeper was beneath their stature, but the lure of his company was almost stronger than their pride. But not quite. In the end, he settled the town's nerves by allowing a young cadet from the college to provide him with valet service. The boy, hardly eighteen years of age, thin as a bean pole, with a gap in his front teeth, caused no brows to rise. The old men at the court house seemed satisfied that this Mr. Parson was better than the others and lived soundly.

The drapes were not closed anymore, but revealed through thin gauze inner curtains a calm interior of dark furnishings, a few candles over dinner, a boy rushing about in his white shirt and tie with a tray for coffee. The grounds glistened from all the attention paid to watering and rose-trimming, lawn rolling, and seeding. Not a single gray or blue weed shot up out of the cropped heads of the Augustine grass. The monkey grass was tight as little fists bordering the front walk. The aspidistra made a green sea around the mulberry trees.

And the Parson Hardware and Lumber Co., Inc., stood on its old footings on lower Main, dominating one corner of an otherwise sleepy, indolent, backward part of town. Cars still came that way but only to park in front of Parson's long enough to procure an odd weight of nail or some peculiarly threaded wood screw unavailable in the chain stores. Otherwise, business was now conducted by phone and fax machine from an ice-cold inner office, and the trucks went out from a depot on the far side of town. The old Parson headquarters kept up appearances from a century before, but only for show.

Beauregard was known as Beau by his friends, and he began to socialize with other East Siders, as they were called. Small cocktail parties were the fashion of the time, and men and women stood on the round porches of the Parson house, sipping tall drinks and taking wafers of cheese and salmon from the tray passed around by the young cadet, whom everyone called Barry. Barry smiled, bowed, said sir and ma'am, and ingratiated himself to a crowd of lawyers, doctors, the police chief, and the taxidermist, and their wives. Barry fascinated the younger women who found him graceful and mannerly. They thought of him for their daughters, and several times he was invited to other houses for a cup of tea and crustless sandwiches, while the new Elviras of the gentry entertained in organdy dresses or pedal pushers.

One such young woman, herself eighteen, a first year student at Baylor Women's College to the north, noted the blankness of Barry's attention when her mother left the room. He seemed to go stiff and cold, and only to thaw in her company. She detected a certain jaded streak in the young man's attitude, as if he had grown up only in the company of older women. She wondered if he were having affairs with women of her mother's generation and decided to keep her eye on him.

But Barry was clever and elusive. He was seen rarely and spent most of his time conveying a silver coffee urn up the stairs to his employer and out in the garages simonizing the Parson sedan and the new red roadster. The women lost touch with him, and the Parson house drifted slowly back to its private ways of before. Barry stayed on after graduation and wore a dark suit and bolo tie, and roper boots. He drove the car for Mr. Parson, as he called his employer, and they went off to Round Top to listen in the front row of seats to the piano pyrotechnics of Mr. James Dick, virtuoso. The two were seen on the Brazos in a canoe by a group of girls headed for Austin. They had stopped to gaze down from the bridge on Route 21 only to find the silver canoe glancing off the muddy waters with two men pulling oars, the one slender and erect, handsome and aging, Beau Parsons, and the other, slumped in his seat, dabbling at his steering oar, young Barry.

"You don't suppose," said a reedy young Jennifer Slaughter, and looked off.

Kimberly Larson looked down again and thought aloud to herself, "I do very well suppose, Jenny."

Others had observed the two men together walking the grounds of Peaceable Kingdom, and on that same afternoon, touring the Anson Jones cabin at Washington on the Brazos. They were mistaken for father and son by a guide, and Beau Parson's neighbor, Mr. Allen, heard Barry correct the man and say they were friends, not relations.

"Friends," Mr. Allen said, over dinner that night. "Can't imagine Beauregard tolerating the airs of that young man boasting of friendship when he is merely in the man's employ." His wife was busy serving her son and daughter and ignored the remark. She had a thought but it could wait.

Workers appeared one morning in a large moving van and spent the morning staggering down a ramp with parts of a complicated assembly they then put together at the end of the enclosed porch. The sound of sawing and hammering went on for days. Then the electrician and plumber showed up and banged around much of a day and left, and finally, a man in a jump suit came and consulted his clip board, tried switches, had lunch and then dinner in the house, and left late in his van. The next day the mailman noticed two men sitting in a Jacuzzi reading newspapers and sipping coffee from little espresso cups. He shared his observation with the television repair man who was eager to pass his information along to the termite control man, who in turn gave it to the meter reader. And each passed the word to the houses they served and the town's eyes lowered halfway.

The Parson house became a curiosity again, and strollers slowed a little to catch a glimpse of the porch or the shadow of men moving about inside. The drapes came down and the enclosed porch was fitted with expensive awnings that hung down low. The lawn boy had the only privileged perspective into the house on Saturday mornings, now that Beau and Barry chose not to be so public in the summer.

More young men were hired to man the windows as the older ones graduated to posts in accounting, billing, and purchasing. Always the young men, young Barrys in the making, achingly green boys from the college with thick arms and tanned faces, who were permitted in the hotter parts of summer to wear shorts and canvas sneakers, and tight-fitting tee shirts. They were the darlings of the new generation of girls, who flocked to the Parson foyer to dawdle, and pretend to shop, and to giggle silently as the boys scoured their bins for the mate to an obscure tack or small screw. The girls ogled and blushed and turned coy as the boys wrote their names on the back of the receipt and hoped for phone calls. Sometimes they were rewarded, sometimes not.

An imperceptible shift occurred in the Parson clientele. The old guard no longer came around for its supplies but drove on to Sears and got their package of nails or screws. Beau Parson was dropped off the social list and sold his membership in the country club. His position in the town remained coveted; his views were quoted in the newspaper, and his thoughts recorded carefully in the minutes of a dozen committees reporting to the mayor. He attended graduation exercises at the college and several times delivered the commencement address, proclaiming the virtues of integrity, service, and the American way. He received standing ovations and accepted the flowers from the hands of pretty co-eds newly admitted to the once all-male school.

Beau was still guest of honor at the Black and White Ball, and the favorite sidekick of the mayor on parade day, and at Juneteenth ceremonies at the north end of town. His portrait hung in city hall, and in the hallway of the insurance company. Beau had lost favor with the females, but the men continued as if he had not broken step in their grand march. He could have recovered female favor had he worked at it, but pride and stubbornness prevented him from kneeling to them. Then fate intervened.

The long summer ended in a blaze of autumn torpor, scorching trees and flower beds and browning lawns down to their roots. The cotton crop failed, and a plague of grasshoppers worked its way up from the bottoms into the prairies and over the last green shoots of the town. September roasted the little brown grid of Bryan until the dogs and cats lay flat on porches, and children cowered inside playing cards, drinking large tumblers of Kool Aid.

The Parson roadster was wheeled out and the top folded down behind the leather seats. The trunk was loaded with beach ware, inflatable mattress, old linen bedspread, a picnic basket, cooler with two bottles of champagne and sandwiches, and a kit full of sunbathing creams and lotions. Beau sat beside Barry as they roared out under the town's gaze, heading for Galveston. Someone had the leisure and interest to get behind them and tag along quietly.

The red roadster bounced over the country roads to the highway and sped gracefully to Houston and wound around its tangle of beltways out to the marsh flats along the coast. A few beach houses stood up on stilts beside the struggling palms. Farther along, salt grass grew thick and driveways of white gravel wound up through dusty undergrowth to hidden estates. The gates stood well back from the road and required a code to open them. The roadster swung into one and disappeared, and the follower parked down the road.

A path headed the same direction as the driveway, and the curious follower raised his arms above the saw-edged grass and made his way toward the sound of rock music. The fence was high, but torn near the ground, and by crawling commando-style through the hole, the follower got inside, obscured by masses of japonica, mesquite, yaupon and a wilderness of thorny shrubs. Flashes of an emerald pool guided him to the edge of the estate, to a vision he had not thought to encounter. There were dozens of men standing on a putting-green lawn with drinks in their hands, naked and wearing little crowns of laurel in their hair. Other men played badminton, their naked bodies glinting with sweat as they leapt about, laughing and batting a shuttlecock without skill. More naked men swam leisurely in the long oval pool, occasionally hugging and kissing, and throwing water about.

It was a small Greek isle of manly lovers, served by other naked men who carted heavy trays of drinks and went to each with refills. The rock music came out of expensive speakers, and purred a precise, low music that enclosed the scene with luxurious artificiality. The man watched closely, memorizing faces, noting the kissing, the rubbing of buttocks, the dancing that broke out sporadically to laughter and a drink broken on the patio. Couples roamed around arm in arm, or holding each other by the waist. Others paused in conversation to lean over and stroke a face or kiss the lips.

From a side door came Beau and Barry, naked, wearing flowers in their hair. They tilted their heads together and embraced by the pool. The little man took out his camera and snapped photos. When he was done, he withdrew into the tangles of shrub and got back to his car. He drove home slowly to Bryan, stopping off at the Chamber of Commerce to use the dark room. He worked carefully over the developing pans breathless with excitement, and then the naked men began appearing in the photo paper, their bleached bodies darkened at the crotch, their faces bending to kiss, hands reaching over shoulders to embrace. Beau stood sideways, then frontally, then with his body pressed up against Barry, their drinks held delicately at arm's length not to spill.

It was all there, the horror, the fearful abundance of sin and outrage. The negatives were placed in the wall safe, and the prints cropped and put into an envelope and taken to the mayor's office. The mayor, called out of a bridge game with his wife and the Bryan Reading Club members, sat down in his meeting room with the shades pulled up. It was still twilight, bright enough to read a newspaper.

He was given the envelope and cleared his throat. He looked up at Mr. Thompson, the follower, with pity. "Is it that bad, Reggie?"

"Badder than that, Mr. Mayor," he said, his voice flat with righteousness.

"Bad as all that, eh?" the mayor said, sliding his envelope knife along the flap. "Well how the hell bad can that be, I wonder," he said, licking his finger and pulling out the photos. They were turned the wrong way and he flipped one over. He whistled, then he turned another. "Holy Christ Amighty, if that ain't Rome burning all over again," he said quietly. "Neros everywhere."

"Neros? Hell, there ain't no Neros, ain't no negros, either. Just old Beau and his valet, Barry the fairy! Both cavorting around like floozies at Lady T's massage parlor."

"Whole bunch of them buggers," said the mayor, turning over photos and spreading them out on the table. "Whoa, son, this is Sodom and Gomorrah times ten. What in the hell are we going to do about it? If this thing gets out, we'll be tarnished for a thousand years! They'll be laughing at us from here to the Panhandle." He got up and brought two glasses from the kitchen, poured dark bourbon into them and handed one to Reggie Thompson. They sipped and then put their glasses down.

"We can get rid of little Miss Barry, for one," said Reggie. "That's just for starters. A friendly visit to old Beau would be second. He needs to know what a little scorn could do to his business. He could get his little palace charcoaled right down to the waste pipe if he don't play ball with us." He took a pause and studied the mayor. "Remember Jake Thorn out at Sulphur Springs? The boy he took in to live with? Hell, he lasted six days in that little game. Got his house torched in no time, and good riddance. Ain't seen him since."

"Who did that little number?" asked the mayor, pushing the photos around without looking up.

"You don't want to know, your honor. That there's a buried tale," said Reggie carefully.

"Hate to see Beau's place go up, though. It's part of history that old house. Wish he hadn't done this," he said sadly. "But he does need a little instruction on town thinking."

"And you're just the man to teach him," Reggie said, laying a firm hand on the mayor's shoulder. "I suspect you know just how to go about it."

The mayor, short, with a large head, and mild dark eyes, gazed about him after Reggie left. The room had grown golden and mellow in the dying heat. The sound of children splashing in a pool made him shrug off his heaviness and pour another drink. He sat at the end of the polished table drumming his nails on the wood, whistling an aimless tune, thinking of how he would approach Beau.

Later that evening the mayor was shown into the Parson house by Barry, who wore a terrycloth robe and a towel wrapped around his head. He apologized for his appearance, but said he had come down from his shower to answer the door. He didn't know the mayor would be coming. Beau was in the long, dimly lit living room reading in a leather chair. He was dressed in a blue suit and tie, and stood up formally.

The mayor took a seat and set down his drink of whiskey on the table beside him. Beau studied his face with interest, looking him up and down.

"I don't recall a visit from the mayor since my daddy's time," said Beau. "It must be important," said Beau, smiling. "All the same you're very welcome."

"It is a matter of some . . . of some unpleasantness, I think," said the mayor. He was looking around the room at the portraits of the family, oil paintings of Eusebius Hoyle, Clayton rendered in merciless detail by a painter who could have counterfeited Francis Bacon, and a romantic full-length portrait of Beauregard standing on a bluff over the Brazos River. A smaller oil surprised the mayor, a face beaming boyishly in cadet uniform bearing the likeness of Barry, which hung in a corner behind the grand piano. The patriarchs were lined up on a wall that would have been visible from the street.

"I have always confronted unpleasantness head on," said Beauregard in a leisurely drawl. "I hope I am not too late and that it is still in the bud."

"Budded out, I'm afraid, a regular blossom of trouble, son," said the mayor slowly. "Seems someone has been taking an uncommon interest in your private life and has come to the conclusion your morals are less than they should be."

"Go on."

"This fellow citizen discovered you in an embarrassing situation down on the coast, at some sort of party where other men were present, behaving in a manner that was less than dignified."

"You mean what, exactly?" asked Beauregard, sipping his sherry.

"I mean strutting about among catamites and fairies of all stripes, and there are photographs to prove it."

"This citizen, as you say, took pictures? He must have gotten through the gate properly and had the code. That would suggest he was himself a member of the party. I couldn't imagine a man like that daring to trespass onto private property to get such pictures. It would require him to burrow under the fence like a pig, in which case you have the evidence of a crime of trespass, and of nothing more. You understand me, don't you Mr. Mayor?"

"I hadn't thought of that. I don't know how he got the pictures, only that they are extremely damaging and would cause you the gravest consequences should this person show them around."

"Yes," said Beauregard thoughtfully. "You have an excellent point. Is this good citizen by any chance Reggie Thompson?"

The mayor took a long, leisurely draw on his whiskey and set the glass down. He patted his knee with his large fingers and smoothed out the crease of his pants where it came down to his knee. "I am not at liberty to divulge names, Beauregard. I am only telling you to look out for yourself, and to improve your private life to avoid destruction. You know the town has no tolerance for such things, not now, not then, not no time. I am here as a friend advising you to mend your ways, or this citizen will take the full measure of his indignation against you."

"Yes, it's Reggie. He burned down someone's house out in Sulphur Springs. I remember reading about it in the papers. He and his pals at the VFW, Scubbie Hughes, and Tommie Blythe, that little gang. Their daddies used to belong to the Klan, if I'm not mistaken. Now they hunt down fairies and burn their property. Nice work, eh? Shall I show you out now, or do you have anything more to say?"

"That's it, Beau. You know, this thing could easily get warped and turn real nasty. That could make it tough to live here, or do business. This community doesn't forget. Hell, it has grudges going back near a hundred years in some cases. Maybe you should consider marrying, Beau. There's lots of gals would take you up in a blink."

"Thanks for coming around," Beau said and showed him to the door. The porch light went out as the mayor edged toward the steps. He felt around in the darkness getting down to the sidewalk. The house sealed itself behind him.

Beau sat in his chair with the drink beside him, preferring the stillness to anything else. He could hear the slough of Barry's slippers overhead, as he put away laundry. It intrigued him to listen to these deliberate little forays to and from the bureau, the drawer dragging open, going shut again, the slippers plodding over to another place to fold, or put away. The closet door, the cabinet, the wicker chest, the tedious array of compartments in which things would have to go. And there were numberless things that came each week from the laundry service, which Barry, in his dutiful way, took care of from an unstinting devotion to domesticity.

Barry was not a woman, and yet he seemed to have distilled whatever is woman into his mind. His mouth was a woman's mouth, his neck was soft and long, almost too tender. But his arms, legs, his waist, his chest were those of a young man, angular and tawny, and rather stiff to the touch. It was difficult at times to pretend altogether that this man in his bed, willing to be whatever kind of lover Beau wanted, was nothing more than a bony kid, not a woman, not a deep lover, not an oasis of desires. Barry was taciturn, inward, perhaps very simple inside his head. The college didn't teach all that much; it was a simple place, and it made simple people come out of it, each greedy for a job, money, a chance to rise a little in the world.

Why did Beau think he loved this human being above him, bending to this drawer, opening that closet, humming to himself? The question was painful to him. It required him to open up, and he chose not to open up often. It was not in the Parson spirit to be frank, or to deal with one's emotions. It was better to let libido erupt and follow it to satisfaction. To think was too French, and to take responsibility too Spanish.

He was from English stock, and what the English had done to womanhood was perhaps the ultimate root of his confusion. A woman in that damp, cloud-heavy island had died out almost altogether, except for her stout legs, round chin, and endless tea drinking. She had been shoved aside so that the slender, rather handsome young men could unabashedly fall in love with each other. They went to little damp schools where they were flogged into a fascination with their own sex, their own raw buttocks and hard little bodies. They tangled up on the rugby field, and found themselves attractive, even lovely on the cricket pitch. And in the showers a certain groping of eyes made one forget to be shy. All this came on the ships bound for Boston, and found their way along the dusty tow paths into the South, or came directly over into Jamestown and then dispersed itself.

Something about a southern male that made you think first of his own sexual isolation, his aloof relation to form and superiority. The women of the South had been pushed to the extreme of their femininity, where they became brittle as spun glass, and shrill of voice. Their flesh was too adorned, too remote inside their ruffles, and their scents. They too had withdrawn, in the name of English fussiness, in slavish imitation of white extremism in all its ornamental forms. So that when a man was introduced in youth to a proper female, she came to him buried in a kind of dark quartz of her own, frozen inside her artificial gender, like a gorgeous Cambrian fly caught in some motion of clay in a prehistoric rain shower. Beyond touch. Something to look at, to be fascinated by, as if the young man were more lepidopterist than anxious young swain.

And of course, most such meetings ended in disaster, hardly any interest aroused on either side. The women preferred their own relaxed company, their own intimacy to this strutting, this madness imposed on both sexes from above. The man turned away at his first chance and went home, perhaps to share his indignation with some accommodating pal up in the hayloft, or out on the river banks. A swim gave back confidence, a naked swim in which to emerge dripping and silvery and to stretch out under the sun to dry. That directness was all, and it was profoundly reassuring to look without blushing at the voluptuous natural geometry of a man's body, a young body pleated, tucked, hard-curved and indented with shadows, with hairy blossoms, with little mounds of flesh at chest, and shoulders, and swooped clean down into the groin. A man lay smiling to himself, thinking his thoughts, while his friend's eyes went over him soft as a daisy's glow.

But restraint was everywhere, and the sky's blueness was a sign of it. The holding back, the margins around which nothing was ventured. It would have been unthinkable.

So they all turned away in time, got dressed, went home to their strict morality and languished. And adopted some mode of southern gentility and hoped that a puppet in hoop skirts and stays and rattling pumps would somehow be as moving to him as was this naked boy on the river bank.

No girl ever was capable of dropping the disguise and coming out of her armature as something natural. She couldn't do it. She might have wanted to, and one almost did, a certain Mary-Lynn Fenton, who squirmed out of her blouse and bra, and tore at her blue jeans, got them down to her knees and lay in the straw of her uncle's hay wagon proud to be exposed. She giggled, in fact, and took his hand and put it gently to her round, plump breast, with its dark purple aureole, dark as a mustang grape. She wanted him to kiss her there, and brought his head down next, and put his lips up to the nipple. He touched it with his lips, just barely, thinking milk would drain from it if he were to press harder.

It was the fear of this event that made him tighten, lose his frankness. The nipple lay creased and intricate against the white skin, and it expressed some dark maternal power that was different from what men are. The door of that breast led to a world of children and old age, of kitchens humming with boiling water and feed bottles, and the ammonia of diaper pails, and something else. Some other dimension which the female kept to herself, a willingness to shut out the world and be content with what was inside. Inside a room, among the chairs and beds, and cribs, the pantries.

A woman was full of moisture and darkness, a house of the future. At her breast was the start of the process by which nature tumbled out into the sunlight, and the man who opened such latches to the female universe must thereafter bend his back and provide. He could feel that in his mouth, having touched the wrinkled spout-end of the whole volcano of fertility. He pulled back, and pulled his belt tight. He gave her such a look that it froze her smile, and darkened everything about her. She *knew*. And now he knew.

And he knew that in a man's body is sand and ledges of crumbling rock, and a few roots that have grown fierce from the desolation of the sun. In that very lack of life-milk was a certain wildness, a freedom. An ancient claim upon the body that bore no contracts, no devious consequence in which other mouths appeared, like little sucking weights that pulled the spirit down into the tangles of the bank and imposed, weakened, and finally ended the career of something hardly even begun. A man's body was simply portals and channels, little arroyos of hair and skin that led nowhere, and gave one the reckless heights of satisfaction—selfishly. But why not? Wasn't this life the only one, and did it require that one must pay a whole life of work and sorrow for one small hypnotic sexual leap?

He saw in the mayor's scotchy face a look of imprisonment, of having been properly yoked to the plow, for the good of the two or three children he had raised. The wife had melted away into that limbo of matronly roundness, in which her sexuality was no longer embodied, but radiated outward into possessions. The nest materialized into a thousand linens and lamp shades.

His thoughts drifted back into the room again, among the paintings on the wall, which seemed to remind him that he lived in a different world from them. He no longer accepted what used to be called the Parson *vision*, whatever that may have been. He had renounced it in the hay wagon, and walked home under a different, greenish sort of sun, under a heaven that had no further allegories than a few stars and some north winds.

Reggie Thompson kept a close watch on the Parson house. Barry remembered a man following him to the supermarket, staying in his car until Barry drove back home again. The little blue Toyota was always parked on the other corner, and Reggie sat there while Barry walked the dogs. The two never spoke or acknowledged each other. Reggie was sometimes with another man, and the two sat there in hunting jackets when the weather turned cool. Sometimes another car was on the street, with two more men.

There were no more parties or opened shades in the Parson house, and no more visits to the coast. The house was dark much of the time, and Beauregard and Barry were said to be traveling lately. Mrs. Robles, wife of the bus driver for the elementary school, received a letter from Cuernavaca from Beauregard, inviting her to become his housekeeper, and to begin cleaning the house regularly. She accepted and let it be known that her employer was now in Merida, where he bought a small house.

Then, in early November, Reggie Thompson and a friend were given a hunting lease in the Yucatan to shoot javelina. They took off in the blue Toyota for a week's vacation. When word came back, finally, from a police station in Campeche, it reported a hunting accident in which a Signor Thomason of Bryan had been shot twice in the head during a hunt. The man with him, Signor Blyte, had been wounded in the head and had lost his powers of speech. They could get nothing out of him but stares. He would remain in hospital in Aguascalientes until recovered, or until American authorities came to fetch him.

Beauregard came back a week later and knew nothing about the hunting accident. He told Mrs. Robles he lamented the death. At the football game, he was seen with the banker and politician Calvin Guest, an old friend of the family, and told him he was sending a thousand dollars to help a Democratic candidate run against the gun lobby in the State House. Mr. Guest thanked him and told his friends about it. The word got around that a Parson had taken a political stand on something and came down liberal. The gossip seemed to push Reggie Thompson's death to a dark corner.

But it was the ritual of the football game that recemented Beau with his crowd. Outside the stadium were long camping vehicles with awnings spread out over tables and chairs, where wealthy alumni could sit nursing a martini and munching expensive cheese before the game. Once in the bleachers, however, things were different. A test of loyalty ensued, where each man, however he might be constituted, became a roaring bull, a fierce partisan of his school and the team. Down in the field, dark green with the blotchy grass and yard lines, were men floating about in padded uniforms, which looked almost like pajamas from this angle of afternoon sun. The men floated about as if they played in a sort of dreamy wilderness, a green mattress. But the game was more serious than that, as the martini fumes helped bring back some distant memories in the tanned, handsome alumni who stood up each time the ball was rushed down field.

On the grid lay the South's hopes, with the new young men taking up arms against their mythological enemies, the north—in whatever guise it might appear, as rival schools, as the "visiting" team, as a newcomer to the league. Each time the Civil War was restarted, brought to a furious climax, and the hopes and dreams, the residue of southern resentments, were brought up again, put to the white fire of memory, annealed, or forged anew into the same old argument: *We lost!* The win was always another minor act of love in which the conception, the fulfillment was only partially achieved. The *thing*, the crucial gesture could not penetrate the boundary of the past and replot the war for southern victory. But a rite was the attempt, the hypnotic solution to an immoveable obstacle of mind. And so the stadium, a ring of concrete terraced from within like a huge head of many baffles and ledges of memory, was the place in which the war was fought over again, with every variation money and equipment could provide.

And the men who stood and shouted their encouragement did so with a tinge of humor, a distance they resented, but tolerated. It was only a rite, a religious festival, the games. They knew it, and it contradicted the practicality by which they lived the rest of their lives. But there it was, the South's endless preoccupation with losses and failures, a ravaged and irredeemable civilization. Now blacks took the field beside their white classmates, and their languorous bodies loped and drifted in the mayhem of white bodies. And the contact, the thudding, the broken shoulders and sprained legs, the pulled hamstrings all occasioned a kind of male worship below.

Beau watched with fascination as a male enclave gave itself wholly to the embrace of men, the wild contact, the shoving and pitching, and cursing, the sweat and fury of their game—which brought them into each other's bodily privacy, where their faces touched. The wounded were touched and carried like women on their honeymoons—tenderness and even weeping were acceptable practice in this cauldron of manly love. The black bodies were gods of their own kind, and the white men shouted with greater fierceness as these gangly giants spread their thighs out into full gallop, and broke the end zone like a frenzied whir of horses.

Even the coaches were no longer merely the angry, unforgiving father, the ghost of some merciless lieutenant at Antietam, sending his boys over the trench heads into the cannon fire. He was their lover, their patron, their loving seducer, and he made them pretend to die out there for love. For *his love*. The game meant that Beau could come back to his own kind, to where men understood the rules and accepted the small variations of morality. The crooks, the swindlers, the embezzlers were discountenanced, but their redemption lay in this ritual of standing to roar and hugging at the mock victories.

Barry remained in Mexico a few months longer, furnishing the new house, learning Spanish. He wrote postcards in Spanish and Mrs. Robles read them, then whispered their innocent chitchat to her husband, who gave it to the men at the auction barn. Beau had restored himself in the community, he was a true Parson again, a pillar and a force.

But Barry did not return. He kept delaying his visit, making excuses in his postcards. He put on a new roof to the hacienda, and was laying a garden, extending the building to two more rooms, a project that would take six months to complete. He wrote from Canada later, explaining his move as a search for plants and shrubs and medicinal herbs only to be found in Ontario province, and would return to Mexico in summer and back to Bryan that fall. All this passed through Mrs. Robles to the hispanic neighborhood and then to the gentry by those who cleaned for them. A collective sigh of relief was heard over this news, and the town went back to its humdrum life.

Business was good on lower Main Street. The stationwagons from the suburbs lined up in front of Parson's Lumber to get the little hard-to-find pieces for hanging traverse rods and refitting old transoms, replacing the big brass hinges on glass doors, and the molding, the large quarter-turn oak molding that nailed to corners in the old houses. Parson's was the place, and the company had acquired the status of an institution. Beau rejoined the country club and played golf with Calvin Guest and his friends. He was welcomed back to the upper circles and was a raconteur of spellbinding eloquence at the better dinner parties. He gave to charity, and he appeared for a long stint at the university fund raiser for the television studio. He let the whole town see his elegant, sun-tanned face, his long neck and aristocratic ears, his mild gray eyes and thin blond hair, his yachting look, and the phones jingled all night with contributions.

He set the tone of the East Side, digging the first swimming pool of the neighborhood, an elegant Beverly Hills-styled oval pool with diving boards and white gravel shoulders, lawn chairs and a little dressing cabin. A fence of white pickets went around to keep out the neighborhood infants. Otherwise, the young people from the big houses were invited to swim in the afternoon. Beau reserved the pool for his own use in the mornings, and sometimes read his books out on the sheltered part of the pool in the evenings. He seemed to have adapted well to Barry's absence. No more was said of him.

But hints did rise from time to time that a certain person was occupying Beau's time these days. He was seen going off in his red roadster to a house in Navasota where a stunning young woman welcomed him in and sometimes sat with him on the porch of the big Victorian mansion. The gossips were delighted and plied their trade with eager, some would say, feverish attention. Then Beau showed up at the golf course escorted by a tall, elegantly slender young woman who rode in the cart with him.

It was a social triumph to find Beau in the company of an aristocratic female from a good family up the road. The marriage date was on everyone's minds, and the notion of a new Parson heir was satisfaction to the old set. They saw the town take on a lease for the next century in that hope. And Beau did not disappoint their desires, at least part of the way.

His marriage was private, as with all Parson affairs, and conducted in a small chapel in Houston. The honeymoon was spent in the Mexican house, and the couple came back to live in the Parson house from then on. But instead of splendid parties and long dinner and dance soirees on the terrace overlooking the pool, as had been expected, the domestic life of the Parson house became sealed from public view. The grand woman inside did little to bring attention to her, but neither did she ask for acceptance by the town. She avoided the teas, the charities, the women's auxiliary, the committee in support of Phoebe's Home, a house for battered wives. None of this drew her out into public life. She remained within, and occasionally drove the roadster down to the coast and back again late at night. Sometimes with Beau, more often by herself.

She was tall for her sex, as tall as a man, some had thought. And she had a bearing that was full of confidence and athletic ability. But the elegant sway of her hips and the effortless femininity of her look, her laughter, her large brown eyes assured the community that a belle of the Brazos had come to grace another Parson. And it was the first time in living memory that a Parson appeared to be happily married, satisfied. There were no passionate nights of revelry at the river house, with the heels of working girls flying in all directions at the end of a gyrating old Parson with drunken eyes and lusting grins. This was a marriage of dignified retirement, a household that had closed its circle on the harmony of good morals and fidelity. The men approved, and the mayor, long absent from Beau's social life, wished Reggie were there to see what changes had swept over him.

The years passed and the couple were no longer thought of as young or attractive, but merely part of the faded elegance and grayness of older Bryan life. The membership was sold back to the country club, and the housekeepers, gardeners, and pool men were carefully screened for employment and their lips sealed by a good paycheck. The rumor mill lay idle and rusty, aroused to work only when the next mayor took a mistress from the north end of town and kept her in a trailer house out on the highway. His car was frequently parked at the ball field and the poor man walked under a thousand eyes to his weekly dalliances.

A certain doctor was asked once at a church supper if he had not had the pleasure or the duty of treating Mrs. Parson ever. It would seem a woman of her stature would keep a private physician, and a man of Dr. Hadj's reputation as a gynecologist exceeded that of his rivals, Drs. Roman and Rasberry.

But the doctor had never had the privilege of treating Mrs. Parson. He asked around in the medical community if anyone had, and the answer was no. Mrs. Parson had not been to a local doctor for any reason and had never visited the hospital. But she did have a doctor in Houston, a man whom Dr. Hadj knew professionally some years back. At a convention they came together briefly for a drink and Dr. Hadj asked about Mrs. Parson.

"I am not at liberty to discuss her physical health," said the doctor mysteriously. "Some day, perhaps, her story will be public, but I doubt it. She is a most interesting case, Dr. Hadj, of that I can assure you."

The tidbit gleaned in this chat was insufficient to turn the wheels of the gossip mills. The matter was dropped. But a curious illness had begun to afflict Mrs. Parson, and she grew thin and gray, and was seen in an ambulance several times hurrying down to Houston. The ghost of her former self sometimes passed the large front windows of the Parson house, stooped now and grasping for furniture to make her way. It was said she had contracted a vicious parasite in Mexico on one of their stays and was now dying of incurable complications.

She sat out by the pool in a large wicker-backed rocker, covered in a woolen blanket on the hottest days. Her large straw hat shaded a pale face drawn up to the skull bones. Her long arms were as thin as rake handles. Mrs. Robles looked after her much of the day, and at night another woman came to sit with her and attend her through long jags of sleepless moaning.

She coughed blood and choked on any but liquefied food. Her teeth fell out and her eyes grew swimmy and red-rimmed. She was dying and the town grieved for her. The minister came by and was politely treated, but it was clear the poor woman had no spiritual hungers either. She drifted west with the sun, and on a long windless night of autumn, she opened her hands with a long hiss of breath and passed out of the world. Beau allowed the Hillier Funeral home to take the body.

Down in the processing rooms of this distinguished undertaker's establishment a student and a master embalmer unclothed the bony ruins of Mrs. Parson and both drew in their breath and widened their eyes. Lying before them was a sort of pickled manhood, a yellowing, delicately faded rose of male genitals buried in white thighs. The long years of being female had not entirely smothered the boy and man that had been. When the mouth was packed with cotton and the cheeks pushed out with padding, the face became recognizable once more, under the glare of the work lights, as Barry's. Old man Hillier remembered him, and came down to observe this phenomenon, this riddle of southern noblesse oblige. He merely clucked his tongue, prodded the loose, silky flesh, and filled in the death certificate with female as the gender.

Some things you can't undo or right the wrong of, he thought. They made up the face to look as female as their arts allowed and dressed the body in a flowing silk gown. The make-up technician adorned the sallow skin with rouges and lipstick and took out the shadows of the neck with foundation. The body of Barry was slowly transformed in death to the beauty of Rebecca Parson, nee Kingsley of Navasota and Bryan. The town turned out for the funeral in Bryan Cemetery, and the mayor and fire chief spoke movingly of their infrequent but precious hours in the company of this noble woman.

Beau wept openly in his pew and followed the casket with head hung down, his cravat and pleated white shirt stained with his tears. A large marble stone joined the other headstones of the family plot, and the glorious name of Parson made room for one more among them. The Parson house of the living became darker and colder than the graveyard house. Hardly a sound was heard from within, and the cleaners and fixers all came and went as if the house were abandoned.

Somewhere among the turreted corners of the house and the steep pitch of the garret ceilings lay a man contemplating his life, picking at the thread of his vest, lying motionless on an old trundle bed. He read the Bible in the evening, and Baudelaire during the long afternoons. He played Tchaikowsky on the old stereo in the livingroom, turned down low, almost inaudible, and sipped his Dry Sack in a tall stem glass, waiting for something to occur.

The lumberyards were sold off to a big supply house in Houston, and the hardware end of the Parson lumber firm was taken over by a franchise. The boys who dug their big scoops into the bins were gone, and now racks of little packaged screws were all that could be bought at the little-old-fashioned emporium. But the old timers kept coming out of habit, out of desperation to preserve some signs of their past, their footing in the world. The stock in the cavernous warehouse behind contained a museum of tools and axes, ashwood handles, and fine, hand-forged posthole diggers. They were still at 1950s prices and the farmers from as far away as Madisonville and Hearne drove down in family sedans to get a bargain while they still could.

Beau went back to the Yucatan for half a year to recuperate from Mrs. Parson's death. He sold the house and returned dark and withdrawn in the company of a young man calling himself Roberto Jimenez. He would look after the house and grounds and drive the cars for Beau. But after a few months it was clear Roberto could not adjust to the drab life of the little prairie town and went back south. A little later, Beau was seen playing bridge at the neighbor's house and walking the streets at night with a woman who had once been a childhood sweetheart. They were both veterans of long marriages and deaths and appeared fragile and ethereal in their little strolls.

The drapes were parted again at the Parson house and occasionally the tinkle of dance music wafted over the japonicas and through the louvered doors of the front hall. A couple swayed and floated by in ghostly outline through the gauze curtains of the living room, their faces staring off at separate worlds. The two played croquet on the lawn and invited other couples to join them for dinner, for quiet nights of reading poetry and sharing a drink. Beau was the old man now, the faded gentleman of his street, and the boys and girls who passed crept reverently to the porch to request Halloween treats and orders for Girl Scout cookies. They were never refused.

Mrs. Cantrell, Beau's companion of these years, learned all his secrets in their long talks together. She smiled and sometimes laughed aloud at the risks he dared to take with the town's conscience, its iron-fisted morality. She wished she had indulged her own whims and fantasies more, she said, and they drank to youth. They danced to Benny Goodman and the Dorsey band, and a few slow tunes by Elvis, and listened dreamily to the Beatles while the ceiling fan turned and the new boy from the college came in with a tray of crackers and fresh drinks.

When Mrs. Cantrell passed away, the world of Beau Parson broke from the town and drifted to the open seas of privacy and silence. He ventured out no more, but dressed elegantly in his various combinations for morning coffee, his afternoon tea, and for the simple, Spartan supper he allowed himself. At nightfall he sat out on the upper deck looking over the pool, with the portable radio tuned to the fine arts station. He wrote in his journal with the lamp balanced on the back of his lounge chair, a cone of yellow light dancing with insects while his pen scribbled down the creamy yellow pages of his diary. Everything he thought or wrote was addressed to Barry, and his Saturday afternoons were spent cleaning up the little plot where Mrs. Parson lay buried. An alabaster vase was given fresh new roses each week, and a small lamp, fed by a gas jet, bobbled its red tongue throughout the night.

Maria Sanchez moved cautiously in the morning when Beau had not yet arisen. Sometimes she found him seated in bed in his silk pajamas tapping noisily at his Underwood portable, writing letters, sorting out his business affairs. Occasionally he would write a column for the local paper, something about wood care or repairing of old furniture, glues to use, and painting hints for handymen fixing up their own houses. He was a good writer, and well liked by the readers. They clipped out and saved his columns, and copies were xeroxed and given away free at the store.

When his doctors informed him he had an inoperable cancer in his pancreas, and had six months to live, Beau went home and sat alone in his dining room with a pad of paper and a pencil. He wanted to write a poem, a love poem, or a poem about visions. He couldn't think clearly. He had a glass of bourbon next to him and sipped at it, and dismissed Señora Sanchez for the night. He sat up and faced the terror of the blank page, and began to hear voices mumbling all through him. He wrote a line,

This gentle hour of dusk, slow as feathers falling,

and scratched it out. He pushed his drink aside and put his elbows out, lowering his head closer to the tablet.

Walk with me down this path, this golden sunset air

and what? He hesitated, began writing again:

And I shall tell you secrets of the heart, great pains

but pain reminded him too quickly of the throb in his gut, the nudging of the vile tumor as it probed around for food.

Of longing, the sweet impossible lightness of a hand

Barry's hand, soft elongated fingers, a woman's hand for sure, a hand to kiss, hold against one's naked skin, a hand true in its way, faithful as a knight's vows. Silly idea, a knight. He knew nothing of knights or chivalry, or love courts.

At night, in the cool of the wind over the oak crowns,
In the joyous moment of a kiss. Sweet love, sweet darkness
Of my heart, come welcome me, wait on the road for me

I join you soon in that fastidious low ceilinged home.

Too melodramatic. He drew an X through the lines and balled up the paper. He sat forward again, choosing a new pencil from the little cigar box on the table. It was of darker lead, and he felt concentrated, ready.

The Enamoring Flame

Dear bold woman who was man, my wife and lover
in whom I gave myself away, and floated downward
in the agony of love, breathless faller into dark,
mere fragment of a star burning to cinders
in your mild earth, your warmth and arms

I took your love in mouth and eyes,
by my scooped hands, by legs and thighs,
and cherished all our heat, our giddy rock-climbing
ecstasies of love, our passions unmodified
by the drab ice of other men's frailty and fear.

I commend my soul to you, beloved Barry,
my wife and seer, my passion and despair.
         — Beauregard Parson

He found an envelope in the sideboard pigeon holes and put the poem in without a note. He licked the flap shut and addressed the envelope to the Editor, Bryan *Eagle*, Briarcrest Drive, Bryan, TX. He gave no return address. He put a stamp on it and clipped it to the outside of the mailbox with a clothes pin. Occasionally a poem was printed from the readers in a little filler column run by a woman named Margaret Ann Zipp. She would print this one by so distinguished a citizen, but it was unlikely she would understand it. Barry was not a name on many tongues these days, and even the name of Beauregard Parson was not familiar to the younger generation. It would go into the "Around Town" column and sit there obscurely for a day. It would only have effect upon a few households where the information would go into an unfinished imaginary puzzle, and the design would be snug and definite.

And the design would include the romping foot work of Eusebius, the yellow fat of Clayton's naked hips, the curious willowy dancing of Barry on the coast, sloe-eyed, moist of lip, weaving in and out of naked men's bodies, a Salome of the burnt sunscape, a work of sweat and tears and salt in the marshy despair of that afternoon, with Reggie firing off his little Pentax in the trembling grayness of the shrubbery, among the decaying leaves of past summers, his dead body rising from a field after Barry delivered the two long bullets to his head, and joining the mural of the puzzle with a swaggering righteous grin. The mayors of the Parson era were all here gazing up to the patriarchal faces hung on the wall, and Mrs. Cantrell would be descending the staircase in her amber housecoat and topaz rings, her hair gathered up over her head in the shape of yucca blossoms.

The cast and crew of the Parson epic would all be on the margins of the puzzle, sweeping, pruning, roofing, and sawing at trim wood, painting porches, laying pipe for the swimming pool, peering into the windows of the Jacuzzi room, withdrawing to whisper at Sam's Barbershop, and passing the word at the auction barn. The Mexican women would be there in the hall, listening to the murmurs of lovemaking above them, and wondering who or what had entered into the dark private chambers of the reclusive owner. And there, on his trundle bed, in old tattered vest and slippers, would lie the elegant length of Beau Parson, reading *Les Fleurs du Mal* in the original, turning the onion skin pages without haste, sipping his sherry and allowing Bryan to push him down stream on the Brazos, toward the Gulf of Mexico and silence.

A brief thunder crackled out of the timbered confines of the Parson house, not enough to disturb a human being, but quick and fatal enough to raise the dogs' heads of the surrounding streets. In a little while, lights would be thrown, and doors opened by force, and cars and panel trucks would crowd the little curb, and the poem would appear beside a picture of Beauregard Thrustle Parsons, late of Bryan. The old Parson store would prosper under new ownership as the days, numberless and alike, rose from the horizon. ✿

Paper Dolls

by Nancy Jones Castilla

All four lanes of traffic crawled to a stop, and I knew I was stuck on LBJ Freeway, frozen in my lane for god knows how long. If I couldn't get to an exit soon, I'd be late for my dental appointment. The Marsh Lane exit was less than half a mile ahead; if the sluggish traffic inched forward just a little, I could exit on Marsh, go south a few blocks and hit Forest Lane, then zip down to Preston Road and still make it to the dental office without being late. I wished for a car phone, a luxury I'd never allowed myself.

Drivers around me wore the same frustrated looks, except for a blonde in the lane to my left, animatedly conversing on her phone, laughing, and simultaneously applying a fresh coat of bright red lipstick. How does she do that, I marveled. If I tried to talk and put on lipstick at the same time, I'd look like a clown, my nose and chin smeared with red. A man in a black Mercedes to her left seemed mesmerized by the performance.

In the lane to my right about four vehicles ahead, a battered red truck piled high with household goods—a dresser, table, some chairs, and boxes—shuddered and smoked. Lord keep that truck running; don't let it stall here in this bottleneck, I prayed. A family moving, I thought. The shaking truck laden with odd pieces of furniture took me back to a time when I was ten on our blackland farm in Northeast Texas, and another family was moving in a battered red truck.

"The Smiths packed up and left this morning." Daddy was talking to Mother in the kitchen. "He came and got his pay for work this week. They're going to South Texas, to the Valley, think they can make a lot of money down there gathering fruit."

Mother sighed deeply. "He doesn't have sense God gave a goose," she said, measuring out flour in a mixing bowl. "They'll be back, come spring, wanting to borrow more money—just you wait and see."

"I told him I could lend him enough to make it through the winter, and they could pay it back when we started planting again next spring. But he wouldn't listen, said he heard about some people who went to the Valley and made a lot of money."

"You've already lent him more now than he'll ever pay back," Mother grumbled. It was an argument I had heard before. "Neither a borrower nor a lender . . ."

"He paid back *some* of it," Daddy interrupted. "Most people pay back when they can."

"Hum-m-ph," Mother grunted and began beating the cake batter vigorously, the spoon clacking against the side of the bowl. Then she stopped and looked up. "Those poor kids," she said. "They've changed schools twice already this year, and now they'll have to change again."

"I know, I know; I tried to tell him. He said, 'Why, some of them kids can already read 'n write better'n me.'"

Mother shook her head and muttered something I didn't understand about a great stage of fools.

"They piled all their stuff on that old red truck and they're gone. Somebody will want the house right away," Daddy said. "We better see if it needs sweeping out or cleaning up."

I looked down the road at the house and thought about it being empty. When Aunt Vera and Uncle George had lived there, Aunt Vera had it fixed pretty with curtains and pictures and all. Red, yellow, and orange zinnias and daisies and petunias had grown in the flower beds. Now tall weeds and Johnson grass covered the beds.

I thought about Tinesy and Ruth. They rode the same school bus that Margaret and I did. Tinesy was in my class at school, and although Ruth was bigger than Tinesy, she was in the grade below. Tinesy's straight red hair was always pulled back with the same dirty pink barrette. Until Mother gave them some of our clothes we'd outgrown, I'd only seen Tinesy wear two different dresses, a blue-checked cotton with no sleeves and an ugly green one with long sleeves. Ruth had two dresses, too, one with a pocket partly torn off. I always wondered why her mother didn't sew it up.

When Ruth had asked me if I would *tote* some books for her, I didn't know what she meant. They said a lot of words funny; Mother said it was because they were from North Carolina. I thought Tinesy was a nickname until the teacher called her up to her desk and said she needed Tinesy's real name to add to the roll. Tinesy said, "That's my real name." "Then how do you spell it?" Mrs. Stratton had asked. "Just like that," Tinesy said, and Mrs. Stratton's eyebrows almost flew off her forehead.

When Tinesy came back to her desk next to mine, I peeked over to her paper and saw T9C Smith at the top. I pretended not to see, but I could hardly wait to tell Margaret after school. "Wonder why they didn't name Ruth 'Biggy'?" Margaret said. "Then they could have spelled her name Big-E!" We laughed so long our stomachs hurt.

After Mother took Mrs. Smith a big box filled with clothes Margaret and I had outgrown, Ruth and Tinesy came to the fields wearing one of our church dresses—the pink plaid ones with the big wide linen collars edged in lace. I didn't think that was funny. A lot of play clothes were in the box, but their mother hadn't told them to wear those. We always had to take Sunday clothes off and change into play clothes as soon as we got home from church; we didn't even get to eat dinner in them.

Now here were Ruth and Tinesy in the fields ready to pick cotton in Sunday dresses. We had gone with Daddy to take fresh ice and water to the hands. They had stood there preening for everyone to see. I didn't say anything, but I sure wanted to. I wanted to say, "You all can't even tell the difference between everyday clothes and church dresses. How can anyone be so dumb! Don't you know *anything*?" But I knew better than to say it out loud. Daddy always said, "Be nice; don't hurt anyone's feelings." That day he had said, "Now don't tell your mother; no sense in upsetting her."

Of course, Mother found out later. But by then, nothing the Smiths did surprised us much. Mother said none of them had sense enough to come in out of the rain, and I guess she was right.

One Saturday we saw all the Smith kids playing in the rain, Ruth and Tinesy, their little brothers, and even their older sister Lucy, who was fifteen. They were all running and trying to jump the ditch in front of their house, Ruth and Tinesy wearing our last year's red velvet dresses. We'd only worn them twice before we outgrew them, once at Christmas and once over to Aunt Maggie's for a family dinner. Ruth and Tinesy were barefoot and spattered from top to bottom with muddy water, and their mother was laughing. Mother just shook her head. I couldn't help but wish I was out there with them, feeling the mud squishing between my toes, trying to catch raindrops in my mouth, laughing about falling in the water, and wearing a beautiful red velvet dress. But Mother wouldn't have laughed like Mrs. Smith did.

Lucy's long red hair was matted against her face, and her wet blouse stuck to her chest. I envied her, particularly her pointy breasts, and wished I were fifteen. "I'll bet she wouldn't be out there in the rain playing if there were any boys around for her to talk to," I told Margaret.

Just last week I had walked in the kitchen, and our big brother Bobby was laughing and telling Mother that he overheard Lucy talking in the field saying she could take a man big as a stovepipe. "And then. . . ." But then Mother saw me and shushed him. "What did Lucy mean, Bobby? What did she mean?" I asked, but he said to never mind, he had to go help Daddy, and he went to the barn.

And Mother just threw up her hands when Daddy reported what Mrs. Smith had said about the garden. When Aunt Vera and Uncle George moved to town, they had to leave their garden planted with tomatoes, lettuce, carrots, cabbage, beans, and squash and had said to tell the Smiths they were welcome to all of it. "We don't *care* for garden vegetables," Mrs. Smith had replied, care sounding more like *keer*. "We like canned goods." Mother, who seemed to always be peeling and slicing vegetables from our garden, wiped her hands on her apron and said, "They just don't have a lick of sense. Think how much money they could save."

But they didn't seem to care about saving money. Once when Margaret and I went with Daddy to the house to get Mr. Smith, Mrs. Smith told Daddy how they couldn't afford to buy a lot of milk for the kids, that she rationed it out to them so it would last longer. I saw Daddy reach in his back pocket for his billfold. He pulled out a folded-up twenty-dollar bill from the place behind his driver's license, smoothed it out, and handed it to her. I wondered what he'd been saving it for. I'll bet he doesn't tell Mother, I thought. When Mrs. Smith said they'd pay it back, he said, "No, no, this is a gift. You go buy those kids some milk; don't be rationing it any more." He sounded mad. He turned, said, "Come on, girls," and we left real fast.

That was on Saturday morning. Monday morning on the school bus Ruth told me their mother had found a radio for $19.98 when they went to town Saturday afternoon and bought it for their room. I felt my stomach sink. We may have had more milk in our refrigerator, but Margaret and I didn't have a radio in our room. Ruth said they were going to listen to "The Lone Ranger" that afternoon after school and asked if we wanted to come and listen with them. I said I had to do my arithmetic homework.

And then they were gone, as if I'd dreamed them all up.

I found Margaret in the porch swing trailing a ball of string for a yellow kitten. I stroked the top of its head. "Guess what—I heard Daddy tell Mother that the Smiths left this morning. They moved."

"Why did they go?"

"For goodness' sake, I don't know, Margaret; they just left, that's all. Let's go look at the house."

"Go ask Mother; it's your turn—I asked last."

"You always say that," I threw over my shoulder as I started for the kitchen.

I always liked to go look at a house when someone had moved out. We never knew what we'd find. When the Littles moved out unexpectedly, we went with Mother and Daddy to the house. When they had moved in, Mother had sent them one of our rocking chairs because they had small children, and Mother said if they had a rocker, they could rock the babies. She had sewn a new blue cushion for it before Daddy carried it down. When we went in the empty house, there were pieces of the rocker on the floor and the rest of it had been burned in the fireplace. They had torn up boards from under the linoleum and burned those, too. Mother looked stricken, and Daddy said, "Well, I'll swear!" Then he told Mother, "The last time I went to cut wood, I noticed they didn't have any in their woodpile, so I told Joe Little I was going to cut some fallen trees in the pasture for firewood, and he was welcome to come with me and get plenty for them." Mother just sighed. Daddy said, "I figured I could use the help and he could sure use the firewood. But he said they didn't *need* any!" He looked around at the trash littering the room and the holes in the floor. "I'll swear!" he had muttered again.

I didn't think the Smiths' house would be like that, but I still wanted to go see it.

Mother was kneading dough, and I knew we'd be having hot rolls for Sunday dinner. "Mother, can we go look at the house where the Smiths lived?"

"Well, go on, but come right back. I need you all to beat the egg whites for the pie and set the table." I whirled around, and Mother said, "Watch out for cars. Keep to the side of the road."

I ran to the porch. Another kitten was asleep in Margaret's lap. "It's okay; we can go, but we have to hurry back and help Mother with dinner." She gently transferred the sleeping kitten to the pillow beside her in the swing. It was the fluffy black-and-white one we had promised to Tinesy and Ruth. But Mr. Smith said they didn't need any cats, and they had to bring it back to us the same day they took it. I remembered the look on Ruth's face. She had stood there, twisting one side of her skirt into a knot, and kept her eyes on the ground while Tinesy handed over the kitten to Margaret. Seems like Ruth's face was always dirty, and I could see where tears had left crooked trails on both sides of her cheeks, like little rivers on her face.

I stroked the kitten again, and it stretched lazily, then curled back up again.

We walked fast, not even stopping to pick any of the purple and yellow wild flowers on the side of the road or to blow fuzz off the dandelions. The sun was bright and hot, even in late October.

Some paper sacks, tin cans, and a broken white bowl lay in the yard. Tall grass and weeds grew in all the flower beds. The front door was ajar, and we pushed it open. I stepped over trash on the floor and could almost hear Mother complaining about how clean the house had been when the Smiths moved in and why hadn't they at least swept it out and taken out the trash. The house smelled like old bacon grease, soured milk, and dirty clothes. When Aunt Vera lived there, it had smelled like cookies baking or apple pies and cinnamon.

In the living room, scuffling through the trash, I turned up a coloring book. "Look, Margaret! A brand new coloring book." I picked it up and turned through the pages. "Come on, let's see if there's anything else in any of the other rooms." Papers, trash, and old rags lay scattered on the floor. In one of the bedrooms a book of paper dolls rested in a corner. The paper dolls were far nicer than any Margaret and I had ever had.

Margaret saw them, too. "Elizabeth, Wow! These are better than ours. A lot *bigger*."

We had little paper dolls because Mother said the bigger ones cost too much. Now here on the floor, amid other pieces of trash, were tall stiff cardboard dolls on fold-out stands that would actually stand up by them-selves—and a whole book of cut-out clothes for them. We picked them up gingerly. They didn't even have any dust on them. They looked new. "Why did they leave them?" Margaret wondered.

"I don't know," I said; "Mother always said they didn't have a lick of sense, didn't know the value of a solitary thing."

"Let's take them home with us, Elizabeth."

I was already mentally locating my scissors at home and trying to decide which doll I wanted and which dress I would put on her first.

I began to sing a song I'd heard on the radio: "I'm going to buy a paper doll that I can call my own," and Margaret chimed in:

"I'd rather have a paper doll to call my own than have a fickle-minded real live girl." Then she asked, "What's *fickle*?"

"I think somebody who has lots of boyfriends, like Lucy," I said. I began to sing again. "I'm going to buy a paper doll that I can call my own. . . ." Somewhere in my head I could hear Daddy saying, *Don't ever take anything that isn't yours.*

"Do you think it's okay to take them?" I asked.

"Why not? The Smiths aren't here anymore. These don't belong to anybody now."

"But what if somebody sees us carrying them home with us?" I argued. "Anybody would know where we got them."

It took only a minute or two to think of putting the paper doll books under our blouses. By crossing our arms over our chests, we held them secure—and out of sight. When Mr. Thomas drove by, my heart beat faster; I couldn't wave because my book would have fallen out.

By the time we reached home, I felt clever and was congratulating myself and Margaret. "We did it!" I said, gleefully. "Nobody saw us!"

"Did what?" Daddy asked, suddenly coming around the corner of the house. "Nobody saw you do what?" Mother came out on the porch and stopped to listen.

"Look what we found—look what we found! Some real nice paper dolls!" and we pulled our treasures out from under our shirts.

Mother looked at Daddy.

"You hid them under your clothes?" Daddy wasn't smiling. "Why did you do that?"

I stole a look at Margaret. "Somebody might have seen us," she said, "and thought that we were stealing them."

Daddy looked at the paper doll books, slightly wrinkled from being crushed against our chests. Mother didn't say anything.

"Take them back right now," he said quietly.

"Take them back?" Margaret's voice didn't sound right.

"But they *left* them," I said. "They went off and left them on the floor!"

"Put them back where you got them. Right now."

"But why?" I asked.

"They might come back to see if they left anything by mistake."

I didn't believe him. I knew he knew they wouldn't come back for some paper dolls, and there was nothing else but trash and dirt in the house.

"I've always told you not to ever take anything that isn't yours."

"But the Smiths are gone!" Margaret said. "They're not coming back, and they *left* the paper dolls!"

"They're gone, Daddy; they're gone!" I protested.

"Take them back," Daddy said again.

I looked at the ground. Tears filled up my eyes, not only for the paper dolls, but also because of something in his quiet voice. I bit my lower lip.

Surprisingly, Margaret didn't say anything either, and I wished we'd never found them.

We put the paper dolls and coloring book back under our shirts and walked back down the road to the house, slow this time. "It's all your fault," Margaret said. "If you hadn't wanted to come down here. . . ."

"You wanted to come, too," I said. "You said you wanted them. You were the one that wanted to take them home."

"You did, too, Elizabeth!" she stormed.

We put the coloring book and paper doll books back on the floor where we'd found them, closing the door behind us.

As we left the yard, I kicked a Campbell's pork and beans tin can; Margaret stomped on a cricket and squashed a brown bug.

They're not coming back, I thought. Even though the coloring book and paper dolls really weren't ours, I hated to put something perfectly good on the floor with trash. I brushed my hands off on my skirt.

A big cloud over the sun shaded the road as we walked home. There was a chill in the air, and I remembered Mother saying that cold weather was just around the corner.

A few days later we went back again with Mother to pick up trash out of the yard. Before we left, we all walked through the house one last time. The floor was clean, and I knew Mother had already been there while we were at school to clean the inside. I didn't ask about the paper dolls.

A cold wind from the north was blowing leaves across the yard, and I buttoned my sweater against the cold. I shivered a little; I wondered where Ruth and Tinesy were and if they had warm coats for the winter. I could imagine the old red truck scooting down the highway on its way to somewhere, Ruth and Tinesy perched on top of their belongings in the back with their hair flying in the wind, off on another adventure.

The blue car in front of me began to move, the old red truck up ahead jerked forward in its lane, a wooden chair on top wobbling dangerously, and I exited onto Marsh Lane, leaving the crush of traffic behind me. ❀

WHAT COWGIRLS DO

by Aimee Lee Brown-Caban

The first time I met Kori Chong, I said mamma out loud and other stuff in private, and Kori understood me. Kori was wearing her best silk kimono and had her stick horse between her legs. She had two black braids and almond eyes, just like mine. We both wore our best kimonos and had on cowgirl hats. I had on black sandals instead of cowboy boots like Kori's, but we both had the same initials. Her name was Kori Chong. Mine was Karen Chen.

I didn't like my name much, and neither did Kori. She changed my name to Korean Cowgirl, KC for short, and I have loved her ever since.

I sleep in the corner on the shelf above Kori's bed. Kori kisses me before bed. I say mamma out loud and tell her I love her in private. I love her because we look alike. I love her because she gave me a good name. I love the feel of her moisture on my lips and her cheek fuzz on my face.

The horses on Kori's posters talk to me after Kori falls asleep.

I am Bronco, says the horse with the cowboy on his back.

I am Clydesdale, says the horse pulling a red wagon.

I am Black Beauty, says the horse with the white forehead.

I am KC, Korean Cowgirl. Someday, Kori and I will live on a ranch. Someday you will not be posters anymore. Someday we will ride you because that is what cowgirls do.

Kori plays with Peter from next door. She always invites me to play too. Peter wears dirty horse t-shirts and has fingers caked with mud. He brings Joe Jockey to play with us today. Sally from across the street comes, too. She wears ruffle dresses and white, shiny shoes. She brings Laughing Linda. Sally doesn't like boys with muddy fingers or girls who wear black braids, but she plays with us today because there is no one else at home for Sally to play with. Everyone except for Sally and Linda sits by the creek. Sally brushes off the top of a rock, and she and Linda sit down.

I want to play cowgirls, I say.

Cowgirls are stupid, laughs Linda.

I will play cowboys, says Joe Jockey. Linda can be our horse.

Kori and Peter want to play cowboys and cowgirls, but Sally won't ride her horse through the creek to escape from bandits. Sally and Linda want to play Scarlett O'Hara, and we can be their ranch hands.

Kori says girls who don't play cowboys and cowgirls are stupid. Sally says girls with slanted eyes are stupid. Girls with slanted eyes can't be cowgirls.

Kori pulls me close to her and puts her horse between my legs and her legs. Peter pushes Sally. Sally sits in the creek bank in her ruffle dress. Kori and me yell yahoo and gallop toward the creek and willow trees. Peter and Joe follow our trail of yahoo's. Our trails disappear under the willows.

Kori and I play dress-up and school when Peter isn't home. I like dress-up more than school because Kori always gets to be the teacher.

Be quiet, KC. What's 2 + 2, KC. Stand in the corner, KC. Don't call me mamma, KC. Call me teacher.

Today, Kori and I play dress-up. Kori unties my kimono and pulls off my pants, sandals, and cowgirl hat. Kori's fingers tingle my legs, my feet, and my head. I sit barefoot in my pink, lace panties and wait for Kori to cover my body.

Kori pulls out a pink ruffle dress and a flower bonnet. She ties the bonnet around my neck and braids.

This bonnet is choking me, Kori.

Kori warms my flesh with her fingers. She pulls my kimono snaps apart with her teeth. Kori's wet breath lingers on my tummy.

I look dumb in this dress, Kori.

Kori unties her kimono and pulls off her pants. She pulls a blue ruffle dress over her naked chest and puts the hat she wears to church on top of her braids.

You look dumb too, Kori.

We look dumb, Kori says. She puts our kimonos and cowgirl hats back on our bodies. Kori and I sink into her bed and dream about our life on the ranch.

Just before bed, Kori nestles my body between her V-spread legs like her mamma nestles her when Kori gets her hair braided.

Cowgirls only wear their hair in braids, Kori says.

I rest between Kori's warm V, and Kori splits my hair down the seam of my head and brushes each section. Her pajama sleeves brush against my head. Kori tickles my scalp with the brush bristles. She splits each section of my hair into three parts while her arms rock me back and forth like the rocking horse at Peter's house. I rock harder and harder between Kori's legs as Kori uses her fingers, then her wrists, then her arms to weave the sections of my hair together.

We rock back and forth, back and forth until Kori finishes. We sink into Kori's bed, and Bronco, Clyde, and Beauty's whinnies lull us to sleep.

I go to Ms. Wallace's class with Kori today. I hear crying and muffled moans from Ms. Wallace's desk. Kori says all the noisy kids go to Ms. Wallace's desk and are forgotten. I don't say mamma once.

At recess, I see Joe Jockey. Joe has bendable arms and legs. He has goggles and leather boots, and he carries a little whip in his hand. Joe's hands are covered in dirt. He yells, Giddy-up, Midnight, but he doesn't have a horse.

Another girl brings Betsy Wetsy. Betsy cries all the time and got my leather sandals all wet, but she is better than Laughing Linda. Linda laughs at my best kimono and my braids, and the ruffles on her dress shake.

Betsy and Linda sing songs about the Chinese and the Japanese. They don't have any songs about the Koreans, but I don't mind because my knees aren't dirty. Kori always makes sure I'm clean.

We go back to class, and Kori says I have to be quiet again. She puts me on a shelf in the back next to Joe, Betsy, and Linda.

Linda asks why I wear a kimono and a cowboy hat. Joe tells Linda to shut up or Ms. Wallace will stuff her in the desk drawer. It's okay, I say to Joe. A kimono and a cowboy hat are what all the Korean cowgirls wear, I say. Linda laughs, and Joe and I shove her to the floor. Linda shakes with laughter. Her white, patent leather shoes fall off her feet.

Mrs. Wallace picks Linda up and shoves her in with the moaning and crying. I never hear Linda's laugh again.

Kori and Peter wear their cowboy boots. I wear my sandals and Joe wears his jockey boots. Kori says we are going to look for the horses that Peter saw down by the creek.

If we find a horse, we will catch it and take turns riding it. Kori and I will get Mondays, Tuesdays, and Fridays. Peter and Joe will get Wednesdays, Thursdays, and Saturdays. We will all sell rides for a dollar on Sundays, but Sally has to pay three.

Kori holds my hand and Peter holds Joe's hand as they wade through the creek water. No horses there. We climb up and down Farmer Brown's hill, and we lay down and sink into the grass carpet and the polka-dot rainbow of flowers. The grass blades tickle my feet where they are not covered by my sandals. I laugh and yell mamma. Kori pulls me close to her, and I can feel the fuzz on her face.

Peter and Kori decide to pee because they think the horses will smell their sugar pee and come to Farmer Brown's Hill. I don't have to pee, so I sit on the ground next to a willow tree next to Joe. Kori and Peter pull down their pants. They race to see who can pee longer and who can pee farther.

Kori moves her hips back and forth. Her stream flows straight down from her squatted legs. Peter stands straight and aims past the mud Kori has made. Peter pees the farthest. Kori pees the longest. Still no horses.

We climb back up and down Farmer Brown's Hill and gallop through the creek water. My kimono gets wet, and Peter puts his lips on Kori's lips. Joe dangles from Peter's hand and his body touches mine. Kori punches Peter in the lips, then she kisses him back. I say mamma. Joe yells Giddy-up, Midnight. Peter and Kori prance toward their houses.

Kori and I play gossip today and talk about Peter.
Peter is so dirty, but he's cute, Kori says.
Peter always plays cowgirls with us, I say.
And he always sticks up for me when Sally laughs at my eyes.
And Peter even said he would ride horses with us on our ranch.
I love Peter.
I do too.
Kori pulls me to her chest and her heartbeats lull me to sleep.

Kori doesn't let her mamma braid her hair today. She says braids are for chinks.

Are we chinks, Kori?

Nobody wants to play with chinks.

I want to play with chinks.

Kori sets me between her legs and unweaves my hair. I rock back and forth and Kori spanks me for not sitting still. She brushes my hair and the bristles scrape against my scalp.

You're hurting me, Kori.

Be still, Korean Chink.

My hair falls flat against my face like Kori's. It sticks to my neck and my face.

I want my braids back, Kori.

Kori and Sally play together today. I sit in my corner and try to join in too, but Kori can't hear me with Sally there.

Kori and Sally put colored powder on their faces.

You need lots of blue to cover your almond eyes, Sally says. Boys like Peter don't like girls who have eyes like yours.

Boys like Peter don't like girls who wear ruffle dresses, I say.

Kori faces me and wipes wet powder from her eyes.

Kori doesn't wear her cowgirl hat today. She wears leotards, jeans, and a baseball cap that holds her straight hair in a pony tail. I think Kori looks better in her hat and braids.

Sally and Kori play the name game again.

Can we play dress-up or even school? I ask. I'll be quiet and call you Miss Chong.

Did you see the new kid with the dark hair? asks Kori.

The one who is good at math, asks Sally.

I will wear the ruffle dress. I think his name is Tom.

No, it's George.

What happened to Peter?

I think he's cute.

Me too.

Sally and Kori play dress-up, and I wait for my turn. Sally takes off her dress and tries on Kori's black jeans and sweater. Kori tries on Sally's dress.

You look dumb, Kori.

Kori takes off Sally's dress and tries on her new black pants and white button shirt. Sally takes off Kori's jeans and sweater. Kori takes off her new outfit.

Sally and Kori look at each other's chests. Sally touches Kori's.

Is anyone going to touch me?

Kori puts her lips against Sally's face, then asks Sally if she can touch her.

Sally and Kori decide to go have a tea party.

I don't have a tea party outfit, Kori.

Kori turns off the lights to her bedroom and closes the door. I never got my turn.

Kori picks me up from my corner. I try to feel the fuzz on her face, but she lays me down in her lap and pulls off my sandals and my hat. Kori's fingers warm my lap and tickle my feet.

Who are we going to dress up like, Kori?

Kori kisses my face. The moisture from her lips covers my lips, my eyes, my nose.

I don't like these kisses Kori.

I love you, Peter.

I'm not Peter, Kori.

Kori and I sink into her bed. Clyde and Bronco look down at us, and I say hi. Kori puts her hands between her legs and the bed bounces me up and down. Beauty asks if we are playing bucking bronco. I say mamma. Kori puts her warm hand around me, throws me on the floor, and calls me dirty.

My name is KC, Kori.

Kori takes me to the bathroom and dunks my head into water that burns my face. She puts stuff on my hair that runs down my cheeks and stains my skin and then dunks me back in water.

I don't like this game.

Kori blows warm air on my hair and brushes her fingers against my scalp like when she used to braid my hair. The warm air stops blowing, and I look down at my hair that falls around my shoulders. My hair is red.

Where's my black hair, Kori?

Now Peter won't make fun of your Korean hair.

I like my hair, Kori.

Kori takes off my kimono and pants. She dresses me in a red jumper and white, patent leather shoes like the ones Laughing Linda used to wear.

I don't like these clothes, Kori.

Kori puts on a pink jumper.

I don't like your clothes either.

Put our hair in braids and let's go find horses for our ranch.

Kori throws my clothes into the trash and walks back into the bathroom.

I want my cowgirl clothes back.

Kori slams her door shut. Her short, black hair swishes back and forth. Kori picks me up and punches me. She screams and cries and says Sally is stupid. Sally kissed Peter and Peter kissed Sally back. Sally sang the Chinese song and Peter sang the Japanese song.

Kori hugs me, and I say mamma.

Kori puts on her kimono and cowboy boots.

Will you put my kimono on too, Kori?

Kori pulls my sandals and cowgirl outfit out of the trash. Her fingers warm my flesh as she puts my favorite outfit on my body.

Kori and I put her stick horse between her legs. We gallop down to the creek and stop by the willow trees. Kori and I sit underneath the willow tree and talk about Beauty, Bronco, and Clyde.

Kori and I ride home. She tosses me onto her bed and pulls back the skin around the corners of her eyes. Kori picks me up and throws me into the corner.

I see Peter's horse t-shirt from my corner today. Joe Jockey hangs from Peter's hand and I say hi. Kori, Peter, and Joe sit on her bed.

I say hi to Peter. Peter says he is sorry to Kori. He is sorry he called her names. Peter says he doesn't like stupid girls like Sally. Stupid girls like Sally only want to play house and princess all day.

Peter asks Kori if she wants to go to the creek and look for horses.

Can I go too?

My arm warms in Kori's hand. We ride horses with Peter and Joe down to the creek. We all sit on some rocks by the creek. Kori gives me to Peter. Peter gives Joe to Kori. Kori looks down Joe's pants and Peter looks up my dress and down my lace panties.

I don't like Peter's hands, Kori. I don't like this game.

The last time I saw Kori, she was giggling. Kori grabbed Peter's hand and they galloped down the creek past the willows. Joe and I sat against our rocks.

I yelled mamma and other stuff in private, but Kori disappeared under the willows. Joe thinks she went to look for the horses. I think she doesn't understand. 🏵

Just Desserts

by Dulce D. Moore

Nobody expected the Board to close the club Saturday just because Rhonda had killed herself with an overdose of sleeping pills that morning. They might close it a couple of hours for her funeral. If what was left of her family buried her Monday or Tuesday. Those were slow days, anyhow. Not if they waited till Wednesday. That belonged to the bridge players and mid-week golfers. Rhonda's relatives wouldn't want to wait that long, anyhow. They were too anxious to find out which of them had inherited what from the huge estate she'd inherited when her husband died a couple of years ago.

If he were still alive, the Board would've shown every sign of respect possible except that of closing on a Saturday. J. J. Rutledge had been far too rich and powerful to offend. But noththing less than a tornado or a presidential assassination was important enough to interfere with that most sacrosanct day of the week. And hell, they'd have assured each other, Ol' J. J. was a businessman, he'd have understood that.

Just as Jerry expected me to understand that since Rhonda and I hadn't been really good friends since high school, nearly twenty years ago for Christ's sake, it'd be ridiculous for us to stay home. Missing the Saturday night dinner-dance would mean missing out on all kinds of business contacts he couldn't make anywhere else. Even a man in his position had to do a little sweet-talking and back-slapping to stay on top, and his wife ought to damn sure be in there helping him do it.

I got dressed. Our marriage was so shaky, one more big blow-up might bring it down. Rhonda was beyond caring, and at least I wouldn't have to stay long. If Kaye would co-operate as she usually did when I wanted to leave early and she was mad or bored. We'd flip a coin those nights, loser to plead the kind of splitting headache that would allow us to cut the evening short without too much of a hassle.

Not that we ever got off scot-free. The husband of the offending wife on that particular occasion either complained, loudly, that by damn he was getting sick and tired of being drug home when the party hadn't hardly got started, and he was of a good mind to take her home and come back to finish it by himself. Or, also loudly, that if what those damn libbers preached about women being equal to men was true, how come it was always some woman who ruined things for everybody else by whining about her aches and pains.

Nor that we risked our luck so often our husbands, oblivious as they generally were to anything less subtle than a two-by-four between the eyes, might catch on. If that happened, Kaye and I would be stuck every Saturday night from 7:OO to 2:OO for the rest of our lives in the hallowed precincts of the Big Oak Country Club—yessir, a fine little club right outside the fine little city of Big Oak, Texas.

When we got there that evening, the Fosters were already seated at our table; Ross, my husband's business partner, already well-oiled; Kaye, my fellow conspirator, already on the ropes in the umpteenth round of their running battle over money.

Kaye said that Ross was too tight to let them live the way they ought to on his income. Ross said they couldn't live the way they did—which was pretty high on the hog if you asked him—if he didn't get the most out of every dollar, and she ought to be grateful she could sit around on her butt doing nothing all day in the four-bedroom-three-bath-brick his hard work had bought her.

We heard that fight nearly every Saturday night. Though this time they'd apparently started it at home instead of waiting for the end of the evening as they usually did. When both husbands had at last wandered back from the bar, where they headed to talk business with their cohorts the minute they finished dinner and stayed till the club manager flicked the lights as a signal for the band to play 'Good night, Ladies."

As we sat down, Ross grinned his big salesman's grin that said all was right with his world, podnah, and he could make it so in yours. Kaye substituted whatever she'd been about to say for, "Go get these people a drink, Ross, they're way behind. And bring me another."

When the men got up to adjourn to the bar after a relatively peaceful meal, Ross squeezed my shoulder and said, "Hell of a thing about Rhonda. Want you to know I'm sorry."

I nodded my thanks as they walked off, and Kaye said, "What a bull-shitter. He's no sorrier than any of these other hypocrites going around moaning about how sorry they are. And why should he be? Why should anybody be sorry she killed herself?"

"She was a human being, Kaye. Somebody we've known since we were kids. If I'd had any idea she was that desperate—"

"Why would she be desperate? She lived in an absolute mansion, drove a Ferrari and wore designer clothes and could flash more diamonds than Liz Taylor. What more could she want?"

What she wanted was to be sixteen forever. Forever in love. With someone who'd love her forever. Not like Lennie Falk, whose forever ceased as soon as he won a football scholarship to A&M.

Rhonda left town a couple of months after he did. Some said she went to the Edna Gladney Home in Fort Worth and put the baby up for adoption. Some said she went to stay with an aunt over near Waco, where her baby was born dead. Lennie's mother said there never was a baby to start with. That Rhonda just made that up so she could force Lennie to marry her. The little slut. I said Rhonda wasn't a slut, and after awhile nobody said anything. But nobody forgot. Small town people never do. Especially when the sinner in question lacks money and influence.

Which was why when I went home for spring break, I didn't tell anyone I'd run into Rhonda earlier that year, waiting tables at one of the rare full-service eating places close to the campus. When the late lunch crowd cleared out, we sat in a back booth, both of us straining to find a safe topic of conversation. We couldn't gossip about home, like old friends meeting by chance somewhere else normally did. We were too young to care about the weather or politics or any of the other subjects that would seem important to us when we were older. After a couple of false starts, we finally settled on talking about the pains and pleasures of living in Austin, discovered that we didn't know any of the same people, and had just begun to relax with each other when she glanced at her watch and said she had to get back on duty. No, they wouldn't fire her, good waitresses were too hard to come by. But she couldn't afford to lose the tips that helped pay her tuition at the junior college where she was studying for an associate degree in food marketing and management.

We hugged and swapped phone numbers and promised we'd keep in touch. But she never called me, and I ignored my conscience till the end of semester, when it was too late. The number I called turned out to belong to the restaurant and the voice that answered my request to speak to Rhonda informed me she wasn't with them anymore.

Kaye jerked me back to the present with an impatient, "Get the hell on with it, will you? I'm tired of waiting."

"For what?" Not another drink just yet, I hoped. She was already slurring her words some.

"For you to tell me why Rhonda wanted to die when she had everything in the world to live for. You ought to know. Y'all were thicker than thieves."

"In high school, Kaye. We didn't see much of each other after that. She was living out of town, both of us were busy going to college, working—"

I at my first job, that very summer, as general flunky for Fields and Foster, Inc., one of the few oil and real estate combines to prosper during the Awful Eighties. They created the job for me as a favor to my father, who, like nearly everybody else in that business, had lost his shirt.

I filed, answered the phone, ran errands, drove prospective clients around and took their wives to lunch at the club while Kaye's sick-as-a-dog-somebody-feel-sorry-for-me pregnancy kept her from performing her duties as hostess. I held her hand all those summer evenings Ross worked late and spent most of my other evenings holding my bewildered parents' hands.

Instead of going back to The University that fall, I transferred to Mary Hardin Baylor so I could live at home. Fees were higher, and I had to drive back and forth to Belton, but it was still cheaper than living in a dorm. Or a crummy apartment where I'd have to cook all my meals because I couldn't afford to eat out anymore. Even at fast-food joints.

There were lots of things I couldn't afford anymore because of my father's financial losses. My sophomore year among them, if my summer job hadn't paid for it. Having to quit when classes resumed would've added to that list, had Ross and Jerry not let me pick up a little extra money wining and dining some client's wife on the weekends Kaye couldn't.

When she could, I sat with Little Ross, such a sickly, cranky baby nobody else would. I took her place when she couldn't, either because she was so looped or so bedraggled-looking from being looped all week, Ross wouldn't let her out of the house—

"Well, I never went to college like you and Rhonda," Kaye said, "but I worked as hard as either one of you ever did. Hell, I'm still working."

"Doing what?"

She polished off her drink, saluted me with the empty glass and said, "You ought to know, babe. Keeping a rotten marriage from falling apart's the hardest work there is."

I didn't want that discussion to get started, so I stopped a passing waiter and ordered two more of the same.

Kaye told him to make hers a double and as he turned away, said, "Now where were we? Oh yeah. You were trying to tell me you and Rhonda drifted apart because of working and college and all that crap, when I know you stayed in touch with each other."

"Yes, but it wasn't the same. Our lives changed—by the time I had to drop out of MHB my senior year to help look after Mama, Rhonda was married—"

"Ummm, yes," she sighed, "to that gorgeous hunk what-was-his-name?"

"Wesley Turner." The ideal good old boy. Tall, handsome, country-talking, with those lovely Southern manners only East Texans still practice. He'd be your truest friend, your deadliest enemy, and he was so crazy about Rhonda—the waiter brought our drinks, I signed the chit, and Kaye said, "Maybe if a guy like that had asked me to marry him—"

"You'd have said no in a New York minute."

"You don't know that."

"Sure I do. He didn't have any money. He was a long dis- tance trucker, what they call an independent contractor, who—"

Lost control of his rig on an icy overpass outside some little town in New Mexico. Rhonda had his body flown back to Daingerfield for burial in his family's plot. Drove back home to her mother's after the funeral and lost control of her life.

She'd come home every three or four months, stay till she was on her feet again, then take off again. Mrs. Horton would call me when she showed up. The poor woman didn't have anyone else. She was a widow, with no kinfolks in town. She didn't want the neighbors to know the shape Rhonda was in. She knew I was Rhonda's friend.

That first year, I'd go over there and help her give Rhonda a bath, get her into a gown, doctor her cuts and bruises, spoon some hot milk down her, put her to bed—then I no longer had the time. I'd married Jerry— keeping two ailing parents in a good nursing home costs a lot of money— and he wanted his money's worth.

Kaye looked up from the designs she was drawing in the mois-ture that had gathered on her glass and said, "How long had they been married when he got killed?"

"About five years."

"And they really were happy the whole time?"

"Yes . . .the way everybody thinks they'll be. Or hopes they will, anyhow."

She slapped the table hard enough to jiggle the ashtray and said, "Now don't you be a bullshitter. We both knew marrying into Fields and Foster, Inc. meant abandoning all hope. But even that's never driven us to drink as bad as Rhonda did or take dope or—"

"Rhonda didn't do drugs. She did stay drunk most of two years and hang out with the wrong crowd, the wrong men—I tried to tell her once she was slowly but surely killing herself and she looked me straight in the eye and said yes, because she didn't have the guts to do it any faster."

"What finally turned her around?"

"I don't know. Maybe she saw what she was doing to her mother. Or maybe she just got tired of living like that. Whatever it was, she signed herself into a rehab center and then moved on to a half-way house—God, how I wish she'd done something like that this time, that I'd realized—"

"Well, you didn't, and it wasn't your fault, so—will you look at who Ross is buying a drink for?"

Bald, old seedy-looking Lennie Falk was standing at the bar, one hand resting on Jerry's shoulder, the other lifting his glass to Ross. "That bastard," I said. "How does he manage to keep sneaking in here?"

"Look at the help we have nowadays. They're all either college kids who couldn't care less about the rules, or illegal immigrants who're scared to question anybody for fear they'll get shipped back to Mexico."

"Roger ought to stay on the door himself."

"Nah, our beloved manager's too busy circulating around sucking up to the high and mighty. The Board's not going to fire him or even reprimand him. He knows where all the bodies are buried."

"Well, regardless, if people would quit letting Lennie cadge drinks—"

"And miss all the fun of listening to him tell how he got cheated out of playing for the pros so they can laugh at him behind his back? Silly ass. Everybody knows he spent most of his time at A&M sitting on the bench—and speaking of circulating, I guess we better do some of that ourselves if we don't want to catch billy hell when we get home."

"I just can't do it tonight, Kaye. I keep thinking about Rhonda—she was doing so well till J. J. came along. She was happy again, really proud she'd worked her way up to assistant manager in Nick Kokinos's famous Athena—it's funny. If she hadn't been living in that half-way house, and he hadn't personally delivered his usual donation of left over rolls and pastries—"

"Yeah, I know. I've heard that story a dozen times—how he was so impressed with the way Rhonda was running the kitchen and dining room that he gave her a job at his place. It's never occurred to you he was more impressed by what a looker Rhonda was?"

"Oh, that probably influenced him some. Rhonda was beautiful. But she knew the restaurant business, too, and she didn't mind hard work. Of course, Nick had to teach her the finer points of dealing with the kind of upscale clientele he was beginning to attract, but—"

"No more 'buts.' The truth is, Nick rescued her from that hole she was in, gave her a real career and treated her like a queen, and what did she do? Kissed him off the minute J. J. strolled in and crooked his finger at her."

"She didn't 'kiss him off.' She was fond of Nick. She respected him and she was grateful to him, but—"

"*But* she was greedy, too, admit it."

"No, J. J.'s money didn't have anything to do with her marrying him."

"Oh, please!"

"I knew her better than you did, and I'm telling you material things didn't meant that much to Rhonda. Besides, by the time J. J. came along, she already owned a high-priced condo, wore good clothes, drove a nice car, had a pretty hefty bank account—"

"All of which looked like peanuts next to what J. J. Rutledge had to offer—hell, I'm not knocking her. Who wouldn't jump at the chance to marry a man that slipped little diamond goodies into the flowers he sent her and—"

"You've forgotten how good-looking J. J. was, what a charmer he could be when he wanted to. Rhonda didn't know him the way we did."

"Yeah, yeah—hey, you—" to a waiter scurrying by "—how about some service over here?"

"You better slow down. You know how mad Ross gets when—"

"Piss on Ross. And piss on all this talk about poor little Rhonda—two more of the same, Pedro, and don't take all night."

"Listen, Kaye—"

"No, you listen. Rhonda used men. She used Nick and she used J. J. and—"

"Nick got what he paid for out of Rhonda. She worked like a dog helping him build that restaurant into the kind of place that you had to book reservations for a month in advance. And as for J. J.—"

The waiter set our drinks down, Kaye signed the chit, took a sip instead of a gulp I was glad to see, and said, "Okay, now tell me how dear Rhonda paid J. J. for what he bought."

"She loved him, can't you get that through your head? She was a good and faithful wife to him, stood by him when any other woman would've sued him for a divorce and walked off with half of everything he owned."

"She had that option, all right. Ol' J. J. was a terror with the ladies."

"It wasn't just his trifling and the way he rubbed Rhonda's face in it. He beat her, Kaye. A couple of times I know of, for sure."

"Well, then. Maybe Rhonda figured she deserved more than half. Maybe she figured if she stuck around long enough, she'd end up with all of it. J. J. being J. J., somebody would've eventually shot him or clubbed him to death with a tire iron—hell, him getting so drunk he fell off his boat and drowned just made her waiting shorter."

"You don't understand."

"I understand that she could've divorced him and lived happily ever after—could have, anyhow, once he was gone, and—"

"No, she was in love with him. She'd thought he was in love with her, that she'd found her forever, and—"

"Well what I want to find is another drink. You see Pedro? Or Kirsten or Caitland or whatever they're named these days?"

"No, not anywhere nearby. But I'll go fetch us a drink from the bar if—look, why don't we have one more, then fix it up to go home?"

"I'm getting bored enough, listening to you make excuses for Rhonda. She had more chances at the good life than most people, and if she didn't have enough sense to take advantage of them, she got what she deserved—and don't look at me like that, damn it—oh, hey—" her nails dug into my wrist—"I'm sorry. I guess I'm pretty tight, huh?"

"Yeah," I said, pulling my arm away, "I guess you are."

"Well, tell you what. You go get us that drink, then I'll do the honors—" scrabbling through her purse—"I know I've got some change somewhere in here."

"Let's flip first."

"Okay. Here we go, with a shiny new penny. What's your call?"

"Heads."

The penny wobbled up, dropped back down onto the table, spun around in a slow circle and fell flat. "Tails," she said, "you lose." ✦

Box Set

by Rob Johnson

"I hope I die before I get old."
Pete Townsend

"I hope I die before I become a box set."
Clemons Juggernaut, lead singer, Brain Circus

Has there ever been a rock band more confounding than Brain Circus? Three guys working a shrimpboat out of Corpus Christi, Texas, who played music with an effect on their listeners that only chocolate brownies and several Lone Star beers could cure, who sold fewer albums in their lifetime than Beethoven did in his, and whose artistic energies peaked recording incidental music for Aaron Spiegelman's mid-seventies police dramas? Obviously to try and contain, in one box set, the music of the ultimate fin-de-seventies band, is an impossible, nay, a foolish under-taking. Still, am I wrong or isn't it true that now, more than ever, we *need* the music of Brain Circus, what with the possibility of their reunion tour, the Tarrantino thing, and the lack of any music out there that people our age can relate to anyway? But I don't have to tell you any of this, not if you are reading the liner notes to this 12 cd box set. Because you already know. Or, to quote Clemons Juggernaut himself, "Do you know that you know?"

Everyone comes, or doesn't come, to the music of Brain Circus in their own way. Maybe you were lucky enough to catch the early gigs during their shrimpboat days, or later off Western Ave in Hollywood. Maybe you ran off and joined the Circus later, perhaps having read about Brain Circus's refusal to leave the stage until headliners KISS agreed to appear on-stage without their make-up—a rock-and-roll filibuster that resulted in Brain Circus jamming out a ninety-two minute version of "Wild Thing" ("You can hear the whole history of rock and roll in Brain Circus's version of that song," wrote rock critic Lester Bangs). Even the uninitiated know the stories—the famous *Cream* photo of Clemons Juggernaut deeply french-kissing Ian Mottle of the Blue Boys; the refried bean balloon drops; the band's impromptu gig on "The Merv Griffin Show," with Griffin sitting in on piano for a bring-down-the-house version of the band's dance sensation, "(Crab Walking) Back to You, Babe" (available on cd here for the very first time).

That's getting ahead of our story, though. *The early days, the formative years.* Corpus Christi, Texas, the little city by the bay. Clemons, Waylon Bones, and East-side accordion-player turned bass player Humberto "Hum" Robles. Three guys barely in their teens hauling shrimp nets in the near-dawn, doing absolutely nothing all afternoon, and learning their licks at night. "The way we looked at it, if you could repair a shrimp net, you could certainly string a guitar," Clemons has said of those days, early on demonstrating characteristic Brain Circus logic. "Our major recreation was having fights with shrimp heads on Captain Pappy's boat," Waylon Bones recalls. "We needed an outlet." It was, initially, Juggernaut who dreamed the dream. "I think we were all drawn to Juggernaut, as an artist, out of some strange pity," Robles has said in his only public statement, the famous Vegas suicide note. "You see, Clemons lived in a lighthouse, and he spent too much time staring into the 300,000-watt bulb. He wore sunglasses even at night. If you could ever see his eyes—he showed them to me once—they looked like the eyes on those fish you find in caves. Brrrr."

If you really want to know those early days, though, just take a listen to the recently uncovered rare demo of Clemons singing the band's first ballad—"Lighthouse Home" (disc 2, track 12). Released on their second album, *Nude Descending a Stairway to Heaven*, which sold only 12 copies before Plant and Page litigated it out of existence, "Lighthouse Home" shows the band never forgot where they came from, even if in later years they wouldn't know where they were. The track, replete with the authentic cries of hungry seagulls, confirms a bit of history supplied by Hum Robles that "Clemons learned to sing listening to Sonny Bono songs on Mexican radio stations that kept fading in and out."

With encouragement and inspiration from crusty old salt Captain Pappy, the boys put together a rip-tide list of briny rockers that still moves butts today—including "Hauling and Balling" (based on Captain Pappy's ribald tales of shrimping and loving; disc 4, track 11), "Doom Buggy" (disc 11, track 11), and the influential pre-grunge classic "Frontloader" (disc 3, track 8), based on the life of Juggernaut's dockworker father. (Soundgarden, Alice in Chains, were you listening? We think you did!) Clemons gave the fledgling band its name: "Brain Circus was a board game I played as a child," he reveals. "It was almost immediately recalled when it became apparent that the 'Ringmaster Says' cards led to poor personal hygiene and precocious sexual activity."

Their music spread like an oil spill throughout the coastal Texas towns. At legendary clubs such as the Sick Porpoise, the Bufadora, and Sam's Flotsam, the band quickly built a reputation for playing music that you could listen to when you were very, deeply drunk, the kind of drunk from which you never fully recover. "You think they're another bad cover band when you first hear them," a reviewer from those days wrote in the *Corpus Christi Herald*. "But then you realize, with a prickly sensation not unlike horror, that these are *original* songs. Their audience seems intent on ridding the city of Corpus Christi of all alcoholic beverages in a single night of drinking."

With reviews like that appearing, Captain Pappy suggested to the lads it was time to ship out. He grabbed a piece of butcher paper, drew an arrow pointing North to a fat line labeled Interstate 10, and told them, "Make a left."

The boys arrived in the City of Angels in a battered Econoline Van, addled and ready to play. Their good-bye to the little city by the bay had been a bittersweet one: a bad shrimp, ingested during the farewell feast on board Captain Pappy's boat kept Clemons' head hanging out the window for the two-thousand-mile trek ("Bad Shrimp," disc 8, track 10).

Success was slow coming in the big city. For a while, they didn't even know where they were. Hum insisted that they had made a right, not a left. These were hard times. The Econoline slept three uncomfortably, and there was always the street-cleaner to deal with, the threat of unpaid tickets.

"To this day, the sound of wire brushes and jetting water sends me into a panic," Hum commented. "We had to get out of the van," writes Waylon in his bitter memoir, *No-Brain Circus*.

During one low period, they ended up sleeping under the deteriorating "Hollywood" sign high in the hills overlooking Los Angeles. Years later, it would be Clemons—not Alice Cooper—who would start the crusade to restore the sign. Says Juggernaut, "I bought the 'Y', which is where I used to sleep. The 'H' offered the most shelter, the 'O' was hard on your back, and I took the 'Y' for philosophical reasons. Waylon—you know he wrote an inexplicable book about all this—of course he had to have the 'H.' "

Their break came when an enterprising booking agent, finally realizing the boys auditioning before him were singing about a bay somewhere, billed them as San Francisco's best new band. The gambit worked: Angelenos loved to think that people from San Francisco looked—-and smelled—like these guys.

That cover was ultimately blown when the boys opened their mouths. Still, their South Texas charm captivated big-city dwellers. Long-time fan Roddy McDowell remembers, "I just simply lost it hearing Clemons pronounce the word 'metaphor' as 'meta-furrr.' You had to love them." "And, oh," says another longtime fan, Dick Van Patten, "their endless dismay at the tiny size of Pacific shrimp. To hear them describe Texas shrimp, you could saddle them up and ride them! I cannot tell you what a tonic they were in those days." Their six-month reign on Tuesday nights at the Below-the-Belt club on Western Avenue would be the stepping stone to the albums and large venues which followed. "The Beatles were a hit at the Cave Club, the Doors at the Whisky," reflects Juggernaut, adding in a bit of Lennon-esque punning, "We hit Below-the-Belt."

Hollywood was more than just home; the rich history of the city began to creep into Juggernaut's evolving music. "I was walking down an abandoned railroad track, scouting locations for a band photo, and I met Buster Keaton, who was still living off his cameo in *Pajama Party*. He took me home and showed me his model railway, which ran all through the house, and even outside." Inspiration was everywhere in those days.

"Keaton was trying to stop smoking," Clemons reveals with a wink, "and he would light a cigarette, place it on an ashtray attached to one of the model rail flatbeds, wait until the little car with the stogey came all the way back around, and then take another drag"—the source, as you can well guess, of Brain Circus's signature seldom-played second encore song, "Addiction Train" (disc 3, track 4).

"That was the beginning of it," writes Waylon Bones in the afore-mentioned sour-grapes account of the band's career. "Juggernaut had started to go Hollywood. It was that crowd of strange old vaudevillians."

Fate would have it that about the time of what Bones considers the beginning of the end, the band would be discovered by Irving Restless, an industry CPA with some revolutionary ideas about accounting. "Write-Off" Records' first single would be Brain Circus's "Addiction Train." "They were very, very good for us during a particularly profitable moment in the industry that led to increased tax obligations." So, they were a prestige band, as opposed to a profitable one? "You could say that. Yes, say that," concurs Restless.

Rolling on the threatening-to-break-into-the-top-one-hundred chart success of "Addiction Train," the band took the advice of a drunken fan in a seersucker suit—"I believe, sir, that you boys would be big in certain bars found in unreconstructed Southern states"—and, in June of 1972, embarked on their only nationwide, headlining tour, the epochal "Mindless Summer" tour.

"I don't remember 1972," Juggernaut says blithely. "I've seen tapes of me in it. I was fabulously dissipated, and the photos from me of that time worked wonderfully in my recent Health Club ads—you know, the Hard Rock/Rock Hard contrast series."

In spite of Juggernaut's apparent stupor, the band racked up forty-nine gigs on the sixteen-day tour, playing flea markets, drive-in movie inter-missions, and gun shows. An unsoiled "Mindless Summer" T-shirt from this Sherman's March through the South now sells for well over ten dollars, if signed by the band's surviving members and if an unvalidated meal ticket is found in the pocket.

Today, it seems as if every music fan of that period caught one of the

Southern gigs. "If you put in one room all the people who say they saw those shows," says Irving Restless, "they would probably make a dent in the seating of the overflow dining room at Cantor's Deli—you know, six or seven booths—really it takes two waitresses to station it properly—the room with the bright orange leaves printed on the plexiglass ceiling tiles?"

It was the beginning and end of headlining, but the beginning of several years of prestigious opening act spots. "They were a band that really made the headliner sound good," recalled the late great promoter Bill Graham. "They were in high demand."

We've represented those salad days with a thick slice of classic studio and live albums, including tracks from *Brain Circus's Big Top* (Write-Off, 1972), *Nude Descending a Stairway to Heaven* (Write-Off, 1973), *Live Brains* (Write-Off, 1973), *The Brain Circus Album* (Write-Off, 1974), *A Very Special Evening and Early Morning With Brain Circus* (Write-Off, 1974), *Send in the Clowns With Chinese Take-Out* (Write-Off, 1974), and *Brain Circus B-Sides* (IRS, 1975). Tasty, no?

Back from the rigorous touring, exhausted by the demanding studio schedule, Juggernaut and the band still had it in them to record what now is now considered their most important work—the incidental music they recorded for Aaron Spiegelman's mid-seventies police dramas and movies of the week. Juggernaut proudly claims, "If it was made for TV in 1975, and if there is music in the background when the cops chase some black guy into a bar full of pimps, that music is by Brain Circus."

"I absolutely refuse to discuss the music of that period," says Bones. "It was really what put Hum over the edge. It's just ridiculous. It was that bunch of broken-down silent movie stars that introduced Clemons to Aaron Spiegelman." To this day, a more-than-a-touch bitter Bones will not watch police dramas on TV, not even *Silk Stalkings*. "I can't believe," he says, "that anyone wants to hear the music we did for those crappy shows."

Well, Quentin Tarrantino, for one does, and now you too, for the first time on cd (or anywhere else for that matter), can hear "Huggy Bear Walking Down the Alley" (disc 4, track 3), "Pimps at the Bar" (disc 10, track 7), "Car Chase (Studio Lot) Parts I-IX" (disc 6, complete), and both "Pursuit Up the Fire Escape" and "Pursuit Down the Stairwell" (uncut long-play version, including dialogue segue performed by Anthony Franciosa—"Down the stairs!" (—disc 7, track 4).

Industry insiders remember the band had a natural knack for such creations. "It was truly remarkable," says a former TV script doctor. "We could say, 'OK, this black guy . . .' and one of the band members, I think it was the drummer, would say '. . . walks into a bar crowded with prostitutes and starts shooting pool.' I mean, it was amazing, they could tell you what was going to be the visual accompaniment before you even completed a sentence."

It was their best work, and it would be their last music made together.

The bitterness, the recriminations. Those who fly too close to the flame. . . . "I really don't understand Waylon's book," Juggernaut says, hand on forehead. "It hurts me. All that time on the road, in the studio, I thought we were having fun. It came as quite a shock to me how miserable he was."

Things fell apart quickly—"the center cannot hold." Yeats said that.

Hum left the band for his own brief but distinguished solo career. "It was really him, not Jaco Pastorius, who changed the way musicians play the bass today," says a still-galled Waylon Bones. "You know, it wasn't thump thump thump thump, it was thump thump thump thump. I think his innovations were mainly due to his background in conjunto accordion."

Hum's last-known appearance was on a radio station in Las Vegas. A tape from this interview (disc 12, track 9) shows that Hum seemed to have no idea when the microphone was on, and when it was off. "I really need you to give me some head now," he tells a college-radio DJ identified on the tape as 'Cindy'. "Hum needs head!" That night, his body was found by Vegas police, crumpled over an unusual device Hum had used to inject drugs—his old accordion! The Vegas coroner never ascertained the cause of death, but did tell reporters that Hum had been injecting fluids that no "normal person would inject—and I'm talking about people who are drug addict normal."

Waylon Bones went on to become an Ezra Pound scholar, specializing in the late Cantos. He teaches at UCLA and misses no opportunity to dismiss his former band and bandmate Juggernaut.

Clemons Juggernaut is, of course, an inspiration to a whole new generation of Brain Circus influenced bands. Everyone's older brother who died young or amounted to nothing or has never been seen again seems to have left behind a well-played copy of *Brain Circus's Bigtop* or *HustleBustle* that their younger siblings inevitably took a listen to. "In the late eighties," says Jon John, lead singer of Holiday Death Toll, "if you wanted to clear out a party, you put on that live Brain Circus album—the one with the giant puppets on the cover."

"I think the real revival of Brain Circus came with the Tarrantino thing," reflects Juggernaut. "Pairing 'Bad Shrimp' with the brothel massacre scene was inspired. Then suddenly, everyone was sampling the old TV stuff, especially 'Chasing the Black Guy Clutching the Paper Sack Filled with Money.' We used to just let people use the songs for free—that's how surprised I was by the whole thing. Not anymore, of course," he says with a laugh, and his eyes must be twinkling behind the dark shades.

Now there's talk of a revival tour, with Paul McCartney on bass. "Do you think this box set will help our chances?" asks Juggernaut. "I know it won't be the same without Hum, and I do think the Ezra Pound thing is just a fad with Waylon. And Paul, if he's interested, he really is a pretty good bass player." For just a moment, Clemons Juggernaut grows moody, but the large tumbler of bourbon quickly mellows him. "You know," he says. "I won't say that we were ahead of our time. We definitely lived *around* the time these records were made. But you get older, and you realize that whatever inspiration you had leaves you, and you're just older and more tired. That comment about box sets, for example. That's a Clemons Juggernaut I simply don't know anymore." Tantalizingly, he looks as if he is going to take off his glasses to rub those famous fish eyes, but instead slides his shades back up his nose. "To be honest, that first song, 'Lighthouse Home,' that's the best song I ever wrote."

And I'm privileged to hear a brief, *a capella* preview of that possible reunion tour:

> *The Brain is like a circus*
> *And your head is a bigtop*
> *Ringmaster! Ringmaster!*

Make it Stop, Make it Stop

"It's really the only half-assed good one at all," sighs Juggernaut. "I can say that now."

And after over a dozen cd's and almost seventy tracks, you might agree with him. 🏵

THE HAMM'S BEAR SAYS IT'S CLOSING TIME

by Donna Walker-Nixon

I'm just about to leave the house when the phone rings. It must be the bartender, telling me Jerry's in worse condition than I think, but it's my son Travis, calling to apologize one more time that he won't be in from A&M until tomorrow afternoon. "I know you need me, but I've got to work a late shift tonight," he explains. And I wish his daddy would bear up under responsibility like his son does.

"No, I understand," I tell him. But I was counting on seeing him, first thing in the morning. To make things easier, I tell myself.

I hang up and head to the Rig to pick up Jerry. As I walk in, his back's toward the door, like he wants to deny that I'm here. I can't help thinking of a song that I used to call the Jerry and Karen theme song before I told him to leave two months ago. So I start saying the words as I walk up to him. "I'm gonna hire a wino. To decorate our lives." He turns around and tries to act surprised. I don't know why he's surprised; every Saturday night since Jerry moved out, the bartender calls when Jerry's gone over his limit and says, "Come get your husband."

The first time, I tried to tell him that Jerry moved out on Monday. The owner got on the phone and said, "That don't matter. He's yours, and I'm not about to take him home with me."

I've been coming to the Rig ever since then to take Jerry home. The owner doesn't want Jerry to get to his Dodge Ram pickup until the next morning when he's had enough time to get sober. About a month before Jerry moved out, he took my keys and drove back to the Rig. He broke in the back door, thinking it was still open, and the police took him into Lindsey to spend the night. The owner wasn't too happy, and now they all figure I can take Jerry home. The next day Jerry calls one of his friends to take him to get his truck.

Jerry laughs at my take on the song and pats me on the back, hard like he thinks I'm a buddy at the bar. "The day when I can't drive for myself. . . ."

I finish the words to the song when I tell him, "The Hamm's bear says it's closing time."

With him a joke works better than fussing, and he says, "I ain't drunk yet."

He begs me to stay until the set is over. I agree to let him stay, so long as he doesn't order another drink. Tonight, I'd rather be at home, getting ready for Travis to come home. It's the first time he's been back since Jerry and I separated and since the trouble with those girls at Lindsey High started. I can't stand to see Jerry sit and talk while we've got a world of trouble to face. So I nod to Rick and say, "Keep an eye on him."

I head to the ladies' room, wishing I had someone pick me up and take me home. Jerry needs someone to take care of him, but I'm tired of it being me. It's been this way since CJ passed on. Jerry has trouble dealing with the fact that we lost our son.

It was an accident. Some folks don't realize that, but it was an accident. Jerry said himself, "A man don't set out to kill his son." It's true, men don't do that. But it's taken most of ten years to get people to believe him. People not letting up, men especially, but women, too.

Tonight, I hide in the stall of the ladies' room while two women in raspy cigarette voices talk. "You see the man at that table next to the bar? The one with the bulby nose."

"Yeah, what of him?"

"Dale went to school with him. He killed his son, you know."

"No."

"Dale says it was no accident."

"I can't see as how a man could kill his son and get away with it."

"Neither does Dale. But that isn't the half of it," she says.

I flush the toilet loud to keep from having to hear them and to make them aware that someone is in the next stall hearing every word. They don't stop. One croaks as she says, "You heard about those girls over in Lindsey, didn't you?"

"What girls?"

"The ones that said the school janitor made them do favors for him."

The other mumbles something about having heard that story, but she doesn't know much about it. Neither one knows much; they don't know Jerry took that job four years ago so he could bring in money to send Travis to A&M. They don't know the toll it takes on Jerry working after he's already gotten off one job, so his son can have a better chance at life than Jerry ever did. That's the kind of man he is, but they don't know that.

"People in Downs Creek where he lives swear by him. Just like a little community to take up for their own. Never saw anything like it in my life."

I flush the toilet again; they wait for me to come out, and their voices turn to whispers. I stay put; it's been like this since CJ passed, and now it's getting worse. The rollers from the paper dispenser begin to creak. The paper crackles as they dry their hands and leave. I stay behind the stall until I hear some girls giggling, and I go to the sink and start pushing the soap dispenser.

The girls with their tight pants and red lips hog the mirrors, and I wait on them to leave so I can check my make-up. My eyes feel puffy; I have to make sure, for Jerry's sake, that he can't see that I'm upset. When I look in the mirror, I see that the old saying must be right: when a man and a woman are married so long, they start to look alike. I've got his bulby nose, and my sky blue eye shadow looks like the black circles around his eyes. What happened to the Assembly of God girl who married Jerry when she was sixteen and pregnant?

Even though Jerry moved out six months ago, it was because of his drinking, not because I believe what those girls are saying about him. If he heard what those old women said, he would go up to Dale and call him out to the parking lot to settle things. I keep it all inward because Jerry behaves when he believes that people have forgotten, but they don't. I can see it in their faces. Still, there are people like Jerry's friends at the Rig who look past what happened to CJ and see Jerry for what he should be—a good man who happens to drink too much, but who can make people laugh and forget themselves.

Tonight, Jerry forgets about himself and listens to Old Man Putnam's stories about serving in Brazil in World War II. Old man Putnam's wife passed on five years back. Once he gets started, there's no stopping him, but Jerry listens while he finishes the beer that he got the bartender to give him while I was gone. That's a Jerry those women will never see.

Most Saturdays, I put up with the talking, but tonight Travis is coming home, and I can't stay until the they shut the doors at two. "Jerry, I've got a headache. Let's go."

He shrugs and keeps on talking to Old Man Putnam. "You say those beaches in Brazil were some of the most crystal clear you've ever seen?"

"Pretty as anything you'd want to see, but they told us not to go out in the water because these red man-eating fish would leave nothing but the bone."

I try to finish the story for him, "Once two boys went out there."

"You know how young folks are. We was no different," Old Man Putnam says, just like I hadn't said a word. "Those boys didn't come back. All we could see on the water was red blood mixed in with the crystal clear blue." He wipes his eyes with a paper napkin.

"It must've been like one of them *Twilight Zone* stories," Jerry says.

Jerry starts talking about the court action against him. "You know how kids are these days. They make up stories. No one believes them," he says, waiting for Old Man Putnam to agree, but then starting again. "In my day, girls like that was seen and not heard. You better believe, their daddies would make sure they knew what was what."

Jerry's friend Bob eases around the table behind us. "Them girls ain't nothing but . . . and I know there's women present, but the truth is the truth . . . they ain't nothing but whores, if you ask me."

Others start joining in, like it's a song they're playing on the juke box between sets. Jerry got them to act the way he wants; he'll stop at nothing till he gets them to agree that not a jury in Lindsey county could see it any other way.

"That gives me hope. You don't know how despairing a man can get. Some days, I wonder what's the use in living. You try to do right, all your life through, and then to be accused of fondling two young girls old enough to be my daughters. Just like I don't got a good woman who gives me all a man could ever want." He slaps me on the thigh and looks lustful, never mind that I don't live with him. And for months before he left, he told me as he patted his private parts, "Jiminy Cricket's too tired."

His words echo false in my ear, and I can't stand listening to him carry on any longer. "Jerry, the Hamm's bear says it's closing time." I can't stop crying. That's not like me, but tonight listening to those women, shut behind a stall door, not able to make them or the world stop, it's different.

On the way home since it's earlier than usual and he hasn't drunk enough to bring on the feeling that nothing matters, when we pass the package store on the county line, he commands, "Pull over."

I keep driving, holding back a part of me that he's never seen.

"Pull over," he yells at me. "Woman, don't you hear a word I say? Pull over."

He grabs the steering wheel, but I push him away, and then I stop in the middle of the road and make him walk across the road to the store while I wait for him to get back. When he gets back in the car, he pats the brown sack just like he used to pat Jiminy Cricket and says, "This'll get me through the night."

I know better than to answer him, and just when I hear the door shut, I take off, jerking him forward. "This ain't no cattle car," he complains, but I keep driving and reminding him, "The Hamm's bear says it's closing time."

When we get to his trailer, he acts like he's too far gone to do anything but sit in the car. I push him awake, and he snarls. "Woman, what do you want?" He says something about FDR declaring the end of the war, like he's back talking to Old Man Putnam.

"Jerry, I'm going to make sure you're tucked in for the night." That gives him hope that I'll stay, and he opens the door and stumbles. If I didn't know better, I'd be surprised he didn't break an arm or a leg, but he never does. Part of me wants to leave him on the parking lot of the trailer park, but neighbors might come home and say I don't do my duty by poor old Jerry who's had a bad time of it lately.

"Jerry, just let me have the key."

He holds his hand to his pocket and says, "See if you can get past

Jiminy Cricket."

I head to my car when he starts acting like he never had a drink in the first place. He walks to the trailer, and he sits down in his chair like he's come in from work and expects to turn on the TV and see the ten o'clock news. The chair and his TV are the only things he wanted to take with him when I told him he had to leave.

"It's Ewell's fault."

His step-father passed on three years ago, and Jerry still blames all the bad things that ever happened to him on Ewell. I'm tired of that, too; for once, I tell him as much. "Jerry, Ewell's gone. He didn't. . . ."

"You don't know all the things he said and did."

I do know. He's told me, from the first date till now, he's told me. Ewell was a nice old man who didn't have any children of his own and tried to do right by Jerry's mom by raising Jerry and his brother Roderick like they were his own, but Jerry wouldn't have it.

"He made Roderick what he is today."

I wait for him to tell me once again that Ewell is the reason Roderick turned queer.

"Queer as a four dollar bill," he says. "Ewell never recognized that fact. He just compared me to my dad and said, 'Apple don't fall far from the tree.' That's what he said every time I didn't meet up to his expectations. That, or he'd call me a dark angel. What can you expect? Growing up with Ewell, I never a chance to become a lawyer like Roderick. The only thing he said I was good for was fixing cars and working like a dog for him."

"Yes, Jerry." I leave him in his recliner to nurse his beer.

When I open the door, his chin starts to quiver, almost like he's going to cry, but Jerry never cries. "You're leaving me, too. Just like everyone else."

I try to remind him that we separated before all this trouble started with the girls.

"You think I'm guilty, don't you."

"You know better. It's your drinking, Jerry. That's the reason I'm gone."

"With a good woman by my side, I could quit."

He knows better, I know better, and people in Downs Creek know better—even the ones who stand by him now and say they've never known a better neighbor than Jerry Clark.

"Jerry, you won't quit. I've waited most of my adult life to see you quit. With CJ's passing, it got worse."

"Why you bringing up that boy's name?" He never calls CJ by name, and most of the time I don't mention CJ. Tonight, those women said nothing that I hadn't seen in people's faces. But seeing a look on people's faces isn't the same as hearing thoughts put into words.

Jerry's face turns ruddy red, like the after-blush of alcohol. The red mixed with the black circles around his eyes makes him look like a hot air balloon about to burst. As I look at him, I want him to burst, like the balloon. I want him out of my life, and most of all I want him out of my other son's life.

"I got nothing to live for. If my woman don't believe in me, I might as well give up—if I don't have my family behind me." He falls in front of his chair, and he crawls to the cabinet where he keeps his real daddy's tools. He picks up the nail gun that his daddy killed himself with, and like he's done in the past he makes his threat. When he pulled out the nail gun right after we got married, filled with hysteria, I yelled, "No, Jerry, don't. I love you."

He wants me to do the same, but I can't. "Don't make threats you won't keep," I say.

"Travis believes in me. Why can't you?" he asks and loses track of what he just said.

I can't because . . . because of CJ, but I don't say it. On that day, CJ was proud to get to go with his younger brother and his daddy hunting, but he didn't take to hunting. Two years before, when Jerry brought in the biggest deer ever bagged in Lindsey County, CJ vomited. And Jerry made fun of him. "Only babies act like that, only babies." He threatened to find a diaper in the nursery where I kept babies during the week for working mothers. That wasn't the only time Jerry threatened to find a diaper for CJ. Each time, Jerry got what he wanted: CJ backed down and tried to do exactly the things he thought Jerry wanted. The only problem, Jerry didn't know what he wanted, so how could CJ know how to please Jerry?

Thinking back, I blame myself. I made Jerry take CJ with him and

Travis. "He's the oldest, and you never bring him along."

"I'd take him if I thought he could cut mustard," Jerry said.

"You don't have to look at his face every time you go with Travis and he's left behind."

I knew better than to threaten, but Jerry didn't treat CJ right, and as a mother, I couldn't make things right, only Jerry could.

"All right already. Deer season begins in two weeks. He's got to practice first before I'll risk taking him to the lease."

CJ smiled when I told him. His blond hair fell over his eyes, and I had seen pictures of Jerry when he was CJ's age: Cottontop, they called him. That's what I wanted to call CJ, but Jerry would pitch a fit because he swore that Ewell took over when CJ was born and never gave Jerry a chance to father his first born. They got up that morning, and they left before breakfast to go to the range that Jerry built beside the house. I didn't get to see CJ off, but he didn't sleep much the night before. I woke several times and heard him in the bathroom, then the kitchen, and finally I passed back to sleep.

That morning, I heard gunshots in the back field; I felt comforted that CJ finally had his chance. Travis ran into the house, yelling that CJ had been hurt. I called the hospital. I put the boys in the Blazer. CJ bleeding from his stomach, CJ unconscious, I told myself. He was unconscious from the shock. When we got to the hospital, when we got to the doctors, they would pull him out of it. And me, I had it all together. I took charge, like always with Jerry. I wanted to blame him. I wanted to say, "You killed my son." But no, I told myself, CJ would pull through.

But then the doctor came, shaking his head, in tears that I never saw on Jerry's face. "He didn't make it, Ma'am. I sorry."

By then Ewell had come. He sat in the red vinyl chairs, crying, saying words Jerry should have said. "My boy, my boy," like CJ belonged to him. Jerry sat in the chair, his thighs bulging against the sides, and even then if I had been honest, I would have wished him dead, not CJ.

Ewell blamed Jerry, but I wouldn't allow myself to say those words. Jerry answered with hollow words that meant nothing: "No man starts out to shoot his son. No man."

I tried to believe him. Ewell said, "What did you think you were doing out there?" I believed my husband. Through the years, with all the stares and looks and people whispering, I believed him.

It was the alcohol that caused me to leave. Every Saturday night standing by for calls. The drinking, something my mama never tolerated and she never showed sympathy when I complained of his drinking. "What do you expect? You let him keep it in the house," she told me more than once.

Tonight, too, it was the alcohol. I tell myself. No man I loved could shoot his own son. No man I loved could fondle young girls. It was the alcohol, and they misunderstood his intentions. Either that, or they lied. Girls lie; they make up stories.

I can't think clearly. Thoughts blur, and I've got to get away from Jerry. "I'm going."

"A man has to lean on his family. If he can't do that, then he might as well call it quits."

"Yes," I say and leave for home.

The next afternoon, Travis comes in from college. I'm glad to see him and just as glad he didn't have to see his dad last night. Travis is a good boy, taking only the good parts of Jerry and me. He'll graduate in December, and he hopes to come back to Lindsey to coach football. From what I hear around town, people want him to fill Coach Potter's place. That's how much they like him.

"How's Dad holding up?" he asks while he pecks me on the cheek.

"Fine." I'm not telling the whole truth, but he knows better than to question.

"Word is around town, those girls have it in for him. The Burson girl moved from Houston, and they say her parents brought her here because she was all over the boys."

When he says those words, he sounds like Jerry, and I can't help shuddering.

"Mom, I'll see him through this thing."

If I didn't know better, I'd think he was trying to make me feel guilty for leaving Jerry. He didn't hear those women last night. When CJ passed, Travis never noticed the looks people gave me in the H•E•B when I bought groceries or at the laundromat when I folded clothes. He didn't notice the way some people, not everybody, but some turned away when they saw his daddy coming.

When I look at Travis, I don't see Jerry. I see CJ, and I know that I had two sons, not one. I picture Jerry in his recliner, holding the nail gun that belonged to his daddy. 🏵

THE HUMMINGBIRD

by Guida Jackson

Marta slammed the door so hard the windows rattled. Jesús, who'd been napping on the couch, bolted up and tried to look alert or at least conscious, wondering what he'd done this time. But he had a pretty good idea that it had to do with Domingo.

"The man is ruining us!" she told him. Her black eyes flashed like agate, something Jesús had considered hermosa in their courting days, but had now come to recognize as the omen of bad times ahead. "We are going to be outcasts from the whole Project! No one will speak to us!"

With great reluctance, he asked, "What's the problema?" Because he would just as soon not know anything else.

She flopped down beside him, sending eddies of exasperation washing against him. "Sangre de Cristo, I do not know what comes over that man! Do you know what he did? He threw a rock through Mrs. Mendoza's window! Just stood there and threw a rock!"

Jesús wondered if there could be a mistake. True, Domingo sometimes acted on impulse, but he was good at heart. He was rash, like Perro Feo, the airplane-eared pariah dog that had attached himself to Jesús. That dog tried so hard to make people like him. Domingo did, too, but like Perro Feo, he didn't think things through. Marta said that dog was nothing but forty pounds of reflex. Same way with Jesús's cousin, only Domingo weighed in at about four times as much. And his reflexes were duller.

Jesús reached for the remote and flicked on MTV. "I'll talk to him," he said, knowing that was not what Marta wanted to hear. She wanted him to send Domingo back to Progreso, the same way she would banish Perro Feo to the pound if she had the chance.

But how could he tell Domingo to go? It was his idea in the first place for Domingo to come to Pharr. There was no future for any man in

Progreso, much less one who walked like Domingo, with one foot turned all the way in since birth. Tía Guapa used to take him to La Curandera in San Antonio every time they had a family reunion. Tía Guapa had assured everyone that ever since he was born, Domingo had worn his deer's eye to protect against Evil Eye, but La Curandera had told her that Domingo had gotten Ojo while he was still in the womb. The family had doubted this diagnosis at first, but through the years, despite being rubbed by the grease of black cats, dogs, and pigeons, Domingo's foot never straightened an inch. The family eventually accepted the truth: Domingo's brand of Ojo could not be undone.

But other than rendering him mute in the presence of a pretty woman, the affliction could not dampen Domingo's outgoing nature. His arrival at Lalo's Icehouse always signaled a round of spirited storytelling among the beer drinkers, with Domingo typically leading off with some escapade in which he got the better of a highly-placed, always inept public official. Gradually, as each man took his turn, the stories invariably came around to the subject of prowess with women. When hunger threatened to disperse them homeward, the storytellers would turn again to Domingo for the capper, for in the three months since Domingo came to Pharr, no one had come close to matching his stories about women.

"...and I mean, man, the woman couldn't keep away from me! I walk into the confessional and shut the door and there she is, man, crouched down in the corner, just waitin' for me, man, and she is pantin' and moanin' and me, I got to give my confession to the priest with this woman all the time climbing all over me. . . ."

And the men at Lalo's would look from Domingo's animated face to his turned-in foot and if they doubted, none spoke. Because Domingo gave voice to all their fantasies. Yes, Domingo earned his keep, but it was not a thing that Jesús could readily explain to Marta.

Besides, how could he have known, at that boozy family gathering in San Antonio, that in the expansive aftermath of the feast, when he had told Domingo, "Hell, man, you ought to come on down and get a job at Calidad Electronics . . . hell, amigo, mi casa es siempre tu casa"—how could he have known that Domingo would take him up on it?

Marta looked out the window and said, "Here he comes now." She got up and snapped off the TV, whipped around and planted herself in front of it with her arms folded like Pancho Villa. Her voice was out of control, like the screech of a wild javelina. It was enough to turn anybody's knees to jelly. "I want you to see to it that he puts a new glass in Mrs. Mendoza's window. And then—"

But before she could say, "I want him out of here!" Jesús had made his escape. Perro Feo, who had carved out a dirt bed for himself beside the front door, sprang to duty and wagged his whole body. Sure enough, here came Domingo, clumping along toward the house, his usually big open face drawn with worry until he spotted Jesús. Then he brightened with a flash of teeth and stuck up a thumb. "Hey man! Qué pasa?"

In the wake of all that wagging and grinning, Jesús was undone. He slapped a hand on his cousin's shoulder and spun him around. "We got to run an errand," he said. Perro Feo trotted diagonally along in front of them in his lopsided gait with ears fanning, clearly believing that he was invited.

When it became obvious that Domingo did not intend to bring up the subject, Jesús said, "We got to buy old lady Mendoza a new window. Why'd you do it, man?"

Domingo stopped in mid clump and then stumbled forward as soon as he'd gotten a grip. He grinned again. "Oh, so you heard. It was an accident, man. I was aiming at a bird."

That was all Domingo would say. What mystified Jesús further, once they reached the crime scene with the new glass, was that the broken window was located clear around on the back side of Mrs. Mendoza's house. It was the only window without a screen. Mrs. Mendoza had hung a hummingbird feeder under the eave and had removed the screen so that she could fill the feeder without going outside.

"What were you doing around here in her back yard, man?" Jesús wanted to know.

Domingo, unconstituted to hold anything back for long, hung his head and said, "You'll laugh."

"I won't laugh, amigo. Tell me what you were doing, man."

Domingo hesitated and then blurted, "Trying to kill me a hummingbird."

"Trying to—" And then Jesús understood. El Abuelo used to tell them that the way to attract women was to tie a dead hummingbird in a sack around your neck. It was a technique that had worked without fail in his family for generations, dating back to early times in Central Mexico.

Without intending to, Jesús glanced at his cousin's turned-in foot and heaved the sigh of the hopeless. "Anybody in particular you got in mind?"

Domingo stared past him at some Vision Glorious and whispered, "Felicia Gonzales."

Por Díos. Jesús looked down at Perro Feo: same dark glistening gaze of adoration. But beautiful Felicia! Domingo was going to need all the help he could get. And more.

He studied the tiny birds darting up to the feeder, wings whirring so fast they were invisible, and wondered how either of them could hope to bring one down without risking another broken window. Especially now, with Mrs. Mendoza glaring from the kitchen door. If only he could get them to slow down. . . .

"I got it!" Jesús said. "We don't have to try to bag one on the fly; we can put 'em to sleep first!"

"How, man?"

"Tequila. Tonight we lace the colored water with tequila, then all you got to do is wait until one drops, and you can pick it up and wring its neck. And you got yourself a dead hummingbird!"

The idea possessed the simplicity of true genius, except that there was no way, when they returned after dark, to prevent Perro Feo from tagging along, running circles around them, tripping them up, and occasionally barking his encouragement. Jesús had to wait on the corner holding Perro Feo by the scruff while Domingo accomplished the deed alone. When Domingo rejoined him, Jesús said, "That tears it, man; this dog is going to screw up the whole deal."

Domingo's bushy eyebrows almost met over his nose as he frowned in thought. Finally he brightened. "I got an idea. You and the dog can distract the old lady in the morning by knocking on her front door while I sneak around back and pick up a bird."

The plan admitted of no obvious flaws, discounting that they were both due at Calidad Electronics the next morning at eight o'clock. But nobody was ever fired off the line for being late.

Two other flaws were to surface the next day that Jesús did not anticipate. The first was evident almost as soon as Mrs. Mendoza opened the door to his knock and said warily, "Well?"

Jesús had neglected to plan what he would say next. He looked down at Perro Feo, faithfully tongue-lolling at his side, and inspiration seized him. "I came to see if you would like to have a dog," he said.

The old woman's eyes narrowed as she sized up Perro Feo. "Does he bite?"

Alarmed, realizing that Mrs. Mendoza was actually considering his offer, Jesús blustered, "Sí! He bites all the time! He's a very vicious dog!"

"Good!" Mrs. Mendoza said. "That's just what I need since all these drug pushers and *rock throwers* moved into the neighborhood." She opened the door wider and favored Perro Feo with a gold-toothed smile. "Are you hungry, pobrecito? Lástima! Just look at those skinny bones! Mama Mendoza will fatten you up with some nice chorizo scraps."

And without so much as a backward glance, Perro Feo, that traitor, wagged past Jesús and into Mrs. Mendoza's house. The old woman gave Jesús a look normally reserved for axe-murderers and shut the door before he could protest. He stood there for a while, trying to think of something he could do to retrieve Perro Feo. But the whole incident had happened so fast that for once his powers of invention failed him. Finally he wandered on off, abandoned and dejected, muttering about the disloyalty of dogs these days, and eventually made his way to work.

Domingo was already there, working on the line. He lifted his goggles, stuck up a thumb and pointed meaningfully at the lump on his chest. Jesús hoped to God the spell worked, after all he had personally sacrificed.

Even so, it wouldn't hurt to light a candle to St. Jude, patron saint of lost causes, and he told Domingo as much when they got off work. But a new assertive Domingo looked at his watch and shook his head. "I can't, man. I got to get the bus over to McAllen. If I don't catch Felicia before she gets off work, I'll never find her in the crowd." Felicia worked in the

Chicky-Bite booth in the mall.

Jesús caught his cousin's arm. "Look, man. I think these things have to build up for a while. I think you got to wear that bird for—well, *weeks*, maybe—" He thought of something else. "Have you got that thing in a zip-lock bag?"

But Domingo was already sidling away to catch the Express, and he didn't answer. Jesús shook his head, feeling sorry for poor naive Domingo, and knowing nothing, as yet, of the other flaw in their plan.

On his way to Lalo's Icehouse, he stopped off at the church to light a candle to St. Jude for Domingo. Then he remembered Perro Feo's recent betrayal and lit another one.

The crowd at Lalo's voiced loud disappointment when Jesús came in alone. The storytellers were so subdued without Domingo's catalyst that the evening just never got off the ground. So Jesús left early and even made it to supper almost on time, as Marta noted with some sarcasm.

"Where's Domingo?" she said.

He pulled a chair up to the table. "I think he had a date."

"Him? He can't get close to a girl without stuttering."

"That was before."

"Before what?"

"Before he got him a dead hummingbird."

Marta set the frijoles down with a thud. "Madre de Díos! Who is she?"

"Felicia Gonzales."

"Oh, que idiota! She's way too pretty for Domingo! Didn't you tell him that? Where is he now, making a fool of himself up at the mall?"

He looked at his watch. The mall had been closed for two hours; Domingo had had plenty of time to get home. He rolled some beans into a tortilla and stood up. "Maybe I better go find him," he said, picturing the impulsive Domingo throwing himself off the freeway just because some mujada had rejected him.

He cruised by Felicia's house, just in case, but it was dark. Then, remembering that Felicia made a daily trip to the Shrine of the Laundromat to pay homage to the vision of the Blessed Virgin stuck on the dryer door, he cruised by there, but the manager had already locked up.

Even Lalo's Icehouse shut down on week nights at ten o'clock. But as he drove down Main Street past the Reynosa Cinema, he saw the two of them, Domingo and Felicia, coming out of the movie arm in arm. And nose to nose. Jesús honked and unlatched the passenger door and called, "Hey, Paco! Want a ride?"

Domingo must not have understood, because he only waved and kept walking. Jesús sat on the horn until everybody on the street turned to look. Domingo clumped slowly over with what Jesús took for reluctance, with Felicia clinging to his arm. She bounced into the front seat, then when Domingo had eased in, she repositioned herself atop his lap like the cherry on a sundae. The two moon-eyed one another while Jesús revised his assessment of her taste.

Without even looking at Jesús she said, "Why didn't you tell me about your cousin before?" Domingo blushed and ducked while Jesús considered puking.

He gunned off so fast that Felicia grabbed the dash and said, "Aguila! Cuidado! Do you want to crush the bird?"

"Oh, so you told her about the bird," Jesús said, and he glanced at Domingo's chest—and gasped. The lump beneath Domingo's shirt fluttered! With disgust, Jesús said, "Shit, estupido! No faltaba mas! You didn't even kill it!"

Domingo fidgeted under his burden and said, "I know, man. I didn't have the heart. Cueste lo que cueste."

Felicia beamed at Domingo while she confided to Jesús, "Is this some kind of guy who doesn't have the heart to kill a bird, hey? He even opened up the bag and fed it juice through a straw."

Aha. Maybe that was why Perro Feo didn't stick around. Maybe, if he had just fed that dog once in a while. . . . ✿

This story is based on a folk practice brought to South Texas from Mexico.

THE VANISHING POINT

by Lee Martin

He wouldn't boast, no, not he, not Mr. Little Washington Jones, but under the right conditions—perhaps on a May night in 1921, when the mimosa trees were pink, and the magnolia flowers had bloomed, and he and his wife, Eugie, had just strolled through their front gate after a trip to RCO's Ice Cream Parlor—he might admit that yes, indeed, he truly did have the finest, most well-kept lawn in the entire neighborhood of Quakertown, in all of Denton, maybe, and, though he hated to have to say it, but there it was, slap in front of his eyes, perhaps the loveliest in all of Texas.

Consider, he might say, the American Sweetheart tea roses, the verbena, the periwinkle, not to mention—well, if he must—the rare white lilac.

And if he paused, then, at the low picket gate and lifted his hand to one of the white blossoms just for the sheer joy of letting the velvety petals brush his work-worn palm, who would fault him? Surely no one who knew how he had found the white lilac growing wild along the banks of Pecan Creek, showy and magnificent among the scrub of mesquite and bramble, how he had uprooted it, wrapped its ball in damp burlap, and hauled it in his wagon the two miles to Quakertown, hauled it first down Oak Street, past the grand homes and their green, green lawns where young men in white linen trousers played croquet, and ladies in ankle-length skirts batted feather shuttlecocks back and forth across badminton nets. Little sat up straight on the bench seat of his buckboard, gave the reins a shake, and listened to the jingle of the mule's harness, the cloppety-clop of its shoes over the cobble street. He heard the pock-pock of the croquet games fall silent, a rocker squeak as someone leaned forward. "I swan," he heard a woman say, that single voice, a voice of amazement and admiration he would carry with him for years. And he knew that what his father had told him was true: a black man with a talent could always make white folks take notice. "Find something they prize," his father had said, "and do it better than they can. You'll always have a place with them. You'll make yourself an easier life."

Washington Jones, Sr., had been a travelling man, a mapmaker who had specialized in bird's eye maps, detailed renderings of communities as they might be seen from the air. He used engineering maps as sources and then replicated every street, railroad track, tree, barn—every object, in fact, that someone might see from a perspective above the city. Once, in a hotel in Lincoln, Nebraska, he showed Little how to draw a horizontal line only a whisker from the top of the paper. That, he said, was the horizon the way it would look to a bird in the air. He drew their hotel. He drew buildings and streets that disappeared at the high horizon. That was the vanishing point, he said, the place where any two lines would meet and disappear. The secret was perspective, knowing what to make small and what to make smaller, what to make close and what to make far away. It was that and knowing how to use darker and lighter shades to create a trick of the eye, an illusion of space and depth. "I can make something so small," he said, "it almost disappears." He touched his lead to the map, leaving two specks in a window of their hotel.

"What's that?" Little said.

"That's me and you," his father told him. "The two of us, sitting right here, right now. There we are, and no one will ever know."

As Little grew, so did his talent with flowers and trees and shrubs, and people in North Texas treasured anything green or brilliant with color, determined as they were to make something grow from some of the worst soil in the world, a gummy mess of clay they called gumbo.

Each morning that summer of 1921, Little ate his breakfast on his front porch so he could watch his neighbors walk up the hill to the College of Industrial Arts where they worked as maids and cooks and janitors. As they passed, he called out to them, "Mornin' Osceola, mornin' Miss Simms, mornin' Mr. Smoke." He sat on a cane-bottom chair, a red bandanna tucked into his shirt collar, and sipped his tea, his own blend of comfrey and sassafras. He waited for someone passing to compliment his lawn, to stop, perhaps, and admire the white lilac or the Chinese Pistachio.

From time to time, Eugie called him a high-hat nigger. "I declare," she told him once. "Look at you. Sitting up there like you owned the world."

That night, when he stood in the dusk near the white lilac, she accused him again of putting on the swank. He lifted his head and saw their daughter, Camellia, who sat near the front window, tatting lace for her wedding dress. She was marrying Ike Mattoon, the barber who had been in the Great War.

"Little, you're a yard man," Eugie said. "That's the true by and by of it. You carry white folks' dirt home under your fingernails, but does that make you white? No, sir. That just makes you a dirtier nigger."

Her father, Captain Jiggs of Boliver, had been a white man, a rancher who had taken Eugie's mother as a slave and had then married her. When Indian raids threatened their safety on the ranch, he moved Eugie and her mother to Denton, into a rented house on Oak Street where Little had begun to work. Eugie was caramel-skinned with lips that formed a dainty bow and a nose that came to a button tip. Camellia's skin was even lighter, and she had her mother's features. Little watched her at the window, looping and knotting the lace, and he felt, as he often did, that she and her mother were bound by a blood he couldn't share.

Camellia was their only child, a teacher at the Quakertown School. Little liked to slip away from his work at the noon hour and drive his wagon by the school yard. Sometimes he sat awhile and watched Camellia, a flock of boys and girls clutching at the folds of her coat, and he marvelled over the goodness of her. She was so easy to love. Nights, she sat at the kitchen table and marked her students' lessons. She encouraged even the poorest, always finding some reason to write "good" in the red blush of her marking pencil. Like Little, she was a dreamer. Once a month, she went up the hill to the college and slipped into the balcony of the auditorium by climbing the fire escape ladder so the audience below her wouldn't know a colored girl had come to watch that evening's travelogue. She came home chattering about Paris, China, South America. "Papa, there are other places," she said once. "Other worlds. All these other lives we could have. Why do we have to settle for only one?" Little imagined that Ike Mattoon had appealed to her because he was a war veteran who had seen some of the world. He talked of France and the wide stretch of ocean, and how long he had travelled over it on the troop ship, convinced he would never again see land.

Little laughed now and said, "Well, maybe my lawn's not the best. Maybe that's a stretch. There is one other contender. Mr. Andrew Bell who lives on Oak Street. Mr. Andrew Bell, the banker. Do you know Mr. Bell?"

"Little," said Eugie. "Quit acting the fool."

She did indeed know Mr. Bell and his fine lawn because it was Little who managed it all for him, Little who had the magic thumb. He could make a brickbat grow daisies, Mr. Bell told him once. "Honestly, Little, you're a wizard." And Little, though he didn't want to be prideful—at least not overly so—could not, for the life of him, disagree.

Then one day, when Little was pruning a live oak in Mr. Bell's back yard, Mr. Bell called him down from his ladder, and he said to him, "I need you, Little. This city needs you. Will you help us?"

"Yes, sir," he said because it was what he always said when Mr. Bell asked him to do something.

Mr. Bell stuck his fat thumbs into the pockets of his vest, and the shiny material stretched across his ample stomach. His gold watch chain sparkled in the sunlight. "Good. That's the spirit. That's just the sort of civic pride we hope your neighbors will have."

"Oh, they're good folks," said Little.

"Of course they are," said Mr. Bell. "That's why I'm sure they'll know opportunity when it knocks."

It was, Mr. Bell explained, a chance of a lifetime. The city wanted to build a park, a magnificent park like the one in Dallas, and someone would have to be the caretaker of that park, and the City Commission—on Mr. Bell's recommendation, of course—had decided that this someone should be Little Washington Jones. "We all want a pleasant life, don't we, Little? Whites and coloreds alike."

Little had heard about the park in Dallas, its waterfalls and ponds, its exotic plants. "Why, Mr. Bell," he said. "I don't know what to say."

"Say you'll accept, Little. Say you're our man."

"Mr. Bell, you know you can count on Little Jones."

"Outstanding. Now listen. Here's the way we think it should go."

When Little got back to Quakertown that evening, he saw the janitors and maids and cooks coming down the long hill from the college. They were laughing among themselves, throwing up their hands, relieved to be rid of work for the day, thankful to be away from the college where they had learned to move about with their eyes cast down to the floor, to mumble, "yes, miss," when need be, or "no, miss," or "sorry, miss."

Now they were back in Quakertown, the neighborhood of homes and businesses their ancestors had managed to build in the years following Reconstruction. On Frame Street, there was Nib's Grocery, and above it, the rooms where Dr. L.C. Parrish practiced medicine. Next door, Poot Mackey operated the Buffalo Bayou Cafe, and across the street, RCO's Ice Cream Parlor advertised Dairy Maid Custard. And there was Bat Suggs' Shoe Repair, and Miss Abigail Lou's Hair Salon, and Billy Moten's Apothecary, and Griff Lane's Hardware Store, and the barber shop Ike Mattoon, Little's soon-to-be son-in-law, had opened after the war when he had come home from the war and left Tennessee because he had heard about Quakertown from the porters on the passenger trains that stopped in Chattanooga. There was this place in Texas, the porters said, a little piece of Negro paradise.

In the evenings, someone out for a stroll might hear the clack of dominoes slapped down on a kitchen table, the call of, "Boxcars. Now how you like that?" Or the voices of the AME Church Choir going to work on "Couldn't Hear Nobody Pray." Or, if it was Saturday night, a blues singer at the Buffalo Bayou Cafe—Mabel Moon, maybe, or Big Mama Annie, Hocey Simms, or Choo Choo LaDeau. Third Sundays, the Heroines of Jericho put out a feed. They laid plywood sheets over sawhorses the length of Frame Street, and everyone came toting kitchen chairs, sat down, elbow to elbow, and packed away catfish gumbo, garlic grits, Cajun cabbage, sweet potato pudding, red beans and rice, pork chops, barbecued chicken, baked ham, hot rolls with peach peel jelly, apple pie, sugar pie, black walnut pound cake. "Lord," someone would say. "This is as good as it gets."

At home, Little stepped up on his porch and saw Eugie and Camellia sitting across from each other in the living room, their knees touching, the folds of Camellia's wedding dress draped over their laps. Eugie was showing Camellia how to sew beads to the bodice. They were sitting in a patch of sunlight, and the silver beads were glittering. Little felt a chill pass over him. For an instant, he imagined that he was a stranger, peeking in at this woman, Eugie, and this girl, Camellia. Only moments before, he had stepped, for the first time, into Mr. Andrew Bell's home. He had sat on a chair covered with crushed velvet, had sipped lemonade from a crystal tumbler, and Mr. Bell had sown him the design for the park, a drawing of flower beds, wading pools, gazebos, footbridges, picnic pavilions, a band shell, a swimming pool. Little stared at the green puffs of bushes and trees, the blue streaks of water. And at the edge of it all, he saw a sketch of his own house: its front porch—the porch he stood upon now—its cedar shingle roof; the beds of marigolds, and alyssum, and candytuft; the tea roses; the pinkie hawthorn shrubs along the foundation; and in the yard, the Chinese Pistachio, the flowering pear, and the white lilac at the picket gate.

Now, Little opened the screen door and stepped into his house. In his head, he carried a chant that had filled him when he had looked at the drawing of the park and had seen it spread between the streets that bordered Quakertown: "Frame-Withers-Oakland-Bell."

"We need that space, Little," Mr. Bell had said.

"But folks' houses."

"We'll move them a few miles east. Don't worry. Everything will work out fine."

Little's shadow fell over Eugie and Camellia, and when they lifted their faces, it was easy for him to imagine that they were looking at him with heat in their eyes as if he had just interrupted something consecrated and hallowed. He knew the words from Mr. Lincoln's address at Gettysburg, an oration Washington Jones, Sr. had recited time and time again. Little knew what the words meant. They meant there were things in the world no one ought to disturb, places only a savior or a tomfool would ever venture to walk.

"Moms, Baby-Girl," he said.

He came closer to them, intending to tell the story of the park the city wanted to build and how he would be the caretaker of that park, but, just then, a silver bead dropped from Eugie's hand and rolled across the floor until it bumped against the toe of Little's boot. He knew she had saved back a dollar here and a dollar there from the money she earned doing alterations downtown at Neiman's Department Store, and she had bought the lace she would need for the bodice. Camellia had pitched in what she could spare from her teacher's salary, and they had gone to Miss Diane's fabric shop and had special-ordered five yards of white satin. Nights, they had worked side by side, first cutting the pattern and then stitching the pieces together at Eugie's Singer, its hum as constant as blood through veins as Eugie pumped the treadle with her foot.

Once, Little woke in the night and found her sitting in her rocking chair by the window, crying. He said to her, "I'd think you'd be happy for Camellia." And she told him, of course, she was happy, but oh so miserable, too, because she could imagine how empty the house would be without their Baby-Girl.

"We'll still be here," he told her. "And Camellia and Ike here in Quakertown, not living off somewhere the way so many do now days."

"You don't think they'd do that, do you?" she said. "Move away? You don't think Ike would ever take a notion to go back to Tennessee."

"Why would he do that? He's set up in business here."

Now Little got down on his knees and plucked the silver bead from the floor. He carried it to Eugie and laid in on her palm as carefully as he had once put their sleeping Baby-Girl in her arms. Something in the delicate motion made him consider the threads that tied them to one another, bound them to Quakertown, and he couldn't bring himself to say what he had agreed to do.

It was late, long past midnight, when he woke and heard Eugie and

Camellia talking in the kitchen.

"Mama," Camellia said in a pleading whisper.

"Hush," said Eugie. "Done is done."

She stepped out onto the back porch, and through the bedroom window, Little saw her go down the brick walkway he had laid just that spring and into the alley where she turned north up the long hill to the college.

He dressed quickly, slipped through the dark house and out into the night. In the alley, he saw Eugie ahead of him, her shoulders pitched forward as she climbed the hill. He kept to the shadows, sneaking along behind her.

At the end of the alley, Little saw a figure hiding in the recess of the back door entry to the Estuary Rare Book Shop. The man's shoulders slumped as he leaned forward on his cane, and Little knew it was Mr. Andrew Bell's son, Kizer.

Little hid himself behind a row of trash cans and saw Eugie step up to Kizer who offered her an envelope. "It's what you want, isn't it?" He gave the envelope a shake. "Fifty dollars. That's what you asked."

"Yes, it's what I want," Eugie said. She took the envelope from Kizer, folded it once, and stuffed it into the pocket of her dress.

"Camellia," said Kizer.

Eugie held up her hand. "This is the end of our business. I'll keep up my part of the bargain. You be sure to stick to yours."

Little remembered, then, how on his trip with his father to Nebraska, his father had made a colored bell man polish his boots with his white gloves. "Do you know who brought me here?" Washington Jones, Sr. had said, when the bell man had balked. "Councilman August Cook, the same Mr. Cook who owns this hotel. I wouldn't want to have to tell him that you made me unhappy. Would you want me to have to do that?" The bell man got down on his knees, and dipped his white-gloved fingers into the boot black. Washington Jones, Sr., smiled at Little. "This is livin', ain't it, Little? High on the hog, hey, little man?" Little felt an ache come into his throat. He knew why his father was happy to spend so much time away from him and his mother. So he could stay in fancy hotel rooms, look down on the cities and let their people treat him like a king. So he could forget, for as long as it took him to draw his maps, the color of his skin, which was the color of Little's skin, and the color of all the people he loved.

Now, in the alley, it was clear to him that, whatever this business was between Eugie and Kizer, she had determined that Little himself wouldn't know of it. He remembered what she had called him that night by the white lilac—"a yard man," "a dirtier nigger"—and he couldn't bring himself to announce his presence. He slipped off through the shadows and made his way home where he pretended to be asleep when she returned.

When morning came, he hitched his mule and left for Mr. Andrew Bell's. On the front lawn, he knelt beside a pittosporum shrub. At the request of Mr. Bell, he was grooming the pittosporum into the shape of the sphinx. From the picture Mr. Bell had shown him, he had built a wire mesh frame that duplicated the outline of the body, which was that of a resting lion, and the head, the head of a man, his face framed by the triangular folds of his headdress. All spring, Little had let the pittosporum grown inside the frame, and he had sheared away the stems and leaves that poked through the wire.

He clipped the stems with small, gentle cuts. The blades of his shears, honed to a sharp edge, gleamed in the sunlight, but he didn't wield them with the reckless abandon such sharpness might have tempted most men to do. He made a few cuts and then stopped to run his hand over the wire mesh, brushing away bits of leaves. As he rubbed his hand over the leaves, he remembered how, whenever Camellia had been cranky or upset as a toddler, he had taken her out into their yard and told her to touch the glossy leaves of the cleyera, to trace the bell-shaped flowers of the forsythia, to smell the clove perfume of the moonflowers opening at twilight. Now, here she was, a grown woman, as delicate as her namesake blossoms which burned in full sun and needed the shade of filtered light.

Years ago, when she had been no more than five or six, Little had brought her to the Bells'. He had told her to sit on a bench at the rear of the back yard while he worked in the flower beds along the house's foundation. When he finished his work and turned to look for her, she was gone. He called and called. Finally, he heard a rustling in a snowball bush. He crouched down and parted the branches. Camellia and Kizer were sitting cross-legged on the ground. She was holding her arm next to his, studying the difference in color. "We got born wrong," she said to Little on their way back to Quakertown. "That boy's leg's too short, and I'm not the right color."

Now Kizer came out onto the lawn, the tip of his cane sinking down into the damp ground. "You're hard at work," he said to Little.

"Yes, sir, Mr. Kizer." Little squinted up at him. "Doing just like your daddy said to do, make this shrub into this lion-man."

Kizer reached out with his cane and flicked at a stray stem poking through the wire mesh. "It must seem ridiculous to you. A silly thing, I mean, for someone to want."

"I've made birds, sheep, fish." Little snipped the stray stem. "What people want is their business. I figure they got their reasons. It's not my place to judge what's in their hearts."

Kizer let his cane fall to the ground; then, he got down on his knees. He reached out and touched Little on the wrist.

"Your daughter," Kizer said.

"Camellia," said Little.

"She and I . . ."

"Yes."

"The fact is . . ."

"You and her."

"Yes." Kizer gripped Little's wrist more tightly. "Exactly."

Little knew how Camellia was always quick to show a kind face to the students who, because they were poor or ill-featured, or slow to learn, needed her love—how, too, she was greedy for adventure—and he sensed that she and Kizer had come to trouble.

"You hadn't ought to tell me this," he said. "Camellia is going to marry Ike Mattoon."

But Kizer, once he had started, couldn't stop the flow of words. The sound of his voice was, to Little, like the sound his shears made against the pittosporum stems, a sharp whistling keen. "Fifty dollars," Little heard, and then something about Eugie and how right now, this morning, she was with Camellia. "Dr. L.C. Parrish," he heard, and then a word he didn't know.

"Say it plain, please, Mr. Kizer."

"Curettage," said Kizer. "Abortion."

The sun was so fierce Little could feel the heat on his eyeballs. He spoke in the quiet voice he had learned to use in the company of the people who employed him. "I don't know why you told me this. I don't know what you expect me to do."

"Won't you stop it?" Kizer's voice was choked and pleading.

"Stop it," said Little. "Do you think I'd have anymore of a chance of doing that than you?"

"She's your daughter."

"She's her mother's daughter," Little said. "That's plain."

He heard the anguish in his own voice, and he knew, then, why Kizer had told him the secret. So he wouldn't be alone. So there would be two of them, closed out by Eugie and Camellia, who had decided.

That evening, when Little came home, Eugie was waiting for him on the front porch. "I was just sitting here," she told him, "thinking how beautiful."

"Beautiful?" he said. How dare she talk of beauty then?

"The yard." She swept her arm out before her. "The mimosa, the lilac. All because of you, Little."

He sat down on the porch floor, his back against a post. He waited for Eugie to say more, to tell him about Camellia and Kizer and Dr. L.C. Parrish, but all she said was, "Do you remember the night Baby-Girl was born? How you said we had to name her Camellia on account her skin was soft and buttery like a camellia blossom?"

"I remember."

"You wouldn't want a thing to hurt her, would you, Little?"

"Has something happened to Camellia?" He stared at Eugie, trying to will her with his eyes to tell him so they could at least mourn together whatever life had gone away from them.

She bit down on her lip and looked away for a moment. When she turned back, she was smiling. "Camellia? Don't you worry, Little. There's not a thing wrong with your Baby-Girl. I'm just talking. Mother of the bride has a right to get soft in the heart."

He was about to come out with it, tell Eugie exactly what he knew, but just then Camellia appeared at the door, and through the screen, he could see that she was wearing her wedding dress, the white satin with the lace bodice sequined with silver beads, and, overwhelmed by the sight of her, angelic and pristine, he couldn't bring himself to say the words.

"Papa," she said, "I'm getting married come Sunday. Can you believe it? Quick tell me I'm beautiful."

Soon teams of horses would come in the night, and with rollers and sleds they would move the houses from Quakertown, and Little's neighbors would believe him when he would tell them that they would build a new neighborhood to the east, a better one, never stopping to think how far they would be from their jobs at the college, from the businesses on Frame Street that would linger for a while and then close down. Everyone would listen because he was Little Washington Jones, and they had watched him grow nearly anything he wanted out of that gumbo clay. He had the touch. Some sort of mojo in those hands. They would bring him into their houses, invite him to sit at their tables, eat their food, all for his touch when he knocked on their doors, the touch they believed would bless them.

"Papa?" Camellia said again.

He knew, at that moment, he was agreeing to seal the secret between them, between him and Eugie and Camellia, seal it out of love because it would be less hurtful in silence than it would be if they ever spoke it. He imagined them in one of his father's bird's eye maps: Eugie bowing her head, Little lifting his face to the white, white, white of Camellia's dress. It would all be so lovely, he thought, if only he were watching from far away, so far away he wouldn't be able to see his lips move or hear the words he spoke, his voice shaking. "Baby-Girl," he said, "I can hardly believe it's you." 🏵

It's The Law

By James Ward Lee

It was a late-December day in Bodark Springs. It was gray and bitter and so unnaturally cold that Judge McCraney sat behind his desk in the little municipal court room with his hat and overcoat on. The judge wasn't holding court; the only other person in the tiny three-room municipal building was Banty Isbell. Banty, along with his twin brother Bunk, shared the roles of city secretary/volunteer fire chief/municipal jailer. Either Bunk or Banty usually sat in the outer office waiting for a fire call. Or for somebody to come in to pay a fine for drunkenness. Or for running a stop light. On the rare occasions when somebody was in the tiny lock-up, Bunk or Banty—sometimes both—had somebody to talk to as they sat whiling away the hours. The third room in the building was an add-on; it had been built by the WPA a year earlier to make a holding cell for miscreants too tame to need sending across the square to Sheriff Hermann Wells's jail in the basement of the county courthouse.

Banty was leaning against the doorjamb that led into McCraney's tiny courtroom talking about Hitler. It was a week before Christmas, 1939, and Europe had been at war since September. Banty was saying, "I-God, when England and Britain both get to fighting, that damned war won't last three months."

Judge James W. McCraney was just pointing out that England and Britain were the same when the door flew open and Isham B. Hayes, the garageman and mechanic from down the street, came in out of breath and shivering against the cold.

Hayes wasn't a man to waste time on preliminaries. He breathed in and out a couple of times and said, "Judge, what's the fine for assault and battery?"

It seemed an odd question, but Judge McCraney made it a habit never to appear surprised, so he looked at Hayes under lidded, bored eyes and said, "Twenty-five dollars." He wanted to say "Why?" But McCraney never stooped to curiosity.

Hayes, who ran the only decent garage in Bodark Springs—some said in Northeast Texas—ran his hand into the pocket of his coveralls, pulled out a roll of bills, and started counting out ones. When he got to twenty-five, he handed the stack of greasy bills to McCraney and said, "Here's the fine." Then he turned to leave.

"Wait a minute, Hayes," McCraney said, "I'll have Banty here give you a receipt."

Banty Isbell seemed lost in thought and confusion. He still hadn't figured out the business about England and Britain, and now Isham Hayes was trying to pay a fine for a violation that Banty hadn't heard about.

"A receipt please, Banty," the judge said, and then to Hayes, "You'll have to wait a minute, Hayes. We can't accept a fine without giving you a receipt. It's the law."

It wasn't the law, but Hayes didn't know that. McCraney was hoping Hayes would mention who, exactly, had been assaulted and battered. But he stood mute, as did Banty. Finally, Judge James W. McCraney said in his most formal and judicial voice, "Mr. City Secretary, please make out a receipt to Isham B. Hayes for twenty-five dollars in payment of a fine for assault and battery."

Banty, torn between the mystery of the fine and the puzzle of the English-British relationship, started rustling through the papers in the old desk looking for the receipt book and a pencil. He got the book and an already abused sheet of carbon paper. Then he wetted the lead of his pencil with his tongue so that he could begin slowly and laboriously to fill out the form.

He worked for a while and said, "All right, Judge, I got the receipt made out to I. B. Hayes"—he couldn't spell Isham—"Now, what do I put in where it says what the fine's for?"

"Assault and battery."

"Yessir, I know, but who did he assault, Judge?"

Judge McCraney was busy dusting off imaginary specks on his blue serge Hart, Schaffner & Marx suit. The judge was a dapper man—some said a dude—with a pencil-thin Errol Flynn mustache. J. W. McCraney was without doubt the best-dressed man in Eastis County. The only thing that marred his looks was the fact that he was one-legged and had to get around on crutches. His left leg was cut off so close to the hip that it was impossible to fit him with a cork leg, but he was so expert with the crutches that he seemed to make them a natural part of him. How he had lost the leg nobody in Bodark knew, though McCraney didn't do anything to quell the rumors that the absent limb had died a hero's death in the First World War and was buried somewhere in the Meuse-Argonne Forest. He had come to Bodark about 1923, so nobody knew for sure how he had got his leg cut off. Everybody was too polite to ask, and McCraney kept his past life to himself. He practiced law for a while, but gave it up when he ran for—and won—the municipal court judgeship. About 1930, he opened a Texaco station on the best corner in town, but he left the running of it to Eugene Schmitt and spent most of his time sitting in the little two-room city office building or hanging out at Ralph Powers's cafe.

When McCraney didn't answer Banty's question about the reason for the fine, Banty came over to the judge's desk and asked again, "Who did he assault, Judge?" Then he pointed to the pad of receipts and said, "There is a place right here to list the name of the person or persons who are victims of the crime. See, here it is right here," and he turned the paper toward Judge McCraney.

McCraney didn't look at the paper in Banty's hand. He said, "You'll have to ask Hayes here. He didn't tell me."

Banty looked at Isham B. Hayes in his filthy coveralls and then at McCraney, who now sat behind the desk with his only leg propped up on the corner of the desk. He looked at Hayes, who stood mute, and at McCraney who was looking off into the middle distance trying hard to affect complete boredom and said, "You been in a fistfight, Isham B.?"

"No."

"Then how come you are charged with assault and battery."

"I ain't."

"Then how come the Judge here told me to make out a receipt for twenty-five dollars?"

"I don't care nothing about no receipt. I just come up here to pay my fine."

McCraney stood up on his one leg and grabbed his crutches all in the same motion and said to nobody in particular, "I'm going on down to the filling station. If anybody wants me, I'll either be there or over at Ralph Powers's."

"Just a minute, Judge," Banty said, "how am I supposed to make out this receipt? How am I supposed to enter this in the fine book?"

"How the hell do I know. I told you—ask Isham B. here."

McCraney paused, but if Hayes didn't volunteer any information, McCraney would have to swing himself out the door without knowing why Hayes was offering to pay a fine for an unsolved and possibly uncommitted misdemeanor. He had gone too far with his boredom to turn back now.

"Melvin Spruille," Hayes said.

"Melv—what the hell are you talking about? Melvin Spru—the postmaster? You hit the goddam post—What the hell do—" the Judge sputtered to a halt and stared goggle-eyed. First at Isham B. Hayes and then at Banty Isbell.

It was too late for McCraney to pretend nonchalance. He had revealed himself and was disgusted at his own outburst. So he turned to Isham B. Hayes and said, his voice now under control, "So you have had a fight with Melvin Spruille. When did this happen? And where?"

"It ain't yet," Hayes said.

"You mean—" Banty and the judge spoke at once, and when Banty stopped in mid sentence, McCraney went on, "You mean to tell me, Isham B., that you are paying a fine for an assault and battery that you plan to commit? That you haven't done anything yet?"

"That's right."

"Well, goddamit, Hayes, you can't just waltz in here to this office and pay a fine and then go off and commit a crime and—" McCraney couldn't find a way to end the sentence.

"Melvin Spruille is a son-of-a-bitch, and if I have to, I am going to go over to the post office and whip his ass right now. Then Banty here can fill in his blank and let me alone. I'd sooner put it off a while, but if I have to do it today, then by God, I'll go do it right now."

Judge James B. McCraney had half walked, half hopped back to his desk and fell into the chair again. He looked up at Isham B., who still stood with his legs apart in a truculent stance, and said to him, "Well, goddamit, Hayes, I know Melvin is a son-of-a-bitch. Everybody in Bodark knows that. Nearly everybody in Eastis County must know what kind of son-of-a-bitch Melvin is, but if everybody decided to whip his ass, where would we be then? That's what I want to know."

Both Hayes and Judge McCraney were careful in their pronunciation of "son-of-a-bitch." Neither one used the more casual "sunavabitch" or "sumbitch," so it was clear that they were serious.

They were taken by surprise when Banty answered McCraney's rhetorical question about "where we would be then" by saying, "A whole lot better off, I'd say!" Banty surprised himself by speaking, but caught himself in a second and said, "Excuse me, Judge, but that just slipped out. But, hell, Judge, you know your ownself what kind of sumbitch Melvin is and how bad he needs his ass whipped."

"Oh, hell, I guess so. Go ahead and record the fine, Banty, but Isham B., you had better not go over to the Post Office and whip Melvin's ass. I think that makes it a federal crime, and you'd find your sorry ass over at the federal courthouse in Sherman staring up at Judge Walter D. McIlroy. And old Walter D. ain't an easy judge."

Hayes walked out to the front door of the jail/city office and spat out some Brown's Mule tobacco juice he had been holding since he came into the office. Then he came back in and said to McCraney, "Old Walter McIlroy was raised on a farm not six miles from Melvin's daddy. Hell, he'd probably pay me to stomp Melvin's ass good."

"Probably would at that," McCraney said. Then he turned to Banty and said, "Give Isham B. here his money back. I'm gonna pay that fine for him."

"Say, Judge," Banty said, "I can spare two-dollars; how about me getting in on this ass-whipping fine?"

"Okay by me if it's all right with Isham B."

"Well, it ain't all right with me. I saved up that money to pay, and I want the satisfaction of paying and whipping." With that, Isham B. Hayes walked out of the office and made for his garage two blocks down the street.

McCraney grabbed his crutches and started for the door but stopped. "I'd never catch up to old Hayes. Besides, he is probably too smart to whip Melvin's ass on government property. But you keep and eye on Isham, and if he starts in on Melvin, run and get me. I'd pay good money to see Isham Hayes whip Melvin's ass."

Before dark, every white male in Bodark Springs knew that Isham B. Hayes was going to whip Melvin Spruille's ass. By the next morning, the rest of Bodark's populace—women and children, black and white—had heard the news. By New Year's Eve every sharecropper and tie hacker and round dancer in Eastis County knew what was in store for Melvin Spruille. On paper, Melvin was perfect. He was a Baptist and a Democrat and a Mason. He was a personal friend of Sam Rayburn and had met Franklin D. in person when Roosevelt had saluted "the Empire of Texas" at the State Fair in 1936. Melvin had been a second lieutenant during the First War but had got no farther than Fort Dix, New Jersey. He was a married man and a stern father to two boys. He paid his taxes and voted Democrat in every election—even when the Catholic Al Smith had run against Hoover in 1928. So, as far as the record went, Melvin Spruille was a perfect citizen of Bodark Springs, Texas, in the year of our Lord 1939.

But there was no doubt in anybody's mind—black, white, poor, rich, honest, crooked—that Melvin Spruille was a son of a bitch. He had proved it a thousand ways. If your post office box rent was a day late, Melvin sealed your box and sent your relief check back to the government. If clerk Charlie Stone came up a penny short at the end of the day, he stayed in the post office till he found his error—once till 10:15 on a Saturday night. If your letter weighed over an ounce, Melvin would can-cel the stamp and then send it back for postage due. He was always the same. A son of a bitch.

Melvin and his brother Lindley ran the Bodark Springs Drug Store, though Melvin only worked in the store a few nights a week to let Lindley off. Melvin had been postmaster for two years during Woodrow Wilson's second term, but when Harding took office in 1921, Melvin was replaced by Jack Hurst and went back to the drugstore that he and Lindley had inherited when Hermann Spruille died from the Spanish flu in 1918. When Roosevelt was inaugurated in 1933, Jack Hurst went back to running his grocery store full-time and Sam Rayburn got Melvin reappointed postmaster.

C. C. Reed, who ran the grocery story next to Bodark Springs Drug Store, once told Grady Dell, the mail carrier, "That son of a bitch you work for is the most stuck up, tight-assed-walking bastard I ever met."

Grady said, "I'm civil service, so I don't exactly work for him."

"But you will admit that he is a mean-spirited son of a bitch, won't you?" C. C. persisted.

"I may be civil service, but I do owe a little bill at the drug store, so I'm holdin' my fire on that one, C. C."

"Hell, Grady, you owe a big bill here at the grocery store and no telling how much you owe Tubby Wallace the bootlegger."

"Naw, C. C., Tubby don't allow no credit. I'll try to pay you a little something on the first."

When Grady left C. C.'s store, he saw Melvin going into Spruille Drugs and what looked like half the population of Bodark craning their necks to see if today would be the day that Isham Hayes made good on this threat.

Two weeks had passed since Hayes had paid his fine, and nothing had happened. For most of that time, Melvin wasn't in on the secret and wondered why there was always a crowd following him around town. Every morning when Melvin parked his car in front of the post office and went in, thirty or forty people were milling around on the street near the post office. When he left for lunch to drive home, several cars set out after him and drove slowly past his house when he went in to eat.

Melvin's brother Lindley overheard Sam Attaway telling his cousin from over at Savoy about Hayes's threat. Lindley, who liked Melvin about as much as everybody in Bodark Springs did, kept it to himself for a day or two before deciding that he guessed blood was thicker than water—even Melvin's blood. One night when Melvin went into the drug store to relieve Lindley for supper, Lindley broke down and told his brother what he had heard.

"Melvin, I don't 'spect you know about Isham Hayes and his fine, do you?"

"What fine?"

"Well, Melvin, I hate to bring this up, but I heard that Hayes went in and paid Judge McCraney a twenty-five dollar fine as advance payment for an assault-and-battery charge."

"Advance payment? Advance payment? Whoever heard of paying a fine in advance? And why do you hate to bring it up, Lindley?"

"Well, the reason I hate to bring it up, Melvin, is because I heard that Hayes said you were the one he—that he was going to whip your—Well, you know."

"No, Lindley, I don't know. I think you are going to have to make yourself clearer. What exactly do I have to do with this mechanic's supposed fine?"

"It's over you, Melvin?"

"Lindley, unless you have been stealing drugs and taking them, you had better quit beating around the bush and tell me whatever you are trying to say."

"All right, Melvin, Isham Hayes said that he was going to whip your ass. There!"

"Lindley, I can't—and won't—abide that kind of talk. I have made it clear that—*My* ass! What do you mean *my* ass?"

"Your ass, Melvin. That is what Sam Attaway from over at Savoy told me that Banty Isbell told him. And he said Banty was over at J. W. McCraney's office when Isham Hayes paid the fine and said—and I quote—'I'm gonna whip Melvin Spruille's ass.'"

Lindley Spruille was scared of his older brother, but he was loving every minute of this. "And another thing that Sam Attaway said was—"

"Never mind, Lindley," Melvin said and took his hat and walked out the front door of the store, leaving Lindley with no supper except for the milkshake that he had Bert Curley the soda jerk make for him.

Melvin talked to Orr Starnes the chief of police, but Starnes, who hated Melvin, said, "Mr. Spruille, there ain't a thing I can do until Hayes makes his move on you. Then, since he has paid his fine already, I can't see much point in arresting him, can you?"

Melvin did, but he couldn't budge Orr Starnes, so he went to see Hermann Wells, the county sheriff, who said, "Melvin, unless he whips your ass out in the county somewhere, I can't touch him. I'd say you ought to stay close to home. You ever had any boxing lessons, Melvin?"

Melvin slammed the door on the way out.

Things were quiet around the Bodark Springs Post Office throughout the months of January and February. Melvin spent a lot of time watching his clerk, Charlie Stone, and Grady Dell, the rural letter carrier, and Tarp Davidson, the walking city mailman, to see if they were taking any pleasure in the rumors that still ran back and forth across the county. Even Brace Jackman, the postal inspector out of Fort Worth, had heard the tale of Hayes's fine, and when he made one of his surprise inspections early in March, he looked at Melvin, grinned, and said, "Don't look like you been in any fights lately, Spruille. You been behaving yourself?"

Melvin turned away and then back to Jackman and said, "Here are the c.o.d. books you asked for."

Grady had a coughing fit, but since he had been gassed in the war, Melvin couldn't prove that he was coughing to suppress his laughter. Charlie Stone dropped his pencil and had to get down under the counter to find it. Tarp Davidson was just getting back from his afternoon rounds and didn't realize that Jackman was making a surprise visit.

Tarp looked around and said, "Hey, Brace, looks like you got everybody looking guilty here. Some kind of crimewave going on?"

Jackman grinned at Tarp and said, "Well, it don't like it's federal; must be some local brouhaha. That right, Melvin?"

Melvin's face had gone from red to white to purple, but all he said was, "Do you need to see the money order receipts, Mr. Jackman?"

After Jackman left, Tarp and Grady and Charlie got more work done than they had since the Germans rolled into Poland.

After that, almost everybody but Melvin and Hayes had lost interest in the threatened ass-whipping until a rainy day in the middle of March. Melvin was still dashing from the post office to his car and from his car to the drugstore. He even drove into his garage and pulled the door down before going out the side door of the garage toward his house. Melvin was very careful, but the rain had been going on for three days and he got careless. Just as he finished locking up the post office on March 15, he took off his glasses, pulled his hat down, and raised his umbrella to shield himself from the blowing rain as he made for his car.

Isham B. Hayes stepped out from behind Melvin's car and hit him with what Grady Dell, who listened to boxing on the radio, called a straight right hand right between the eyes. Melvin's hat flew off, he dropped the umbrella, and Hayes hit him with a left hook to the nose that caused an explosion of blood to hit Hayes and get all over Melvin's windshield. He hit Melvin with another left hand and used his right hand to keep Melvin from falling. He held Melvin up against Melvin's own car and kept pounding him with his left hand. Hayes later told Grady Dell that he had nearly busted his right hand when he hit Melvin so high up on the forehead with his first punch.

Grady Dell was giving Tarp Davidson a ride home and had already started his car when the fight—or rather the beating, since Melvin had never raised his hands—broke out. Tarp said to Grady, "You reckon we ought to get out and stop I. B. before he beats Melvin to death?"

"Yeah, I guess so, but hold on a minute. I've got to turn the car off and find my umbrella in all that mess on the back seat. I can't afford to catch a fresh cold. I just got over the last one. I don't guess there is a big hurry is there?"

Tarp grinned and said, "No, not too much, but I guess sooner or later we are going to have to get out in this rain and stop old I. B. unless he wears his arms out from hitting Melvin."

"You are right, Tarp, but all that mechanic work has built up Hayes's arms. Hell, he's got the biggest arms in Bodark, so I guess we got a minute or two before he wears out."

Tarp and Grady got out of Grady's 1936 Chevrolet and walked over to Hayes, who had his victim laid out across the hood of Melvin's 1939 La Salle and was now reduced to slapping the inert postmaster.

"That'll do, Isham," Grady said, and pushed Isham away from Melvin.

Hayes was completely docile now. He looked at Tarp and Grady and the crowd that had gathered but stood back against the post office wall until Grady stopped the fight. Now they all crowded around the hood of Melvin's La Salle to see the damage. Hayes looked around and said, "Well, I guess that's about twenty-five dollars worth, ain't it?" and walked off in the direction of his garage.

Charlie Stone slipped out of the crowd and helped get Melvin across the street to Dr. Clayton's clinic.

Grady and Tarp stood hatless and umbrellaless in the rain talking to one of the most festive groups Bodark Springs had seen since the war started. Everybody asked the same question: "What was Hayes after Melvin about. And why did he wait so long?"

Grady said, "Maybe he was waitin' for the Ides of March," but that didn't get a reaction, and finally everybody drifted off with a story to tell at supper.

It was a month or two before old man C. B. Isbell, Bunk and Banty's father, got Isham B. Hayes to tell him the story.

Hayes said, "It is in 19 and 14, and Melvin didn't have so much money then. Remember? He drove that old T-Model Ford with the Isinglass curtains? Well, Mr. Isbell, he sent his brother Lindley after me one night about 10:30 to come and fix that car, said he thought it had a busted magneto. So I drove out to where Melvin was broke down and saw right off what the trouble was. The son of a bitch had run out of gas and was too stupid to know it. So I drove back in and pumped up five gallons and put it in my can and takened it out to Melvin and poured it in his car for him and even cranked the T-Model so he could take that Brasher girl he was sparking home. Next day, when I went to settle up, I told Melvin that he owed me seventy-five cents for the gas and two dollars for mechanic work. Wellsir, that son of a bitch give me six bits for the gas, but wouldn't pay me a dime for my work. Said his car wasn't broke and didn't need a mechanic. What it needed was a gas man and I had been paid for that. Well, I decided right then and there that I was going to whip Melvin Spruille's ass. And I done it."

Old man Isbell had laughed so much that tears ran down his face, but he finally recovered enough to say, "but you waited twenty-five years or so, Hayes. How come."

"I waited exactly twenty-five years. To the day, though that was sort of a accident. That son of a bitch cheated me on March the 15th of 19 and 14, and it was raining, by God. So I waited until I had twenty-five dollars saved up—one for each year—and I waited for it to rain so that son of a bitch would have to take his glasses off. It just happened to be raining on March the fifteenth, exactly twenty-five years to the day from when he cheated me. See I had to wait for it to rain because Texas don't let you hit a feller with glasses. It's the law."

THE SNAKE WOMAN

Susan San Miquel

Marta Inez moved about the room so quickly that her shadow never had time to take on the form of a woman. First she was up on a ladder that reached the top shelf of the bookcases putting away books that her daughter Dolores had left piled on the desk the night before. Then she was opening the windows, almost toppling over the trays of seedlings that Dolores had so carefully placed there and labeled with both their Latin and common names.

Dolores must have been digging into her father's things again, Marta Inez thought. Those seedlings could only belong to Salvador. He had brought some seeds from Mexico to this ranch in San Antonio, Texas, just after they married over fifteen years ago. Those seeds were all that remained from Salvador's days as a curandero back in Mexico.

At the desk again, Marta Inez brushed aside notebooks filled with sketches, complicated diagrams and tedious notes, as she reached for her own daily planner and ledger of accounting figures neatly aligned in rows and columns. She paused for a moment when she glimpsed the handwriting, like loose threads scrawled across the page, the way her husband wrote, and the ink looked fresh. How could Salvador have been writing in his notebooks when he was not even here? For the past five years he had been away fighting in that damned Mexican Revolution.

"What are you looking at? That's mine." Dolores came alive from where she had planted herself in the corner of the room. She snapped a notebook closed as she snatched it from the desk.

Since Salvador was gone, each woman had attempted to claim his study as her own. That they were there at the same time meant unspoken guerrilla warfare, for nineteen year old Dolores at least who cringed while her mother attempted to erase any trace of her presence without even acknowledging that she was doing so. All the while Marta Inez sang softly to herself, in a pitch that contradicted the fervor of her movements because it was so sad. It was the same song Dolores had listened to all night long while she listened to her mother's footsteps on the wooden floors just above where Dolores worked. There was something dreadfully wrong with her mother. Dolores was sure of it.

Marta Inez would not allow anyone to look at her long enough to see her eyes. The tiny lines at their corners that flared out like sun's rays said that she was tired, but her dark eyes darted here and there, unreadable. Marta Inez was so pale that in the sunlight, her skin became transparent and the blue and green veins showed through. She was rapidly losing weight. The old faded cotton dress that she wore every day now and that had fit her well only a few months ago hung off her nimble body like a thick spider web. It seemed even that her feet did not touch the floor, the untamed waves of black and gray hair that fell below her waist somehow kept her afloat.

"You were listening to me all night, weren't you Dolores? I could *feel* you eavesdropping." Marta Inez didn't bother to conceal her irritability with her daughter as she usually did. And so she provided Dolores with the opportunity to calmly take note of her mother's uncharacteristic anger. Dolores had been keeping a diary of her mother's behavioral changes. She would definitely write this down.

"Mamá, you know you haven't been acting like yourself lately."

"How dare you say that. You don't even know who I am."

At first, Dolores didn't respond. She just stood there, her black eyes fierce but quiet, her expression as still as if her face had been carved from the trunk of an ancient oak tree. That is the way Dolores looked, dark and as thick skinned as tree bark with two ropes of long black hair that elongated her oval face and seemed to pull her down to earth.

When Dolores finally spoke her voice was so calm that she seemed hardly to open her mouth. There was no need for Marta Inez to be outside with the men, herding and roping cattle, Dolores told her mother. They didn't require her watching over them all the time. She should rest.

"Rest? But Dolores," Marta Inez began breathlessly, "those men didn't even know how to walk a calf. If I'm not there they spur the calves, rope them and drag them to the branding fire. It's bad on the horse, the saddle and the poor squalling calf. They should do it my way so that the calf thinks he's pulling the horse to the branding fire. It's much more humane."

"You're so clever Mamá." Dolores was amused that her mother thought she knew more about cattle than those men who had spent most of their lives working ranches all across Texas and northern Mexico. "I've heard them complain that they don't rope as many calves, that they have to let too many go when you're around."

"What do you know what they say?"

Dolores simply walked over to the window as if the answer lay some-where outside. It was late afternoon, a quiet time when the whole house was at rest and the men were usually in the barn taking their siestas since it was December and mildly cool even in the sunniest portion of the day. But from the direction of the gate came the sound of mens' voices. A group of eight or ten of them had assembled together. Dolores recognized them as the mainstays of the ranch; some had worked for her father since she was a child. A few had even lived on the land since before her parents arrived from Mexico. The voice of Pete Lopez could be heard over all the rest, which was surprising since Pete was known around the ranch as a man of few words. But there he was, arms waving and gesturing toward the house. He happened to glance at the window where both Dolores and now Marta Inez stared down at him. That is when he motioned for the group to follow him, and together they strode deliberately toward the house. A few minutes later there was a knock on the door, and Pete Lopez could be heard asking to see the senora. The housekeeper escorted them right in, since Marta Inez never refused to see anyone.

"I wonder what they want," Marta Inez fluttered about the room with a feather duster, not a trace of concern in her voice. Then she stopped. "They have news of Salvador, or perhaps, do you think Dolores, that he could be among them?" She ran to the window to look for him but by that time the men were already just outside the room.

"Not likely," Dolores muttered under her breath as she went to the door. Pete Lopez stood in the forefront with ten men behind looking down at their feet. Having a roof over their heads and being in the same room as two ladies had quieted them down some.

Pete was almost seventy years old and the years in the sun showed. His thick dark skin fell in folds beneath his eyes which watered down his cheeks from squinting. He had been in charge of repairing and building fences on the ranch ever since they first started building. He camped out on the land, hunted for his food, occasionally brought game up to the house which he left in the kitchen for the cook. Sometimes he would decide to be sociable and sit down to dinner with the family and the other men, but usually he spent all his time alone in the brush.

As soon as she saw Pete, Marta Inez became the capable business woman that she could be because something must be seriously wrong, she realized, to bring Pete Lopez to the house.

"Buenos tardes, Pete Lopez. The fence you built for the horses looks fine. Was that pine that you used?"

Pete squinted at her and she detected little rivulets running from the corner of his bloodshot eyes down his tanned face. He nodded yes indeed that he used pine boards, the hardest he could find, ordered special all the way from Fort Worth and he made the fence especially tall so that those wild mustangs wouldn't even think of jumping it.

And then in the same breath he said, "Don't you go out there anymore. You have no place with us." The men behind him fidgeted and mumbled and nodded in agreement. When Marta Inez didn't respond at all and her daughter just stood there in the corner with her arms crossed as if this were all very intriguing to her, he added feebly, "There's rattlesnakes out there. They're gonna bite you one of these days." The men behind him did their best to look concerned for her. That was the excuse they had apparently agreed upon to be the most acceptable to a lady.

"Nonsense. It's winter time. They're hibernating. Besides rattlesnakes are everywhere, even in the yard. We couldn't step outside if we were afraid of a snake. My youngest daughter Luz shot three last August, didn't she Dolores?"

Dolores said George helped her and that Luz had always been terrified of snakes, screaming loud enough to break an ear drum if she so much as heard a baby's rattle which sounded like a rattlesnake.

This answer pleased the men, who usually didn't much like Dolores, though they respected her.

"I'm not afraid of them," Marta Inez retorted.

"It's not just that," put in Jo Clifton. "We don't like you telling us what to do. The new guys just passing through don't seem to care too much but we've known you all these years, seen you all dressed up with your hair in those curls on the top of your head and all that jewelry. To tell the truth it's just plain ugly seeing you wearing rags and acting like you're the boss of us."

"See Mamá, what I've been saying is true."

"If you don't want to work for me then leave," Marta Inez told the men, ignoring her daughter's comment. But she was the one who left. She marched outside, the door slamming behind her, grabbed a hoe that had been propped up against the wall of the house. Since the men had done what they had set out to do and had no more business inside, they followed her, curious as to what she might be up to. Dolores followed too, in spite of herself and her sister Luz came around from the front of the house where she had been playing with her new litter of baby raccoons to see what was happening. Was Marta Inez going to hoe the garden in the dead of winter, or would she seek out a snake and kill it just to show that she could. The men had put their hats back on and stood with their hands in their pockets snickering to themselves. Outside, they were in their own element and feeling sure of themselves once more.

Near the well was a pile of limestone, the residuals of Salvador's additions to the original structure of the house. Luz once mentioned that she wanted to create a garden with those stones, but she had not gotten around to it yet. As far as anyone knew, the mound of rocks had not been touched since Salvador piled them there ten years ago.

When Marta Inez kicked aside the largest rock at the top of the heap, a familiar dry droning sound sprayed into the air, like splattering rain on hard packed earth, except more subtle than that, more sinister—the sound a rattler makes before it strikes. A diamondback roped along the jagged stones, opened its sleepy eyes, showed its fangs, stretched its neck to bite, but Marta Inez was too quick for it. Its teeth sank into the handle of the hoe.

A hush fell over the men as they watched, so stunned that it did not occur to one of them to help. They expected that she would next slice that damned snake's head off, as every one of them would have done, as any man in his right mind would. But Marta Inez didn't kill the snake. She allowed it to curl itself around the handle of the hoe like a vine and then, to everyone's amazement, she held the hoe straight up, toward the sky so that the snake slithered down toward her, wrapped around her neck, flicked its tongue at her ear.

Luz screamed, wanted to run away, but couldn't find the strength to move her legs. A few of the men fell to their knees and crossed themselves. Others just stared because they didn't believe what they were seeing.

At her feet, another snake had curled around her ankle, and several more slithered out of the crevices in the rock pile. They crawled up her body until she was completely entangled, dripping with snakes. The snakes hissed and rattled as if the sky had spilled a thunderstorm of rain, but behind her the dying December sun silhouetted her body like a halo. And the air had gotten colder, the temperature dropping twenty degrees. The men pleaded with God and prayed aloud because whatever was happening, it was either a miracle of God or a trick of the devil.

When Marta Inez saw that all of the men were on their knees and that even Dolores had fallen back against an oak tree until her presence was all but invisible, Marta Inez nestled each snake back into the crevices of the rocks, lulling them to sleep by humming her sad song, until they were just as she had found them.

Dolores ran to her, told her that she needed to come with her. She would put her to bed so that finally she could rest, but her mother only flung her away. Luz also tried, but Marta Inez just looked at her youngest daughter sadly, pushed her aside and began to walk. There was just so much work to be done she said, so much to do before Salvador returned. When she grabbed an ax from the toolshed, the men felt that surely they had seen the last of her and perhaps it was for the best. Marta Inez swung an ax in one hand and a hoe in the other as she strode through the gate without looking back.

She had come to know the contour and shape of the land well. It appeared to rise and swell before her as she walked away from the house, but she knew that this was an illusion. The house had been built on a slight incline so that rain water flowed away from it, irrigating the field as the rain water drained southward into the Medina River. She knew that the soil was reddish brown, almost silty clay with lime deposits north of the Medina river and that as she neared the flood plain the earth changed in color to a grayish brown as the lime became more prevalent. She remembered that the best place to cross the river was about one hundred yards east of the old Apache encampment where her daughters as children, scavenged for dart points and arrow head, bits of clay pottery and tools. The ground was hardpacked there, as if moccasins and bare feet still padded the earth into a floor. As she came to the narrowest section of the river, she remembered that in the spring beneath the roots of that willow tree whose branches drooped low over the murky water, was the best place to fish for perch. Pete had once brought home a string of twelve, caught in less than twenty minutes without any bait, he boasted. As she stepped across the embankment she was thankful that she was not on a horse. She knew that these steep ravines had caused more than one man to be thrown to his death. On the south side of the river the earth became dusky white with sandy loam and lime deposits, soil that barely supported anything but brush, thorny shrubs, trees with shalllul roots—scrub oak, huisache, and mesquite. This scraggly tree, with its tangled low limbed branches stretching out to a width that exceeded its height, thrived because no one had ever tried to stop its prolific growth.

Wintry gray, bare bone limbs reached for Marta Inez's neck; thorns jabbed into her arms and tore at her dress. She heard a low moaning that sounded almost human, like a woman crying up ahead through the brush. She had heard this sound before on nights when she lay awake with the window open. She began to follow a cattle trail that seemed to lead in the direction of that sound. Here in these woods was the best place to see a white tailed deer, a javelina or shoot a wild turkey for Christmas dinner. She saw tufts of reddish hair caught on the brush, a coyote nearby in pursuit of that rabbit still and gray as the shrubs around it. She stayed on the trail, because with the sun hardly an orange rim above the horizon and the air becoming hazy with low lying fog, she could hardly distinguish the outline of the limbs stretched out in front of her. A flock of doves cooed in the trees above. She walked until the color of everything was gray and the cattle trail stopped because not even cattle could penetrate this thick brush anymore. She had come to the densest part of the brush country. More of the same, low and twisted mesquite and scrub oak saplings, brazil bush, dwarf huisache trees, so wild that this land had hardly been touched by man since her ancestors, the Spaniards, first arrived bringing longhorn cattle which ate the brush and defecated the seeds that spread the thick foliage, rapidly diminishing the value of the land. But Marta Inez knew that the land could again support cattle if the brush were cleared and a hearty breed of wild grass were planted to choke it out. She picked up her hoe and began.

Stars now sprinkled the night sky while the wind ballooned Marta Inez's dress around her, freezing the sweat that coated her body as she slashed through black barked trunks and brambling undergrowth. Her legs and arms bled from so many scratches; her palms stung with blisters, but she felt none of that. She had discovered a soothing rhythm to her labor. The harder she worked, the less aware she was of her body. She had cleared the better part of an acre, while the sound of the woman crying up ahead had steadily grown stronger then occasionally lulled into a fitful whimper that grated at Marta Inez's nerves.

She promised herself that she would not think of Salvador. Five years he had been gone without a word. There were stories. People talked. They said that he had abandoned her, that at forty-five she was still a beautiful woman and should think of remarrying. A man passing through who had worked the border ranches spoke of bandits who had staked out the cattle camp where he worked on a cool winter evening last year. They stole their horses, frightened the cattle, shot two cowboys. The amazing thing he said was that the leader came back with his hands in the air; he would never forget him, a small man, little slits of eyes that sparkled in the moonlight, and the darkest leathery face he had ever seen. He laid his gun on the ground, knelt beside the dying man he had just shot, took a powdery substance from a pouch he had strapped to his waist and sprinkled it onto the gaping bullet hole in the man's chest. Then he placed his hands on the wound, small hands the narrator recalled, like a woman's. At first blood gushed through the fingers while the dying man screamed in agony and fear. All those present that night were awestruck, staring at the hands that calmed the man and absorbed the blood. No one thought to shoot this man who healed. No one dared because all at once the dying one was no longer dying; he was sitting up. The next thing they knew the healer had mounted his horse, and had faded into the dusky landscape.

Her Salvador. Who else? Killing a man then trying to erase his mistake. Fighting for a revolution that he couldn't claim, riding across land that wasn't his, waving a flag that should mean nothing to him.

As the wind rose, the woman's howl again increased in intensity, a shriek that soon died into hushed crying. Marta Inez cut at the brush viciously, bitter tears rolling down her cheeks. She didn't realize that she had left bits and pieces of her dress and hair on the ravaged brush behind her or that so much time had passed that it would soon be morning, not until she spotted a glint of sunlight through a thicket of trees up ahead. There, at the southern most tip of the de la Paz property was a mott of mesquite all writhing and twisted in the perpetual motion of growth. Probably some brutish man had dragged a poor woman into those trees to have his way with her. What a terrible place for a woman to be, all tangled up and choking in briars and prickly pear cactus. Someone had to free that woman.

The sound of that cry touched Marta Inez deep within her breast, and seemed to reflect exactly the way she felt. She cut her way frantically through the brush, until she had arrived at that thicket of trees where the woman's cry was so painful. There were two trees, or perhaps they were one tree with two trunks, their roots crawling, intertwined above the ground and their limbs outstretched and embracing. As a gust of wind struck their twisted trunks, whistled through their limbs, that bone chilling cry swept across the field and sky.

Marta Inez knew at once what she had to do. In one swift movement she severed the trunk of the mesquite in front of her from its companion, if only to put them both out of their misery. With a quiet swoosh it fell to the ground leaving a gaping wound in the trunk of the other so she cut it down. Then she chopped down the next tree and the next until the whole thicket was gone and the pasture completely cleared. She was finished there. It was time to go home.

As Marta Inez came to the gate that opened to the yard, tears still streamed down her face, but she didn't notice them. The crying had only grown more severe. When she saw that Dolores waited for her at the front door of the house she self-consciously wiped away her tears and composed her face. She would not give Dolores the satisfaction of seeing her like this.

"Go tell Pete to come and see me. I have a new job for him. And Jo Clifton and at least three of the others," she said as she met Dolores on the back steps.

Dolores only looked at her pitifully. Didn't she remember that today was Sunday. "He's at church, Mamá. All the men went to church."

"But Pete hardly ever goes to church and when he does he comes to our chapel. You say he and the rest of the men went into town to attend mass?" she asked incredibly.

"This morning they all went. They left at sunup."

It vaguely occurred to Marta Inez that the padre would be arriving soon, the chapel had to be made ready, Sunday dinner had to be prepared. She glanced around her, saw the chapel doors opened and the altar adorned in honor of Christ's birth. She smelled the aroma of brisket cooking in the kitchen. Dolores had taken care of everything.

"When Pete and Jo return from mass tell them I wish to speak to them."

"You look very tired mother. Let me fix you some tea to help calm your nerves and rest."

While Dolores prepared the tea, Luz ran down to the gate to wait for the men to return and Marta Inez went into the study. Her books were in even greater disarray than they had been the evening before. Rich green leaves sprouted up from the trays of dirt in the window sills where only yesterday there had been seedlings. Marta Inez almost tripped over a row of clay pots, where Dolores was growing some type of thick viney plant that Marta Inez had never seen before. The room was so hot that she could hardly breathe.

She sat down at the desk where Dolores had left her papers scattered about, filled with that familiar handwriting—notes, diagrams, recipes and prayers. Just then Dolores entered with a cup of steaming hot tea. When Dolores realized that she had left her papers out right in front of her mother, she quickly scooped them up, holding to them protectively.

"Dolores, I believe I've changed my mind about the tea. It's much too hot in here to drink it."

"But Mamá, you're probably running a fever. The tea will cool your body. I'll set it right here on the desk in case you change your mind."

"I don't think I have a fever Dolores. This room is dreadfully hot."

"Well," Dolores said sweetly, "if it's too hot in here for you, you could always go upstairs to your own room."

"My *own* room? That's so thoughtful of you, Dolores, but I think I'll stay."

As Dolores left, Pete Lopez and Jo Clifton entered smelling of lye soap. They wore starched white shirts and thin neck ties and tight fitting jackets from twenty years gone. They took off their cowboy hats and looked down at them, rather than at Marta Inez who was a terrific sight. She had not combed her hair or bathed or changed from her soiled and torn dress. The two men hung back, near the door visibly frightened of her. She pretended not to notice their fear.

"I have cleared the southern most pasture. Please put a fence around it and in the spring you all can plant the grass seeds."

"You've done what?" Pete looked directly at her, his mouth wide open. "But that's impossible. It would take thirty men at least two weeks to clear that pasture. You couldn't have done that."

"I did it and there is more work to be done. Today is Sunday, a day of rest. You may start on Monday at sunup."

With that she went upstairs to her bedroom, where from the balcony she had a much better view, now that the pasture was clear. When Salvador came walking through those fields on his way home, she would be the first to spot him. ❀

Out of Egypt

Lee Merrill Byrd

MARY GAYE MARTIN in her purple sun dress pulled an over-grown boy wearing a mask down through the back alleys of Galveston. It was her own boy—seven-year-old Riley Martin—and she was feeling the sweltering death and decay of Galveston's early summer heat and the pinch of brand-new white rhinestone-studded sandals—all the fashion this season. Oh, why did I go buying these crazy things? she kept asking herself. She couldn't have planned things any worse if she'd sat down and said to herself, Now, Mary Gaye, let's make this the most miserable day of your life, let's fill this day with prickly thorns and hoary thistles and enough heat to kill all the black people in Africa!

It was three in the afternoon, the very hottest part of the day anywhere near any ocean in the whole world. You could have taken a bath in the sticking salt water that filled the air. Mary Gaye shook her head once and quickly, a habitual motion meant to clear out the dark caprices of her mind—a claw-footed tub had popped up in her head, quicker than she could suppress it, and herself in its bubbly waters with one leg thrust in the air, bright-polished toenails—Fire Engine Red—exposed for all to see. Oh funny funny!—herself in the middle of the street stark naked! Well, it wasn't much worse than hauling along a much-too-big boy whose face was covered with a brown elastic hood—Mary Gaye Martin, former Miss Shelby County, in her birthday suit!

They were wandering, Mary Gaye and her son Riley. No sure place to go right now except back to the hospital. The doctor had said for her to get out, take her son—her only son, her only child—get him used to being outside, get him used to being stared at before they went back home. Mercy. Let him have his fill of that, all right. She groaned down to the soles of her feet just to think of it. She would have just taken him out in the car—in the *air-conditioned* car—except that *Brit* had said when he left that she didn't need a car, being in a rooming house only three blocks from the hospital and all and having nothing else to do besides walk back and forth to that infernal place, so he, instead of flying back to Memphis, took *the* car back home with him. *Her* car sat unused in the garage in Memphis, and Brit could have used it to get around and left *his* car with her. But no, not Brit. He didn't see the point of spending money on a plane when he could drive, and he didn't see the point of her riding three blocks up and three blocks back every day when anyhow it cost for parking.

And she would have rented a car except that *Brit* had said that renting a car for one afternoon was a foolish waste of money.

And, pray tell, what is money for, sir?

Mary Gaye Martin dragged Riley down along the dark edges of Galveston trying to kill time, making sure, if it was at all possible, that no one saw either one of them.

Stared at! Get him used to being stared at—Jesus Jesus! Not if she had her way.

Don't come back until four, they had told her at the hospital. And y'all enjoy yourselves. Uh huh. Uh huh.

Can't you walk any faster? she snapped at the boy. You've been laying in bed now for three months, you ought to be strong by now. I don't want to just creep along. We'll draw attention.

I can't, Mother, fussed the boy, his whiny voice muffled by the brown hood and the white plastic life mask the hood held in place. I'm tired, I tell you.

You're tired, I'm tired, I'm so goddamn tired, she chanted as she pulled. Three months of sitting by your damn bed. No one to talk to except a bunch of niggers and trash, nothing to do, that ratty damn apartment with the gas leak nearly ready to kill me, and it doesn't even have a TV. Miss my friends! I am so bored! I am ready to go home, I am so ready to go home! Where is your father, do you suppose? She stopped abruptly. Where oh where is your goddamn father?

I want my father, the boy cried loudly.

Oh you, always want what you can't have. Always always always

always! Great big boy like you crying for his daddy. Now hush! They turned a corner. He's working, your father is, Mary Gaye said suddenly, at least that's what he says he's doing. Making all that money that he won't let us spend. Wonder does he think what I'm doing isn't work? How comes he isn't helping out with this deal? She pinched her face up—*Costs too much for me to be flying back and forth, Mary Gaye.*

Out of a side street a man appeared, no way to avoid him. A medical student in a long white coat. He was black—she put her hand to her throat—but he was tall and his face was handsome. Mary Gaye in her purple sun dress slowed down a minute, cocked her shoulders forward just a hair and sucked in her stomach.

Shut up, she hissed at the boy out of the side of her mouth, cut out your goddamn whining. She smiled big and pretty at the student as he approached—*Now, how you doing? Bless your heart and in this heat, it's something else, isn't it?*—and leaned down toward Riley so her big straw sun hat with its wide lavender grosgrain ribbon was in front of the boy's face.

Now, do I need to fix your face? she said so loud to Riley, all sweetness and solicitation. She looked up at the student until he was well past, then glared back at the boy. I want you to shut up. I don't want you to say even one more goddamn word, I don't care what you want.

Riley Martin began to wail, tears tumbling down and making wet and dark the thick stitching around the eye sockets of his brown hood. Someone opened a door somewhere—Mary Gaye heard music and voices—but before she could turn and locate it, the door was shut again.

Listen to you, crying just like a baby. Stop now! What *is* your problem?

Riley sucked in a deep, shuddering breath. He'd been out of the hospital for the first time in three months, wrapped in ace bandages and wearing a mask, trudging along through alleys filled with old garbage cans, his mother calling the shots and not doing at all what he thought the doctors had told her to do—he, a boy who had sustained third degree burns over fifty-eight percent of his body. This percentage had amassed itself for the most part on his face and head, though there were significantly large burns on his chest, arms and legs. His features—long the pride and joy of his parents—which had been as nearly perfect as God Himself could make them, had relocated to places where eyes and noses and mouths did not belong, pulled at the whim of foreign skin that was defiant and furiously red. The new skin—grafted when possible from Riley himself, when not possible from a skin bank and who knows what person—had its own rules: rippled and twisted where it should have laid flat, lay down smooth and taut and shiny whenever it felt like it, rode roughshod over old familiar territory, obliterating the normal lines of demarcation so you could barely tell when Riley was smiling—where his cheeks began or where they ended—or if he was smiling at all. His head, once resplendent with thick auburn hair from Mary Gaye's side of the family and comely waves from Brit's, was now, but for a few small singed wisps, entirely bald, his scalp paper-thin. He had lost both his ears and something had happened to his nose in all this—the fire or the grafts or the doctors or the whole malignant creation itself had stretched it or pinched it or seared it or sealed it off completely, some godawful thing, so that you could hear him breathe—he had to breathe through his mouth. And damned if he wasn't breathing all the time. He sounded like an old sewing machine, a sewing machine that needed oiling, badly.

In a fitful dream which Mary Gaye Martin had two months after her son's fire, she understood completely that the fiercely patched-together face which he was now acquiring before her eyes was his real face and that the face which she had thought was his—the flawless, so-nearly perfect one she had tried at times to recapture in her mind—had been a mask which Riley had shed forever—a mask and an ugly trick designed just *specifically* to string her along and fool her.

She could barely remember what he had been like before the fire, that petulant and oversized boy she loved—her son—who seemed sometimes just like an old man to her. Already grown before his time—looked like four when he was two, looked like seven when he was hardly five. Now that he really was seven, he could have passed for ten or twelve. All those overbearing tight penny-pinching Martin genes. His size had always bothered her, it really did—he always looked too big to be such a baby, even though he was just that: a baby. She knew all her friends thought the worst of her, that she spoiled him, but it was because he was so big—they just thought he was older. And Brit didn't even get it—all the Martin men were huge! They were all like that—just great big babies.

Mother! Riley had been forever demanding of her as he bustled around the house, wanting this and wanting that. He drew enormous pictures of outrageously arrayed dinosaurs engaged in violent battle that she could only assume mirrored the way he intended to deal with the world. Fire shot out of the dinosaurs' mouths, and tiny men died with their feet in the air all around them while the scaly creatures stared stubbornly into each others' brittle and unforgiving eyes.

And his voice. That voice which alternated between a sullen, stubborn sulk and a droning chatter—that voice now—finally!—had a face to fit it. In her dream she thirsted to know how he would get by with the new face that he had acquired. He would have to change all right. No one would listen to him anymore, would even give him the time of day. The life work that she had long felt was hers and dreaded—the making of a big spoiled self-centered baby, so much like the men in Brit's family, into a human being—now fell to the fire. The fire, which had been so determined to claim him, could have him. It could be his mother now—it could raise him. And though outwardly she swooned in ongoing and melodramatic grief—*Oh, I can't stand it. It's so ugly. He can't even move his lips. Doctor, isn't he ever going to look normal? God, he's just such a mess*—and indulged herself in conversations that dealt with her impossible burden, inwardly—in the dark and secret places of her heart—she exalted, as if the felicitous intersection of her life with this fire had somehow relieved her of all responsibility for this boy, her only boy, her only child.

Riley's father, Brit—trying to avoid dealing with the whole affair by plunging himself into work back in Memphis—was adrift, too. He felt like the joy of life had been sucked right out of him. He and Mary Gaye had put all their eggs in this one basket: their only child, but what a child! Good-looking—the fruit of their combined beauty—rambunctious, shooting up like a weed—at seven as tall and as strong as a ten-year old. Husky! Bright! Near-genius! Athletic! Why have more when the one you have is perfect, was how they often talked to themselves. And so much to do besides raise more kids, Mary Gaye had said so often. Busy busy!

Since Riley's birth, Brit Martin had lived at the very center of a dizzy kaleidoscope of possibilities concerning him. He'd laid Riley's whole life out for him: Riley on the soccer field, Riley at the tennis courts, Riley at the head of his class, Riley playing football—the big guy! like all the Martin men—Riley on the swim team, Riley at the prom, Riley at Harvard, Riley playing polo!, Riley getting married—he'd have a beautiful wife, the daughter of the richest man—Riley with children, Riley as a lawyer in the same law firm as his father. . . .

But try as he might, he could not put his son's new face—the face of an absolute stranger—into all the old pleasant daydreams. It didn't fit. It was shamefully out of place, like a . . . like a . . . like the waiter would be if he suddenly sat down at a country club banquet. Just the thought made Brit tremble.

In an uncomfortable and awkward interview, the social worker and the psychiatrist at the Burns Institute suggested to the Martins that—for Riley's well-being—as soon as Riley was allowed to leave the hospital for good, they should resume their normal life, that round of comings and goings associated with well-to-do lawyers who lived in the lush green suburbs outside of Memphis. They were to include Riley in everything they did, they were to take him wherever they went. But Brit, though he indulged them, did not listen. These people didn't and couldn't understand. There was no normal life for them anymore. Let the poor resume their normal life. Let the riffraff who surrounded him at this charitable hospital resume their normal life. Let them who took charity continue to be pitied. If it had not been for his physician's insistence that the work going on at the Shriners was the best in the country—and the pressing emergency of the situation—he himself would not have brought his son here. And when these charitable people were done with Riley, Brit would not bring him back. Expensive plastic surgeons in private hospitals would mold the crumbled Martin future now. And they would put Riley, they would put Riley, they would put Riley . . . where no one would see him. Tutors, private tutors, maids when they went out, a great big wall around the house— maybe he hadn't actually said the words out loud, maybe he didn't know how it would work, how it would be possible to hide his own son, but for certain, Brit Martin knew he would accomplish it. He would make it happen. He didn't want anyone seeing his son with a face like that.

But today these issues which plagued the hearts of Riley's parents took a back seat.

It was June and hotter than the hinges of hell itself. Riley Martin had been in the hospital for three months and was about ready for discharge in one week. The doctor had suggested to Mary Gaye—in front of Riley, for godsakes—that she take him out on a three-hour pass after lunch and the psychiatrist had pushed further. It will be appropriate, she told Mary Gaye in that overly-solicitous voice she had, for you to take him out in public before you get back home to Tennessee, and it will do you both a world of good, but Mary Gaye didn't at all see the point and thought that she would avoid the issue altogether by just staying home that afternoon and taking a nap.

But Riley had heard and Riley wanted to go! Just as if he were a normal boy! Just as if he had no idea whatsoever what he looked like! And he made such a big fuss. He wanted to walk. He wanted to get out. He wanted to see what was going on outside the hospital. He'd heard about the ocean. He'd heard about the beach. He wanted to go to the beach. He wanted to go swimming. He wanted his mother to go buy him some pants, a brand new pair and a new shirt and he wanted shoes. Shoes that tied, with socks. Brown socks, Mother! And a swim suit.

She asked the psychiatrist if the hospital furnished a car they could use, but that all-knowing woman was quick to point out that being in a car would not accomplish anything—as if being stared at were the accomplishment they were after. Something you could get a gold star on your forehead for!

She called Brit's office from the pay phone across the street from the hospital. I don't believe it, she cried. He has no idea what he looks like, he wants to go everywhere and do everything just as if he's a normal boy. That psychiatrist is not his mother. She has no idea what I'm going through! What am I going to do?

Tell them you're sick.

Riley will never let me hear the end of it. If they just hadn't brought it up in front of him. Oh Brit, they want me to take him to the mall, they want me to take him to get an ice cream cone. Imagine being inside the store? I'd have to take his mask off so he could eat the cone! I can't do it. I think I'm going to die. Oh I wish you'd left the car with me! But she knew she was pushing it before the words were out of her mouth.

That would have been a useless extravagance, Mary Gaye, he said, just like he was her father.

It was then that Mary Gaye—grabbing at any solution, despite the consequences—suggested she rent a car, no matter what the psychiatrist said—that woman wouldn't have to know—and just drive Riley around to see the sights without letting him out.

Where are you going to get a rent car from? Brit wanted to know. His voice let her know that she was pushing him much too far. The nearest airport is fifty miles away. How will you get to it? In a shuttle? The shuttle costs twenty dollars. The car would be close to fifty dollars by the time you add everything up. Just for the afternoon? And then you'd need to take the shuttle back. It's much too expensive, Mary Gaye.

Don't we have the money?, Mary Gaye wanted to know. They were the only people she knew who would have had this conversation—any one of her friends would have rented a car without thinking about it for a minute. Brit made a fortune, but where was it? Hidden away in stocks and investments, pinched aside for the future. Well, when was the future, is what she wanted to know.

Not that kind of money, Brit was saying. Not the kind to be just throwing around.

Well, what am I going to do?

Just take Riley back to your apartment. It's right around the corner, isn't it? Stay there for three hours.

That ratty place, he won't stand for it, Mary Gaye said. Brit hung up. She went on talking huffily to herself. He wants to go to the beach, he wants to go to the mall, he wants to go to the Baskin Robbins, he wants to go anywhere and everywhere where there are people so they can . . . stare at him! And me!

Between the morning and right after lunch, while she was at the

Holiday Mall next to the hospital buying Riley some new clothes (on sale), and the ill-fated rhinestone sandals and the purple designer sun dress and the straw hat with the lavender grosgrain ribbon (she felt she needed something to cheer her up), Mary Gaye came up with a plan. She knew that Riley would never be satisfied with her apartment, the first place she was going to take him. He'd want more—she knew the way he was. He'd want to take everything in. But since he didn't know where anything was, she'd just walk him along, just wander with him through all the mean dirty dew-dripping back alleys of Galveston until the three hours were up—just tell him that was all and everything there was to this nowhere town until he was thoroughly exhausted.

RILEY TALKED ABOUT what *he* wanted to do the whole time she got him wrapped and dressed, only stopping to point out inconsistencies in her purchases in that flat voice of his. They don't fit, he said, while she pulled his new pants on. And they're not very good pants, Mother. Did you get them on sale? I wanted shoes that tie, he insisted, and his face got all screwed up.

Just looking at him upset her. She laid no claim to him.

I didn't want flip flops! I wanted socks, brown socks!

Shut up, Mary Gaye finally snapped. That's what you're getting whether you wanted them or not. Put on those shoes and shut up. For a minute he stopped complaining and even brightened up. Then continued. Now Mother! he said, the nurses have been telling me about the ocean, it's not far from here, and I'd like to take a swim. Did you bring a swim suit? She would have slapped him right then, burns or no burns—the outright audacity of his statement and those damn nurses and their foolish suggestions—taking a boy whose skin is burned to stand out in the hot sun before God and all creation in his swim suit—except when she stood up from forcing his flip flops on him, she saw the doctor and the psychiatrist watching her from the nurses' station. Seemed to her everybody was watching her these days. Her hand fluttered in front of her. They waved back. They came to the door. Y'all have fun, hear? they said.

Have fun have fun have fun, she spit out as they rode the elevator to the lobby. Oh we're going to have a ball, aren't we?

Over by the hospital were the busiest streets, the most people. She calculated them in her mind as she stood peering out of the glass door in the hospital lobby and made her plans: cross the street in front of the hospital, cut across the lawns toward the UTMB hospital—no one ever cut across the lawns, they took the sidewalks, so on the lawns you wouldn't meet any curious eyes wondering what an overgrown boy was doing out on the hottest day of the year wearing a mask—cut across the lawns on the other side of the hospital, away from lunch-time Rusty's restaurant. In the next block, there was an alley and that alley would take her to another alley which would bring her right up to 10th or Church, she couldn't remember which, and she didn't care as long as there was no one walking there, and then they could get to that old tree-top apartment of hers on the third floor of Mrs. Griswald's boarding house. And she prayed that that fair lady would be out somewhere, not wanting to come and pour her syrupy pity all over Riley. Mary Gaye had had enough pity—syrupy and saccharine— to last the rest of her whole forever lifetime.

The automatic sliding doors to the drug store in the bank building across the street opened up, and a group of women suddenly appeared like a pulsing vision before Mary Gaye's eyes. There were about ten of them, elegant and stylish in that off-hand way money has. They paused a minute to turn and talk, then one of them gestured over toward the hospital and they continued on, heading right toward Mary Gaye Martin and her son, her only son. A bunch of do-gooders, come to tour the hospital.

Ohhhh, ain't this gone far enough, Jesus, Mary Gaye muttered under her breath. Ain't this just about gone far enough? She gritted her teeth together. You're pushing me, sir, yes indeed you are. I don't have much rope to play with here.

Let's go, Mother, said Riley.

She jerked Riley by the hand. We're going out the other door. She pulled him down past the elevators and out the side entrance toward the parking lot.

They inched along—truly it was hard to walk in flips flops when your feet and legs were wrapped in ace wraps—to a droning litany by Riley. Mr. Louflin, he declared just as steadily as if he were lying in his bed in an air-conditioned room, told me that this is hurricane season. Now during hurricane season, hurricanes come every day or so and when they come everyone in the hospital has to leave they have to get out and go somewhere some go to Houston and some go home to their mothers and fathers and some go somewhere else as long as they don't stay here because during the hurricane the ocean jumps the Seawall jumps up over the Seawall even though it's made of—what's the Seawall made of? Mother?!

I have no idea, I've never seen it, she lied.

—it jumps the Seawall waves bigger than houses bigger even than ten-story buildings bigger even than the hospital it jumps the Seawall and comes rushing down through all the streets of Galveston sucking in all the houses in its paths all the restaurants—are we going to a restaurant to eat?

You already ate.

I'm hungry. Can't we go somewhere where I can get a hamburger and some fries? I want ice cream—And then it comes up along toward the hospital the waves hitting and banging and crushing everything they touch and then even if they have a surgery going on even if the doctors are doing a graft on someone's face and the lights are on bright and shining in the operating room or even if Carnell Hughes is getting his dressings changed or all the big boys including Melvin are down in the playroom playing pool everybody just has to stop whatever it is they're doing and get in the helicopters which are waiting on the roof and go straight up to Houston or they'll be killed by the hurricane which is coming at them faster and faster every second—

Then finally they were at the apartment and Mrs. Griswald, thank God, was nowhere in sight.

—I think that they would have to have at least ten helicopters don't you because there are four of us in our room and two over across the nurse's station then there's that boy in isolation they brought in last week I think that's all though I'll have to ask the tub men tomorrow if there are others and then there's all those kids over on the Reconstruction Ward and I don't know exactly how many one helicopter can hold—

She unlocked the front door wishing he would hush and ascended the old creaky stairs to the door of her own apartment. Riley roamed around from room to room while she sat exhausted on the end of her bed, taking her sandals off and hoping that he could entertain himself for the next three hours. Maybe she could even take a nap.

—they would have to have something beside helicopters something bigger like the airplane they brought us over here in right after I got—

She could tell by the sound of his voice where he was, first in the kitchen—he must have climbed up on the built-in seat by the kitchen table to look out the street-side window—then he was over past the stove to the back door, standing maybe on tip toe to look down into Mrs. Griswald's mumbly-peg garden—though he was probably tall enough by now to just look out. She shut her eyes and lay back on the bed. She felt his knee brush against her hair—he was kneeling on the top of the bed near her head so he could look out through the little dormer windows above her pillow. Lord God, he's so big. And that see-sawing breathing of his enough to drive her nuts.

—where is Melvin? The helicopter is here and no one can find Melvin and here comes the hurricane all the trees are twisted up the waves are pounding on the beach everyone is going everywhere looking for Melvin oh Melvin where are you there he is down stairs in the basement hiding in the closet—

Then he was in the alcove, standing on the twin bed to catch a glimpse of Mrs. Griswald's side yard and the huge magnolia tree that ruled over it and last he went into the bathroom. His voice stopped.

Mother!

Mary Gaye wanted to sleep, really she did, but Riley would never give up once he wanted her attention. She knew that much.

What?

I want my mask off.

He'd found a mirror, she guessed. There weren't any in the hospital. That so-smart psychiatrist was supposed to bring one around eventually and explain to him what had happened to his face. As if he didn't know. Well, hell, thought Mary Gaye, he's going to have to look at himself someday. It might as well be today. He can't keep that damn mask on forever.

Get here, she told him. She sat up on one elbow, released the velcro at the back of the brown hood and pulled the hood and the white life mask off together. The white rubber mask had a sweet smell that made her feel sick in her in every part of herself. He went looking for the mirror again. She lay on her side and waited to hear what he would say.

But he didn't say a word, at least not a word that she could hear.

Riley was considering his transformation in silence. His face surprised him at first, took him off guard, shocked his system—but once he got used to looking at himself, he was excited. He'd been looking for a disguise for a long time. He'd felt it in his long gangly limbs, this urging to be full grown and gone!—out of himself. He was tired of being called the baby and the big boy—Oh my, what a biiiig boy! He's such a baaby! He hated the sound of it. Now he was tougher than nails—he could see it—like a dinosaur, like GI Joe, like the Bionic Man—plastered all over with layers of skin. He admired himself around from all sides—his eyes were drawn down, his lips were swollen, no hair, no ears, something about his nose, just like the aliens on Star Trek—not a trace of the old Riley. That boy was gone, like a dead man, just disappeared off the face of the earth never to be heard from again—and good riddance. No one at all would recognize him. He could be just whoever he pleased. He could scare the living devil out of all the kids he met—those stupid kids he knew back home—and they wouldn't for a minute—for even a minute—know what he was thinking, because his new face hid everything, like a mask—it was rigid and fixed. He was safe behind it. He could order his mother and father around with it. He tried making it move in the mirror, raising his eyebrows. But he had no eyebrows! Good! Only his pulsing eyes showed his displeasure.

—All right now all of you, he said, marching boldly out through his mother's bedroom and round and round the kitchen, you too Melvin you bad boy get a move on it do you hear me we're heading out of this hospital on the double this is an evacuation the hurricane is coming and I'm here to save all of you Melvin get out of that closet! If you miss the helicopter just jump on my back and we'll fly all the way to Houston in a flash we'll fly right into the eye of the hurricane we'll blow it to kingdom come—

Riley? Riley! What are you doing?

I'm ready to go, he declared.

Ready? she fussed. It's barely half an hour.

I want to see the ocean, he said. I want to get an ice cream at the 31 Flavors. I want a hamburger with fries. I want to get those shoes that tie. These flips flops are not right at all.

Hold your horses, young man, said Mary Gaye, sitting up. None of these places are at all near by (that was a lie—they could have walked to Rusty's, right around the corner, to get a hamburger before you could shake a stick). This place is bigger than you yourself have ever imagined, I don't care what those nurses and doctors told you. There's no way we can get to any of those things this afternoon, not walking, not even in a car. She stood up. This heat would kill us before we ever even hit the door. No sir, we're staying put. She headed for the kitchen to look for something to occupy herself.

Staying put! he wailed. Tears leaked out of his eyes. That's not what the doctor told you to do, Mother! He stamped his foot. He told you to take me out to get an ice cream, weren't you listening? I heard him! There's nothing to do here. You don't even have a TV!

There was a knock on the door.

Good Lord, look what you've done, said Mary Gaye. It's Mrs. Griswald!

They heard the low drawling of that bug-eyed woman at the door. Yoo hoo, everthing all right?

Shut up! hissed Mary Gaye to Riley. She went to the apartment door and opened it just a crack. Why, we're fine, thanks ever so much, Mary Gaye cooed. Just getting ourselves used to things. Riley's indisposed right now, we'll come visit y'all some other time, she went on, but Mrs. Griswald's eyes, which had shifted from Mary Gaye's face to a lower place right in back of her, raised up just barely enough for someone who was looking to see. Mary Gaye felt Riley breathing hard at her back.

Well, there's the young man, said Mrs. Griswald. How you, fella? Come to keep your mother company? Bless his heart, she said, sucking in her breath. We've been waiting for you to come on home, she said, and there followed a torrential monologue about all the folks that had lived at her boarding house over the years and all their various aliments and how they had grown up and come back to visit and were doing good despite all the tragic things that happened to them why there was even a boy who'd lost his nose—Riley listened to Mrs. Griswald with his motionless face turned up while Mary Gaye shifted her feet, waiting for Mrs. Griswald to retreat. Why how old are you? You're such a big boy. You must be going into fifth grade, are you?

Second, Riley said.

My my. You *are* big! Well, if you're just going to hang around here, why don't you come on downstairs and have some pie with me and Arnold. He'll show you some of the junk he bought at the flea market this morning.

Pie? said Mary Gaye, searching hard. She knew nothing would be dearer to Riley's heart than a look at Arnold's junk and a piece of Mrs. Griswald's pie. He was, in fact, breathing even harder to show his intention, but Mary Gaye could not bear the thought of Mrs. Griswald's dingy old kitchen or the idea of making melancholy small talk or of having Mrs. Griswald and Arnold stare with abandon at the face of her son.

Pie, no, thank you, we were just going to take a little spin around town, Mrs. Griswald. Weren't we, darling? She stared with all the force of her motherly authority at Riley's face, specifically his eyes, until she was sure he had got the message.

Mother and son fled shortly after Mrs. Griswald clumped back down the stairs. They set out on Church Street, heading away from the hospital, Mary Gaye pushing and pulling Riley by the shoulder of his shirt. Mary Gaye took it block by block, watching out ahead of her to avoid any area that looked like it might have commerce or traffic or people. That first block, overshadowed by towering liveoaks, was quiet, as empty as a tomb, but on the second block, she saw a man rocking in a chair on his front porch. They shifted to the alley oceanside of Church, a place presided over by metal cans and old fish, broken shells, and people's disposable items. It wasn't shaded deeply by trees like Church was—why waste a good tree on an alley? It was just dirt and smells and heat, but it had this to recommend itself—there wasn't a living breathing soul anywhere to be seen along its entire length.

It ended temporarily in an old school playground whose buildings held no kids—for it was the beginning of summer.

There now, there's a swing, said Mary Gaye, pointing to a jungle gym sitting in the middle of the dirt yard. Swing some. Go play.

Are we on our way to Baskin Robbins, Mother? Riley wanted to know. I'm getting awfully hot and tired.

We're on our way, all right, she lied. Right after you swing a little.

Truth to tell, if she'd been with any other person in the universe, she would have liked a little stop at the Baskin Robbins, even though its bubble-gum-pink school chairs were always smeary with sugar, and it was generally full of bare-chested teenage boys. She would of liked any dark cool spot right about now, sugar and skin or no.

But the metal swing set, unshaded in the hottest part of the day, was much too hot for Riley to hold onto, even if he'd been able to hold on to it at all. But he was not. His hands, wrapped in splints to keep the grafts there from pulling back, had no way of grasping. She knew it all along.

They went on, creeping toward God knows what, up one street, and down one alley, circling upon themselves till Mary Gaye felt completely lost in the still and heavy heat and worse! like she was in a not-very-good neighborhood. Keeping to the alleys had made her lose sight of the houses on the nearby streets—they were no longer three-story Victorians with gingerbread lattice, but only run-down shacks, some boarded up, others covered with obscene graffiti. What's more, she began to feel faint and remembered that she had not actually eaten lunch, she'd been too busy getting things together for Riley and buying that outfit for herself. Breakfast had just been a Diet Coke and a sticky bun. And Riley was still muttering out from the confines of his mask, going on and on about—now what was it?

—the helicopter's getting ready to take off for Houston the hurricane is coming in faster and faster waves pounding on the beach Wonder Woman is going to carry that big kid from the Reconstruction Ward because he's still playing pool have you checked the landing gear have you checked the IVs have you checked to see if Ronnie Tate is breathing does the pilot understand what Melvin is like—

Where are we? Riley complained. We're lost. Where's that Baskin Robbins? I'm hot and tired. This isn't any fun at all. I can't keep going on like this. I need to sit down. Do you know where we are, Mother?

I'll tell you where we are, exploded Mary Gaye. We are in the middle of nowhere is where we are. And do you just want to know, young man, exactly how we got here?

How?

We got here because *you!* thought you were such a smarty-pants and such a big boy and because *you!* had to do exactly what you were told not to do and because *you!* decided that you would like to learn a little something about gasoline like you've been told not to do one hundred times before and because *you!*—she turned and glared at him—decided to play with matches. We are here, young man, because *you!* decided to set yourself on fire! That's why we're here. For that reason and no other. You just decided to ruin everything because *you!* wanted to do what *you!* wanted to do. Oh I could kill you, I tell you, there are days when I could just kill you.

His breathing came hard and heavy.

Do you hear me, sir? She pushed him on the back. Huh? Huh?

Whooo wee! she heard soft and low to her right. Three tall black boys wearing no shirts at all stood together like ascending pillars on the stoop of an old gray house. Something gold glinted out on the chest of the tallest; it caught her eye, forcing her to squint closer to look—his nipple was pierced. God almighty! escaped her lips and her eyes fled for a brief look up at his face—his tongue was out and wagging languidly back and forth like a snake's, rubbing against his teeth. Hardly fifteen! He winked at her. The hum of slow laughter. Had they seen Riley? Had they heard her fussing at him? What were they laughing at? What were they looking at?

They crossed the street but there were men there wearing very short cutoffs with their legs propped up against the banister—you could see right up their pants!—on a porch two houses up, then an old woman out sweeping the dirt in front of her house on further who stopped, arrested by the sight of Mary Gaye and her son, wanted to talk. Mary Gaye pushed ahead. They crossed the street again, went down an alley but didn't get far—toward the end of it she saw men bunched together in a rumbling clot against a car, drinking beer—at three in the afternoon! She turned around quickly, but not before the men began to stir and fume, roiling out in separate pieces from their center to wave at her, make her some kind of an offer. Was it Riley they were staring at or her own self—Mary Gaye Martin with her ivory-white shoulders exposed? A hot wind blew out of nowhere, her hand up so quick to grab the top of her straw hat, standing there at the end of the alley posed like a *Playboy* center-fold and in front of all those men. Was she seeing things? Or were things seeing her? She'd lost track.

THE CHURCH APPEARED out of nowhere, an ancient stone building, cozy with green grass, sweet-smelling pitisforum bushes and fat oleanders, a wiry old man tending the yard with a push mower. The front door was open, it was dark and cool and inviting inside, a refuge from the heat and a place for her to rest from the prying world around her. It wasn't Baskin Robbins, but at this point Riley didn't care. They walked up the flagstone steps and went inside.

The church was filled with astonishing pockets of cool air. She sat down in the first pew her eyes took hold of, slumped against red cushions, her feet propped up on the padded wooden kneeling bar below—and groaned in relief. Her body pulsed with exhaustion. Riley went ahead as she knew he would, up the center aisle, his head bobbing along like a cork in a black-green ocean of colored light and deep shadow. She was glad to be free of him. In front of the altar, he turned and began to lace his way back toward her, in and out of the pews, touching every little thing as he went along. She could hear the flip-flop of his plastic shoes on the marble floor and pick up bits and pieces of the ongoing, intense and grueling discussion he was having with himself and half the known universe about hurricanes and how he would single-handedly bring them to a satisfying order.

As she was trying to decide what she could do next, a man walked up to Riley—he seemed to come from a door near the altar. She guessed it was the priest or pastor or rector or whatever person or thing was in charge of this place. She tried to stir herself, jump up and get Riley away, but she was too tired to move. The man wore a black coat, had glasses and gray hair that he had tried to whisk away with some black dye, but to no avail. He had his hand on Riley's shoulder. Pervert, was the first word that came to Mary Gaye's mind—they always had bad dye jobs—and for a minute her most motherly and protective instincts surfaced, but fell away in the shadowy silence. She was there, after all, and watching, and a man who was a priest, even if he did have vile instincts, would be careful inside a church, of all places. Mary Gaye shook her thick auburn hair. She must be going perfectly crazy to let her mind go on so.

Riley was talking. She could barely hear him, droning on within the muffling confines of his mask and his taut lips, his breathing whirring along with him. Hummmmmmmm hummmmmm is what her ears picked up mostly. The man was listening, talking back, asking questions, probably about the fire and Riley, she knew, was giving his version. She was sure it was all wrong. At a certain point, they both turned—the man in the black coat whose face now that she could see it was completely unmemorable, and Riley, her son, her only son, her only child—to look at her. They looked and they kept on talking—was the priest giving Riley instructions?—acknowledging her only with their eyes. Then they turned away and continued.

Mary Gaye's impatient soul fretted: that priest was only talking to Riley because he couldn't see his face. He wouldn't pay one ounce of attention to him if he knew what Riley really looked like, least ways she wouldn't think he would.

An arm came up around her shoulder. She shut her eyes. It was a— oh, she didn't know—a soft arm, a strong arm, it was the arm that needed to be there, for sure, the one she had needed for such a long time. She didn't think a thing about it, not then. It was an arm to rest on while she watched the priest kneel down in front of her son in such a way that Riley's head and the priest's were almost even and then the priest began to circle his hand, just so easily, around Riley's head, peeling away layers of white bandage that covered it—she didn't remember having bandaged him like that—while Riley, as patient as an old dog, stood—she hadn't heard him so quiet in his whole life, nor so waiting, so himself. She didn't think she'd ever loved anyone as much as she loved Riley right at that minute nor seen anyone's life laid out so sharply—every detail of the sorrow and intense joy that would come to him—as the priest's hand wound round and round her son's head, then came to rest again on Riley's shoulder, the top of the priest's head leaning lightly against Riley's chest. The unraveled bandages lay all around Riley's shoulders like a celebration wreath.

The arm that was around her own shoulder rejoiced. She felt the warmth coming out it—how tender it was, like a mother's arm. This is the most important thing that's ever happened to Riley, someone said. Now anything is possible. Do you know that?

She turned her head just a hair. It was that man, the priest. He was right beside her—though she thought he'd been there next to Riley—and it was his arm that was around her, the most perfectly natural thing that had ever happened to her in her whole life. She sighed, savoring the essence of Riley's life: it would be sweet. He would be the most handsome boy. His beauty would rise up out from the very center of his body to be tasted by anyone willing to wait—they would have to be very patient. How refreshed they would be by it! It made her hungry just to think of it with a great and satisfying hunger.

The priest—she turned to look at him: ohh! he was very ugly, his mouth wide, his ears too big, and the shape of his face as square as any face she'd ever seen. It made her laugh. I'll fix the color of your hair if you'll let me, Mary Gaye said, putting her face up close to his. He smiled. There was something in and around his nose that made her wonder if he'd ever been burned and the minute she thought that, he agreed. He knew about fire. She could see it in his lovely eyes. Oh, he said, it *can* burn. . . . He shook his head back and forth so slow. His thoughts shimmered and settled in waves all around them until everything was very quiet.

There is never any point in trying to change things yourself, he told

Mary Gaye. Everything must be put in the fire. She accepted what he had to say—it was perfectly clear.

It was amazing, too, how much he loved her—it seemed to pour out of him—even in her store-bought dress and sandals. They had given her blisters—their only function! She had been close to naked walking through the streets of Galveston in her fancy-foolish clothes, her head bent in shame because of her son—her only son, her only child, her dearest boy—flaunting herself, like a loose woman. She was the spectacle! Yes! The priest agreed with her the very moment she said it, his eyes fixed on hers, but . . . no father could love a daughter more than he loved her. That she knew. She rested there. His hand touched her hair.

Mother!

Mary Gaye Martin started up, her mouth thick and dry from sleep. Riley stood next to the pew.

Who was that man? she asked him.

What man? Riley asked impatiently.

You were talking to a man, telling him about the fire.

Riley shook his head. I'm hungry, Mother. And I'm hot. I want to go swimming.

Her disappointment was intense. I need a minute, she said. Just give me a minute. Clearly she had been dreaming. It was the heat, she knew, this oppressive heat, heavy enough to undo a person, and the fact that she hadn't eaten. Her feet were killing her. And she had no idea how they would get back to the hospital.

THEY SET OUT EAST, moving through the heat like swimmers navigating a dense swamp. It surrounded them, a solid molten mass emanating up from the broken seashell covered paths, a nearly impenetrable wall. The neighborhoods through which they passed were even more unfamiliar than the ones they had gone through before. Had she gotten turned around? Why was it so dark and dreary? And yet not quite dark and dreary, because the sun shone somewhere she knew, its heat but not its light riffling down through the gigantic towering trees. There didn't seem to be anyone anywhere, as if all the earth's inhabitants had disappeared while she dreamt the afternoon away on her red-cushioned church pew. She could not hear any traffic, she did not see any stores nor the tall buildings that would indicate that life was being carried forward in the usual fashion. All she saw was a field full of too-tall grass on one side and some old run-down houses on the other, their front yards filled with broken cars.

I want to go home, Riley cried suddenly. I just want to go home. I want to see my father. I'm hot and now I'm tired and I can hardly breathe.

Mary Gaye was sorry. She should of thought to get a taxi somewhere along the way, maybe when they left the church, but she didn't recall having passed through any part of town where a taxi could be hailed. She hadn't seen a pay phone to call one.

She was still dazed. She heard a sound, just a little sound at first, someone crying, a child somewhere crying and her heart began to pound furiously. She was positive that there had been an arm around her shoulder, more real than any arm she'd ever felt, no matter if she had been dreaming. The arm had held her and had been telling her everything about herself— but that was all the time she had to think about it, because the child crying somewhere got closer and his voice got much louder.

Help me! Somebody help me! She pulled Riley along until she could find where the noise was coming from and there on the corner near a stop sign and just beyond the field of grass was a boy with blond curly hair no more than four years old dressed in a jaunty little sailor suit and he was screaming his head off. I'm lost!

Oh, Lord, said Mary Gaye and she raced forward, leaving Riley to stand alone. She caught up to the boy and bent down on one knee so she could be face to face with him. What's the matter, dear heart? she said. I'm lost, the boy wailed. I'm lost. I can't find my mother. Oh help me, he screamed, louder and louder, I'm lost.

The lost boy would not be consoled. Why you're such a sweet little thing, Mary Gaye crooned. Your mother would never leave you. She touched the little sailor suit. It was made of the finest seersucker with the loveliest little red piping that went around the bib. His little shoes were a perfect match, natty blue denim tennies with brand-new red laces. His cheeks were rosy red and his yellow curls could each be wound around your finger, they were so thick. You poor thing, she said. But he cried on. His crying affected her so strangely. Oh please stop, she said. We'll find your mother.

She started seeing things floating in front of her eyes, little bubbles and suddenly she felt faint—was it running to grab the little boy and then bending down so quickly and in this heat? She heard Riley crying—how odd, like birth pains—but when she looked up to find him—straight into the light—his groans turned into a great shout—was it joy?—somehow. He was a giant of a man—of course, he was always big. He was surrounded by other men as big as he was. They were leaping up up up and their bodies were peeling off of them like the skins of apples—unwinding and unwinding.

Mary Gaye wanted to have her hand there on the unwinding. She stretched it out, but it couldn't reach somehow. She felt a deep sorrow and then a hand reached out to help her—that tender hand—and she had hold of Riley, was unwinding with him, and a woman was talking to him and there were people standing in a circle all around her looking down and one of them was that man, she knew it was, the priest—that very bad dye job, he was by far the ugliest man she'd ever seen, he would lead her back—and she realized then that they were in very familiar territory, a corner near the hospital and that the woman was the lost boy's mother, come to rescue her. But when the people standing all around and staring got her stood up and her dress all patted back in place, the priest was gone.

SHE COULDN'T HAVE explained it to anybody in a million years, the whole thing, the walk, the priest, the wandering, just like she was in some place that only existed in another world, some antediluvian place— nor the absolute certainty of it, that arm around her shoulder, much more certain than any other thing—

Riley was mad at her. You could have just told that little boy to go find his mother, he fussed at Mary Gaye. He didn't need your help—he began in on a fresh litany as they started for the hospital—really he didn't, Mother, he had *his* mother right there.

Now Riley was in the lead, marching along in front of Mary Gaye and fussing at her.

—He was just a baby that little boy he didn't need to cry like that his mother was right next to him and here he was making all that racket just like a little baby what a little baby he was those kind of kids make me sick. Riley turned to see if his own mother was close behind and paying attention.

Mother! Mary Gaye was stuck in her daydreams. Mother! She looked up.

Mother, you could have just told that man from the church to get us a taxi and then we wouldn't have had to walk. Didn't you think of that, Mother?

Mary Gaye stared after Riley.

What man are you talking about?

You know what man, Mother. Riley turned and marched up the street.

You did see that man! Mary Gaye called to him. You talked to that man, didn't you? I wasn't just dreaming I really saw him what did he say to you why did you tell me you hadn't seen him it would have made all the difference in the world if you hadn't lied to me right then—

But Riley had gone on ahead, was still lecturing her.

—if you'd told that man—he said his name was Nate—to get us a taxi you wouldn't have fallen down like that and all those people wouldn't have stood around you staring I wish you'd just talked to that man and got us a taxi Mother sometimes you make me so mad— ✿

Saturday Night is for Losers

By A.C. Greene

Newspaper people don't get rich. Not from the newspaper business. I'm not talking about newspaper owners, or syndicated columnists who are on television round tables every night, or byline writers who fly all over the world and bring a book out every year. I mean the men and women who put out the paper, the ones you never see in print who make it happen. They work the city desk, the copy desk, the rim. They sit on rewrite all day wearing headphones and doing stories somebody else gets credit for. It's the kind of newspapering I did most of my career. But one time . . . a funny once . . . I almost got rich doing it.

I was in a new town looking for a job. No point in going into why I was looking for a job in a new town, but I was. It was one of those newspapers that went to bed at 2 A.M. and nothing short of the Second Coming could cause a remake. The managing editor's name was Dolan. He finally offered me a job on the nightside rim and asked me if I thought I could handle it. I said, "Sure."

"We've got a pretty fast operation here," he said.

"No faster than I am," I told him.

"I hope you're as good as you talk," he said. It always hacks an M.E. for a desk man to be cocky.

It was tough, I'll grant him that. You came on at 5:00 P.M. and you didn't stop until the "red streak" edition shoved eight hours later. After that you could slow down some and look over what you'd written.

There were five of us on the local desk. A fellow named McGraw was City Editor. He was a good sixty-five years old. He never said much but you could ask him the name of the mayor's wife's sister, or who was Miss America of 1967 and he'd spell it for you out of the side of his mouth without looking at a directory or an encyclopedia. That old man knew everything. It didn't take me but a couple of shifts to see that he was the reason the paper came out on time.

Then, when I'd been there a month, he died. Heart. There wasn't anybody to fill his shoes, either. Newspapers never think about filling people's shoes. They're afraid they're going to have to pay a bigger salary to a replacement.

McGraw died and for the next two weeks we did bust a gut trying to get that four edition rat race out of the chute every night. The guy in the City Editor's slot was a wimp named Claudell, and he was scared to death management was going to find out it had been McGraw who was putting out the paper all the time, so he drove hell out of us without it doing any good.

I finally went back to the managing editor's office and said, "Look, Mr. Dolan. I've been here six weeks . . . no, seven. It's been so fast I've lost track of time."

"I told you this is a tough operation," he said, in that proud-to-be-difficult way managing editors have.

"It's not tough, it's just screwed up. McGraw held that carnival together and when he died the merry-go-round broke down."

"Claudell tells me everything's going along fine," Dolan said.

"Claudell would have said the same thing to the captain of the *Titanic*. You've got a real loser in the slot when you've got little Mr. Claudell there."

The M.E. leaned back in his armchair and stroked his chin, which is a universal sign the big man is about to take you into his confidence.

"How would you like to go into the slot?" he asked me.

"Instead of who?"

"Claudell. It didn't take you to come in here and tell me what's wrong. McGraw dying made us realize we've got to have a good, dependable swing man; a pro who can handle anything. You're a pro."

This is another line a managing editor uses on the person he wants to stick into a fifteen-hundred-a-week job that pays seven-fifty. But it always works, and it worked on me.

The swing man in the slot is halfway between a brown-nose and a press-gang contractor. He's not the City Editor but he has to do the city editor's job without his authority. He tells fifty guys and gals what to do and makes them do it with nothing to force them but his tongue.

I caught the slot two days, swung to the copy desk for two days and rode the slot again on Saturday night. That was why they needed a pro. What they really wanted was somebody without a wife and home who could come early and stay late any time the M.E. whistled.

I fitted the picture pretty good. The wife and the home had both played out on me about the same time. All I had to do now was read magazines and watch television in the cheap hotel room where I lived. I didn't even want to go to the movies alone, and I hit the city without so much as one friendly phone number.

Saturday night I came on at 5 P.M. to get out the Sunday paper. I worked until there wasn't anything else to do and if it was still 1 A.M. I was lucky.

The usual run of tavern customers began making their calls about seven, after they'd had time to get five or six beers down, cussing the paper because their old lady had run off, or wanting to fight "whoever that smart son-of-a-bitch was that wrote that lie about me las' week..." or las' month, las' year or las' century.

You acted dumb, you got tough, or you sobbed with them, according to how drunk they were. Then the work got too fast for you to fool with that kind of shit and you turned the outside calls over to some cub, or maybe the staff souse—which was about the caliber of manpower you drew on Saturday night.

That Saturday it had been quiet. The sections were all printed up and collated, only sports was still open. On the news-side there was nothing but a mugging in Federal Park, some wife beatings, a drive-by shooting, and a drug bust or two. The politicians were settling down after the mid-term elections.... I even managed to sneak out to the Brass Rail for a roast beef sandwich and a draft beer with one of the rim men.

Ten o'clock we were working on a police brutality story when I smelled something rich and heady—the kind of perfume you don't smell in a city room, ever, and not often in the Entertainment department. There's been a little perfume in my life, good perfume, so I recognized it.

I turned in my swivel chair and a big, fine looking blonde was looking down at me. She wasn't young, but she hadn't lost anything as she picked up her years.

"Where's the city editor?" she asked.

"He's off," I said, "I'm in the slot."

"Who the hell are you?"

"I'm Ed Vayne."

"V-a-i-n, like a woman?"

"No, V-a-y-n-e. Like John Vayne."

She didn't laugh. She took a drag off the filtertip cigarette she had in her hand, inhaled, then blew it out. The thought crossed my mind that the "No Smoking" sign was getting fly-specked.

"Duke would beat hell out of you if he had heard you making fun of him," she said.

"I doubt he'll know about it now," I said.

"If I had told him . . ." she stopped, looked around, and asked, "Where the hell's the ash tray?"

"We have a No Smoking sign," I said, nodding my head in the direction of Mr. Fly-specks.

"That's for the staff," she said, "and I'm not staff."

I pulled out the drawer were we kept such items, put it on the desk, and she crushed out the practically new cigarette, She looked back at me, finishing her thought, " . . .and Duke Wayne sure as hell could have done the job."

"You're probably right. On the other hand, Duke might have walked away talking soprano if I'd gotten in close. I've have some mean ways."

"Duke Wayne would make two of you the best day you ever saw," she said slowly.

"That I wouldn't doubt," I said, "but if you'll pardon me, Duke Wayne's dead, this isn't the best day I ever saw, and I've got two more editions to get out, and I'm running into that time. Maybe one of the reporters can be of some assistance."

She walked around to the other side of my desk.

"You know who I am?" she asked.

"No, ma'm, I don't."

"I own this paper."

I looked at her and thought that she was just the kind that would be telling the truth.

"Well," she said, "what are you looking at? I own it: every stick of furniture in this goddam office, every ton of newsprint in that warehouse across the street, and all six floors of this building."

"I didn't know that," I said, because there wasn't anything else I could say.

"I know you didn't," she said. "You were too anxious to make wisecracks about people who are bigger than you are to find out. You've got to shoot off your thousand a week mouth about a man who could buy you out the rest of your life with what he made for one picture."

A man can take so much, of course. If she owned the paper she had more to lose than I did if she fired me from this job this night. So I stood up.

"I don't know your name and I don't know if you own this paper. You probably do. But one thing I do know: you don't own Ed Vayne. And that's V-a-y-n-e, *not* as in John Wayne." I paused, "And it just so happens I don't even make a thousand a week."

She puffed on another filtertip and looked at me through the smoke.

"You don't like this job?" she asked.

"No, by God, right at this moment, I don't." I said back.

"If this were any time but Saturday night I'd pay you off in cash from my purse and send you the hell back out on the street. But Arno said never fire a man on Saturday. The big Sunday paper is too full of ads."

"Look, Mrs. . . . owner. You started this whole thing. If there's anything to be sorry for, I'm sorry. But if I'm going to get this big Sunday paper out then I'm going to get it out my way—and right now."

She reached into a gold cloth clutch bag she was carrying and pulled out a piece of folded blue paper.

"Run this," she said, "and don't bury it on the local runover."

She walked out of the office. I noticed again what a good-looking woman she was.

All of a sudden, when she left, there were guys and gals all around my desk. They'd been somewhere else during the shooting.

"Wow. You've had it now," a lanky copyreader said, looking at me as if I'd fallen into a vat of plutonium.

"Who was that?" I asked.

"It was just who she said it was. It was the owner."

"What's her name?"

"My God . . . you mean you've been at this paper for six months and don't even know the owner's name?"

"I've been here nine weeks. I thought Thurmond was the owner. He's the publisher."

"Thurmond doesn't own enough stock to swap for a home edition. That was Mrs. Markley. Her husband was Arno Markley."

Arno Markley had been the big cheese of the paper for forty years before he died. There was a statue of him in the lobby, and all kinds of utterances of his chiseled around the building.

"She must be a lot older than she looks if she was Arno Markley's wife," I said.

"Trophy wife. She's in her forties. He married her late. He settled with his first one a long time ago when they divorced. This one got everything he had."

"I'll bet she did too," I said.

I'd forgotten about that piece of paper she gave me. I unfolded it and it was written in longhand. Nice writing. It said she was going to marry T. Preston Matthews. There was a lot about what he did and who he was and who she was, and it was written in fairly good news style.

We ran it page one, right under the fold. I wondered if I wasn't making a pretty stout play of the story, but I decided a woman like her would want it that way. It got in 557,898 copies more or less; trucked, flown, pedaled, and tossed, all over the state.

Sunday morning, 8 o'clock, me deader than a poisoned shad from the late shift, and the phone rings. It was Dolan.

"What th' bloody hell did you do?" he yelled.

"What do you mean, 'What th' bloody hell' did I do?"

"That story on pI about Mrs. Markley."

"Wait a minute, Dolan. I'm not good awake. What's wrong with it?"

"This is what's wrong. Thurmond just called me screaming. T. Preston Matthews's lawyer got him out of bed fifteen minutes ago to tell him T. Preston Matthews is suing us for ten million dollars for printing that story. How much wronger would you like it to be?"

T. Preston Matthews's lawyer advised Thurmond the story was a complete fabrication. A suit would be filed just as soon after 8 A.M. Monday as a fast clerk could get through the courthouse door.

Thirty minutes after getting Dolan's phone call I was in the city room. There were just the three of us: Thurmond, Dolan and me. It was spooky, being in city room in the broad daylight with nothing happening but a police radio blabbing somewhere off in a hallway room.

Thurmond had gotten up nerve to call Mrs. Markley's home, but it didn't work. The butler said Mrs. Markley was asleep and she wasn't to be waked; not by a lawyer, a publisher, or anybody else, but most especially she wasn't going to be waked by a butler. He hung up. Lord God, I thought, watching Thurmond's reaction, it would be nice to hang up in a publisher's face.

Thurmond turned to me when he put the phone down.

"Where in hell did you get that monstrosity of a story?"

"She came up here and gave it to me."

"Who gave it to you, Mrs. Markley?"

"I guess it was Mrs. Markley. She said she owned the paper."

"Don't you know Mrs. Markley?"

"No, I don't know Mrs. Markley. Why should I know Mrs. Markley? I don't even know you."

"When in God's name did he come to work here?" Thurmond asked the M.E.

"Vayne's been under a lot of stress, Mr. Thurmond. He's been through a lot since McGraw died."

"Well, by God, as long as I'm paying his salary he's going to speak decently to me," Thurmond said without looking at me.

"He didn't know," the M.E. said.

Thurmond turned to me. He's a big man with a bushy mane of silver hair which you can tell costs a lot to keep silver.

"Vayne," he said, pausing to see if he had heard the name right, "On this paper we clear things through someone with authority. We don't stick stories on page one every time some tramp drops in. . . ." He realized what he had said, "That is, ah, presuming whoever gave you the story turns out to be, ah, an imposter." He frowned just a second trying to figure whether he had said it right, then asked, "Goddamit, why didn't you call me?"

"Now wait a minute, Mr. Thurmond," I said, "In the first place, I've got twenty years of this business under my belt. I know about running stories in the newspaper. In the second place, the guys on copy told me who she was. They said she was the owner. And in the third place, you haven't talked to Mrs. Markley about it."

"I wish to God my phones were working," he turned to Dolan, "Why in hell are the phones in my office the only ones in the building that aren't working? I hate to use these." He looked around the room as if it were littered with the dead from an outbreak of bubonic plague.

"Because you ordered your phones shut off every night, Mr. Thurmond. You said the custodians were using them."

"Oh," the publisher said.

"Here, I'll call Mrs. Markley," I said. "I've got nothing to lose."

I dialed her number and got the butler, too. He was telling me I couldn't talk to Mrs. Markley when I heard someone cut in.

"Who is this? Is this Bradley Thurmond?"

"This is Ed Vayne, Mrs. Markley, I am. . . ."

"What the hell are you doing calling me at home? Get off this phone."

"Mr. Thurmond wants to speak with you," I said—and stepped back.

The dignified silver mane was caressed over and over as Thurmond talked; or listened: "Good morn . . . yes, Mrs. Mark . . . but Mrs. Mark . . . T. Preston Matthews is suing us for ten million dollars, Mrs. Markley. There was . . . there was a story on our front page that . . . that you and Mr. Matthews were to be married. His lawyer says it's a . . . yes? Of course, Mrs. Mark. . . ."

He looked at the receiver, then at Dolan.

"She says to not bother her. She says the story is ridiculous. She'll call me tomorrow."

He turned to me. "Vayne, if this thing blows up the way it's looking right now, your career in journalism is over. I'll see to it no newspaper on the North American continent will let you in the door. You won't even be able to draw a bundle for street sales."

"I'm afraid he's right, Vayne," Dolan, the M.E. said, shaking his head up and down wisely. But they didn't have the guts to fire me yet.

Monday morning I was down goosing the mail edition. The copy-readers and reporters were talking about Mrs. Markley's engagement story, glancing at me as they did. I played cat's-got-my-tongue.

I'll admit, with T. Preston Matthews on my mind, I was afraid for the first call to come in from the courthouse press room. I drifted over by the rewrite bank to see if I could overhear somebody talking to Barnaby, our beat man, but there was nothing.

I sweated the courthouse call through the first street edition, and when I cleared the copy for it, I leaned back and closed my eyes. Still nothing.

I opened my eyes and who should be standing there by my chair but little Mr. Claudell.

"What are you doing here? Isn't this your day off?"

"They called me to come down," he said, looking satisfied about something.

"Who called you to come down?"

"Mr. Dolan. He said he wished I would replace you in the slot."

"I'll bet he wished you could," I said, but only half aloud.

"I am to take the slot and you are to go to his office immediately."

The bleached blonde who secretaries for Dolan told he was gone and I was wanted right now in Mr. Thurmond's office. And hurry.

"I don't know where it is," I told her.

"Oh, Mr. Vayne . . . you mean you don't know how to locate the publisher's suite?" She frowned, perplexed.

"Honey, I don't even know how to locate the executive crapper."

She giggled and said, well, they weren't far apart, on the second floor. She said I'd know Thurmond's office by the door. "It doesn't look like any crapper door I ever heard of," she giggled again. She was right. It was hand carved and looked four inches thick, and the hall was carpeted. It's amazing the difference in the way a newspaper office looks around where the money is.

I knocked and Dolan peeked it open. "Oh, come in," he was almost whispering. There was another man inside with Thurmond and Mrs. Markley. She was sitting at the publisher's desk, smoking a cigarette and looking at the other man. I sat down on an orange colored suede sofa. Damned if I was going to die standing up.

"Pres, ten million dollars is ridiculous," she was saying. "Your honor isn't worth that."

When he spoke T. Preston Matthews's voice had a smooth-mean tone to it like he had been used to firing people since the age of twelve.

"Something better be worth ten million," he said, "because I don't intend to settle for a dime less."

"You surely can't hope to collect," she said.

"Don't be a fool, Rita. I'll own more of this paper than you do before this is over."

"Not for a measly ten million you won't," she said.

"Mrs. Markley. . . ." Thurmond kept trying to get a word into the conversation.

"What?" she turned to him annoyed.

"Here's Vayne," Thurmond pointed to me on the sofa. She looked at me again the way she had looked at me Saturday night.

"Did he run the story?" she asked Thurmond.

"Yes, he did. He said you gave it to him."

I opened my mouth to say, "Don't you remember?" but she turned back to T. Preston Matthews, tossing over her shoulder, "I don't know where this guy comes in."

Well, I could see this was a real plate of scrambled eggs, although I wasn't actually afraid . . . I mean about running the story. That stuff about never seeing me before in her life was window dressing.

She was ranting along about how ten million dollars wouldn't buy the ink for our Christmas edition when T. Preston lifted a hand and stopped her.

"Dear Rita, shut your mouth. You're acting silly. I know how much this paper is worth and how much you own. You'd give every cent of it to get me. That's why you did it . . . and I know you did it."

The rest of us held our breaths. Dolan, Thurmond and me.

She quit smoking and laid her filtertip carefully on the edge of Thurmond's twenty thousand dollar antique desk.

"It hasn't been long since I heard you were offering *two* million just to get me in bed."

"You never heard that and you know it. Anyone who knows me knows I don't buy, or beg, women. I don't have to."

T. Preston Matthews had an admirable detachment.

She looked around the room. "None of this crowd knows you, Pres. That's the trouble. They're not in your league. I own all of them, even Thurmond. They have to believe anything I say. If I say you have done some begging, they'll believe me."

I waited to see if Thurmond or Dolan would speak up, but when they didn't, I decided there was no use in my commenting. T. Preston Matthews shrugged it off, anyway.

"The point is wasted on me, dear Rita, because whatever they believe or whatever you say, I'm suing you for ten million dollars." He looked around like he might be looking for an ash tray. Thurmond hurriedly slid one across to him, and he continued. "You printed a story on the front page of your newspaper that we were going to get married. It was outlandish, childish—and it was a damn lie." He elevated his eyebrows and took a long drag on his own cigarette, then released the smoke slowly.

"You want to marry me," she said, "I know you do. I decided to say 'Yes' in public."

"Oh my God . . . then it *was* you. . . ." I heard Thurmond sob. I guess he had hyped himself into believing she could not have done such a thing. She kept on, not even hearing him.

"Your lawsuit hasn't got a chance, Pres, because if I have to I'll deny I ordered the story run. You said yourself it was outlandish." She turned and pointed to me. "I'll say he did it. For spite. Has a secret passion for me but he hates me. Psychopath. They'll believe me."

Before I could protect myself with a protest, T. Preston snorted: "For God's sake, Rita; you don't think that will shield your paper, do you?"

"What the hell do I care about 'shielding' my paper? Nothing can hurt my paper."

"There's that ten million I'm going to get. That's a nice little thorn, if nothing else."

"And what the hell do you care about ten million dollars, Pres? You *need* ten million dollars? I'll loan it to you."

He shrugged his shoulders and leaned back in the wingback chair he had carefully seated himself in. "You're crazy," he said, without heat.

"I'm not crazy," she said, "I want you for my husband. I told you that a month ago. I sweated out ten years of Arno Markley so I could have this paper and get any man I wanted. I want you, now, and I'm going to have you."

"Well, you weren't waiting for me all that time. My wife didn't die until four years ago."

"I know when your wife died. I wasn't waiting on any man all that time. I didn't let a man put a hand on me. I wasn't going to have any rumors going around that might cause Arno to change his will. I wanted this paper."

"Well, you got it."

"Yes, and I waited another five years after Arno died to be sure I would keep it. Now there isn't anything can take it away from me. All the 'ifs' and 'howevers' are over. I've passed that, and now I want something else. I want a man."

"Rita, look around you," T. Preston said, seriously. "You're saying things in front of people, things you have no right to say. It's too big a responsibility for them."

"What can they do? I did what I did to get what I wanted. And now I want you."

T. Preston Matthews got to his feet and put out his cigarette carefully in the porcelain ash tray on Thurmond's desk.

"Tell the rest of them to go," he said, waving at us.

"I'm not going to do it. I told them to come here. This is a company matter."

"You've made it more than a company matter," he said.

"I don't care what they hear. They can't live without my pocketbook. And I couldn't care less what they think."

T. Preston looked at her and shook his head. "All right, Rita. I'll call off the lawsuit. You run a retraction and explain it any way you want to. But I won't marry you."

"Why not?"

"It's blackmail, if nothing else."

"You should be flattered," she said, "I want a man enough to blackmail him."

"Well, marry someone else. Not me."

She looked at him. "By God, Pres, maybe I will. Maybe I'll do that very thing. I can, you know."

She got up from behind Thurmond's big desk and came right over to the sofa where I was sitting. Everybody was watching.

"Vayne, how old are you? In your forties, right?"

I shook my head yes.

"By God, I'll take it. I'm going to marry you."

I smiled, "Mrs. Markley," I said, "I might be married already."

"Oh, go to hell. Don't you think I checked up on you before I had you called down here? Why the hell do you think you're here? Do you think you're just a natural big shot? I know you're not married. I know all about you."

That time I couldn't think of a thing to say.

"I'll marry Mr. Ed Vayne; Vayne, as in John Vayne," she laughed. "We'll do it this week. I'll get Judge Ledbetter to waive the waiting period, whatever it is. I'll tell him I'm pregnant."

"I'm sorry, Mrs. Markley. . . ." I started saying, but she turned to me and there was smoke and brass in her eyes.

"Shut up, Vayne. If I want to marry you, you'll do it, so keep shut up."

Then I knew she meant it. She God damn sure intended to marry me . . . and I realized, too, that I would do it. I started exploding inside. My God. That kind of money, that kind of living. A woman like that saying she will . . . and she WILL.

The things I would be when she married me—they all hit me; hit me hard and spread out over my body in a warm rummish glow. Even if it didn't last but a while, I could have some of what I thought I'd never get any of. I knew something about that kind of life because I had interviewed them and written about them. Now, I'd have it. And maybe it wouldn't have to go away. I was as good a man in bed as any of them. The old democratic process. After a couple of months . . . who knows? She might not take it away at all.

I smiled. I couldn't help smiling.

"See there?" she said, pointing, "he's going to marry me," and to T. Preston Matthews she said, "And you can go to hell."

She walked over to her bag and took out a cigarette case and took out a filtertip and put it to her lips. "Here," I said, and jumped up, but T. Preston beat me, holding a gold Dunhill's flame near her cigarette.

She leaned against the desk and I was already beginning to wonder about those wonderful legs under her suit. She took a deep draw on her filtertip and let it out easy, looking at T. Preston Matthews.

"Pres," she said, "I'm as serious as I've ever been in my life. I'll marry this Vayne and you know it. I wanted you, but I want a man, too. He'll sure as hell do. I've planned this whole thing out; running that story, getting you here—even checking out Mr. Vayne, as in John Vayne. I've done whatever I've planned my whole life."

"You don't bluff, do you Rita?" He smiled.

"I always hold the cards. I don't like to gamble when it might mean eating my words. Either you marry me or I marry Ed Vayne who doesn't make a thousand a week. He'll do it in a New York minute. He'd be a fool to turn down a proposition he'll never come close to again in his life. He's such a hot newspaper man I might make a little profit off him. I'll make him publisher. He'll take any deal I make him. He's one of those men who despise money so much they have a low sell-out price."

T. Preston shook his head and smiled. "Damn it, Rita, of course he will. But I can't stand to see you pull something else crazy."

"You think the story was blackmail. You'd like to have me but you're too full of pride. So I'll take Ed Vayne here who's got no pride if the price is right."

She hadn't looked at me through the entire speech.

T. Preston frowned. "Damn if you're not the most. . . ." He looked down at his shoe tips, then up again quickly. "Come over here. I'll marry you."

She went to him and planted one on his mouth that hung there for a good twenty seconds. Before it was over, T. Preston was reaching and grabbing pretty hard, too.

It boned me out; starting with the top of my body everything began dripping like an icicle, down to my feet. I dropped back on the sofa.

"That damn silly story . . . right on page one." T. Preston Matthews was getting boyish. "People don't run engagement stories on page one anyway."

"I'm not *people*. I run things in my paper any damn way I want them run," she said, still up against him.

"But I really was going to sue you, you know that?"

"The hell you were. You were going to marry me."

"No, Rita, I wasn't when I came over here. I was mad as hell when your boy Thurmond asked me if I'd meet with you. I wasn't about to marry you."

"That was the trouble, Pres. I knew it would take big dynamite to get you started." She pushed up some hair. "Pres, darling, we're not quite young enough to wait until things start themselves."

She gathered her bag and her jacket off the desk. I watched her body slide around, just right, in the gold silk suit she had on—but that was copper I could taste in my mouth.

I saw that her first cigarette had left a nearly two-inch burn on the edge of Thurmond's desk. There went a refinishing job; more than I'd make in three weeks. I almost cried.

Dolan and Thurmond were easing their way toward the door and I was right behind them. Thurmond smiled chillily at me. That crack about making me publisher still had him unblocked, even if the threat had passed away.

"Well, Mrs. Markley . . ." he dragged it out, hesitating. "We'll keep this, er, quiet. We sure will. But congratulations, er . . . I mean, to both of you."

I started out the door behind him and Dolan but she called out, "Vayne . . ." and I turned.

"Vayne, as in John Vayne," she wasn't joking, she was sneering. "You almost got more than you could say grace over, didn't you, Ed Vayne?"

"I don't know," I said, "it depends."

"Yeah, it depends." She reached back and took the filtertip out of T. Preston's mouth, dragged on it, then blew the smoke in my general direction with a little toss of her head.

"Now you take my friend, Duke Wayne . . . he'd know," she said.

I opened my mouth but she cut me off.

"'You don't own Ed Vayne.'" She leaned against T. Preston Matthews (who was smiling) and mimicked me. "Why didn't you jump up and holler the way you did in the city room about me not owning Ed Vayne? Hell no. I put a million dollars on the line and you paid off like an insurance fire."

Standing half in, half out of the doorway, I blinked. A man can take so much—but this time it didn't mean what it had before.

"Okay," I said, soft and choked down, "that's the ticket. I guess it never was a question of me being for sale. It was just my price. Whichever it was, you won."

She stubbed her cigarette, then looked me right in the eye. "You know, Vayne . . ." she paused to watch the effect her words were having "if you had. . . ." She stopped, but kept looking, "You might have come closer than you know."

Then her face turned back into that look: stone cold and a thousand years old.

"Run, you gutless wonder. Get back up there and make some more money for me." She spat the words right in my face, and I could feel them running down . . . running down.

Back in the city room I told Claudell to beat it, and I took over the slot while he fussed and fumed that I couldn't do him this way. I didn't listen to a word he said. ✿

SPEAKING IN TONGUES

by nia akimbo

Amber Maylene Martis supposed that speaking in tongues was something akin to having multiple orgasms. At least, she supposed that speaking in tongues was like what she imagined multiple orgasms to be, but she wasn't for sure, being only twenty, virginal, and lacking the necessary experience to validate her supposition.

Similarly, Amber Maylene had not supposed she would get so happy as to actually speak in tongues when she first visited the New Zion Hill Pentecostal Church and Assembly, located three doors down from her mother's front porch. That Sunday evening, right before the dark snatched all the light from the road, Amber Maylene was sitting on that same porch, enjoying a lull in spring's thirsty heat, when the chimes of vibrant tambourines and the dark monotone of drums—*ba-dum ba-dum*—drifted past the Millers, who lived two doors down from the New Zion Hill Pentecostal Church and Assembly, then slivered through the dense row of thorny bushes her mother, Meora Martis, planted to separate their place from Viola's, the negress next door (who had been Meora's childhood play-mate and who now served as a permanent symbol of a kind of disorder wherein just about every sort of being was permitted to purchase the newly divided lots of what had once been her family home) to rush at Amber, upsetting her balance, as if to drag her from the porch. That time, Amber Maylene had succeeded in righting herself; but her curiosity sprang from a deep well.

In the days before disorder won out, the Martis's were gatekeepers. But things become unsettled, get out of whack. The seven-foot tall marble columns that stood at the plantation's entry (complete with gargoyles, ancient imps, and offering a view of the fifty or more slave shanties that dotted the Martis's seventeen hundred acre homestead) once marked one's front-door invitation into East Texas Society. For more than thirty years now, those marble columns have announced one's arrival in Martisville, population one thousand; their portal view provided courtesy of the state and consisting of fifty or more signs that dot the seventeen hundred acres, advising travelers to avoid low roads during spring (which locals know runs from March to May in some years, from May to March in others, and can't be avoided except to relocate from the area).

After the last of what everyone hoped was the last of the upset, the Martis's found themselves in a fix. Those shanties not already burned to the ground and washed away by spring rains were toppled by bulldozers acting at the behest of the Texas Reassessment, Reimprovement, and Reintegration Association. Meora Martis, from age twenty until two short days before, on her fifty-sixth birthday, watched with growing despair as her private playground decreased in size. When she was forced to rent the half-acre just parallel her own to a couple she suspected of being white trash (what was she to do?), Meora cursed the negras. Lazy and dirty, they were, every single solitary one, with the possible exception of Viola, and even she was suspect, being so black—almost blue—and taken to telling lies like they were gospel.

After that first Sunday, even caution was not enough to slow her pace, for Amber Maylene—despite stories her great granddaddy repeated regarding the negras, their ways and most especially, their music, and despite her understanding that the negras and their music were part of the general upset that plagued the area these past thirty-odd years—made her way to the front gate where she stood and peered in the direction of the New Zion Hill Pentecostal Church and Assembly, when the chimes flirted, her weakness sighed, and she left the safety of her mother's gated yard to walk around the dense row of thorny bushes, skip past the Millers, and enter the New Zion Hill Pentecostal Church and Assembly for the first time. As she slipped into the sanctuary, the chimes of tambourines met her discretely at the door, slyly reached underneath her dress, and tugging at the crotch of her freshly-washed cotton panties, guided her to the center of the third pew. The drums became bolder: They reached past the cotton lace at Amber Maylene's panty leg to implant a song at her core.

"Ye Ma Jah," Amber Maylene whispered.

"Ye Ma Jah," the tambourines responded, and kissed Amber Maylene full on the lips, hushing her outcry.

Viola sang everywhere she went, so when Meora didn't hear her voice behind her on the dark road that led from the shanty where Viola and her family lived to Meora's home, she stopped cold and began to whimper the girl's name.

"Viola," she breathed into the dark air. "Viola."

Again and again Meora called, with no answer, until she decided to go on ahead by herself, and report to her dear mother what a mean and hateful negra gal that Viola was, leaving her all alone, when Viola put out her hand and touched Meora on the shoulder.

"Pouf," Viola said. "Here I am."

Meora screamed and took off so fast she ran smack into the wide round trunk of her granddaddy's prized pecan tree, the oldest in the state. It was not true, as Viola reported, that the tree hasn't yielded the same since. Besides, the whole mess was Viola's fault—her being so black that night could cloak her like that. And when Meora thought about it at all (and she thought about it plenty) she had no doubt that that mess with Viola was just one single solitary sign of an upset that has carried forward to this very day.

Continuing through mid-spring of the following year, Amber Maylene visited the New Zion Hill Pentecostal Church and Assembly each day the doors opened for services. And who among us can blame her? For Amber Maylene found there the connection for which she had long searched. The tambourines chimed in her ears; the drum's dark monotone wrapped her in a seductive comfort, and the recent bounce in Amber Maylene's step matched the drum's *ba-dum ba-dum.* The rhythm rose in Amber Maylene and filled in all the empty spaces. What was more, the music understood the nature of Amber Maylene's physical needs.

By all counts, Meora was at least thirty-four years-wise, about half that otherwise, when Joe Doe, a tenant farmer newly resituated, set his eye in her direction. Viola knew the exact hour—eleven p.m.—Doe sprinted up the twenty front steps (two at a time) to tap tap tap at Meora's front door; she knew too the hour (just a second before the sun released light all over the dark road) that Joe Doe would drag down the twenty steps (one at a time). Viola recognized Doe's type because she'd seen that kind before (never matter colored or white, slave or master): Joe Doe was one of those easy talking fellows who could charm the fat out of butter; fellows who were possessed of a radar that honed in on well-situated virgins.

So, there was never any doubt in Viola's thinking regarding the whole matter: Joe Doe came to Martisville searching for a being in need of comfort (who might provide another comfort in return), and he found Meora, kept her wrapped in the wide round span of his arms for the space of a year before Meora's granddaddy grew annoyed with every single solitary aspect of the arrangement and cut off all Meora's funds until he was sure he had wrung Doe dry. Meora was six months gone when he left.

At six in the evening on the first Wednesday after Amber Maylene's encounter, she participated in feet-washing services at the New Zion Hill Pentecostal Church and Assembly. The ritual of humility was as if it were a natural part of her life. The movement of her fingers matched perfectly the drum's dark tone. Amber Maylene spent four hours on her knees with a basin of water that had to be emptied and refilled countless times. She tenderly cradled the rough brown feet of one and then another of the Elder Sisters in her smooth pink hands. Rubbing her pale fingers over the Sisters' blackened heels, she used her nails to slough off pieces of dead skin, working a miracle and receiving another in return. Her head swayed side to side as she washed, and a low moan escaped from her lips. She rocked back and forth as the chimes encouraged, finally entwining her pale fingers between the toes of an Elder Sister and squeezing—hard— when the music finished. When Amber Maylene rose from her place at the Elder Sister's feet, she felt not all there, shaky, and unsure of time or place, like she was coming out of an upset, or going into one, it was hard—at first—to tell which. So the Elder Sister made Amber Maylene sit down, fanned her with the white paper fan that she drew blood red roses all over to imitate one she'd seen in a fancy catalogue, and hushed the girl's outcries, upsetting Amber Maylene's going in (which was what every other member of the congregation figured was happening at just that moment) and generally denying the whole of them (gathered there for night of the new moon services and in powerful need of a miracle) the sight of the pale thin white woman in the throes of their Holy Ghost.

Meora wailed like a woman possessed when it was for sure that Joe Doe was long gone. Every single solitary night for a solid week Viola suffered as Meora paced the dark road, wallowing in grief, wringing herself dry of tears, her flesh puffy and raw at hands and knees as if she had crawled about on brimstone. On the soft dusk on the eighth evening, Viola met Meora in the dark road and planted a jumble of dark herbs in her hand.

"Make yourself a tea, girl," her voice chimed. "Let innocent folks rest one night out of eight."

Meora, as far as anyone knows, drank the tea she made from the jumble of dark herbs, for shortly after her encounter with Viola, she took to her room, staying there until late spring when Amber Maylene cried out, announcing her arrival.

The year of Amber Maylene's birth was the year that even spring conspired in the general upset. Meora waited for spring in March, and when April's late frost came and went with no sign of new buds or green blades, she suspected something was amiss. Her suspicions were confirmed when spring arrived in late July, for it brought with it dark rains, winds that chimed throughout the day, and thirsty heat that sucked the rain out of the air before it could offer comfort. Then, as if to make up for its late arrival, spring continued on into early October, each day alternating winds, dark rains, and thirsty heat, or serving the three up in a single twenty-four hour period. As the weather alternated from heat, to rain, to wind, spring all but killed Granddaddy's prized pecan tree—the oldest in the state. Meora cursed the negras—every single solitary one of them, but Viola in particular.

Thursday night, Amber Maylene took a pecan pie (store bought) to share at Bible study. She wore the ankle-length dress and panties from before, the dress stained and crumpled now from the toils of the prior night's encounter. Amber Maylene swore to wear nothing but these items from that time forward, vowing to spend each evening hand washing them in preparation for the next day. At Bible study, she learned of the Assembly's need for volunteers, so she volunteered to come in twice a month, on Saturdays, to clean the pastor's study and mop the floors. As Amber Maylene discussed with other Assembly members the upsets of Job, she came to understand the old man's feelings of despair, came to understand the dark cry of yet another who begged not to be forsaken. As Amber Maylene studied, the drum's dark monotone stroked her cheek, and the congregation whispered *how dear, how dear*, but not once did the music reach under the ankle-length hem of her sanctified dress to slide up the inside of her thighs and enter her through the lace leg of her freshly washed panties.

That Thursday night, if Amber Maylene was upset, it was not by the music's presence. Still she rose before the sun spread light Friday morning and began to pray. But without the chimes, the words of prayer crammed in her throat. Without the drum's dark tone ringing in her ears, the words choked her, made her gag and cough, causing her to seek solitude in her room where she knelt in the farthest recess of the easternmost corner and wept. She remained so situated until nightfall cloaked the room in dark moonlight, whereupon Amber Maylene rose from the floor and dragged her spent body to bed.

Viola called on her most powerful prayer that eighth night. She sat in the darkened easternmost corner of her home and swayed, her voice chiming throughout the house. She prayed for Meora's deliverance, yes, but for her own as well, and for the deliverance of Joe Doe to those who judge such. Viola's voice became dark as the sun raised in the sky; her outcries wrapped themselves in the wide round span of Martisville and echoed from each piney tree. As she prayed, Viola's tongue grew limp, falling from the opening in her face to languish at either side. Sweat consumed her being, matting her hair, chilling her, until Viola transcended the realm of ordinary beings and floated above Martisville. When the woman came to, it was midnight of the next day, and Meora was not wailing on the dark road. Viola drew herself a bath, scenting the water with a jumble of dark herbs.

The next Saturday was the first Saturday of many that Amber Maylene spent cleaning the New Zion Hill Pentecostal Church and Assembly. But, when she entered the sanctuary, the music was nowhere to be found. She moped about the empty building, searching for the music in the dark corners of pews, using a strongly scented pine cleaner to coax the chimes from their hiding place. She looked for the *ba-dum ba-dum* in the pulpit where she dusted, swept, mopped, and waxed the pastor's stage. She sought out the music in the baptismal shrine. But Amber Maylene was completely alone. She drained the water left from the last baptism and used her sanctified, hand-washed dress to dry the tub area. She put the mop pail and dust mop away, and as she prepared to leave, a sound, the faintest of calls (a call only the truly devout could be expected to hear) came from the piano.

Amber Maylene lifted the cover which hid the piano's keys, striking a black key, then a white one, a white one, then a black one, repeatedly, alternating the strokes and her tempo. Nothing happened. Amber Maylene ran her fingers from one end of the keyboard to the other then back again. Still nothing. She closed the cover, knelt in prayer before the piano, and began to polish the rough, brown piano legs, slowly rubbing up and down each leg. She lay on her back and rubbed the underside of the piano. Slowly Amber Maylene leaned forward and placed a kiss on the hard wooden bench before straddling it, her teeth clenched, her hands on either side of her gripping the sides of the bench.

But the music, content with things as they were, saw no need to reveal itself further, and Amber Maylene left the New Zion Hill Pentecostal Church and Assembly that Saturday evening without noticing Viola who stood in the dark sanctuary, silently watching

To be sure, Viola would stand by and watch it all no longer: It was she who sent ole Miss Miller's half-idiot boy up to Mason County.

"Tell ole mister, he better do something quick like," she instructed the boy, "else he gone be sorry*er* for sure."

And her words were the same as gospel, for Granddaddy Martis was already sorry: sorry he had to parcel out his land to negras (although he didn't have to live within walking distance of them) and would be sorry*er* still if he waited too much longer, for Joe Doe (a type of being bad enough left alone, but hell-fire when situated amongst his kind) would surely own Martisville and in no time flat, those marble columns would extend yet another invitation.

Viola knew ole mister's fears, and shared with him at least one: She had no need, neither any desire, to live among a village of white trash (those cross from Meora's place was more than enough), so bright and early one morning, just before the sun spread light all over the dark road (and a split second before Joe Doe wove his body down Meora's front steps —one at a time), she had made her way up to ole Miss Miller's to stand impudently at the front door, beating upon the door-frame as if she were God's right-hand servant come to deliver news of great importance.

On the next day, Sunday, at eleven a.m., Amber Maylene sat in her usual place in the center of the third pew and waited for the music to acknowledge her. Timidly, she announced her presence, raising her hands in supplication as the sound of chimes lifted from the pastor's stage. Amber Maylene mouthed the words of the hymn Assembly members were singing until the drum's dark *ba-dum ba-dum* swelled, filling the Assembly. The music announced itself in every mouth, pressed itself onto every mind, then devoted the full force of its attention on Amber, pressing itself so hard against her breasts that her nipples stood erect and her panties flooded.

"Ye Ma Jah," Amber Maylene pleaded, but the music was finished.

After that, Amber Maylene's visits to the New Zion Hill Pentecostal Church and Assembly increased. She added Friday nights to her routine, joining in with others who prepared meals for shut-in Assembly members, or helping to deliver those meals prepared by others. Each Wednesday she washed the feet of the Elder Sisters; on Thursdays she joined in discussions; every other Saturday she cleaned the Assembly building, and on every single solitary Sunday, at eleven a.m., she could always be found in the center of the third pew, joined there now by Viola, who smiled to herself throughout service and left immediately afterwards.

Viola hadn't intended to spook Meora, and besides, Viola liked listening to the chimes crickets made when calling out to their mates, so she kept herself quiet, floating above the path that led from her home to the big house where Meora lived. Viola had tried to pay attention to Meora's rambling tongue that went loose about everything as they walked, but the music won out and before long, she was wrapped in its wide round span, rising higher and higher until Meora's dark whispers pulled her back.

Viola thought Meora *saw* her, or at the least *felt* her standing in the pathway between Meora and her granddaddy's prized pecan tree, so wasn't nobody more stunned than she when the girl lit into that tree. Viola had to use rainwater she dipped from a puddle at the tree's base to coax Meora back into her senses.

In early spring, before the rains came, residents of Martisville trekked into town intent on stocking their pantries in anticipation of yet another spring-time upset. It was then that an Elder Sister ran into ole Miss Miller at the market and asked the woman why she didn't visit New Zion Hill Pentecostal Church and Assembly sometimes, especially since it was just a hop, skip and a jump from her place.

"And, you don't have to worry none 'bout being the only white person there," the Elder Sister whispered just loud enough so that the cashiers and other customers standing there in line might hear. "That Martis girl comes every Wednesday to wash the feet of the Elders, and Thursday nights for Bible class, too."

Before the Elder Sister could tell ole Miss Miller about the wonderful work Amber Maylene did on Fridays and Saturdays, or her presence in the center of the third pew every single solitary Sunday, ole Miss Miller dropped her two-pound bag of Imperial Pure Cane Sugar, quick-dissolving, and the two-liter bottle of 7-Up, on special, onto her foot. The 7-Up fell funny (chiming as it fell) and cracked the bone in her baby toe, but Ole Miss Miller did not find that out until the next day after her toe had turned different shades, and she had to go back into town in search of a doctor to set her toe right again.

That broken toe had not stopped Ole Miss Miller from walking from the market straight to Meora Martis to tell her the news. It was in this way that Meora found out how her daughter had been spending her Wednesday evenings and Thursday nights.

Viola knew that as long as she sat quietly among her mother and the group of women gathered in the dark yard of one or the other's homes, she would be permitted to stay, thereby learning, in the early spring of her life, the value of keeping one's tongue. From the time she was barely ten years-wise, but thrice that otherwise, Viola's ear was privy to the secrets that wrapped wide and round the Martis's plantation. Although Meora was to inherit the gate, it would be Viola who inherited the key, so, of course, she could not stand idly by while ole Miss Miller conspired to unsettle things. But Viola's aim was off: she had intended that two liter bottle of 7-Up to hit square in the middle of the ole miss's instep.

"It's a blessed shame." Meora said to Amber, when the girl came in late from Saturday clean-up service. While Amber Maylene had not tried to keep her comings and goings secret from her mother, who rarely left the privacy of her room (not even to tend to personal needs for she kept a bed pan in her tiny, cluttered bedroom) neither had Amber Maylene thought it necessary to confide in her mother.

"A blessed shame," Meora said the next evening when she carried the bed pan from her cluttered bedroom to the bathroom where Amber Maylene was getting ready for church.

"A blessed damn shame," she testified and spilled the contents of her bed pan onto the bathroom floor in her haste to be out of the girl's presence.

"How could you stoop so low to wash the feet of negras?" Meora Martis asked her daughter, but Amber Maylene knew no answer would explain the chimes of the tambourine and how those sounds had slipped, uninvited, underneath her ankle-length dress that first time, and how, after that, she'd had no choice but to return, just as the rains returned each year, from March to May or from May to March.

By late spring, the rains gave way to icy winds that slowed the flow of music from the New Zion Hill Pentecostal Church and Assembly. Every single solitary service was canceled, and without even sporadic attention from the music, Amber Maylene wallowed in a mute grief. She paced the wide round porch of her home and hummed. But without the music, the songs were as cold as late spring's icy wind. Without the music, the songs reached just midway Amber Maylene's thighs, leaving her dry and flustered. It was in late spring that Amber Maylene learned the magic her own pale fingers possessed. In her bed at night during the music-less month, Amber Maylene's smooth, virginal fingers tugged and teased at her panties, imitating perfectly the dark music.

When spring returned—humble and chaste—the ice melted and the music again flowed. Cool and distant at first, the music wafted about the newly refilled New Zion Hill Pentecostal Church and Assembly as if it intended to ignore Amber. However, once Viola joined Amber Maylene in the third pew, the music stretched out, jumbled the pulpit, rocked the ceiling, and rediscovered Amber Maylene in the spot where it had last loved her—sitting in the center of the third pew, expectant, waiting. The day the music returned was the second time Amber Maylene spoke in tongues.

"Ye Ma Jah," Amber Maylene's voice rang out when the music reached her in the third pew.

"Ye Ma Jah," the drums responded and parted Amber Maylene's thighs.

"Ye Ma Jah," Amber Maylene repeated, clenching her teeth and gripping onto the hard edge of the pew.

"Ye Ma Jah," the drums answered and quickly entered her.

By mid-spring, Amber Maylene caught hold of a realization that made her smile. The knowledge of her now perfect state jumbled her body and face with an awful joy. The bounce in Amber Maylene's step became more apparent, and she acquired a way of walking that caused men, and women alike, to stare and whisper as she swept past, just as nearly every single solitary one of Martisville's one thousand residents had watched and whispered while Joe Doe spent up Meora's life, mumbling disapprovingly to themselves about how poorly things was looking, but lacking energy, power, or nerve to reset things.

Right before the end of mid-spring, Meora Martis also noticed the bounce in Amber Maylene's step. Meora noticed too that the ankle-length dress that once hung from the girl's shoulders now hugged her coming and going. Remembering that she had purchased a one-hundred count package of sanitary pads right before the storms in February, Meora rushed to count the pads left in the one-hundred count package only to discover there were exactly eighty-seven left.

Viola counted the hours until ole Miss Miller's half-idiot boy returned to Martisville. She knew the exact second he arrived, having located the sound of his stumbling gait shortly after the moon stole all light from the road. She had not rushed out to meet him, but waited, counting to herself as he made up his half-mind who to report to first: His own mother or the impudent negra who had sent him out.

Finally, after exactly eighty-seven seconds had passed, the boy passed out in the dark road in front of Viola's home, peed on himself and lay there in the moist dark dirt for some hours before he came to. It was to Viola he whispered the news of Granddaddy's imminent arrival, for it was her face alone he saw when he awoke, although the boy lay in the dark road surrounded by his mother and other residents of Martisville.

As Amber Maylene sat with the body of an Elder Sister (surrounded by the Sister's friends and family who were situated along the lines of those who believed the woman's death signaled her claim of heaven's reward, and those who maintained any reward due her resided in a much warmer climate) Meora again counted the pads. She counted them by twos, then by threes. She counted every single solitary pad, lifting it from its place in the pile of pads and beginning a new pile with the one most recently counted. She laid the pads out before her in a circle and placed a mark on each one she had counted so as to not count it a second time. Each count revealed there were eighty-seven pads left in the one-hundred count package.

By that same time the next spring, Amber Maylene's body had become fuller still. Her pale skin glowed like a ripe mango—flush and red even on rain-jumbled days. Meora was no longer content to keep to her cluttered bedroom at night: she began to roam about the house, muttering and swearing under her breath, cursing Amber Maylene should the two meet in the hallway, on the porch, or in the bathroom.

"A blessed shame," she said when she met Amber Maylene coming in from Wednesday night feet-washing services.

"A blessed damn shame," she reproached Amber Maylene when the girl checked in on her after Thursday night Bible class, or when the two of them met in the bathroom on Sunday mornings as Meora emptied her bed pan and Amber Maylene prepared for eleven a.m. services.

But Meora did not throw the contents of her bed pan on the girl again, nor did she slap Amber. Instead, Meora visited with Viola, walking around the dense row of thorny bushes that Meora planted to separate her property from the woman's, returning to her cluttered bedroom with a small dark bag jumbled with herbs and stones.

Meora Martis took the eighty-seven pads that remained in the one-hundred count package and constructed them into an altar that she placed at the easternmost edge of her cluttered bedroom. She sprinkled the herbs before the altar and for the next two weeks, from sunup to sundown, Meora could be found prostrate before the dark altar, praying, and offering herbs jumbled in sacrifice.

In mid-spring, Meora gave her daughter an ultimatum: Amber Maylene could leave the New Zion Hill Pentecostal Church and Assembly, or she could just move all her things out of Meora Martis's house—"I'm a proper woman"—and move in with the negra whose baby she carried.

Meora threatened to cut off what remained of the girl's tiny trust, declaring her intent to wring Amber Maylene dry before she saw a penny of Granddaddy's money used to give comfort to 'ary a one of those lazy dirty negras.

"This ain't no negra baby, mother," Amber Maylene said. "I swear to you, ain't no body touched mine." Amber Maylene's words, and the altar's to-date slow response to her prayers, sent Meora back to her neighbor's house. Racing through the thick row of thorny bushes as if the chimes of secrets thrown wide and round were in pursuit, Meora showed up on Viola's porch out of breath, upset, scratched, and bleeding from the thorns, only to return home empty-handed. Viola, her voice chiming, told her childhood friend that she knew of nothing else that could help. Viola suggested, her tone dark, that Meora's faith was not strong enough, and her prayers before the altar of pads insincere.

By late spring, Amber Maylene had not relocated from her mother's house, neither had she stopped attending Wednesday night feet washing, or Thursday night Bible class. Nary a single eleven a.m. Sunday service was conducted without Amber Maylene's presence in the middle of the third pew; neither was there a solitary Friday night-meal cooking service where she was not to be found.

"A damn shame," Meora said to Amber Maylene each Wednesday evening when the girl returned from feet-washing, lifting her full body up the steps and into the front door.

"A blessed damn shame," Meora said to Amber Maylene when she returned home, spent and damp after her encounter with the music during the eleven a.m. Sunday morning service.

"A damn blessed shame," Meora said when Amber Maylene reported that the baby had kicked so hard during Thursday night Bible study that it had almost knocked the hymnal from her lap.

"A damn blessed shame," Meora said every other Saturday when Amber Maylene returned from clean-up service, clutching the dust rag in her hands as if it were a satchel of gold, until Meora was driven, in the predusk evening of the first Wednesday in early August, to change the locks on her front and back doors.

When Amber Maylene returned from feet washing that Wednesday night, damp and spent after another encounter with the music, she went straight to bed, neglecting to remove her sanctified, though saturated, ankle-length dress, or her freshly washed panties. As the girl slept, Meora rose from her cluttered bedroom and bolted the girl's door from the outside. The next morning, Amber Maylene rose and found she was unable to leave her room.

"What has settled here?" Amber Maylene's dark chimes demanded, upset, from behind the bolted door, but Meora did not respond. She continued praying, prostrate, before the eighty-seven pad altar she had built in her tiny, cluttered room, offering herbs in a jumbled sacrifice.

As Meora prayed, the chimes of the tambourines rose from their place in the New Zion Hill Pentecostal Church and Assembly, drifted past the Millers, said a quick hello to Viola, glided untouched through the dense row of thorny bushes, and wafted through the crack between the floorboard and Amber Maylene's bolted door to slowly slide up the inside of the girl's no longer virginal thighs, past the lace at the leg of her panties and enter her, causing Amber Maylene's dark cry "Ye Ma Jah" to chime out through the unsettled night.

After that time in early spring, the first time since late spring that Amber Maylene had not attended feet washing service at the New Zion Hill Pentecostal Church and Assembly, Meora purchased herbs from Viola on a regular basis. Meora arranged to have the dense row of thorny bushes cut down and a patio built over the roots to discourage their regrowth, and now she and her childhood friend spend long hours on that patio, talking, sharing recipes, the stuff that neighbors (who were once childhood playmates) do. Any passer-by so inclined can readily distinguish Viola's laughter from Meora's dark chuckles as the sounds waft through Martisville late into the night. Meora uses the herbs, and some recipes as well, to offer a jumble of dark sacrifices before the altar of eighty-seven pads. She kneels before the altar—each Wednesday evening, every Thursday night, every other Saturday, each Sunday at eleven a.m., and recently, she has even begun to go before the altar every single solitary Friday (except when it's a Friday the Thirteenth, in which case she waits until after midnight) scattering herbs and praying for Amber Maylene's release from the upset that orders her. All the while, Amber Maylene calls out in tongue after tongue, while another voice (a voice clearly possessed of gospel quality) chimes into the dark, settled night "How dear, how dear." ✹

JACKHAMMER

by Robert Phillips

The day he found out who he was, jackhammers woke him up. That early summer morning, his bedroom window wide open, Francis leapt naked out of bed and went to the window. He was thirteen, and secretly sleeping without pajamas made him feel grownup. Down at the highway, where their front lawn ended, a group of four men, one black, had begun to break up the road. They all wore jeans and work shirts except one, who'd already stripped to the waist. From behind the curtain Francis stared at the half-naked young man: he had broad shoulders, biceps like grapefruits, and a well-developed chest. His skin deeply tanned, his short hair was blond. Wielding his jackhammer made his body shudder.

Francis dressed in tee shirt and jeans. After breakfast he returned to the bedroom window to watch. It was going to take weeks to break up the old road. Then there would be a new cement to pour. He stood there a long time. At one point the blond young man glanced up toward the house, and Francis was certain he saw him beyond the curtain. He almost stared at Francis, he thought. Then the man resumed work. Francis had been told that if you stayed on that road to the very end, it would take you to New York City. He knew he would take that road to the end someday. He never had been farther away than Laredo. The young man looked up toward the window a second time, then looked away.

Towards noon Francis went to the kitchen. He filled a tall glass with water and ice and, unseen by his mother, who was watching a "Wheel of Fortune" rerun in the family room, he slipped out the front door. He walked down the lawn. The Texas sun was brutally hot. Underfoot the grass felt fried. As he approached the blond young man, Francis could see he was covered with sweat. It rivered around his nipples. He must be very thirsty.

"Here," Francis said timidly, extending the glass. The young blond man turned off his jackhammer, smiled broadly at Francis, and said, "Much obliged." His eyes were very kind, like in the picture of Jesus that hung in Francis' Sunday School room. His teeth were very white. Then he looked over his tan shoulder and said, "What about the others? They've been working hard, too."

Suddenly all the jackhammers were silent. The men stared at Francis. "Hey, we're just as thirsty, pal," one barked.

Francis realized he should have brought out a tray of four glasses.

"We don't matter. Gene's such a looker, the ladies are always after him."

"Yah, and a few of the guys."

Gene's face turned red. "I've told you guys to cut that out!" he said angrily.

"Well, it's true, ain't it? Look at this little cocksucker giving you water. The little queer wants to suck your cock."

The black man groped himself and said, "If this sweet thing brings us all a drink, maybe he can suck *all* our cocks." They laughed.

Gene drank the water in one gulp, his Adam's apple bobbing. He thrust the empty glass toward Francis and said roughly, "Now get on back home to you mama, cocksucker."

They all hooted uproariously, including Gene.

"That Gene, he's all right," the black man said. Jackhammers were turned back on, work resumed. And Francis, mortified, retreating up the hill, wished he were taking the road all the way. ✿

Nest Eggs

by Sallie Strange

Lulamae opened her eyes. She couldn't think what day it was. She hoped it wasn't Thursday. She didn't like Thursdays. She'd have to have all her wits about her if it was Thursday, but maybe it wasn't. Her frown relaxed as she watched the sky turn from pale orange to a bright pinkish orange.

As she usually did just toward dawn, she turned to lie on her left side, facing the window to the east. That was important to her. She had told her son, daughter-in-law, and daughter—when they decided to move her to this apartment in the old folks' home that they called a "retirement community"—that she required, then told them she needed, and finally told them that unless she could see the sun rise every morning, she would not go. And so she had prevailed—her success had made her happy for a few days till the thought surfaced that she had won a battle but lost the war. For the last seven weeks she had turned on her left side to watch the sun rise every morning—and that too made her happy. As quickly as she had smiled her happiness at this dawn, which was particularly colorful, she squinted her eyes in concentration. There was something missing—on the bedside table.

She looked carefully. There were the lamp, her glass of water, her glasses, but no hearing aid. She worked her left hand between the pillow and her head, found her ear, felt. Sure enough, there it was. She sighed and turned on her back and unscrewed the thing from her ear. She held it close to her eyes to look at it. God knows she hated that squealing, hissing piece of plastic!

She blinked at the light, now pouring below the raised blinds of the window, then realized she had also seen a piece of paper on the bedside table—her lottery ticket? She reached for it. She never had bought lottery tickets till that seven weeks ago when her daughter-in-law drove her to this place—they were following the moving van—and, pausing in her explanation of how Lulamae would enjoy her new life, told her—also they were passing a gas station with a Texas Lottery sign in front—that she was so very happy that Lulamae never wasted the money they gave her on gambling and that she was sure that no matter what the other people in the community did Lulamae would not be so foolish. So the first thing Lulamae did—after Charlotte had seen to the arrangement of the furniture, helped her make the bed, and left, vowing to return the next day and finish the unpacking—was to go next door and inquire of the woman there about the Texas Lottery.

Three days later Lulamae bought a ticket. Thereafter she bought two tickets a week, a ticket for each drawing. She didn't really expect to win. She knew the odds were better that she die on a Wednesday or a Saturday than that she win millions of dollars on those days. But she wanted to win to prove Charlotte wrong.

For nearly thirty years she had put up with Charlotte and was willing to spend two dollars a week of her secret money in the bare chance that she might prove her wrong because she and Bill had tried to deceive her when they married. Charlotte was pregnant. Lulamae could understand why Charlotte would want to deceive the world about her condition, but it was insulting to treat her that way, as if she was not even related and, even worse to her way to thinking, as if she was the stupidest woman on the planet. But Charlotte had done that, had even ignored Lulamae's hints that she knew about the baby and, with a smile, that she thought it was really okay. The last time Lulamae tried to be honest with Charlotte was on her and Bill's tenth anniversary. She had told them both—and truly meant it—that they had made the most out of what could have been a stormy marriage headed toward divorce. Bill did not answer his mother. Charlotte said she had no idea what Lulamae was talking about. So Lulamae gave up on Charlotte. She hadn't expected any more from Bill.

Now looking at the lottery ticket, she knew she had to destroy it—you had to destroy evidence of what you were forbidden to do, didn't you?—but it would be foolish to destroy her ticket if the winning ticket had not been drawn.

She stared up at the ceiling. Was this Wednesday, the day of the midweek drawing, or Thursday? Again she concentrated on the day of the week, but this time more desperately. Did she watch the drawing last night on TV? A blank. What had she done earlier in the day? In the morning, she had—the ploy did not work; it wouldn't come to mind. Sometimes it did if she sneaked up on it. Lunch? Still nothing. For supper she had breast of chicken sprinkled with paprika and poached in a little butter and a potato from the microwave. There. She smiled. Then other details tumbled out. She had gone to the store with Pat. She had picked up groceries—

She threw the covers back, got out of bed, and hurried into the living room. Her Bible was on the end table and there on top it was—the three dollar bills and some change. She put her hands to her mouth in horror at a near slip-up—her near slip-up—and felt the hearing aid on her lower lip. She looked. It was in her left hand, the lottery ticket in her right.

She put the hearing aid next to the Bible and went to the bedroom to put on her glasses. Returning to the living room, she leaned over the table to count the change and saw the lottery ticket by the hearing aid. Picking up the ticket, she hurried to the kitchen and lifting the lid on the garbage, stood over it, picked out the skin of the potato, put it on the counter, and tore the lottery ticket into little pieces, placing them in the potato. She folded the skin into a tight ball which she dropped back into the garbage container.

After washing her hands, she returned to the living room and counted the change—a quarter, two dimes, and three pennies. She scooped up the coins and went back to the bedroom, to her dresser, and opened the middle drawer, picked up her purse, opened it, got out her billfold, clicked open the change purse and dropped the coins in, put the wallet back in her purse, the purse back in the drawer, closed the drawer and went through the living room to the kitchen. It was breakfast time.

She opened the door of the refrigerator and saw the milk carton, but there was something else in her line of vision. Something red and shiny— a beautiful color. The cranberry juice. She didn't much like cranberry juice, but Dorothy had given it to her. A penny saved is a penny earned.

She smiled. What a brilliant idea! She would save at least a dollar by drinking that jar of cranberry juice, instead of the orange juice she usually bought, so that money belonged with the rest. After breakfast she would go the bedroom and get a dollar from her billfold and put it with the rest of her money—her nest eggs. She nodded her affirmation, then smiled at the thought of increasing the number of her eggs.

She got out the red glistening jar and poured a small glassful of the juice, got down her pillbox, popped open the WED lid—the box was empty—then opened the THU lid and smiled. All along she had a suspicion it was Thursday. Then she frowned—Charlotte's day. She poured the THU pills in her hand and downed them with the cranberry juice. She returned the juice to the refrigerator and took out the carton of milk, got the cereal and a bowl, and fixed her breakfast. She got a spoon out of the drawer and stood at the counter eating till she remembered she was not supposed to do that. You are supposed to sit down and eat your meal; otherwise, how can you digest it properly?

She carried her bowl out of the kitchen to the dining alcove, set the bowl on the mat that was facing the TV, got the remote from the table beside the wing chair in the living room and switched on the news. She stood and watched the weather. Another hot one. Ninety-eight degrees, the sign said.

Charlotte wouldn't like that, especially on her day to check up on Lulamae, though Charlotte would not put it that way. Instead: "I go to visit my mother-in-law every Thursday. She's in a retirement community. We are paying for it, of course, and it's our pleasure. Bill's so busy that it's up to me. But I don't mind." Here Charlotte would look down at her wedding and engagement rings on her plump fingers. "Lulamae gets so lonesome, you know. It's the least I can do."

The anchor stood and shook hands with somebody. Behind them was a large window with a scene of a bright green lawn with two trees, whose leaves no breeze disturbed. Lulamae used to look out the window on a scene like that. She lived in a regular house with a yard, and the mowing service would come once a week, and sometimes she would have them clean out the beds and trim the shrubs. And before that she had mowed the yard with her electric mower. And before that her husband. And before that Bill. Had Sheila ever mowed the yard? She tried to remember her daughter behind the mower.

She looked at the TV. The anchor was telling everybody good-bye, the picture window behind him. She turned off the TV. Her spoon lay in the empty cereal bowl. She took bowl and spoon to the kitchen and put them in the dishwasher, put the cereal box and the milk up. But then, heading toward the bedroom, she stopped suddenly. The three one-dollar bills were still on the Bible. She thought she had put them up. She shook her head, picked them up and put them under the fold of Henry's khaki pants that lay atop her sewing basket by her wing chair. She patted the fold and smiled. Charlotte would never snoop there. Charlotte bragged that she had never threaded a needle. Then she remembered the dollar she owed herself. She hurried into the bedroom, got a dollar out of her billfold, was returning to the living room, when the phone rang. She walked to the gateleg table and lifted the receiver.

It was Sheila. She had just finished talking to Charlotte. The two had agreed—as had Bill by default—that their mother should have her eyes checked and go for the second mammogram. Lulamae sighed. She wished they would drop it, just drop the subject, so that's what she told Sheila: "Why don't you just get off that for once? Just get off it. Pretend it never happened." She was unusually irritated with her daughter, who had turned into a terrible nag and refused to honor her mother, in fact went on to say, "If you hadn't told the technician that the lump was in the right breast instead of telling her the left **where you felt it**, then we wouldn't have to do it again, would we? So **you** just get off it, Mother, and listen to **me** for once. Charlotte's going to make appointments for next week when **I'm** in town, so **I** can take you." She paused. "Charlotte's feeling put upon again. I know it's not your fault but—"

"I don't need any more tests and examinations. I see as good as I ever did, and the lump has gone away. So there. No need to see anybody for anything. You can just tell that to Charlotte for me."

"You're just saying that, Mother, because you don't want to go. We're just thinking of you. **Why** can't you understand that? Why can't you just go along and stop arguing?"

Lulamae sighed. She knew they weren't thinking of her, they were thinking of themselves. They ran her life, every bit of it. They locked her up in this place and thought she should be happy. They even put their noses into her own private financial affairs. She laid the dollar bill on the gateleg table by the phone and smoothed it. It was old and rather faded. It was very pretty. She was going to win this struggle, and that would give them a turn. She would show them, ganging up on her like that. She laughed, imagining Charlotte coming on a Thursday and being told by the receptionist in the lobby, "Why, your mother-in-law moved out last week. She had a lot of money. No, she left no forwarding address."

"Whatever you say, Sheila."

"You're being sarcastic again, Mother."

Lulamae was counting: four dollars and seventy-five cents added to the rest was almost eighty. She had saved eighty dollars in less than two months. At that rate in a year she would have—She needed to use paper and pencil.

"I'm coming Thursday next week, so Charlotte won't have to, but she's having us for dinner that night. I know you'll like that. It'll be nice, won't it? You'll get to see Bill. He's so busy. So she'll arrange the appointments for Thursday and maybe Friday. I've got to come home—"

She wrote on the scratch pad. She divided 80 into 2 and got .015. "That can't be right," she muttered.

"Mother, are you watching TV or something?"

She divided 2 into 80 and got 40. That was right. Now times 10 more for the remaining months and got 400. My, my, my. She smiled broadly. She would leave in a cab and tip the driver a ten.

"**Mother**, answer me."

"I was just figuring something."

"I'm calling long distance, **Mother**." Now Sheila was angry. Well, she deserved it. You reap what you sow, Miss Buttinski.

"I know you're calling long distance. You don't live here, do you? I may be old, but I don't have Alzheimer's. Yet." She frowned and knocked on the table.

"I'm sorry," Sheila said.

"Your apology is accepted," Lulamae said archly, "but don't do it again."

I'm sorry, Mother, but you can be so difficult. See you next week. We'll have fun. You'll see. Bye."

"Bye-bye," Lulamae said and hung up the phone.

She picked up the bill and looked around the living room. What had she done with the other money, the three dollars? It wasn't on top of the TV. It wasn't on the Bible, but it had been. She remembered that clearly. She looked on the sofa, in the wing chair and the club chair. She went to the alcove. It wasn't on the dining table. She went in the kitchen. Nothing on the counters, the stove. She opened the refrigerator. Surely she wouldn't have put it in there. Her desk! She started back towards the bedroom and stopped. She might be a little forgetful, but she certainly wouldn't put it put it there. Charlotte checked her bank balance ensconced at the desk, the checks Lulamae had written, her bills, what she had spent for groceries. Had to show her the receipts. Nosey old bitch! Now there was a Miss Buttinski for sure.

Then she thought of the sewing basket and when she lifted Henry's pants off the basket, the bills fell out. She stooped and picked them up. She put the four bills together and counted them again. One more and she would change the ones into a five like she always did. Less bulk that way. Then she would roll four of those fives into a spool and wrap them in yarn. Around and around and around until she had a perfect oval.

She went back in the bedroom and opened the left-hand, bottom drawer of her desk. The smell of mothballs was strong. The right-hand drawer contained the acrylic yarn, but she preferred the wool. It took color better, she thought. There they were. Her nest eggs—all bright, beautiful colors. She picked up the red one. It was her first. She patted it and held it to her cheek. Her first twenty was in there. She picked up the royal blue and gave it a kiss—the second twenty. Then she took the lime green and straightened the end of yarn—the third twenty.

The other balls were there waiting: purple, pink, emerald green, lilac, orange. The collection was exquisite, a potpourri of soft jewels. So quiet. So receptive. And below that gorgeous display were other balls of other colors, all waiting for their part in the plan, waiting to be unwound, waiting to accept the new bills from the Bible, from Exodus, chosen for an obvious reason, then rewound and returned gently to their companions. Five hundred dollars and she would be out of here. She surveyed the balls and decided the color of the next egg would be yellow. She patted the yellow ball, blessing it for being the next chosen vessel, nestled it gently back with the rest of the chosen, and closed the drawer.

She returned to the living room. The bills. The four bills. What had she—She could feel the terror, the hollow feeling in her stomach. Twenty years ago when she had left her credit card at a department store, she felt the hollow in her stomach and since then, every once in a while, when she forgot something, lost something—She sank into the wing chair and closed her eyes. She tried to think OHM but she couldn't. She could only think of Charlotte coming into this room and seeing the money, finding it, and then taking all of it, all of the eighty dollars, all of the five hundred she could stash away, and keeping her prisoner forever. A tear ran down her cheek, then another, and another. She coughed, opened her eyes. She needed a tissue. As she started to rise from the chair, she saw the bills. Right there on the arm of her chair! She picked them up and kissed them and cried some more.

Then she told herself severely that she must think exactly what she was doing when she was handling her treasure. She had to put these four ones some place and get a five dollar bill from the grocery store tomorrow and pick up at least one item for someone in her wing. Then she would exchange the bills for a five and put the five with its three companions in Exodus and wind them carefully in the yellow yarn. She loved that ceremony. Until then—

She looked around the room. Why not put them where she had put them before—in the fold of Henry's pants? She wasn't going to hem them till tomorrow afternoon anyway. She had to go to Cloth World tomorrow morning during her grocery run with Pat to get some thread that matched the pants. She reached over and unfolded Henry's pants, put the ones in, closed the fold over them and said aloud so she would remember, "The money is in Henry's pants."

It was kind of like a miracle or a coincidence the way her financial plan had come to her. Like casting bread upon the waters. She and Gloria used to go to the store together and quite often picked up something—a dozen eggs, milk, bananas—for some of the other people in their wing. Upon returning, Lulamae presented her grocery receipt to the people she was buying for, showed them the cost of their items, and they would give her cash. The second time she did that, she thought of hiding that money and collecting from Charlotte for the entire receipt. She thought they called that "graft" or maybe it was "fraud." She was sure it was not on the up-and-up, but it really didn't bother her till Gloria poked her nose into it.

Thinking back on it, she knew it was a mistake to tell Gloria about it. Gloria, who was a holier-than-thou if she ever saw one, told her that she should be grateful to her son for putting her in this place and that what she was doing was stealing and she ought to be ashamed of herself. Lulamae was not in the least grateful and furthermore knew it was not stealing. It was only graft or fraud, but Gloria would not know about those things. So to keep Gloria from bugging her, Lulamae started going to the store with Pat. She wanted to tell Pat and even to tip Pat—after all it was her car and gas—but she was afraid to. So she kept her mouth shut and salted away her money.

Lulamae started to get up. She needed to get dressed for Charlotte's visit, when she remembered Gloria's death. She was there. They were playing Aggravation Rummy in the Game Room, when Gloria laid down her hand and fell out of her chair with a stroke. It happened not two weeks after she called Lulamae a thief. Lulamae thought maybe God was on her side and punished Gloria for her mean words and maybe God also didn't want Gloria to spill the beans to Charlotte. Realizing that now, a month later, she bowed her head and thanked God for his protection and for the sign of his approval of her. She then went in her bedroom to get dressed. She didn't like for Charlotte to see her in her nightgown.

At exactly eleven o'clock the doorbell rang and Lulamae opened the door for Charlotte, who leaned forward and brushed her heavily rouged, fat cheek against Lulamae's. Lulamae wanted to wipe the side of her face but restrained herself. "My, don't you look pretty!" Charlotte said.

"I do what I can," Lulamae replied. "It's not as easy as it used to be."

"Isn't that the truth," Charlotte laughed. "Bill's getting gray. You'll see. You and Sheila are coming to dinner a week off. I wrote it down for you. And your doctors' appointments. They're on the same sheet." Charlotte opened her purse and began rummaging in it. "I know I put it in here," she said. "I remember quite clearly."

"That's nice," Lulamae said. "Won't you have a seat? You can look better, sitting down."

Charlotte sat in the wing chair, propped her purse on her knees and began taking things out of it.

Lulamae sat in the club chair. "You sure carry a lot of stuff in your purse."

Charlotte glanced up at her. "I'm a busy woman." Then she sighed and began putting the things back in her purse. "I'll mail it to you," she said. "I want you to have the sheet and put it under the telephone like we discussed. You remember that, won't you? Then you could just look at it and see. So when you get it in the mail, put it under the phone, then you'll have it."

Charlotte looked to her left side, saying, "What's this?" and lifted Henry's pants off the sewing basket. The bills fell to the floor. Charlotte faced Lulamae, holding the pants up, the bills on the floor below them. She looked puzzled. "This is a pair of men's pants."

Charlotte's reaction had more impact on Lulamae than the discovered money. Almost incredulously, she watched Charlotte's expression change to horror, as if she had uncovered a snake. Changing her grip, she held the pants by thumb and forefinger. "Where did these come from?"

"They're Henry's," Lulamae said, wondering what reaction that piece of information would evoke in Charlotte.

"Who's Henry?" She draped the pants back on the sewing basket, then looked at Lulamae. Now she was angry.

"He's one of the residents here," Lulamae said.

"That's not what I meant and you know it."

"I think his last name's Jacobs. Something like that. I don't know. I don't know much about him."

"You don't know much about him, but his pants are on your sewing basket?" Charlotte picked up the money from the floor and showed it to Lulamae. "He's giving you this money for mending his pants. You're taking in sewing now? Bill and I have put you here at great expense, and you go around trying to make money by sewing on other people's clothes. I can't believe this. It's so humiliating. Do you do it in the whole place? Do you go around asking for business?"

Lulamae was fascinated at Charlotte's imagination. She never knew her daughter-in-law thought up things like that. Wonder what other things went through her head?

She was beginning to try to figure out what Charlotte imagined about Bill, about Sheila when Charlotte's voice cut through her thoughts. "You did not answer me, Lulamae. Do you go around this—this lovely community offering to take in darning, sew on buttons? Why don't you just take in laundry? I imagine some of these seniors would pay you for that, too."

Lulamae could feel her own temper rising, but she spoke as calmly as she could, considering what she had been accused of. "He's not paying me for hemming his pants. I offered to do it. That's all. As a favor. I'm going to Cloth World tomorrow to get some thread that matches."

"Then what's the money for? Where did it come from?"

Lulamae's radar went off: there was an enemy out there with torpedoes loaded and her in the sight. "I'd rather not say." Maybe Charlotte was hung up on sex things. Maybe that pregnancy—

Charlotte drew in her breath sharply and her eyes bulged. "I can't believe this," she said. "I just can't believe it. I heard of things going on in these communities, but I thought—I just can't believe this. Dollar bills for that. Oh, Lulamae, how could you? And at your age?" Charlotte began to cry.

Seeing her opportunity quite clearly, Lulamae smiled. "I didn't want to, but you don't know what it's like to have to ask for money to buy food and toiletries and even pay for utilities." Then she checked her feeling of triumph and sighed, shaking her head. "It's awfully hard not to be able to treat Pat to a sundae at Braum's or go to a sale on a lark and buy something you don't really need. I just want to be able to do that. I want to do it again."

"But this." Charlotte took a tissue from her purse and wiped her eyes. "I just can't hold my head up. What will Bill say? Sheila?"

"I can't imagine." And she truly couldn't. For a moment she wondered whether Charlotte had a thing about sex. Was that why she couldn't be honest in the beginning? But she couldn't think about this now.

"Can you stop? This isn't some kind of addiction, is it?"

Lulamae dropped her eyes to her lap. "I think I could stop. Do you think you could give me an extra ten dollars a week?"

"If you promise, never, ever, to do that again. To take money that way."

"I promise." Then, "You want to see my grocery receipts?"

"I don't think that's necessary at this juncture," Charlotte said, opening her purse. "It was fifty-six dollars last week, so I'll just give you that again."

"And the extra ten makes sixty-six."

"Your mind seems to be working very well today," Charlotte snapped.

"Why, thank you, Charlotte, I try." That forty dollars extra a month added to her other forty—Eighty dollars a month. Times ten—She smiled as she took the money. "And thank you for being so understanding."

"That's what daughters-in-law are for." Charlotte's eyes teared.

Lulamae remembered to be contrite. "I hope you don't have to tell Bill and Sheila."

"I don't know," Charlotte said. "Maybe it has something to do with circulation. I might mention it to Dr. Wells."

"As you think best." Lulamae leaned forward for the brushing of the cheek. 🌸

FALL FROM GRACE

by Jim Sanderson

After Walter Boone and his ex-wife had married off their son, Michael, Walter and his best drinking buddy spend a night cruising the sleaziest bars in Pumpjack. Bobby nearly lost his marriage to Lorrie, but Walter helped save it by talking sweet to Bobbie's wife, Lorrie. Still it was one of those nights that has the ingredients for bullshit. So that Sunday evening, still feeling like he had been eat by a wolf and shit off a cliff, Walter met Bobby at The It'll Do to compare what each remembered from the night before and sanctify the memory.

Micki, the waitress, laughed at Walter when he ordered a coke; then looked at Bobby and said, "You want a sody water, too?"

"Hell, no," Bobby said. "Hair of the dog what bit me." He had a bottle of bourbon and ordered ice and a glass of water.

"Shit, Bobby," Walter said. "You got bit by the whole pack." Bobby poured a little less than a finger into the plastic cup of ice that Micki brought him. He only sipped at it and drank glassfuls of water.

"Looks like the meeting of the goddamn Ladies' Temperance Union," Bill said as Bobby and Walter sipped their water and soda waters. He came up to their table and sat beside them.

"Don't tease them," Micki said as she went to wait on another table, favoring her bandaged right arm. "They just got out of Sunday school."

"You're right, Micki," Walter said. "It's so bad I'm thinking about joining the Baptist Church."

"Hell, I wouldn't do it," Bill said. "Then you couldn't fuck standing up."

"Elsewise, the Lord might think you're dancing," Bobby cut in to steal Bill's punch line.

"You all's dicks are gonna get you in trouble," Bill said. They sat around the table, Bobby's bottle of bourbon in the middle of the table, like it was a shrine, and they offered prayers in the form of the exaggerated memories that they told Bill.

Mamma Brody sat at the bar and munched her orange rat trap cheese and stared at them through her yellow eyes. She was old enough to be beyond all of this foolishness. Though she could let loose a smile and a giggle at some of their stories, life to Mamma was much more serious and miserable than it was to Walter and Bobby. With Elaine Cleburne's help, Walter had lost the seriousness and the misery that got a hold of him the night before, and Bobby was still living under the same roof as Lorrie, so Walter felt sorry for Mamma Brody and relieved for himself and Bobby.

After an hour, an unshaven man with dark circles under his eyes walked in the door, bellied up to the bar, next to Mamma, and looked over at Walter and Bobby. Bobby noticed him first and nodded his head. The man didn't return the gesture. His gimme cap was squished down on his head so that his brown hair curled out and up in ringlets from underneath it. His hair and face looked dirty. He had on a western shirt, jeans, and Nike jogging shoes. "Bill," Mamma yelled. "You got customers." Bill got up from Bobby's and Walter's table and went behind the bar to get a drink for the man.

"What'll you have?" Bill asked once he got behind the bar and in front of the man.

"I'll have me a piece of Walter Boone's ass," he said. Walter turned to look at him and squinted. Bobby scooted his chair out from under the table. Both Walter and Bobby curled their hands into fists.

"Now, you wait on," Bill said. "If anybody's gonna be getting some ass in here, it'll be me."

The man stepped back from the bar stuck his hand into his shirt and down to the edge of his pants. Walter turned to Bobby and asked, "What the hell's he doing?"

"He's trying to grab his dick," Bobby said. But the man brought a tiny .22 pistol out of his pants and pointed the pistol toward Walter and Bobby.

Walter and Bobby heard a plop and looked behind themselves to see that Micki had dived onto the floor. She groaned, probably because she broke another bone. "Which one of you is Walter Boone?" the man asked.

No one said anything. "I know it's one of you bastards." Bill started scooting down the bar, probably to go for the bat he kept behind the bar or his own gun. The man whirled around and pointed the gun at Bill.

"I'm Walter Boone," Walter said.

"Me too," Bobby said. "I'm Walter Boone."

Walter turned to look at Bobby. Walter wasn't sure if Bobby was playing around or had a strategy. Bobby wasn't sure either. He shrugged his shoulders. Then, from Micki, down on the floor, hands over her head so that her voice was muffled, they heard, "Like hell, I'm Walter Boone."

The man whirled around again and levelled the gun at them. "Smart asses. You're all just a bunch of smart asses, aren't you?" Both Walter and Bobby wanted to kiss Micki. Perhaps they should have years ago.

"Shut up. Think you know so goddamn much. Think you can just take a man's wife." Now Walter and Bobby each had an idea of what he was but not specifically whose husband or ex-husband he was.

"Makes no difference to you, you ruin a man's family. My name is Ray Palmer and my wife is Deborah Jo Palmer. I want to know what she's been doing with you."

He twitched a little, switched his aim from Walter and Bobby to Micki lying on the floor, to the other two guys drinking back by the shuffleboard table, and to Bill behind the bar. "If you can't keep her at home, what am I supposed to do?" Walter asked.

Ray Palmer steadied the gun at Walter. "You destroyed her soul," Ray Palmer said.

"You did what?" Bobby whispered to Walter.

Ray went on: "She confessed to me. She said she couldn't live with her sin no more. So she called me and confessed. Then she called the preacher and confessed to him."

"Who the hell didn't she confess to?" Bobby muttered. "Next time find one doesn't talk so much."

Ray started shaking. "Shut up. Shut up. All right for you to talk. But she left me." He looked back at Walter, "You made her leave me." Walter knew two things: Ray was confused, and Deborah Jo Palmer was a really dumb mistake on his part.

"Get your scrawny ass out of here." It was Mamma Brody. She threw her cheese at the man and hit him in the back. He turned his back to Walter to point the pistol at her, but he didn't know what to do about Mamma Brody. "Go on, get your ass out. You don't come into my bar and do this kind of shit."

"Shut, shut up," Ray said. "I'm here to do what should be done. I'm here to do God's will." He turned to Bill. "Make the old lady shut up."

"You goddamn watch your mouth," Bill said and began to move toward Ray. Ray panicked and shot once toward the ceiling. He jumped, then let off another shot. It was clear to Walter that Ray was not going to shoot anybody.

"You goddamn, silly-assed, pencil dick, son of a bitch," Mamma yelled and squirmed on her bar stool.

"Enough of this shit," Walter said, got up, and grabbed Bobby's whiskey bottle.

He walked up to Ray, and as Ray spun around, Walter caught him with the whiskey bottle on the side of the head. Bourbon ran down the side of Walter's hand and arm, and he licked at it. Ray glanced up at the taller Walter and slowly lowered his gun. His mouth worked, but no words came out. He looked like a fish gulping for air. Then a few garbled words came out of Ray's mouth. "Kill your ass" was all that Walter heard. So Walter whacked him with the whiskey bottle again. This time a crack opened up in Ray's skull and spurted some blood. Poor ol' Ray Palmer fell to the floor on top of the bourbon that Walter had dribbled, and Walter licked his fingers and sat the bourbon on the bar.

"Hit him again," Mamma Brody said.

Bill knew that he had to call the police, but he told Walter and Bobby to leave and then tell the police they'd never been there. But Walter knew that sooner or later, someone would knock on his door and want to know what happened, so he stayed, and Bobby stayed too, to support his drinking buddy. So Ray Palmer went to the hospital, and

Bobby and Walter went to jail.

Walter's ex, Sarah, Michael and his new wife, not yet out of town for their honeymoon, and Lorrie, Bobby's wife who nearly divorced him the night before, bailed them out. "My God," was all that Sarah said, then *tsked*. Michael looked at his father then at his mother and tried to figure out how he should go about scolding them. Kimberly ducked her head as though, now that she had Michael, she should cut a few of her links to Walter and Bobby.

"We just checked into the Iron Bar Motel for the night," Bobby said. "No Big Deal." Lorrie hugged Bobby anyway. She tried to wrap her small arms all the way around him, but could only get a little of him in her grasp.

The next day, Monday, Bobby found a note from his principal, Lucas Daigle, in his mailbox. And, since the cops closed The It'll Do down for a couple of days (Mamma bitching, no doubt, because it was really Ray Palmer's fault), Bobby met Walter at Johnnie Jones' Lajitas North for a beer and to tell what had happened to him.

Johnnie Jones propped a foot up on his cooler and leaned across his bar to talk to them. First, he told them about how he got all three of the killer bees to his house to smoke a little dope and how he tried to get them all to jump into bed with him. Then, when Johnnie got in early Monday morning and checked his crude, haphazard bookkeeping, he came up short. Some of the waitresses fessed up about what they saw: Paula closed down and skipped out with the cash. Johnnie didn't even have to fire her. She never came back, just kept running with Johnnie's cash.

Then, Johnnie said, "I read about you guys in the paper" to let Bobby tell about what was going to happen to him and Walter.

"My note said we 'reflected negatively,'" Bobby said first.

"Gonna catch any shit?" Johnnie asked.

"Don't know," Walter said, then added, "Hell, who gives a shit. Let's drink a beer."

But Bobby hung his head and let it bounce off his chest. He reached down and pulled out his shirt tail, so he could get comfortable before he told Walter the news. "They showed me two contracts and told me to sign one or the other. One says I resign. The other says, I'll sign up for some kind of de-tox or counseling or some such horseshit and stay out of bars."

Johnnie let out a whistle. "So what did you do?" Johnnie asked.

"You told them to stick their contracts up their asses," Walter said, tilted his head back, and took a long gulp of beer. He sat his beer down, turned to look at Bobby, and cocked his head to see out of his one good eye.

"I asked for a night to think about it," Bobby said.

"You gonna tell them to stick it up their ass?" Johnnie asked.

Bobby rubbed his cheek and then scratched both sides of his head, leaving his hair wild and unruly. His eyes were red. "I got a family. I'm gonna have to eat shit."

"What kind of counseling?" Johnnie asked. "Some of it ain't bad?"

Walter answered: "Some limp dick with a psychology degree will tell you how to get in touch with some out of kink part of your psyche." Bobby tried to explain some more, but Walter was on a roll, "Or you'll go to some kind of camp where they'll treat you like a boy scout who peeked up his mamma's dress or some shit. Or some AA outfit, which is no better than a church revival for drunks."

"Maybe, we are drunks," Bobby said.

"Not that kind," Walter said and stared hard at Bobby.

Bobby turned to look at Walter. "You are single." Walter's shoulders hunched up, and his head hung down. "You can afford dignity," Bobby said.

"It ain't that," Walter said. "This is chickenshit." Walter banged his half-full beer bottle down on Johnnie's bar.

"I know a lawyer," Johnnie said and stared at Walter.

Bobby just kept his head hung and stared into the small round hole on top of the neck of his beer. It was like he was saying good-bye to it.

Walter looked at his best buddy staring at his bottle and said, "Yeah, you're gonna have to eat shit. Damn, I hate to see that."

"I know lawyers," Johnnie said.

"What do I do in the meantime?" Bobby said.

"Yeah," Johnnie said. "They got you by the ying yang. "

"What can I do?" Bobby said as though he had spent the afternoon straining himself to think of an out.

"Nothing," Walter said. "You're gonna get fucked."

Bobby had thought and worried himself until his brain was tired. Walter was surly and pissed off, like he wanted to pick up a whiskey bottle once again and take another swipe at somebody. But he was sorry he had hit poor old Ray Palmer, not because he was catching shit from his boss, but because poor ol' Ray wasn't so much dangerous as ignorant and scared.

The next day, Walter met Lucas Daigle in the Principal's office, surrounded by the photos of the great football teams from Robert E. Lee High. Walter folded his hands as he stood in front of Lucas' desk. Behind the desk sat Lucas.

"Walter," Lucas tsked. "You put my ass in a ringer this time. What the hell can I do?" Lucas ran his hands along the wings his hair made on the sides of his head.

"Hell, Lucas," Walter said, "This sounds like a divorce."

"Let's try to act reasonable." The "let's" pissed Walter off this time. Lucas pushed himself up and smoothed back his hair. Walter glanced down at his shiny black boots, than back up at Lucas. Lucas walked to Walter and patted his shoulder. "I've got no arguments with what you've done. But the board doesn't want a jailbird and drunk to teach our kids."

Walter, for one of the first times in his life, got tongue tied. He could not say anything because he was so mad that all the blood was rushing up into his head and jamming his vocal cords, because he was imagining Bobby sitting at home but wanting desperately to get out for a beer at The It'll Do, because in his imagination he also saw Lorrie with her arms around Bobby, soothing him because she truly loved him and was sorry because of the turn their lives had taken. "You gonna do it, Lucas? You gonna fire me?"

Lucas patted Walter's shoulder again, "You had a really nice nest here. But you messed in your piece of that nest." Walter wished that he had another bottle of bourbon to swing.

"Am I fired or not? You tell me, then tell my lawyer."

"You're fired, Walter. You knew what could happen from the beginning."

"Where's my two contracts in case I want to take the pledge like

Bobby?"

"I made some notes all about this affair. Bobby Baker is still a family man. He. . . ."

"He still has hope," Walter said. Walter looked at Lucas who hung his head, "Hell, Lucas, I wouldn't have signed it anyway." Walter patted Lucas' shoulder.

Lucas forced his head up, "Fired or not, you're going to have to leave this place. You'll miss it. Me, all I ever wanted to get out of West Texas was my ass."

Lucas Daigle was right. Pumpjack changed for Walter. Walter began to think that maybe he *had* wasted his life. He began to think that, while he had been drinking and bullshitting and running women, he had lost Sarah, Elaine, Michael, and a bunch of others. At night, he couldn't turn off his brain, so instead of sleeping, he re-thought himself and these women. He hopped bars, and toward closing time, usually at the It'll Do, the only bar that kept him interested enough to drink more than one beer, he became something of a problem drunk, the kind that babble on about what's bothering them and end up cussing something. Several times bar owners had to kick him out. Mamma Brody told him that he was disgusting. Bill said that he always knew Walter's dick would get him in trouble.

The way Walter and Bobby got fired could have provided the material for a really good story, one he could tell in a bar, one that would match stories about the oil field, welding, or roofing. But Walter could not work this reality into a story.

Only dear Lorrie knew about the demons hiding in Walter's accelerating brain because Bobby was having the same problem. Bobby's getting fired helped his marriage, made him a better member of the community, but being a better family man was making him edgy and nervous. Even Lorrie, at first glad to have him home early every night, began to scold him for his depressions and told him to get out of the house more. She suggested bowling, a trip to the Dairy Queen for ice cream, miniature golf, a cup of coffee. But romance was gone without liquor.

Walter had dinner at Bobby's once or twice a week, and Bobby and he would drive to a small town across the county line for a beer. Bobby had a full two months to try to find a drying-out facility or a counselor, so he was looking for the most innocuous one available. Sometimes, he hung his head and pounded his fist on the bar or the table. "Goddamn. I wish the bastards had enough respect to let me go to hell in my own chosen fashion." When he said this, Walter bought him a beer, or if Lorrie was with them, she'd wrap her arms around him and kiss him on the cheek.

So Walter wanted out. Walter wanted to make tracks, simple motion, as in jogging, not to get away from anything or to something, just movement seemed to be soothing. But there had been enough good in West Texas that Walter wanted to take something from Pumpjack with him. He didn't want to go alone. Elaine, again, was the solution.

So Walter drove to P.C.C.C., Pumpjack Country Community College, and waited outside its one large Stalinist-looking building that sat in the middle of one-hundred acres of mesquite (room for the expansion that never came) and saw Elaine coming out, staring down at her feet, her shorts rolled up to mid-thighs, her hair blowing behind her face. "Elaine," Walter said.

She smiled, walked slowly up to him, and kissed him. "You're fired, right?"

"Come with me."

"Where?"

"Anywhere."

"You mean for good. Like leave town. Not just a drive or a drink?"

"I'm getting the hell out of Dodge. Distance, man. Motion."

She juggled the books in her arms and cocked her head to one side. "What about all the preaching about my own distance and space, about my own pilgrimage?"

"I was wrong."

"How do I know you're not wrong now?"

"Trust me."

She hung her head. Walter stepped a bit closer, and she let the side of her fist gently bounce off of his chest. He tried to hug her, but she twisted out of his grasp and backed away, back toward P.C.C.C. The sun was behind him; Elaine squinted, and put a hand over her eyes to see him. "What about all your bullshit? You know, everybody is alone?'"

"It was just bullshit," Walter said.

Walter stepped toward her, but she moved back. "I feel like screaming."

"Go with me."

"Why?"

"Because I'm desperate. Bobby's changed and stuck. You're all that's left. The bullshit is just, just . . . bullshit."

"You son of a bitch," she said. "How can I know what to believe? How do you know what to believe?"

"Please, just come to my place. Let's talk."

"No," she said. "I've made my choice. You're not in it." She moved slowly toward him. When he reached for her, she stopped. Walter kept his hands to his sides and didn't move. She walked past him, and he turned to watch her. From behind her, seeing her move away, looking just at her back, Walter watched her pull one hand up to wipe her eyes.

Like certain women would do for certain men, Elaine had endured Walter's stale whiskey breath and kissed him, then made love to him. She had remained full and substantial the whole time Walter had run with her. Her body was always uniquely hers, not like any other woman. But she wouldn't leave with him. She was smart enough to know she was only twenty-three, and thus couldn't get smarter and yet keep Walter. Walter really knew all along that an affair with Elaine couldn't last. It would have been a perfect arrangement for Bobby.

Walter figured that his scarred, worn old heart was rougher than an outhouse toilet seat. Nevertheless, he called Elaine every night for a week and begged her to go anywhere with him.

Walter took two days to say his good-byes to those who gave a shit. Kimberly cried, and Michael hung his head when Walter had his last dinner with them. Then, he started stuffing his ancient Porsche, and the night before he left, Sarah came over to say goodbye.

Sarah Boone had heard from her friends that her husband was leaving. Ever since Walter had come to Pumpjack to live in the same town as his wife, Sarah had heard from customers and friends what they had heard Walter had done and with whom and in what old bar. In a way, she was glad to have her friend's gossip. What they said seemed closer to some "hard" truth. Walter had a problem with the truth. It was not so much that he lied (Walter always owned up to everything), but when he explained what he had done to Sarah, he made it sound inevitable, interesting, even logical.

Since Walter had come to live in the same town as her, Sarah had learned that she was still susceptible to her ex-husband, so she stayed away from him as much as possible. But when she heard that he was leaving, she thought that she ought to try one more time to give him some clear, more realistic idea of himself in relation to the real world. "I heard that you asked a girl half your age to go with you," was the first thing Sarah said to Walter.

Walter had given his rented furniture all back, so Sarah looked around the barren apartment, put her back against a wall, then slid down it to a sitting position. "News travels fast. I can't imagine what you heard," Walter said back at Sarah and squatted in front of his ex-wife. "Yes, Sarah. I'd like somebody to leave with me," Walter said. "What about you?"

After she giggled and said, "Get serious," Sarah studied her ex-husband's face because she felt like it would be a long time before she saw it again. She was glad to see him go but would miss the gossip, the excuses, and his face. "Walter, she's a baby."

"What do you know about love?"

"Walter, in the end, finally, what do you know about love?" Sarah did not laugh. She did not say it with condescension or pity. It was a real question, and it shocked her husband.

Walter sat in front of her in the play of shadows and light and stared at her. "Where are you going to go? What are you going to do?"

"I don't know," Walter said. "But I've been here before."

"Oh, Walter," Sarah said and stretched herself toward him. "You have never been 'here' before. You always had somebody to move with you or be there to meet you."

Walter's brow wrinkled as he thought, and when his brow grew straight and he smiled, they both knew that she was right. "Yeah, always you."

"You really have reached the bottom. This is going to hurt you," Sarah said and touched the side of Walter's face.

Walter raised one brow and asked, "How about a good-bye," he hesitated, "kiss," he said and winked.

Sarah kissed him. "Goodbye," she said, pushed herself up, smiled, and left.

What Walter couldn't cram into his ancient Porsche, he stacked up outside on the balcony of his apartment. Bobby pulled up behind Walter and walked up to the Porsche as Walter shoved a baseball glove and old jogging shoes into the car. "What you doing, Walter?"

"I'm getting outa here," Walter said.

"Just like that?"

"Hauling buns."

"You mean for good?"

Walter pulled up and said, "You got a better plan?"

Bobby looked around and squeezed the sides of his arms. "At least you're going to fight them."

Walter looked at Bobby, "Bobby, there's no 'them.'"

"You can't just leave," Bobby said and reached for his arm. "Come on. Remember what it was like," Bobby pleaded. "Walter . . . Walter. We're cowboys, goddamn it."

"Yahoo!" Walter said. Bobby needed more. "The job isn't the point. *It's* all gone. Everything that made this place worth a shit is gone. Or it will be soon. What do we owe it? What does it owe us? It's turning into a goddamn wimpy country. Everybody wants a guarantee, wants a signed contract, an easy life, egg in his beer, peace, and happiness."

Walter stepped back away from him and leaned against the Porsche. Then, as he climbed in, Bobby smiled and said, "They'll never see any beauty, will they?"

Walter scooted in the driver's seat, then poked his head out through the window. The smile that made him filled up his face: "Never will. They've got too many things to believe in."

Bobby stuck out his hand, and Walter reached through the window to shake it. "Give Sarah a call. Tell her to hire some guys to move what's left to her place. I'll pay the bills."

"I respect you too much not to let you go to hell in your own fashion," Bobby said and smiled.

Walter turned the keys. The Porsche backfired, sputtered, then roared out of the parking lot.

When Walter was teaching at Sul Ross State University, some of the cowboy students told him that Pumpjack was the most fuckingest and drinkingest town in Texas (what else was there to do?). There are other sayings about Pumpjack. Like Lucas said, the best thing to get out of Pumpjack is your ass. The best view of Pumpjack is in your rear-view mirror. Lubbock is the asshole of the universe and Pumpjack is one hundred and thirty-four miles up it. So Walter got his ass out of Pumpjack with his liver and dick still intact.

But for a while Pumpjack was heaven for Walter, for Walter and Bobby, as fully mature men, formed but far away from infirm old age, were as close to gods as anyone in the Bible Belt, oil field West Texas could possibly have been. They had created their world out of the debris that others had left. They found joy in it. They were reverent toward their creation.

After Walter left, Bobby wrote to him about Pumpjack. Bobby was trying to stay married and decent. He spent a lot of money to go to a de-tox center in Carlsbad, New Mexico. He jogged, played tennis, lifted weights, ate healthy food, and met a genuinely better class of people than he knew in Pumpjack. When he got back to Pumpjack, he snuck around to bars at sundown and got home before ten p.m.

Johnnie Jones stayed up too long after two a.m., and he got shut down and fined by the county sheriff, even though the sheriff was a buddy. He never quite recovered financially, and his dream about sitting on the bank of the Rio Grande down in Lajitas with the right woman or women got dimmer and dimmer. He sold Lajitas-North to a Lubbock banker who changed the menu, brought in plants and went broke within a year. Johnnie used what skills he had—bricklaying, carpentry, sheet rocking, drinking, and picking up women—to get by after he sold his bar.

Sarah wrote, too. The oil bust got so bad that Sarah finally pulled her business out of the decaying mall and moved her art boutique to the Albuquerque airport. Michael and Kimberly got fat and happy, stayed in love, and started having grandkids for Walter and Sarah. Elaine wrote or phoned Walter to tell him what she did. First she went to school in New Mexico, then graduate school in Colorado. Then she stopped writing and phoning.

Micki kept getting older and breaking more bones. Eventually, she'd just have to die; she'd have nothing left. The It'll Do started losing more and more money.

One Christmas, a Pumpjack husband learned that his wife had been sleeping with Bill Brody. He marched down to The It'll Do, bellied up to the bar, pulled out a pistol, said "Merry Christmas," and emptied the chamber into poor ol' Bill. Mamma had nobody else to take care of her and got put into the county old folks' home. The Pentecostal Church across the street from The It'll Do bought the bar and turned it into a day-care center.

When Bobby phoned to tell Walter about the fate of the It'll Do, Walter concluded two things: The Lord works in mysterious ways, and Bill's dick got him in trouble.

As for Walter, when he left Pumpjack, not knowing where to go or what to do with himself, he thought about driving west, toward California, but because he'd never seen the hill country, because the sun was in his eyes, he turned east and wound up in San Antonio.

He got a job exterminating bugs. He figured that no one cared if a bug killer got thrown in jail. He tried to avoid anything that vaguely smelled of horseshit. He moved just south of Downtown and made himself a fixture in the San Antonio icehouses and neighborhood bars. He discovered brown skinned waitresses with big butts who were willing to teach him a little Spanish. He liked sitting under the shade of oak, pecan, or cotton-wood trees in the earlier evenings and listening to and telling stories. When it was his time to tell stories, he told the waitress and the other bar patrons about Pumpjack. But because Walter was a bullshitter, he mixed the real Pumpjack that kicked him out of town and the Pumpjack of the It'll Do, Bobby and Lorrie Baker, and Ray and Deborah Jo Palmer, so Walter, as always, told the best stories.

To keep himself going, Walter, for a while, thought he would write down the Pumpjack bullshit. So he hit the computer keys that made little dots that in turn made letters, but when he read the words, he realized what he had written was dog shit. After several attempts, he shut off his computer and sent that dogshit to computer heaven where unsaved documents go to die.

But the Lord sent an archangel with a message to Walter in the form of Henry Armendariz. Henry was a tiny, wrinkled man whose face looked like a raisin. With his straw hat pulled low on his forehead to keep out the sun, Walter could just barely see his eyes. Henry met Walter at Neal's icehouse and told him what he remembered about Mexico. Henry was as good a bullshitter as Walter.

With Henry's prophecy, Walter would sit in his apartment and look at a Rand McNally road map of Mexico. He drew red circles around the towns in the small black type within one-hundred miles of the U.S. border. (Don't be completely impractical, Walter told himself. With the Mexican economy and politics on a roller coaster, he'd be wise to keep an American bank and the border close by.)

Walter meant to look at all the towns. An old man with a little money could have a good time spending the rest of his life in Mexico. In Mexico, a poor old American man would have enough to buy most anything he wanted: booze, whores, or dignity. Anything else is egg on your enchilada. Walter realized that the Lord had allowed him to create his own Eden in Pumpjack, and now, Walter figured that the best way to thank the Lord was the make another Eden, and Walter felt the need to be about the

Lord's business.

So he wrote Bobby and went to the San Antonio icehouses and bars, bullshitting his way to Mexcio along with other drinkers. He'd probably never make it, but he could imagine himself and Henry Armendariz in Mexico telling bigger and better lies to Bobby, who would retire and come down with Lorrie in tow. And Elaine and Sarah would visit him, and when they were gone he'd see if his dick could still get him in trouble. *Adíos.* 🏵

Plastic Cowboys and Rodeo Dreams

by Betty Wiesepape

Plastic cowboys, twelve to a package. I bought them on sale at Perry Brothers for twenty-nine cents. Made from molds of cheap plastic, the only variation from cowboy to cowboy was the color of the plastic and the position of tags of plastic overrun that protruded from their bodies. Identical boots, identical chaps, identical six-shooters and wide-brimmed hats were pressed onto the cowboys' bodies, so I couldn't remove their clothes and redress them the way I redressed Barbie.

All twelve pairs of legs bowed out to exactly the same degree. The clerk at Perry Brothers told me the reason. The cowboys were made to sit astraddle plastic horses that came twelve to another package for an additional twenty-nine cents. The cowboys couldn't stand on their own without the horses. This disability created a dilemma. My allowance wouldn't cover the cost of both packages. If I bought the cowboys, I'd have to wait until the next week to buy the horses. I stood in front of the toy counter for the better part of an hour, contemplating my choice. Finally, I carried the package of plastic cowboys to the checkout counter.

When I returned for the plastic horses the following Saturday, Perry Brothers had sold out, and I was stuck with twelve bowlegged plastic cowboys who couldn't stand up on their own unless I propped them. Without the plastic horses, the plastic cowboys were almost as useless as the cheap plastic prizes in Cracker Jack boxes.

Eventually, I put the plastic cowboys in a shoe box that I kept on the top shelf of my closet and turned my attention to celluloid cowboys. Celluloid cowboys turned out to be a much better deal. For twenty-five cents children under twelve could get into the Saturday matinee at the Rex Theater and watch larger-than-life cowboys gallop from adventure to adventure on larger-than-life horses. For the price of a three-cent stamp and a return envelope, we could join the celluloid cowboys' fan clubs and receive autographed pictures in the mail.

We were all under twelve then, that last generation of children who spent Saturday mornings beside the radio, listening for the sound of the *William Tell Overture*, the Masked Man's "Hi Ho Silver," and his Indian friend's "Kemosabe," brought to us by Wheaties, the "Breakfast of Champions." I preferred Malt-O-Meal, but on Saturday, I ate Wheaties. That was the least I could do for the Lone Ranger.

After the Lone Ranger and Tonto rode off in a cloud of dust, my father dropped me off at the Rex Theater, where I stood in a long line of children that stretched from the theater ticket booth, down the 200 block of Main Street, and around the corner onto Market. Each time the door to the Rex opened, the scent of popcorn wafted out and another child with a ticket disappeared into the lobby. I stood on tiptoes to count the number of children who remained between me and the ticket booth. It was a contest to see if I could reach the end of the blue velvet ropes and plunk my quarter on the counter before the usher came out of the lobby with his plastic megaphone and announced that seats for the Saturday matinee were sold out.

The first fifteen minutes of each episode was a recap of the entire adventure up to that point, so one missed episode was not a big deal. It wasn't what happened next that I dreaded missing so much as the opportunity to spend two hours in the presence of real heroes whose photographs lined the walls of my bedroom. I had them all—Tom Mix, Tex Ritter, Monte Hale, Gene Autry, Rex Allen, Hoot Gibson, the Cisco Kid, Lash La Rue, Red Ryder, Rocky Lane, Hopalong Cassidy, and the king—Roy Rogers.

If I arrived at the Rex early, I got a front row seat, where I alternated between standing on my knees with my fists clenched in my lap and slumping far back into the velvet seat with my boots sticking straight out. My position in the seat was directly related to my heroes' chances of winning their battles against Indians, bank robbers, cattle rustlers, and other assorted bad men.

In black-and-white film the good guys and bad guys were easy to tell apart. The good guys wore white hats, fringed leather jackets, and fringed leather chaps. If the bad guys didn't wear black hats, they rode dark horses–unless they were Indians. Indians didn't wear hats. They wore feathers and moccasins and, if they were bad Indians, war paint on their faces. Sometimes bad guys donned feathers and moccasins and war paint and pretended to be Indians, but I could always tell they weren't real Indians.

Fake Indians weren't the only problem with those western serials. Mountains and palm trees appeared on the plains of West Texas, and the good guys fired more shots at the bad guys than their six-shooters held cartridges. But none of that mattered to those of us seated in darkness in the Rex Theater on Saturday morning. We were more than willing to suspend our disbelief so long as our heroes won. And win they did, Saturday after Saturday after Saturday. The bad guys put up a good fight so that the outcome was in doubt, but in the end, the good guys always managed to win and to rescue whatever damsel happened to be in distress that particular Saturday–usually the beautiful daughter of some wealthy rancher.

The beautiful woman's part never amounted to much. She was never on the screen for more than a few minutes, and the cowboys never took her along to catch any bad guys or fight any Indians. Even so, no Saturday matinee was ever complete without a beautiful woman. A beautiful woman was to the western serial what a cheap plastic prize was to a Cracker Jack box. Without a beautiful woman in the picture, the cowboys had no excuse to go on an adventure and no reason to turn and tip their hats for the camera before they rode off into the sunset–or straight into another adventure, depending upon which number in the serial we happened to be watching.

The way I remember, Dale Evans was the only female who ever got to ride alongside the cowboys, and she was relegated to the margins of the screen as soon as fighting broke out. I don't remember the name of a single actress who stared in those Saturday serials except Dale Evans. I remember Dale because I dreamed about her. I dreamed she died of pneumonia, and Roy Rogers invited me to ride the range alongside him on Dale's horse.

I don't remember exactly when the windows of the ticket booth at the

Rex were boarded over, but sometime between my last kick ball game and my first sock hop, my obsession with cowboys shifted from celluloid cowboys to a specific bullrider on the Junior Rodeo circuit. He had broad shoulders and a flat belly, and he was every bit as unattainable as the celluloid cowboys, because he already had a steady girlfriend whose father was part-owner of the famous H&H Ranch. But I had every confidence that I could unseat my competition. This was the United States of America. Everybody was created equal, and I could be anything I wanted to be.

I ran this reel over and over in my imagination. I was dressed in a red satin shirt, tight fitting jeans, and red boots, and my shoulder-length hair was tied with a red ribbon into a pony tail that bounced against my back when I came bursting from the chute, leaning low over the stallion's neck headed for the barrels. My bullrider was on the sidelines cheering me on, as I circled the barrels and dashed across the finish line at the sound of the buzzer. In this reel, the daughter of the H&H rancher always fell

I had almost everything I needed to turn that reel into reality. I had the boots. I had the curves to fill out the tight jeans and red satin shirt. I had the ponytail, and I had the red ribbon. All I lacked was a horse.

My father was not a wealthy rancher, and no matter how hard I pleaded, he refused to buy a horse. I wanted a horse more than anything, but unless some talent scout discovered me and paid me a fortune to star in a Western movie, I'd be an old maid long before I saved enough money from my weekly allowance to buy a horse.

I suspected, even then, that my father's refusal to buy me a horse was related somehow to the behavior of the Salt Trail riders who congregated in my hometown each year on the first Saturday in February. In a small Texas town where entertainment was limited to drive-in movies, high school football games, and cruising Main Street in the family Buick, the Salt Grass Trail Ride was a big event. My father would not allow me to go anywhere near the Washington County Fair Grounds where the Salt Grass Trail riders camped out, but he did allow me to attend the parade on Saturday morning.

I arrived an hour early to stake out a spot in front of the Rex Theater where my young bull-rider would be sure to see me in my new black boots, button-fly Levis, and black Stetson. I hooked my thumbs through my belt loops and parted my lips the way I'd seen Dale Evans do when she was waiting for Roy to ride up on Trigger. I stood like that until my lips dried out and my mouth felt like cotton. The parade hadn't even started.

When the parade finally did start, the first entry was not a cowboy or a covered wagon or a rodeo clown. It was a big black Cadillac filled with city officials who were running for re-election. Cowboys-for-a-day was what I called them—these old potbellied men dressed western for the occasion in leather vests, bolo ties, and wide brimmed Stetsons on loan from Bode and Tonn's Western Wear Shop. They smiled and waved at everyone in sight, but I never took my thumbs out of my belt loops. No sense waving to a bunch of old men who didn't even know which side of a horse to mount.

I did take my thumbs out of my belt loops to wave at my little brother. He was one of a large group of Boy Scouts who had donned moccasins, feathers, and war paint for the occasion. Girl Scouts dressed like pioneer women in aprons and bonnets followed along behind the Boy Scouts. Then came students from Miss Kim's School of Baton Twirling and Modern Dance, miniature baton twirlers in graduated sizes who wore identical pink tights and white boots, no two boots or batons in exactly the same position.

Shriners from Houston, dressed in maroon hats with maroon tassels, raced miniature cars around in circles for no apparent reason, and on a float behind them, more Shriners pretended to be cowboys and Indians, firing cap pistols and arrows with suction cups on the ends at one another. Two rodeo clowns with over-sized boots and painted faces rode in a covered wagon behind the Shriners. When the mule pulling the wagon decided to lie down in the middle of the street, the fire truck driver had to slam on his brakes, and the entire parade came to an abrupt stop. One of the clowns had to get out of the wagon and coax the mule to his feet with an apple. The crowd roared with laughter, and the Salt Grass Trail Parade started up again.

As soon as the sound of approaching snare drums filled the air, spectators rose to their feet, folded their plastic chairs, and began to clap.

With my thumbs back in my belt loops, I leaned forward and looked down the street to see what all the clapping was about. A drum majorette dressed in white from the toes of her leather boots to the plume on her fake fur hat, was prancing down the center of Main Street in a way that was giving the hometown crowd plenty to cheer about. A row of twirlers in short green skirts marched along behind the drum major, doing a high kick routine with movements so synchronized that the tassels on their boots swung in perfect unison.

Half a block behind the high school band rode the main event, two hundred horses and horseback riders from across the State of Texas. The riders were decked out in leather vests, fringed leather jackets, and fringed leather chaps. Their costumes, decorated with rhinestones, sequins, and silver, sparkled like diamonds in the sunlight.

In the center of the street, a couple of horse lengths in front of the others, rode the Grand Marshal, the silver screen cowboy that the residents of Brenham had come to town to see. The Grand Marshall of the Salt Grass Trail Parade was always whatever Western star was to appear at the Houston Fat Stock Show and Rodeo the following weekend. Most of the Western stars whose autographed pictures lined the walls of my bedroom served as Grand Marshall at one time or another.

If these Western stars didn't sit quite as tall in the saddle as they had on the screen at the Rex, if their stomachs lapped over their belt buckles, if their pancake makeup was so thick it resembled war paint, I was too blinded by the glitter of rhinestones and silver to notice. These were my heroes, and for weeks after the Salt Grass Trail parade, I envisioned myself riding down the center of Main Street on a beautiful stallion beside each one of them.

By my senior year in high school, I found a way to participate in the Salt Grass Trail parade that didn't require a stallion. Dressed all in white from the toes of my boots to the plumb on my fake fur hat, I was the drum majorette prancing down the center of Main Street in front of the high school band. I was aware, as only a teenage girl in a short skirt and satin tights can be aware, that every male in the crowd was watching me prance. I tossed my baton high into the air, whirled so fast that my short skirt stood in a perfect circle around my hips, and landed in a split in the middle of Main Street at the very moment that the baton fell back into my hand. People on both sides of the street burst into applause, and for that brief moment, I knew how it felt to be a star.

Main Street was shorter that day than it ever was before or since. I pranced and twirled like I had never pranced and twirled, and all too soon I reached the end of the parade.

As I made my way between fat politicians, moccasin-clad boy scouts, decorated floats, and hundreds of horses, I discovered that the Salt Grass Trail riders were not as shy around women as the celluloid cowboys on the screen of the Rex Theater had been. The riders didn't stop with a tip of the hat and a "Howdy ma'am." They whistled, made off-color remarks, and asked if I was coming to the dance at Fireman's Pavilion. I smiled and shook my head and kept walking.

I didn't attend the dance that evening. The honkytonk nature of the event and the fundamentalist beliefs of my parents prevented me from going. The closest I got to the festivities taking place directly across the street from my house was my bedroom window.

From the window box in my bedroom on the second floor, I watched the arrival of the Salt Grass Trail riders. I sat in the darkness with my legs folded Indian style, my grandmother's quilt wrapped around the shoulders of my flannel gown, my face so close to the window pane that my breath frosted the glass.

The trail riders' leather and rhinestone outfits looked even more splendid in the orange glow from the streetlight than they had looked in the sunlight. Each time the doors of Fireman's Pavilion opened, I pressed my nose against the windowpane and strained to hear the beat of the music. The thump of the bass guitar, the whine of a fiddle, and the twangy voice of the western singer made me feel like an exile, seated all alone on that window box while couples, silhouetted against the glow from colored lights that hung in swags from the ceiling, swayed arm and arm across the dance floor. I must have dozed off, because sometime after midnight, I awakened to what sounded like a gunshot followed by the rattle of a beer can, scraping the wall of our house. With my fist, I rubbed a circle in the frosted glass and peeped out.

One of the doors to Fireman's Pavilion was propped open, and I could see band members packing up their instruments. The dance had ended, and cowboy after cowboy staggered through the doorway, so drunk they had to lean against the wall or hold onto a brick post for support. One inebriated cowboy's knees gave way completely, and he fell on all fours on the concrete. The next cowboy who stumbled through the door, tripped over the first one's legs, and fell face down on the concrete. Then a third cowboy tripped and fell on top of him. The three cowboys rolled and tumbled, and got their legs so tangled that I had to cover my mouth to keep from laughing out loud.

Then one of the cowboys untangled his legs, struggled to his feet, and swaggered across the street to our front yard. The next sound I heard was him, relieving his bladder on the shrubbery beneath my window. I shrank even farther into the darkness and listened to the sound of his splattering.

I did not see the trail riders again until the band bus pulled into the parking lot in downtown Houston the following Saturday. A cold front had moved into the area, dropping temperatures below freezing. Sleet was falling intermittently with rain, and the band's participation in the Fat Stock Parade was doubtful.

My mood was as dismal as the weather. All week I had savored my success at the Salt Grass Trail Parade and had anticipated even greater accolades when I tossed my baton into the air and landed in a split in downtown Houston. Where hundreds of people had applauded my performance in Brenham, thousands would be cheering in Houston. Some Hollywood talent scout might even be watching. These were the thoughts that filled my mind as I sat, staring out the window of the band bus. I prayed, I wished on planets, I placed a lucky penny in my boot, and something must have worked, because fifteen minutes before the parade started, the rain stopped and the clouds parted to reveal patches of blue in the western sky.

Dressed only in a short white skirt and satin tights, I was half-frozen by the time I blew the whistle for the band to start. The metal whistle stuck to my lips, my toes were so numb that I couldn't feel the lucky penny in my boot, and my fingers grew so stiff I had trouble gripping my baton. To make matters worse, whoever assigned parade positions had made a terrible mistake and placed the Brenham High School Band behind the Salt Grass Trail Riders and their horses.

Dodging half-frozen water puddles was nothing compared to navigating a path through piles of loose horse droppings. A couple of blocks down the parade route, the pavement was so coated that I was convinced every horse on the Salt Grass Trail Ride had developed a major case of diarrhea between Brenham and Houston. My white skirt and satin tights were covered with yellow splatters, and the soles of my white boots grew slicker with each step. Long before the band reached the reviewing stand, band members gave up marching in straight lines, and majorettes ceased kicking their legs in unison and tilting their heads at exactly the same angle.

As for me, performing my prancing routine on slippery concrete was next to impossible. Just remaining in an upright position on a street that resembled a giant Slip-N-Slide required total concentration.

The gap between the band and the trail riders grew wider and wider. Not once did any of them turn around to look behind them. They were too busy smiling and waving at the crowd to be aware of the havoc their horses were causing. By the time the band reached the end of the parade, most of the cowboys had loaded their horses into trailers and headed for the matinee performance of the rodeo.

The Saturday matinee performance was sold out, but the ushers took the bands, the horseback riders, and everyone else who had marched in the parade to reserved seats on the west end of the arena behind the starting gates. The seats wouldn't have been all that bad, if you didn't mind looking at the rear ends of horses, but I had seen enough horses' rear ends for one day. I collapsed into a plastic seat and closed my eyes.

When I opened my eyes and saw that I was seated in semi-darkness surrounded by people wearing cowboy boots, leather western wear, and wide brimmed hats, I thought, for a moment, that I was back in the front row of the Rex Theater. Then two spotlights swirled around the arena and came to rest on two horseback riders seated on white stallions. Dressed in white boots, white jeans, red satin shirts, and white Stetsons, the cowgirls looked better than the celluloid cowgirls in the Saturday morning serials as they carried the United States and Texas flags into the arena. They galloped their horses around in a circle, manes brushed, coats glistening, tails braided with red ribbon. People stood up, folded their plastic seats, and applauded as riders, stallions, flags, ribbons, and spotlights came together in the center of the arena.

As I stood up to sing the "Star Spangled Banner," I was overcome with the unfairness of the situation. What had these cowgirls done to deserve applause?. What was so great about riding a white stallion around a warm dry rodeo arena? So what if their boots were polished? So what if their white jeans were spotless? Why did they deserve to have their moment in the spotlight when I had been denied mine?

All my life I'd done what I was told I was suppose to do. I'd shared my toys, said my prayers, obeyed my parents, and practiced my music lessons. I didn't drink, smoke, attend honky tonks, or sleep with cowboys. Yet there I stood in semi-darkness in the worst section at the rodeo, my clothes covered with yellow splatters, and me smelling like a septic tank, while the daughter of the wealthy H&H rancher, the one I was almost certain had slept with my junior rodeo bullrider, was seated on a white stallion in the center of the spotlight with half of the people in Houston applauding.

I had come to a moment of truth. What I had been told all my life was a lie. I could not be whatever I wanted to be. I wanted to be a Western star, a rodeo queen, or at the very least a champion barrel racer. More than anything at that moment, I wanted to be seated on a white stallion at the center of the arena with the spotlight shining on me. Without a horse, those things were never going to happen.

The moment passed. The cowgirls and stallions exited the arena. The spotlight shifted, and I slumped back into my plastic seat. Lost in self-pity, I was only vaguely aware of the rodeo events that took place in the arena that afternoon. The calf roping, the bucking broncos, the bullriding event melded together. I was in no mood to laugh at clowns with their painted faces, and I certainly had no interest in watching the daughter of the H&H Ranch win a first place ribbon in the barrel racing event. Several times I stood up, folded my plastic seat, and prepared to leave the arena, only to sit back down again. One of my favorite silver screen cowboy was to make an appearance, and despite my depression, I didn't want to miss him.

No sooner did the announcer say his name than I was on my feet, applauding and cheering. Because of what happened next, even now after all these years, I can't bring myself to say the names of the cowboy and horse who rode into the spotlight at that moment. They were magnificent. The horse had a mane like silk and a chocolate colored coat that shone like satin, a white blaze on his nose and four perfectly matched socks. The cowboy wore a silver Stetson, a blue bandanna around his neck, and a silver guitar strapped to one shoulder, and the rhinestones on his satin shirt flashed like a thousand tiny mirrors.

My childhood hero lifted his hat high above his head and held onto the saddle horn, as together horse and rider circled the arena. The more the cowboy smiled and waved, the louder the crowd applauded. Then the horse reared up on its hind legs, the way the good guys' horses reared up in the Western serials before they took off after the bad guys, and for a moment my hero and his horse looked exactly like the image on my brother's flannel pajamas.

The image was spectacular, the moment glorious. And just as quickly as the image appeared, the moment was over. My hero tilted sideways, lost his grip on the saddle horn, and hung suspended at an angle, not able to pull himself up, not able to dismount. He hung for what seemed an eternity, before he tumbled to the floor and lay flat on his back in sawdust and horse droppings.

The spotlight shifted to the antics of clowns at the far end, but I couldn't take my eyes from the center of the arena. I didn't want to look, but I couldn't keep from it. The cowboy pushed himself up from the ground, staggered, and fell again. A clown with fake hair and a red plastic nose helped the Western star to his feet and dusted the seat of his pants. The clown placed the silver Stetson on the cowboy star's head, lifted his arm and waved it at the crowd. The crowd roared with laughter.

Slowly, the cowboy placed the toe of his boot in the stirrup and pulled himself halfway into the saddle. Once more the spotlight shifted to the center of the arena. Once again my hero toppled from his horse. This time he landed face down. The stallion stood beside its fallen master, nuzzling his ribs, pawing the ground, swishing its tail from side to side. Two clowns in a covered wagon rode in from the west end, hoisted my hero into the wagon, and drove him from the arena, the cowboy's bowed legs dangling from the back.

Once again the spotlight shifted to the clown with the red plastic nose as he picked up the silver Stetson and placed it on his own head. With an exaggerated wave to the crowd, he placed the toe of his oversized boot into the stirrup and hoisted himself into my hero's saddle, facing backwards. The clown meant to be funny, but the image was grotesque, and all around the arena, people fell silent.

In that moment, I experienced a second epiphany. My favorite Western star was not a hero. He was no more a real hero than the plastic cowboys in the shoe box on the top shelf of my closet were real cowboys. None of the celluloid cowboys were who they pretended to be, not Tom Mix, or Tex Ritter or Monte Hale or Hoot Gibson or Lash LaRue or the Cisco Kid or Red Ryder or Rocky Lane or Whip Wilson or Hopalong Cassidy. Not even Roy Rogers. Take away their hats and six shooters, take away the horses, and they were ordinary middle-aged men with ordinary names like Alfred, Edmund, Woodward, Harold, Clayton, Leo, Lennard, Maurice, Guy, Franklin, Duncan, and Donald.

The clown with the plastic nose lifted the silver Stetson in a final salute before he rode out of the arena, and for some reason that I cannot explain, I raised my hand. I stood, hand in the air, and watched as horse and rider disappeared into the darkness and the rodeo gate swung shut behind them.

When I got home, I took the shoe box filled with plastic cowboys from the shelf of my closet and gave them to my little brother. Then I removed the autographed pictures of western stars from my bedroom walls and helped him thumbtack them to his. Later that spring, my father painted my bedroom a soft pastel color, and I used the money I had saved to buy a horse to purchase a white wicker desk and a typewriter to take to college.

Along with the plastic cowboys and autographed pictures of celluloid stars, I gave up my Western dreams and accepted reality. I was never going to be Junior Rodeo Queen or a champion barrel racer or a Western movie star, riding the range alongside Roy Rogers. What I'd been told about holding onto dreams wasn't true either. Some dreams are as useless as plastic cowboys without horses. ✯

ADVICE

by Cindy Bonner

It's funny how a thing as simple as moving those safety rubbers out from underneath the bed and Papa's eyes, can change your life. I'd stashed them high up in the kitchen cupboard, hidden behind a sack of buckwheat flour, but I forgot to move the safeties down and back under the bed after Papa left. And when Gil came the next Monday, things got too carried away and too heated before I remembered. Neither one of us wanted to leave each other long enough to go all the way across the dining room and into the kitchen to reach high into that cupboard. We just got careless and a little lazy. And we kept on being careless for another three nights before I finally pulled a chair over and climbed up to fetch the box down. By then, though, Gil was spoiled to going without, and he didn't want to use them anymore.

I knew how easy it was for me to get pregnant. It never had taken much more than a wink and a whistle and a handshake, and Gil and me were sure enough doing more than that. It was unholy the fierce desire we both had, and it wouldn't go away, wouldn't calm and get less. It just seemed to grow bigger and stronger, like we had all that lost time without each other to make up for.

Him and Abigail had been fussing more and more, so that he came to me tense and fidgety; and it seemed to take me longer and longer just to ease him down. He'd started talking, again, about leaving her, about snatching Martin, and us running off to France. But that type of talk just scared me because I was content with things how they were. I was learning new vocabulary words, how to keep a ledger, Gregg shorthand, and filing by the alphabet—things I'd never dreamed I could ever learn. And I treasured my little house on the hill, and I adored Austin, too, looking down on the capitol dome and the tower lights at night. Nina was as happy as a little pup, getting big and smart and learning to talk. I didn't want anything to change. But I let Gil go on a few more times without using those safeties, and in my heart I knew it was already too late for things to stay the same.

On the ninth of August, my time of the month came and went. My breasts swelled up and stayed swollen. My belly bloated, my feet puffed out. I got crampy like the blood was fixing to flow, but then it didn't. That whole week, I couldn't concentrate on anything. During classes I sat with my mind wandering out the window. At night I tried to study what I'd missed daydreaming. Every time I went to the bathroom I watched for blood, longed for it. By the twentieth, the puking started, every morning first thing out of bed. I hadn't been so sick since Isabel, and I knew, I knew it without a doubt: I had Gil's baby growing inside me.

I'd heard all the stories about children born to parents too close kin. Babies with twenty fingers and their organs growing on the outside. We'd had a woman in McDade—old Mrs. Previne—who'd been raped as a girl by her own brother. The brother killed himself afterwards, or so the story went, hung a rope around his own neck and threw it up over the barn rafters. But the child conceived of that rape, old Lucien, had been the town idiot as far back as I could remember. Everybody liked him, but not enough to tend to him once his mama passed on. He got sent off to a home for simpletons somewhere down around Wharton.

Cousins weren't the same thing as brother and sister, though. I had DeLony blood to dilute whatever Lange was in me, and Gil had Dailey. Lots and lots of Dailey. He'd always favored Uncle Nolan's side much more than he ever did Aunt Prudie, or Mama. Anyway, I wasn't ready to face what all it meant, me being pregnant by Gil, him a married man and me married, too, not to mention, my first cousin. Once the wonder of it set in—the certainty and the glory of a baby made from my heart, Gil's baby, a child created in true love—I couldn't ponder much on the consequences.

In my mind, I practiced breaking the news to Gil. I tried to imagine every reaction he might have, both good and bad. But once he'd get to Austin again, driving up in that new Templar roadster, smiling happy, whistling "Wait Til The Sun Shines, Nelly," I couldn't bring myself to say the words. And I didn't want anything to spoil my secret joy. Nothing could taint it so long as nobody else knew but me.

The weather turned bad, hot and wet, a storm from out in the Gulf. His leg wound deviled him. He had bad headaches, still, from the mustard gas, dreams that kept him awake nights, remnants of the war. In September, he caught a slow fever that left him with a little cough he couldn't shake. He couldn't make it to me that week. On Sunday he put a telephone call through to tell me he'd been shut up for twelve days with Abigail and Martin, and that she wasn't happy to have him at home and underfoot. Martin was teething and fretful, so Gil couldn't get any rest. He needed me. He missed me. He whispered it to me over the telephone line. I wondered who else up and down his line might've been listening to the words he said. My end was private, but he had a ten-party line, and he was usually more cautious when he called.

The next time he came to me, he looked gaunt and glassy-eyed. I drew him a bath, boiled water on the wood stove to make the bath hotter. I washed his back. I made a pie for him—Mama's buttermilk pie—and I fed it to him with my fingers. I wore the lacy slip he'd bought for me in France—Valenciennes lace. I sat in his lap to pamper him, rubbed the base of his neck. My breasts were ripe, popping out from under that lace, and I expected him to notice, to say something about their size, or about how my waist was thickening up. I expected him to recognize it when I woke up too queasy for breakfast or even coffee, but he didn't. And I couldn't find a way to broach the subject, either.

That Friday, he didn't want to leave. He lingered in the bedroom, watching me get ready for school. I was having trouble finding something to wear. Everything strained at the seams. He came up behind me and linked his arms around me. He said, "I feel so easy here with you, Sunny. Don't make me go."

I looked at our reflection in the mirror. We didn't look like cousins. We didn't look like we were any kin at all. His hand wandered down over my belly, the little mound that was already there. No revelation came to his face, though, and I wondered how he could not know.

I reached back to pat my hand on his cheek. "Maybe you can come back sooner," I said. "You can tell Abby you got behind on your work, and now, you've got to get caught up, again."

He pressed a kiss underneath my ear. "Maybe I won't listen to you anymore. Maybe I'll just go back and tell her it's over with us, and bring all my stuff here for good. Huh?" He kissed my neck again, harder, digging in, trying to tickle me with his morning whiskers. "What would you say to that, huh? If I just did it without telling you."

I squinched my neck tight, because he *was* tickling me, and I turned around to face him. I opened my mouth to tell him I didn't care anymore, that if he wanted to leave Abigail it was all right with me, that the only thing that mattered was our love for each other, and it didn't make me one bit of difference if we couldn't ever get married legal the way other folks could. Some laws were just higher than manmade laws, and love like ours was one perfect example, so far as I was concerned. And I wanted to tell him, finally, about the baby—our baby I was growing inside my body—but all those words got stuck in my throat somehow, and I couldn't shake them loose no matter how hard I tried. I just stood there giggling like a little girl over his whiskers on my neck, and over how happy I was feeling just then.

Nina hollered from the other room, "*M'ere! Dattagu! M'ere!*" She wanted him to come help her with the new shoes he'd bought her—new shiny patent leather T-straps too fancy just to wear to the babysitter's. But he went in there to do up the buckles for her, and another chance for me to break my news to him passed.

Saturday morning, the telephone rang, and my first thought was that it must surely be Gil, calling to say it had all dawned on him finally; that he had recognized the tight mound of my belly; and that he realized I was having morning sickness. I was so certain it was him calling—for who else could it be?—that after the operator connected us, I answered in a silly, singsong voice, "This is heaven, which angel did you want?" expecting his laugh to come to my ear. Instead, there was nothing but silence. And so I said, more serious, slow and questioning, "Hello?"

"Sunny. . .?" came a voice. "Is that you?"

I started to tremble. "Yes?" Crackling popped over the line.

In the other room, Nina was trying to sing the little French song Gil had been teaching her— "Frera jocka, frera jocka. . . ."

"Your aunt told me how to reach you," the voice in the telephone said. "She told me you're living in Austin . . . Sunny?"

"I'm here," I said, my voice a raspy whisper.

"You must be feeling much better," his voice said, the voice I recognized, even despite all the crackling and popping of the long distance connection . . . Ira's voice . . . my husband.

"I am feeling better. Thank you." I sat down at the desk, or more, my knees gave out, so I plopped down. I put the telephone set in front of me, fiddled with the wire. "I wrote you a letter." I cleared my throat. "You didn't get it?" Of course, he didn't, since I never had mailed it. I'd even forgotten all about it, with everything else that had been on my mind lately. I thought about it then, tucked neat inside my purse.

"No . . . no, I didn't get a letter," he said.

A silence came, engulfed us. Then the popping; louder. Nina's little voice, off-tune, floated through her open doorway.

"It surprises me to hear you're in Austin," Ira said.

I swallowed, and nearly strangled myself. "I'm going to a business college. Learning to typewrite."

"That's what your aunt told me."

Aunt Dellie. It had to be. She was the only one Ira would've known to contact, and she was the only one who would've been polite enough to answer his questions. She wouldn't have known I didn't want him to find me, that I'd been hiding from him all these months, pretending to be sick, heartsore from losing another baby. It gave me chills to hear his voice.

"You had a long talk with her?" I said.

"Not so long. She told me how to reach you. I was curious as to how you're faring. And I wanted to ask after Nina."

"She's fine. We're both of us fine. Ira . . ." My armpits were sweating, and underneath my breasts was wet. I felt woozy ". . . you can quit sending money to us."

Another silence came, a longer one. Finally, he said, "When are you coming *home?*" like home was what he had to offer me, or had ever given me. "I think it's time. You've had a long enough rest."

"I just told you, I'm going to business college. I already paid for a whole term."

The crackling got so loud it hurt my ear. I changed to the other one. I heard him say, "We're losing our connection."

"I said"—I shouted, straining towards the mouth horn—"don't send any more money! We don't need it! We don't want it! We're getting along just fine!"

"I'll send you enough for train fare," he said, and then the noise got terrible, like the crystal radio set at Mr. Harvey's store. I couldn't make out anything. No voices. Nothing but electrical static.

"I can't hear you!" I hollered. "Can you hear me! I said, don't send money! Don't send train fare! I've left you, Ira! Do you hear?! I'm not coming back up there! I'm not coming back to you! Do you . . ." I stood up, taking the phone set with me, pressing the ear piece tighter, listening, a little out of control. I sounded like my vocal cords might snap in two. "Can you hear me?! Ira?!"

Nina peered around the edge of her door, her eyes big, like she thought I might be yelling at her. I set down the telephone, tapped the lever a couple of times, but it was no use: The connection was gone. I hung the ear piece on its hook, and set the phone back down on the desk. I stared at it. Nina crept on out into the dining room, still careful, still watching me.

"Get your shoes." I'd gone almost panicky. She blinked at me. "You want to go bye-bye? Get your shoes. Let's go bye-bye."

She ran back to her room, and I ran into mine. I started throwing things into a bundle on the bed. I wasn't staying here. He might call back, and I didn't want to talk to him again if he did. I couldn't. I didn't want to see him again, or talk to him—ever. My hands rummaged through the drawers for clothes—the first things I touched. I wasn't going back up there to North Texas. No matter what, I wasn't going back to that. The whole long year and a half I'd spent miserable up there came to me in one big, sickening memory. I didn't love him. I'd never loved him. And the baby we'd lost still hovered around me like a ghost.

"Get your shoes, Nina!" I called out. She was taking too long. "Get the ones from Daddy Gil! We're going to go see Grandpa."

The choking fumes and hot air from the open windows on the train made me puke. I had to go to the water closet and let Nina just stand there watching as I did my business onto the tracks running by underneath us. It probably upset her to see such a thing, her mama sick and gagging, but I couldn't help it. And I didn't have a choice either: I couldn't leave her by herself untended. Once we were back to our seat, though, the noise and the motion of the train seemed to lull her, even while it was flushing over me in waves. She got me sweaty, laying against me, but she slept most of the way, and I was grateful for the quiet time, at least.

Nobody was at the McDade station to meet us since nobody knew we were due. I wasn't wearing the right shoes for walking the mile and a half out to the farm. Nina was cranky by then, so I had to carry her part way, along with the draw-sack of clothes I'd brought us. I thought about the baby in my belly while I was straining under Nina's weight. I tried not to consider the trouble Ira could make for me if he found out I was pregnant with another man's child, but it was almost all that was on my mind, walking that distance out to the farm. It was fiery hot, humid. Sometimes September will be the hottest month of a Texas summer. The sun made me feel weaker than I already was.

When we got to the farm, Blank came running out to greet us, prancing around in our way, excited over company, his black tail waving like a fancy flag behind him. Two of the laying hens were sitting on the porch steps. Blank ran at them, chasing them off, but he wasn't really trying to catch them. Papa would have got rid of him by now already if he'd been a chicken-killing dog.

Nobody was at home. I called out and got no answer. I walked around to the side yard, but still no answer. I went inside the house, and made Nina get down from my arms. She fretted about it for a minute, but then she spotted something in Ding's room that took her attention. I wilted down on Papa's easy chair, caught my breath. I could smell the Wildroot hair oil on the dishrag draped across the chair back, and it was comforting to me. Even the juice can on the floor where he spit his tobacco seemed comforting just then. I didn't mean to doze off but I must have, because the next thing I knew, Nina was patting me on the face. She had a piece of school chalk she'd been scribbling with, all over the wood floor in Ding's bedroom.

I started to give her a whipping for it. But I never had done that before, and I couldn't bring myself to now, either, even though I was nearly to the end of my tether, what with the baby I hadn't told Gil about, with Ira calling out of the blue after all this time, and with feeling so poor in my guts. My nerves were shot, but I wet a rag and got down to scrub the marks up off the floor. It was just about dark by the time I finished.

When Papa's wagon came rattling up the road, the sky still held a trace of light. He didn't even act like he was surprised, or particularly glad, to see me. But Ding jumped down and came running, gave me a big bear-hug that liked to have knocked me off my feet. I couldn't get over how much he had grown. From nine years to ten he'd sprouted four inches at least, into a rangy, sun-dark kid.

"Been with Dellie all afternoon," Papa said, his mouth set in a firm, grim line.

Ding butted in, "Uncle Danny's heart attacked him."

I said, "Oh no, Papa," and he nodded his head. He put his arm around me, and I didn't know when I'd ever seen him looking so forlorn. Uncle Daniel and Papa had been friends since they were shirt-tail boys.

"He passed on about four hours ago," Papa said, his voice ready to break. "Wasn't nothing anybody could do. Dan hadn't had his health for a while. Ever since he took that fall last winter." I thought I might start crying myself, to hear Papa sounding so sad.

I didn't know what to say. All of the sudden my problems seemed so small and selfish. And I wondered when death was going to stop picking on this family of mine. I didn't understand it, yet, that death was part of living, that our losses shape us into who we are—a thing Mama had wanted me to see, in her quiet way, all that time ago when my first baby, Isabel, had died. All I could think about was the misery and the grief, what

I saw on Papa's face, and what I saw doubled on Aunt Dellie's later, when we went to her house the next morning.

All my cousins were there—Julianne came with her husband and their four-year-old twins, all down from San Antonio, where Sterling was stationed now, training aviators. He had made Major, and he wore his uniform, and somehow he seemed taller than everybody else. He went around with a box camera taking pictures of everything.

Letty looked almost as bad as Aunt Dellie did. And when I went to hug her neck, she whispered in her broken English that she'd lost this last baby, too. Just couldn't seem to get more than a couple of months along with any one of them. Gabriel thought it was on account of the war, her family starving about half the time before they escaped to go live with her Uncle Marcel in Paris.

"The goddamned Kaiser bastards rationed them to three slices of black bread a day," Gabriel told me, in a moment away from everybody else.

I noticed he smoked one ready-roll cigarette after another, and he drank too much—bootleg whiskey that had somehow gotten past the Revenuers at the border. Papa drank some of it, too, and he made Aunt Dellie drink a few cups. She didn't take too much coaxing. She might've even been drunk when she pulled me down to her level, where she sat like a queen in a high-back chair with gold braid and polished wood. I know I could smell the liquor on her breath. She said, "Your husband called here for you." Her eyes were swimming, and glistening, either from the whiskey or from too many tears.

"I know. I talked to him." I patted her arm, and she latched onto my hand.

"Time goes by quick, Sunny," she said. I nodded, and she looked deep into my face. She took hold of my chin. "Value yourself, girl."

And then she did the strangest thing: She reached her hand out and laid her palm flat against my belly, the same way she would have if she'd been checking my forehead for fever. She didn't say anything else, just smiled, a slow, sad smile that seemed to mean so much more. I bent to kiss her on the cheek, and she made a smacking noise back at me. But no matter how hard I tried, I couldn't shrug off her words, or the swollen look in her red eyes.

That night at the farm, I laid in my old bed trying to sleep, and I thought about what she had said. I wondered what she meant by it. I put my hand where hers had rested over the child I had inside of me, the little polliwog nestled in there. Did she somehow know about this baby? Did she sense it? And how could she be thinking of me at all in such a time of grief? Value myself, she'd said. *Value myself?* But hadn't I been doing that already?

I forced my eyes closed and felt the comfort of home around me. I didn't want to think and wonder. Just live and be, that was what I longed for. Live and be. And value these moments in time. The baby in my belly let go of a kick, a long flutter like gas, or butterfly wings. Life . . . value. . . . Bless Aunt Dellie. And bless this child, too. Now I lay me down to sleep. . . . Peace. ❦

THE WOODEN BOX

by Yvette R. Blair

All I could hear was "she's going home to be with the Lawd," and I kept wondering where was that home, and how come I couldn't go, too. I didn't much understand what my big sister Nora was trying to tell me. Something about Mamma was out of pain and didn't have to suffer no more. Mamma had gotten real sick; they said she had cholera. Every night I would hear her in there screamin', "Lawd, no, who's gone look after my Josiah," and then she would turn from side to side and close her eyes. I could barely see what was happening. Nora would stand over Mamma, patting her on the head with a white piece of linen that she would soak into a wash basin that sat by Mamma's bed.

Nora was tall and had big dark hands. She wore a red rag 'round her head, but some of her hair would stick out. She was real mean. I guess that's why she ain't have no men calling on her in the evenings 'for supper. I couldn't do nuthin' without her hollerin' and runnin' after me screaming "Boy git yo' behind outta here."

And now here I was sitting beside her on this old hard bench. I looked around the room and I saw all of Mamma's friends fanning and wiping sweat from they face. Mrs. Harris was one Mamma called her best good friend. That woman made the best pies, and I guess that's why I liked her, too. One time she made a pie all for me on account of I did all my 'rithmetic problems just right. She said it's real important for a boy to know how to count, so when he grows up, won't nobody cheat him out his money.

She was dressed in a black dress that was real tight around the arms. Must have been too tight 'cause the buttons was loose. She had on a black hat with shiny lace and it hung over her face. She waved her hands and shouted Amen just like she did on Sundays at regular church. I 'member I asked Mamma why Mrs. Harris always shouted and passed out sometime. Mamma said it was 'cause she could feel the spirit of the Lord moving in her. I told Mamma I was glad I didn't never feel it, 'cause what if I passed out and couldn't nobody get me back up. Mamma said I was talking foolish and told me to turn around and just be quiet. She always said chirren is s'pose to be seen and not heard.

A whole lot of Mamma's friends was here. Some of them was hugging each other and wiping tears off each other face. I sho' is gone miss Nettie, I heard one of 'em say. I really wun't for sure which one it was 'cause so many of 'em was gathered together. Then I seen our neighbor Ms. Willie Mae Pearl. She screamed and some of Mamma's friends had to carry her out. As they was carrying her out, she reached over and patted Nora on the hand and told her, I knows yo Mamma gon' be looki' down on you and little Josiah. Girl, don't worry 'bout nuthin' for God goon' send his angels of mercy to watch over y'all I wonder what kind of angel God gon' send. I ain't never seen no angel, 'cept for the ones Mamma showed me in the book she call the Good Book and the one that hang in the Sunday school class. That one in the Sunday school sho' do look a lot like our preacher. Only thing is, that angel got wings, and the preacher ain't got no wings.

Well, that day sitting next to Nora I ain't do hardly no talking. It was so hot in there and I felt sweat running all down my back. It made me tingle and I was fidgeting to keep the sweat from settling on my behind. I don't know if it was hot everywhere, but it sho' was hot here in Marshall.

The music started and I was glad. That was really the best part about church. I wanted to play the tambourines like Elam big brother did. The men's who stand in the church and let everybody in walked Mrs. Willie Mae Pearl to her seat. She was shaking her head and stretching her hands up, stretching 'em to who, I don't know. Then she got to her seat and started singing. "One of these old mornin's it won't be long, you might look for me and I'm goin' home to live with my Lord." People got up and started shouting and dancing. See this is what I liked about church. We could dance and stuff. But Mamma said it was different than regular dancing. She said this dancing was for the Lord. Well, I sho' had a thing or two I wanted to show the Lord. But I sat there looking at everybody. One of the old men in the church, Elder Barnes, said the church needed to take up a love offering for Mamma. "Ev'rybody bow you head so we can ask God to bless this here offering. Lord we comes to you right now asking that you will bless this church, this church family, and the money that we is about to take up for our dearly departed Sista Nettie. Lord we just pray and hopes that this money will be used for your glory and for how you see fit for this chirren to have it. All together let the church say Amen."

I felt in my pocket and pulled out a marble. I dropped the marble and let it roll between my shoes. I looked at Nora. She had a big tear drop hanging on her nose and I figured I better tell her 'fore someone say it, and wouldn't no man want her for sure. "Nora, you got something on your nose," I said, pointing it out to her. "Boy," she said with her teeth clinched together, "our Mamma is dead. Dead. Do you understand me? Now shut up and sit still." Did I understand? How could I? I was seven years old and sitting with people who were all crying and screaming "Lawd." I just wanted to see Mamma.

I looked down for my marble, and it had rolled across the room to where the preacher was. He kept right on talking and hitting his fist on that stand in front of him. There wasn't no reason he shouldn't of seen it. It was clear as day and he didn't even see it. The preacher was big and had on a big black thing that looked like a dress. I figured maybe he musta wanted to look like a woman or something. He did have red lips. They was real big. He had hair kinda like a woman, and it looked like he was wearing some of that Madam Wade stuff on it, the same stuff Nora be putting on her hair so her nappy part won't look so bad. But you can still tell it's nappy 'cause all that Madam Wade stuff do is just sit on her head and make it look like the sun is shining on it.

The preacher, Reb. Brown, opened up his Bible and started talking about some man name David. "Yea, though I walk through the shadow of the Valley of Death, I will fear no evil. For Thou, I say, for Thou, come on church, talk with me, for Thou are with me. Amen. That's right, Thou are with me. The Lord tells us that he is with us always. He will never, what church, he will never leave us, nor will he forsake us. Umph! What a mighty God we serve. He is with us even until the end of time. And I come here to tell you today that Nettie might not be with us in body, but she with us in spirit. Church, I wants y'all to know today, that the Lord done prepared a place for Nettie. And you know how I know, 'cause it say so right here in the Bible. He say in my father's house there are many mansions and I go to prepare a place for you. If it were not true I would have told you so. Can I get a Amen." Amen, Reb., preach on, somebody hollered out.

Some fat ladies was singing old spirituals. I counted three, maybe four, because there was a skinny one about Nora's age standing behind the fat lady with the curly hair. All of a sudden the singing stopped and ev'rybody's head was down, and they eyes was closed. I turned around and started looking at the people, but soon as I did, Nora slapped my arm and ordered me to shut my eyes. "Shut my eyes," I thought to myself, "what for?" I put my hand over my eyes and peeped out to see if ev'rybody else had they eyes closed.

The preacher's voice got louder and people started shouting. I said, "Uh. I, I, I said, uh, "Jesus said just believe in me." Ahhh, huh? Uh, uh. "For you will not perish. For I will give you everlasting life. Let the church say Amen."

Nora grabbed hold of me and shouted Mamma, oh Mamma. I managed to squirm away from her and directed my eyes to that wooden box that was at the front by the preacher. Some men, about six of them, had carried it in. I recognized one of 'em. The tall skinny one was called Cleotus. He lived in the same project as us. He looked different than usual. Back at home, he always sat on the stoop with pants and no shirt, eating on a little stick. Standing beside him was Billy Ray. My sister liked him, but he was sweet on somebody else. He had a good job. I heard Nora say it once. She said he would make a good provider 'cause he was real stable. Billy Ray was really tall and had a strong body. He worked down at Mr. Bobby's construction site and always had a musty smell. But that didn't make Nora no mind, she still liked him.

My thinking was interrupted by Mrs. Harris. She got up and started talking about the good times her and Mamma used to have. She talked about how every Sunday she would make a sweet 'tato pie. I got hungry just thinking about it. Nettie was my best friend. Can't find no woman more God-fearing and Christianfied than Sister Nettie. Somebody in the back kept hollerin' out, "Oww, right now, praise the Lawd." You see, I knows just where Nettie is gone, she gone home to be with the Lord. Ev'ry Sunday, I went by after church and ate supper with Nettie and her beautiful chirren, Nora and Josiah. Nettie made the best pork chops and gravy you ever want to eat. And I always brought over a sweet potatoe pie. And she always said to me, now, now, Lillie, girl, you ain't got to bring no pie over just cause you havin' supper with us. You's my friend. You ain't got to bring nothin' over. But I always did.

I tugged Nora on the leg and asked her if we would be going home soon. But Nora didn't hear me. Aunt Lillie had here arms around Nora, rubbing her back, and telling her everything was gonna be all right. I directed my eyes back to that wooden box and tried to see what was in it. I sat on the end of my seat with my hands pressed down on the bench to balance me. I moved my head to get a closer look. IT WAS MAMMA! She was in the box. I wanted to know what Mamma was in that box for? I turned to ask Nora, but she was busy crying in Aunt Lillie's lap. I asked the man who was next to me, and he said Mamma was preparing to go to God. I asked if I could go with her to see God, and he gave me the meanest look. "Boy ain't you got no better sense than asking all them questions?"

I sat back and started fidgeting with the piece of loose thread in my britches. I tugged at it, and the more I did, the longer it got. I was aiming to see how long that thread would get. A few minutes later, I had a bunch of crumpled thread. I looked down at my britches and one was shorter than the other. I knew if Mamma would of looked up out that box, she would of got a switch to my back side. She bought this suit from a big store uptown. She had saved up for two months to get it. It came from Busby's store and it musta costed her a lot of money 'cause she said don't never get it dirty on account of how long it took her to get it. I guess she liked it a whole lot too 'cause I wore it every Sunday to church, including today.

By now people started getting up and they walked up to where Mamma was in that wooden box. They walked around it. Many of 'em said good-bye, Nettie. You is in good hands now. Others wiped tears from they eyes. One woman even reached down and kissed Mamma. All them people, and not once did Mamma move or say nothing. She just laid there. Still. They was acting like they wun't gonna see Mamma no more. When everybody got through looking and crying over Mamma, the preacher said it was time for the family to come look. A bright skinned woman sitting behind me, put her hand on my shoulder and whispered: "Be strong. You not a little boy no more. You a man."

Me, Nora, Aunt Lillie and some more of Mamma's kinfolk was next. Aunt Lillie grabbed my hand in her big hand. It was wet with tears, some of them hers, the rest Nora's. Together we walked up to the box. Somebody had put the prettiest smelling flowers I had ever seen on Mamma's box. Inside the box where Mamma was, was a white sheet. And right underneath her head was a small white pillow.

I looked at Mamma. Her eyes was closed, but she was smiling. Maybe she was thinking of something that made her happy, like sweet 'tato pies on Sundays. Or maybe she was thinking about the time I brought home a nickel that I found. Or maybe she was happy because she was getting to see God. Every night she used to read from the Good Book about a man who took a bunch of animals on a big boat. I laughed. And she would look me straight in the eyes and say "Josiah, that's the Lord's work. It ain't nothing to laugh at."

Whatever the reason was, she was smiling. It was good not to see her in pain. Her arms were folded on top of her chest and she held a little silver cross clutched in her hands. Her face looked funny. She had powder on it, just like on those fancy donuts. I reached out to touch her hair, and Aunt Lillie pulled my hand back. Nora leaned over and touched Mamma's hand, and nobody told her to quit. I guess Nora was so mean that they were scared to tell her no. I just stood there stiff and watched as tears rolled down Nora's face. And they rolled Mamma away in that wooden box. ✿

WOODCOCK—PROPER INTRODUCTION

by Steven Tye Culbert

(Set around a Victorian mansion on the Gulf Coast of Texas, The Woodcock Summer, the novel from which *"Woodcock— Proper Introduction"* is excerpted, celebrates the return in 1972 of young Jules Woodcock, fresh out of prep school in Switzerland, to the ancestral estate he stands to inherit upon the death of his grandmother Iris, a once-insatiable debutante who inhabits the mansion alone, and Jules' love for his first cousin Beatrice "Beanie" Woodcock, an amber-haired pussycat with wildcat propensities.)

Between Tristessa and Esperanza on the Texas Coast, where the Great Plains peter out into the deep green sea, we find a dinky town called Woodcock. Using South Plains slang, it don't amount to a popcorn fart. But it's beautiful in a cruel, private sort of way, with its luxurious past empalmed and oaked in empty buildings where people used to sit and shit, sit and think, sit and eat, sit and work, sit and drink, sit and talk . . . Tradition died when they hauled off the Duchess of York from the Shortgrass Tannery. Cats vanished. On Friday nights sometimes a beer would explode in the Circle C convenience store refrigerator, some of Chet Chesterfield's home brew, you see, but he wasn't there. There was no reason for him to be there after they hauled off the Duchess of York. It was like the final fragment shorn against the ruin of a zombie town, a town like Frankenstein's monster, made of the unhatched hopes of a few hundred drifters at various stages of wealth and personal development. And all these fragments was sewn together into a powerful, lonely, rotten body still beautiful, embalmed in hope. Their hope had little faith. It was trapped in the medium called drifting. Perhaps that makes too little sense, but that doesn't matter. Not to us to whom it does make sense, the nameless types who notice when cats vanish. The smell of seafood rotten in red-hot dumpsters in the sun. That's hard to capture. Woodcock was built on cattle first, then leather, then shrimp, then alcohol. I haven't seen a baby in Woodcock, except the occasional tourist baby, since the summer they hauled off the Duchess of York. Sometimes a road-beat tourist will get lost and wander off the main road to Madre Island, and wind up in Cockroach Lodge for the night, wake up and find his way to the shower and a faceful of rust. That'll sober him up. Teach him to feel his way to the shower in a ghost motel . . . It used to be Shotgun Lodge, and Stud Mingus owned it. That's Big Stud Mingus. He had a son called Little Stud, though his boy was a dead ringer for his father. For Stud. Somehow, if . . . if we stick to facts we won't get lost. But one wonders what they did with the Duchess of York, where the hell they put it, and who for. And if it had anything metaphysically to do with the kids' disappearance and Jules Woodcock coming to town. One wonders all kinds of shit that don't amount to a popcorn fart in one of them old abandoned outhouses back of the unfathomable slave quarters like wooden sighs still checkered around the property scrub-oaked behind the mansion, when the sun goes down on the Fourth of July and you just wanna go back there and take a dump where the slaves used to sit and think and wonder in the drift of hopy faith or dreamy certainty about things metaphysically correlated in the material world. Ever once in a while. Or maybe just once in a while. God, if we could just see a baby not a tourist baby in Woodcock . . . But in fact it's been fifteen years since young Jules Woodcock showed up with his grandmother, Iris Woodcock, to hear a completely uncalled-for wild sermon shouted almost incomprehensibly from the cypress pulpit of St. Theresa-by-the-Sea Noncongregational Church o' the Inscrutable Rapture (once Catholic) down on swampy, romantic Whooping Crane Island where the Big Oak grows. Shit, it was a Mexican Baptist preacher itineratin' around Texas between Persecution Point, Esperanza, and Tristessa, that triangle, and the man was wild, perfect in his role, and inappropriate for the likes of Jules, a quite highly cultivated youth, and his delicate grandma, the stately namesake of our town both before and after they hauled off the Duchess of York from Shortgrass Tannery, which, as

I've hinted, sort of killed everything Woodcock. "That's really Woodcock," they'd say in the towns around. As far as up to Persecution Point and down to Brownsville, once, I've heard it: "That's really Woodcock." And the Woodcock mansion, where Iris lived all her life and Jules had come that summer to visit, stood a yellow block fronted by noble palms a hundred feet high, it seemed, where a cattle baron and his bitch alcoholic wife once lived and bucked under a brown coppery slate mansard roof under pure stars with a million acres of oaky bush sandy worthless land roamed over and trampled by disemballed bulls become steers mooing for all the want they missed after the oyster knife, surrounded by cows right up to the door in the popular Woodcock imagination, and out front about a hundred yards away from the ingenious seashell and limestone marble foundation stood the slate-green shallow sea where an occasional spider monkey'll wash up in the sudsy tide. It happened then. It happens now. The stars. The monkey. The drunk bucking under the shiny mansion roof . . . "That's real Woodcockian," I heard once at the Circle C. Some crazy itinerant shrimper *cum* entrepreneur suckin' a bottle of Wild Irish Rose and lookin' the place over. Not the manse but the Circle C. But Chester wasn't there. Chester's never home. He'll never sell. That's what I told the excruciatingly drunk shrimper dreaming in his new white boots: "Chester'll never sell. He don't want his life's work turned into a fuckin' bait house." Then, for the cruelty, I handed him a clean, dust-free bottle of something dimpled, and he quoted something forgettable from the Bible, and tucked his shirt in— a blue sportshirt thin as kleenex—and he split, waving good-bye in the dim-littered parking lot. Chester had great litter, old as the hills. I won't mention it again intentionally, probably. But it was real Woodcockian. Rubber ants. Cigarettes put to lips afire a year ago, then. Treble hooks lost in dandelion cracks, finally rusting, waiting. Spilled salmon eggs, illegal, far from home. A plug from a flip-flop. A hair net. Too much to name. Too much to name the unimportant lost trash in the Circle C parking lot. Too much period . . . Another rubber ant. Rarely if ever will you see one rubber ant. It's like one cougar, one coyote, one anything. We drift in the hope-like faith there's more than one.

The Duchess of York. 🏵

THE EDUCATION OF MELANIE BEAUFORT

by Judy Alter

Fort Worth, Texas, early Spring 1857

Melanie Beaufort stood at the window in her sister's small house and pulled back the lace curtain so that she could look out on the dirt street. There was precious little to look at. Two other houses were within sight but neither was as nice as the one Ben Thompson had built for his wife, with its board sidings painted a gleaming white—now dulled with dust, but Melanie would never have mentioned that—and a white picket fence enclosing what might someday, with struggle, be a garden. Knowing her sister Sophie as she did, Melanie could not imagine why she had chosen to marry a man who wanted to be a banker in Texas. Every time Sophie looked at the hot, dusty street with no trees lining it, she must think with longing of Linden, their Georgia home, with its towering pines and magnolias and the green lawns that stretched out beyond forever.

Melanie pulled back the lace curtain that covered the front window.

Some six months along in her first pregnancy, Sophie sat in a rocking chair, complacently taking neat, even stitches on a tiny garment. "Anything worth looking at?" she asked idly, her attention riveted on the small garment.

Melanie shrugged. "Two men on horseback. They look . . . well, unkempt, to say the least." She stared at them again. Unkempt they may have been, with long hair spilling out under hats with wide brims and their cotton pants and boots covered with dust, but they were laughing and gesturing as though they were having the time of their lives. Melanie watched them intently and felt a twinge of envy at their freedom. Even here in the wilds of Texas, she was bound by what "a lady" should and should not do.

Sophie rose, a little laboriously, for her new shape was still strange to her, and came to the window. "Farmers," she said. "From the west. Sometimes they come in for . . . well, I guess for some excitement, but they have to come a long way. A hundred miles or more. We don't associate with such people, of course."

Ignoring her sister's last prideful statement, Melanie asked in disbelief, "They ride a hundred miles for excitement?" To herself, she thought she too would ride that far for a little excitement. So far, after three weeks, life with Sophie and Ben had been more than a little dull, and she had promised to stay until the baby was three months old. A long six months stretched before her.

Intent on getting a better look, Melanie pulled the curtain back even further. She was a tall young woman, with reddish-brown hair she parted in the middle and pulled back into a chignon, though tendrils always escaped to frame her face. Her almost severe hairstyle only accented her high cheekbones and large, dark eyes. Her father always said there must have been a Cherokee in the woodpile someplace who had given his dark good looks to Melanie, while Sophie clearly took her rounder, softer blond appearance from their Celtic ancestors.

The riders were by then abreast of the house, still laughing, when suddenly the one nearest the house happened to glance at the window. Seeing Melanie, he tipped his hat in a jaunty gesture and smiled broadly.

The curtain was quickly replaced, but not before his look was burned on Melanie's memory. He was older than she—in his late twenties she judged, and they had been years of hard living. Even at a distance she could see a certain firm set to his chin, a directness to his gaze that bespoke someone beyond callow youth. She couldn't tell for certain since he was ahorseback, but he looked tall—and there was that thick dark blonde hair that hung to his shoulders. For a reason that Melanie Beaufort would not identify, her heart skipped a beat.

"Melanie, what is it?" Sophie asked.

Red rising in her face, Melanie replied, "Nothing. I just find such men . . . such, well, interesting. You know, they're so free to do what they want to do."

With all her fine Georgia breeding rising to the fore, Sophie said preachily, "They're not the kind of men we will ever know, Melanie. Even though we are in the wilderness, we must try to live as we did at home. And that includes the people we associate with."

Melanie was tempted to tell her she was tired of the people they always associated with, and since few of them were in Fort Worth, they'd been associating only with themselves, which was getting boring. But she held her tongue, reluctant to upset the mother-to-be.

"Ben says he'll take us to dinner at Hutchin's tonight," Sophie said without looking up. "It's probably the finest dining room in Fort Worth." Then she giggled, sounding just a bit as she had not too long ago when she'd been but a girl and Melanie had liked her better. "It's the only one decent enough that Ben would take me there."

Fort Worth was then not quite ten years old, a town that began as a military fort for protection of settlements from the Indians. Having never seen any Indian activity, the army soon abandoned the place and left it to civilian squatters. Now, some five years after the army's departure, the city showed signs of growth—a doctor, two lawyers, several saloons, a cotton yard, Steele's Tavern, where ladies could wait in a secluded parlor for the stagecoach which stopped there, the Hutchins Hotel, hardware and mercantile businesses, and, of course, a new bank. Newcomers these days were not squatters but men like Ben Thompson, men of wealth who came from the South and brought their slaves with them. There was even talk of building a courthouse but so far that had not materialized. But the squatters and the farmers and the drovers—those with not enough money to own slaves and drive fine carriages and build new houses—had not been driven out. They mingled easily with their wealthier neighbors in this frontier city.

They even mingled at Hutchin's Hotel. Ben, Sophie and Melanie had only just seated themselves—they chose the table with the cleanest looking cloth on it—when two men dressed in rough clothes entered.

"I tell you, it was Providence," one said to the other. "Meant to be that we came to Fort Worth today."

"If you say so," the second man replied, his voice considerably lower. He was dark-headed, not quite as tall as his companion, but stocky and solidly built. Now he took off his hat and held it nervously in his hands as though uncertain what to do with it. His hair bore the indent where the hat had been sitting all day.

After one quick glance at the men, Melanie quickly turned her full attention to her dining companions who were, unfortunately, totally silent. Then Sophie, too loudly, said the last thing Melanie wanted her to. "Aren't those the two men we saw riding into town today, Mel?"

Before Melanie could shush her, Ben turned his head, then said heartily, "That's Lyle Speaks and Sam November, new clients at the bank." He was instantly out of his chair and across the room.

Ben, Melanie thought somewhat angrily, is a good banker because he flatters his customers. But how, she wondered, had these two men found enough money to deposit in a bank? The next thing she knew, the two men were following Ben back to their table, where the banker made the proper introductions.

The taller, blonde one—the one who had raised his hat to her—was Lyle Speaks. His companion was Sam November. Speaks knew no embarrassment, probably never would in his life. "Ma'am," he said, "I saw you at the window today. You, well, for just a minute there, you reminded me of someone, someone very special."

Was she imagining it or were there tears forming in the eyes of both men?

"I guess, then," she said haltingly, "that it is a good comparison."

"Yes, ma'am, it is, a very good one," Speaks said, his voice cracking. And then, recovering himself, "Well, we won't interrupt your dinner. Just wanted to say hello. Thompson, we'll be in to sign those papers tomorrow."

Melanie felt disappointment—and a thousand questions—as the two men turned away. She kept her attention focused on her dinner the entire evening, never—well, almost never—looking their direction, though the roast beef tasted greasy to her and the potatoes were burnt.

The two men stayed buried in deep conversation, even while they ate. Melanie did sneak enough of a look to see that their table manners were pretty good, somewhat to her surprise. She also noticed that they drank more than a little whiskey with their dinner. When Ben announced that it was time to "get poor little Sophie some rest" and they rose to go, a cheery "Good night, folks!" followed them out of the dining room. She knew it came from Lyle Speaks, and on a bold impulse, she turned just enough to send him a smiling thank-you.

"Sam," Speaks said, "I'm gonna' get to know that woman. I may marry her."

November laughed aloud. "Lyle, you get crazier ideas than anybody I ever saw. We come to town to sell our farms, and you decide to get married. You do that and we can't go to bounty hunting for that sheriff, like we discussed today."

"I ain't saying I'm for sure getting married. I'm just saying she . . . well, she attracts me more than any woman I've ever seen."

"Most of the women you've known have been whores," November said. "This one's a lady, a real southern lady. You wouldn't know how to treat her."

Speaks sobered and his voice softened, "Mama was a lady, and she insisted we learn our manners and learn how to treat women. And Beth, she was fixin' to be a lady." Suddenly his voice got a hard edge to it. "But I don't want to talk about them."

"Man," his friend said, "someday we're gonna' have to talk about them, or they'll haunt us till we die."

"They'll do that anyway." And Speaks left his companion behind.

It had been twelve years since Lyle Speaks found his family massacred. Since then, November, who'd planned to marry his sister Beth, had become his partner and constant companion. They'd farmed, they'd wandered West Texas looking for Comanche to kill in vengeance—and killed a few, they'd even served under General Samuel Curtis Ryan in the Mexican-American War, but none of it had brought them peace. During the day, they laughed and rode and fought and carried on with the best of them, but at night both men were haunted by memories—Pa and Mama and Caleb with their scalps gone and the cabin in flames, and especially Beth, brutally treated before she was murdered on the road. Jeffrey, the youngest, whom Lyle had managed to rescue, had been sent to Tennessee for relatives to raise. It was more than Speaks could do to shoulder the responsibility of a growing brother even while he tried to work his own way out of despair.

☆ ☆ ☆

"Melanie, where are you going?" Sophie's voice had a whiny tone to it.

"For a walk," Melanie said. "I'm feeling cooped up." She tied her bonnet under her chin and picked up her parasol.

"It's . . . it's not proper for a young woman to walk unescorted," Sophie said.

"Oh, bother, Sophie. We're not in Georgia. We're in Texas, and it's all different here."

"Well," Sophie moaned, "it shouldn't be. You wait, someday it will be just like Georgia."

Melanie resisted an urge to say "Heaven help us!" She also managed not to slam the door as she left. She was soon aware that Sophie's words were not idle. The rutted dirt street was almost empty but the few people she saw were men. Were there no women in this town? She decided to simply walk the length of the street to the bluff where one could look out over the Texas prairie forever. Then she would turn back, having had her fresh air, dusty as it was. But the going was not easy: she had to pick her way over ruts, dodge wagons careening down the street, even watch out for stray dogs.

When she reached the bluff, she stood for a long time, staring out at the plains, wondering that she found herself in such a strange place. But the view intrigued her, and she felt a longing to ride out on that lonesome land. It was April, and the prairie was covered with wildflowers so that from the distance it looked like a yellow carpet spread over the brown land. She had never seen anything like it.

"Ma'am? Are you all right?"

The voice startled her, and she whirled to find herself staring at Lyle Speaks who stood with his hat in his hand.

"I . . . I'm just admiring the view. Those flowers. . . ."

"You shouldn't be walking alone," he said. "No telling, with all these ruffians in town, what could happen to a fine lady like yourself." His eyes stared directly into hers, and she felt something deep inside her jump. She didn't know if it was alarm or pleasure or embarrassment, but she sincerely hoped her face was not turning red.

"Thank you, Mr. Speaks. I'm sure I'm fine."

"Well," he said, holding out his arm, "I'm not so sure, and I'm going to escort you wherever you're going."

Slowly, she took his arm. "Home, I guess," she said.

And so, her hand linked in his arm, they paraded the length of what was then Fort Worth. He told her, unbidden, some about himself—though he never told her about the massacre of his family. "We came to town to sell our farms. Didn't know what we were going to do, but farming wasn't it any more. Just happened the sheriff was looking for bounty hunters. Now that we can do—tracking men down."

"Why would you track men down?" she asked innocently. Bounty hunters were not something she knew in Georgia.

"'Cause they done—uh, have done wrong and need to be apprehended," he said righteously. "And we'll get paid for bringing them in."

The idea appalled her, she turned to stare at him. "You'd turn men in for money."

Something along his jawline hardened and his eyes turned dark. "Yes, ma'am, if they've killed somebody, I surely would. Wouldn't hesitate an instant."

"Something bad has happened to you, hasn't it?" she asked, having watched his face change.

Without even thinking, he turned toward her, putting his hand over hers that rested lightly on his arm. "Yes, ma'am, it has. But I don't want to talk about it." His eyes were dark and hard.

They walked the rest of the way in silence, his hand all the time covering hers. She made no move to dislodge it.

At Sophie's house, she thanked him for escorting her safely home, and he made a funny little half-bow. Clearly, he wasn't used to such gestures.

She didn't see him again for two weeks. Oh, she saw him, when she looked through the curtain—she was embarrassed now to pull it aside—

but she did not see him to talk to. For days, just after the noon meal, he would ride by, and he would always look toward the house. But he never stopped. Then there would be a string of three or four days when he didn't appear. After that, he'd be back again. Once he appeared at the Sunday meeting a visiting preacher held in the tiny schoolhouse, but they had no chance to speak.

Melanie had no way of knowing, of course, that when he didn't appear, he and November were off chasing this desperado or that. Nor did she know that November teased him unmercifully. "'Bout time to go for your ride, isn't it?" he'd say as they rose from the table at whatever saloon they'd chosen for their noon meal. Speaks would just grin and reply, "Guess it is."

What Melanie did know was that Sophie disapproved, loudly, of even a mild interest in "that wild man," as she called him. "I don't know why you keep watching out the window for him," she said, fanning herself. "He's not your type, and he knows it. He best not ever stop at this house."

Of course, that was just what he did. Boldly stopped at the house one afternoon when the two ladies sat over a cup of tea.

Sophie answered the door. "My husband is not at home," she said loftily. "I believe you can still find him at the bank."

Hat in hand, he stood tall, straight, and not the least intimidated by her. "I didn't come to see Mr. Thompson," he said. "I came to speak to Miss Beaufort."

Sophie opened her mouth, but Melanie was too quick for her. "Why, Mr. Speaks, do come in." Her heart fluttered a little but she kept her voice steady. "We were just enjoying tea . . . might I offer you a cup?"

Must be a southern habit, he thought. Aloud he said, "No, ma'am, I never was much for tea. If we could talk for a minute. . . ."

"Of course," she said, "Sophie will excuse us."

Sophie made a broad show of picking up her cup and leaving the room, pulling the pocket door almost but not all the way closed behind her. Then she sent Penny, the maidservant, to listen at the door, but as the poor girl reported later to her angry mistress, nothing much was said except that he asked her to ride out on the prairie with him the next day, and Miss Melanie had agreed. Sophie sent Penny for the smelling salts.

"I'm afraid any buggy I could find would be pretty rough," he said apologetically.

"I would much prefer to ride," she said. "Sidesaddle, of course."

He grinned. "I'll see if I can find one of those contraptions. Don't wear your best gown." And he was gone, still grinning.

Next day, he appeared leading a fine chestnut horse with a sidesaddle on its back. Melanie, wearing a muslin morning dress and matching sunbonnet, met him at the door. "Sophie would greet you," she said with a revealing smile, "but she's resting. She's feeling poorly."

He understood perfectly. At the fence, in a most gentlemanly manner, he placed his hands on her waist and hoisted her into the saddle, backing away as soon as he was sure she as safely situated. She hooked her knee over the horn, draped her skirts appropriately, and nodded at him as if to say, "I'm ready."

"I want you to see those flowers," he said, as he turned his horse westward, away from the settlement.

Soon they were by themselves, the town a speck in the distance. The flowers, she discovered, were not all yellow but all kinds of colors—there were deep blues and bright reds, a few delicate pinks, but the biggest and boldest were yellow. "Do they have names?" she asked.

"My mother could have told you," he said with a shrug, "but I can't. Some are Indian names."

At the mention of the word Indian, she looked around in all directions. They were in totally open land, with only here and there a clump of mesquite or black oak, surely not cover in case of an attack. In the distance, she could see a fork of the Trinity River edging toward Fort Worth, but its banks offered no comforting trees. "Is it safe to be out here alone?"

"Indians?" he asked. "There's been no trouble near here since the army came. Indians are to the west." His eyes turned hard, a look she had seen only briefly once before and found frightening both then and now. "Sometimes I wish they'd try," he said. "I . . . I . . . well, never mind." He smiled as if to reassure her and then said, "Only thing to worry about here is outlaws, and I can sure to God take care of them. No, you're safe."

She had known all along that she was.

They rode slowly, talking of nothing of consequence and everything of importance. He asked about her home, and she described Georgia and her family—two brothers and a sister, all younger, still at home. She told him she'd come to help Sophie with the baby and then, as though someone else had her tongue, she confessed that she was growing impatient with her sister's complaints and bored with the narrowness of their lives. "Sometimes," she said, "I just want to ride as far and as fast as I can. Isn't that awful?"

"No," he said, "I've known that feeling a whole lot of late." Then he grinned. "But you can't do it on that saddle," he said.

"Men," she pronounced, "have all the fun just because they can wear pants."

He chuckled. "There's a woman or two 'round here, early settlers they were, that wear pants and ride astride just like a man." He watched for her reaction.

"Why, I'd never!" she gasped. And then, with a slight smile of surprise, "or maybe I would."

Their rides became a regular thing, two or three times a week, except when he was gone. And then he always sent a message to tell her he was leaving town. When they rode, they laughed and were silly in ways that neither could be in town when others were around. Once he took her to a plum thicket and helped her load her apron with the juicy fruit. Then they laughed because they had no way to carry the plums home.

"You put them on the ground," she said, "until I'm mounted, and then I'll make a bowl of my apron again."

"It would be like riding with a lapful of eggs," he said. "One mis-step, and you be purple from head to toe."

She laughed aloud again at the picture that drew up in her mind.

Lyle never talked to her about where he had come from, and she knew intuitively not to ask. But he talked a lot about his plans for the future. "Rich," he said. "I'm gonna' be rich. Gonna' have a big place somewhere—not in West Texas—and live like a king. Gonna raise a family just like mine was, a lot of kids, teach 'em all how to work."

"How are you going to get all this money?" she asked, eyes alight with merriment. If she had noticed the past tense in reference to his family, she chose to ignore it.

He shrugged. "Haven't figured that out yet. If they ever put a bounty on Comanche scalps, I'll do it that way." There was that hard look again, the one that frightened her. "Meantime, I'll wait and see. Too late to go to California for gold." What he didn't know, of course, was that within another ten years, Texas beeves would turn into their own kind of gold and there he would find his fortune. But neither of them had a crystal ball those days on the prairie.

Sam November would have been amazed by the difference between the laughing, relaxed Lyle Speaks who rode out with Melanie Beaufort and the Lyle Speaks who rode with him after outlaws. Chasing a horse thief or a suspected murderer, Speaks was cold, analytical, all business with never a smile or a joke. When he caught his prey, he tended almost toward cruelty, and November sometimes wondered if Speaks didn't take his deep anger at the Comanche out on outlaws. Once, when a sniveling coward of a stagecoach thief tried to sneak away from their campfire in the night, Speaks shot him once, cleanly, through the head. "Got what he asked for," was all Lyle said.

"You think that southern lady is going to marry a bounty hunter?" November asked him one night.

"Not going to be a bounty hunter all my life," he said. "Neither are you. We . . . we're headed for something, Sam. I just haven't figured it out yet."

Sam November was always ready to let his friend do the "figuring." He just followed along. But always, he wondered where revenge on the Comanche would fit in the scheme of things.

One day as Melanie and Lyle were returning from a ride, they met Ben Thompson, coming home after a day's work at the bank.

"Thompson," Speaks said, raising his hat."

"Mr. Speaks," came the reply. "I've been meaning to talk to you.

Melanie, could you leave us for a minute." He made no effort to help her dismount, and Melanie wondered with a hidden giggle if he meant her to leave still ahorseback. That would have scandalized Sophie, if she'd gone off riding alone through town.

Lyle was off his horse in a second, throwing the reins to Thompson, who looked surprised and somewhat indignant at having to hold the other man's horse. But Speaks was already helping Melanie dismount, his hands around her waist, her hands on his shoulders.

Was it Thompson's imagination or did they stay that way just a fraction of a second too long? And did their eyes really meet and lock for just a minute? Before he could be sure, Melanie was thanking "Mr. Speaks" for the ride, and Mr. Speaks was bowing from the waist—a gesture he was getting better at. Then she opened the gate, went up the dirt path and vanished into the house.

"My wife," Thompson began, "is upset."

"I heard she is in the family way," Speaks said.

"No, no, that's not it." He wanted to add that even between men such a subject was not politely brought up, but he refrained. "She is upset at this . . . this relationship between you and her sister."

"I'm finding her company delightful," Speaks said, not at all relieving the other man's anxiety. He considered adding that he intended to marry the girl but thought he'd spare this nervous banker that much.

"It's not proper for her to be riding with you unchaperoned," Thompson said, speaking through his nose as though that gave him authority.

"Well," Speaks said, talking slowly as though to one who might have difficulty understanding, "Mrs. Thompson surely can't ride with us. And I can't see that you'd want to take time from the bank to do it. Now maybe I could ask Sam November. . . ."

"That would hardly solve the problem," Thompson said. "I want you to discontinue the rides and stop calling on my sister-in-law."

Speaks was polite but firm. "I'm afraid I can't do that, banker." With that, he raised his hat again, grabbed the reins of Melanie's horse, mounted his own, and rode off, leaving an indignant banker behind him.

The next time he came for Melanie, she appeared wearing a muslin skirt and white shirtwaist.

"You're a mind-reader," he said as he helped her mount.

"Why?" she asked. "And why do you have a third horse. Is someone else going with us?"

He chuckled. "No, but your brother-in-law thinks that would be a good idea. You'll see what I have in mind."

They rode south this time, where the land dipped into culverts and hidden valleys. At a stream he called the Clear Fork of the Trinity, there were trees and shade from the sun, which was now almost summer-hot. Carefully, Speaks unrolled a bundle from behind his saddle.

He watched her as he spoke. "If I turn my back and stand on the other side of the horses, will you put these on?" He unfurled a pair of pants, sizes too large for her. Then he handed her a length of rope. "For a belt," he said.

She stared at him in disbelief.

"Well," he said, now uncomfortable, "I thought maybe you could ride astride, and then we could race over the prairie like you been wanting to do. If you don't think it's a good idea. . . ."

Without hesitation she went to him and took his face between her hands. "I think it's a wonderful idea," she said. "And the sweetest thing anyone has done for me in . . . I don't know when."

He was tempted—sorely tempted—to kiss her, what with her face just inches from his, but he didn't want to step beyond the boundaries of propriety. He was saved by a stern command from her.

"Get behind that horse, and turn your back," she said. "I'll tell you when I'm ready."

"Yes, ma'am!"

In minutes, she called to him, and he walked around the horse to look at her. At first, it was all he could do to keep from laughing. The pants could have held two of her, and the rope she had knotted through the loops made them pleat so that they were bigger than some of the skirts she wore. The dainty white pleated chemisette she had worn with her skirt looked purely ridiculous on top of the outlandish pants. But, not having a mirror in which to see herself, she looked inordinately proud.

He couldn't help it. He laughed, and then he couldn't stop laughing. And then she, looking down at herself, began to laugh. Finally she had to sit down on the ground, panting. "I . . . I think next time you should bring me a shirt," she said. "And could you find a smaller pair of pants?"

"Those are mine," he managed through gasps. "It never occurred to me but I guess I could go get some pants made for young boys."

"A capital idea!" She stood up, having finally regained control. "What do we do with my clothes? Just leave them here?"

He nodded. "We'll come back to this spot, and you'll have to change again."

"What is some Indian comes along and decides he wants a muslin skirt and petticoats for his wife?" That idea set her to giggling again.

"You'll have to go home looking like that!" he said, and when he imagined the looks on Ben and Sophie's faces, he too was off on hopeless laughter again.

Finally, they sobered. Lyle tied the sidesaddle horse to a small tree by the creek, draped her clothes carefully over a bush, and held a hand for her to mount. She was awkward at first, riding astride, and had to fight the urge to sling her right leg over to the left side of the saddle. But when he slapped her horse's rump with his hat and they took off across the prairie at a gallop, she shouted with delight.

They rode, the world whirling by them in a blur, until Lyle caught the reins of her horse and slowed them both down. "The horses," he said, "they're getting winded."

"Me, too," she panted. "But that was the most wonderful thing I've ever done. You've given me a gift, and I thank you." And then, with a smile, she added, "Besides, the pants are cooler than all those skirts."

He looked at her, uncertain whether to smile or not. Even Lyle Speaks, untutored man of Texas, knew that women didn't ordinarily talk about their skirts with men to whom they were not married. He changed the subject. "We'll walk the horses a bit, and then we can ride back to . . . to, ah, your clothes."

"And hope they're still there," she said mischievously.

The clothes were there, and so was the tethered horse. After a last hard ride across the prairie, Melanie was as winded as the horses, and when Lyle reached to helped her dismount, she fell into his arms. Without Ben Thompson there to watch, they stood that way for a long minute, and then, forgetting his mother's admonitions about the way you treated proper young ladies, Lyle Speaks bent down and kissed Melanie Beaufort. Her lips were cold and still, having never been asked to respond thus before, but then she answered his kiss tentatively . . . and Lyle suspected she might get a lot better at it with practice.

"You best get those clothes on," he said, pulling away. "I'll step over here and turn my back."

When they rode sedately up to the Thompsons' house, Melanie Beaufort knew that something had happened that would change her life forever. She would never again be the same person who had ridden away from this house only hours ago.

But when Lyle Speaks helped her dismount, he held her properly at a distance. And he said, "I have to go away. I maybe gone three weeks or more. I'll be back as soon as I can."

Impishly, she looked up at him. "Will you bring three horses next time?"

He grinned. "I will." And then he was gone.

Bad things, they say, always happen in threes. Melanie Beaufort came to believe it in early August that year. Lyle Speaks left for three weeks or more, that was the first. Then Sophie's long-overdue baby put in an appearance that involved prolonged labor and much gnashing of teeth and screaming on the part of the new mother. And, finally, Melanie received a letter from her own mother.

About Lyle, there was little she could do but worry, and worry she did. He and Sam November were trailing horse thieves to the north, up to what he called "Red River country." She had only the vaguest idea of what that meant, but she was fairly certain it was also Comanche country. The realistic part of her mind knew that what Lyle did was dangerous and that he could just not come back from any of his trips, but that part of her mind also recognized that he was more capable of self-protection than most and that he and Sam November were an unusual and impressive combination. The imaginative side of her mind constantly saw Lyle staked out on the prairie—hadn't she read somewhere that Indians did that?—or hanging from a tree limb because the horse thieves had lynched the bounty hunters, instead of the other way around. Indeed, if Lyle Speaks could have been privy to her wildest imaginings, he wouldn't have known whether to laugh at their extreme nature or to be angry at her apparent lack of confidence in his ability to take care of himself. For Melanie, it would be a long three weeks and she would spend much of it pacing, albeit sometimes with a crying baby in her arms.

The baby was all reality and her presence required no wild imagining, although Melanie suspected that Sophie had suffered through some wild imagining during the long hours she labored to bring the child into the world. It began late one night, when Sophie complained of indigestion. Melanie wanted to suggest that she had eaten a rather large dinner for one in her delicate condition, but she bit her tongue. Within an hour, indigestion had turned into labor pains.

Melanie had honestly tried to prepare for this moment, for she felt that to be of aid was the whole reason she had suffered through a hellish long trip by steamer and stage from Georgia to Texas. She sent Ben for the doctor, hoping he could be found. And she called to Penny.

"Penny, we must get Mrs. Sophie to bed," she said, her voice calm with practicality.

"Lord, Miss Melanie, I don't know nothin' about birthin' babies. When my maw had her babies, she made us young'uns leave the cabin. Sometimes we was gone two days."

Melanie rolled her eyes heavenward, while Sophie continued to moan. "You don't have to know anything, Penny. Just do what I say. First, put her arm over your shoulders and together we'll get her to the bedroom. Are the linens clean?"

"Yes, ma'am, they are."

Getting Sophie to bed proved more difficult than Melanie had anticipated, for she was limp, dead weight. But at last they had her in the bed, dressed in a flannel gown, even though she had wailed for one of her pretty silk gowns.

"I want to look pretty for the baby," she panted between moans.

"Not now, Sophie," Melanie said, realizing she would have to be stern with her sister.

She sent Penny to boil water and bring clean sheets. At home in Georgia when her mother had the younger children Melanie remembered that one of the housemaids had tied ropes to the posters at the foot of the bed and given these to her mother to pull on. Improvising, she pulled the draw-cords from the bedroom drapes, allowing them to hang limp over the windows, and tied them to the rail at the foot of Melanie's iron bedstead.

"Here," she said, "pull on these."

"I haven't the energy," Sophie said, her tone indignant.

"Sophie, you'll have to have the energy or you'll never get that baby out. It won't come by itself. You'll have to do the work." Her voice was deliberately harsh.

"Why are you so mean to me?" Sophie wailed.

By the time Ben returned with the doctor, Melanie was tearing sheets into strips to be used for bandaging or whatever. It seemed to her a logical thing to do, but Ben was indignant.

"Those are good linens!" he cried. "What are you doing?"

"I think you have enough bandages," the doctor said mildly. "Might I have a cup of coffee?"

She sent Penny to brew a pot of coffee— "Be sure to put an eggshell in it to settle the grounds!"—and sent the doctor into the room with Sophie. Ben hovered at the door of the bedroom until Melanie suggested that he go out on the porch and see if the night air didn't offer the slightest breeze.

"And leave Sophie?" He was aghast.

"You won't be far, and I'll get you if you're needed." Melanie could see that this would be a long night.

The first loud, piercing scream came about one in the morning, startling Melanie from the rocker where she'd been dozing. Her dream had been of Lyle on the prairie with a broken leg, his horse having spooked and thrown him, his companion having ridden on. She could hear Lyle saying, "No, don't worry about me. You go after them." She was almost relieved that it was only Sophie screaming in childbirth.

Things went on that way through the night. The doctor left, saying he'd be back at daybreak, and that there was nothing to do but give her sips of water and lots of encouragement. "Urge her to pull on those ropes," he said. "She doesn't seem inclined to help herself."

Melanie spent the night sponging Sophie's forehead and praising her few feeble pulls at the ropes. By daybreak, when the doctor returned, she was more tired than Sophie. The doctor ordered Penny to take her place at the bedside and sent Melanie to sleep, but it was at best a fitful sleep punctuated by Sophie's screams.

By noon, Ben had decided that Sophie was going to die. "It's my fault," he said. "I should never have...." Then he blushed, to think that he was speaking of such intimate matters to an unmarried woman.

Melanie was tempted to put him on the spot by asking, "You should never have what, Ben?" But she didn't. Instead she said, "Nonsense. Most women have this much difficulty with the first baby . . . and they say afterwards, with the baby in her arms, she'll forget all about the pain."

"Not Sophie," Ben muttered.

By suppertime, even Melanie had begun to worry. Sophie was exhausted and nearly crazy with pain. The doctor had come and gone all day, but when he returned in the evening Melanie asked, "Is there nothing you can do?"

"She's almost there, Miss Beaufort," he said. "She has not . . . ah . . . been the most cooperative patient. And. . . ." He hesitated as though not sure he should finish the sentence, but then he plunged boldly on. "Her extra weight does not make this any easier. I can hardly feel the baby."

Sophie, claiming she was eating for two, had put on more pounds than Melanie cared to think about. She had gone from gentle and round to overwhelmingly fat, and Melanie knew their mother would have had a few things to say about that if she'd seen Sophie.

The baby arrived shortly after dark, a squawling, healthy baby girl with a headful of dark hair. Melanie helped to sponge off the baby and then to get Sophie into a clean gown—silk this time, thank you—and fresh linens, while Penny stood cooing at the tiny handful.

"We done it, missy," she said in a singsong voice. "We done brought you into this world hale and hearty."

Melanie wanted to whirl and say, "What do you mean 'we'?"

With mother and child clean and in fresh clothes, Melanie invited Ben in and shooed the doctor and Penny from the room. Ben stayed no more than five minutes before he came rushing from the room, apparently still uncomfortable about the screams he'd heard. His first, indignant words were directed toward Melanie.

"It looks more like your baby than hers. Where'd she get all that dark hair? Sophie's blonde!"

Melanie gave him a withering look. "But not everyone in our family is," she said. "Your daughter is beautiful, and I hope you told her mother that."

"Yes, yes, of course I did." Nervously, he went out the door to pace the veranda again.

They named the baby Emily, after Mrs. Beaufort back in Georgia. The doctor had said that Sophie would need to rest a day or two and then could be up and about as long as she did no heavy housework. Melanie wanted to assure him there was no danger of that! But Sophie seemed to require much more rest—days stretched into weeks, and she was too weak to rise from her bed. Ben hovered over her when he was not at the bank, and Penny labored over energy-building meals—fried chicken, mashed potatoes, stew, all the heavy dishes she'd been taught were good for building the blood. Melanie was left with Emily, a responsibility she delighted in.

Sometimes she'd stand on the veranda, the baby in her arms, and look to the west out over the prairie, as though she'd see Lyle riding in. And she'd imagine him admiring the baby and looking deep into her eyes as though to say he hoped one day they, too, would be the parents of such a beautiful child. But then she'd bring herself up short by remembering that Lyle Speaks was probably not the marrying kind and that the differences between them were as great as a canyon which could not be jumped. And sometimes she'd looked at the contented sleeping baby in her arms and wonder how those two people had ever produced this beautiful, happy child.

"Mean, that's what you are, Melanie Beaufort," she said to herself when those thoughts came unbidden to her mind.

The letter from her mother came the day that Emily was two weeks old, which also happened to be the day that Lyle had been gone three weeks. Melanie knew better than to expect him back punctually on the day he said—his was not work which followed the calendar—but she also knew the longer he was gone, the more she would worry. So she was not in a good frame of mind when she slit open the envelope.

Dear Daughter,

> *We are anxiously awaiting the news of the arrival of our first grand-child. I know that you will be of great help to your sister, and I am grateful to you for undertaking that long journey to be with her. Ben will, of course, be of comfort to her, but it is not the same as having a woman from your own family with you at that hour of need. I am only sorry that I could not be with Sophie, as by rights I should have been, if that husband of hers had not seen fit to take her off to the wilds of Texas.*

"You should be grateful," Melanie thought, "that you are not here. Sophie would have embarrassed you—or driven you wild."

Then the letter got down to brass tacks.

> *Sophie has written us about your 'preoccupation' with a gentleman from Texas. We are given to understand that you are infatuated with a man who is not your social nor educational equal. While I have always had faith in your good judgment, Melanie, I know that you are sometimes given to impetuosity. I expect you to break off this friendship at once and no longer see this man. I am sure there must be suitable men in that place for you to meet. Surely Ben would not have taken Sophie to a total wilderness.*

> *Your father joins me in sending love and wishes me to tell you that he expects you to behave in a way that will do the family credit. By that I mean, of course, no more unchaperoned rides across the prairie with this rough, uncouth Speaks person.*

> *Your loving Mother, E. Beaufort*

Melanie held the letter in shaking hands, uncertain whether to laugh or cry, whether to storm into Sophie's sickroom and accuse her of snitching—and slanting the truth—or ignore it. Knowing that actions taken in haste were often regretted, she slipped the letter into her pocket. But every word was emblazoned on her memory, and she carried those words with her day and night.

Lyle Speaks returned to Fort Worth: corralling a herd of fifty horses and packing three dead men on led horses. He and November had caught the horse thieves herding the animals north to sell to the Comanche. Two thieves died on the spot; the third, halfway back to Fort Worth.

"You want to go in another way, so you don't go by her house?" Sam asked at one point.

"Nope. I ain't putting on any pretenses."

And so Melanie Beaufort saw Lyle Speaks return to town, and all that registered in her mind was that there were three dead men draped across the backs of three horses. She fingered her mother's letter in her pocket.

He sent word that night that he would come for her in the evening, being as the days were so hot now. When he arrived, he had only two horses.

Melanie, carefully dressed in a muslin skirt and the plainest shirt she owned, threw propriety to the winds and met him at the gate. "You only have two horses!" she accused.

He laughed aloud. "I'm glad you missed me too!" Then, more seriously, "I decided it was silly to have three horses for two people. I've got a plan."

She believed him, and they were soon cantering out of sight of the village. As they rode, she told him all about Emily's arrival, and she spared nothing about what she saw as Sophie's weakness.

"You won't be like that?" he asked.

"You bet I won't," she said. "Mama always said doctors and midwives are scornful of women who scream."

He chewed on that thought and liked what he heard from her.

When they reached "their spot" on the Trinity, he handed her pants and a loose shirt and walked around the horses.

Once changed, she demanded "Do I have to ride sidesaddle dressed like this?"

"No, I'm gonna' ride bareback, and you can ride my horse."

She smiled at him and, without even thinking about it, she walked into his arms. He kissed her but gently, and then pushed her away. Lyle Speaks was a man who knew about propriety . . . and understood that if he didn't things could easily get out of hand right here on the prairie.

They rode fast and hard for only a mile or two, and then she pulled her horse to a stop. "I want to sit," she said.

Obligingly, he helped her dismount, ground-reined the horses, and put the saddle blanket from his horse on the ground. "Don't want to sit on ants," he said.

"I've had a letter from my mother," she told him. "She's as much as ordered me to stop seeing you."

"Does she have some kind of second sight?" he asked. "I mean, all the way from Georgia!"

"Sophie wrote her, the snitch!"

He laughed. "I bet Ben Thompson put her up to it. I'd pull my money out of his bank if there was another bank in town."

"I don't know what to do," she said.

His hand reached to cover hers. "Well, you have two choices. You can stop seeing me, or you can keep on riding the prairies with me."

"It's not that simple," she replied, averting her eyes from his. "I saw you come in yesterday. . . ."

"And you know we killed three men." He said it flatly, without looking at her. "I do my job. I'm paid to bring men in dead or alive. I'd rather bring them in alive, but I'm not going to risk my neck—or November's—to save some outlaw. Men who break the law make a deliberate choice—they know the risks. If I didn't go after them, someone else would. And if nobody did, Melanie, we couldn't live in his land."

"But couldn't you . . . " She almost smiled, "couldn't you be a banker or something where you didn't have to kill?"

"Nope. It's not in my nature." He wondered if now was the time to tell her about how he'd lost his family, as though that would in some way explain the anger that almost forced him to do what he did. But Lyle wasn't used to confiding, and he particularly didn't want to talk about that day twelve years ago. Instead, he asked curiously, "Do they ever kill men in Georgia?"

"Not the people I know!" she said indignantly.

"I bet you'd be surprised," he said. "What about whipping slaves? Is it worse to kill an outlaw than to whip an innocent slave?"

She grinned at him. "Why do you presume the slave is innocent? They're people. They do bad things."

"What an admission from a southern girl!" he exclaimed. "Slaves are people. Do I take it that you don't approve of slavery?"

"It's not a question of approving or disapproving," she said slowly. "It's the way life is in Georgia . . . and always will be."

"Then you've not been keeping up with the news," he said. "And I suspect you've not read *Uncle Tom's Cabin.*"

"That awful book," she exclaimed. "I wasn't allowed to read it. Have you read it?"

"No, but I'll get you a copy," he promised. "The North is up at arms about this slavery business, and I'm afraid there's more power up north than in the South. I'm no politician, but I think they'll go to war."

"They? Isn't it your country too?"

"Naw," he laughed. "I'm in Texas. That war won't touch us out here."

"You wouldn't fight?"

"Texas will need to take care of its own problems if war comes. Think about the Indians for instance. If the army pulls its soldiers back east to fight, the Comanche will try to take over this country again."

"And you'd fight the Indians but not the Yankees?"

"Reckon so," he said.

It was a loyalty—or lack of loyalty—that she couldn't and wouldn't understand. To her, the South was home and demanded allegiance. Texas was . . . well, frontier, not a country. How could one be loyal to Texas? She stood up abruptly. "Let's ride." It was almost an order.

She set the pace, riding so hard and fast that Lyle Speaks began to wonder about the wisdom of his bareback ride. But he kept up with her, afraid to let her go farther on her own, and at last, as winded as her horse, she pulled to a stop.

"I feel better now," she said triumphantly.

"I'm glad." He would never have admitted that he felt a lot worse.

They walked their horses back to the spot on the river, talking about nothing serious, avoiding her mother's letter, his killing of the outlaws, even the possibility of war. She told him about the baby and how spoiled Sophie was—"I don't know how she'll manage when I go back."

"Do you want to stay?" he asked.

She shrugged. "I don't know."

Speaks was the first to spot trouble. Melanie's skirt was not hanging on the bush where they'd left it. He looked around to make sure he had the right spot, but it was his business to note signs like bushes and trees, and he had little doubt about which bush was which. Without a word to her, he pushed his horse into a fast trot. The sidesaddle was gone too!

Melanie approached to find him dismounted and doubled over in laughter. "Whatever is the matter with you?" she asked. Her attention was so riveted on him that she hadn't noticed that her clothes were missing.

When he finally straightened up and calmed himself, he said, "I'm picturing you riding into town that way."

"This way? Why?" Only then did she look around. "My clothes! They're gone!"

"So's the blasted sidesaddle, and I bet the livery will charge me a pretty penny for that," he said.

She slid off the horse, took one look at him, and began to laugh herself. Finally, choking, she sputtered, "Sophie! She'll die of embarrassment."

Lyle Speaks knew at that moment that he loved her. Any other woman would have been furious and would have likely turned that fury on him. Furthermore, most women would have thought of their own embarrassment. She didn't seem to give a fig about what people would think of her.

"We can wait till dark to go in," he suggested.

She began to giggle again. "Then Sophie will think we've been killed by Indians, so she'll have two reasons to be angry—because we made her worry and because I'm a disgrace to the family."

Neither one of them knew how it happened, but the next instant she was in his arms, and he was kissing her gently on the forehead, the tip of her nose, and finally on the mouth. His gentle kiss turned to one of real longing and passion, and she responded much more than she had during their one brief kiss before. Wordlessly they sank to the ground, their mouths locked together.

It was Speaks who stood up. "I don't think we'll wait for dark," he said. Over the years, he and November had visited more than once with the soiled doves in various West Texas towns, but he had never known the desire that raced through him now. It frightened him—for himself and for her.

Equally shaken although less understanding of what had happened, she sat on the ground. "You know those two choices you gave me before?"

He nodded.

"I know which one I want."

He drew in his breath and waited.

"I want to keep riding with you."

Exhaling slowly, he said "I'm glad." And almost added, "And I want to marry you." He didn't know what made him afraid to say the words, but he was. It was as though she were a doe that would spook easily. Instead, he said, "Well, damn, I guess I'll just have to find another sidesaddle."

She rode proudly into town, head high, slid off her horse at the fence, and handed him the reins, letting her hand linger in his just a moment. Then, with a wry smile, she headed for the door, calling over her shoulder, "I'll return the pants tomorrow."

The lace curtain moved back into place.

Sophie waited, her hands planted on her hips. In another part of the house, the baby wailed loudly. Before Sophie could attack, Melanie said, "What's the matter with Emily? Why aren't you seeing to her?"

"Don't tell me how to take care of my child, Melanie Beaufort. You're a disgrace to this family."

"I knew you'd say that, and I don't want to hear it," Melanie said crisply. "Nor will I tell you why I happen to be wearing a pair of men's pants." She stormed out of the room, leaving her sister behind babbling to herself. But Melanie thought she heard the words, "Wait till Ben comes home?" and resisted the urge to ask, "Why, will he spank me?"

That night, while Lyle Speaks lay on his bunk, heads behind his bed, eyes fixed vacantly on the ceiling above him, Sam November went to Steele's Tavern. When he came in two hours later, smelling of whiskey, he shook Speaks awake.

"Man, you've done it now," he said, his voice full of laughter. "Everyone's talkin' about how you brought that southern girl home wearing pants. Lyle Speaks, is there something you aren't telling me?"

Speaks sat up. "They're talking about it? Who?" He reached for his boots.

"No, no," November said, "You'll not go defend her honor against a bunch of drunks. And I'm too drunk to help you."

"She's too good for the likes of them to talk about." Then his face reddened. "Besides, it was all very innocent."

"You need to go to Miss Sadie's?" November asked.

Lyle threw a shoe at him.

The next morning, dressed in his newest breeches and a freshly laundered shirt, his hair clean and plastered to his head, Lyle Speaks rode up to the Thompson residence. For once in his life, he wished he owned a suit like the ones Banker Thompson wore to work every day.

Sophie opened the door when he knocked. "You're not welcome here," she said.

He wondered how two sisters could be so different in looks and temperament. Politely, he said, "I came to see Miss Melanie."

"Miss Melanie is busy tending the baby," Sophie hissed.

Melanie disproved her words by appearing behind her. "Mr. Speaks," she said formally. "May I help you?"

"Yes, ma'am, I came to talk with you if I might . . . in private."

"Mr. Thompson has ordered me not to allow you in this house after you disgraced my sister," Sophie said, her voice rising in agitation.

He almost bowed. "Then perhaps we can speak on the veranda. Mrs. Thompson, I have come to make amends for embarrassing your sister. It's the last thing in the world I wanted to do." He hated himself for fawning over this bothersome young woman.

"Fiddle, Sophie! If anyone's embarrassed, it's you. It didn't bother me a bit. Now go see to Emily, and I'll speak to Ly . . . Mr. Speaks." She stepped out on the veranda and pulled the door firmly shut behind her. Then, looking at him, she had to cover her mouth to keep from laughing. "Isn't she foolish?" she asked.

To her surprise, he didn't even smile in response. Instead, looking down at the hat he held in his hands—she noticed his still-wet hair—he said, "I came, Melanie, to ask if you would marry me."

Taken completely by surprise, she learned against the veranda railing for support. Finally, weakly, she muttered, "I don't think that's what Mother had in mind in her letter."

"Do you mean that your family would never give permission for you to marry me . . . or for me to court you?"

"I guess that's what I mean." She wanted to throw herself in his arms, tell him she didn't care about her family, beg him to take her away right then. But she stood rooted to the floor.

"And you need their approval, their permission?" He spoke formally.

"I don't know," she said slowly. "May I have time to think about it?"

"Of course." He too felt the strangeness of their situation. He wanted to hold her, laugh with her as he had done on the prairie. Instead, he stood before her, feeling like a wooden doll. A speechless wooden doll.

He inclined his head just a little—the best he could do towards a bow at the moment—and bid her good-day, ramming his hat on his head as he went toward his horse. Although she stared after him, he never looked back.

"Well," Sophie said when Melanie went inside, "I certainly hope you told him you'd never see him again."

"I think," Melanie said, "that I will probably marry him."

"Marry him!" her sister screeched. "You can't!"

"I can." She wanted to add, "He's a lot better than the fool you married," but she kept that thought to herself.

She sent him a message with the simple word "Yes" and her name. He came, dressed in his finest and still wishing for a suit. They sat in the parlor, like strangers.

"I guess I'll have to go to Georgia," he said.

"Why?" She was appalled at the thought. It conjured up visions she'd rather not contemplate. Mostly visions of her mother, who could be as uppity as Sophie.

"To meet your parents, and ask your father's permission."

"Ah, I didn't think we'd do all that. I thought . . . well, maybe I presumed . . . but couldn't we just get married here?"

"I don't think that would be proper," he said. He was remembering his mother and imagining what she would have said to him. The one thing she never would have said was that this girl was too good for him, and that thought never occurred to Lyle Speaks. She was different, he knew that, but they could overcome differences. He didn't know, as she did, that her parents would find him wanting in education, in social graces, and in future prospects.

"Well," she said, rising impatiently, "I'm not to go until October, and it's only August now." Then she exploded. "Lyle Speaks, I don't want to sit in a parlor and speak formally with you! I want to ride and laugh and be like we've always been. Marriage comes up and look what happens!"

He was startled at first, and then he began to laugh. Standing, he grabbed her hands and whirled her around the room. "Will you be ready to ride tomorrow?"

"Will you have a sidesaddle?"

"Yea," he promised. And wondered why he felt apprehensive.

She wondered why she felt sad.

They rode on the prairie almost every day. Sometimes when they left Sophie stood on the veranda, her arms folded across her chest in a belligerent way, staring stonily at them.

"What's the old saying," Lyle asked, "about if looks could kill?"

"We'd wither like prairie grass in the summer heat," she said.

"You're starting to talk like a Texan," he laughed. "That's good."

"It is?" she said, genuinely puzzled. She never intended to talk like most of the Texans she'd met.

Other times they'd arrive home near dusk to find Ben Thompson sitting on the rocker, pushing it back and forth with one foot, his fingers drumming impatiently on one of the chair's arms. Once he saw them, he'd rise and enter the house without ever having spoken a word to either of them.

They'd become accustomed to their routine. Lyle brought "her" pants—a smaller, boy's pair—and a cotton shirt for her, and he turned his back in a gentlemanly fashion while she changed, though he had to fight back waves of longing that went over him. They never did find out what happened to the stolen clothes and sidesaddle, but now they were simply more careful about hiding things. They had found a plum thicket that did nicely for that purpose.

By late afternoon, now that it was September, the air had cooled some, and sometimes there was enough of a breeze to ruffle Melanie's hair as she rode. They had survived the beating sun and ferocious heat of the Texas summer, but in spite of the bonnet she had worn faithfully her face had tanned. Lyle thought she glowed with a look of health and happiness, and he told her so, in words that made her blush and look away. She thought he looked handsome as always, but she was embarrassed to tell him . . . or didn't know how.

"Next summer," she said, "I want a hat like yours."

"You'll have it," he promised.

Sometimes they rode without talking, letting the horses amble along companionably; other times, they raced across the prairie, chasing each other and shouting like Indians. Well, at least Melanie thought they sounded like wild Indians. Lyle never would have made that comparison.

Other times, they ground reined the horses and sat watching the sky change as the sun went down and light clouds trailed across the sky.

They never talked of serious things like marriage, for they had found the subject turned them both into speechless wooden dolls. Once he felt obliged to tell her about his family. He didn't tell her it was something she had to know if she married him. Instead he just said, in his blunt way, "My family was massacred by Comanches. My mother and father and one brother scalped; my sister . . . well, she was terrorized before she was killed. I saved my littlest brother."

She knew what he meant by "terrorized," and she knew that what he had just told her explained the hard look he sometimes got in his eyes, the look that had puzzled her all along. But it left her speechless. "I'm sorry" seemed empty and trite, though she did lay a hand on his arm and say it.

He shrugged. "I've learned to live with it."

And then she knew he hadn't. She couldn't say "How awful!" nor could she tell him that now she had two visions in her head that would not leave: one of a family she'd never seen, lying scalped in the yard of a house she'd never seen; the other of three dead men across the backs of three horses.

One day as they walked their horses toward home, he said, "In October I'll go east with you. Speak to your father."

"I guess so," she said.

"You don't sound like you put much stock in the idea." He stared straight ahead, as though afraid to look at her. Maybe, if he looked at her eyes, he'd see that she didn't love him.

"I . . . I can't imagine it," she said. "Oh, Lyle, there's so much I can't imagine."

"You don't have to imagine anything," he said. "You just let what's going to happen come."

She shook her head. "I always have it planned out before . . . and I always know if it's going to work or not."

His voice almost broke as he said, "And this isn't going to work?"

"I don't know," she said miserably.

Two days later, she received a letter addressed in her father's bold, scrawling hand.

Dear Daughter,

Your mother is ill. You are needed at home. Please come at once.

Your Father,

William P. Beaufort

When Lyle came for their ride, she tucked the letter in her pocket and went to meet him with her usual smile on her face.

When she had changed in her pants, she came round the horses, grabbed his arm, and reached up to kiss him, a light, teasing kiss.

"What's that for?" he asked, obviously pleased.

"For being you, because I love you," she said. And then, without waiting for his help, she was ahorseback—a trick she'd learned over the summer. "I'll beat you to that far tree!" and she was off, leaving him to leap into the saddle and gallop after her. She beat him, a triumph that set her to laughing.

"You're sure full of yourself today," he said.

"I have to be . . . or I'll cry." She had put the letter in the pants pocket, and now she fished it out and handed it to him.

He read, then looked at her. "You'll go?

"I have to."

"And it's not a good time for me to go with you."

She shook her head to say "no." Then, "I'll come back."

But they both knew at that moment that she would never come back to Texas.

Lyle drove her to the stagecoach. When she walked out of the Thompson house, Sophie followed, wringing her hands. "Poor dear mother, whatever can it be?"

"Serious, if Papa wrote me," Melanie said shortly. "Try to take good care of Emily, Sophie."

"She's my daughter!" was the indignant reply.

To Ben, Melanie said briefly, "Thank you for your hospitality," words so formal that they almost conveyed her distaste. She hugged Sophie quickly and felt a pang over the distance that had come between sisters once close. Then she turned and walked around the wagon, where Lyle waited to help her up. He had already thrown her baggage behind the seat. When they drove away, she never looked back. You see, Melanie Beaufort was wondering if her mother was really sick or if she, herself, had been caught in—or rescued by?—a trap of Sophie's making. She would only know when she got to Tennessee, and she couldn't risk calling Sophie's bluff in case her mother really needed her.

"I'll let you know what's wrong with Mother and when I'm coming back," she said to Lyle, and he replied "I'll be waiting." Then he kissed her lightly on the forehead and handed her into the stagecoach. He drove off in the wagon long before the driver cracked the whip over the horses that pulled the coach.

"Let's go. We're movin' on." Lyle Speaks charged into the room he shared with Sam November.

Caught napping after an afternoon beer or two, November struggled awake. Sitting up and rubbing his eyes groggily, he echoed, "Moving on?"

"That's what I said. I told you we weren't going to be bounty hunters forever."

"What about Melanie?" He asked before he thought, and the minute the words were out he would have done almost anything to take them back.

Speaks' jaw tightened, and his eyes took on that hard look that November knew better even than Melanie did. "Never would work out. We're too different."

"I hope she's not heartbroken," Sam said.

"She's not." Lyle Speaks didn't believe in heartbreak, but this was the second terrible wound to his soul that he would carry the rest of his life.

They rode north at dusk, in spite of Sam's timid suggestion that they wait till morning. Speaks was determined to go then, though he didn't say where.

"Where we goin'?" November asked.

Lyle shrugged, as if to say, "Don't know."

Sam November just sighed and prepared to follow his friend.

Sophie and Ben Thompson were among the many for whom life in Texas was too much. Within a year, they returned to Georgia. With them gone and Lyle Speaks gone north, there was no one in Fort Worth who remembered Melanie Beaufort. But folks talked for a long time, and children heard the story of the wild lady from Georgia who rode astride in men's pants.

A FEW GREAT BOOKS: A FEW GOOD MEN

by Donley Watt

My brother was twenty-two when he came back home early from the Marines. This was some years after Viet Nam, in the uneasy safety of the Cold War, and during his abbreviated tour Perry had not confronted anything more threatening than the precariousness of a troop helicopter or the darkness of a smoky Philippine bar. The latter turned out to be more dangerous than the former.

In the Marines he had learned nothing more vital, my mother afterwards said, than how to kill another man. For that he had done, killed a man in that nameless, faraway island bar, struck dead with a cue ball held tight in his fist, a Marine not much different from himself, a man hardly more than a boy and not the enemy at all, but a boozy Lance Corporal from Stillwater, Oklahoma, named Mouth by those who served with him. The fact that Mouth died with a locked-open Buck knife in his left hand saved Perry from Leavenworth, but the Corps no longer wanted him. A dishonorable discharge.

This much I know from the little my father told me and from the rumors and gossip that for a few weeks seeped and circled through our small east Texas town. Perry himself never talked about it. A letter from his commanding officer had earlier arrived at our door, so by the time Perry slipped back into town much of our father's fury had in its own way shook and spewed and then mostly dissipated.

But those first days that he was home, in the aftermath of what my father called Perry's disgrace, were not easy. For our house became a silent battleground of strong wills and temperaments too much tangled by blood, and the battles became a way for both father and elder son to rail against a suddenly realized and detested likeness. The Lord was not ungenerous with the Lambs, my mother would say, when he handed out stubbornness.

During those weeks my mother hardly left the house. She even stopped going to church although she was a devout Nazarene. Leon Lamb had grown up in a not-take-it-too-seriously Baptist sort of way and now had fallen away from religion altogether. Not that still being Baptist would have saved him. "He will go to Hell," my mother told her sister Ruthie. "But it's his own burning."

She told Perry to his face, with me looking on, that he, too, would go straight to the devil for killing another man. "Repent and be baptized," she threatened. I grinned at Perry and my mother whirled on me. "And you, too, young man. If you're not baptized. Don't either one of you believe in your Savior, Jesus Christ?"

I was willing to live with my soul in mortal danger, to take my chances, for there was no way I would ever get dunked in front of a bunch of people I hardly knew. And by inclination, if not by temperament, I was more attracted to my father's robust ways that by my mother's long-suffering piety. And now that Perry was back at home and had flagrantly broken one of the Ten Commandments the heat was off me, and for that I was grateful.

Sunday mornings my mother stared out the kitchen window for hours, immobilized, her only movement to dab the puffiness under her eyes with one tissue-wrapped ice cube after another. She talked hardly at all and then in aphorisms. "Life is a long road from which there is no turning," being her favorite.

I am ashamed to say this, but at the time the killing did not bother me one bit. At least not as much as having to share what had become my bedroom with Perry once again. Maybe I can blame my indifference to what my brother had done on being fifteen and not able to see the world as much larger than a basketball. That, and a feeling that the killing must have been just a fair fight gone bad, a beating that had gone too far, one that got tipped over some frontier into territory where no one would have wanted or desired it to go, a foreign place that two young Marines could not with honor withdraw from.

I felt, but could only imagine, that the fight had nothing personal to do with that Oklahoma boy at all. For although Perry always had taken on the world with an aggressive stance, he had to my knowledge never acted in a deliberately mean or vicious manner.

Anyway, Perry was my brother, and I looked up to him without a whole lot of questioning, which is how it should be, I suppose. To me, early discharge from the Marines seemed to be a break for Perry, and not a bad one at that.

For my father it was different. Leon Lamb was not the kind of man who could, like me, accommodate the killing with some excuse or the other. But the echo of one hysterical "Thou shall not kill" from my mother still rang relentlessly through the house, and my father took on a look of desperation. The Church could not condone a killing, she said, although a half century of wars never had seemed to bother her or her church. My mother's anger towards Perry seemed to spew from somewhere deeper than that, a place that I could not then imagine.

Leon Lamb was not able, either, to withdraw into the sad comfort of blame and self-pity. Our father could tolerate Perry's return only by avoiding it, by refusing to live with it. So my father gave Perry thirty days to find a job and get out of our house.

"Thirty days? What a piece of crap," Perry complained.

So the Lambs' cold and private war began. My father took me aside for a talk, wanting to say more, it seems, than he was able. I followed as he strode across the backyard and out past the pen where Happy, our Irish Setter, whined. I had sprung up the last year, and now had passed my father's moderate height. This genetic accident, a gift from my mother's side of the family where all the men are long of limb, was one that at the time I took complete and unabashed credit for. But my father, even in his early fifties, made it clear that he was still in charge. He bounced on his toes with every step, as if he were wading against the current of some invisible river. What he lacked in height he made up in strength, his upper body thick, his thighs still solid.

We stopped under the winter bareness of a magnolia tree and next to the chain link fence that marked the boundary of our narrow lot. From there I looked back at the house I had lived in all my life and suddenly felt amazed to see how small and ordinary it was, with yellow paint peeling from the wooden siding, and a roof of curling asphalt shingles. It looked as if ordinary lives should be lived there, perhaps even with some semblance of scruffy contentment. It surprised me to see my bedroom on the back of the house and realize that I was the ordinary person who slept there every night, when I had always thought that I was different and perhaps even special.

My father glanced towards the house to see where my attention had wandered, and then checked all around to make sure we were alone. He then raised himself up and leaned close. A blood vessel in his temple jumped and twitched. For a moment he seemed startled that he now had to look up to me, and in that same moment I sensed for the first time an uneasiness that afterwards I never saw leave him. But then the air filled with his familiar mix of Chesterfields and Old Spice, and I owned my smallness once again.

"Now listen carefully," he said. "This stuff with your brother." His voice was little more than a hiss. "It's just like this. Perry joined the Marines. He got discharged early. That's the whole story. The rest is nobody else's concern. Do you understand?" I nodded. "And don't pay any attention to your mother. She's just taking it all pretty hard. She'll come around." His business with Perry had ended, at least with me.

Earlier, with the damning letter fresh in his hand, he had spit out a few angry and sketchy bits of information. And now this admonishment to let the matter be, to keep it in the family. He moved back to the house, arms swinging at his sides. We had had our man-to-man, our father-to-son. Probably because my mother demanded it. Now Leon Lamb could get back to selling Ford pickups at the local dealership, which, I thought at that time, was his true calling in life. For the way I saw it, my father does consider his vocation an almost holy calling. Leon Lamb *believed* in Ford pickups.

But at that moment in our backyard, out beyond the hearing of neighbors and through the brittleness of his anger, I could see that there was more, although what exactly the more might be I wasn't able then to express or define. But I could see that he loved us, his family. Although now I understand that he never really was able to like Perry. He loved us, and it was important at fifteen for me to know it, for me now to say it, even though what went on among our family a stranger might not have described as generously as love.

So Leon Lamb loved his work and loved his family. He also loved to hunt, and an image still hangs in my mind, one of him striding through a field, his twelve gauge Ithaca pump cradled in one arm, encouraging Happy as the dog tirelessly worked ahead, sniffing out pastures and woods for birds.

Perry liked to hunt, too, especially ducks, but would never hunt with my father, either not wanting to compete or afraid of wanting to compete too much—which I'm not sure. But now that it's mid-December and Perry is back, he and I hunted when we could.

We spent one Saturday in the upper reaches and backwaters of Cedar Creek Lake, trespassing freely through barbed wire gates that kept in scatterings of skinny, mixed breed cows. The day had moved beyond drizzle, the light rain cut with a little sleet that pinged and bounced softly off the pickup's hood. We sat in the truck with the heater up high, the wipers on intermittent, and hoped for ducks to skim over and light on the choppy grayness of the lake. If the wind died we planned to ease out of the truck right at dark and get a shot or two.

But because of the cold, my hope for ducks was half-hearted, and at the time, Perry seemed content to watch the blankness that stretched out in front of us and talk. His talk was not ungenerous, but of small successes. An ex-girlfriend who left town for a Dallas paralegal job, an old high school buddy who now drove George Strait's tour bus from show to show. I nodded, hardly listening, my mind sorting out stuff of its own.

Then right out of nowhere Perry asked, "You think he means it, the old man, about the thirty days? About me having to get out of the house?"

"Maybe you could start going to church," I said. "You know, just for show, to get Mama on your side, and it would be okay."

"Naw, that's not it. Mama doesn't care. To her I'm already history. It's Daddy. He resents me. He always has. You know that, don't you?"

I shook my head.

"Why's the old man a damned car salesman? Why didn't he finish college so he could get a real job?"

I shook my head again.

"You're looking at him. Right here," and Perry jabbed himself in the chest with his thumb. "Reason number one."

"Aw, that's crazy," I said. But down deep the possible truth of it struck there hard and hung.

Then right out of nowhere Perry asked, "You remember Will Stanton?" He leaned forward so he could look out to the west, towards the Trinity River bottom. I had never met Will Stanton, but had heard the story from our father for years. Will Stanton was one of Leon Lamb's folk heroes, someone he idolized for reasons that ran much deeper than I knew back then.

So I told Perry sure, I'd heard that story a dozen times, but Perry just ignored me, and it was unreal the way he started repeating it. He sounded just like our father, and I let him go, didn't try to stop him. He started in the beginning as if the story held some importance beyond itself, and at the time I couldn't figure out why.

"Will Stanton was a young man back in the thirties," he said, "about my age, maybe a little older, when a doctor over in Corsicana diagnosed some fatal disease, tuberculosis, I think. And Will Stanton, in the face of that death sentence, retreated deep into the Trinity River bottom, not a half dozen miles from here," and he pointed out into the shadowed afternoon to the west.

Then Perry kept on going with the story, but the words were no longer his. They were the words of Leon Lamb's with his voice and his saleman's eloquence, and it became, once again, our father's story. "The river bottom was then in its last stage of wildness, thick with brush and rumors of big cats and wolves and even a last black bear. And Will settled in the center of the wildest, most remote part, right where the Trinity makes a big loop and a spring flows from a bluff above its bank. The only high spot along the river, they always said, though no one ever went there. River overflow all around, and with the big spring rains it became an island. Will built some kind of a shack to live in, hacked a canoe out of a log, and hunted and fished.

"Of course, this was before the Trinity became an open sewer running south out of Dallas. Will carved gun stocks by hand from black walnut and hickory and native pecan and traded them for flour and bacon and salt and coffee. Except for that he lived off the land. And he didn't die. Not then, anyway. The TB went away.

"In the early fifties Will's brothers-in-law, just back from the war and bored, would fish and camp weekends on the river. Will always wandered by to help out, pitching a squirrel or a rabbit into the common pot of stew. He ran a string of traps and grew a garden . . . everything. He was a purely self-sufficient man. They say he even read Plato and Aristotle and. . . ."

Perry stopped a minute and looked sideways at me as if he were puzzled, or maybe had just waked up. "He would have done the same as Will. Daddy would've. If it hadn't been for me, him having to marry Mama. She probably was half-crazy even then."

Perry stared out straight ahead for a minute. A flock of blackbirds rose and fell on a long, winding stream, as if they were all strung together by invisible thread. Then Perry banged his gloved fist hard on the dash. "It's a bullshit story," he said. "A pickup salesman's bullshit story. A loser's fairy tale."

Perry stared out into the gray for a minute. He got this look on his face that I'd never seen before, and it scared me a little. A look that I imagined he might have got in that bar in the Philippines, when he stood over Mouth with the cue ball still clenched tight in his hand. A frozen moment when he must have sensed through the clamor and smoke and confusion that the MP's would be on their way, and he knew that he could run, and if he was going to run, that this was his only moment.

Perry's hand gripped the door handle. Run was written all over his face. Then he pointed. "Ducks," he said, "A pair."

I hadn't seen them. "Bullshit ducks," I said under my breath.

But Perry had slipped out of the pickup with his gun. I stayed put and watched. From the back and bundled up he could be my father, the same thickness of body, the same sureness and strength, or perhaps the anger of his walk. In a moment Perry had disappeared into the mist.

It was dark when we got back to the house with supper for us on the table. Our mother had retreated somewhere deep into the house and was quiet. The sweetness of bourbon hung in the heated air. Our father paced in the next room where the TV flashed. Perry watched him from the kitchen table where we sat. I watched Perry. Something from the day had changed him. Or maybe it was just the harshness of the overhead light.

Perry swallowed, wiped his mouth with his napkin and placed it, folded like a tie, beside his plate. His hands were rough, his fingers thick, but not fleshy at all, just big of bone. I tried to visualize them wrapped around the white of a cue ball and wondered if Mouth saw that hand and cue ball coming at all. Perry spoke softly, but his voice carried evenly into the next room.

"Let's find Will Stanton's cabin," he said. He was speaking to me, but he watched our father, knew that he could hear. "We'll take our guns, walk up some ducks, and find his place."

Our father stopped his pacing and stood in the open doorway facing us, attentive. I knew what he must be thinking. *Tomorrow is Sunday. The rows of shiny Ford pickups will have a day of rest. The Cowboys will play at Tampa Bay. Tampa Bay, for God's sake. A laugher.*

"You'll never find it," our father said. "No one's ever found Will's cabin and no one ever should. It's just the way he planned it."

Perry grinned. "Too bad," he said. "Not everything works out the way you plan it." He shoved back from the table and looked right over at our father, straight on, as if to make some silent kind of dare. Of the thirty days he now had only twelve remaining to get out. Perry moved to the sink and stared out at the night. "Hell," he said, "who gives a damn about Will Stanton, anyway?"

And I wondered, yeah, who would care about an old recluse of a hermit who's been dead for twenty years? And I could see from the way our father hesitated it might not be that easy to say. Not with Perry there, knowing the truth, and our mother surely listening from the bedroom. Or maybe he had never been asked the question before.

"I guess you need to have been around him to understand." Our father still stood erect and solid in the doorway, but I looked up, startled when he spoke, for his voice had slumped as if it had exhausted itself. I watched to see if his body would follow, but it didn't.

"Maybe if you could have been around Will Stanton, especially after being in my boots for a while, after peddling pickups to dumbass roofers and would-be cowboys day after day, then you might, just might, be able to see."

These were new words, ones that I had never heard, and I looked back up at our father, this Leon Lamb I hadn't known, and felt as if I were a stranger in that house.

Perry drew a glass of water. I could feel his uneasiness. Our father had gone off somewhere that my brother had never been. I could sense it, but only after he came back.

Our father gathered strength, snapped back from where he had slipped. "But a little duck hunting sounds okay. Yeah, maybe I'll go along. We can walk out the river bottom. Maybe get a few ducks. We might even run across some black walnuts, bring back a sackful to have around for Christmas."

"Okay," Perry said. "In the morning, early. And we'll find the cabin?" He pulled on his jacket and moved toward the door. "With Will's library full of Plato and all his philosopher pals?"

"I'll tell you what," our father said. He pointed a finger right at Perry, and his words were slow, pulled out from somewhere black and deep. But before he could finish Perry was gone.

It was dark, the air heavy and cold. Leon Lamb's pickup eased through town, passing under signal lights still flashing early morning yellow. The side streets were polished black and smooth, gleaming from the drizzle that had fallen all night. At every corner, giant Christmas candles lit our way out of town.

Our father drove and fiddled with the radio. Ag news. A gospel quartet. C & W. A fragment of a mellow and earnest prayer.

I sat in the middle. Perry leaned away from me to be close to the slit of open window. He watched the smoke from his cigarette curl away.

We stopped at the end of a gravel road. Just light. The northern sky coiled with thick ropes of clouds. A cold front had rushed down from the Panhandle in the night, but a little pink still gleamed in the east. We unsheathed our shotguns. Our father rubbed the stock of his old Ithaca pump with his gloved hand and pulled his cap down tight, then led the way. Perry was quick to follow, and I hurried to keep up, my eye fixed on Perry's camouflaged back.

The land stretched flat, dotted with only a scattering of mesquites. The black gumbo sucked at our boots, so we picked our way towards the river by zigzagging from field to field, choosing a route where dead grass lay matted across the soft ground.

It took a hard hour to reach the river. Crouching low, we slipped down the bank and made our way quietly around a bend. A dozen or so ducks drifted downstream, out of range, bobbing with the current. Perry lifted his gun to his shoulder and sighted. I heard him, an angry "dow, dow, dow," a hard whisper, then lowered his gun. He shook his head. We straightened up. My boots had grown into a gobs of black clay, and I wiped the sides against the rough bark of a pecan tree.

Perry leaned against a tree and lit up. Our father found a fallen log and kicked his boots against it. The drizzle floated around me. It hardly seemed to fall, but hung lightly against my face. I longed for the warmth of the pickup and thought about going back, letting the two of them go on with this stupid chase. But I knew I couldn't.

Perry moved to the river's edge. It flowed thick and green and sluggish. It steamed like a pot of stew. "We'll never even get close," he said, pointing down river to where the ducks had disappeared. He turned to face us. "Which way now?" he asked. "To Will Stanton's old cabin?"

Our father looked up river. "It's been a long time," he said. "An awful lot of years since I've been here. But Will always seemed to come from below our camp." And then he turned and, without another word, headed south, following the flow of the river. We slipped and slid along the narrow bank, splashing across the shallows of gravel bars, working around the bare thickets of bushes and briars that flourished down to the water.

Our father stayed out in front, pushing hard. Perry followed close. "Humping again," he said back to me with a laugh. "Just like the Corps."

His movements were sure, almost effortless.

The wind had picked up from the north. I could hear it in the sway of tree tops above. Clouds now tumbled overhead like bundles of wool.

We moved through the drip and splatter for an hour or more. Then we stopped, our father looking up for a sun that wasn't there, then all around, trying to get his bearings. His breath rushed out quick and hard. I could see his disorientation, then new determination in his face.

Perry stayed distant, like he moved in another space. He held back, content to let our father lead the way, his movements still smooth, without effort.

I hated it. The slickness of the mud, the heaviness of my boots, the numbness of my face, the aching in my legs. I started cursing to myself, all the words I'd ever heard. I cursed Perry for what he'd done, and for the first time, perhaps because I was cold and vulnerable, I felt anger at his killing another man. And our father got his, too, for his pride and hard-headedness.

I didn't want to be there with them. I didn't want to be like either one of them. I didn't, at that moment, even want to be Perry's brother or my father's son. But I followed.

We climbed a bluff coated with slick leaves. Pecan husks hung from tangled webs of limbs high above. Suddenly Perry started to run. He gave a little whoop and passed our father who had stopped ahead. Then I spotted it. Will's cabin stood right there, no more than twenty yards away. But it was hardly a cabin at all, at least not in the way I had imagined, but a peeling tar-papered shack with a patchwork of tin scraps for a roof.

Perry was inside by the time I got there, but our father hung back. We weren't the first to have found it. Broken jars and empty tins covered the plank floor. On one wall someone had scrawled "R.D. and Jerrel 1978." A bundle of burlap sacks and a filthy sleeping bag lay stiff against one wall. Scraps of yellowed papers clogged the corners of the one room. Perry kicked his way through the rubble. I moved across to what must have been Will's kitchen. A two-legged table hung from one wall where it had been nailed.

Our father eased in through the door and looked around. He shook his head, then moved towards the far side of the room where a couple of apple crates had been hung for a pantry or for shelves. The wad of a rat's nest filled the corner of one.

"Hey," Perry shouted. "Look at this." He held up the remains of a magazine, waved it like a banner through the air. In a glance I could see it was a *Hustler* or *Playboy* or the like. "Maybe Plato's not so bad after all." He laughed, and I looked over at our father, but he was busy pulling aside the rat's nest, a tangle of paper and rags and twigs, with a stick. Behind the nest was a stack of books. They were small and mildewed, and the glue from the bindings had been chewed off, but they are what my father has come to see: *The Republic* and *Leaves of Grass* and *Walden* and a couple more about medicinal herbs and plants. Although Leon Lamb had never read them, possibly never even seen them, he turned their fragile pages as if they were his own.

Our father held them out to Perry. "Here, take them," he said. "This is what a man could do with his life. What a man could have done."

Perry waved the pages from the girlie magazine. "What about these, old man?" he said. "Life could be lived like this, too. Couldn't it?" And I was afraid Perry would shove those faded pictures in our father's face. But after a minute Perry threw them down. "This place is a pig pen," he said. "Only a bum would live like this. A bum and a pervert. He never read that shit," he said, pointing to the books our father held. "He probably couldn't even read."

But the books were there. Perry knew it and I knew it and our father's face told the whole story, as if Leon Lamb had just made his greatest sale. Then Perry started circling through the room, kicking at the junk scattered around the floor. He knocked the legs from under the table and it fell halfway, hanging by bent nails from the wall. I backed away towards the door.

"Hey, there's no reason for this," my father said. He moved towards Perry, put a hand out, grabbed Perry's arm and swung him around.

"Come on now, you two cut it out," I said in the same way my mother would have said it, full of conciliation, empty of effect.

Then Perry backed away. He had gotten that numb look on his face, what I thought of as that standing-over-the-fallen-Mouth sort of look. He crossed his arms, reached them as far as they would go around himself, hugging himself as if his were someone else's arms, as if he wished he were being held by someone who could never hold him.

"Why didn't you?" he asked, turning to face our father, "if you believe in all of this—living this way, back in the woods, reading this philosophy shit, and kissing off the world—why in the hell didn't you live this way? Why didn't you ever at least tell us or show us or something?"

Our father wouldn't look up, just thumbed through a piece of a book he held in his hand. "Don't say it," Perry said. "I already know. It was me."

Then Perry stumbled a little, but moved to the book shelves and with one quick motion had his lighter out of his jacket pocket and in a moment the rat's nest was aflame

"Damn you!" my father shouted, first moving towards Perry, then towards the flames. "You destroy every damn thing you touch!"

Now Perry's face was the one to light up. Its glow came from more than the fire that had started to crawl up one wall. Our father grabbed the sleeping bag from the floor and started beating at the flames. Smoke began to fill the room, and I backed to the door of the cabin.

Perry grabbed handsful of the old paper and rags from the floor and pitched them on the fire and laughed. Our father cursed and beat at the flames even harder. Perry jerked the table from the wall and broke it across the floor. He threw the pieces at the fire, which by now had climbed out of control up one wall.

I eased back outside and waited in the cold drizzle. I heard our father grunt as he thumped the sleeping bag against the walls. The brittle wood crackled from the heat; the tar paper sent black smoke up through the trees. Perry stumbled out the door and his face held something so elemental, so frightening, that I had to look away.

Our father backed slowly out, then stopped and slung the sleeping bag back in. He still held three of the books in one hand. He had lost his cap and his face was streaked black. We all moved away from the heat.

Then suddenly Perry moved next to our father and with one swift motion grabbed the books from his hand. He ran the few steps to the cabin and hurled the books into the flames.

Our father cursed again, with sounds more animal than human, and with a rage jumped Perry from behind and locked onto his neck with both arms. Perry staggered backwards with the weight. "They're just goddamn books," he gasped. "Just goddamn books."

And then he turned and with three strong steps, our father still clinging to his back, he charged backwards, slamming our father against an ancient tree, and just that quickly the battle was over.

We cut saplings and strapped them together for a pallet and carried Leon Lamb out. He was conscious and in pain, I could tell, but he never spoke a word.

It was dark when we made the pickup. Perry drove and I scrunched down in the back where our father lay all the way to the hospital. Perry dropped us off.

My brother had crushed something inside of our father, it turned out, and a rib had punctured a lung. That was serious, but a few days later Leon Lamb was home from the hospital.

The rib and the lung would heal. Perry had crushed something else that wouldn't heal. Leon Lamb could no longer sell Ford pickups. He tried for a while, and a few folks, mostly old customers, bought from him out of loyalty or out of habit. But he had the look of a man who had dropped something he needed and knew where it lay, but could find no way to retrieve it.

Perry lost himself somewhere—Houston for a while and then on to Atlanta. I got a note one Christmas, then the next. That's all. I guess I understood.

It is now 1996. My sons are five and three. They go with me when I visit my mother at the Golden Care Home. It is a clean place, the nurses have a false cheerfulness that I hope they never lose. Mother seems content to be there, her Bible by her side, one eye cocked towards her future, her heaven.

Afterwards, my two sons go to the cemetery with me and I show them the grave of the grandfather they never knew. I sit in the shade of a juniper tree and tell them about Ford pickups and Happy and Will Stanton and all the books there are to read. While I talk they find secret places to hide among the tombstones. When we leave I hold their hands tightly, for now I know how easy it is for sons and brothers and fathers to slip away. ✿

THE CLEANER

by Jill Patterson

Three days after her arrival in Phorney, Ms. Peggy Showers answered her front door and found Irving Johnson, the 'Gators starting pitcher and student council president, poised on her porch. His right hand popped to a salute, and his left clapped a baseball cap over his heart. Then he whisked a magician's bouquet from his sleeve. The feathery pansies shimmied in the humid August breeze. "For our new Vice-Principal." Winking, he palmed a key from behind Peggy's ear. "To my heart," he said.

All morning, Peggy stood before her vanity mirror and practiced magic. She stuffed the flowers up her bathrobe sleeve then yanked them free. Each time the bouquet rustled against her wrist, she giggled. The nosegay, her first, left her flushed and weary of unpacked boxes, dusty cabinets, utility connections, and moving vans. Her new life stretched before her like an empty diary, and her lungs filled with potential the way the auditorium at Jackson Community College had teemed with her classmates' tossed mortarboards only three months ago.

She shook her flowers and smiled, thinking how one domino triggered others to tumble into place. Graduating *cum laude* had given her the confidence to fell the job at Phorney High, and already her career had thumped her personal life into action, too. She imagined every male student, every male colleague—teachers, coaches, counselors—would bristle before her power the way men were always roused by *femme fatales*. Still, dusting the small town habits of Phorney High would require a diligent custodian, one who kept her own home tidy, so Ms. Showers spent her last weekend before in-service mopping floors, washing windows, and assigning her knick-knacks and books their proper places.

Monday morning, she discovered the key to Irving's heart unlocked the front door of the school building. When Ms. Showers asked the secretary, she learned that no one had assigned Irving to the Welcome Committee, and she should probably call the police.

"Irving's a truant," Abigail said. "Ought to be in juvi-hall."

Anger knotted Ms. Showers' hands into fists—not because Irving had access to bootlegged keys and school property, but because her stomach trembled the way it always did whenever a blind date stood her up. "How did a truant become school president?" she asked.

"He promised to outlaw the TAAS. It was a landslide."

Ms. Showers blushed, remembering that Irving's sham bouquet sat on her dining room table, enthroned in her only crystal vase.

"You want I should pull his file?" Abigail opened a drawer and skimmed the labels. She tugged free a thick manila folder. Several Post-It's waved from the contents like warning flags.

Just as Ms. Showers suspected, a family of malcontents had hatched Irving. His grandparents carted around his mother, Jeanette, in a lavender VW Bug through most of the sixties, exposing her to Woodstock, marijuana, and sexual promiscuity. Later, several misdemeanors pocked Jeanette's academic record, preventing her from attending college. Though the dates didn't add up, she named Davy Jones as Irving's father, swearing he sired her son at the old Rangers stadium after the Monkees comeback concert in 1987. Upon Jeanette's arrival in Phorney, the Ladies' Circle denied her membership because they claimed her love beads, braids, and tales of hippy fornication conveyed an immorality inappropriate for the Circle's political agenda. Jeanette planted herself anyway, and because she worked as the town's only florist, her business thrived though her social life suffered drought. Full of vengeance, maybe she'd encouraged her son to defy the sanctimonious leaders of Phorney.

Whatever Irving's motive, Ms. Showers' heart hardened toward him. When he sparked a brawl on the first day in Mrs. Henley's English class, she fought to sanitize the school by expelling him. "He's a germ," she complained. "Germs spread. A senior in a sophomore class! What if he infects the new kids." Dr. Whitfield, Principal at the high school, instructed Ms. Showers to undergo anger management or start a soothing hobby. He himself had learned the art of origami and, locked in his office, would fold elegant sculptures whenever that thread he hung by threatened to snap. "You can't scorn the son of the only florist in town," he said. "Jeanette might close shop. Who would complete our homecoming orders?" He finished creasing a mum from tissue paper and poked it behind Ms. Showers' ear. "We wouldn't want to ruin the festivities." Irving continued to torment Ms. Showers, writing X-rated essays in English and torturing girls in Biology with frog limbs and earthworm organs nipped during dissection labs.

Then, after Christmas, he vanished.

Though Ms. Showers should have celebrated, a depression tainted her victory. She fancied that she maintained an on-call stance, ready to mop the spill should Irving return, but truthfully, she let herself go. Sometimes she forgot lipstick. Sometimes she wore dainty church dresses to work instead of her sleek A-line skirts and heels. She thought her despair was the sign of a good teacher: shouldn't she have worked harder to cleanse her flock's one dirty sheep? Occasionally, she could smell Irving's presence. It wafted across the courtyard between classes, sharp but sneaky like the odor of a well-hidden, floral Stick-Up. The familiar bouquet left Ms. Showers fumbling through her purse for lipstick and rouge though she didn't understand why.

Irving reappeared the morning of the TAAS exams. Announcing his resurrection as a true Houdini always demanded a drum roll, he had a package delivered to Ms. Showers' office at seven a.m. Peggy's stomach lurched as if she'd dropped over the first hill of a roller coaster. Her hand's trembled as she untied the ribbon.

Abigail crouched behind the file cabinet and sheltered her head with an attendance notebook. "That might contain a bomb. I've seen this kind of thing on TV."

Too anxious to heed Abigail's warning, Peggy wrestled with the lid. When she finally popped it open, potpourri burst from the box, and the explosion of petals slammed Peggy into laughter. She tossed the flakes into the air like confetti.

"Get ahold of yourself," Abigail ordered. "This is no time for hysterics." She checked Peggy's coat closet and peered under her desk. "Suppose Irving intends to fulfill his campaign promise?" She slapped the box's lid in place. "Suppose he besieges the school, peppering students and faculty with bullets while we labor over the TAAS exams?"

Peggy's giggling shut off. She brushed the potpourri from her hair. Was that how Irving intended to demonstrate the danger of standardized tests? Holding the exams in the cafeteria, at one time, one place, was she sweeping the sophomore class into a dustpan, precise and tidy? One rap against the can, and an angry outcast could dump their lives in the garbage. Ms. Showers peeked inside the package again. The potpourri smelled like fresh buttercups, but when she shook the box, the dead petals rattled like tiny bones broken.

By the time the students arrived, Ms. Showers had stationed Abigail in the kitchen, armed with a fire extinguisher. She posted herself at the cafeteria door, checking pockets and frisking jackets for calculators, cheat sheets, explosives. She confiscated two volumes of the *Encyclopedia Britannica*, one slide-rule, and a spray can of mace. Still, despite her careful purging, someone—or maybe several co-conspirators—smuggled in Irving's spirit. Ms. Showers sniffed the hint of carnations when a group of kids bundled in woolly coats jostled passed her, but a loud crash in the kitchen and the flush of a fire extinguisher sent her skittering to Abigail's aid.

During the exams, Irving possessed the students. Though they hunkered over their test booklets, diligent as scholars, Ms. Showers doubted their fervor for their eyes shifted mechanically like kaleidoscopes twisting under a powerful hand. Two weeks later, the scoring center in Austin returned the tests as evidence that a mutiny had been managed. The students had answered every question, blacking the bubbles with their number two's per instructions, but they were intent on nothing more than stippling pretty pictures. Lane and Lacey—seniors who had repeatedly failed the TAAS exam—dotted big hearts and words of true love in their booklets, and Kent Williams dimpled a musical composition for bass drum. Neal McKray chiseled a polka-dot representation of Mount Rush more, though the answer sheet didn't provide a wide enough tablet of rock and he had to lop off Lincoln.

It didn't take two days for the *Phorney Pulpit* to publish the TAAS scores. Abigail skittered around the office, blubbering that Darlene, the paper's star reporter, might as well hammer down their coffin lids. Everyone would blame the staff for its laziness, poor training, and lack of organization. The sophomore class would have to retest next year and a handful of students wouldn't graduate, but otherwise TAAS failures went unpunished. The school board would fire teachers and kill careers, but they would pat the students' heads, preserving the self-esteem of America's youth.

Quiet as midnight, Dr. Whitfield perched himself in his captain's chair and pleated the front page article into a pirate's hat which he propped atop his balding head. A patch shaped from a memo pad and fastened with a rubber band cupped his left eye.

That's when Ms. Showers first understood her role as Vice-Principal: like George Bush, she'd been voted in to clean up the garbage left behind by the fool with Alzheimer's. Recognizing that only some fancy maid-service could launder this mess and that only she possessed enough skill to twirl the broom and addle the press, she prepared a statement that shifted blame away from faculty and staff. She signed Dr. Whitfield's name to it because it wasn't right to bow in the spotlight of fame and admiration when the curtain call belonged to someone else.

One hour after Ms. Showers messengered the release to the *Pulpit*, Darlene stormed the main office. She thrust a mini-recorder at Dr. Whitfield and waved the release under his nose. Her head tilted, thrown off-kilter by the weight of skepticism. "You saying this school's average TAAS score of a 42—a score denoting mental retardation—is a direct result of poor PTA morale, out-dated band uniforms, and a Japanese con-spiracy to contaminate the drinking water of America's school children?"

Dr. Whitfield, still dressed in his buccaneer drag, could only point a bony finger at Ms. Showers and stammer, "Pa-pa, pa pa—" His cheeks puffed, black as thunderheads, but he couldn't spit out Peggy's name.

Maybe he couldn't remember it.

Ms. Showers panicked. It never occurred to her that a spin job could reel too tightly. Her thoughts pivoted, and she felt dizzy as if caught in the eddy of a toilet bowl rinse. She staggered toward Dr. Whitfield and draped an arm around his shoulders.

Dr. Whitfield's pirate hat trembled and slid off his head. "Pa, pa, pa-pa," he stuttered.

Ms. Showers yanked a tissue from the box on Abigail's desk and blotted Dr. Whitfield's brow. She sent Abigail for his heart pills, and when Abigail rattled them in her face, she noticed for the first time that the prescription wasn't a blood thinner or some other medication for cardiovascular disease. Dr. Whitfield was taking valium. Those letters—V-A-L-I-U-M—formed the bubble of an idea for Ms. Showers, and she worked it into a full lather. "Truth is," she said, "Phorney High is ravaged with addicts. Dr. Whitfield wanted to spare the city a narcotics scare, but now that the story has burst free, he pledges to fumigate the school of those blood-sucking dealers."

Dr. Whitfield slapped Ms. Showers' arm from his shoulders and snagged his valium from Abigail. A daft Blackbeard, he cranked his wrist in Ms. Showers' direction as if brandishing a sword.

"That's right, Captain. We'll pillage the dealer's brig." Ms. Showers flourished her pencil. "On guard!" she squealed.

Darlene jerked the recorder from Dr. Whitfield's grasp and surrendered it to Ms. Showers. "You have a master plan?" she asked.

"Do I." She smirked. She figured Irving dealt dope or smoked it himself. What else besides money, power, and a drug-induced high would allow arrogance to fester in a young man. A Just Say No campaign would lure him back to campus. It was like daring Copperfield with handcuffs, two coffins, a watery grave, and an HBO special. And when Irving did return, he wouldn't be able to break the shackles Peggy planned to bind around his ankles.

That afternoon, the school librarian taught Ms. Showers how to search the Web for dope slang and other streetwise knowledge. Scavenging among the drug culture made her feel worldly, hip. She even found a website, maintained by Irving and his proselyte Kent Williams, that explained how to manufacture crack cocaine. Though she knew she should report the site to Dr. Whitfield, she found herself fascinated by the pictures of crack and the description of its instantaneous euphoria. The crystals looked sheer as water, and when she imagined holding some in her palm, she could feel herself lift then drop as if rolling on clean ocean waves. *I'm surfing the net*, she said to herself.

Equipped with her new drug literacy, Ms. Showers shaped a Just Say No campaign around five slogans which would attack one narcotic per day. Her slogans reminded her of the pep rally battle cries spun by the cheerleaders when she attended high school years ago. The student body had mustered around that group of girls, and even the players gave them credit for the team's winning streak. Ms. Showers dreamed her campaign would capture a little respect from the social elite, but when rumors about her crusade bloomed and local businesses and the Ladies Circle begged to participate, she grew bored with the victory. Instead of parading her conquest, she spent her afternoons, when school let out and the office quieted, logging on to Irving's website. By the time she shut down her computer, the ecstasy had faded anew, and she drove home depressed.

Sunday, before Just Say No Week kicked off, Ms. Showers plastered the school halls with decorations and posters honoring the first day's slogan—*Put a Cap on Speed*. To slow the crowds between classes, she hung yield signs the size of tuba bells, tacked up speed limitations, and rigged traffic lights from strings of Christmas bulbs. On her drive to work Monday morning, she noticed that several businesses had displayed traffic signals in their front windows, and the mayor had set the intersections blinking yellow. To show further support, every 'Gator fan saluted her, pointing to the slew of caps crowning their heads: berets, coonskins, fedoras, shower bonnets, and one sombrero. Even the mayor's wife lodged a football helmet on her bouffant and paraded downtown to the Piggly Wiggly.

But the kids at school stared. Ms. Showers' gimme cap from the

Git 'n Gallup station didn't compliment her new skirt and heels. Dr. Whitfield didn't even notice the hullabaloo of decorations in the hall. Instead, he hid in his office, molding a replica of the ark from an old refrigerator box. "You're gonna get hat head," he warned. Then he stretched his measuring tape, checking the dimensions of his cardboard vessel.

By lunch, Ms. Showers' gimme cap had triggered a headache. Her temples pulsed like they did after she'd spent a weekend cleaning house only to discover on Monday morning that she'd forgotten to dust one room. That botched chore belied her tidy homemaking, and afterward, she imagined dust carpeting the top of the refrigerator, mold fuzzing the bath tile, and lint herding under her bed. Now, without Irving's white flag of surrender, Ms. Showers' anti-drug campaign hardly seemed shipshape. Fed up, she stalked the payphone near the cafeteria, waiting for the lunch crowds to subside so she could place an anonymous call to the *Pulpit*. The piece of foil she clamped over the mouthpiece rattled as she informed Darlene that the Vice Principal at Phorney High had outdone herself and the town paper ought to hustle over and snap her picture for tomorrow's front page. "She's a tough cookie," Ms. Showers buzzed, "and has some words for the local drug lord." She slipped the receiver into its cradle and wadded up the tinfoil evidence.

As she stood there, luxuriating in renewed anticipation, Irving Johnson scurried by, scorning the nearby traffic lights that stared down at him, red-eyed and angry. His T-shirt flashed an advertisement for Motor Speedway in Dallas. Spotting Ms. Showers, he jammed on the brake, kicked his fist to his shoulder, and twisted it like he was revving a Harley. "Brrm, brrm," he growled. Then he winked, flirty-like. "You want to make an arrest, Peggy. I got outstanding speeding violations. I'll bet you could arrest me real good. Got any cuffs?"

Though Ms. Showers blushed, her mouth pulled into a flatline. He couldn't just highball onto campus after such a long truancy and tease her into forgiveness. He'd called her by her first name! But she knew how to rebuff arrogance. "You're a real Speed Racer," she said then flipped her back against him and stomped to the main office where she planned to file a report as soon as she stopped trembling.

Later, during sixth period, Darlene lined Ms. Showers, Dr. Whitfield, and Abigail in front of the 'Gator Spirit Pole to take their picture. She ordered everyone to say *Cheese*, and when the bulb fired, Irving barreled by again, rumbling his fake engine. Abigail pumped her hand to her brow, trying to see past the flash still blocking her vision. Darlene nearly dropped the camera. "What the Hades was that?" she demanded. "You allow go-carts in the school courtyard?" But Irving had disappeared by then, leaving a puff of floral exhaust in his wake. "And what's that smell?" Darlene asked. Though she propped her fists on her hips, Peggy breathed deeply, savoring the fresh aroma. It reminded her of fabric softener.

Tuesday came, and Ms. Showers stretched a banner across the front lawn: *Dress Against Snow.* She spritzed the windows with fake frost and hung cut-out snowflakes from the air conditioner vents. The Trane would blow all day because she lowered the thermostat to forty. When the students arrived, the snow flakes pirouetted like ballerinas, and though it was 95 and humid as a boy's locker room outside, inside it was perfect for the winter gear they were supposed to wear. A few students dressed the part, but most giggled when they saw Ms. Showers bundled in her leopard coat that she wore instead of her bulky sweatsuit which magnified her rear and camouflaged her better curves. She wanted to look smart should Irving show his face again. She had his APE form ready to go if he did.

At two o-clock, Irving still hadn't reappeared. Instead, Joe Rivers hobbled into Ms. Showers' office, ignoring Abigail's demands that he needed an appointment. He bulked against Ms. Showers' desk. His tool belt banged the cherry wood finish, and his wrench dropped in the middle of her papers, peppering next year's course schedule with oil and muck. A camouflage jacket swaddled his body. A woolly scarf snaked up his throat, and a toboggan clung to his head so that only his lips, spitting profanity, and his eyes, blinking tears, remained uncovered. "It's cold as a three-dog night in my shop class," he barked. "You trying to freeze me out?" The stench of cigarettes chugged from his open mouth.

"It's cold in all the classrooms. That's the point."

"You don't fool me. Ms. Peggy Showers. You're working on taking over as Principal, just like you confided. You ain't forgetting what you said, are you?" He picked up his wrench and acted like he was going to tighten her ear, tweak her memory. "You promised to recommend me as your successor, but this highbrow campaign you're running makes me think you'll forget the little people."

Ms. Showers hadn't forgotten. After Christmas, when Irving disappeared, her melancholy began to blot her social life. Some evenings she didn't feel like dating, and when she did, she pulled dirty blouses out of the hamper and wore them, wrinkled and stale. Her search for a husband had grown tedious, and she would have stopped worrying about her future altogether if Abigail hadn't pointed out that Joe Rivers was the only single man in town who didn't still live with his mama and she'd better get to flirting. Eventually, Peggy spent a weekend with Mr. Rivers, attending the 1999 Texas State Auto Show, where drunk on Cadillacs and BMW convertibles and pumped full of margaritas, she not only modeled her Wonder Bra for that grease monkey but blabbed about her desire to climb the Phorney school district ladder, swearing to drag him along.

Back at home, her passion for engines and Quaker State withered. She wanted a man brimming with masculinity, but when that manliness slopped out of the cup and onto the saucer, it overwhelmed Ms. Showers' fastidious tendencies. She couldn't help but notice that rust and grease caked his tools and that his freezer had grown icy walls three inches thick—a defrost nightmare. His breath, sooty with cigarette smoke, began to gag her. And suddenly, when his mechanic hands tinkered with her bra, sour spit gathered in the back of her throat. Awakened to the reality that Mr. Rivers far surpassed her tolerance of bachelor ways, she brushed aside his continued advances as gently as she could. She told him she was suffering dizzy spells, and her doctor had diagnosed them as a sign of equilibrium malfunction requiring a breast reduction. "No more steamy lingerie," she whined. "It's Wal-Mart training skivvies from here out." Joe Rivers squirmed for a few days but lost interest pretty quick.

Now, he rapped his mittened knuckles on her desk. "I've got valuable skills, Peggy. I aim to leave the shop monkeys behind. I want an office." He shed a mitten. "These paws can match the grip of any fussy administrator."

With those filthy fingers waving in her face, Ms. Showers endured a genuine sensation that the room was tilting and her breasts were rolling like loose ballasts. "Now, Joey," she managed to coo, "you know I cherish our tryst at the State Auto Show. It's my dreadful affliction that's thwarted our happiness." She hoped he couldn't spot her healthy breasts beneath her fur coat. "I promise. I'll never forget you."

Reassured, Mr. Rivers tugged on his mitten, knotted his scarf tighter, and headed for the tundra of his shop. Ms. Showers sprayed her office with Lysol and was preparing to clear her desk and scrub it with 409 when Irving Johnson strutted in sporting Bermuda shorts, a muscle shirt, and sandals. A lei made from fresh carnations hung around his neck. "Aloha!" he said. His toes were frozen pale as vienna sausages, and goosebumps speckled his legs like he'd developed the pox, but he'd proven his point. The day before, he was a hot rod, addicted to speed, and now, snow didn't scare him. A chill skidded down Ms. Showers' arms. She suspected the trickster was ready to palm a stash of cocaine from behind her ear and charge her with possession. So when he whipped a plastic baggy out of his shirt pocket, split the Ziploc, and dumped the contents on her desk, she was stunned. Two rectangular tubes of Pez and an Easter Bunny dispenser clattered onto her desk.

"I caught Neal McKray, in the boy's restroom, pumping Pez from this dispenser, crushing them on the windowsill, then snorting the line." He raised his eyebrows, daring Ms. Showers to do something about this outrage. "He's got a drug problem. Snorting candy—that's slang for dope. I read about it in Biology." He opened his textbook to a highlighted page as if to prove his knowledge about drugs stemmed from honest education and not personal experience.

"Am I to understand you highlighted these pages while pouring over your biology lesson?"

"Yes, ma'am. Cramming for finals early. They're around the corner, you know." He grinned at her and rubbed his arms as if erasing the cold. "I'm thinking someone should call over to the *Pulpit* and report this drug activity."

"Mr. Johnson, it's illegal to deface school property. I'm afraid you'll have to pay for your textbook." Ms. Showers opened her file cabinet, pulled the price list and showed it to him. "That'll be $86.95. You can pay cash, or I can call your mother and have her come write a check."

Irving twirled his lei. He stared at the sullied textbook then the Easter Bunny. He grinned and nodded. "You're a quick one, Peggy. We'd make a great team."

"Or—" she paused, "—you can hand over the Pez, get a new textbook, and I'll clean the log saying this defiled one belonged to you."

Irving swaggered to the supply closet and yanked out a new textbook. He flung the lei on her desk, a shed gauntlet, winked then left. His flipflops clapped like castanets against his feet. Later, at home, Peggy shed the leopard coat, stripped to her lingerie, christened her lei with some bottled water, and hulaed around her living room. The carnation petals glistened like polished furniture.

By Wednesday, everyone—except Dr. Whitfield—grasped the slogans. In honor of *Back Away from Crack* Day, the student body wrestled with their jeans so they zipped over their butt. The male teachers strung their ties on backward, and the female teachers reversed their dresses and skirts. Absorbed in his ark construction, Dr. Whitfield didn't notice when Ms. Showers ran the day's schedule counter-clockwise, starting with sixth period and ending with first. That morning, Ms. Showers walked her beat, puffed with success. She touched the students' shoulders and caressed her colleagues' ties as if giving them the white-glove test. She kissed her fingertips. Her plans for Phorney High were finally hanging clean and straight.

During lunch, the cafeteria moms launched the food lines with dessert and saved the utensils for last. Unimpressed with the lunchroom shtick, Irving harassed the volunteers, insisting they plop his steak fingers on the tray because he shouldn't get a plate before the food if they were going to play by the rules. Ms. Peggy Showers marched to the cafeteria, feeling strangely euphoric that for the third day in a row Irving hadn't been able to resist her Just Say No campaign. Though she meant to punish Irving's disrespectful attitude, she told herself that her scheming had probably spared him the life of a drop-out. When she found Irving, she saw that he'd donned his T-shirt backwards. He saluted her, quick and clean, then flipped his baseball cap around, too. As he passed out the cafeteria door, he maintained the salute and even walked backward, keeping a steady gaze on Ms. Showers, the unlikely steward who'd broken the spell of the school's sorcerer.

But later, during last period, while she patrolled the front doors, ready to wrangle any ditchers, Ms. Showers caught Irving huddled near the pay-phone, his cap cupping the receiver and his voice grunting like a man who'd smoked for years. On the back of his T-shirt—or the front—the side he'd kept hidden when he paraded past her earlier, a marijuana leaf stretched open like an octopus minus some tentacles. The slogan said, *Make Mary Jane Legal.*

Ms. Showers sprinted to the phone, slammed down the receiver, and gripping Irving's beltloop, drug him into Dr. Whitfield's office. The principal had started folding animal couplets to board his ark. A pretty duo of swans shaped from the day's attendance sheets floated across his mahogany desk. Their necks curved gracefully.

Irving bowed his head, imitating the paper waterfowl. When he flapped his arms like wings and said, "Quack, quack," Ms. Showers gripped his belt loop again and scooted him to her own office. "You think I'm ignorant about the dress code? I'm phoning your mother right now. She won't appreciate her little daydream believer's shenanigans." She waited, pondering her next move, her trump card. "Bet you didn't know, your mom is helping with Friday's Just Say No activities. That's right. She's joining my side."

"*I'm* on your side, Peggy. The TAAS joke caused you some problems. I came back to make things right." He reached across the desk and twirled a strand of Ms. Showers' hair around his finger. "Didn't I hand over Neal?"

Ms. Showers clicked on the intercom and told Abigail to phone Ms. Johnson.

Irving flailed his hands in mock dismay. His mouth crumpled into an exaggerated frown. Then he stood, slithered out of his T-shirt, and gave Ms. Showers' desk a little one-two bump of his hips as if preparing to striptease.

"Good God." She clapped her hand over her eyes. But she felt her mouth peeking open, ready to grin, and had to slide her palm down to quell her giddiness. Her view uncovered, she saw that Irving had turned his T-shirt inside-out. The Fruit-of-the-Loom tag wagged at his Adam's apple. "Well. Good then," she said. "Straighten up and fly right all the time, you might make honor roll."

He pointed his finger at her. "I think someone's a little peeved because I forgot to bring her flowers."

Darlene showed up after school let out, toting her tape recorder and notepad and insisting that Mr. Rivers had called to warn her that the drum major was dealing dope to the entire band. She recognized his scraggly voice. "That man must smoke two packs a day. Really. You should sign him up for the patch. His health is going to cost the district thousands in hospital care."

Ms. Showers saw right away she'd been hoodwinked by the class president again. His gruff telephone voice was a forgery of Mr. River's. She would have to keep a more snug eye on him if she hoped to avoid being fooled by his sleight-of-hand maneuvers. She smiled and offered Darlene a seat. "Cup of coffee?"

"Now, Ms. Showers, genteel gestures can't distract me. Everyone saw the drum major run the band into the bar ditch during homecoming parade—like some pied piper tooting a tempting tune on his dope whistle. We all saw it."

While Dr. Whitfield had laughed during the parade, Ms. Showers knew that fiasco would haunt them the same way hard water stains lingered in her shower though she'd doused it with X-14. Quincey had never led a parade before, and he swore the band director gave the signal for a counter march, although maneuvering one with the rest of the parade following the band didn't seem sensible. Still, Quincey obeyed orders. And it wasn't his fault that the senior class 'Gator float had slid too close to the band, violating the thirty yard formation. When the woodwinds filed out the back of the brass section, those snapping jaws threatened to chomp instruments and fingers, forcing Quincey to give a quick left flank. When the band turned, Quincey realized they were headed off the blacktop. It didn't help that the band was playing the alma mater. Panicked, Quincey stood on the shoulder of the road, waving his baton in a 4/4 pattern, too stunned to blow the whistle. The band, instruments banging, collapsed into the ditch.

"No one was bit," Ms. Showers said. "Seriously, you got false information. But you can print in tomorrow's paper that I've called in drug dogs to sniff out narcotics. That should prove Quincey's innocence and calm the fears you'll rouse unnecessarily if you print that silly story. Quincey's parents might sue. If you don't have any more proof than some phone call you think Mr. Rivers made."

And though Darlene swallowed Ms. Showers' whitewash about drug dogs and she did manage to find a private investigator whose canine squad could come on short notice, that phone call Irving made taunted her. Obviously, he was a stalker, obsessed with her. If he knew about Mr. Rivers, he knew about the State Auto Show and maybe even about her flashy brassieres. She squirmed, maybe with worry, and a bra strap slid from her shoulder, dangling like a white flag from her sleeve.

On Thursday, the student body protested the use of heroin: *Kick the Horse Habit* the banners demanded. Between classes, Ms. Showers heard cowboy boots and ropers stomp through the halls. The sassy tap she detected was Irving, who showed up wearing a three-piece suit and white patent dress shoes. He bought the outfit at St. Anthony, he boasted, a thrift store over in Montoya. Cut from plaid fabric, the suit drooped off his shoulders like a pancho, but the sleeves stopped short of his wrists and tangled around his elbows when he tried to move his arms. A boutonniere dangled from his lapel.

Ms. Showers pretended to ignore him for she'd learned by now that disdain hooked his attention better than outrage. Sure enough, while the drug dogs searched the lockers and dressing rooms, Irving visited Peggy's office. He propped his white shoes on her desk. He'd caught Neal in the bathroom again. "Snorting Smarties," he said. His index finger clamped one nostril, and he inhaled like he was whiffing cocaine.

"Seem to know the routine, Irving. Had lots of practice?"

"Mock me all you like." He tugged his suit jacket straight and buttoned it. "It's my Presidential duty to inform the authorities about this problem in the men's room. Smarties and Pez today, but tomorrow, Neal could o.d. on bluebirds, angel dust, XTC. You're obstructing justice if you don't tell. And what if Mr. Rivers found out? Could he dirty your chances for the Principal's job?"

Peggy's left cheek twitched, but she held a steady gaze. She thought her voice might jitter if she tried to speak, so charged was she with their game. It reminded her of the impatience she felt when fighting the weeds in her garden. They grew as fast as she yanked them, her garden never spotless but always a challenging chore. Crushing the dirt in her hands, she felt a power she couldn't experience just holding a dishrag or duster. "Irving, your *A* in shop is the only star preserving your position on Student Council. If I tell Mr. Rivers you're impersonating him, you're liable to end up an impeached President."

Irving's face hardened. "I keep saying I'm on your side. I thought you were sharper than that."

Ms. Showers stared at Irving's boutonniere. Though she knew it offered a soothing scent, her breath tightened like it did when her bathroom tensed with the odor of Comet, Vanish, and other chemicals. She sensed she was on the verge of sanitizing Irving's interest, but she didn't know why. "You've worn rebellious costumes everyday. You're mocking me."

Irving shook his head. He walked around her desk and brushed his lips against her ear. "Damn it, Peggy," he whispered. "I have an image to maintain."

Ms. Showers escorted Irving back to English and when they arrived, they discovered the drug dogs were inspecting his classmates. Mrs. Henley had jumped in front of Cathy Bryant who cowered in the corner of the room, screaming that a dog tried to molest her. "He humped my leg. I swear."

The dog shuffled away from Cathy as if her frigid reaction yanked no fur off his back. He swaggered around the room, sniffing desks, legs, feet, until he bumped into Neal McKray. Slumped in his chair with his head propped against the chalkboard, Neal slept through the whole incident. The dog whiffed his backpack. He licked it. Then he grumbled, breathed, licked again, and stretched his bark into an angry howl. Neal popped awake. Snatching the canvas in his teeth, the dog slung it. The zipper unstitched from the fabric. The contents spilled on the floor: pencils, pens, calculator, saxophone reeds, *The Scarlet Letter*, and a small Ziploc. The dog pounced on the baggy. His teeth tore at the plastic until the trainer yelled, "Heel!" The trainer slapped Neal's shoulder and shook the bag in his face. Inside, several rectangular pills and a round mirror jiggled.

Irving elbowed Ms. Showers. "Told you."

"Officer, may I see that please?" She opened the baggy and held the pills in her hand. Colored a pastel orange, pink, and yellow, they smelled like fruit. She popped one in her mouth. The class gasped. "They're only Smarties," she said, handing the contraband back to the trainer. "Maybe your dogs need a refresher course."

The officer insisted on taking the candy for testing. Before Ms. Showers left, Neal started snoring again. Cathy sat back in her seat, writing her English assignment though her hands trembled. Irving hunkered behind her sniffing her hair like a dog in heat. Ms. Showers could hear him whine. "Carry on," she told Mrs. Henley. Then Peggy scurried out of the room because she could feel a strange choking in her throat, almost like tears but more like one tiny weed worming around her tongue.

Friday's activities focused on the idea Irving's mom had volunteered. Since she owned the floral shop in town, she suggested Ms. Showers hold a sixties dress-up day. "Sniff the Roses, not Glue," she answered when Ms. Showers asked what the slogan could be. "Everyone can dress like flower children."

"Wasn't the drug culture started in the sixties?" Dr. Whitfield stammered when Ms. Showers arrived at school that morning. "Aren't flower children infamous dopers? Some religious right-wingers might think we're sending subliminal messages."

Ms. Showers glared at him, and he skittered back to his godly origami, shaping a male and female bunny from a pack of Charmin. He'd become pretty easy to bully.

Irving's mom scattered rose petals and carnations down every hallway. Potpourri sat in little containers in the bathrooms. Ms. Showers took turns walking into each lavatory, breathing in the dewy scent. The cheerleaders stapled posters of The Monkees over the old traffic signs, and they planned a special pep rally to cheer everyone to clean living. They promised to perform a dance routine to The Monkees' theme, in honor of Ms. Johnson's floral donations, and the band, wearing tie-dyed shirts and headbands, would play several Monkees tunes.

When the bell sounded to dismiss classes for the pep rally, Ms. Showers stationed herself near the gym, waiting to see if Irving would be holding Cathy's hand. She'd report their relationship to Cathy's mother: no decent woman would want her daughter dating a future con. But Ms. Showers didn't see Cathy. Instead she spied Irving and Kent Williams, giggling near the trophy case. Irving wore an old pair of Blue Snap jeans that Ms. Showers recognized from the 70's. They barely clung to his hips. A pair of platform shoes gave him extra height, and a pair of shades with aqua lenses made him resemble John Lennon. He snapped the glasses off his face, gave Ms. Showers the peace sign, then handed his shades to Kent who was begging to wear them.

Kent sported flared jeans and a suede vest with fringe shimmying around his butt. Ms. Showers wondered why Kent wasn't gearing up with the rest of the drumline. She didn't like the two earrings stapled in his left ear or the Zildjian tattoo that punctured his right bicep. Someone had told her Zildjian was a brand of cymbals, but she thought it looked like gang insignia.

Then, Cathy Bryant waltzed by, her white go-go boots shuffling a rhythm down the hall. Kent called to her. "Here, here, my little papaya." His hand reached out like he wanted to pick some produce. Ms. Showers imagined his palm was already tacky with fruit juice. She hated sticky messes.

"Hey, little pomegranate." Irving licked his lips.

Before Ms. Showers could interrupt this pick-up, she spotted Neal McKray holding open the door to the gymnasium. His shaggy hair splintered around a tie he wore as a headband. Jimmy Hendrix leaned across his T-shirt, playing a guitar. Neal's mouth slid into a smile, and he sang, "*Hey, hey, we're The Monkees. People say we monkey around.*" He slapped a textbook against his hip and then his palm, like he was banging a tambourine. She thought his deep-set eyes, pointed nose, bulbous chin and skinny lips resembled a chimpanzee's face. He staggered and fell to the floor, wiping his brow. For a moment, Ms. Showers thought he'd erased the color from his cheeks, for she'd finally noticed his soapy complexion.

When Ms. Showers turned to ask Irving what was going on with Neal, Lane and Lacey stumbled into her. Their matching tie-dyed shirts and torn jeans turned Ms. Showers' stomach. Lacey caught her balance against the wall and pulled Lane to safety too, as if they dangled on a ledge. Then they began fondling one another. Lacey giggled, and Lane grunted like a pig. He nuzzled Lacey's underarm and smiled as if the smell satiated his desires.

Cathy Bryant skipped to Ms. Showers and kissed her cheek. Ms. Showers could feel the stamp of frosty lipstick. "I feel sooo good," Cathy said. "This can't be right." She slunk to the floor, woozy and apparently drugged.

The paramedics arrived in ten minutes, and by then, Irving, Kent, Neal, Lane, Lacey, and Cathy lay stretched on the floor in gaudy costumes. "Looks like a damn Woodstock reunion," one of the EMS men said.

Neal gripped Ms. Showers' arm and pulled her hair when she squatted to feel his forehead. "Someone in shop said it was candy. I snort candy all the time."

Lacey sat up and squealed. "Candy! That's what he said. I thought I was swallowing candy, too!"

"I'm sure," Ms. Showers said, "because one always swallows candy. It tastes better if you down it with a glass of water."

Lane reached over and placed his bulky hand on Lacey's back. It spread over her spine like that marijuana leaf on Irving's T-shirt. "Does my little Easter Bunny like candy? How about a Hot Tamale?" He started to unzip his pants, but a paramedic clamped Lane's arm to the floor.

Mr. Rivers hovered over Cathy Bryant, taking her pulse and spitting stats to the paramedics. "Nice way to end your Just Say No campaign. What a climax. Guess you showed those drug dealers." He smiled, leered almost, and Ms. Showers thought he might be on dope, too. But when he fingered Irving's throat, watching the clock that hung above the gym door, he looked like an expert in CPR, and Ms. Showers laughed at her paranoia. Then he leaned over Irving to check his breathing.

Irving popped upright. "He touched the hatch! The candy man tried to open my hatch!"

Kent clasped his head in his hands. "Mine too!" he yelled.

Mr. Rivers grimaced and plugged his ears. "I'm not deaf," he screamed at them. Then he slumped, his eyes rolling backward and his head collapsing on Kent's shoulder.

Ms. Showers shoved him off and slammed him against Irving, promising Kent that Mr. Rivers would be severely reprimanded. Ms. Showers glared at Irving. "See?" she asked. She wanted to tell everyone that Irving was the candy man, but her tongue felt knotted again, and she knew tears would choke her words if she tried to speak. She leaned against the wall, exhausted and panicked as if she'd just been dumped. This drug frenzy in the middle of her Just Say No campaign would permanently soil her tenure at Phorney High.

But while Ms. Showers pondered her inevitable fate, watching Mr. Rivers' chest heave, Irving clasped her hand and whispered to her. "Peggy," he said. He said she knew how to bleach dirty situations, and it looked to him that Mr. Rivers was not only high on candy too, but probably lived the secret life of a pedophile, desperate to maul the hatches of every male student interested in mechanics. She could ship him to rehab in Dallas. She could fire him tomorrow. She could be the custodian who spared the Phorney teens years of repressed memories, therapy, marred relationships.

Irving's arms, like puppeteer strings, bound Mr. Rivers into an upright position. He tweaked Mr. River's nose as if gripping a wrench.

"You going to remember the little people like me, right?" For just a second, Irving's eyes cleared the way fog can lift momentarily before dropping its heavy curtain again.

And Ms. Peggy Showers knew, could see it in his eyes, glassy as crystal balls. He'd framed Mr. Rivers. For her benefit. His mouth spread into a dopey smile—he thought it was love. Then he palmed a rose in full bloom from his sleeve, a real flower this time. Winking, he tucked it over her ear, inside her hair, and his hand caressing her cheek as it retreated, brushed soft as a feather duster swishing her worries away. ✿

THE POSSUM

by Mark Busby

As I reach the place where I usually cross the street on my way to the park, I'm forced to stop and wait for an emergency vehicle from a nearby fire station. I jog in place impatiently, looking down at my running shoes and noticing that I'm straddling a yellow line that marks the edge of the street. I'm trying to follow my usual routine when I am home for a visit, so I jog down to the city park nearby, where the jogging track circles a small fishing pool and several baseball and soccer fields. I live now in a small town and can run with ease on back roads where I see maybe a single car on a ten mile run. I don't like people; that's why I moved my computer consulting business out of the city. When I'm in Dallas, I try to run early and miss the weekend families out in the park. But I can't miss the sounds of city life, for the park is just over the hill from the fire station and even on Sunday mornings, or perhaps especially on Sunday mornings, the sirens of these EMS units going out to treat injuries pierce the morning air and roll down the hill into the park with screaming vengeance just as this one with its flashing lights shrieks past.

The route from my mother's apartment takes me by the small cemetery where my sister Catherine lies buried. I usually don't run through there because I'm afraid that mourners might find it disrespectful for a sweaty body with a t-shirt that says "Shit Happens," "Quayle Is a Dick," or even "Go Buffs" to sully the serenity. And I don't much like cemeteries, but I've promised my mother to look at my sister's grave and make sure everything is all right. A mugger tried to grab Mother's purse on her way into Dillard's, and when she resisted, he jerked it away from her. She fell and broke her hip and can't get out yet.

At the park, I round the track, cross the bridge over the gentle stream, pad beside the little league field that seems almost miniature, pass the swing and seesaw, go by the tennis courts and am showered by more shrieks of the sirens as the EMT's race out to the shootings, stabbings, and car wrecks that constitute Sunday morning worship service in America at the end of the century. I put on headphones from my walkman but even its loud volume will not drown out the screech. Soon it fades somewhat into the distance but remains a presence in the morning air.

On my second lap I pass two boys about ten in animated argument near the swings. I'm relieved that my headphones drown out their words. Jogging on, I realize that autumn in Dallas is more colorful than my hill country community whose live oaks and cedars are unaffected by the seasons. North Texas has a much greater variety of trees, and now the yellows, reds, browns, and oranges of the changing elms, oaks, bois d'arcs, and pecans flame across the area and especially in this planned public park. As I make my last lap around the track, I try to count the different varieties but lose count halfway.

On the way back I turn into the cemetery and jog back toward the new section with Catherine's grave. I go slowly through the older section on the right that lacks the uniformity of the new area. Lots are of a varied size, and markers range from modest stones to gaudy rising angels. Here flesh become words as the markers try to offer some lasting comment on the dead. "In Loving Memory," "Asleep in Jesus," "Rest in peace," "Gone but Not Forgotten," "Dearly Departed." In the older part, I note the monuments marking Civil War and World War I and II vets, and their headstones document their experiences: "Member, Company B, Terry's Texas Cavalry." One small grave is distinctive, for the marker reads: "It's a little grave/ But O have care,/ For worldwide hopes are buried here;/ How much of light, how much of joy/ Are buried with our darling boy."

The new part is across a small road. A hill rolls down to a street that marks the boundary, and across the street is a railroad track beside a stream. There are almost no trees in this part and almost all the graves are single ones. No family plots are squared here. Markers lie flat against the ground. Only a small holder for flowers rises above the mounds, and almost all of them here are filled with colorful plastic flowers. Some cemeteries, I understand, discourage plastic flowers, but not this one. I suppose it's because they're easy to maintain. No wilted stems to remove. I think the plastic flowers are a good idea. You don't have to check on them as often. Still it's a jolt on a cool late autumn day after the first freeze to find the blaze of colors splashed across these graves. At first glance it looks like flowers have cheated death and altered the natural course of things.

I search for my sister's grave; I haven't stopped here but once since she died. I know it's on the second row about mid-way down, but without bushes or trees to distinguish the area, I have to walk along reading the markers. In this area most of the graves are of younger people. No miniature graves for babies, but most of these dead are people in their teens, twenties, and thirties—people without families since they're buried singly here. I find my sister's grave. Mother has left yellow silk flowers, not plastic ones but not real ones either. Catherine's marker is simple: her name and "Sister and Daughter, October 2, 1951–March 15, 1987."

I'm about to leave when I realize that I'm not alone. I look up and notice a squatty man sitting on a bench under the canopy-covered cement slab near the edge of the new section. I'm surprised I hadn't seen him when I came up, but I see now that there's a pickup parked out at the curb. Most people drive into the cemetery, but this guy must have walked up the hill. As I look up at him, he stands, tips his cowboy hat to me, smiles broadly, and begins to limp over toward me. He's short and broad, a fireplug with a hat and a smile. I start at first to just wave and jog off. I'm definitely not interested in company, but I can tell from the guy's face that he wants to talk. Maybe the good humor is a mask for his anger at someone jogging in a place reserved for serenity. That smile looks genuine though. He extends his hand. I notice that he's wearing black, hightop Keds, the kind I used to wear in junior high school.

"Howdy. Howdy. It looks like this here sun's going to warm it up this morning, don't it. Damn these corns. I can just barely walk."

"Yeah, I reckon it is," I answer, wincing as I drop into a regionalism without being able to stop myself.

"You got a loved one out here?" he asks, sweeping around the area with his arm.

"Yes, this is my sister." I point and then notice that he's holding a small spiral notebook. He writes briefly in it with the nub of a pencil as he looks down at Catherine's headstone.

"That's my son over there," he gestures. "Fell out of the pickup truck when I was driving down Gaston Avenue, 1986. Hit his head on the cement. Seventeen years old." His comments are guileless, straight-forward. There's no particular sadness or guilt in his voice. He could be telling me about some cattle he has for sale as easily as he is about the death of his son.

"C'mon. Let's git out of this here sun. I been out in it so long it's eating up my skin. Doctor says for me to stay out it as much as I can."

"I really have to be heading home," I protest.

"Naw, c'mon now." He takes me by the arm and guides me over to the canopied area and points to one of the benches there. I notice that his sunglasses look like the kind welder's wear with protective glass curving around the edges and all the way to the skin.

"This here one is mine. See there, 'Ledbetter,' it says there on the side."

I hadn't noticed that these granite benches have names on them until he sits on one.

"Yep, I come out here and sit right here on my bench. Not that one there, that's Forester. Their daughter is buried over there." He points. "See that one with the big yellow flowers.? That's Sherry Forester. She died in a headon up I-35 just beyond Lewisville. Some guy was drunk and coming down the wrong way. She never knowed what hit her. Closed casket. The car, one of them little foreign Jap jobs, got cut right in two. Awful."

I nod, uncomfortable with his intimacy.

"Well, I ought to be taking off," I say and start to get up, but he ignores me. "And you see that other bench down yonder. That's Tommy Swindell. He's the one down there with them purple ones.

"Tommy got shot by the po-lice." He pronounces it with the accent on the first syllable, I notice, the po-lice. "Some kind of a drug deal. Tommy was kind of dumb. After the po-lice let him know who they were he reached into his pocket real quick, and they let him have it. He shouldn't a done that. He didn't have no gun. They didn't know what he was reaching for. Just dumb."

I mumble something about that being too bad and stand up. Ledbetter doesn't stop.

"And that other one just next to Tommy, the one with them plastic roses, that's George Harris. Now he was a Vietnam vet. Lived through the war. Got back here and couldn't get off the sauce. Drank hisself to death. He wasn't but thirty-nine. Still young."

I'm ready to go and start walking out from under the canopy toward the street where Ledbetter's truck is parked, but he won't let me go. He comes out toward me and grabs my arm.

"C'mon over here. I want to show you something."

He walks me around the canopy and back into the line of graves, narrating along the way.

"That's Lance Guyton right there with them purple flowers there. Died of AIDS. Wasn't but thirty-one. His friend, a fella named Louis, used to come out here regular, but I ain't seen him in a long time. Right nice. He'd change them flowers ever time he come out. Yellow one week, red the next, then all different colors. Lance has been purple since the last time Louis was here."

"Now, c'mon over here. This is what I want to show you. This here is Sharon Oldfeather, killed by a rapist. She was an Indian." (He pronounces it "Indyun.") Died at twenty-four. See that there, he says pointing to the headstone. See?" He bends over and touches the marker. "This here is Indian words they put on this stone. See." He rubs the words on the granite slowly and lovingly. "Choctaw, I think, but I don't know for shore, all them Indians look alike to me."

"Well, it was nice talking to you," I say, again trying to leave.

"Now, come on back here and sit on my bench under the canopy. I cain't stand this sun, you know. I want you to tell me about your sister now." He looks again at the notebook.

"You know I come out here all the time. That's how I know about these other folks. I ask about their loved ones when they come out here to visit. I like to know about the other folks out here with Bennie. So you come on over here and tell me about Catherine."

I am jolted by his sudden familiarity as he calls my sister's name. I hadn't come here to think about Catherine. I just wanted to make sure that her grave looked okay. I did not want to talk about my sister.

"Oh, well," I say. "There's no big story here. She died of cancer," I say, but the image of her on that last Christmas cuts through me like the north wind.

"The big C, huh," says Ledbetter. "That can shore be a bad way to go. Did she suffer?"

I want to walk away from this little man, offended that he's trying to get me to talk about something that the family has tried to forget.

"Look, I'd rather not talk about this if you don't mind. I've got to get home."

Ledbetter keeps on as if I had said nothing. "It was pretty bad I guess. What kind did she have?"

"Breast cancer," I answer despite myself. "Spread to her pancreas and liver." And I remember her announcing that she'd asked for both breasts to be removed and how she'd become obsessed with yoga and heathy diets after the operation. How she became paranoid and couldn't go back to work, accusing her coworkers of conspiracies to take credit for her work. How we all would get together and shake our heads about Catherine and wonder when she would have the implants and try to live a normal life again. How we all thought that her obsessive bathing and sleeping were all in her head.

"Did she have them cut off?" Ledbetter asks.

"Leave me alone," I blurt out, pulling away from him. "This is none of your goddamn business."

"No harm meant," he says, smiling. "You know what they say. There's so much bullshit in the world, a fella's bound to step into some of it some time."

"I've got to go," I say and start down the hill.

"That's okay," he calls out to me, "I'll see you again sometime. Me and Bennie and Catherine will be here next time you come by. So long."

As I jog down the hill, I am forced to think about Catherine and recall the day she got the results of her first biopsy. She was working in Houston and had an apartment down near NASA, just beyond the string of chemical plants that dot the Houston ship channel. She had called me to drive down and be with her during the procedure and wait with her for the results. It was springtime, just before tax time, my busiest season. I thought she was being an alarmist, but I took work with me and went.

The feeling in her apartment was so oppressive after the doctor called and told her the test was positive that I had to get out, so I went jogging though the campus at Clear Lake. Just across from the Student Union, I noticed an opossum lying in the roadway, and on an impulse I stopped, wondering if it was playing possum. I remember how I squatted down and looked at its still body. Its long hairless tail, rope-like, lay across it. I rolled the possum over with my Nike, and it was clearly dead. Rigor mortis had begun to set in, stiffening the corpse. Suddenly I noticed movement in its pouch and saw two babies, eyes closed, mouths moving in a sucking motion. Startled, I had run quickly away and had forgotten about the experience until now when it is suddenly unearthed and comes unbidden to consciousness.

As I reach the street where I turn to Mother's house, my eyes blur, and I must stop and lean against a chain link fence. Behind me an emergency vehicle screams past and turns toward Central Expressway. ✿

THE LAST DEER EVER SEEN IN THIS PART OF THE COUNTRY

by L. D. Clark

Year after year the old man repeated his deer story, and his neighbors always welcomed it, often as they'd heard it before. Because over time it became a ritual: a tale solemn beyond the telling in that during the old man's lifespan one era succeeded another so quickly that the epoch of the story receded into a mythic past whose echo resounded in the voice of the storyteller. A group of men would gather and wait in silent anticipation which never failed to rouse the old man into repeating the ceremony. His story was no yarn. It was simple and earnest and varied hardly a word from one telling to the next:

"I killed the last deer ever seen in this part of the country. A big old buck. I was about twelve at the time. One morning right at sunup me and Pap stepped outside, and there that monster stood, head up and broadside under a big old elm tree on the hill above our homeplace out yonder."

"Now Pap he reached easy back inside for the old muzzle-loader he kept leaning again the door jamb. He fetched it right out and, I want you to know, he handed it to me. Nor he didn't say nothing. Just give me a steady look.

"Well sir, whichaway to turn next? Pap, he just stood there awaiting. Finely I made my move. A mighty risky one, too. I stepped right soft over to the wellbox—a few foot over thisaway—for a gunrest. I knelt down and laid the barrel along the lid, taken good aim and squeezed the trigger. And blam! down he went. For a little bit I couldn't believe my own eyes, because I dropped him smack dab in his tracks."

He would pause then, draw a deep breath and relish the silent pleasure of his hearers. . . .

That shot was fired in eighteen hundred and something. The old man lived far into the nineteen hundreds, while so much happened in Compton

County that the time gone by appeared too brief to contain it. This was where the old man and his story came in. What a calendar could not touch in the passage of time, the shape of a unique event could: a moment at sunrise, a boy with a rifle, a creature the last of his kind shot dead: not just the last remaining deer but the last wild animation of the land itself. This event, as voiced by the old man, seemed a perfect joining of time-is and time-was, with years reaching back to the coming of the first white settlers to Compton County, which to the people alive in the old age of the tale-teller was like the beginning of time itself.

The parents of the old man were among those first settlers. They built their cabin of hewn logs on the homestead where their son was later born, and where the buck eventually fell. Before settlement the country hereabouts had lain undisturbed since the true beginning of time, except for a few Indian tribes drifting through: a land of hills heavy with timber, in places flats of oak and hickory and elm extending a smooth brown leaf floor among a regular spacing of tree trunks to the limit of vision. Here and there lay glades as trim as parkland, teeming with wildflowers in the warm months. Springs at the base of the low hills sent pure streams across many glades to gather into small clear lakes. Beetrees stood thick in the woodland. Deer and a multitude of other game broke cover at every hand.

Once plows had sliced into the turf of the glades, the wildflowers vanished, many never to return. The tallest and straightest of the oaks the settlers chopped down for cabins and barns and firewood, the rest they felled and burned on the spot. Every foot of land with good soil was turned into fields. What was too rocky or hilly, or too soggy in the bottomlands, was turned into pastures soon filled beyond capacity with livestock.

So the land started to erode. Gullies appeared. Springs filled in. Most of the streams went dry, and the few left became polluted. The game that was not killed off died out. The time when a deer became a rarity, and then with a single gunshot a thing of the past, was upon the people before they could absorb their own history.

The teller and the tale kept pace with all this. The population of Compton County swelled, doubling from one decade to the next. Talk of twenty thousand inhabitants at first sounded unbelievable. But once that number was reached, then forty thousand was no longer out of the question. Or, as some dared to dream, the county seat might be transformed into a metropolis. And who could tell the limit of that? Five hundred thousand? Or why not a million: a number with real magic in it?

Inside this rush to the future the memory of killing the buck became momentous as prophecy fulfilled. More yet, the prophet himself was still alive to remind the people that his deed stood for thousands like it by which the pioneers had prepared the land for its present condition of plenty. Without those deeds summed up in his own, the roads could never have threaded the county, the farmers never have brought in their harvest, the stores never have filled their counters and show-windows with the good things of life.

So the satisfaction of a great mission accomplished trembled in the voice of the story-teller as he silently took credit for what he and his listeners took such pride in. Beyond this echo of marvelous achievement another was forever heard: the passage of a deed beyond the measure of time into the sacred aura of myth.

The old man and his wife had only one child, a daughter who died young. In due course he traded the homestead for a house in town, and not long after they moved, his wife died, too. From then on he lived alone. As for the homestead, once he had surrendered it to the new owner, he refused to set foot on it. Imagination took over. The homestead was no longer ten miles from his front porch in Milcourt where he most often told his story. It took on the distance of memory. The hill where the buck had fallen slipped into the faraway just as the event did, fashioning a marvel glimmering before the inner eye of the old man and his listeners as if out of a fabulous age and a fabulous geography where a tree as tall as a thunderhead sheltered a buck with antlers like a fork of lightning and haunches that rose like an ancient upthrust of boulders.

Then, all at once, a change came over the world.

In much of Compton County the soil proved too thin to support the years of overuse. As a living grew harder to grub out of it, many left their farms either for Milcourt—no metropolis after all—or for one of the cities now sprawling not far away. The deserted fields filled with weeds. Thickets and second-growth saplings and cedar brakes invaded the cut-over timberland among the few big trees too knotty or crooked to use. The cleared land did begin to recover slowly as thin pasture, but the owners of the cattle grazing there lived mainly in town, so the old houses caved in one by one. In the country two or three miles might intervene now between occupied dwellings.

But the true astonishment was that the deer came back. That is, the game commission trucked in a few head from wilder parts of the state and released them in the creek bottoms, from which they spread and thrived. Within a few years Compton County had a deer season.

So now the men could become real hunters. And they sought out the old man with their hunting stories, as if in repayment for sustaining them during the long deprivation. He gave a close ear to all they said, planted square in an old metal lawn chair softened by a ragged cushion, a firm and wiry presence for all his years. But he offered little in reply, and, strangely, he seldom told his own story anymore. The hunters got used to this, came to look on it almost as homage: as acceptance of their own stories into fellowship with one that had long been unique. Or, as a look or a chance word might convey, some hunters treasured their own stories as superseding the old man's, exhibiting the triumph of a later over an earlier generation.

The truth was that the old man puzzled constantly over emotions new to him. His story had always given form and clarity to the history of his world. But now that seemingly finished world had collapsed. The species whose extinction had been essential to the creation of modern times: the species whose obliteration he had accomplished single-handed, had unaccountably reappeared. And had multiplied by the hundreds. But how could a game commission—the government!—produce at will a herd of descendants of the legendary creature he had annihilated? If history could be so easily abrogated, then what could his singular deed mean, or with it the whole sequence of events from early settlement to the present day? And so in silence and dismay he simply refused to believe that the deer of this day and age could even belong to the same species as the gigantic buck he had brought down. He had no desire even to see a modern deer. So although hunter after hunter invited him to join them, he only gave a negative chuckle and a headshake.

Now one young man in Milcourt had not paid the old man a visit for a long while. Because, for reasons peculiar to his nature, he had as yet no buck to his credit, no story to offer. Growing up in town, he'd had no woods of his own to roam. Still, next to his outlying house was a creek bottom with dogwood thickets and a cedar brake. There he played at hunting from early boyhood, from the day when he talked his mother out of an air rifle if not any shot for it. But he found a way past that. The cedar berries were the size of BB shot. Dropping one down the barrel and cocking the lever, he would flush a bird, take aim, pull the trigger and thrill to the weak *pow*. That the berry fell to the ground a few feet away, and the bird flew on unharmed, was all the same to him. As yet he made no great distinction between shooting at a bird and dropping one.

When he reached the age for a .22 rifle, and finally a shotgun, he hunted on the farms of friends what there was to hunt: squirrels, rabbits, quail, possums, rarely a fox. All this was before the return of the deer, and he took it for granted that such big game would remain forever beyond his grasp. As with many others, all he knew of that vanished animal came from the old man's story, to which he had always been an avid listener. What passed before the eye of thought then was a kneeling boy and a giant buck at each end of a rifle shot's distance, a scene to which he gave silent reverence till it faded, as he would to any recurrent and inviolate wonder.

So the reappearance of the deer astounded the young man as much as it did the old man, if in another fashion. All at once what he had thought out of the question was here before him: he could hunt deer, and in his own county at that. Soon after he began to ponder this, however, he discovered in his mind a curious but compelling twist: that he had no desire to hunt anywhere except on the ground to which the old man's story belonged, which brought him to the perhaps insurmountable necessity of matching physical against imaginary reality.

He knew the countryside well. He had driven past the old man's farm many times. The present owner lived in a city and seldom came to see about his property. The young man greatly envied him, and with that feared he could never persuade him to lease the hunting rights. It took over a year of negotiations, until at a price the young man could ill afford the prize was his: the sole privilege of hunting the woods and glades of the great buck.

On the first day of the season he pitched his tent in the deepest woods of the farm. The glades outside the woods were old fields eroded away, or scanty meadows and pastures, all derelict and ragged with brush and weeds. Even so it was no more than a few hundred yards in any direction to the edge of his domain, and on one side a blacktop road announced its nearness periodically by the hum of speeding tires. Any direction he considered revealed clearly how cramped were the limits of his hunting grounds.

But he had prepared himself for this, and his camping place, in a draw among gray rocks at the head of a deep ravine, under a few postoaks, could still call up wilderness enough to justify expecting an incarnation of the great buck in the next clearing, over the next rise, out of the next clump of saplings. Not in reality, maybe, but as he hunted he sensed the shadow of that presence: let the shadow hover beyond reason, let it be of his own invention, expectation still clung that the actual gigantic creature might in an instant spring out of it.

Day by day he retraced every pocket of his hunting grounds. He saw droppings recent enough to keep his hopes glowing. He heard shots from deer leases close by. The third day, in a creek bottom a little beyond the fenceline of this farm, he saw a standing deer. By the time he could focus his binoculars, it was gone. The fourth day what was surely a large deer bolted unseen out of a cedar brake ahead, with a swish and crackle of branches and a quick clatter of rocks.

On the fifth day it happened. Daybreak came through bands of cloud rolling low and dark with light furrows between. Brushes of rain sounded now and again among dead leaves hanging thick on the blackjack trees. But no drops touched him as he left his draw in the first light of dawn and stole along over the leaf floor, glad to have the noise of his steps softened by the moisture underfoot. Not until he crossed a notch between two rises and came into an old field did he truly notice how the closeness of the gliding clouds drew all the horizontal of earth nearby into a sphere of dark clarity that seemed to move along with him: a sphere within which he could see in exact relation, better than in bright sunlight, each tracing of the earth and its growth. But then, at a deceptive distance, that clarity went murky under the low clouds, and as these lightened or darkened, objects appeared to shift closer or farther away. Now and then the sky let down shreds of mist that drifted against distant trees in ever-changing shapes.

His senses were tensed into such alertness that he did not know whether a sudden conviction of the proximity of a deer came from within or without. He felt that presence so powerfully that he stalked along with every muscle straining, rifle gripped against his chest.

He stopped, the thump-thump of his heart loud in the stillness. Then a tiny noise. He darted his eyes around to catch any movement. Only a weed, after all, touching his pants leg with a faint scratching transmitted from the uncontrollable trembling of his whole frame. Another sound, so like the cautious advance of deer hooves through pebbles and brush that he held his breath—but it was only the gurgling of his own innards.

He stood facing a narrow arm of thin timber, through which he could see another overgrown field. The light on that farther clearing came and went at the dim border of his sphere of clarity but near enough for him to be assured that he now saw the head and antlers of a large buck protruding from a mass of underbrush, with a tatter of mist sweeping the horizon behind the antlers. He was not looking this way. He stood with lifted head, intent on the space directly before him, in that arrested and engrossed and wary attitude that only a wild animal can assume.

The young man raised his rifle slowly. He strained to steady the bead of the open sight on the base of the deer's neck. He drew in a deep breath and held it. Still the gun wavered. He could only hope when he squeezed the trigger that he had chosen the right moment in the barely weaving motion of his arms. He took the recoil of the shot firmly, remembering not to lower the rifle too soon. When he did lower it, he worked the lever quickly to reload, flicked on the safety, strode forward, troubled in that he had caught no movement, no sound, after the burst of the shot. His heart pounded with the hope that his prey had dropped where it stood: like that buck from another age.

He came to the spot. It was void of evidence that a deer had ever set foot on it: no scuffing of the low thick clumps of brush, no dirt kicked up by dashing feet, no sign of blood.

He sank to his knees, hugging the rifle planted before him. Minute by minute he studied the distance, as though waiting for some click in time to snatch back the instant of squeezing the trigger, to recover before him the presence of the deer. . . .

The countryside started coming to life: the first flight of crows in a clamor overhead, a scuttling squirrel, the awakening mink-mink of a blue jay, the coyotes giving their end-of-the-night signal yelps across the hills. . . .

Of course! What was wrong about all this was that the old man was not here. . . .

When he reached Milcourt, that warm and clearing afternoon, he drove straight to the old man's house. Scowling on recognizing Lon Busby's pickup in the driveway, he parked and went on toward the porch anyhow.

Lon crowed out, "Hey, ole buddy."

The old man sat perched on his lawn chair. Lon lounged closeby with legs dangling over the edge of the porch, his pot belly protruding over the beltline of his khakis, his pale round face thrust forward with a toothy grin, his gimme cap barely clinging to the back of his head.

"How're you, Eck?" the old man said.

"Not bad, Ab. What you up to?"

"He's about got enough of these hunter fellers, I reckon," Lon put in, nodding to lead attention to a brown paper bag standing between him and Ab.

Eck sat down cross-legged on the floor to Ab's right. Lon repositioned himself to face them both and plunged into the subject cut off by Eck's arrival: "Ab, I wish I'd'a brought his rack to show you. Three big old points on either side. Counting his eye-crooks, that makes one hell of an eight-point buck!"

Prodded out of his silence, Ab went, "Huhh. You call that a buck.

About like the rest I hear tell of these days. Why, they say some of 'em're tall enough to see over a jack rabbit's back—if he ain't standing too close."

Lon toyed with the bill of his cap and gave a wheezy laugh, "Aw, he's just showing his appreciation, Eck. You see, I brung him some deer chops."

He flipped a thumb toward the paper bag.

Ab had gone back to the silence he ordinarily kept these days when the talk was about hunting.

"Been out this year, Eck?" Lon hurried on to ask.

"Sort of."

"Any luck?"

"If you call seeing one luck."

"Get a shot at him?"

"One."

Lon gave Eck a bug-eyed stare, putting more teeth yet into his grin. Then he made a gesture filled with great satisfaction: he set the gimme cap low over his eyes.

Silence. But that soon brought Lon to his feet. "Well, I gotta be moving along. Go by the beer joint and see how the other fellers're making out this year. Better luck next time, Eck. And uh . . . Ab, don't fall all over yourself thanking me for them chops."

As Lon strutted away, Ab called out, "Shore nuff, I do appreciate the meat, Lon. Don't pay no 'tention to my sour face."

Lon flipped a hand upward without turning, "More'n welcome. More'n welcome."

As they watched Lon drive away, Ab spoke, "I hear tell you got the deer lease on my old place."

"I have, for all the good it's doing me."

"You say you did see a deer?"

"Seen him, yaow. Shot at him too. Missed him."

"Any size to him?"

"Oh—I can't rightly say."

No need to go on. Both knew the only true measure: the size of the ancient buck.

Eck now took his time: "The thing is, Ab, I been studying about it, and I wonder if you'd like to go out with me next time."

"Me! What in the world you talking about?"

Again Eck waited, let Ab go back to his silence. But then Ab came out of it all at once by giving the paper sack a kick that nearly sent it off the porch. "Oh no! You expect me to go off in the woods chasing critters the size of that. I'm too old for any such farting around."

Eck continued to wait. Until Ab spoke up again, slowly:

"I sorta wish you'd tell me what taken place, though. Where you seen him and all like that."

Knowing this might come, Eck had tried to lay out coming into town what he would say, but had hit on no pattern he liked. As he spoke now, he groped for words to be faithful to every detail. But uneasiness gripped him, and soon bordered on panic that Ab would never join him unless he built the event of this morning into a vivid and compelling order, into a manner of telling to convey a gripping certainty that the buck he had fired on existed outside the distortions of his own imagining. . . .

The crucial point came: to describe the buck standing against the undergrowth, the wisp of cloud drifting. As he floundered after precision, he went on talking, straying for a moment from awareness of his own tongue. When he heard again the words flowing from it, he was appalled and yet for all that helpless to control the rush of them:

"Now here I was away back deep in the brush at the foot of a ridge"— 'ridge?' whispered the voice of fact, 'what ridge?'—. "And yessir, he bolted up right under my feet and went crashing away like he meant to tear them woods apart. No sight of him at first. Just that loud thrashing. I like to jumped out of my skin, but I did have the gumption to make a dash over to my right where it was open enough maybe to get a glimpse of him."

"Now you know how a buck'll freeze sometimes, just when you least expect it. Right out in the clear, too. And stand there eyeing you. Well, he done that. And not fifty yards off. He was as tall as a sapling. The sun come out from behind a cloud right above him. And what a sight! The reflection on his coat near blinded you, with a tracing of fire all around him. And what a fork he had! First off it crossed my mind I wasn't seeing antlers atall but a dead tree smack behind his head, with big old bare limbs sticking out.

"I unslung my rifle. But before I was halfway ready he took off. He went bounding straight up that ridge, through timber, leaving a little glimpse of him now and again in some opening: a glimpse of them antlers as big as a hay cradle, or his rump flag up and snow white, or a time or two of his whole body, bright gray and speeding. Crashing on like a runaway team of mules. And still for all that noise, like he was floating. Like maybe he was two bucks at once. Like while he was one buck making all that racket, he was another one skimming along quiet. That last one hit the top of the ridge aflying and disappeared like into the air, like he didn't have no body atall. . . ."

Eck stopped, horrified, too petrified at last to push headlong beyond himself, wondering if his face was as red as the tingling of his skin made him think it was.

Ab's voice was cool and calm: "But then you did get a shot at him, you say."

"I did. Just as he went outa sight for good."

A pause now that stretched longer and longer. Eck would not open his mouth, lest he succumb again to rash inventions.

Finally Ab said, "Let's see, tomorrow and the next day, that's all they is left of the season, ain't it?"

"Yaow."

Another pause. Then Eck knew he could risk it, that it was hardly even a risk: "Any reason why you can't be ready before daylight in the morning?"

Ab slouched back in his chair and let out a big sigh, "No. None as I know of."

As the silence returned, Eck thought, 'Oh God. Oh my God. What am I to do next?'

Next morning when dawn brightened on the two hunters driving out to the old farm, high thin fingers of cloud had begun to reach across from the northwest, slowly thickening and lowering. They had time to reach the farm and pitch the tent on the south side of a timbered ridge before the north wind came, clacking the bare limbs of the trees, hissing along the leaf floor, and soon afterwards flinging snatches of rain from hurrying clouds.

All day they sat in the tent, while the wind jostled it and the now steady rain drummed on the canvas: weather certain to keep all deer bedded down. Otherwise they would have been glad to brave a drenching. During that night, waking to hear only the wind, they had hopes for the next day. And dawn did come with the rain gone, with broken clouds and great patches of bleak orange light, but a cold north wind tossed and whipped among the barren trees.

So it was hunt today or put it off a whole year. That is, Eck could hunt while Ab went along. For when Eck had suggested they pick up a license for Ab and borrow Lon Busby's rifle, Ab only snorted and said, "Let's get on the road."

What to do next was still no great problem for Eck so far this morning. For the time being he had only to attend to immediate events ongoing of their own accord. The camp was near the south boundary of the farm. They walked along the line fence going east to the corner of the property, then wove northward upwind to the northwest. At that corner they worked their way zigzag south, to have at least some advantage in going slantwind.

Slowly they threaded the abandoned fields, the branch-course thickets, the cedar brakes. Through any bit of woods they crept along, surrounded by hiding places that could send a buck leaping any second, counting on the wind to smother their noise.

About mid-morning they drifted to the old houseplace, now marked only by a scattering of hewn logs and rotting planks from the caved-in wellbox. They inspected the ground between the houseplace and where the giant elm had stood. All sign of the tree was gone except for a charred rind of stump. From this they walked in a straight line back to the ruined wellbox, Ab gravely pacing off the distance. Then he stood by the well gazing away toward the tree site. For a long time he gazed, Eck standing by.

By noon they had covered all the ground and seen nothing: no droppings since the rain, no recent tracks in wet earth. Gradually they drifted back to the tent, glad to have temporary shelter from the wind. Not talking, they ate sardines and crackers, and pork and beans cold out of the can—.

"Listen!" Eck said, all of a sudden.

But it was not a sound he felt an urgency to share. It was silence: the wind had fallen.

So they rested for an hour in the quiet. And when they stepped outside they met with what could have been another day altogether. The sky bleak from the north wind was gone. Lower, heavier clouds had slipped across from the southwest, the air was warmer, and now and then a thick drizzle blanked out the atmosphere around them.

They got into slickers and rain hats, in which they were sure to perspire, but it was either be soaked by sweat or by drizzle. Eck carried his rifle with the barrel slanted down under the slicker to keep the action dry.

And so they picked their way through the dripping timber, with little hope, but still with only brief halts to catch their breath, they tramping on through the whole afternoon. All the while it grew darker and mistier. Thickening gloom at day's end found them still in motion, sweating in earnest now, and though Eck worried about Ab's endurance, he showed no sign of tiring.

When they came to the south fence for what must be the last time and swung back toward camp, Ab spoke: "Say, we ain't yet been by that ridge where you seen him. Why's that?"

Eck had hoped this dilemma would never come, yet how could it not? He was afraid to go near that ridge, as though the terrain for which he had invented the buck might betray him, might transmit the lie to Ab out of the very air. Yet how could he justify avoiding the one place where he claimed to have sighted a deer? But then with sundown near and vision dwindling, perhaps he could hide his dread as he maneuvered Ab past the spot. And that did work. They skirted the foot of the slope, Eck halting momentarily a time or two to peer into the timber uphill. And at least Ab refrained from comment. Did he suspect? Eck wondered.

Once they were safely past that ridge, a brief thinning of the mist revealed that dark was not so near as they had thought. Right away Eck decided to circle past a location they had skirted often today but never combed: the far end of that dry ravine gashing a slope among gnarled postoaks where Eck had pitched his tent the first day out.

So they entered the mouth of the ravine and wound their way upward, with dusk rapidly deepening. Now they could see dimly over the banks above into the trees, now their view was hemmed in by protruding boulders or by red clay overhang—.

The buck stood before Eck's eyes, on the lip of a high bank as they rounded a sudden bend of the ravine: stood half-turned away, head swung toward them poised and alert, the great spread of antlers thrust high, the clear, wide, black staring of the eyes picking up the faint light of final dusk. He could not have been as big as he looked, towering over the wet brown earth beside a rotted snag, among stunted trees, his coat shagged out glistening with water droplets, wisps of steam drifting from his breath.

"Kneel down," came Ab's grating whisper. "Kneel down at the wellbox and aim."

Not that he needed to kneel, Eck realized. It would require only seconds to disentangle the rifle from the slicker and bring it to his shoulder, and even if in those seconds the buck bolted, at this distance he could not conceivably miss. Yet Ab's voice was so compelling that he took the extra instant to sink to one knee and crook the other leg to support the elbow under the hand gripping the forestock of the rifle. An image of the wellbox came dimly to mind. He got a bead on the buck with ease, and still he had not budged. Along the notch of the rear sight and over the tiny, barely visible dot of the front bead, the massive furry body appeared only a few feet away. Eck squeezed the trigger with all care, still keeping the throb in his veins and the thumping in his ears under control.

Explosion. Kick. A moment's loss of perspective.

The buck hit the air as if the earth had tossed him. As dark as the air. Did not engage the earth again, it seemed. Or no more than to touch it with hoof tips for another spring, another purchase for a flight so rapid that he vanished instantaneously, as though in no direction at all. And the bank and the air he had occupied lay silent and dark as if they had never known his presence. . . .

"Thunder and damnation!" Ab bawled. And stumbled ahead to stop below the ravine bank. And snatched off his rain hat. And drew back and sailed it up the bluff. As though it might reach the buck and bring him down, since the rifle had not. Then he whirled and howled at Eck, "How in the name of johnny hell could you miss a shot like that? And why, oh why in the name of good Godamighty didn't I bring a rifle!"

Eck had turned away, intent on working the rifle lever, slowly ejecting not only the spent casing but shucking the five remaining cartridges from the magazine through the chamber, spinning them out in glinting arcs onto the dark ground. Finally he rammed home the action uncocked, knelt and groped around to find and pocket the five cartridges—.

So that was it for this year. And all the while Eck was thinking, out of a deep hollow of sickness: I put him there, didn't I? He stood there in a place like that day before yesterday on that other ridge, didn't he? In the lie, in the lie I told. And here he is today. Here he was, that is. More or less, was. And because of that tale I made up I didn't deserve even to get a shot, let alone hit him. . . .

So now he stood waiting for Ab and saying nothing.

"Why you unloading?" Ab said. "We have to look for blood up there. Maybe you wounded him. Maybe we can find him. Maybe we'll run across him again on the way back to camp."

"No such thing," Eck said.

Yet they did climb up and inspect the ground for blood—and found none. Eck had known in his heart they wouldn't.

They had to hurry now to reach the tent before darkness overtook them. Neither said a word. As they went, the drizzle turned into a hard driving rain that oozed and trickled under their slickers. With the night growing blacker by the minute, they had to slow down and pick their way haltingly among the rocks and trees. Longer and longer the way to camp seemed, as if they were crossing some broad and alien region. Full darkness had settled in when they at last crept up to the tent and groped their way inside.

They got into dry clothes, but as they could not build a fire to ward off the chill that had returned with the night, they could only crawl into their sleeping bags to keep warm, unwilling to face cold food just yet. . . .

The rain hit the canvas in torrents: Eck was aware only of that. . . .

Until with a jolt he found himself wondering, "What! have I really been asleep?"

Asleep or not, the time had come. He was pierced by fear in knowing that the time had come. . . .

Still he delayed. The rain came across the tent in sweeps. He felt warm, dry, safe. Why not sleep, then, really sleep?

It took that: a balance between the sound of rain and the temptation of sleep to remind him again that the time had come, the time for him to say, almost under the swish of the rain: "Well, I don't guess he was that big. . . . Or do you reckon he *was* that big?. . . ."

No, that was not what he had meant to say. He could not do that. Touching on the ancient buck would not allay the lie he had told. And if he waited any longer the time would pass, be lost forever. He would go on. He did, he came out with it bluntly: how he had made up the story about the buck on the ridge the other day, had not even known he was spinning that yarn till he was deep into it: told then what had really happened, as near as he could recall, ending with, "If you was to ask why I made up such a windy—well, the best I can say is I done it trying to coax you out here with me."

So now Eck lay waiting for an answer, and as the moments passed he strained his ears for fear Ab's voice would be lost in the peppering of the rain—until after a while he saw that Ab meant to say nothing. At first this made him more uneasy than protest or accusation would have. Then, all of a sudden, he thought: 'Why he don't care how that buck got on that ridge, no more'n he does whether today's buck was where we seen him or not.'

Rising above the silence, then, was only the sound of the rain, which came to Eck still as the perfect companion for his thoughts. But then the feeling stole over him that yes, he did have something more to say, and the time had come for that too.

Except that Ab spoke just ahead of him: "I can't get over it. I never thought I'd be on this earth long enough to see a sight like that again."

Then Eck broke in: "You reckon if we come out here another year he could still be in this territory?"

"Oh. . . . You may find him here another year. By that time I may be dead and gone."

Eck knew the perfect response to that:

"Say Ab, that story you used to tell about shooting that big old buck under the elm tree, I've sort of forgot some of that. How does it go again?"

❀

A Frog's Bath Water

by Tom Doyal

Lois wanted to be adult about everything. She knew life settled into routines, some pleasant and some not. She knew nobody liked a forty-five-year-old whiner who thought life should be a perpetual thrill; those kinds of thoughts were for adolescents, naive adolescents who believed real life was like television. Still, her life with Harvey these days seemed like a kind of sleep-walking, not painful, just kind of dead. I mean, she thought, how many times a year do the kitchen curtains need to be washed and ironed, especially when I hardly ever cook anymore?

The kids were good. They called every week. Their daughter Brenda had married Robert, a career officer in the Air Force, and they were stationed in England for two-years, and their son Jeff was holding down two jobs while studying architecture at the University of Texas in Austin. Lois felt proud of them and how well they had started out to build their own adult lives.

Harvey's insurance agency had finally turned the corner. He went to work every day and the money was better than it ever had been. He played golf twice a week when the weather was good and slept in front of the television most evenings after supper. Lois thought that his interest in sex had dropped off kind of fast in the last couple of years. Last night she asked him if he was seeing another woman. She thought it was a provocative question; it might even be true. He looked over his reading glasses at her and said, "Have you quit taking your hormone pills?"

"No. I haven't. I just think our lives have gotten pretty dull and I wanted to be sure that was true for both of us. I mean these are supposed to be our best years and they just don't seem to be measuring up."

"Measuring up to what? Some episode of *Dynasty*? Jeez, Lois, our kids are fine, the business is doing good, and we're both healthy. What do you want?" His tone said that wanting anything more was clearly unreasonable.

"I want romance. I want to know that you love me. I want to know that our lives are not over. I want a home where the television is not blaring all evening every evening. I want us to talk to each other."

"What in the world has gotten in to you? I think you're just bored. Take a class. Do some volunteer work. We've got it made here. Don't mess it up by imagining some ideal life that nobody really lives." Harvey felt a little guilty as he made his speech. He knew that his idea of love had merged inseparably with his deep belief in comfort.

"What about sex?" she asked.

"What about it? I'm generally in favor of it. Do you have some complaint?"

"Forget it," she said and went in the kitchen. She loaded the dishwasher and then peeked through the louvered shutters to see Harvey sleeping in his recliner with the newspaper spread across his chest, his pot-belly rising and falling with each breath.

Lois took the phone from the kitchen wall and dialed Myrna Schutze. She and Myrna had been best friends since eighth grade, back when Myrna Schutze was Myrna Vogel. It was only 9:15, not too late to call.

"Myrna, I'm bored out of my skull."

"Let's take a class," chirped Myrna. God, had Myrna's voice gotten even squeakier and more annoying lately?

"I don't want a class. I want a life. How many bad ashtrays, macramé planters, and decoupaged prayers can one house use?"

"The instructor said your ashtray was earthy and elemental."

"He's a homo, Myrna, and he's paid to say crap like that. Besides, I haven't been off the farm so long that I don't recognize a replica of a steaming pile of cow plop when I see it, and that ashtray qualifies."

"Look, Lois, let's go in to San Antonio tomorrow. Shop a little, have lunch someplace that serves frozen margaritas, and maybe catch a movie. I think there is a new movie with Mel Gibson's bare butt in it. I'll pick you up at nine in the morning."

"You are an incredible movie reviewer. Body parts only. Okay. See you in the morning."

They had a good time. Myrna bought her husband Lester a pair of boxer shorts with pictures of red chili peppers on them. She drank two margaritas at lunch and then talked about everybody in line at the mall movie theater.

"Don't you think it is interesting to see what kind of people will stand in line to see Mel Gibson's butt?"

"Lord, Myrna. Some of them may have come to see the whole movie."

"Oh, get real," said Myrna.

When they came out of the movie, Lois said, "Well, we did see his butt. That certainly was the high-point of that little cinematic adventure."

The half-hour drive home was filled with Myrna's speculations about why Alta Faye Willis's Mexican yardman, the new one, had started showing up at the Willis house every Wednesday afternoon wearing starched khakis and pointy shoes, going in the house for about two hours, and then making a quick trip around the lawn with Alta Faye's new Toro riding lawnmower. "I tell you, their yard is looking like shit. You'd think Hardy Willis would notice."

"Maybe he's just grateful he doesn't have to do the job himself."

"Which job?" asked Myrna. And they both laughed.

On the access road just after the Mahler exit off the freeway, Lois noticed a homemade sign in front of a little frame house sitting in a bare sandy spot beneath some oak trees about twenty yards off the road. The white sign had a big red hand painted on it with the words "Sister Luisa— Reader and Advisor" painted in white across the red palm.

"Let's get our fortunes told," said Myrna.

Myrna pulled her Buick into the sandy yard. As Lois and Myrna stood on the tiny porch and knocking on the screen door, a woman appeared from the dark interior of the little house. She stood peering out at them for a moment and then said, "Good afternoon, ladies. Please come in. I am Sister Luisa."

Sister Luisa had on tan slacks and a loose blouse of a black shiny material patterned with orchids. On her feet were fuzzy pink slippers. Sister Luisa was of medium height. Her face was deeply wrinkled, though she didn't seem to be old. Her hair was an improbable black, the blue-black color of new stovepipe. Lois thought Sister Luisa looked nothing like she thought a fortune teller should look like, except maybe for her eyes which were almost black, like glittering black stones.

The windows of the room were draped with import-store bedspreads and the doorway into the next room was curtained in the same orange and brown fabric. Sister Luisa asked them to sit in kitchen chairs at a small table draped with a black and gold scarf. She took the chair opposite her guests. On the table were a deck of ordinary playing cards, a pack of Kool cigarettes, and a clean glass ashtray.

Myrna went first, carefully cutting the deck of cards with her left hand as instructed by Sister Luisa. "What does my future hold?" asked Myrna. Sister Luisa carefully dealt cards out on the table in the pattern of a cross and then added more cards in the spaces made by the cross.

"You have abundance in your present, abundance of love and material goods. These things have made you comfortable. Your next challenge is to continue your own growth despite your high level of satisfaction with the current way of life. You have abilities which you are not using." Sister Luisa's voice was low and calm. Her hand moved above the cards, pointing at various cards as she spoke. Myrna asked a couple of questions and got back equally vague responses. At the conclusion of her answer, Sister Luisa said, "Please place a love-offering of twenty dollars or more in that basket beside the door as you leave."

When Sister Luisa turned her attention to Lois, she studied Lois's face for a long time, several minutes at least. She then instructed Lois to cut the cards. "I need to speak with her alone for a few minutes," Sister Luisa said to Myrna.

"Oh. Well, I see. I'll just wait in the car," said Myrna. "Is that okay with you? I'll just be right outside," she said to Lois.

As Myrna self-consciously bustled from the room out onto the porch, Sister Luisa once again dealt the cards into the same pattern as before. She studied the cards before speaking. "You have some trouble in your heart now, about a man. You are lonely, but have not spoken of this to anyone." Tears came into Lois's eyes.

"I think you can help wisdom appear to you by a ritual. Do you want to know about it?" asked Sister Luisa.

"Yes," said Lois.

"Find a frog, not a toad, but a fresh-water frog. Do no harm to the frog, but rinse the frog in distilled water. Then fill a one-quart jar with distilled water and dip the frog in the water three times while holding an image of the man in your mind. Return the frog to its home or a safe place like its home. Each evening for seven days fill a red glass with about a cup of the water. Place it where the morning sun will strike it at sunrise, in your kitchen window, on a fence-post, or wherever. On rising in the morning, drink the water. Come back to see me on the seventh day. Come after noon on that day."

"Will it help?" asked Lois.

"It might," said Sister Luisa. "You and your man have lost touch with something elemental, something from the reptilian mind. Please leave a love-offering of thirty or more dollars in the basket by the door as you leave."

When Lois got in the car Myrna asked fifty questions before Lois could answer one of them. "I mean, why did she have to see you alone? She just said all of my stuff in front of you and then kicked me out. What did she tell you?"

"She prescribed a ritual to keep me and family from harm," said Lois.

"What kind of ritual?" asked Myrna.

"I'll tell you later. Right now we need to get a frog."

"A frog! There is no place to buy frogs. The old downtown Woolworth in San Antonio used to sell little alligators, but I don't think I've ever seen live frogs for sale," said Myrna. Lois was thinking that Sister Luisa had made fifty dollars in less than an hour.

The next morning Myrna called about nine. "I've got a frog."

"That was quick. How did you get a frog so fast?" asked Lois.

"Mattie next door has her grandson visiting for the summer. He's nine. I told him I would pay him a dollar if he would go down on the creek and catch me a small or medium sized frog."

"What did you tell him you wanted a frog for?" asked Lois.

"I told him that you and I were conducting an experiment."

"Oh, lord. Everybody will think you and I have become witches."

"It'll make us seem more interesting as people," said Myrna. "I'll be over there in about thirty minutes. The frog is in a shoebox and I don't know diddly about the care of a frog. We better just give him a bath and turn him loose."

In Lois' kitchen, both wearing rubber gloves, they rinsed the little greenish brown frog and dipped him as directed. Myrna took the frog back home in the shoebox after promising to take it back to the creek and turn it loose herself. No use in involving that kid again. If he talked to his grandmother, Mattie would have it all over town before dark.

After all the questions in the car on that first day, Myrna had not been curious about the whole matter of the ritual. She participated enthusiastically as she always had done with their craft and volunteer projects, but she asked no questions and never mentioned her own reading by Sister Luisa. Lois wasn't surprised. She always thought that Myrna was one of the kindest people she knew, but Myrna had the attention span of a speckled pup.

The next seven days seemed long to Lois. She performed the ritual carefully each day. She was surprised that she didn't mind drinking the frog's bath water at all. It tasted just fine. She set the red glass on the window ledge behind the curtain in the kitchen window above the sink. Harvey never noticed it and their lives moved along in the familiar sleepy rhythm. About the third day Myrna called to say the neighbor grandchild was coming by daily to ask if she needed more frogs. When she told him no, he asked about tadpoles and crawfish.

"I told him that I was now collecting arrowheads and would pay five dollars apiece," said Myrna.

"Don't get too creative," said Lois. We'll just seem that much weirder."

"Well, damned if he didn't bring me one this morning. This is getting expensive."

"I'll pay you back, Myrna."

The seventh day fell on a Wednesday and Lois drove out to Sister Luisa's place without inviting Myrna. An old blue Cadillac was sitting beside the house. When Lois entered the front room of the little house, she saw cardboard boxes everywhere. "Are you moving?" asked Lois.

"Yes. One of the people I have been providing with spiritual counsel turned out to be the wife of the Hulsey County sheriff. She is a very literal woman and not at all spiritually evolved," said Sister Luisa. "I am relocating my ministry to the West coast. I have many wealthy and influential clients there."

"When are you leaving?" asked Lois.

"Probably tonight, right after dark. My son Jesse who was also assisting this woman left on the Greyhound during the night last night. He's twenty and may have been too enthusiastic in this instance."

Lois didn't know what to say. She knew there must be some strange story behind these events, but thought it might be impolite to ask anything. "You asked me to come back today. You know, after seven days of drinking the frog water."

"Have you completed the ritual as I directed you?"

"Yes."

"Well, now I just want to give you one more easy exercise and then you will be on your own," said Sister Luisa. She shook a cigarette from the pack and lit it with a silver lighter which she took from her pocket. She took a deep drag, leaned back in her chair and blew a thin stream of smoke at the ceiling.

"What do I need to do?" asked Lois.

"We don't have a lot of time here so I'm going to abbreviate this, but you seem like a smart lady, able to take everything in. Anyway, years ago, before I became a spiritual adviser, I worked in a branch of the entertainment industry. I was fifteen when I started and real ignorant, especially about men. An older woman helped me by telling me what I'm about to tell you."

"Is it something about my husband?"

"Yes, if he's the man you want," said Sister Luisa. "Do you perform oral sex on him? Do you know what I'm talking about?"

Lois felt herself blushing. "I know what you are talking about. Twenty-five years ago he mentioned it once, but I was too shy and we never did anything like that. I mean our sex life has been good, but lately there hasn't been much of it."

"Well, I don't think it is possible to over-emphasize the importance of this to most men," said Sister Luisa. "I suggest you learn to do that for your man."

"I don't know if I can."

"Sure you can," said Sister Luisa. "It's easy. Go to the grocery store and buy two plums, one small and one medium. Unless your man is exceptional a large plum is not necessary. Wash the plums and pull the stem, if there is one. Then, practicing first with the small plum, put it in the front of your mouth with the stem hole pointed toward the back of your throat. Be careful that your teeth do not break the skin on the plum. Then lick the underside of the plum with your tongue. About every fourth or fifth lick, stick your tongue in the stem hole. Then do the same drill with the larger plum. Do this until you are comfortable. As you grow more experienced, feel free to discover your own variations. Are you understanding what I'm telling you?"

"Yes," said Lois. "I don't know if I can move from plums to the real thing."

"Honey, anybody that can drink a frog's bath water for a week can do it," said Sister Luisa. "Do you have any money on you?"

"I've got a hundred dollars," said Lois.

"Let me have half of it. I'm facing some challenges here in the next few hours and some money will help. Besides when everything works out for you, you'll wish you had given me all of it."

Lois fumbled through her purse. "It's in twenties. Let me give you sixty."

"Hey, I'll not fight abundance when it presents itself," said Sister Luisa.

"I appreciate the things you've told me and I'm going to try to do everything just as you said. I'm sorry you are leaving," said Lois.

"You are kind to say that," said Sister Luisa. "My destiny seems to involve lots of mobility. Good luck. Now get on out of here. I've got to finish packing and load the car."

Lois helped Sister Luisa load the roadside sign in the back seat of the Cadillac and then left. She drove to the Mahler Food Festival and bought several plums, just in case she damaged the first couple. Harvey wouldn't be home until about six o'clock. She had time to practice for a while. At first, she felt that her jaw would come unhinged, but then it seemed easier. She practiced several times over the next two days.

When Harvey came in on Friday evening, Lois had the baked chicken and rice dish that was his favorite. After dinner, she said, "Harvey, take a shower please. I want you to hold me for a while." He looked at her closely, but said nothing and took his shower. Although it was only eight o'clock, he put on his pajamas. They lay on the bed together with her head on his chest, his arms around her.

"Lois, I know you have kind of been having a tough time lately, but I don't really have any idea how to help," said Harvey.

"This is a nice help. You know, you holding me and talking."

Harvey turned to face her and kissed her. The second kiss was longer and by the time it ended Harvey was breathing more quickly.

"Please lie back," she said. He did as she asked. She sat up in the bed, leaned over and took Harvey's plum in her mouth. Each time she brushed her tongue across the plum, Harvey made a little sound, and she enjoyed that sound.

Afterward, she lay back into his arms, and Harvey hugged her to him tightly. He was silent for a while and then finally said, "Lois, where did you learn to do that?"

"Don't worry. I learned it from an article in *The Ladies Home Journal*." She hated lying to him but she didn't want to explain about Sister Luisa.

"Damn," said Harvey quietly. "That is a much better magazine than I ever dreamed. Baby, I do love you. It just feels awkward for me to say it. I don't know the kind of words people use, about rainbows and flowers and all that kind of stuff. There is not much poetry in me, but I do love you."

"Just tell me in your own plain words when you can. I really need to hear it sometimes. I feel awkward with your thing in my mouth too, but I want to do it because I know it pleases you."

Harvey was quiet for a minute or two. "I'll do better about it, Lois. Lois, I'm really sleepy. Is it all right if we don't talk anymore tonight?"

"Go to sleep," she said. "You've done just fine and I thank you." She rubbed his back until she heard his purring little snore.

In the next few weeks, Harvey brought home some cut flowers one evening, took her to dinner in San Antonio, and fumbled around trying to decide how to say "I love you" on several occasions. Once he even shouted from the driveway as he was leaving for work, "I love you, Lois." Even when he made mistakes—like the gift-wrapped blender wand, she loved the efforts he made.

One evening when he came home from work, he said, "There is nothing good on television. I think I'll read a little this evening. Do you have a *Ladies Home Journal* around here?"

"No, Honey. I changed my subscription to *Family Circle*," Lois said.

Myrna called the next morning. "Just when you think you have got them figured out, they do some other crazy thing."

"What are you talking about?" asked Lois.

"I got a postcard in the mail which says that Lester has given me a gift subscription to *The Ladies Home Journal*."

Lois laughed. "Let's go to San Antonio tomorrow. I'm sure you can locate a movie for us with some good body parts in it," said Lois.

"I'll pick you up about nine. Lois, you've been acting like you are feeling better lately, a little more yourself. Did the spell work? You know, the frog thing."

"Yes," said Lois. ✿

The Bellhop Calls for Mr. Crofford

by Ewing Campbell

"You knew that was no place for a child," Thea said. "I—" his mother went on bitterly while Hunt stood between them, thinking, *please, please stop this*, confused but understanding she faulted FJ for exposing him to a pagan creed, as she called that mocking pageant of taupe-daubed, greasepainted men in mourning, lit by fireworks and celebrating outworn. He missed his father's reply because two gulls, squabbling over a tattered scrap of shrimp bleaching in the sun, distracted him. They snatched the remains, pulling it apart and deciding the issue in time for Hunt to hear his mother start again, speaking with the slow soft accent of South Texas.

"This is how we're punished for our failings."

"A night on the seawall, Thea, people having fun. It had nothing to do with what's happened."

She stared hard at FJ, her eyes wild and bright. They were talking past each other, hardly noticing what the other said. Hunt could not bear the look of pain he saw there. It, his loss of speech, had nothing to do with the seawall or the night he and FJ went out among the celebrating people. She was wrong about that, but he was glad he couldn't say it, relieved he couldn't tell them about Maximo the Dwarf's magic lantern and what he saw when he looked inside. It didn't matter if he never spoke again as long as he avoided that. An illusion of light, it must have been, his father—it looked like FJ—with the pretty woman. That and the dwarfish death's-head grimace had done something to him he didn't understand, and now they were bickering.

"We had a fine one, we did," FJ was saying in his own defense. "Just the thing for a boy, getting out with sporting folks and having fun. Too long in coming."

"I won't have a child of mine grow up like that." A strand of hair fell over her eye. She pushed it from her face with the heel of her hand and blinked away tears.

Hunt wasn't sure what she meant by the words *like that*, but the image of men in black dresses and veils stuck in his head. There probably was a connection. Not wanting to listen, he gazed at the horizon where the bay and the sky came together. Broken threads floated in his sight, drifting motes gently falling, rising, wheeling slowly, and bobbing in the eye's humor, floaters against a pale blue sky. A whiff of seaweed came to him on the breeze, and one of the gulls walked sideways ahead of a ribbon of foam running up the beach. The bird eyed them boldly.

"Come along, son," FJ said. "Let's see what the surf's turned up."

Hunt glanced toward his mother, but she didn't say anything when FJ moved ahead along the playa, stooping to take up a turreted casing with a hermit crab inside. Farther on he found a fluted shard delivered by the tide from shell beds offshore, its curved surface worn smooth, soft to the touch, and translucent like some exotic sea petal lying in a bed of coral twigs delicately branched and jointed. He seemed interested in every bivalve, whelk, and slipper shell he found while curiously calm about the boy's silence, but Hunt knew better. His father had taken him out of school, where the situation had become a distraction and everyone had an opinion.

"My uncle said something frightened you." This from Hooter Pease. His uncle knew a dockworker who lost his hearing after a falling cotton bale nearly killed him.

"It's a disorder," Angus Moody had countered.

"What disorder?"

"Nervous fatigue," Angus replied.

Hooter eyed him closely. "How would you know?"

"My mother read in the newspaper soldiers brought it back from the war."

Hooter Pease liked his uncle's notion that another scare could make a mute talk again. It gave him an excuse for popping a bag behind Hunt's back to make him jump and utter a startled cry, but it didn't work. Other kids tried to talk with him, then went away making faces, frustrated, and resenting his handicap. It set him apart, excluding them from his world, though that was not his fault. So they bullied and teased, giving him the same treatment they heaped on rag pickers and odd old widows, but it also gave him a privacy no schoolyard tough could penetrate and, with the privacy, a vague power that conjured up memories of his lost voice, now enhanced by an experience no one else among his friends could match. He had crossed over to a farther shore reserved for veterans sent here to recover from the nervous disorder Angus Moody had linked him with. It overcame the weak ones, if Angus could be trusted, when artillery shells exploded all around. Maybe Angus Moody was right. Maybe he knew what he was talking about since some older boys had pictures of men in field dress, heads bandaged, eyes staring into space. Hunt didn't mind sharing that with patients from the Army Convalescent Hospital who came to the shore to recover and sat all day under umbrellas and gazed in silence at the bay.

"Sad to see," his father said, shaking his head and glancing at the ranks of invalids recuperating in beach chairs between the Breakers Hotel and the exposed playa. The government had requisitioned rooms at the hotel for the overflow from Europe and North Africa. You weren't supposed to make disturbances near them, though the mewing seagulls didn't follow the rules anymore than the surf or the trains in the switchyard across the strand jutting out between the two bays. Some had lost limbs and carried scars from the fighting. Many stared at the horizon with no wounds you could see. If they could talk, what might they reveal? Did they see floaters, too? Not moving or speaking from the time they were led out in the morning until they were guided back to their rooms, they seemed dispirited and in a permanent daze.

"Your mother's not herself, son. It's no one's fault, but the two of us have to do what we can to ease her fears."

Hunt looked at the firm wet sand beneath his feet, feeling guilty and concerned about his mother. He lifted his eyes and gazed across the water. A boat was crossing the bay, trawling beyond the ship channel near a marked sandbank. A jet of diesel smoke shot from the exhaust spout. The boat went across the water, its bow nodding to the south off the Naval Air Station. After a while it came back, its smoke a tattered, dirty smear on the sky.

"This, too, will pass," FJ said. "Everything will be back the way it was. You'll see what the sun, the sea, and time can do."

Hunt cast a look over his shoulder and watched his mother walking behind them, her head down, unaware of his gaze.

ii

Forced inward by his condition Hunt shared the beach with silent invalids who, unaware of his presence, stared through him at nothing he could see when he turned around to look. Unpainted storm shutters—weathered gray by sun, sea spray, and wind—stood above the untended flower bed, where a patch of sea oats and withered chrysanthemums rattled in the breeze. Squat and ancient salt cedars rooted themselves in the sand above the surf, their warped boughs supported by trestles, and held against the breeze coming off the bay. Raking last year's mulch of needles into windrows for the flower bed or sweeping the sand beneath the trees that marked their cottage boundary, he noted tidal rhythms, daylight phases of a pale weak moon—slivered crescents, gibbous, full by turns—the unwelcome change in his mother, which he associated with the moon. Some evenings, when the moon was full and shining down, dogs howled together in the distance. Then with FJ gone to work his mother would start to cry as if abandoned, no longer trying to blink away her tears. It was a season of discovery and distraction. Even FJ's shifts at the carousel, alternating with those of Sam Graggs, week nights, days or nights on the weekend, were repeated until they too had a rhythm all their own. These formed a pattern for Hunt's solitude, separated from his mother by her despair, from his father by the demands of work, from the convalescing soldiers by a barrier he couldn't see.

He had paused in the shade of a salt cedar. The shore, as white as caliche dust under the sun, released its store of moon snail and channel clam after the tide went out. Sand dollars littered the sand and were a common find, but a feathery sea pen was rare, something to be cherished if discovered. He rose and, shading his eyes with his hand, stepped into the light, walking toward the convalescents in beach chairs at the water's edge. One young invalid who had been staring out to sea got unsteadily to his feet, a hand lifted to his chest and lying against the lapel of his rumpled linen suit. He wore a panama hat and a tie knotted loosely at the collar as if arranged by a nurse or the orderly who moved among the young men and kept an eye on them.

The surf pushed up the beach, puddling around the young man's leather street shoes, wetting the cuffs of his pants, but he seemed unaware of what was happening. Then staring in amazement at the man stepping awkwardly toward the next breaker coming in, Hunt saw something he had never encountered before. He saw this young man's misery rise from him like the aura of backlighting cast against a solid object. The veteran was already up to his knees in the shuffling waves and moving somnambulistically outward when the sharp sound of a whistle broke in on Hunt's rapt state and he heard the lifeguard's voice amplified by a megaphone.

"Sir, sir," the lifeguard shouted, "you in the straw hat. Sir—orderly, see to that patient."

His reaction was quick, a bound to the sand from his elevated chair even as the hospital orderly hustled toward the wading man.

"Lieutenant," he was shouting at the back of the figure in his light-colored linen jacket, which had ballooned upon the water's surface like a trailing cape. "Wait, sir." All of this too late because the distraught veteran had already slipped beneath the waves and could not hear them, leaving only the panama floating as a marker where he had been just a moment before.

Hunt saw the lifeguard go past the splashing orderly, saw him dive, saw the strong strokes increase the distance between them and the plunge as the second figure disappeared beneath the surface. Two heads came up, and the inept orderly was there by then to help, the pair of them tugging the third man to shore while the crowd moved between Hunt and the men struggling up the beach.

In those hours immediately after this attempt, Hunt's confusion increased. Even after he went to bed that night he couldn't sleep because the image of the invalid slipping under the waves stayed with him. Why would someone do that? All night he lay awake staring at the sky. The moon was in its crescent phase with Jupiter, Saturn, and Venus aligned in a row at right angles to the cusps. He lay there and wondered until the sky over the bay began to grow light. Exhausted, he at last fell asleep, dreaming he was suspended under water and looking up from the depths at the moon, pale and distant, but he wasn't afraid. Just the opposite—he felt a sense of euphoria suffuse his whole being, an ecstasy of peaceful depths where he had the power to float to the surface any time he desired, and yet he didn't want to lose this feeling of power or sense of well-being.

He wanted to stay there forever like that, floating until the day he woke and found orderlies from the Army Convalescent Hospital loading duffel bags and trunks onto baggage cars, escorting veterans from the Breakers Hotel to the train that would take them away. Tuesday they were there, bivouacked as usual on the shore. Wednesday they were gone, a sign that something was up. The *Caller-Times* reported dirty weather in Atlantic sea-lanes west of Cape Verde Islands. Rough seas almost swamped the tramp steamer *Lisboa* on its way to the port of Santa Cruz de Tenerife, but Corpus Christi so far away remained clear and basking in a hallucinatory light reflecting off the sand and bay.

Hurricane hunters flew from Miami for a look and brought back storm warnings. Two days later high seas and strong winds struck Hispaniola and the barometer started dropping along the southern seaboard. Breezes died away, as if sucked out to sea. A low tide exposed an ugly band of muddy sea floor between the beach and the shell beds offshore, leaving clumps of brown seaweed for all to see. The sun bore down in an excess of light as the air grew thick and clammy. That night an intolerable weight pressed upon him and, strangest of all, the clamor of the sea fell silent with the going of the breeze and tide, silent too the patch of sea oats beneath his window. He listened to the crash of trains coupling in the switchyard and felt the earth shake as a freight train passed through on its way to the border. You could set your watch by its arrival.

The next morning two boatmen on the pier fought over a pack of cigarettes. Dockworkers on the waterfront seemed listless and irritable. Smoke spilled out of a tugboat funnel and spread like ground fog, stinking of diesel fumes. It left soot everywhere, on decks and hatches and car windows, and put down a film of grime that turned linen suits a dingy gray.

Hunt stepped inside the cottage, wishing a breeze would come up but glad to be out of the sun. His father had just returned from breaking down the merry-go-round and helping Sam Graggs load the large van with horses. "Everything's ready," he was saying. "Sam's driving the truck. They'll take the machinery as far as Del Rio to avoid this storm."

"Is it going to hit us then?" his mother asked.

"Who knows? But we'll probably catch whatever's coming." There was an edge to his voice. He looked through the screen door at the exposed seabed. "I never saw the bay go out so far."

"What caused it to do that?"

"The moon and storm, I guess, pulling together. Must be big to do a thing like that."

Hunt watched his mother bite her lip, her face expressing more than she could ever say out loud. FJ stood opposite, leaning on the door frame, sucking his teeth, and staring toward the southeast where a brickdust sky hung above the horizon. The temperature had gone up and the mercury was stuck at a hundred degrees. When the sky had turned, shore birds flew up and filled the hot heavy air like a long black ribbon waving overhead until the air quivered with flapping wings and darkened above the salt flats and estuary.

"Sam'll take the two of you to a shelter," FJ said.

"Why can't we go with you?"

"I'm going nowhere, Thea."

"You're staying here—why?"

"Somebody has to be with the house. It won't look after itself."

"But what could you do? You can't change anything by staying, FJ."

Crofford's gaze strayed to the pattern of sunlight on the wall. "I can try," he said as if to himself, but after a moment he glanced back and added, "You and the boy can shelter at the Nueces Hotel. You'll be safe there."

"It's the heat making you talk that way, the humidity." She begged him to drink something cold and went off to get a glass of iced tea from the kitchen.

FJ mopped his head with his sleeve, muttering something Hunt couldn't hear. He faced about, turning his eyes on the boy. "There you are. Listen, son, they're evacuating the North End. So you and your mother will have to leave." He paused, then added, "You take care of your mother and don't give her any reason to worry."

She came back with two glasses of iced tea. "This should help," she said, handing one to each of them. Her smile seemed forced and unconvincing. Cold sweat beaded the glass, tea cold enough to make Hunt's teeth ache, but it also gave relief from the heat and humidity as a car pulled up out front.

His father set the cold drink aside and crossed the room. "Pack a bag, Thea. Sam's here."

When Hunt followed his father out he saw Sam Graggs standing beside a Nash, pushing his hat back, looking at the sky. As the engine idled beneath the hood, the sedan and the air above it shivered in the heat. Graggs took off his jacket and put it through the open window of the car.

"Everything's just about ready, FJ. Maybe another hour. You changed your mind about staying?"

"Let's keep this short, Sam."

"Fine, the shorter, the better. Anything I can do? Name it and you got it."

"See Thea and the boy to the Nueces. Look up Gianni Po. I talked to him already and he'll set you up. You have time for that, don't you, before you pull out?"

"Sure, FJ. I got time. I got nothing but time for the next few days. Leave it to me. Anything else before I point the rig toward Del Rio?"

Before FJ could respond Hunt's mother came out with a small cardboard suitcase. His father took it and placed it behind the front seat on the floor board. They embraced, not speaking. Finally he turned to Hunt and said, "This is it, sport. You take care of your mother until this is over. Can you do that, son?"

Hunt wanted to say yes, but the word could not get past his impediment and would not come out, not even in a stammering murmur. So he nodded, then went with his father to the car and climbed in beside his mother. As they drove away he looked back and saw a hand go up in a wave of "So long, take care."

iii

At the Nueces Hotel they were met beneath the green awning that shaded the Chaparral Street entrance by a little man in his red bellhop uniform, frogged and braided with gold trim, white gloves on his hands, and a pill-box hat tipped jauntily toward one ear. No mistaking his importance, his air of confidence, as he stood before the hotel, a living copy of tobacco's most famous trademark. This was Gianni Po, longtime carnival barker and now captain of bellhops at the famous Nueces.

A problem in his pituitary gland had stunted his growth and left him at the boyish height of four feet, but his voice, forever young, big, and with bell-ringing clarity, had made him the most important barker on the Midway in his time. Who knows? If Johnny Roventini had not beaten him to that lifetime contract with the Philip Morris Company, he might have become the favorite of smokers everywhere, bearing a pack of smokes on his silver salver and saying, "Your cigarettes, sir, and four for your friends." It might have been him everyone was hearing that night on the radio.

When Sam Graggs stepped forward with the cardboard suitcase, Gianni Po saluted him with two fingers lifted smartly to his little cap. "Samuel," he said, greeting the group and regarding Thea's case without offering to take it. "What brings you this way?"

"Hello, Gianni," Sam replied. "FJ thought you might find a spot for his wife and boy here, someplace safe till this dirty weather blows through."

Gianni Po's head bobbed as he said in his high clear voice, "Sure, Samuel, sure thing. Anything for the old times and pals like you and FJ, anything at all." The wink that accompanied these words reminded Hunt of his encounter with Maximo the Dwarf and the magic lantern.

Gianni Po waved them forward. The air was cool inside, with none of the humidity that weighed you down outside. Square columns supported a high ceiling and mezzanine. Floor tiles formed the pattern of a key, and overstuffed leather chairs filled the space beneath Corinthian capitals. There was a marble-faced self-winding clock hanging above the front desk. The bellhop gestured toward a corridor leading off the lobby, where a set of stairs went down to the basement.

"This way," he said. "Come right along. We already set up cots down below. Watertight, windproof, safe as a bunker in peacetime. You folks'll be fine, high, dry, and snug, all right. Snug as a cub in hibernation," he added, glancing at Hunt.

They followed him into a vaulted region beneath the extravagant lobby, mezzanine, and sun parlor businessmen used when closing their most important deals. People had already gathered below, whole families staking out five or six cots at a time. The basement was poorly lit, with half a dozen iron lanterns on the wall and near the landing. There were windows high up the wall at street level, steel shutters shoved into place and fastened with bolts. From the looks of this subterranean room you might have thought it was a dungeon, but it was only the basement of an expensive hotel.

Gianni Po swept an open hand outward, indicating their temporary quarters. "Pick the spot suits you best, wherever you like."

The air was stale and Hunt was sick of it already, wanting to be with his father and not in a room full of strangers. He took a deep breath. A memory of cool breezes came to him. It was all he could do to hold back the tears. His mother set the suitcase down next to a cot and turned to Graggs.

"Thank you, Sam. Thanks for everything."

"Don't mention it, Thea. I'm happy to do this." He glanced past her. "This suit you, Hunter? You going to be okay?"

All he could do was nod, a reflexive response by then. People wanted a sign and he gave it without thinking. There was an awkward moment before his mother said, "This suits us fine, Sam. Be careful driving to Del Rio."

"That's the attitude. This will be over soon enough. I'll see you when this is over." With that he turned and followed Gianni Po up the stairs.

iv

The front edge of the storm came without warning and swept in the rain. It pelted the shutters and drummed on the outer walls of the building. Then the wind began to rise and a whistling outside could be heard even below in the basement. The lights held steady and bright for a while, and the other families kept up a steady patter of talk until the noise outside grew and overwhelmed all speech. The howl of the wind filled Hunt's ears like the roar of a train.

He sat there on the edge of his cot and waited, but not for long. There was a jolt and a flash of bright light, followed by darkness. A child started to scream. Others took up the cry. In the rapid flashes of lightning Hunt saw frightened faces, eyes wide with fear staring around. Someone made an effort to light the storm lanterns. They flared one by one, throwing shadows over the walls, making the basement seem more like a ship's hold or a dungeon than a shelter. His ears felt ready to burst with the pressure. So he covered his ears and curled up on the cot as the wind and the waves drove hard upon the shore, shaking the earth like a quake. Explosive claps struck the shelter, rattled its storm shutters, and shook the bunker as if it were straw instead of bricks and concrete. Hunt buried his face in the crook of his arm, but nothing he did could shut out the noise. Had his voice returned at that moment, he would have cried out with the other refugees every time lightning strobed the darkness, revealing those faces. In the end their looks turned him to the wall where he stared into the eye of the storm with his eyes shut.

The boom of waves against the seawall produced a vision of rock jetties awash in spume, heavy sheets of rain driven horizontal to the earth, the Gulf of Mexico surging into the bay, turning the Nueces River on itself with a flood that rushed inland away from the sea. He heard the roar overhead and pictured boathouses smashed, fishing piers broken up, lumber tossed like match sticks on the steps of the seawall. He saw it all in spite of himself. He had grown used to his own silence. Now he yearned to be blind and deaf, free from the bursts of lightning, from the inhuman shriek of the wind overhead. He tried to scream with a voice that wasn't there and could not even whimper.

Heavy blows fell on the hotel, tree limbs, the shock of a transformer ripped from its pole and hurled against the building with the blast of a bomb. Metal awnings wrapped light poles in their heavy foil. He could hear the rip, rap-rap of slate shingles and roof tiles drumming the wall like a scatter of rock flung at a shed.

His mother had pushed her cot against his and lay beside him in the dark. Protective, she bent her body to him, her arm tense and holding him tight. The building shook. It trembled with each concussion in the air, and Hunt had no idea how long he stayed that way, trying to shut out the terror. At one point the storm seemed to move off, growing quieter for a while. Then it came back louder, stronger, more furious than before, and he was swept into the maelstrom. He heard a high voice calling out, articulating the words with precision, slowly drawing them out:

"Call for Mis—ter Crof—ford."

He saw a small figure in a red and gold-trimmed uniform going away, one white-gloved hand holding a silver tray aloft as if carrying a message for some distinguished recipient. Hunt saw this and heard the words once again. There was no mistaking them. They were perfectly formed and drawn out, as clear as the toll of a bell:

"Call for Mr. Crofford," the voice rang out. "Call for FJ Crofford."

But when the caller turned and revealed his face Hunt saw it was not Gianni Po who was calling for his father, but Maximo the Dwarf, the malicious little man's death's-head rictus gaping spitefully at him, and water was falling with a deafening roar, the ocean swollen and surging over the land, snapping off water pipes and gas lines like twigs and string tethers, shaking the cottage in its little grove of salt cedars. And that was not all. The walls of the cottage, like the old tamarisks that formed the boundary around it, were moving slowly back and forth from the pressure, buckling, cracking plaster and lathing all along where the walls joined the ceiling, nails popping out. Pieces of plaster dropped into the water that was filling the room. Hunt heard boards splintering and snapping like sticks, parts of the house already collapsing under the weight of the sea.

The east wall opened for a moment and the sea rushed in before it could close. Everything was giving way to the brute force of the surge while water rose rapidly inside, blocking all exits. Nothing could keep it out.

His father was under water, trying to reach a submerged window, but the house began to roll, going over in the waves, forcing him back. Hunt couldn't breathe. He felt the cold spray and the wind as his father came up, gasping for air, his head bobbing beneath the cracked ceiling. Suddenly the cottage gave a loud moan, joists and beams tearing from the frame, floor boards popping their joints, the whole structure going over, tumbling in the tidal surge. It rolled, pushed by the crest of the flood toward the railroad tracks, where waves pounded the embankment and battered the roadbed, washing out ties and rails, breaking up houses, and heaping the flotsam high on the raised tracks.

Hunt saw it all—he saw his father face down in the filth, his clothes ripped away, his naked figure lacerated and lifeless on the massive waste. He saw destruction and desolation in every direction and came up from the cot. "Father!" cried the boy, suddenly awake, as the image of his father dissolved with the dream that had created it, leaving only specks floating in his eyes as he blinked at the dim light of iron lanterns hanging on the walls. His mother lay beside him, her body twitching in troubled sleep while the wind keened overhead and shook the brick walls. Slowly he lowered himself to the cot once again and gazed up into the dark recesses above. "Father," he whispered and felt hot tears scalding his cheeks. He was shaking like the walls of this dungeon. The thought that there could be nightmares such as this filled him with dread, and high in the darkness, hidden vaults formed hollows of inexplicable sorrow.

V

There was no life or sign of it this time after the storm. Now only muck, thick upon the shore, stinking of corruption and drawing flies where once fresh breezes stirred and salt-cedar bungalows, motor courts, pavilion piers had stood on piles. Gone now—except the Hotel Breakers, which had weathered the storm intact—all gone, unlike earlier structures that had withstood other storms. Now a wasteland divided the two bays, lying like a beached corpse rotting in oppressive heat and summer drizzle, aftermath of devastating force, its spine all that remained of the broken railroad berm. Black flies swarmed in clouds to feed from and lay their eggs on the fouled surface while a boat, approaching so slowly it seemed not to move at all, crossed Nueces Bay, bringing back the mangled body of FJ Crofford from the farther shore.

In that vespertine drizzle the sky took on a greenish glow above three men crouching within the boat's nodding bow. They waited till the last moment before leaving the boat for the water and running it up what was left of the beach. They'd tied scarfs round their faces and wrapped the body in a blanket to keep the flies from getting at it, but when they shouldered the remains and rushed forward, flies rose out of the muck and went after them, enveloping both the living and the dead in a dense cloud. So many. Where did they all come from? Just as they shoved their burden into a waiting van, the shroud fell away, exposing feet discolored by death and water and the filth that had produced the look and smell of an open sewer. Then the flies came back in the rank dead air to the original effluvium. Soon it would be alive and roiling with maggots devouring every trace of organic matter heaved up by the sea that surged across the strand, taking Hunt's father and their home and everything else.

It was the end of childhood, too soon in coming, but experienced before in a dream that had the strength of premonition and was so intense it had restored his lost powers of speech. Now he and his mother had to join her parents in the housing project called La Armada, where the two Theodosias, mother and daughter, prepared to wash and dress FJ for the last time. Long ago before the boy was born they had resolved the difficulty of two people sharing one name. They had done so by dividing its distinct parts between them, each taking half for herself and modifying it appropriately—his grandmother Dosia accepting the suffix and relinquishing all claim of the prefix to her daughter Thea. Now again they shared, were sharing the labor of preparing the boy's father for his funeral rites since there was no money for undertakers whatever the law demanded, no insurance or death benefits. They would have to make do as best they could with soap, hot water, and oil of lavender.

Strangers had brought the body to the door of the dwelling, which was one in a series set side-by-side in a long brick barracoon facing the street. It consisted of small functional rooms—parlor, kitchen, bedroom, and bath. They had laid him out in the parlor, sending the boy to the bedroom, where from the doorway he watched his mother draw back the blanket and shudder at what she saw there. His own chest was heaving as he tried to swallow air, making an effort to force it past the knot in his throat. He had wept in fear and despair at the height of the storm, the nightmare of losing his father pushing him beyond what he could bear, but now that all he beheld had come to pass, there were no tears, only the physical knotting of grief in his throat and his chest heaving against the outrage and injustice lying motionless in the other room.

"Come away from there, boy," his grandfather called softly to him. "Leave that to the women."

The old man was already keeping a strict mourning, sitting in patriarchal rigidity at his writing table, wearing a dark coat over his nightshirt, and filling quires of paper with looping flourishes and slanting lines as he refined his penmanship. In another time he had been, if you could trust gossip, a member of a Masonic Lodge and privy to secret handshakes although he rarely went out these days or shook hands with anyone. Hunter had been given his Christian name, but the old man never called him anything but boy, as if the family patriarch couldn't bear to say his own name to anyone else. He had been a private in the Spanish-American War, when only eighteen, without ever seeing action because a single misstep had driven a nail through his boot and into his foot. Medics evacuated him before the assault on El Canay.

"Let me do that, Thea," Hunt heard his grandmother say as she placed a pan of warm water on the floor. Each month she managed, unfazed by the paucity of her husband's war pension and old-age benefits, to eke out a frugal existence for them, doling out money as needed to the grocer, the housing authority, putting off payment for as long as possible. The two women had pushed back the furniture to make more room in the tiny parlor.

"I'll wash him, mother," Thea Crofford said, kneeling beside the body and taking up a sponge. There was no need to strip the body. The storm had taken care of that, ripping away all he had been wearing, right down to his shoes. "You lay out a fresh shirt and one of dad's old suits."

"He won't look like himself in that."

"It'll have to do." She was soaping his grime-clotted hair, lifting the head to get at his neck and shoulders, scrubbing at the filth, her voice on edge as she said, "It can't be helped with everything gone save what was in our—" Wearily she let it trail off. No use repeating the obvious in the stifling, airless room.

When she had rinsed and sponged him and scraped the three-day stubble from his cheeks with her father's safety razor, she opened the container of lavender oil, releasing a fragrance Hunt could smell even where he was, beyond the door. In a trance his mother set about anointing her dead husband from head to foot, rubbing the herbal oil into his flesh. The two fought his deadweight into clothes the grandmother had taken from the closet and laid out, never once asking the old man for help.

Then they replaced the blanket with a fresh sheet, pulling it up and covering FJ, now fully dressed in his father-in-law's suit and collarless shirt, fastened at the throat with a mother-of-pearl stud. On his feet were the old man's shoes. When Thea turned her eyes full upon the boy he saw for a moment the eyes shining in solitude, seeing not him but someone, something else not there—and then it was gone, the look, replaced once again by the eyes he had known his whole life long, but with something strange, a little unhinged in them.

vi

Sam Graggs came back from Del Rio that night and with Father Salinas, from the Church of Our Lady, Star of the Sea, made arrangements for the funeral. He had driven through the wet evening in a borrowed Ford and was there when they roused Hunt from the pallet put down beside the bed of his grandparents. Thea had sat up in the front room beside her dead husband, waiting for Sam.

So they dressed him in a dark shirt and pants and together in a group went to the church. Though small it had a nave and side aisles, where vessels of votive offerings promised during the storm still hung in the damp dim air of the chapel. Gray light filtered down through the stained windows and, except for the dripping rain outside, silence filled the darkened vault. A man came in and lit candles in the sconces on the walls as Hunt knelt, his head bent in sorrow beside Thea, and stared at his black shirt front.

On the bier at the chancel the coffin of cheap yellow pine lay draped with a black pall and flanked on each side by candles burning in the over-hanging gloom. A young server came forward bearing a vessel and followed by Father Salinas in his loose surplice. The priest halted at the foot of the casket and began to chant a prayer. Pale candlelight flickered in the gloom to the rise and fall of his voice intoning above the deceased, and the drizzle outside fell on the already sodden earth. Dampness and shadows. The first halting words of the solemn canticle petitioned for eternal rest, for perpetual light:

"Requiem æternam dona eis, Domine: et lux perpetua luceat eis."

Vaguely aware of late mourners coming in, Hunt raised his eyes to watch the priest walk round the coffin, sprinkling it with holy water and intoning the *Pater Noster*.

"Requiescat in pace."

And was answered, "Amen."

"Domine, exaudi orationem meam."

"Et clamor meus ad te veniat."

"Dominus vobiscum."

"Et cum spiritu tuo."

The oppressive scent of incense hung in the air of the chapel, an odor of sanctity so heavy and thick he couldn't breathe. His mother stifled a sob, and he felt her rise to go forward, head bent, fists clenched at her throat. She approached the bier and, looking at FJ—closely shaved for the last time by her own hand, his face powdered with talc—she sank to her knees. The boy could see her eyes staring into a future reft of her husband and his father, and all the while Father Salinas was making the sign of the cross over the body and returning to the sacristy, where he continued intoning the *Kyrie Eleison*. *Now he is dead*, Hunt thought, *and we can bury him. But why? And for what purpose?* For a moment he was lost, unaware of what was happening. Then he felt Sam touching his shoulder, motioning him forward to take his place at the casket, which had been closed, the top screwed down and fastened for eternity or until the wood rotted in the moist coastal caliche. He was positioned in the middle across the modest coffin from his grandfather when he saw in amazement that Starlight, Primo the Giant, and a roustabout he knew by sight had returned from Del Rio to be pallbearers for his father.

They went out the side door with the coffin, to the churchyard, and into the gray steady drizzle. An awning stood among the tombstones. Hunt saw the new caliche clay turned up beside the grave and the diggers with their muddy boots and corduroys, leaning on their spades and standing under some dripping salt cedars and mesquite trees, watching the short cortège come into the cemetery. Other men he didn't know stood there too, some with stubbled cheeks and jowls already blue this early in the morning as if dusted with steel filings from a machinist's shop, their heads bared in the wet air. Seeing those rough faces in mourning, he remembered masculine widows in their black cloaks and veils on parade during his first festival with his father. *Never again*, he thought. There would be no more festivals with him now. Gnats clouded about his face as the line of people approached the mound of damp earth next to the trench, nets of the pests hovering above puddles among the gravestones and under the canopy.

Prayers began again for the last time when they reached the graveside and placed their load on bands supported by trestles. It took an effort to position their burden exactly over the hole. As if on signal from Salinas and as the words rose into the gray air, the sexton at the gravehead began to winch the pine box into the ground, lowering it until the bands went slack, after which he retrieved them and moved the trestles to let the diggers get at the clay. Into the grave to be walled up with him went Crofford's insistence that solar winds had shaped the conception of his only son. There was no one left to advance that notion. Hunt saw the men come from where they sheltered under the salt cedars. Without haste they began shoveling dirt into the hole.

It fell in muffled clumps upon the coffin, flushing a cloud out of the pit. Hunt saw an iridescent speck caught in the net of flies hovering before him. It was only a floater, which reminded him of the nacre stud buttoning his father's collarless shirt. *They should've put on a collar. At least that,* he thought, *if nothing else.* But in reality he knew there had been no collar for FJ. Brushing the flies away and looking at his mother he discovered in her face a sleepless night beside the body. His gaze drifted, then settled on Starlight's frayed cuffs. During their labors the diggers had to pause repeatedly and knock their spades against the trestles, dislodging damp clods of caliche clinging to the metal.

Across the flooded ground a long line of broken Canary palms was barely visible in the heavy drizzle that flicked at the canvas tarp. It fell softly on the other graves and on the puddles of standing water from which a stench rose while the men worked to fill the hole. His head ached, and he felt ill. He was sweating, and then his headache blossomed into a throb as he listened to the sound of spades cutting into wet hummocks of clay and the damp earth falling on earth until the trench was filled in again, these sounds punctuating the last words of the priest:

". . . for the soul of thy servant Francis Joseph Crofford, who at thy bidding has today departed from this world. Do not deliver him . . ."

Sam Graggs took a wreath from the server helping Father Salinas with the ceremony and handed it to the boy, beckoning him to step forward and place it on the grave. He took it, went forward, bent and laid it against the headstone. Then he lifted his gaze to those gathered and saw her immediately, the pretty face last seen in Maximo's magic lantern on the first day of spring, saw that she was already averting her face, turning to leave, and slipping back toward the church as he thought, *There was a girl too and she is here.*

vii

It was then that Starlight stepped forward and, clearing his throat, began speaking to those assembled.

"Friends, grieving comrades and family, a few words in remembrance of a good colleague when he was at his sporting best and always a friend even at his all too human worst. We folded up our tents to return from Del Rio in order to see our dear old friend off in a fitting manner. For he was a sporting man whose intangibles can only be measured by the affection he stirred in all who knew him. In deference to custom and feeling, I stand here before you, paying homage to our late comrade and sometime benefactor, known to each of you—whether showman, entrepreneur, roustabout, or what-relation-soever—and feeling an obligation to share these poor remarks conceived in bits and starts over the better part of an hour on the road between the outskirts of Brackettville and the flooded Sabinal where it crosses US 90. A hundred to one, if you're present, he rendered a service on your behalf. And were it not for a storm and the sea, a bad decision on his part to stay put in the face of adversity, inspired by a fit of spleen against nature or from a want of good sense, he might be among us still, still serving our best interests or, at worst, saying a few chosen words over the remains of some other misfortunate creature washed up on the shores of this place. Generous to a fault, and a list of his deeds would be too long to recite on this solemn occasion and then only hint at that generosity. For he contributed to the Order of Benevolent Friars in troubled times, sponsored a subscription to the Retired Bargemen's Relief Fund, wrote letters of recommendation on behalf of Gianni Po and a host of others, supported many by word of mouth, a hint dropped in the right place, a comment of praise expressed soberly, without recourse to hyperbole, flattery, or pressure so that his word carried weight with the recipient far beyond any hoped for results. I see Gianni Po before me, paying his last respects. Who better to confirm my testimony? I see all the many beauty queens gathered before the grave, not a dry eye among you. You'll miss FJ with feelings notable in young ladies of your tender years. I will never quite be able to suppress the quiver in my lips when I pass the seawall of a moonlit summer eve from now on or fail to think of your loss and ours. Such were the joys."

He paused as if to collect his thoughts and looked at Hunt, his mother, his grandparents, and the priest.

"I speak for Maximo, too, when I tell you we are thinking of those who remain. We've made an offer to Samuel Graggs for all the machinery of the merry-go-round and for all the goodwill he and FJ built up over the years so that FJ's surviving widow and boy will not go hungry in these troubling times which are upon us."

A murmur of approval could be heard among the barkers, midget wrestlers, roustabouts, and operators who had come there to pay their last respects.

Starlight raised his hand, exposing a ravelled cuff, and gave a surprising command, "Now bring on the band," which summoned a gaggle of horn blowers from round the corner of Our Lady, Star of Sea. As the band broke into a jazzy rendition of "My Blue Heaven," he quickly added, "Let's hear it for the dearly departed, you sentimental boobs, and in the spirit of a sportsman's last best dance and ditty—or not at all."

The back fringe of mourners embraced, starting up a series of shuffling steps and hops meant to celebrate the end of something long cherished, now gone and never likely to be seen again. They groped and mimed a dance of disintegration that quickly devolved into chaos and uncertainty while Thea, her parents, and Father Salinas gaped at the wild gavotte and ghastly band. The dancers splashed and stomped in a muddy frenzy as if the tempest had been only a prelude to the real storm that was about to break across that city and over its law-abiding citizenry. Hunt saw Father Salinas clutch his rosary and begin to move his lips in prayer against the revelry exploding before his eyes in the graveyard. Even the diggers had joined in.

Starlight, bombastic, profane, persuasive with his mascara lashes and raddled cheeks, worked his magic on the fringe, whirling and snapping his fingers overhead as if clicking castanets and dancing a moist flamenco on the grave, his mouth stretched in a grotesque grin.

"What a face you're pulling, Padre. Dost think they cry above? Say it ain't so. Lift your skirts and give us a spin. Nobody ever went broke under-estimating the public's taste. You can take that to the nearest bank and deconstruct old wives' tales to the contrary."

Certain mourners laughed when the priest shook his head, his face growing red. They offered themselves instead and swirled with Starlight to the ragged music, first one, then another, on down the line, their mirth out of all bounds in a small churchyard by the sea and yet paraded before the astonished eyes of the widow and her parents. At last Graggs stepped into the breach and collared the band leader, motioning for a moment of quiet.

"Wait a minute, Starlight," he said. "Just a minute, everybody. Let's take this to the seawall where the public can join in. It's not like you to limit access to a good time, and this is no place for an Irish wake. For God's sake, man, share the festivities and do it on secular grounds." He turned on the band leader. "March yourself and this band to the seawall. Go on, you know how it's done. You've done it before."

The man looked to Starlight, who waved him on. "You heard him, old comrade. Strike up the music and lead us on." He goosed the leader as soon as he did an about-face, causing the poor fellow to hit another false note when he tried to blow his horn. The others followed his lead as he went out of the churchyard, all arm in arm, hopping, skipping disjointedly, Maximo even leaping to Primo the Giant's back and spurring him on with rapid kicks to the kidneys until at last they passed from sight around the corner of the church and were gone. Hunt looked up and saw the slope of the zinc roof glistening wet under the fall of light summer rain, smelled dark odors of the storm's aftermath, choked back a sob. Then all was silent once again in the gray streaming light, and his father was laid finally to rest. ✤

Won't Somebody Shout Amen?

by Joyce Gibson Roach

1952

Half of the whole second page of the newspaper was covered with the advertisement. Almost everybody in town—at least those who was saved—knew about the Easter Pageant before the paper come out, but the announcement made it official with no doubt about it.

My daddy read it out loud sitting at the table waiting for supper.

"No need to go all the way to Lawton, Oklahoma, to see Jesus crucified! The Pulpit Preacher's Organization acting in one accord with their respective congregations' elders, deacons and/or leaders will join together in the spirit of the Living God to put on an Easter Pageant with try-outs for Jesus being on Wednesday at the school auditorium right after prayer meeting."

Daddy read it in a real serious voice. He pushed back balancing on the chair legs and gave the rest of the particulars about how each church was taking on responsibilities such as making costumes, clearing the site, putting up a stage and providing refreshments.

"Uh-huh. Refreshments are too important to be left hanging loose," he added. "An inter-denominational choir would be forming."

The last part of the announcement was in fine print but it said that some volunteers were needed to play major roles such as Judas, Pontius Pilot, and Barabas.

"I allow as how there will be a little trouble in that department."

We was all sputtering near to laughing by that time and Mama stepped in.

"Hush that up. It isn't nice to make light of such a holy time as Easter. Folks are at least trying to do something special. Blessed are they that . . . that . . . "

Not being able to find a beatitude that fit happened a lot to Mama so Daddy jumped in, "Blessed are they that crucify Jesus."

Daddy winked his eye at us and, while Mama was sputtering, went back to reading. The last sentence said that the lumber for the cross would be donated by Jefferson Lumber. It never mentioned who was going to do the building, but I knew. My own daddy was building the cross. It was all so right. Jesus was a carpenter and, well just look how things turned out for him.

Then Daddy explained about the denominations that weren't joining in. We'd heard it all before and we looked forward to it ever single time.

"It goes without saying that the Catholics, Church of Christ, African Methodist Episcopal and us Holy Rollers won't be joining in. It is common knowledge that the Catholics use real wine for the Lord's Supper instead of Welch's grape juice." More laughing.

"Now, the Church of Christ keep to themselves, too, and have no truck with the rest of us," my daddy went on. "It has something to do with their being the only true church and refusing to go to hell. Now, I figure even hell has a piano and that would keep 'em out of there."

I never understood the remark but repeat it among my own kind every chance I get. It draws a laugh. We are a happy people and laughter always means folks is happy.

"Naturally, black folks can't come around the whites especially at their worship. It's because the coloreds can out-sing, out-preach and out-glory everybody else. You can't have such as them about. And you can't have such as us—Glory to God! Praise the Lord! Amen!—hanging around."

Talk of what others believed caused Mama to turn and smile at Daddy over her shoulder while she was standing at the stove dipping up our supper.

"Orville, hush up talking so in front of James and the girls. You're saying way too much for them to know about let alone understand.

Thou shalt not bear false witness against anybody."

Daddy grinned back at her. "Now Sarah, I'm not bearing false witness. I'm telling a lot of the general truth about folks. And I'm not calling names. Don't you think it's kinda funny. I see you're smiling at me."

"No, I don't."

"Then quit smiling at me."

At this, Mama had to laugh out loud. And she raised the spoon at him like she was going to swat him.

We belong to a church without a name. Some call us Pentecostals, some by other names, but mostly they call us Holy Rollers. In our bunch we believe that some have the gifts, speak in tongues when the Holy Spirit says to. Others have the gift to interpret what the speakers say. We raise our hands in praise, sing strong songs in strong harmony, and receive the baptism of the Holy Spirit which makes a person either shout, dance, or just fall flat in the floor for sheer joy. We call our place Glory Church.

The people in Toad have less to do with us than even the blacks. They make a lot of bad remarks, too. But Mama says it is because they don't understand. Even if we wasn't included in the Easter pageant plans, it wouldn't, she said, keep us from having a glory hallelujah time on Easter morning just like we always did.

"Blessed are they that are persecuted for my name's sake?" my Mama would say, asking. "Amen!" we said back to her when she put a question mark at the end of any sentence. At church the preacher always had to ask, "Can somebody say amen?" after saying something he wanted us to agree with. Mama didn't have to do that.

Like I was telling, my daddy was building the cross. He said they just asked him to give our church something to do. It didn't mean nothing, but I felt like it was the most important part whether anybody knew it or not.

And we was certainly invited to come to the pageant. They wanted a crowd bad enough to invite everyone including us and the black folks.

You understand I am not saying there is anything wrong with us at all. We are different. Our women dress real decent, never showing their arms and keeping most of their legs covered up. And the way the women wear their hair—their crowning glory—is really right.

My mother has the most beautiful hair you ever saw. Daddy tells her that all the time and it is so. Her hair is black and shiny because she washes it every Saturday night and my sisters, too. They are pretty like Mama and just as good and decent, more valuable than rubies. Ruthie wears her hair down real long, but Pearl is putting hers up just like Mama now because she is a woman.

I'm thinking like I always do that it is just a pleasure sitting at the table with my two sisters, Ruthie and Pearl, and her baby boy, Joshua. Joshua doesn't have a daddy. Well, he does, but Pearl won't talk about it and Mama says it don't matter. "He is precious in the sight of the Lord?" Amen!

Daddy don't say anything about it either, but I think he is hurt that Pearl don't have a husband, but he's not ashamed of her or nothing. He just seems sad and sometimes mad, but Pearl won't say anything. I think him and Mama talk about it at night, but I don't really know what they are upset about. Daddy acts like Joshua's daddy, though and I'm Joshua's uncle so there's men for him to count on and look up to.

We have a good life and all of us work to make it so. Daddy can repair or build most anything. Mama and my sisters clean houses like a lot of the women of our faith do.

Ruthie is fifteen and Pearl nearly seventeen, but they don't go to school anymore. I don't know why, but I think it may have had something to do with Pearl being with child although nobody ever knew it because she quit before she was showing. Ruthie stopped the same time as Pearl did.

Daddy said we could all quit anyhow when we learned to read and figure numbers good. I'm thirteen years old, and me, I'm still in school and plan to stay. I don't have but a few friends at school, but I sure do have friends at church. Every single person young or old likes me. So I'm not lonesome or anything. And, I like school real well and do best at memorizing and reciting.

I work after school cleaning churches—Baptists on Monday, Presbyterians on Tuesday, nobody on Wednesday since that's prayer meeting night and I just don't work on prayer meeting night. Thursday, I take up the Methodists and Friday, the Church of Christ.

The Catholics never use me. Something about having plenty of their own folks cleaning up for penance and there being a bunch standing in line to get to do it. Penance is some kind of money I think.

On Saturday I clean my own church, for free, naturally. In the summer me and my daddy mow such lawns as need it done like at the bank, Masonic Lodge, the courthouse square—important business places like that.

And we have a big ol' garden that keeps us all busy. There is plenty for us, our neighbors, and some to sell. "God's plenty?" Amen!

My name is James Arvin Stout and yes, I aim to be a preacher. Been doing a little of it since I was six years old. Whether or not I was going to preach regular was up to the Holy Spirit. Mama said God would reveal it to me. She and Daddy want me to be a preacher and surely if they think it is a good idea then God would want me to do what my parents say. I just keep waiting and waiting for a sign, and preparing myself the best way I can.

But, you know I've never been to Lawton, Oklahoma, to see the famous Easter pageant where some man playing Jesus gets crucified. Lord, cars pack up to cross the Red River like they was giving away something free on the other side. They take picnic baskets and blankets and do a whole lot more than watch the pageant. There is sin and wickedness just across the Red River. My daddy said folks could stay at home and crucify Jesus themselves. I didn't get it, but Daddy said I'd understand it better by and by.

But it wasn't that I hadn't been nowhere. Me and my family went one summer to Tennessee—I forget just where—to see 'em handle snakes at a revival. We didn't like it as much as we thought we would, but it was interesting and exciting all at the same time. There was no denying the power of God and that was worth witnessing. Amen!

We went on lots of trips around here to revivals, some of 'em in tents which could be moved about, but most in tabernacles which can't be moved. Sitting on benches under a good roof with the sides open for God's sweet air to blow through and singing, praying, dancing, and shouting is a fine way to pass the summer.

But back to my story. This Easter Pageant business was about to get in full swing. This is the way it come about. On Monday evening after the announcement in Wednesday's paper the week before, I went about my regular duties at the Baptist church after school. Mrs. Poe, the undertaker's wife, come downstairs to the basement where I was mopping the floor. She was a heavy-set woman who always wore dark dresses, smelled of Evening in Paris perfume—that's what Pearl said it was called—and marched instead of walked.

"James, is that you working so hard?"

"Yes'um," I said. "Can I do somethin' for you?"

"Well, matter of fact you can. I had these new fans made. The weather will be gettin' warmer soon and revival season is right around the corner. Do you reckon you could take a handful of them to the other churches when you clean? It's good for Christians to share with one another and I do this out of Christian charity."

"Yes, Ma'am. I'd be pleased to, Mrs. Poe."

As she was leaving she stopped on the bottom stair and turned around to me. "James how is your mother and father, and your sisters?"

"Fine," I said. "Daddy is working on the cross every spare minute, and. . . ." But I never got to finish.

"Yes, yes. You are hard working people. I'll give you that. Did you know our son is in the running for the part of Jesus? There's a million things to do. Don't forget the fans, James." And she went on up the stairs kinda stomping with every step she took.

Mrs. Poe didn't even know or care about the cross. Maybe Daddy was right about just giving us something to do that didn't seem important.

Since I was stopped I picked up one bundle of fans and broke the string that bound them. On the front was a picture of Jesus standing and knocking at a door. I understood what the picture represented. It meant that Jesus was knocking at your heart's door. A person ought not to keep him waiting, but let him in.

Just when I was thinking on what a fine thing Mrs. Poe was doing, I turned the fan over. On the back was a message about Poe's Funeral Parlor and how they had burying plans and did long distance shipping. Long distance shipping to where? Heaven or Hell? I was thinking like my daddy did and laughed out loud to myself. Mama would have had my hide if she could'a heard me.

The last line give their names—Arlie, Marvene, and Tuffy Poe—and then said they supported the Easter Pageant. Why did they say that? Didn't everybody support the Easter Pageant?

Next night I went to the Presbyterians, cleaned up and put the fans on the pulpit chair just as their preacher, Reverend Campbell, came in.

"James, what are you doing up there?" His asking sounded like he thought I'd done something wrong.

"Just some new fans Mrs. Poe asked me to bring over. The chair seemed like a good place for someone to see 'em."

"James, you come down from there and let me see what you're doing."

"Yes sir." I didn't go down the stairs but jumped off the platform. Reverend Campbell took the fans from me and began to look at 'em real close turning them front to back.

"James, I can't believe you'd be a party to this."

"A party to what, sir? I was just doing what Mrs. Poe asked me to do. Is there something wrong with that?"

"Yes. No. Never mind, James. Just return them to Mrs. Poe tonight after you leave."

"What should I tell her?"

"Tell her we don't need any fans."

Things was gettin' complicated. But I did what the Reverend Campbell told me to do. Presbyterians are a stern lot. I ran most of the way because it was after dark and I needed to be home or else my folks would worry. And I still had chores to do.

When I got up on the porch I could hear the Poes arguing about something. "Marvene don't make Tuffy run for Jesus. He doesn't want to do it."

"I don't care. It won't hurt him. And I'm his Mother."

"What does that have to do with anything? Jesus's mother's name was Mary, not Marvene, as I recall."

"Oh, Arlie! You are so cruel to me."

I knocked loud and cleared my throat at the same time. Things got real quiet in the house and then Mr. Poe came to the door.

After looking at me kinda surprised, he said, "Is that you James? What do you want?"

"I brought these fans back that Mrs. Poe asked me to take to the Presbyterian church. Reverend Campbell told me to give 'em back. Here." I dropped the bundle at the door and ran.

Not sure what happened after that but things got in a terrible mess with carrying gossip back and forth and such. The whole town was in an uproar. As it turned out, the Presbyterians didn't have any candidates. The Methodists had three and had to decide between them. Anybody who wanted to do anything was okay by the Methodists. They weren't stern enough. The Church of Christ weren't involved in it except to talk about everybody else. More business about going to hell. But since they thought we were all going anyway, how could one more "wickedness," as they called it, make any difference in the outcome. The Catholics was just laughing.

I knew all along that people in one church didn't have a lot of use for people in the other churches. That was natural. You had to feel like your bunch was the best or else you'd go somewhere else. But it come as a revelation to me that some folks had no use for others in their very own churches either. There was a lot of murmuring like the Israelites of old. Course, I heard every single word at every church, mostly by what they were offering to the Lord in prayer in the groups that was beginning to gather.

I shared ever bit of information I got with all the others at my cleaning rounds. And I asked folks to pass it on so every church could keep up with the plans. Pretty soon my name got mixed up in it somehow.

By Friday night of the next week the plans had changed. The try-outs were not going to be held for Jesus. Instead, folks was going by the cafe and vote on paper for their choice. It was told that Jasper Farley, who ran the cafe, was probably an atheist since he didn't go to any church. He didn't have no special interest in any of it. There was three standing for election and no mention was made of church affiliation.

They were going to announce who was playing Jesus on the Monday before Easter so the lot of 'em could practice the whole week. The ballots would be counted by the PPO and the results revealed on the first night's practice.

I will allow as how each church had fine representatives. Course, I knew them all from school. Tuffy Poe was a graduating senior and an all-around athlete—football, basketball, baseball, and track. Billy Joe Jefferson was going to be the valedictorian. He was real smart but he didn't play sports. Called him Brains for his nickname. His daddy provided the lumber for the cross and it was in the paper every week. Finis Grissum could play the piano, quote poetry from memory and went to the Interscholastic League competition every single year since he was in the eighth grade. The pageant was being held on the Grissum ranch so he stood a good chance.

The one qualification they had was that they were young, younger than Jesus. Everybody knows that He was thirty-two when all the trouble started. But they needed someone that wasn't married yet and was still pure, if you get my meanin'.

By the end of the next week I was standing in the need of prayer myself. Had listened to too much tongue wagging, as my Mama called it. And lost my jobs. How that happened, I just don't know, especially since I tried so hard to be helpful.

Mama said to never mind when Daddy was about to say something strong to me. Things would come right. We could get by for a time. I could watch Daddy work on the cross, maybe help him, work the garden to get ready for Spring planting and even spend some time on my knees talking to the Lord about preaching. And I was admonished to ponder the wages of carrying tales. I knew what the wages of sin were, but couldn't remember where in the Bible it mentioned the wages of talking. I did what I was told to do, though, even when Daddy said it was a little late to do anything but think about it. The damage was done, he said.

Daddy had a lot of work to do for folks, some of it at the churches. But late in the afternoon he would come home and go straight to the shed by the barn to work on the cross. He spent a lot of time complaining about the lumber Mr. Jefferson gave him to work with. Said it was bad quality and all. Mostly I just watched him. Something was eating at him. Tried to help him all I could but he got cross with me, and my sisters wouldn't come about at all. Seems like my Daddy knew things I didn't know and he wasn't sharing his burdens with me.

One afternoon after school when I went to the shed, Daddy was harnessing the mules to the wagon, had his ax, cross-cut saw, and other needments loaded in the bed and was in an awful huff about something.

"What's the matter, Daddy? What's wrong?"

"Nothin' son, nothin'. If you want to go with me get in. I'm sick of that lumber of Mr. Jefferson's. They don't care about the cross anyway. They as good as said so. But I'm going to the breaks and cut down two of God Almighty's beautiful cedar trees for a proper cross."

I was already up in the seat before he jumped on and hollered the mules into their traces. He never stopped talking either. Most I'd heard my daddy say all at once in a month of Sundays. Sure 'nuff, he was steamed up with the power of the Holy Ghost upon him about something, I guessed.

"You'd think folks would give some thought to betrayal and death on the cross instead of electing Jesus."

"Amen!" I shouted to match my daddy's mood.

"God, smite their hard hearts and sinful ways. Their hateful gossiping ways. Just like the Pharisees, they are. Blessed are they that are persecuted for no reason at all."

I was puzzled by what he said, but when the power of God is upon a person, it's best to go along with it. "Smite 'em. Yes, Lord!"

"God of Abraham, just let me do my job, play my part, even if they don't want me to do it anymore. Give me strength for I am about to do!"

What was it, I wondered, did he have to do except go cut down two cedar trees for a cross that nobody wanted anyway. What in the world was he so stirred up about? He was lashing the mules with nearly every breath he took.

"Daddy, what is troubling you?"

"James Arvin . . . can't you understand? The church-going people in town just asked me to make the cross to give us some little something to do. That was all right with me because I was going to make a cross to glorify God, not to glorify myself. And then you went and got messed up in it and brought shame to me—to all of us. We are despised and rejected, scorned. We always have been, and now you make it worse!"

And with that my Daddy hit me so hard I tumbled off the wagon seat and rolled til my head hit a tree or something.

When I came around, Mama was cradling me in her arms speaking in her prayer language. Her hands were sticky with something but still cool against my face. I could hear Pearl and Ruthie crying and praying like they were off in the distance somewhere.

I couldn't get my eyes open or make my brain quit spinning. When I moaned from the effort of opening my eyes, Mama's tears were washing over me and she was wiping my face and head with her hair just like Martha's sister, Mary, cleaned up Jesus one time.

"Girls, he's alive. It's a miracle?"

"Amen," I mumbled.

She said all this quiet like over me. "Ruthie, go tell your daddy to come."

Daddy got up from kneeling in the dirt beside the wagon and walked over to us. I could see him plain with my head propped up in Mama's lap.

Daddy came to me and picked me up in his arms and carried me all the way back to the house crying "James, I'm so sorry. God forgive me. God forgive me. Oh please, God, forgive me."

I ought to have said something but I couldn't. I still didn't know what caused him to say what he said and do what he did. Vengeance is mine, sayeth the Lord, but my daddy gave him a lot of help.

Except for a terrible headache I wasn't too bad off. My clothes covered scrapes and bruises and my hair hid a knot on the side of my head just behind my ear. Nobody said anything at school mainly because nobody paid me much mind anyway. But then I got in trouble, as if being on the outs with my family and the people in town wasn't enough.

I was always good at reciting and didn't let trials and tribulations of any kind stand in the way of memorizing my pieces. My head kept hurting a lot but I stayed away from the shed where Daddy was working on the cross to keep memorizing Longfellow. He didn't want me around anyway, I figured.

On the day of reciting I was called on first. That didn't scare me. It was an honor to be first because Miss Rosalee knew I could put the others to shame. Isn't it written that pride goeth before a fall? Well, it does.

I commenced every line just right but for some reason put a question mark at the end of every sentence and then followed with something. *"Tell me not in mournful numbers, life is but an empty dream?"* Amen! *"For the soul is dead that slumbers, and things are not what they seem?"* Glory!

I went on getting in deeper and deeper until Miss Rosalee just asked me to quit after *"We can make our lives sublime?"* Yes, Jesus! *"And, departing, leave behind us footprints on the sands of time?"* Hallelujah!

And she told me to go home. I went and didn't entertain any notions about going back til after Easter. Maybe not then.

Misery. Lord, have mercy! It must have been kinda like this for Jesus in the final days. I began to study on the things that happened and decided prayer was the answer. I didn't have the Garden of Gethsemane, but I had my Daddy's workshop where we all gathered again after our hurt feelings eased.

It doesn't do no good to talk a thing to death. That's what Mama said. Mostly, we just all stayed quiet with one another and didn't talk at all. Lean not on thine own understanding, it said in the Bible. We needed to lean on the Lord and one another.

My sisters sang the sweet songs of salvation with Pearl on the strong alto while Daddy sanded, worked the wood, and held up the tune with bass. Mama, with little Joshua in her lap, held his baby fingers around the rim of the ringing tambourine to keep the beat.

I guess it was because Daddy was working on the cross, but the song I loved the best was the one about *"Must Jesus bear the cross alone and all the world go free? No, there's a cross for everyone and there's a cross for me."*

God give us all the peace once more and we looked forward to going as a family on Monday night of Easter week to take the cross, see who was going to be Jesus and watch the practices.

And because of the forgiving, peaceful feelings, my whole family walked blind right into hell.

Late afternoon Daddy called us all to the shed. He couldn't get the cross in the wagon without help. And it took us all to do it. Even Mama. She put Joshua on a pallet under the springboard seat and the little fellow set up an awful howl. We laughed and Mama got him out from under there and put him by a tree. He was happy with that.

If it crossed our minds that the cross was too heavy for us to carry then it was too heavy for Jesus, we didn't speak of it. I think it would have been more than Daddy could stand. Besides, it seemed plain that they didn't want the cross anyway.

The cross was a regular work of art. He had stripped the cedar to bare wood, dried it and then stained it so as to bring out the dark reds and blonde tones. Then he sanded it and varnished it to a high gloss. And after that he fitted the cross piece by cutting a groove to hold it on the upright piece and pegging it instead of nailing it; then lashed the cross piece on with leather strips.

There were handles for Jesus's hands and leather pieces to tie over them; and one peg at the bottom to put the feet on and tie them on, too. Then at the top of the cross he had carved the word, "Glory," and on the bottom, "Forgive." It was about the best piece of carpenter work I ever saw. God looking down from his throne must'a thought the same thing.

We finally got 'er done and sang all the way to Mr. Grissum's pasture. We met some on the road but nobody said anything to us, not even hello. It was my fault, but my family didn't seem to mind. There was good humor among us.

Daddy pulled the wagon up close to the platform and we finally unloaded the cross and leaned it up by the edge. I couldn't tell what the plan was and I know now there wasn't any plan. Nobody had the least idea what was going to be done. But maybe Jesus was going to pick up the cross but not try to walk too far with it. There wasn't a hole dug or anything.

At first it looked like there was a lot of people there, and lots did come but left after they satisfied their obligations about refreshments, costumes and the like. With all the milling and noise, it was an hour after the appointed time before anything official got underway. We put our wagon a little piece off under some trees so Mama, Ruthie, and Pearl could be comfortable and take care of Joshua. Me and Daddy stood respectful like at the edge of the trees. Some of our brethren from Glory Church were there; some colored folks too. There were a number of unchurched people who had come, maybe to get saved. But Daddy said they had come out of curiosity. I thought he was wrong about that, but said nothing.

We heard that the candidates and their families were coming and as they got near the platform Jasper Farley whose cafe was used for the balloting called for quiet. My choice was Tuffy Poe, hands down. He was popular and such a good sports player, and I knew for a fact how bad his mother wanted him to play Jesus.

Mr. Farley introduced each candidate and there was a nice round of applause for every single one of them. These folks were doing what was right, I thought. They were being Christian all the way. For some reason Pearl took interest and got down off the end of the wagon with Joshua in her arms and started walking toward the platform.

"Without any further ado, I will read the winner's name from the ballots counted by the PPO just this afternoon. I was there and it was done fair. The man elected to play Jesus is Tuffy Poe."

Mr. Farley said it flat like, and, without another word, got down off the platform.

I should have known that something was funny when instead of wild yelling such as I was doing there was only a little applause. Daddy shut me up in a hurry. It made me mad, too, and I started to get loud right then and there. I was under some conviction from the Lord that loosed my tongue. "Tuffy is the best man, Daddy. Everybody knows what a hoss he is. He really is. What's the matter?"

"Don't go working up a head of steam, James," he said.

Others in the crowd around us heard and began to turn toward me and my family.

"James, you'd do well to be quiet and your whole family clear out of here. You're mostly the cause of all the trouble anyway. I can't believe you showed up, the whole lot of you." This from Reverend Campbell.

Daddy was pushing me back to the wagon and told me to get up in the seat. The crowd was closing in now. Our brethren began to gather round us but not knowing what to do.

Now, every eye was turned from the business at the platform to us. I was scared but becoming stronger in the might of the Lord at the same time. The power of the Holy Spirit was coming over me.

Daddy got up in the wagon beside me and we stood there waiting. Nothing happened but insults and the worst kind of words were used on us. It was like a dream. Daddy got with Mama and Ruthie and put his arms around them. They started praying and calling on God's help.

There was some movement up on the platform about that time where only Tuffy was left standing. It really was like watching a dream. I saw Pearl standing looking up at Tuffy and saying something to him. Then she held the baby up like she was asking Tuffy to take the little fellow. Then Tuffy shook his fist at Pearl! Yessir, shook his fist at my sister. Then he jumped down and commenced to running. Mrs. Poe was watching it all and she screamed. Then Mr. Poe started pulling her to the car. They drove off and everyone else began to leave too, real quick.

Pearl started walking back fast toward the wagon. Folks scattered and parted the way to let her through. I offered my sister my hand and pulled her and Joshua up into the wagon with me. Before I could ask her why she was crying and what it had to do with Tuffy, Old Brother Horner started speaking in tongues.

By the time he finished, I was full in the armor of the Lord. It was revealed to me what he said and I interpreted for those who gathered round the wagon pulpit. My first sermon poured out of me even if only a few stayed to hear.

"I don't understand what exactly went on here. But likely God found fault with it. He found fault with me and fault with others. I sort'a understand what I did, but I don't know about others. And I don't have to bear the burden of understanding them. God will or won't take care of it. God is God. That's in his hands, not mine? Amen? Maybe we don't understand much of anything until each of us gets a'holt of the cross for hisself? Amen?

As to electing Jesus. Here and now, I elect each one of you to play Jesus. Glory! Every man here has got my vote. Yes, God! Each one of you take up the cross, carry it by yourself. Nobody else can do it for you. You got to carry it for yourself. It's yours! Jesus! It's yours! Jesus!"

I wish I could remember what else I said, but I don't, though it probably had a lot of words from songs in it. The baptism of Holy Fire rained down on me and I parted the veil to the other side and swooned in the very presence of the Lord for five minutes, they told me later.

On Wednesday night Mr. Farley and two black men came over to our church just about prayer meeting time. They had Daddy's cross in the back of a pickup truck. They said a few words to him in private, shook his hand and prayed together with Mr. Farley leading them. I don't think Mr. Farley was an atheist at all. Then they all set to work digging a hole in the front churchyard and putting the cross in it.

After that, Mr. Farley came over to me. "James, you're . . . well, you're a funny kid. Your daddy says you are going to be a preacher. I've been going to Lawton to see the Easter Pageant for the last six years. I'd like to take you along. Would you like to go? Your Daddy says it's okay."

We crossed the Red River late afternoon on Saturday. There was a crowd pouring into the grounds at Lawton, just like the mob that entered Jerusalem. The sun was beginning to set on three big crosses made out of old creosote telephone poles. What a sight! I looked at Mr. Farley and said "Amen?"

"Amen, brother," he shouted back at me. "Amen!" ✿

EVENING

by Elizabeth McBride

I touched my finger to the dark ivory disc and rang the bell. Steven lived on the second floor. A heavy wooden door opened and his face appeared. He leaned over the railing, grinning and a little embarrassed, then took my arm and pulled me up a flight of silvery wooden steps. He was excited. He wanted to show me around, he said, every room. So he gave me a tour. The living room was large and the kitchen was small, and the dining room only a wide space in the hall. The bathroom was lovely. I felt as if I had entered a dream. The walls mirrored down the blue and green Italian tiles, and behind the bathtub was a white marble shower stall.

The bedroom he showed me was large and spare. The bed was brass with black sheets. On a small table to the left of the bed was a lamp and a telephone. On the floor was a stack of magazines. *Latin America Speaks.* *The New Marxism.* It was dark in the room. But when Steven opened the curtains to show me the courtyard, I saw the sky was only then turning to shadow. When he closed the curtains the room grew dark again. It gave me a strange, thrilling feeling as if I were in a cave. I might be reborn, I thought. I might be starting another life.

I asked him about the upstairs, was it full of things?

"I'll show it to you," he said. "It's like an office. Come on, I'll take you up.

"Not yet," I said. "First I want to get used to this."

In the living room I turned a circle, still holding my bag. Two couches were placed perpendicular to one long wall, and on the other there were shelves, very plain, very ascetic. On the floor between them he'd placed a rug, a geometric design with rich colors—Moorish looking—which didn't quite match the couches, and on the rug a small table, bare except for pieces of fabric. The shelves were comfortably messy, full of books and personal things, things that looked like they meant something. An African basket, a Chinese bowl, a collection of old barbed wire.

Steven came in from the kitchen and glanced at my bag, which I had set on the floor.

"There's something I don't understand," I said. "How can you live like this? You said you were poverty stricken."

"I said I didn't make any money."

I put my hand on his arm, out of sheer delight at being so close. Then I turned suddenly shy and dropped my hand. "Well, where does it come from?"

"I don't think I'll answer that question. You'd probably like me better if I never tell you. And anyway, I don't want to tell you everything on our first date."

"Date? Is this a date?"

"I'd call it a date," he said and leaned down to kiss me. His kiss was as brief and light as a cloud.

"I'll open some wine," he said, and disappeared.

I walked back and forth in front of the shelves with my hands behind me trying not to step on the fringe on the rug.

When he returned, Steven sat down on the couch to pour the wine. He winked at me when he saw how I was walking.

"It's a beautiful rug," I laughed. "It's amazing."

"It's a rug," he said. "It's meant to be walked on. Maybe we'll sell it, then I'll get another one. It's from Guatemala. They *come* dirty. If you saw them being made you'd be shocked." He held up the beautifully hemmed pieces of striped fabric left on the coffee table for napkins. "These are from Guatemala, too."

He handed me a glass of wine.

"I want to see everything," I said, feeling tipsy already. "I want to know why you have barbed wire on your shelves."

"Oh, the barbed wire. My grandfather collected that. Do you know how many kinds there are? Talk about amazing," he said. He put the bottle down and went to the bookcase for a sample.

"My only experience with barbed wire was trying not to get stuck when I was crawling through, when I was a kid going blackberry picking."

Steven had a proud look on his face. "My grandfather was one of the trail riders—of course it was nothing but a trumped up event that didn't last any longer than twenty-five years. My grandfather called it driving cattle up to Indian country. When I know you better, I'll tell you a story about him."

"I know some stories. My mother tells stories. When I know you better I'll tell you one."

"Come here," he said. I was still standing. He pulled firmly on my arm until we were both on the couch.

"You're scared to death," he said.

"Do you know everything?" I asked.

"Just about you. I don't know what it is. I seem to know all about you. Put your glass down," he said. "That's enough for you. You don't drink very much. I figured that out the first time I met you." He put his arm around me and pulled me close. "You smell good," he said, his face in my hair.

He moved quickly. When he placed his hand on my breast I felt I was sinking into the couch. The first thing that happened when I started to feel desire was that my stomach would hurt. After that, my shoulders would burn and my face would feel hot and my ears would ache. And then that familiar, strange excitement would flow. The feeling became unbearable, an unbearable pleasure. When he touch my breast, I could almost feel him between my legs.

I pulled away for a moment so I could look in his eyes. "You think you know all about me," I said. "But you don't. I'm the one who knows about you. Now that I've seen this place you're completely transparent."

He didn't argue with me. I was disappointed because I wanted to argue. Before I slept with this man, I wanted to fight with him.

"Forget about me," he said. He put his hands on my shoulders and turned me against the arm of the couch. I was sick with passion. I wanted him then, that very minute.

"Now," he said in a menacing voice, like the bad guy in a movie. "I want you to tell me about that bag you brought."

He was leaning over me and holding my arms. His hands were so strong I couldn't turn away. I was thinking about my husband, about the lie I had told him. That I would be at the medical library doing research on hyperactive kids. It was a good excuse. I had plenty of those in my remedial classes. I was thinking about how often my husband was gone, how silent he was, how often I wanted to scream to cut that silence. I was marveling that I had never done this before, and if I could get Steven to talk to me it might be worth all the nervous stomach aches, all the anxious waiting for the phone to ring, all the lies upon lies I would tell.

"I want to say something," I said. "I understand that it's a cliche but I want to say it. You probably think I do this all the time." I was thinking about my husband.

"I certainly wouldn't think a thing like that. You're shaking all over."

"Well, I brought this bag," I said. "It's got in it a nightgown and just some personal things in case I want to take a shower or make up my face or something. You might say it makes me feel more secure."

"I don't get it about the nightgown." He looked back at the bag. "Nothing for birth control?"

"Steven," I said, and then I stopped. "Don't worry about it. I'll take care of that. But you're right, I'm afraid. I know I can make you feel good, but I don't know how you'll think I'll look."

"Why is it," he asked, "even the most beautiful women think they're ugly?"

I put my hands on his face. His beard was soft and colorful, gold and brown and gray and a little red. I smoothed the hair back from his lips to draw with my fingers the outline of his mouth. "I like your beard very much," I said. "Ever since Castro hit Houston in the sixties, I've thought that growing a beard was the right thing to do."

"You're skirting the topic of conversation," he whispered.

"What *is* the topic of conversation," I asked.

"Whatever you want," he said. He was kissing my neck. He had become more and more quiet with me, tender even.

"I guess what I want to say is please be careful with me about the nightgown."

"Is that all?"

Steven leaned over and kissed me, and held me against him. He kissed my eyes and my face and my neck and my mouth. He kissed me until I thought if he let go of me I would collapse. Then he laid me against the back of the couch, and I raised my body to help him as he pulled my shirt out of my jeans. His hair was tied back with a string of leather. I stopped him long enough to undo the knot, and when he pulled my shirt up and put his face to my breasts, his hair fell over my skin, as smooth as a piece of silk. If I had been naked then, I would have been ready for him.

"You know what you're doing?" I breathed. "Do you really want to finish off this fast?"

"We can do this again. We can do it plenty of times. We can do it for weeks. I'll put you down in my date book for a daily appointment. Or maybe you lead a busy life and it'll have to be weekly?"

I started to laugh.

"For instance," he said, "we could begin now. I could carry you into the bedroom, you look like you weigh about a hundred and ten, and leave you there with your magic bag, and when I can't wait any more I will return and join you."

"Join you," I said, "what an expression!" My arms were around his neck, and my mouth at his ear. "You are so wonderful, Steven," I said, giggling, feeling drunk and thrilled. "I know the minute I saw you in that Guatemala shirt that you were without a doubt the most wonderful man in the world. But I want you to tell me what grade you will give me for this assignment."

"I can't tell you until you do the assignment."

"Yes you can, you said you know everything, and I believe every word that you say." I hid my head his shoulder then, feeling suddenly cold. What was I doing? If there was anything I had learned from Ray, it was not to believe a man.

"I have three hours," I said, and touched my tongue to his lips. "Do you think that we could make this last for three hours?"

When Steven came into the bedroom, I was lying in bed with the sheet pulled up all the way up to my neck. After all that talk, I had given up on the nightgown. I had gone into that marvelous bathroom with the clean white marble and blue and green Italian tiles and taken my clothes off. I had looked critically into the mirror. I could have counted my ribs. My breasts just hung there, they were so thin. All of America seemed to want to be thin, but when I get thin, I just get skinny. I could see myself all the way down to my belly where the stretch marks from Tina and Andy were thick as ribbons. I started to cry. I really didn't think I could do it. I looked at my shoulders. I had always believed that one was higher, that I was deformed. When I was twelve, I'd spent hours comparing.

Then I remembered seeing a movie starring Sigourney Weaver. Her chest was bony. She was a beautiful woman but her chest was bony. Of course, we had seen her through her lover's eyes and through the eye of a camera and every inch of her body was lovely. I knew I didn't look like Sigourney Weaver, but I was pretty sure I'd look better to Steven than I looked to myself.

I snuggled down into the bed. He stuck his head around the edge of the door. "Is this how you go to bed at home?" he asked. "With sheets around your head?"

"I don't want to talk about what I do at home," I said.

"Oh." He smiled. "The 'don't want to talk about it routine'."

"I don't intend to tell anyone there what I'm doing here, either. You will never have to be afraid I am kissing and telling.'

He grinned. He seemed always cheerful, always patient. Ray was impatient with me all the time. But then Ray couldn't send me home to my husband when he was tired of me, or schedule our "dates" at his own convenience. I was beginning to see why a man like Steven might want to involve himself with a woman like me.

"Steven," I said, "Can I ask you a favor?"

"What's that." he said. "I'll do anything, ma'am."

"Don't call me ma'am, Steven. That's pure Texas bullshit and it makes feel old. And this is serious. Can we turn out the light?"

"Turn out the light? Not only the nightgown, but turn out the light?"

"I ditched the nightgown in the bathroom." I gave him a nervous grin and lifted the sheet, letting it drop too quickly for him to see anything.

"You think I won't like you," he said. He came close to the bed. He looked at my eyes, he looked straight through me. Then he went to the door and turned out the light.

"That's nice," I said. "I grew up wanting every room as bright as the daytime sky. And then I grew up some more."

Steven lit a candle on the dresser and stared undressing. The more I saw of his body the more I liked it. He was strong and thick, with a mole on his left chest to match the one on his wrist. He was gentle and blond and solid and funny and serious. I was glad that he wasn't thin. I wanted a man I could lean into. I wanted a man who was solid.

He finished stripping and stood by the bed. "Sheila," he said. There was an urgency in his voice. "I want to look at you."

I couldn't say anything.

"You see," he said. "You're staring at me. You can't help it. You want to look at me, but you don't want me to look at you. I feel like demanding equal rights."

I reached up and ran my hand down his leg. "You feel like demanding equal rights," I said. "I feel sorry for you, Steven, I am such a confusing woman. I even confuse myself. I feel like I've spent the first half of my life angry for being a sex object and I'll spend the second half angry because I'm not."

"What that got to do with us?"

"I don't know," I said. I placed my hand behind his knee and with a gentle pressure tugged him toward me. I couldn't help laughing. "I want to be sympathetic," I said, "but you lost me with all that stuff about equal rights."

Steven moved to the very edge of the bed and lifted the top of the sheet into the air, higher and higher. "Goddamn," he said. "The things you worry about."

He dropped the sheet slowly around my body, covering me from my head to my toes. As it settled in folds around me, softly, my fear diminished. I felt sure and uncertain, brilliant and yet unable to speak. I was caught in the wild whirl of romance, in the excitement of it. I had known all along that this act of the body would surely destroy me. But I was ready for it. It was what I wanted. ✪

THE SMELL OF TOBACCO: THE FEEL OF BREAD

by Charlotte Renk

Night after night He came. Tamer had not slept. She could not wake Elton. She could not tell Aaron; she had not seen him since they had discovered the vigil of the Red Tobacco Man, sent by God to punish them for their sin. Her belly was growing again, and she was tired.

Red Tobacco Man had parked his green pickup at the edge of the pipeline a little way up the road. Tamer had heard His truck motor cut off one night since He saw them since they saw Him. She heard it again the next night about the same time. She saw light on the window shade and heard a motor cut off. The light stayed on and she knew. She rose from bed where Elton lay sleeping, slipped out to the front porch where she saw the headlights stay a while and go out. Looking toward the truck, she saw a brief orange glow from His cigarette, and in the clear night from her darkened screened porch, she smelled His harsh tobacco. He was waiting.

Eleven nights like this. Tamer was tired.

So when Elton nudged her to get up on this Sunday morning to get coffee, to fix breakfast, and to get ready again to go to Willow Springs, she opened her eyes, rubbed her swollen hard belly, and felt her heaviness press deeper into the dip on her side of the bed. She stretched, tensed, flexed her feet so that they might relax a second more before they touched the drafty cold wood floor. Sighing as she raised to sit slumped with her feet hanging, not reaching the floor, she dreaded.

Then she remembered her plan.

And in her remembrance, she smiled. And though her eyes were still tired from her willed brief sleep, they rolled right and up searching her mind for the details of her plan.

"Well? Are you gettin' up, or are you goin' to sit there 'till we're late to church again? How is it that you're always the last one dressed and the kids and me'll be sittin' in the car honkin the horn while you're still puttin' on your make-up or your shoes or somethin'! I hate walkin' in late; you know that. So get the lead out, okay?"

"Okay."

She had tried as her mother, who had meant well and who had loved God, had urged her to do, but she knew she could never last as long as her mother. She had not loved God, for as some would say, she had never "found Him." She had tried. She'd been to Willow Springs most Sundays for years, had taught the three and four-year-olds in Sunday School to sing "Jesus Loves Me" and to color the coat of many colors, but the children never really understood. And neither did she.

Any other time, she might have fussed back even though she never really liked to fight and felt she often lost because she couldn't or would-n't stoop as low as Elton would, and she really didn't want the kids to hear them fighting, especially on Sunday morning. She was neither a "mighty peeping mouse," as Elton had called her, nor a "bitch," as he also said. She was born with too much "spunk," her mother said; her "will was never broke."

According to her mother, reared Primitive Baptist, Tamer was ruined by her father, half Choctaw Indian, and who had named her Tamer when he heard her birth cry and who indulged her haughty spirit.

So she argued with Elton in spite of herself.

"Why don't YOU get up and get the coffee? I get tired of it. Let ME lie here while you walk out to that cold kitchen, make the coffee, and while you're at it, why don't you throw a pan of biscuits in the oven! Oh and when you fry my egg, make durn sure that the yellow's soft, and the white ain't got none of that slimy shit all over it."

She liked to say "shit" or "damn" or words like that to provoke him. She got tickled every time she recalled the first time she called him a bastard after he had called her a bitch repeatedly. She couldn't remem-ber what the fight was about, but she remembered how he stopped mid-yelling when she said the word "Bastard!" Both stunned, she repeated for effect, "Bastard!" His eyes bulged, his wide shoulders hunched over her, his hand squeezed her cheeks to absurd fat lips, and he rasped,

"Don't EVER let me hear that filth comin' out of your mouth again, do you hear me? I'll not have the mother of my children talk like that in this house. Do you understand?" His teeth clenched, his hand squeezed harder.

Elton did not know what was happening. He and Tamer had worked so hard! For thirteen years he had hated that paper mill, its stench, the shift work. But he went and he came home to work the garden, to put up that paneling, sheet by sheet, put oil and anti-freeze in the wagon . . . and he never once fooled around on Tamer.

He had always wanted to come home to a wife, children, chicken fried steak, biscuits and pepper cream gravy. He only wanted to watch a little TV or to run his hunting dogs now and then with his brother A. J. or to tussle around with his kids. And to top it all off, he just wanted a warm fuck with a willing Tamer at the end of the day. "Was that asking too damned much?"

"Yes!" She said.

"Yes," she said, understanding how bad swearing was but relishing her way of needling him, and so to hide the smile that threatened, she slid the corners of her mouth into a sneer, which seemed more appropriately hateful for the moment. Then she did not hear his words anymore.

She did not hate Elton. He often bragged about her cooking. No man could have been more tender than he, as he stroked her hair from her face when their babies were born or when they almost lost their youngest child. He worked hard. He was faithful. What then?

She just hated her life . . . the neverendingness of it: the cooking, cleaning, kids whining, the toilet and tub backing up everytime she washed clothes of soured washrags, sweat soaked T-shirts, ammonia drenched diapers from the pail, her new oval weave rugs, wet where the runt of the latest puppy litter had pissed on it. The rug she got for her thirty-second birthday to cover the wornout mock-brick tiles in front of the kitchen sink. She hated the telephone disconnect notice on the counter, annointed by rat pellets in spite of the half dozen jar lids full of D-Con designed to kill the rats that skittered and ate and bred.

The telephone seldom rang for her anyway except from somebody giving a baby shower or bridal shower or Tupperware party. Tamer had seen enough weddings and births to know that they, like the brilliant trumpet blossoms of yellow summer squash amid lush green leaves, like most beautiful promises, turn to bland mush with time.

Or it could be June, her nasal-winded friend, fretting again because her second husband was running around on her . . . he had even come on to Tamer . . . but, of course, she could not tell June that. Or June might rave about her latest find at K-Mart or Wal-Mart or that new Crafter's Mall on the Square where she had found that gorgeous long denim coat with its fake fur collar and its pockets and belt studded with rhinestones. Tamer would not hear June's strident voice anymore.

Tamer could not hear Elton's words anymore. His red face and big eyes stretched; they contorted in a kind of comic strip silence. She stared. He released his hold. He spit the wad he could not hold in his mouth anymore.

She went to the kitchen.

She could always go to the kitchen, for there were always potatoes to peel, dishes to wash, sometimes a slick blue-pink gutted squirrel in the sink to clean and freeze, which reminded her of the rats. And then there were biscuits to make. Elton never found fault with any of that because one thing he liked almost as well as screwing and chewing was eating. His latest joke was that he went to the Dr. with a stomach ache, and the Dr. said he really had a problem, needed a lapsectomy. The Dr. said he needed that operation because he had a bad lap condition—his belly lapped way too far over his belt. (Ha, ha, ha!) Tamer fed him well and laughed every time he told his joke.

And so it was this Sunday morning; she did not mind heading to the kitchen, for she knew it was her last trip.

She heard Elton rousing the kids; he was always hateful with it. Her thoughts ran contrary to his: "Seems some people get pleasure out of wakin' people up. Looks like they'd let kids sleep; Lord knows they'll be plenty tired later on, so what's the harm in restin'? Ain't this a day of rest?" She resented his meanness, his impatience.

"Jed, if you're not up in two minutes, I'm comin' in after you with the belt! "Ruth Ann, git on out here and help your mama with breakfast. Who do you think you are, layin' there like you was queen of the hill or somethin'!"

Then he'd yell from the bedroom after he'd awakened the baby, "Ain't anybody gonna see to that baby? If I have to go in there to get 'em, I'll tear his little butt up, give 'em somethin' to cry 'bout."

"Oh Elton, he'll have enough to cry 'bout 'fore this day is done. Nevemind, I'll get him."

And she did. And as she stepped toward the babybed where brown straight hair and wide eyes rose like the sun over the rail, his face still wet and red from crying, the baby's eyes lit with glee at the sight of her. Her legs went limp as she held fast to the rail of the bed. She chuckled as she lifted the bar that lowered the side, "Well, if you ain't the beatenist thing I've ever seen! You sure changed your tune when you got me in here, didn't you?"

She lifted him and felt a pull in her lower belly as she hoisted the damp urine-soaked boy to straddle her right hip. He laid his head on her shoulder. She felt sad. He trusted her.

But she knew . . . she knew she did not deserve his trust *nor* him. She had almost killed him once. She'd slipped off to meet Aaron, the best and worst person to have ever touched her in the world that she was given. And as she was easing back into the house after her sin, Elton was waiting at the kitchen table for her. He rose, and bracing Tamer's shoulders with his big hands, his eyes met hers. As if his tongue were glued to the roof of his mouth, he uttered dry and cracking, "Oh Tamer, where have you been?"

And before she could answer, he sucked in his breath and when he relesed it, he cried, "It's Baby! He fell . . . his head . . . blood . . . must have scooted that chair up to the sink while I was dumpin' them peas out of the bucket on the back porch . . . Grandma's with him at Glenwood; they're watchin' him. . . ."

"Where was you, Tamer? We needed you." And they cried some more. "So how am I gonna leave you again, little man?" Nobody can love you better than I do . . . but I done ruined all that." A lump knotted in her throat. She kissed his snotty cheek, straightened her back for strength. Her stomach bulged larger, pressed beneath the toddler's leg clamped around her.

She took him to Ruth Ann and told her to bathe and dress him in his little blue-denim jumpsuit. "So how am I supposed to help you in the kitchen, bathe the brat, and get ready before Daddy starts yelling at me again?" Ruth Ann snorted, but she took the baby to her right hip and headed to the bathroom sink. Ruth Ann had spunk, too. She would be okay . . . long as anyone could be okay.

Tamer cut the shortening into the flour with her fingers, pinching flour and grease, separating lumps until the flour was like coarse corn meal, adding a tablespoon of sugar and pouring milk into the well, circling the well for flour, mixing it from the sides until the dough could be rolled by hand into biscuits. Cool and wet as mud, earth, clay ready to mold. She pinched and rolled each biscuit and lay each one like a gift upon the greased pan. Elton and Jed would eat three apiece, Ruth Ann would eat two, Junior would eat one with sugar melted in the butter. And in her favorite blue crock bowl, she set aside a mound of raw dough for later. She pushed it to the back corner of the counter near the lid where the D-Con lay.

Tamer cooked sausage that morning even though the grease and smell made her queasy. She opened fig preserves that her mother had given her this past summer. And she stared out the kitchen window past one last struggling pink cluster on the Crepe Myrtle and past the yard to the browning pasture, past leaning stunted corn stalks on to the soft gray centers of clouds that hinted of a rain, much too late to water what was already dead.

Mama said that it always rains when a good man dies. Even the angels mourn their passing. Tamer clouded at that.

She was neither man nor good; they could not cry for her.

There had been Aaron—gentle, smart . . . black—who'd helped her smile one day as she bought a book of stamps at the road. He'd been to college, passed his Civil Service tests, liked "feistiness," laughed at the whelps from the redbugs she'd gotten as they were supposed to be picking blackberries nowhere near Critter's Creek where they were. With time, Aaron taught Tamer that making love was different from screwing.

He taught her that the brief peace and warmth that follows love fit well with the scent of pines—male and female—as they swayed and whispered in the breeze. And as the trees swayed, they slept green freedom, neither black nor white. And they agreed that the hawk that swooped above them was her father who forgave her.

Aaron was quiet and sad, his voice as deep and stirring as a base fiddle's rhythmic pulse, constant beneath a blue lullaby. He had studied forestry at Southern, and he could name every vine or fern or moss or bug around. He had planned to be a ranger, but there were, of course, "no openings" in East Texas. And there were by then, his wife Irene and with Irene, two daughters.

She had not meant to love him. She had gone to the mailbox like she had done every day of the week except Sunday just to get out of the house. She hadn't combed her hair, put on her shoes, which bound her and slowed her down. She waited to buy stamps to mail bills. When the mail car stopped, she asked, "Could I buy some stamps?"

"Yes ma'am, Ms. Tinsley. How many do you want?"

Startled that he knew her name, she jerked her head toward him, wide-eyed.

"You are Ms. Tinsley, aren't you, or is she your mother?"

"Lord no, she's not my mother. I'm Tamer Tinsley. How'd you know my name?"

Chuckling, he pointed to the name on the light bill: Mr. O. E. Tinsley. "I guessed you to be the Mrs. O. E."

"What a dummy I am," she laughed. "I reckon you know everybody on your route."

"Well, yes'm, nearly 'bout."

"Well . . .thank you for the stamps!"

"But, Ms. Tinsley, you never got any stamps. How many did you want?"

"A book."

"Here you are."

"Thank you, ah . . . Mr . . . "

"Harris. Aaron Leon Harris."

"Yes, thank you Mr. Aaron . . . Mr. Harris . . . uhh . . . Aaron Leon!"

Tamer blushed and hurried to the house. She sent the kids to the box from then on until one day when they were at school, and she heard the horn blowing from the mail car. A package of seeds ordered from Tyner Petrus had arrived C.O.D. for $1.11.

"What are you planting, Ms. Tinsley," Aaron asked.

"Same as other folks, I 'spect. Corn, peas, 'tators, tomaters: you name it; Elton'll plant it. Now plantin' it's one thing, but hoein' it, gatherin' it, and puttin' it up gets to be a pain in the bu . . . ack!" she said hastily, laughing at what she had almost said in front of a total stranger.

"When you laugh, Ms. Tinsley, I hear the sparkling of clear waters around the rocks at Critter's Creek."

But there had been that other man, the red-faced, sweat-soured fat one who had watched them from behind a stand of hickory nut trees draped thick by muscadine vines, surrounded by reddening black sumac and thorny briars.

First, Tamer had smelled him as she roused from a dizzy light sleep on the pallet in the shade. She smelled tobacco. Prince Albert. She smelled sweat. Armpit and crotch sweat that had dried and warmed and wet again without washing. She heard breathing and stirring, perhaps a scratching of red rash from the crotch of the Red Tobacco Man.

By the time she nudged Aaron from his dozing, she had raised on her elbow toward the odor and the sound, and she glimpsed a red-faced, double-chinned man with a flat full balding forehead. She saw the broad khaki back of the man turn after he saw her see.

By the time Tamer and Aaron were dressed, they heard a truck start and pull away on the loose gravel. They studied the place where He had watched; cigarette butts, a Prince Albert can, and two dirty white handkerchiefs lay where he had waited . . . more than once.

Night after night he came in his green pickup waiting . . . waiting . . . She could not sleep. She could not wake Elton. She could not tell Aaron, for she had not seen him since they had discovered the watch of the Red Tobacco Man come to take her.

In fact, some new man was running Aaron's route. Perhaps Aaron was finally promoted to Postmaster. Perhaps he had been frightened away. Fear often overrides "love" under threat of disclosure. Could the Red Man have set the Klan to rectify the wrong that they had done? Had Aaron simply grown tired of her and the trouble accompanying their secret? Maybe he recognized the futility of a relationship that had no future, could not possibly have a future. "Birds of different feather cannot flock together . . . Unnatural!" her mother had always said. Maybe he rededicated his life to Christ and Irene, for both Aaron and Tamer acknowledged the sin and the shame of their love. Whatever. . . .

Aaron was gone, and Tamer was alone.

Her belly was tight again, and she was tired.

And the child within her must never. . . .

"Tamer, are you gonna get ready for church? What's going on with you this morning? Looks like you're about to fly right out that window. Come on, girl! We're gonna be late again."

While they ate, Tamer dressed for church.

Tamer wiped the sugar and butter off Junior's face and hands, hugged him, and handed him to Ruth Ann. When she did, she let out an "Ohh!" and doubled forward holding her belly. "Go on, Elton, I'll be all right . . . just havin' a few growin' pains I suppose. Go on without me; I think I need to rest a bit."

Elton mumbled something "'bout waitin'," but she motioned them all out.

Elton had given Jed and Ruth Ann a quarter each for the offering. Ruth toted the baby on her right hip to the car. As she got in the back seat, she bumped the baby's head, and he started crying. Jed told her how dumb she was. Elton revved the engine and started blowing the horn.

Tamer heard the squakling, the squabbling, the horn.

Jed came to the front screen and called, "Mama, you comin' or not?" At thirteen, he squaked more like his daddy everyday. At three, he sang in his little-big voice, "You picked a fine time to leave me, Lucille, with 400 children and a fox in the field. . . ."

"Oh, Jed. Oh, Lucille," she sighed.

She waited for the sound of loose gravel as the car backed onto the road. When it was gone, she retrieved her blue crock bowl from the kitchen and laid it on the bedside table. She took a deep breath, which she let like the swish of the hawk or the whispers of the pine.

She smoothed her pink floral smock over her heavy self, lifted herself to sit, feet dangling from the side of her bed, slid swollen, tired feet under the wonderful weight of the Lone Star quilt that her mother had made her when she married Elton.

And propping herself with pillows, she reached beside her to lift the bowl she loved from the bedside table and laid it in her lap. She kneaded the dough to mix the added powder. Then she pinched a ball of biscuit dough from the mound, rolled it, placed it inside her mouth and chewed. A little dry and salty then, a little bitter, but not bad. She pinched more and patted it to her cheeks—the dough so soft and cool. And when it warmed, she ate it. She ate and she ate, for this was the bread her hands had made. ❀

CLOUDHUNTING

by Robert James Waller

After a week or two of not feeling right, as if something large and badly complected were creeping up behind me and about to pounce, I went to see the bone lady. Her main squat was a three-room adobe way out in the high desert of southwest Texas, forty miles on pavement below Clear Signal and twenty-five miles east after that on a road camouflaged as a bumpy dirt track. Far down the afternoon I went, trailing into heat and silence and scarlet-blooming ocotillo, and when I thought I was lost, I was there. In Hydra. Or what used to be a town of that particular name.

Hydra, so talk went, had never been known as an outright celebration of art and wisdom. Still, fifty years ago there were veins of silver in the hill-sides, and three-thousand people clung to the desert floor when nearby Cheechako Creek ran deep and fast. That was before the mines petered out, after which the miners left, followed immediately by those who had serviced the array of needs miners are said to have. A few stay-behinds toughed it out for another thirty years, until a dude ranch two sections over dammed up the creek to create a five-acre fish pond for the amusement of its guests. And that was the end of Hydra. Except for the bone lady.

On the way down, passing Gallagher's Store and hot from July sun and no air conditioning in the pickup, not to mention being beer thirsty and most of that coming from my jitters about seeing up close the bone lady of some renown and legend, I'd stopped and bought four bottles of Lone Star before making the turnoff onto dirt two miles farther along. By the time I low-geared into the crumbles of Hydra and crossed the dry wash formerly known as Cheechako Creek, only two bottles were left, and they were sweating their way into warm.

A little farther on was the bone lady's dusty-pink adobe house, with a small wooden porch jutting out like a bad chin. Twenty yards south of the house stood a corral containing a handsome sorrel gelding and two burros. Cottonwoods surrounded the place, and inside the corral was a good-size dirt tank with plenty of water in it. I considered the cottonwoods and tank, thinking that amount of available water was odd, given that Cheechako Creek was dry and desert wells were notoriously weak.

Behind the adobe was an old single-wide of the variety formerly known as trailers but now called mobile homes, the designation shifting as a result of several decades of moving people and things into classier-sounding categories and that occurring without any real changes being made in their essential goodness or makeup. (In case you think that's a superior attitude, let it be known I still live in a rented double-wide precariously rooted to Lot Number 14, Cactus Mobile Home Village, formerly, the Cactus Trailer Court, on the west side of Clear Signal. I like living there, doing my evening reading and looking up interesting words when I find them, and I have no problem calling it a trailer, as in: "Hey, Rita, let's get a six-pack and go on out to my trailer.") To my way of thinking, things are what they are and never what we're told they are, and if that seems a little vague, it's only because I've always had trouble stringing multiple thoughts together.

The trailer at one time had carried a silver finish, but now was mostly scoured down to rusty primer by sun and sand. Squinting into hard light, I was momentarily fascinated by a contraption on top of it. Roszakian and pure of form, and recognizing such because I took an art history class at Sul Ross State University during my 3.7 semesters there, it consisted of a warped television antenna bolted to a '57 Cadillac tail fin, which, in turn, was welded to the roof. And across the antenna draped a run of telephone wire coming up from behind the trailer and snaking down the front into the adobe.

Curious structures of apparently random design are common in the lower high desert, yet this one had a engaging winsomeness of sorts, a texture and shape that bespoke of other times and better ways. I became increasingly taken by it until the bone lady opened her front door and said, "Whaddya want, Pancho? Got a problem, or on your way to rub gravestones up in the old cemetery?"

I told her I might have a problem and had come all the way from

Clear Signal to discuss it with her. She seemed unimpressed by that quantity of travel, but she invited me in and indicated I should sit at a round table with a green felt cloth over the top. Feeling edgy and needing to talk a little by way of breaking ice, I commented on her abundance of water.

"No conjuring there, if that's what you're thinking," she said. "Some years ago, I ran two miles of FasLine through the cactus and plugged into the dude ranch fish pond, down in a swampy area where they wouldn't notice it. Fair's fair. They dammed up the creek, after all. Took me three weeks of working nights to get it done. Carried my Smith & Wesson Model 14 in case I stumbled across any dope runners or tourists doing dirty things out in the desert. Didn't, though."

The bone lady drummed her fingers on the table top. "So, any idea what your problem might be?"

I started to tell her that things just didn't feel right, that some shadowy presence kept talking to me at the level of my cells and was disturbing my sleep along with my general sense of well-being. But she interrupted and asked, "That bobcat pee, or what, I smell on your breath? If it is, you got any more?"

Out to the truck for the last two sweaty bottles of Lone Star, which were not even beaded up by this time, just slimy wet. The bottles had twist-off caps, but the bone lady angled hers against the table edge, dug the cap teeth into the felt, and banged it twice with her left hand till the felt ripped, the cap popped, and foam ran onto the floor. I twisted off my cap and took a quick, hard pull so the foam wouldn't go anywhere except down my throat, which needed beer even more than it had a half hour ago.

The bone lady was sitting in a swivel chair having a slatted back and a torn Persian cushion on the seat. She took a slug of beer and wheeled around, tugging open a drawer on the highboy behind her, all the while humming a snatch of Schoenberg to herself. Since we tend to remember what we hate and love, all the while managing to forget the hesitant middles, I remembered how much I hated Shoenberg after suffering through a music appreciation class as a freshman. In the entire semester, I never did hear one song with a decently heavy backbeat lending itself to a Texas shuffle.

But the bone lady had her own tastes and continued humming, a little quavery in pitch, it seemed to me, and somewhere near the middle register of a clarinet. Yet, and somehow, in this context the sound was not unpleasant, even to the ear of a Waylon Jennings deadhead.

The highboy was walnut from what I could make out through about a thousand hacks and other various wounds to the face of it, including what looked like a bullet hole from a large caliber rifle near the upper right corner. The bone lady rummaged a drawer and then swung around to face me again, both hands cupped around whatever she'd taken out of the drawer and saw me looking past her.

She flipped her head rearward toward the highboy. "Nice piece, huh, Pancho? What's your real name, anyway?"

I told her.

"Well, Delmore, you must be from the third star north of Pluto or some place, 'cause I never heard your surname out here. And I been out here a long time, ever since I graduated from Sarah Lawrence."

I was trying to guess her age and having trouble making an estimate, since the desert climate with its hot wind and laser sun had a way of making people look somewhat older than they really were, me included. Her face and hands were the color of burnt sienna, and the face, in particular, carried lines and deep creases of indeterminate history.

She could have been a youngish seventy or an oldish fifty or anywhere along that continuum, though if it had come down to betting, I'd have put my heavy money slightly toward the upper end. Her hair was mostly gray, half-assed into a bun and with about thirty-seven strands hanging loose around her ears and neck. While I was involved in those keen observations, I managed to tell her I'd come out from the hill country twenty-three years ago for purposes of going to college and never got around to leaving once I'd arrived.

The bone lady nodded. "Happens. Place gets a hold on you. Saw you looking at the highboy. That rode on a westbound train with my grandmother in 1890, when she and her husband, Timmer, settled up on the Llano Estacado, few hundred miles north of here. The highboy's a nice example of the Anglo-mania that swept the furniture industry in the mid-nineteenth century, a period of what was called 'truthful construction,' where all the joinery and whatnot were supposed to be manifest to the eye of the beholder; no cards down, in other words. It and the old Victrola over in the corner eventually tumbled south to me after everybody else in the family had picked over the stock and decided they didn't want anything that wasn't in top-notch condition. I call the highboy Tatum, and Sonia's the Victrola, both having served me well. Now, on to the problem you think you have but aren't sure about."

While I was still looking at Tatum, the bone lady shook her cupped hands over the green felt and let fall the following mix: four javelina vertebrae and one fang from a black-tailed rattlesnake.

"See," she said. "Two of the jave's verts point southeast and the buzz-worm fang is pointing due north. Given that Venus is rising and Mars is descending, that means something more than it might rain a week from Wednesday."

"What's it mean in 'something-more' terms?" I asked.

"Means you might be on undulating ground, Delmore. Bones say Riley Boggs is returning to the high desert, and he's bristled up. In fact, he's downright pissed off concerning six parts of everything. That mean anything to you?"

"Aw, shit," I said, took a deep breath and let it out, stared at the ceiling. I'd been hanging out with Riley Boggs's wife ever since he got a rough-necking job over in the Gulf six months ago. Rita Boggs had said he'd left her for good. That's exactly what she'd said. He hadn't, apparently.

I told the bone lady as much, all the while noticing the other two vertebrae seemed to point roughly west by southwest. "What about those two?" I asked, twirling the forefinger of my right hand over them.

"Them's merely additional guides, telling you which direction you might want to go, pronto. By the way, you ain't telling me nothing I don't already know. The going opinion in town is that somebody I'd never heard of—you, I have come to discover—and rutty Rita have been goin' bump in the nighttime, partaking of the wife of Riley, so to speak."

That much was true. I hadn't been hiding out on the subject, since

Rita had sworn Riley was gone and wouldn't ever be seen again in these parts, and along with the general run of cowboys and cowgirls, she and I had been close-dancing down at the Cholla Bar every Saturday night for the past couple of months. Rita said after they closed the rig on which Riley was working, he took up with a carny outfit and ran the nail-hammering game. Somehow though, and Rita thought this was real funny, Riley couldn't master the gaff and kept mixing up the good nails with the soft ones designed for bending over when hit by the strong arms of carpenters who were sure they could beat the game. And they did beat it when Riley was in charge, which he wasn't for very long.

The bone lady was still studying the pointer verts. "Maybe ya'all ought to think about forting-up in the ghost caves near Terlingua," she said, adjusting one of the verts so it headed almost due south toward the caves. "Riley's curly-wolf mean, but he must be afraid of ghosts, that's why the verts are pointing toward the caves. In fact, I seem to remember Donnette saying that after she'd spent a night in the saddle with him, up at the Paisano Motel in Millennium. Said, 'You know that big ol' Riley Boggs? He may be big and all that, but he ain't worth spit between the sheets. Besides that, he's afraid of ghosts.'"

I patted my left breast pocket, located the Marlboros, and shook one out. "Who's Donnette?"

"She's daughter number two by my second husband. Two pair. Gimme a smoke."

"Poker Jim used to say 'Two pair no good,'" I told her, shaking out a cigarette and holding the pack toward her.

She took three Marlboros and put them in her apron pocket. "Piss on Poker Jim. Goddamn northern Indians don't know nothin'. By the way, Donnette's not doing anything but hanging around awaiting career developments, so she might even go down to the caves and keep you company, make common cause with you if you're any good between the sheets. You any good?"

I shrugged, and what else could a man do when asked so directly about matters hard to judge and having no witnesses along to testify? I was sure Rita, had she been there, would have given me at least a seven on a scale not extending more than several points beyond that. Anyway, if I said yes, I'd be bragging. A no would be a little hairshirty, I thought.

The bone lady leaned forward to get a better look at me and rolled on. "You must be okay if Rita's tolerating you. Word is, she don't put up with no minor talents in that venue, and she's collected enough evidence in her thirty-some years to be allowed as having considerable expertise in such matters. That's why she and Riley never could get anything going beyond temporary. From looking at you, though, and having no other evidence to go by, I'd be skeptical about your inherited gifts. Always possible, I suppose, that nurture somehow overcame nature and made you into a Roman candle. Also, and on the other hand, you thin guys tend to have lots of energy, which means only a fleck of panting at the end and no belly to work around in the process, way my second husband did on both counts. So, who knows?"

Finishing her evaluation, she wriggled her eyebrows and grinned in what I took to be a suggestive fashion with her mouth and eyes.

I hadn't come all the way down there on a Saturday afternoon to discuss my abilities along the trails of darkness and sideslipped over to the main thread of the conversation.

"Ma'am, I can't just up and run for the ghost caves. I've got an indoor job at Western Auto over in Sampler. That's four-eighty-five-an-hour work, with a fifty-cent raise coming in two months, which is hard to come by out here and beats billy hell out of what I used to do, day-handin' for some rancher who starts you off at sunup, lays out a baloney sandwich for lunchtime, and sends you home before supper."

"Murderously leaps the serpent on this July day, Delmore, and when it comes to making decisions, y'all got a bad case of slow. After Riley rearranges your somewhat delicate and patrician features, he's liable to strap you down spread-eagled across the Southern Pacific tracks, way he did with two Mexicans who tried to roll him one night after he wobbled out of the Cholla. Hadn't been for their screaming and hollering and the beneficence of a passerby, they'd have been burrito mix by dawn."

She paused for a moment, then added, "I can also unequivocally state that Riley's got himself a new, white Ford 350 pickup with two big antennae waving from the cab."

"The bones tell you that?" I asked, incredulous at her powers and planning my future or lack of it all at the same time.

"Hell no. The bones have their limits. It's simple: Riley Boggs always has a new pickup. Everybody knows that much."

She shook her head at my stupidity and curled her hands into loose fists, holding them up to her eyes like binoculars and slowly swinging her head from side to side. "You can see him coming down the road, some-where out there, probably a little west of Marathon and moving fast. Better decamp and dust trail, Delmore. Not that it'll do you much good over the big haul. Riley's got a short temper and a long memory. Developed the latter by memorizing labels on canned goods during eight-month winters when he was cowboyin' up in the northern ranges and was snowed in with nothing to do. Donnette says he can tell you every ingredient in any Campbell's soup you care to name."

I was acutely aware of the Regulator clock hanging and ticking, slightly off to the right of Tatum-the-highboy. Five-thirty in the after-noon and a date with Rita at nine. Aw, Rita, Rita, Rita. I could feel her rubbing slow against me while we danced to Waylon's voice thrusting its way through the smoke and yelling at the Cholla, later on. And even more later on, doing the same thing for higher stakes. When it came to bedtime, Rita was a real cloud hunter.

A surge of something, testosterone or whatever, hit me hard and fast, and for a quick moment I was saying to myself, to hell with Riley Boggs. Maybe waltz Rita downtown and face up to the consequences.

That quick moment passed like a gust of border wind. Riley was sloppy-gut fat, but he outweighed me by a hundred pounds and carried a lot of old-time muscle under the slop. I'd once seen him in action at a Fourth of July street dance up in Fort Davis, when he'd cleaned up on three of the West Fork hands all by his lonesome. And the West Fork boys were hard as running irons when it came to all-out brawling. In full spate, it was commonly said, Riley Boggs was tough as a hog's snout and rank as they came. So there I was, flopping around somewhere in the middle ambiguities, nervously wringing my hands on the green felt.

The bone lady had swivelled ninety degrees in her chair and was looking out a west-facing window. "There's one other option," she said, with a subdued but ominous bend to her voice.

I waited for her to say something more. She didn't, so I did. "The other option, what might that look like?"

"I could put a juju on your *bête noire*."

Crinkling my face and not understanding at least three of the words in her last sentence, I asked if she could chew it a little finer.

"A hex. I could hex Riley Boggs for you. Problem is, it's hard to control the intensity and quantity of the hex; never know where it might lead if I overdo it."

I was down to practical matters, grabbing for the gold ring of salvation, and didn't give a crap about hex intensity or anything else, long as Riley Boggs exited my life and even if he took Rita with him on the way out.

"How much would it cost, putting a hex on him?"

She whipped back in my direction and looked me hard in the eyes. I returned the look and noticed something I hadn't noticed before. Since I'd arrived, the bone lady seemed to be getting younger, and I couldn't figure that out. The creases in her face were softening, the lines of her body placing up and getting firmer.

"Got no use for money and such," she said. "Got enough for what I need in that line." She waggled her head and grinned. "The miners missed a good vein in the hills south of here."

After thinking for a few seconds, she went on. "Since Donnette borrowed my Bronco and has been gone with it more'n week, what I ain't got and sorely require is two six-packs of Tecate and three limes for squeezing into it. Ya'll head on up to Gallagher's and fetch the beer. I'll do the hexing while you're gone. Deal?"

I thought for a moment. The whole verts and fang thing seemed pretty loony by itself, even though people swore the bone lady knew her stuff and could be trusted. But hexes? Juju and spells? That was King Arthur shit or—who'n hell was it?—Hecate and something about three roads crossing? Whatever, some goddamned nonsense from Introduction to Literature during my aborted studies at Sul Ross and earlier scholarship at

Junction High when I was spending my time in remedial English trying to hustle Manuela Granado, who was the black-eyed, fifteen-year-old daughter of one Manuel Granado, who turned out to be an illegal and got shipped back across the border, Manuela with him.

On the other hand, I had only three options in my sum total of choices, two of which involved unpleasant consequences: standing up to Riley, thereby suffering certain and possibly irreparable damage to my person; or running for the ghost caves, thereby losing my day-job at Western Auto, though the possibility of Donnette going along had made me waver on that alternative for an instant. I'd never met her, of course, but anyone who talked down Riley Boggs had to have high standards and other things of equal value.

Standing up and digging for the truck keys buried in the left pocket of my Wranglers, I said, "Let's go for the hex. It'll take me about a hour and twenty minutes to get up to Gallagher's and back. That enough time for your juju work?"

"More'n enough. Watch for Arthur when you step off the porch. He's a big old diamondback that's lately taken up residence under there. He sleeps mostly, but gets cranky if you step on him. Call him Arthur because he reminds me of my philosophy teacher from my baccalaureate days. Had a brief affair with said professor during the second semester of my junior year, and Arthur-under-the-porch bears a riveting likeness in style and attitude to Arthur-behind-the-lectern. Something to do with deep-seated paranoia, I think. Anyway, and different from the original Arthur, he's got practical skills, such as keeping the rats at bay."

The bone lady was standing there in old cowboy boots, jeans, denim work shirt, and an apron tied around her waist. And the way she was smiling and with late sunlight splaying through a window and touching her on the slant, I couldn't help noticing again how some kind of latent youth had emerged and washed over her face and body. Couldn't quite figure that out. A fade-out and fade-in, from desert crone to uptown passable in an hour, that was her route of climb, and the velocity of her ascent troubled me. The transformation was either in my head or in the flesh, and I couldn't make out which.

Next to the door was a broomstick with a length of coat hanger wrapped around it two thirds of the way up, the remainder of the wire protruding in a generally upward direction about two feet out from the stick. In hurrying to open the door, I knocked the stick and wire to the floor and picked it up, examining it for a moment.

"That's my dancing partner," the bone lady said quietly, turning wistful.

I looked at her, confused.

She took the dingus from me and walked over to Sonia-the-Victrola. Cranking the machine and placing the needle gently down, she held the broomstick in her left hand about six inches from her body, then grasped the far end of the protruding wire with her other hand. Up came the "Westphalia Waltz," a little scratchy but entirely recognizable and a dulcet fiddle carrying the melody, as always. Smiling to herself and then at me, the bone lady gracefully danced the broomstick around and around and across the living room, her boots making only barely discernible scrapes on the mesquite floor as she disappeared into the kitchen.

"When you're all alone out here and nobody to dance with, got to make do." Her voice from the kitchen was disembodied, floating as light and pure through dust motes as the bone lady had danced. "The broomstick, which I call Baylis in honor of my first husband who was an elegant dancer, lacks certain dimensions, such as a man's arm around you and sweet talking in your ear. But it's a dancing fool, just the same. Now get on up to Gallagher's. I have work to do, and I'll be thirsty afterward. Hexing is hard labor."

I made Gallagher's Store a little before six-thirty, got the Tecate and limes and headed into the desert under a quarter moon going to work again, dust rising high and fast from the roll of my tires. If Riley Boggs had been west of Marathon when the bone lady said he was, he would have hit Clear Signal sometime ago. And, as was his custom, he'd be drinking Old Charter and chewing Beechnut and driving around town, probably looking for me, ol' thin Delmore, who, so the going opinion had it was working Rita overtime on weekends plus an occasional Wednesday night. For once, the going opinion was dead-on accurate.

When I drove across the dry bed of Cheechako Creek, a light breeze swept the cottonwoods around the bone lady's squat, and I noticed the sorrel was no longer in the corral. I knocked on the door. No answer.

I was about to rap again when I heard the sound of hooves coming from somewhere to the east. My first thought was Riley had figured out my general location and had decided to ride the high desert until he found and confronted the bandbox dandy with an indoor job at Western Auto, the Delmore who'd been doing his beloved Rita while he was off trying to make ends meet by running a nail-hammering concession.

Then, and talk about apparitions, out of an arroyo and down over a hill toward me came what I took to be the bone lady, moving the sorrel at a high lope and holding herself featherlight in the stirrups. Too small for Riley Boggs, I figured, and nobody else way out here. For a moment I wasn't sure, but that was because she'd undergone a further transformation, wearing a black skirt reaching over her boot tops and a starched, white blouse that was long in the sleeves and loose fitting. Topping off her outfit was a straw Stetson perched on gray hair done up neat and fancy in the back. In the twilight and shadows through which they came, she and the gelding seemed one together.

She reined in the sorrel and executed an effortless Comanche dismount all at the same time. Stood there grinning at me. "Well now, it's the revenant Delmore. Ya'll get the beer?"

I had trouble talking for a click or two, thinking how she seemed rune-like and shape-shifting in the semidarkness of a high-desert nowhere. A youngish seventy one second and an oldish forty-five or fifty the next, then a slow dissolve back to seventy, all of it depending on the light in which she stood and the way she held her body.

The sorrel snorted and snuffled around for anything grazeable in the yard, while I glanced over my shoulder toward the porch, checking on Arthur's whereabouts. He was crawling forth on a night hunt, leisurely traveling in the general direction of the single-wide out back.

"I got the beer. Hex go all right?"

"Think so. Felt good. A little strong maybe; that worries me some."

"Where do we take it from here?" I asked and heard a telephone ringing inside the adobe.

The bone lady said nothing, moved by me and went into the house, leaving the door open for me to follow. She picked up the receiver, listened for two seconds, and said, "Howdy, daughter. Nice to hear from you."

For the next three minutes she listened, nodding to herself occasionally, face serious at first and then smiling after that, finally and slowly shaking her head as she said goodbye and hung up.

She took a can of Tecate, popped the top, and handed it to me. After repeating the process on a second can for her, she held the beer up in salute. "May your days be peaceful, hombre."

I instinctively echoed her salute and wondered what was going on.

She leaned against the door frame leading into the kitchen and said, "Here's the straight goods, Delmore. That was Donnette on the other end, saying she was taking the Bronco up to Odessa for a barbecue dance, and if that wasn't all right, I should say something firm about getting her ass back down here. But, and here's what's important to ya'll, she also told me that, sure enough, Riley Boggs hit the city limits of Clear Signal about two hours ago, pretty much on schedule according to the bones. And, sure enough, he was doing the following things: driving a new, white pickup and drinking Old Charter and chewing Beechnut, all at the same time and leading to the following event chain.

"Seems, according to onlookers, Riley needed to spit and didn't want to chance getting any of the chaw juice on the side of his new truck, so he opened the door and leaned down and out, all the while moving along the main drag at something approaching forty-two miles an hour. Apparently the Old Charter had done its work, *ergo* causing Riley to lose his grip on the wheel and, furthermore, causing him to fall out of the pickup, which continued on its way down Front Street. And, in turn, the pickup's wayward path caused a Quality Products feed truck to swerve in a direction taking its left rear dualies right over Riley Boggs's skull, which was immobilized either by the fall or the unredeemable sin of drink, or some combination thereof. In sum, it can safely be said your *sturm und drang* has reached closure, and unless Rita is in earnest mourning, which apparently she isn't since Donnette saw her five minutes ago drinking Lone Star and shooting eight ball at the Cholla, she's all yours, amigo."

I half-lowered, half-collapsed onto a chair, looking first at the beer in my hands then up at the bone lady, who was still leaning against the door frame, black booted and silver spurred, hands behind her back and boots crossed at the ankles below her riding skirt. She didn't say anything, merely smiled a strange little smile.

After a while, I stood up and shuffled my feet around for a second or two, trying to figure out what I might say. Eventually, I simply said, "Thanks . . . I guess."

Then I asked her, "Think the hex really did that, getting Riley killed and all?"

She canted her head and waved her non-drinking hand as if she were dismissing the whole affair. "Hard to say. I went for a broken leg or hepatitis A, something of that magnitude. Forgot to take Riley's fondness for Old Charter into account. A multiplier effect must have obtained, maybe that's why it felt a little strong. I'll assume responsibility for temporary incapacities, nothing beyond. Men are self-destructive enough that they're hard to hex without things getting more serious than you counted on. Anyway, death is just Nature's way of creating additional space."

She looked thoughtful for a moment, brushing at the sleeve of her shirt. "So it lies, along with Riley Boggs," she said quietly, as if gently closing a book on things best forgotten.

I felt a little less guilty after what she'd said and fished out my keys. "Think I ought to be going. I appreciate your good work, even though it went a little beyond what we were shooting for."

She lifted her can of Tecate in another salute, looking late-forties-descending-to-twenty at that moment. "Go with God, Delmore. By the way, got any of them little stereo deals at your Western Auto? Sometimes think about getting myself something to augment the Victrola. This continual cranking has a way of destroying certain moods."

I said we did and if she'd like to stop by sometime, I'd be pleased to help her pick something out and make sure she got a nice discount on whatever she chose.

West of me, the bounce from an orange sundown was still peeking over the Del Nortes as I hit the pavement south of Gallagher's and started high ridin' for Clear Signal. Should have had a unadulterated purpose on that Saturday night, which was to head on up to the Cholla, console Rita about the afternoon's events, and convince her that complete and utter nakedness was a sure cure for grief, not that she'd probably need much convincing.

Kept rolling things around in my head, though, but not making any sense of it, like billiard balls when you toss them on the table before racking them up. I pulled off to the side a mile the other side of Santiago Peak and thought about as hard as I'd thought since my intermediate welding class at Sul Ross. Started talking to myself: Seventy, fifty, forty, but age has nothing to do with it, shouldn't make any difference. I shoved a Waylon tape in the deck and made a U-turn.

When I hit the bone lady's front yard, it was full dark, and there was only a dim light coming from the adobe's north windows along with the sound of the "Westphalia Waltz." Running a comb through my hair and then preparing to knock on the door, I tilted back a little in surprise when it seemed to swing open of its own accord. The bone lady stared straight at me, chewing on her lower lip in a strangely sensual way. Taking my hand, she smiled and said, as if she'd been expecting me all along, "Ya'll come dance with me, Delmore."

And she felt warm and fine and sweet in my arms as we waltzed around the green felt table, with me wondering for a moment about the amplitude of the hex she'd invoked. Pulling me a little closer and looking up at me, seeming to be seventy and twenty all at the same time, she spoke softly and almost in a whisper, "Let's do some cloud hunting tonight, Delmore . . . and call me Lillian, if you like." ✪

MERCEDES

by Sylvia Manning

If he had sometimes slept in the fields in the years before he met her, and, of course, he had, but that was not to her so unusual because if he had been sleeping beneath the stars sometimes even on this side where people do not so often do that to still know time by how the sunlight is when day comes, to know to go to school, as he had, because the light had come (how obvious?) then how could he become unkind so soon to her when he knew full well that she had lived many times with her family in whatever spot of ground they could smooth with their hands and feet, in whatever little house they could make with sticks and ashes? Was it through living in the fields, was it through having been a true campesino, was it that which makes the person? Then how could he forget her personhood, she wondered, and so quickly and so harshly? This hardness, ¿porqué era?

"Yo de veras me he acostado en el suelo, de veras. ¿Entonces?" she asks herself. So? I also have slept on the ground.

Now she wakes him at four o'clock in the still dark mornings, but first has ready his breakfast tacos of whatever there may be, even if only the warm and soft tortillas de harina which all persons deserve if they are to leave the sweet of sleep to do anything but especially to go work all the day and into the night.

He is so thin in the morning. He leaves something of himself in the dreams maybe? But he is softer at this time than any other, soft eyed like a deer, maybe like a baby or a child. Maybe they will have a child someday and his eyes will be like Paco's. But ah, she cannot think of babies.

"Gracias, vieja," he tells her, thanks. There are good things in the tacos, not just the tortillas today. He eats his taco of potato and egg, and he has one besides to take for later. She brings him a glass of milk and sits a moment while he drinks. She thinks what it would be like if he drank coffee. How nice it might be, the smell of coffee. But then they would need to buy it, and they have so little money. It is better, like he says, to have no need for coffee. Still. Maybe he will remember to bring her a Coca-Cola at night when he returns.

But he said, thank you. And he has eaten. And even if he hates to work with the garbage truck, he is going another day to do it.

"Cuídate," she tells him softly. To take care for the glass and the knives in the garbage. Sometimes he gets cut.

"Sí, vieja," he tells her. Like a boy talking back to his mother it sounds to Mercedes when he calls her "old woman" this time. Like a boy not taking his mother seriously because what does she know? With his "vieja" saying "What do you know?"

"I am too young for that," thinks Mercedes. "I am not really una vieja, anyway, so if I let him call me old lady with anger back for it, doesn't it mean that he will remember when he says it that I am not an old lady, not his mother? How does his mind work with that? He knows I am seventeen. I am young. I am his friend. We are married. Is he still asleep? But if I said it later. . . . ?"

Mercedes decides that his tone to her has nothing to do with the early hour. She decides it is something to understand through long thought in the long day ahead.

In this early dark morning she feels cold. Paco makes fun of her if she says she is cold because he went once as a child to the far north, far past San Antonio. Mercedes is as far north as she has ever been, here on the South Texas border, here in El Valle. On this dark morning she thinks she is as cold as she has ever been, but maybe not. Maybe he would be right to make fun of her if indeed she told him that to her it is cold.

Paco could still go north if he wanted. Back then he had some special papers, and now after many years of being just as illegal as she is, he got some special papers again. But not for her. The new law didn't give them to her even though she was his wife, even though they were married in a real church, a Catholic church.

If Paco went north he would leave her here in El Valle for her to live with her sisters. But Mercedes has decided to go back to Ciudad Victoria in Mexico if he leaves, although she has not told him.

Now Paco is leaving just to go into the darkness, not to the north. He will walk three miles to where he meets his garbage crew. Sometimes they can come for him in the truck and honk, but not if the boss is to be with them, and today Paco thinks he will be. Sometimes Paco is wrong, though, and the men pick him up walking in the dark.

"¿No tienes miedo de la obscuridad?" she asks him.

He is happy with that question. No, he tells her, he is not afraid of the dark.

"No tengo miedo, niña. Soy hombre."

So simple. So easy to say what makes him feel good. He feels so good that he calls her little girl instead of old woman. He feels so good that he smiles at himself when he says, "I am a man."

But so confusing. He did not smile about the knives and glass in the garbage, that he should take care for that, the garbage he would load all day for twelve hours, with only a few minutes to eat the taco she now puts in his hands in its brown paper sack.

"Qué vayas bien," she offers.

"Gracias."

"¿Hasta luego?"

"Ándale."

It would be dark again when he came home. What could she do all day?

Clean. Clean really well. Cook beans. Care for her ranchito, the chili plants by the kitchen door. Watch the novellas on television. Sleep.

Maybe her sisters would come by, either Lulu or Dina, and maybe bring her a Coca-Cola.

She could wash clothes in the sink.

Paco's church (was it hers?) didn't like the Coca-Colas, and they told her it was wrong to have a Coke. Adventistas aren't supposed to take caffeine. That's why Paco wouldn't bring her one every night, except sometimes. That's why they couldn't have any coffee even if they had enough money for it.

And she couldn't walk all the way to the little store to buy one, using bottles or cans for money. Paco had told her she was too good a girl to do that. (Niña, he had called her, before leaving.)

Still, maybe Lulu would come, and they could have a Coke and watch the novellas. Maybe Lulu who had a car would think of her.

But now it was too early, and she was cold and sleepy. Mercedes went back to bed, to sleep until the light should come. ❀

THE BETRAYAL

by Ronnie Claire Edwards

My Uncle Homer was worried sick over the flea's refusal to perform for William Jennings Bryan. He told everyone, "I haven't slept for weeks. I am exhausted with nervous prostration." His livelihood depended on the political career of William Jennings Bryan and the fleas. Their mutiny threatened it. It was not a matter of temperament on the part of a couple of his best performers. He could have sympathized with that. The little buggers were overworked the closer it came to Election Day. But the whole cast was sitting down on the job, filled with ennui. He thought, "Maybe the little blood suckers are off their feed." Recently, some country boob had referred to his flag bearer, Caesar, as a louse. He knew it had hurt and offended Caesar. He always knew when something was troubling him because the height of his jumps were off and he refused to breed for protracted periods. He'd not touched Cleopatra for weeks now and that was affecting her performance as well. It had undermined her confidence and self-esteem.

Homer had traveled all over the Southwest with a medicine show, hawking an alcohol-laced product called Grove's Tasteless Chill Tonic. He met a Mexican in Duval County, Texas, who was looking to sell his flea stock. Because the Mexican's host cat kept having litters of bob tailed, eight toed, hairless kittens, the fleas were starving. He figured he could do as well exhibiting the cats as the fleas and they were a lot easier to keep track of. Homer watered down Grove's Tasteless Chill Tonic and traded the Mexican a case of it in exchange for the anemic fleas.

Five years later, he was still operating with the same stock. He had lost track of how many Caesars and Cleopatras he's had, but it was a strong, talented breeding line and he set great store by them.

Homer had taken up with a Madame Adam, a bearded, fire-eating dwarf. Homer was always having to corral the fleas out of her beard until she commenced squirting it with citronella. But disaster hit in Pine Bluff, Arkansas, when hung over from the night before, Madame Adam became careless and her beard caught fire. They threw her into a nearby horse trough, but it was too late, not just for her beard, singed beyond recall, but some of the fleas perished in the fire as well, thereby depleting the herd. Unable to stay away from the siren song of danger, Madame Adam took up knife swallowing.

As is so oft the case, show business and politics commingled, thereby taking Homer to the top of the ladder careerwise. Homer and Madame Adam had barely been able to eke out a livelihood until that fateful day, on his campaign swing down through the Southwest, William Jennings Bryan caught the act. He immediately sensed the fleas' commercial potential, put Homer on a retainer, and signed the circus to an exclusive contract. New costumes were designed, the better to draw crowds before his rallies. So, Homer bade Madame Adam, who was beginning to sprout a scrofulous beard, a fond farewell, packed up his livestock and hit the campaign trail. Billed as "The Tiny Mights" (Homer refused to allow their billing to be spelled m-i-t-e-s because the fleas were as insulted by that as being called lice) they drew record crowds.

Homer billed himself as Professor Pulex Irritants, after the scientific name of the species hosted by humans. He began his introduction with a quote from a medieval poem: "Ha, the flea born to range the merry world/ To rob at will the veins delectable of princes? To lie with ladies, Ah, fairest joy!" He claimed he'd never met a dull flea.

In his educational lecture prior to the act, Homer said, "Ladies and gents, step right up. May the members of the audience wearing spectacles, please be allowed the courtesy of the front. For your edification and enjoyment, Caesar and Cleopatra, our stars, accompanied by the entire troupe, will perform, in unison, a flying leap over the equivalent of London's St. Paul's Cathedral and they will do it not once, but six hundred times in an hour, if need be, for three days, in a row. Trivial, their grandson, possesses the fastest single switch mechanism of any organism. He is also the proud owner of the most elaborate set of genitalia in the animal kingdom, hence, proportionately, enjoys a complex and active love life. With prodigious energy, you will observe him lift off at one hundred and forty times the force of gravity and soar to an apogee of ten inches. I must request, ladies and gentlemen, that those closest to the stage, please refrain from any coughing or sneezing during the act. Thank you. Let the games begin, Caesar!"

Homer sold cards, "FOR GENTS ONLY!" with a drawing of "The Merry Flea . . . whose Sexual Parts occupy one third of his body length while in repose and come equipped with Spines, Lobes, Tickling Devices for the Lucky Missus! This Amazing Organ takes a meandering route of often-wrong turns, entering taking ten minutes and Copulation oft-lasting three to Nine hours! 'Marke but this flea, and marke in this/ It sucked me first, and now sucks thee/ And in this flea our two bloods mingled be!!' John Donne."

Homer created a new act in preparation for Election Day. The climax came when the whole troupe, like a twenty-mule team of atomies, pulled a walnut shell chariot, topped by a flag which read, "VOTE FOR WILLIAM JENNINGS BRYAN." When William Jennings Bryan saw it in dress rehearsal, he feared it might even surpass his Cross of Gold Speech.

Disaster struck when the fleas were in costume, waiting in the wings. When their music cue came up they refused to enter. The cue was played again and still they refused to perform. Homer was apoplectic with rage at the "little moochers." He began threatening them, hoping to throw the fear of God and a strong wind into them, but they remained immobile.

Homer knew "the fate of a nation was riding that night," and when William Jennings Bryan lost, Homer took it as a personal tragedy. His fleas had altered the outcome of the election and forever changed the course of history.

Homer wired the Mexican that he'd sell the fleas back to him cheap, but the Mexican wired back that he couldn't use them because his cats were still turning out hairless litters.

Despite their betrayal, Homer couldn't find it in his heart to have them put down, no matter how painless. They had provided him with many good years of income and companionship. He released them all on to a passing bloodhound as he did not want to break up the family. The mystery of their mutiny was never solved. Homer always suspected it was because they were Republicans. ✵

The Hands of John Merchant

by Paul Ruffin

Any time I'm back over that way—which is not often, since I've come back to Texas, where I should have been all along—I drive along the beach road and look out over the Gulf toward the islands, which, when the sun is high enough, give off a little glare so that you can tell exactly where they are without actually seeing them. Like an aura, you might say. It's ghostly. And if I let myself, in those brief glimpses before I have to turn my eyes back to the road, it's not so hard to imagine that I see ol' John Merchant reaching a hand up to me from out of that green water, cupping it toward me, with bright red and yellow spices slipping out between his curled fingers like sand, and I can smell the spices so distinctly that my nose burns and my eyes haze over. And I can't wait to get back to Texas.

So here John Merchant was again, his skillet almost red hot and smoking, spices singing on the air, while just outside the screen door evening was softening into night.

I was slouched over his kitchen table working on my fifth or sixth beer of the evening and feeling it from head to bladder while he prepared our dinner, redfish we'd caught in the surf at Petit Bois Island the weekend before. The broad fillets and a few odd little nuggets lay on a piece of wax paper at the end of the table, and an assortment of spices trailed out in a long line of jar lids like something for a witch's broth, carefully measured out, mostly reds and blacks, some greens and yellows. It would all be dumped together in a bowl when he was ready to roll the fillets and throw them into that hot skillet where they'd sizzle and pop until the smoke that rose from them would take John completely and his feet and hairy legs would drop out of that cloud like some sort of very human god just touching down to earth.

Then his lean, sun-darkened hands reached out and whisked up the fillets in one run, like a card dealer, and sooner than I could focus on the flurry of fingers the spices were gone and the skillet shrieked and smoke billowed up until finally I could see him only from the ankles down, just a great cloud with two hairy feet.

This was the way it always went. Most Saturdays we'd get up early and make a run to the islands, spend most of the day thrashing the surf, and come back in and feast. And if we didn't catch anything to eat, we'd just drink beer and get drunk as coots and sprawl out on the floor of his living room or den or wherever and sleep it off—without dinner. It was a point of honor with him, a little less with me. If we didn't catch fish he wouldn't touch a solid thing, just beer or whiskey, and not eat until the next day, but likely as not, I'd wake up during the night hungry enough to eat the linoleum tiles I was stretched out on and crawl to the refrigerator and graze through the bottom shelves—cheese or left-over meat or lettuce or a jar of olives. Hell, it didn't matter as long as it filled the hole in my stomach enough to let me sleep through till dawn, when I knew he'd get up and fix a manly breakfast.

John wasn't married—*had* been but wasn't when I knew him back then. His wife ran off with somebody very different from him, which was the way he wanted it, he said. If she'd grabbed on to somebody just like him, he would have taken it hard and probably tracked down and killed both of them. It was that honor thing again. The overweight used-car salesman with his gold necklaces and polyester leisure pants over which his belly hung like a double scoop of ice cream spilling over the edge of its cone was exactly what she needed, he figured, and he could live with the image of her bearing up under him night after night like a terrible smothering dream. It was better imagining that than shooting her, he said.

He lived in a drab little house at the end of a drab little street in Gautier, Mississippi, about three miles from a trailer I shared with a couple of dogs, which I was fairly confident would never abandon me for a used-car salesman, and even if they did, I'd just get two more. Dogs are easier to come by than women and a hell of a lot less expense and trouble to get *and* keep satisfied.

We worked at the big shipyard in Pascagoula, in the Electrical

Department, pulling cable mostly, since neither one of us had been there long enough to work our way up to anything better. We were academic dropouts from the University of Texas waiting around for some sort of easy life that just never seemed to show up. He'd talked me into coming to Mississippi with him, since he'd grown up there, but there wasn't much light work around. John had tried his hand at reporting on a Coast newspaper for a while, and I substitute taught in math in area high schools and did some night security work at a mall, but all that was meaningless and didn't pay enough to live on. Not a year after we moved over there he knocked this waitress up and married her and stayed married long enough for their trailer to turn green. When she left him, me and John had a one-beer discussion about going back to Texas and finishing school; a six-pack or so later we had decided on the shipyard. Next day we bought some rugged clothes and hard-nose boots and went to work.

Weekends, we fished. Seriously. Like it was a religion. If the weather didn't lay us in, we took off on Saturday morning in John's sixteen-footer, the only thing he kept from the marriage, and stayed at the islands all day, sometimes spending the night out there and sleeping on the beach. We ate what we caught. You can catch fish if you know you're going without food if you don't.

This was one of those Saturdays, though, when the weather threatened early, blowing like a sonofabitch from the east with low white clouds trundling along under darker ones, and you don't want to get caught out there in a sixteen-footer in heavy weather. We already had the beer iced down and the rods stowed when John said he reckoned we'd better wait, so we unloaded the ice chest and spent the day lounging around watching baseball on the tube and drinking beer. Now the only thing between us and a hell of a meal of blackened fish was John's magic with the spices and that skillet. There was a big bowl of salad on the table already, but the fish was what mattered. Jesus, what he could do with those spices.

After a few minutes in the thick smoke he dipped down and out of the cloud and said, "They're about done. You wanna eat outside?"

"That, or we're gonna have to eat on the floor, where we can see what we're eating and where there's air."

"Arright, you get that bottle of red wine out of the refrigerator and the salad and a couple of plates and glasses and silverware, and, shit, some napkins—you know what to get—and I'll meet you on the porch."

Half an hour later, high on the earlier beer and half a gallon of cheap red wine, we finished the last of the fish and studied the weather, which seemed to have washed out over the gulf like a faded flag.

"I guess we should have gone out," John said.

"Yeah, but we'd have missed out on this miracle you've wrought here, Sir John. You dropped down out of that cloud like God Himself and broke fish with me, enough for the multitudes, and turned beer into wine."

"Nope, I couldn't a-done this out there." He sighed and leaned back in his chair. A crusty piece of fillet lay on his plate.

I pointed to the piece of fish. "You gon' finish that?"

"Naw. You want it?"

I reached over and speared it with my fork. "I reckon."

"Uh-hunnnh," he said.

Now, John Merchant was one of those folks of few words. He just never talked much. But when he used that "Uh-hunnnh" as a lead-in, something was coming, something big, something significant.

I held the piece of fish on my fork, balanced it between the plate and my mouth. "What? What is it, John?"

"Well, I was just thinking that most folks believe that all you can blacken is redfish or snapper, but fact is, you can blacken almost anything. It's the spices, of course, and the hot skillet. I'll just bet you could season anything that swims or walks or crawls or just lies flat on the highway and fry it like this and you'd like it just the same. Like barbecue. You can barbecue any Goddamned thing in the world and it tastes good. Rat or snake or squid or—hell, like I say, *anything.*"

I finished off the piece of fish and picked up the glass of wine and sipped. "You reckon, huh?"

"Well, back at UT there was this wormy little guy—a business major, marketing, I believe, short and stringy and mousy looking—and a bunch of the jocks in a sociology class got to where they picked at him regularly— just for the pure hell of it, because he never done anything to'em. Except he made some remark the second week about athletics and athletes being the bane of American society, setting all the wrong role models and stultifying the American mind, establishing a ridiculous value system, and ball clubs paying millions to people with minds like mites.

"Hell, they set in on him like bad yard dogs. They'd do things like track in dog shit and step on his foot, you know, high school stuff, put Elmer's glue in his books and paste the pages together, goofy stuff. All silly, juvenile stuff, but they really kept on him and didn't let up all semester.

"And he never said a word back, just kept on with his studies. And just to show these ol' boys there were no hard feelings, he invited them to a party at his apartment the afternoon before their exam. Now, they wouldn't have gone to any party of his, of course, except that there wasn't any way *he* could be a threat to them and, after all, he said he'd have a keg of beer, and then everybody wanted to know how to get there.

"What he did was, he got with a medical-student friend of his and the two of them slipped into the anatomy room one night and pulled out this ol' fat gal that had died of natural causes—or, hell, *un*natural, whatever— and cut a big thick flank steak off each thigh, underneath, where it wouldn't be missed for awhile."

"Jesus Christ, John, what kind of shit is this you're—"

"Ol' Gerald marinated the meat for a couple of days to take out the taste of any kind of preservative. Barbecued strips of that fat woman's thighs and fed'm to that gaggle of jocks. They shot the beer and wolfed that fat woman and said it was the best meat they'd ever had anywhere, tasty and tender, and wondered what it was, but he never said a word except that the meat was a rare delicacy, and rare it certainly was.

"News of a mutilated cadaver hit print two days later, but the jocks never got the connection, or if they did, they were ashamed to admit it. That would have made them cannibals, you know, which is one of the few things you can't just offhand accuse jocks of being."

I downed the last of my wine and stared at my plate. "What's your story got to do with this fish?"

"Nothing, nothing, only how do you know what you've just eaten?" His eyes were glittering like sun on a sea rod. The wine soothed my burning tongue.

"The only reason you think what you ate was fish is that you saw me get something out of the freezer and take it to the stove," John said. "But you didn't see what I got out. I could have thrown anything into those spices and blackened it. It's all in the hands, and in the spices. And you don't have any earthly notion what's in the spices. Might be ground-up frogs or bat wings or dog shit or anything."

I smiled.

"You think I'm kidding." He tilted his glass back, swallowed deep, and looked away at the moon, just coming up over the edge of the Gulf. "There's more things in Heav'n and Earth, Horatio. . . ."

"Bullshit, John—"

"You never noticed any difference, did you?"

"Any difference in *what*?"

He was smiling, a secret, dark smile. "Well, I've told you I could blacken anything and it'd taste good. The theory's just been tested."

"Bullshit, John." I stared down at my bread-polished plate. "Just bullshit." I was thinking about a slice of fat-woman's thigh, barbecued and served with beer. "Besides, I never did anything to you."

"Those fat-woman thigh strips didn't hurt the jocks. They enjoyed them and came away kinda liking ol' Gerald, I'd say. Probably the best piece of woman they'll ever get. A good joke's a good joke, even if the one playing it is the only one that knows about it."

The fat moon crept up higher in the sky as I sat leaned back in my chair, smashed on beer and wine, looking over at John. The grin on his face told me he was lying. But who could be sure with John Merchant?

He drowned in the Gulf the very next day during a squall when the last thing I saw of him was his two big hands reaching up out of the tumbling sea toward me while I clung to the side of his small boat, unable to turn loose to extend a hand or throw him a line. The joke was that I never knew he couldn't swim. In all the time I knew him, he never told me.

They pulled his body out just inside the cut between Horn and Petit Bois almost a week later, after he'd probably washed way out and come back in with the tide. And I was there. After the Coast Guard picked me up and they checked me out at the hospital, I came right back out and borrowed a boat and helped them search, eating when I had to and sleeping in snatches until on the sixth day someone spotted him riding the currents in the channel.

He was dreadfully bloated and a strange purple and white color, like a blow-up toy that kids punch on, and all kinds of fish had been at him. I wouldn't have known him but for his shirt and pants, and his hands. Everything on him was swollen like a balloon, but his hands—somehow they looked the same, same color and shape, his fingers curled like they were reaching up for my hands or down to pick up fillets.

I live in Galveston now, but I stay away from the Gulf. I have tried to blacken fish since, but I can never get the spices right. I get close enough, though, and the spices and beer and smoke always take me back to John Merchant and that evening when he may or may not have played a big trick on me. Who could know what thing with wings or fins or scaly legs he had waved his dark hands across and transformed with magic spices and fire and served me with blood-red wine? ✿

INCIDENT AT THE BORDER

by Pat Carr

She watches the digital clock above the bullring scene on black velvet. The clock unrolls numerals behind four glass panes, European style, and she waits for thirteen.

When it appears, she immediately rises, lays a ten-dollar bill beside the mug whose coffee she's sugared and stirred without tasting, and walks into the one o'clock glare.

A parking valet stands under the restaurant portico, erect and official, yet discomfited, as if he's conscious the red jacket and corded trousers resemble those of a costumed monkey rather than the major domo he presumes to recreate.

"I have a forest green Pontiac," she says, and he sifts among his fistful of keys, murmurs, "*Sí, señora.*"

Nothing shows in his face, but she doesn't look closely, doesn't offer a mild pleasantry when he gestures vaguely and says, "I have parked your Grand Prix beside the market."

She's been assured traffic will be light, that she can pick up the car and drive across the Pronof Bridge in less than twenty minutes, but as she reaches the pedestrian crossing, it's obvious traffic is incredibly heavy.

Four lanes of vehicles—not only sedans, but pickups, vans, even Juarez city buses—whiz by at taxi speeds. The cars seem to be hurtling into Mexico and carouseling around the market square to recross into Texas, their passenger seats and truck beds crammed to capacity with men in suits, women in flowered dresses, abuelitas in molting scarves, and children flapping miniature Mexican flags.

She turns back to the valet under the stucco arches of the Puerto del Sol. He's staring at her. "There's a lot of traffic," she says.

"*Sí, señora,*" he repeats without expression. "Today is Cinco de Mayo."

Before she betrays consternation, the silhouette of a pacing man flashes into the signal square, four lanes of traffic halt, and she crosses the street against a flow of celebrants ducking their heads under the heat.

Sunlight radiates from the yellow bricks, softens the tarmac, and roasts the strategic, decorative saplings in the parking lot. She screens her eyes with lowered lashes as she searches the sun-blasted cars for a green Pontiac.

A current model Grand Prix has been parked half a dozen rows from the main market, and tiny suns reflect from every metallic curve. She inserts the key, the locks spring up, and she swings open the door to the kilned air. A bottle of Cutty Sark lies baking on the passenger seat.

The motor starts as smoothly as the door unlocked, and she begins to nudge the car toward the exit through tourists and shoppers. But other drivers in overheating vehicles block the lot, and it takes three interminable signal changes from red to green before she can pull into the street. And since traffic is too clogged to time the lights, the car idles during equally long intervals at each intersection. By the time she nears the Juarez booths with their access to the Pronof Bridge, cars are backed up for a mile. The air conditioner becomes futile, but when she turns it off to lower the window, exhaust fumes shunt palpable carbon around her. The scotch she's been instructed to declare at the border effervesces in the direct sun as if it might start to boil.

The car clock reads 1:46.

2

"Did I tell you I got Mafia connections?" He took a confident swig of the draft.

She glanced at him in mild reproof as she dipped two deliberate fmgers into the steaming rinse water.

"You hear what I said?"

She nodded, extracted a stemmed glass, and flicked off residual drops. "But I wouldn't think it was something you'd broadcast to strangers in a public bar."

"Hell, Kate, you ain't no stranger. I been coming in regular, three, four weeks now." He surveyed the bar, which was actually an enclosed patio between two neighboring businesses and whose once exterior walls still exuded lichen spores. The only light came from an electrified Mexican chandelier and a single red bulb indicating rest rooms and back exits. "And this ain't what I'd call public."

"'You ain't no stranger,'" she mimicked. "You don't know a damned thing about me, Vince." She dried and inspected the goblet before she hung its glass foot in the overhead rack

"I know you're a damned good looking woman, too smart to be tending bar in this sorry-ass joint."

"If I were so darrmed smart, I'd have a trade. When you major in art you're qualified to host cocktail parties or mix drinks in some sorry-ass joint like this."

He watched her delicately boned hands rinse and polish another glass. "You could get a better job than this."

"Maybe I don't want a better job than this," she said sharply.

His mane of dark hair tilted, conceded to her private motives, and he said with plainly unaccustomed conciliation, "I didn't know people could major in art."

She gauged him briefly, and her jaw relaxed before his unmistakable desire not to offend. "You didn't attend a toney girls'school in New Orleans either."

"You from New Orleans?" He positioned his empty stein near her hand in a polite refill bid. "I been there a couple of times."

"See what I mean. You didn't even know that about me. Or that I've got a nine-year-old and a seven-year-old this very moment walking home from Mesita Elementary School."

"No shit? You got kids?

"No shit." Her blue eyes and flinty echo dismissed further probing. She centered a fresh beer on the La Cantina coaster. "So just why were you so anxious for me to learn you knew somebody in the Mafia?"

"I wondered if you wanted to go to the dog races with me."

"What's that got to do with the Mafia?"

"That's what I do for them. I train and race their greyhounds."

She accorded him a moment of tempered scrutiny. "I'd never have taken you for an animal person. Or a dog trainer."

"You think I was going to say I'm a hit man?" One nail-bitten thumb jabbed lingering ice crystals from the stein. "Ain't nothing about greyhounds I don't know."

"No shit?" This time she imitated his incredulity.

"You ever been to the races?"

"I thought you were married."

"The wife don't like the track. I found the one woman in El Paso who says greyhounds look wormy. She don't care who I take to the races just so I don't badger her to go."

She glanced away from him to watch two men in expensive suits choose a table in an obscure corner.

"So how about it?"

"I'll consider it."

In the shadows, the two men intertwined their fingers on the marble-shard table top. Neither looked up as Kate approached.

"Two double Cuervo Gold margaritas." It was the older man, whose flawless accent indicated he'd been a native speaker since childhood.

Vince studied them with oblique unconcern. "They come in often?" he asked as Kate selected bottles from the shelves.

Why?

"The younger one does legal work for the boss. I never pegged him for a queer."

She clattered shaved ice into a metal shaker across his observation and leveled him a silent reprimand while she salted the rims of two Margarita glasses.

He seemed to recognize renewed disapproval, and he said, "So how come you ended up in El Paso? It ain't the first place I'd consider after a swinging town like New Orleans."

"'My health. I came for the waters,'" she quoted sarcastically.

"Come on. El Paso's smack in the middle of them dirt hills." He took a deep swallow of beer and added seriously, "And by the time the Rio Grande trickles down here, it don't cover your ankles."

She didn't explain the quote he obviously hadn't recognized, and as if to keep him from registering the derision, she said, "Actually, my sister's husband is stationed at Ft. Bliss. When I vacated swinging New Orleans, I decided a six-week Texas divorce would be as good as any."

He nodded. "It didn't use to take six weeks. Thirty years ago, over in Juarez, they handed you a divorce across the counter with a shot of tequila."

"Ah, the story of my life. I'm always a few decades too early or too late."

"So how about it?" His hand wreathed her wrist before she could move to deliver the gold margaritas. "We going to the dogs together?"

She contemplated his stubby fingers, moved her gaze across the bar to his silk shirt before she looked into his eyes beetled darker by abundant black brows. Then she shook off his hand and picked up the glasses. "Why not?"

3

Despite the fact that coolers had pumped refrigerated air through the ceiling vents since early afternoon, the atmosphere of the dog track remained gelatinous, and Kate had to peer closely at the Mexican waiter extending two tumblers of scotch and water, had to clear her throat of the haze. "Gracias."

Vince swept up the other glass without acknowledging the waiter.

He'd been unexpectedly taciturn during the drive to the track, and Kate sipped the barely diluted scotch as she gave him a caustic stare. "So why this charming murkiness? Did the track officials forget to pay their electric bill? Or is it to prevent hard scrutiny of the dogs?"

"Ain't nothing wrong with the dogs," he said shortly. "That shit you hear about mistreatment of hounds ain't true."

"Oops." She took another swallow of the drink she never ordered for herself and murmured with exaggerated sweetness, "Did I trod on some toes there?"

He scowled. "You got to think of greyhounds as top athletes. Trainers work like hell keeping them in shape." He took moody gulps as if he were drinking straight Juarez tapwater. "You don't pay good money for athletes and then beat them down so they ain't worth shit."

His voice and posture were morose, and this time she forebore goading him.

But when he finished the scotch and set the glass down as if he'd been alone, she rattled the betting sheet. "Which well-trained athlete are we putting our money on?" She gave him a mocking smile. "One of those you keep in shape for your Mafia connections?"

He didn't acknowledge the raillery. "My hounds ain't here tonight. One old Mexican owner from Chihuahua keeps fixing races when he's in town, and I don't pit the boss's dogs against him." He flexed his shoulders, and his shirt rippled lavender auras. "I pegged the bastard the first time he hit the track, but I ain't sure how he dopes them hounds at the gate without one trainer nailing him."

"Those Mafia acquaintances of yours let some hustler from Chihuahua get away with fixing their races? I'm shocked."

He glanced at her, and for the first time that evening his testiness became ameliorated with indulgence. "Couple a grand ain't worth the hassle."

"Dog races make only a few thousand?" She took another sip of scotch. "That hardly seems enough money to interest the Mafia."

"What can I say? The boss likes dogs." He began folding his own racing form into smaller and smaller squares. "I put a tenspot on one called Maximilian's Blade for you. He's fifteen to one, like he ain't got a chance. But he's the only dog belongs to old Villalobos in the first race, so I got a hunch he'll finish out front." Then he lunged forward eagerly. "They just came up to the post."

The racing lead, its mechanical arm secured at the end with a surrogate rabbit so patently fake that it could never have fooled a stationary or sauntering dog, swung toward the row of gates. A static-riddled announcement in Spanish crackled over the loud speaker, and a retort, which may have come from a blank or, since they were in Mexico, from a roof-aimed bullet, puffed out smoke and the scent of gunpowder.

The gates lifted, and the dogs burst from the shoots.

Six variegated greyhounds, buckled into vests of garish colors, sprang toward the metal pipe bearing the simulated rabbit.

As the mechanized pole bobbed around the track, the dogs sheered after it, the flaps of their dog saddles whipping blue, red, orange, too fast to show the numbers on the cloth. Sleek-tendoned fore and hind legs bunched, separated, strained into practiced lengths before the paws tipped again, yawned wide, and propelled the dogs with bounds that didn't seem to touch the earth.

Streaking kaleidoscopic harnesses, tails, and panting tongues, the dogs careened around the curve, sped down the opposite arc, and crossed the finish line.

Kate stared at the track from which the dogs had disappeared. "Is it over? That's it. That fast?"

"Dogs ain't slow."

"Did the dog you bet on win?"

"Who knows?" He indicated a wooden scoreboard from which all trace of paint—if it had indeed once been painted—had eroded. "They post the winners."

"What was my dog's number?"

He angled the sheet to read. "Twenty-four."

The crowd shifted, muttered impatiently as inept hands behind the scoreboard finally opened a slot and slid a wooden shingle into the vacancy. Twenty-four, in blue enamel, had been stenciled on the raw wood.

Vince turned to Kate. "You just won a hundred and fifty bucks."

She looked at him. "Did you bet on any more?"

He rescued his glass and beckoned the waiter through the colloidal air. "On every race running a Villalobos dog."

4

"But you knew the races were rigged." A hillock of twenties mounded in her lap, and she riffled them in the dash light of the Cadillac.

"So?" During the races, he'd re-established the affability he displayed at La Cantina, and now he grinned, his complexion and teeth yellow in the discreet glow of car dials. "All's fair in war and at the track."

She refolded the bills into her jacket pocket. "Well, I suppose Lily doesn't need to know exactly how she rated new Gap jeans."

"Your kids asleep?" He ducked his chin toward the modest stucco facade.

"They're spending the night at my sister's."

"Then why don't you ask me in for a nightcap?"

Without appearing to contract a muscle, she managed to recoil. Her mouth hardened beneath its immobility. "I didn't realize there were strings attached to the evening."

"Hey, no strings." He patted the shoulder pad of her jacket with clumsy reassurance. "I like your company, Kate. You're one educated broad who don't put up with guff. I wish my old lady had the kind of class and—" he groped, "—and confidence you got."

"You don't know me."

"Who knows anybody? But I like to hear you spout them sixty-four-dollar words." He nodded through the windshield. "And since I wouldn't mind getting to know you better, I'd like to see the kind of stuff you got in your house."

"I didn't have the foresight to secure furniture or cash before Marshall Tujac canceled the credit cards." She stared sullenly toward the dwelling flanked by the ubiquitous El Paso twin junipers. "The stuff you'll see is Goodwill's best. Lacquered bright green because Ian's seven-year-old decorating skills declared green the most cheerful color for this damned desert."

"Hey, I can tell a lot by green."

She adjusted her jacket sleeves. "And I don't have anything to drink but *aguardiente.* "

"You're kidding. That shit's as bad as it gets." He registered distaste.

"Take it or leave it. *Aguardientde's* the house drink."

He immediately switched off the lights, opened the car door, and came around with his gait that resembled a bear teetering on hind legs. "Well, I can drink it if you can."

She allowed him to make the gallant gesture before she climbed onto the broken sidewalk. Then she steered him past the wired cedars, their limbs mutilated into columns. "Since the front door of this crummy rent house latches only from inside, we have to enter through the kitchen."

"Hey, as long as it's green."

"It's not."

Morning revealed the efficient appliance white, but now the stove, refrigerator, and metal cupboards glistened sulfur yellow from the alley streetlight.

She didn't turn on the kitchen overhead but led him to the living room where a sixty-watt bulb duplicated itself in the gloss green lamp base and tabletop.

"This is more like it." He flung himself onto a sofa with an undefinable color and texture in the seagrass gloom. "What's with saying this ain't the real you?"

"Stuff a sock in it,, Vincent."

He grinned while he watched her open a cabinet built into the stucco wall and take out a liter-sized bottle.

"If I were entertaining you in my book lined study in New Orleans,, I could offer you Benedictine in crystal snifters. Here, you get licorice-flavored Mexican 'water-with-teeth' served in scrubbed-out cheese glasses."

She tendered the neck of the bottle toward him, and he obediently broke the seal, unscrewed the cap. "Like I say, I can drink it if you can."

She poured them each half a glass and handed him one. Then she dropped into an overstuffed chair that matched the blurred couch. "*Salud*"

A complaining growl accompanied his initial mouthful, and they sat a moment in silence holding the little glasses of 90-proof liqueur before he said, "what's with this husband you divorced keeping your furniture but not his kids?"

"He's not worth talking about." She took another licorice swallow. "He's the oldest cliché in the book. Too much of daddy's money, unrecognized alcoholism, absolute self-absorption."

He wagged a hand sympathetically. "Alcoholics ain't easy to take."

She didn't answer for a second, then, "Fifty years ago, I'd probably have put up with his turning into a turnip by seven o'clock every night. I'd have made do with all that filthy lucre and an affair or two."

She stared across the room, but mused as if she didn't care if her words reached him or not. "That's the funny thing about today though. Both 'funny' as in *boutade* and 'funny' idiosyncratic, in case you wondered," she added nastily. "Every woman I know is so independent, so self-sufficient that she can throw caution to the wind and take off on her own. Somehow I couldn't do any less." She drained the cheap liqueur but went on at once before he could intersperse a comment. "I was shamed into fleeing a marriage that, of course, wasn't worth salvaging, but that made my life one hell of a lot more felicitous than living in this stucco dump and tending bar."

He lifted the bottle from the floor beside the lamp table and poured them each another glass. "Like I say, you could get a better job any time."

"That's the other absurdity about divorce. You convince yourself you're saving your sanity, but by the time you've made up your mind to go, your sanity's already vaporized. Your self-esteem's as breakable as those worthless Mexican plates with the lead paint, and your confidence is so splintered you take the crummiest job you're offered—just up from prostitution—in self abasement. And sometimes after you've talked to your wealthy husband, who reminds you how much you used to enjoy Arnaud's *pompano en paper*, you think you should cut out your tongue so you won't have to debate him ever again."

He grimaced at the *aguardiente*, the shade of creme de menthe in the reflected light.

"Oh, but don't try to give me a pep talk, Vince," she said coldly. "Just because I'm situated here in Kern, onto which the Asarco plant spews its weekly toxic emissions, doesn't mean I'm trying to destroy myself or Marshall's children. I didn't know about Asarco when I rented this damned place. And the bar job is only temporary despite the fact that I love serving Long Island teas and syrupy piña coladas to all those college kids who wander into La Cantina and never leave tips." She let her head fall back and glumly adjusted her neck on the overstuffed curve.

He waited another few seconds. "What about child support?"

"What about child support?" she mimicked viciously. "Would you believe that's something you can't get until the divorce is final? My dear not-quite-ex is refusing to sign the papers, and I've got to fight like hell to get that independence I'm not sure I can handle."

He watched her finish the second *aguardiente*. Then he stretched across the cheap area rug and poured her another. When he thudded the bottle back to the floor he fumbled in his shirt pocket. "Here. Cheer up." He tossed a hand-rolled cigarette into her lap. "You just made eight hundred bucks on a wormy bunch of Villalobos mutts."

She fingered the fat stuffed paper with its texture of a dried goldfish.

"You got a match around here anywhere?" He took out another bulging cigarette and put one end between his teeth.

"Kitchen drawer, left-hand side. Would you believe the abortive stove they put in lacks a pilot light and has to be lit every damn time you turn it on."

He trudged to the kitchen, shoved utensils noisily around the drawer, and returned with the box. His shadow loomed over her,, and a match flared. "I'd put them higher with kids in the house if I was you."

She narrowed her lids, but rather than challenging the admonition she put the cigarette in her mouth. He held the flame steady on the dry paper braid until a scarlet ember glowed. Then he dropped onto the couch again and lit his own.

The blackened curl of wood reached his gnawed fingertips before he blew out the flame. "This shit's top grade."

She inhaled, held the sweet smoke in her lungs. "Some of the boss's stash?"

She'd barely uttered the question, however, before his outline bled seaweed into the green grotto of the room.

"Nothing but the best." His words muddied into a slowed recording.

"A just reward for training those top athletes?" But she may not have said it aloud in the spiraling emerald light.

Two more inhalations,, and roman candles scattered brilliance before her eyes. Blood orange, magenta, vermilion splashed across the jade of his bearlike form, across the verdigris tapestry of couch and wall.

"She-e-it." But she may not have spoken that into the swirling green gauze either, and she sponged her teeth with her tongue. "What the hell is this stuff?"

"Acapulco gold."

"No way." Her head rolled back and forth in ropy negation, and the lava walls gathered, oozed toward the floor. "I've had my share of Acapulco gold."

"The boss likes it jazzed up some."

The house tipped and molten rock crept toward her. "With?"

The sentinel cedars burst their wires, and juniper branches sprouted and deformed their symmetry. El Paso stars boomed, pulsed against the midnight sky.

"Heroin."

"No shit?"

And the floor slid away under exploding glass vials of gentian violet and Mercurochrome gold.

5

"Naomi? I just wondered how the kids were doing."

She held the meringue-white phone and poked the fat cigarette. A replica of those from the night before, it lay showcased on a page from Ian's Big Chief tablet and looked even more like a desiccated minnow.

"Kate! It's seven o'clock Saturday morning!"

"I thought the kids'd be up."

"*They're* up, but Jesus, Bryant and I aren't."

"Sorry. "

She shoved the cigarette aside to read the strangely precise, almost feminine, handwriting on the lined paper. *In case you need a pick-me-up.*

"It's the one morning we could sleep in. Bryant's got maneuvers all month."

Kate didn't alibi that she hadn't known about her brother-in-law's training sessions, and in the emptiness of her silence, her sister added, "The kids are watching cartoons. They'll eat at least a box of Fruit Loops before I get up."

"Thanks, Naomi." She tried to swallow the viscosity in her throat. "Did Marshall call last night?"

"Marshall would allow himself to be immersed in shrimp boil before he called me, Kate."

"He left a message on my machine that he wanted to talk to the kids."

"You know he didn't want to talk to the kids. He just wants you back."

"I thought maybe he did want to hear their voices this time."

She unrolled the cigarette, began to crumble paper and leaves into the sink.

"It's a hard thing to say, Kate, but if Marshall were cutting Ian and Lily loose rather than you, he'd have signed those papers yesterday." She sounded both cynical and sad, and when Kate didn't protest, she asked gently, "Did you have a good time last night?"

"It was okay."

She didn't elaborate, and when she hung up, she watched the disposal grind leaves and paper into compost. "My kids know not to play with matches, Vince, but they don't need this kind of doctored shit lying around."

6

She strained against the brace, lifted the crate to her shoulder, and wobbled upright. She kneed the cooler door shut and the latch fell into place by itself.

"Hey! You ain't got the muscle to be lugging that!"

A man vaulted to her side and seized the case before she'd turned to identify that the voice belonged to Vince. He squared the crate neatly under the bar.

"And what do you suggest I do when a knight isn't here to help me?"

"Bring in a couple of six-packs at a time." He hunched into an elbow-lean on his usual barstool. "But, hey, I got a proposition for you."

"I hate that word."

"Cute." Even in the faulty air-conditioning, which the maintenance man insisted would be repaired by mañana, Vince's silk sleeves were french-cuffed tight at the wrists. "It ain't that kind of proposition. I got something I could throw your way to help you get that divorce."

"Part-time employment at the track?"

He shook his head. "A one-time job for some extra dough."

"What kind of job did you have in mind?" She set a beer before him.

"You sure got a suspicious mind." He drank with determined rapidity. "It's a quick drive. Maybe a half hour behind the wheel."

"Driving from where to where in half an hour?"

"Across the border."

She stared at him. "You're kidding!"

"Why would I kid about driving a car across the border?"

She gave him a withering look. "Because both you and I know anybody who needs a car driven across the border is bringing something in."

"*So?*"

"Drugs sewn into the seat covers, *paisanos* in the trunk, plastic explosives or test tubes of anthrax taped inside the hubcaps."

"Come on, Kate. You seen too many movies."

"Jesus, Vince, I thought we were friends."

Hey." He became instantly aggrieved. "You needed some bread. I was trying to help."

"Thanks one hell of a lot."

7

"When will you have enough of this nonsense and come home?" His faintly Southern drawl through the colander of the receiver was petulant but sober.

"I can't breathe in New Orleans, Marshall."

"Nobody breathes in New Orleans. We've mutated to soda straws and gills."

"Nothing's right there." Her voice made an attempt to be kind.

"You thought things were all right for fourteen years."

"Not exactly. I just didn't articulate what was wrong." The kindness began to fray. "But once you tick off the failures out loud, you have to work too hard to pretend. There's nothing in New Orleans for me any longer."

"What do you have in El Paso? Suitors falling out of the trees like apples?"

She didn't answer.

"You're thirty-eight, Kate. One of these days you're going to fade, and then you'll miss all the money you've been used to." When she still remained silent, he added, "I want you back now, but maybe in a year, I won't be interested."

"Is that a threat or a promise?"

"You can forget about a divorce and custody incidentally. Any judge will see I can do more for the children than you can with your two-bit bar job."

"I've got to go. I'm late."

"Do you have any idea how much knowledgeable lawyers demand, Kate? Do you have any idea how much it's going to cost you to fight for Ian and Lily?"

"Maybe it's not my tongue but yours we should consider amputating, Marshall." She crashed the receiver into its metal stirrup.

8

"I have to warn you, Kate, Marshall means it this time." Her sister's voice was grave. "You could lose the children if you're not careful."

"Marshall never carries through with anything, Naomi."

"This time's different. He's already talked to Bryant about testifying."

"Bryant?"

"You know he doesn't approve of divorce."

"Who *approves* of divorce?" When her sister didn't answer, she said, "Marshall doesn't want the children."

"Of course he doesn't. But he's afraid he's lost you and he's making a last ditch stand to get you back. If I were you, I'd think about getting a better lawyer than that ambulance chaser you've been using, Kate."

9

"Just out of curiosity, do you see anything wrong with driving a car across the border?" she asked as soon as he showed after an absence of nearly a week.

He shrugged. "It was just a thought. Forget it."

She glared. "I mean it. Just how do you reconcile yourself to the fact that your boss runs every crooked and lethal business in the country?"

"Nobody runs *every* business, Kate," he corrected gently.

"Don't quibble. You know what I mean."

He bit at a nail already chewed to the quick. "The boss is one of the few people who loves them hounds like I do."

"That's no justification."

He sighed a bear-like sigh. "Most of the stuff he's into is legit, Kate. Restaurants, office buildings, land deals. He buys places in trouble, either takes up the slack or lets them go bust. You wouldn't believe how many guys out there ain't got a lick of business sense, ain't got a clue they got the wrong sow by the ear."

She watched him a moment. "Even you have to concede, Vince, that the mob has a finger in every racket and drug deal in America. Drugs are hardly legal."

"Sure, drugs bring in a lot of cash."

"So how do you rationalize ruining all those lives?"

"Kate," he said patiently. "Drugs bring in dough because people pay it. Nobody's dragging guys in off the street, putting guns to their heads, stuffing them full of coke or horse. Nobody's forcing them to shoot up or snort. People want a quick fix, and they're willing to pay big time. You can't change human nature. Wanting to feel good's the way of the world."

She shook her head, miming appreciation. "Now why didn't I think of that?"

10

"You've got to get a good lawyer, Kate, before it's too late."

"You keep saying that, but what am I supposed to use to pay one of those high-powered firms who can fight Marshall?"

"Bryant was sure—"

"I got here with credit cards, but all Marshall had to do was call up and insist they'd been stolen."

"You always had savings."

"In a joint account that Marshall cleaned out before I realized it." "But I thought—"

"I don't have a penny. And you've been in El Paso long enough to know what my chances are of getting any kind of quick credit." She took a breath. "Could you loan me something? Just enough for a retainer."

"Oh, Kate, I just hate this. You know I don't have anything in my name."

When Kate was silent, she added defensively, "I'm an army wife. Remember?"

Kate waited another few seconds. "What about my talking to Bryant?"

Her sister became quiet. Then, "He thinks—" She broke off, began again. "You know how he feels about your leaving Marshall. He thinks divorced women are sluts, Kate."

"I guess I knew that."

"Oh, Kate, I'm so sorry. I wish I could help."

"It's all right, dear. I'll think of something."

"You were always the resourceful one, Kate."

11

"Do you know whose car it is?"

He sidled onto the barstool. "Belongs to a guy I know."

She went to the freezer, returned with a bag of cracked ice."What's inside?"

"Who knows." He watched her slit the plastic. "Maybe the guy's just stashing the car because his wife in Chihuahua wants it in the divorce."

"Yeah, sure."

"Could be, Kate."

"And he's going to sell us the Pronof Bridge while he's at it."

"Come on."

She poured his draft, straightened tables, flicked a duster at the powdery wall. When she came back,, she put her palms on the bar top. "How much is this friend of yours willing to pay to save his car from his avaricious wife?"

"Thirty thousand."

"Dollars?" She stared at him. "It's no divorce case."

"Hey, you know how people needle each other in divorces."

"Thirty thousand's not a needle. It's a drilling bore."

The two lawyers came in and sat in the back of the room.

Kate approached their table and studied them a moment, but their absorption in each other seemed to make them oblivious and after a few seconds, she took their order for double golds and went back to the bar.

Vince watched her pensively. "You needed some cash, and I remembered this guy. He can find somebody. But you could drive a car across cool as a cucumber. A classy dame in a classy car, nobody'd think twice."

"A classy car with a mysterious cargo which is, of course, not dangerous."

"He can find him somebody else. But like I say, you'd be a cinch to drive it. And it could be carrying nothing."

"For thirty thousand cash, it's probably not carrying 'nothing', Vince."

12

He stayed away for another week, but when he came in, she said, "When's this infamous ride of Paul Revere supposed to come off?"

"Friday week."

She began to chop limes, the only garnish requested in La Cantina—and then only for Tecate—into ragged, amputated sections. "Is this classy car a convertible?"

"Hell, I don't know."

"I always thought one might be elegant." She shoved the lime triangles into a bin. "I'm leaming to pocket all those fabulous tips without declaring them so I can fudge on my income tax as readily as Marshall can. Look at all those businessmen without a shred of conscience who make millions on questionable market shares. Why shouldn't I consider making a bundle for a simple drive?"

He shrugged.

"So what if it's a trifle shady. Why shouldn't I make some extra bread as you so unerringly call it?"

"One of these days you got to make up your mind, Kate. A week from Friday ain't far off. He's got to fmd him somebody P.D.Q."

13

"Mom, it's Aunt Naomi." Lily dropped the phone to twist on its cord as she raced toward the backyard.

When Kate lifted the phone, her sister said without preamble, "Bryant and I both got subpoenas this morning."

Kate lowered the smooth plastic of the phone, clasped it against her denim shirt, and when she finally returned it to her ear, Naomi had hung up.

She stared at the yard from which the grass had burned away and in which only yellowing kudzu still clung to the wall that separated chipped dirt from the pebbles of the alleyway. She put her forehead against the surprisingly warm glass and focused on the children in the worn sand pile, shoveling moats and poking each other with the plastic handles of theit trowels.

"I didn't think you'd go this far, Marshall."

His voice was too muted to carry through the window, but Ian and Lily nontheless looked up and brandished toy shovels.

She managed to wave despite the involuntary tremor of her hand.

14

When Vince came back the next afternoon, she asked at once, "Has your friend found a driver for his hot car?"

Her voice held such an unmistakable flicker that he squinted at her. But he merely said, "It ain't hot."

"Well, has he?"

"Not yet." He studied her. "But don't say you'll do it and then change your mind. Somebody says something, I hold him to it."

"In your charming jocularity are you intimating that a renege could be dangerous to one's health? Are you insinuating your friend is a hit man?"

He shrugged.

"Why shouldn't I be the one to make thirty thousand for a spin across the bridge? Why shouldn't I be like all those politicians, musicians, athletes with their thousand dollar an hour fees that drive up the price of cocaine?"

"Kate, I hate to say it, but you got a hyper look. You been jabbering like the old lady when she's about to beam off."

"Why shouldn't I jabber and look hyper if I feel like it? I'm ready to join America's free enterprise system of supply and demand. I got my own subpoena in yesterday's mail. I'm contemplating a money-making scheme so I can fight the good fight against good old-fashioned Marshall. And Bryant."

Concern momentarily stamped itself on his dark features. "You got to take this serious if you agree to it."

"As you so aptly put it, I can drive across the border with no sweat. Why shouldn't I take my lunch hour and make a few extra thousand?"

"Okay, calm down."

"Can't you tell? I'm calmed down." She abruptly hurled a sodden cloth into a laundry sack under the bar. "I've made up my mind."

He watched her. The profuse black brows knit together briefly.

"I'm ready to accept my mission impossible."

"This ain't a joke."

"I'm not joking. I'm ready to drive your friend's car across the border in exchange for thirty thousand dollars."

"He ain't somebody you want to make mad."

"I've decided."

"Okay. If you say so."

She stood at mock attention with a paring knife.

He looked at her steadily a moment. "Okay. Here's the deal. You go to the Puerto del Sol Restaurant, Friday, and when you come out—at one sharp—you ask the guy who watches cars—"

"He's called the parking valet."

"Yeah. You ask him for a forest green Pontiac."

"Oh? Is it your opinion that I look like a dame who'd drive a Pontiac?" She somersaulted the paring knife into the sink and asked, slightly more calmly, "Am I supposed to ask him in Spanish?"

"Cute. No, not in Spanish. You think I'm going to trust this to some guy who needs to know Spanish?"

She exhibited feigned surprise. "I think there may be a racist remark in there somewhere, but I'll be damned if I can make it out."

"A forest green Pontiac parked in the market lot. He gives you the key, you get in, drive through customs like you been over for lunch. That's it."

"What do I do with this hot forest green Pontiac then'"

"There'll be a bottle of booze on the seat. You pull in and declare it. A guy'll be waiting just across the bridge, and when you stop to pay the tax, he'll stroll over like some old friend to ask for a ride downtown."

"And he'll be wearing a green carnation and a red fright wig?"

"It don't matter what *he* wears, Kate. He'll recognize you."

"Oh, of course."

"That's it. A free lunch." He laid two bills on the bar top and pushed them toward her. "Twenty minutes across, and you'll be thirty thousand richer."

"How come I have the feeling my instructions have already begun to self destruct?"

"Cute."

15

The cars inch forward, but the brown-clad Mexican officials don't bother to scrutinize anyone heading toward the U.S.—as if what's taken from the country isn't their concern—and she looks past them toward the vendor strolling between the logjam traffic with plastic whirligigs, cellophane bags of something resembling caramel corn, and translucent suckers molded into cones of rainbow stripes. She shakes her head, and he moves leisurely toward stalled cars containing children.

Still a quarter of a mile remains between the Mexican exit and the glass booths of the American side, and his flat assertion echoes from the dashboard, "*Somebody says something. I hold him to it.*"

Her fingers twitch, and she makes white-knuckled fists of them around the steeringwheel as she watches the approaching signs in English and Spanish, *Welcome to the United States.* The lanes advance, but the space seems undiminished, as if the border eases backward before the cars can narrow the distance. She shifts into "Park" and lifts her quivering foot off the brake.

The Pontaic rolls, stops. The welcome sign is nearly overhead now. She reads it softly in English and Spanish, and the family in the car beside her glances over. The parents in their Sunday best smile while the two small children in the back, for whom the father has just bought the conical, multi-colored lollipops, elbow each other and study her.

A membrane in her temple thickens.

Eight cars remain between the Grand Prix and the border patrol kiosks.

"*He ain't somebody you want to make mad.*"

The car on her right with the happy Mexican family stays parallel. The little boy and girl alternately poke each other with the sticky cone-tips and gaze at her with solemn brown eyes.

Border stoplights shutter from red to green to red through transparent ribbons of heat while drivers declare their nationalities and customs officials nod them on. Red blinks to green, the cars lurch forward, and the waiting line is reduced to six.

Abruptly, she presses the lever of the turn signal and inclines toward the Mexican father. "*Perdón.*" She points to the parking lane. "My radia-tor." She motions with her hand and when suddenly the word for "hot" surfaces, she says, "*Caliente,*" as she signs to cut in front of him. "*Por favor.*"

He smiles, his gold replacements gleaming where incisors have been. "*Sí,*" he says in commiseration.

He doesn't edge forward when the space opens, and she swerves the Pontiac ahead of him. She gestures in the rearview mirror. "*Gracias.*"

Few cars stay long at the border pedestrian building, and she manages to slide the Pontiac into an opening at the curb. Her parking is uneven, and the front tire bounces against the raised concrete, but she slants the car in, turns off the key and slides shakily into the sun. She reaches back to grab her purse, then locks the door against the green metallic surfaces with their miniature suns.

Since a greater than usual number of Mexicans are walking across this afternoon, she stands in line surrounded by their holiday clothes and exhuberance, for what seems a long time before she reaches the counter.

"American," she says while the border patrol official glances at the key in her hand and at the purse, which she's pried open for his inspection.

The bag contains nothing but a slim wallet, and the border patrolman dismisses her after a few cursory seconds. She passes through the stile with a group of Mexican revelers fluttering tiny green, orange, and white flags.

They bunch into the sun again, shoulder politely through the metal revolving gate onto the sidewalk that slopes up, then down into the U.S. The crowd thins over the bridge under which the Rio Grande flows in sluggish backwash, and only a few pedestrians come over the concrete rise with her.

And there at the foot of the bridge stands a bearlike figure in a vivid green silk shirt and black slacks.

He's intent on the traffic, scanning the cars for the forest green Pontiac with its simmering Cutty Sark, and there is nothing nonchalant about him. In direct sunlight, it's obvious that he's more coiled, more muscular than he appeared under the subtle half-tones in which she's always observed him.

He squints against the savage glare, and one powerful hand ledges horizontal above the black brows. The silk, the same foil green as the Grand Prix, collects and flings dazzling sunspots from its buttoned sleeves and shirtfront.

The other pedestrians pause or veer toward the banisters above the scummy water, and suddenly she's walking toward him alone. As if he's heard her footsteps, he drops his hand from his forehead and looks directly at her.

His eyes are so dark they appear pupilless, and his expression abruptly changes. They stare at each other, and it's clear from his face that he knows she knows.

But the spasms of her knees and spine have ceased, and she's calm—more calm than she's ever been in her life—as he watches her with hard obsidian eyes and she walks toward him at the end of the bridge. ✿

Rough Girl Rufina

by Adelina Anthony

Rufina keeps vigil from the top step—perched—like the stuffed *pajarito* on Mama Luanna's *altar*, the only things Rufina and that bird have in common are skinny legs and eyes as green as his dusty feathers. Her thin fingers sift through a yellow plastic bowl of milk-less corn flakes, filling the otherwise silent room with a ruido like tires crackling over gravel, or as if someone were whispering Qúe? Qúe? Qúe?. If Mama Luanna was well, "Eating again, mi'ja?" she would say. And then she would rub Rufina's tummy as if she were a Buddha statue and add, "Te lo juro, tu tienes gusanos . . . puro worms en ese tummy." But unfortunately for her children, Mama Luanna is far from her days of *salud*.

And even though the hunger makes her stomach and intestines twist and clench like children's fingers when they play the painful game of "mercy," Rufina feels too guilty to eat while Mama Luanna's tears drip-slip along her crimson cheeks. Remembering what Mrs. Connors said in health class Friday about the body being made up of gallons of water, Rufina figures Mama Luanna has cried at least three gallons. "Have some mercy, Virgencita," whispers Rufina as she flicks a corn flake down the stairs. It lands by the shiny broken ornaments of blue, green, and red scattered on the checkered tile floor.

They were decorating the borrowed Christmas tree Abuelita Lydia had sent them. Rufina and her baby brother, Jorge, fell in love with the tree's artificial snow frosted limbs, as scraggly as their grandmother's braids. But the holiday spirit was crushed when their father, Don Don, came home Saturday evening in a bad mood and smelling of *putas*, as Rufina heard Mama Luanna say. Don Don was known by the local *chisme* network as a hammer of anger.

They fought. And afterwards, her mother was left lying on the wine colored couch like a throw rug. The blood on her face drying like the raw piece of meat in the sink. Rufina inhales the rich scent of burning candles she lit several hours ago when it started to get dark. She watches the yellow light from the candles on the altar patting her mother on the chest, as if to console the woman. Mama Luanna is still whispering prayers frantically, occasionally jabbed with a shrieks of "Me voy a matar, Diosito!" These suicidal words cut Rufina. She can not imagine surviving without her mother. And how would she care for the little brother who sticks to her like a sweaty T-shirt?

Outside the cold air is an intense lover, pressing its thick misted body against the tenement bricks. It will leave a slick sweat in the morning. It slips one of its fingers through the cracked window and fondles Rufina's naked neck and tickles her bare feet. She endures the torturous touch and refuses to abandon the stairwell. If Mama Luanna is going to really kill herself this time, Rufina wants to be awake to stop her. So in the end,she doesn't mind having to shake her feet like *maracas* every couple of minutes to keep the blood circulating. Besides, it keeps the roaches away. Rufina is always amazed at the boldness of city roaches, especially at night. They're nothing like the roaches that scatter away at the flicker of light in Abuelita Lydia's casita in the hills. Maybe it's the sleepiness coming on, but Rufina thinks she even sees one *cucaracha chocante* smile greedily at her while he runs away with a crumb of Christmas cookie. "La muerte is a rotting sweetness," Abuelita Lydia tells her every time they bury one of Rufina's goldfish won by Don Don from one of the game booths at San Jose Park. As the growing army of roaches ravage cookies and dinner to be in the sink, Rufina murmurs, "No, Abuelita Lydia, it just stinks." Dinner and dessert are dead.

Next to the busted Christmas lights, Rufina spies the imprint of her father's boot on a red-sugared cookie, the same triangle that marks the right side of her mother's temple. Rufina prays her nine-year-old fists left the same kind of vicious marks on her father's back; but by the way he flung her on the couch, she knew her kicks and punches might as well have been issued by the wings of a butterfly. Sometimes she hated him not so much for being violent, but for cheating on them with another woman—

Dolores. They found out the other woman's name when Rufina volunteered to go and play detective at Dolores' beauty salon. Dolores trimmed Rufina's hair without ever figuring out she was Don Don's daughter.

Rufina's body cramps from being curled like a crumbled ball of paper. "Mamí," she calls. Silence. Rufina knows Mama Luanna is ignoring her. If it wasn't for the occasional movement of the rosary in her hand, Rufina would have to wonder if somehow her mother fulfilled her wish of suicide and had only left her broken body as a painful token. " Por favor, don't let her kill herself, Diosito!" prays Rufina, "Take *him*, instead."

She has no choice. She climbs the sterile stairs to seek her brother out. Jorge will be where he always is when he cries, in their mother's closet. Though only seven, he knows not to cry in front of others, especially in Don Don's house. Only sissies cry, and Don Don does not raise girls.

Rufina opens the closet door where Jorge is draped by the polyester dresses and cotton skirts. The black and blue striped dress Mama Luanna wears to church has a wet stain near the hem, where Jorge has been blowing his nose since their father left. She hears him sniffle and sees the ripples swim across the clothes as he sways his head from side to side. The caresses from the soft dresses comfort Jorge. Abuelita Lydia, who on several occasions has had to drag Jorge out her closet, confided in Rufina that if they didn't keep Jorge from hiding beneath women's skirts, it would cost him his life one day.

"Jorge, salte. We gotta do the scene for Mamí."

"¿Horita?" He could come back." said Jorge.

"Don't be a tonto. Hurry."

Rufina pulls her brother out of the closet, head first. It is easy for her to grab his head of dark wavy curls. They are the length of a girl's. Jorge recently began to protest that the older boys around the Victoria Projects were calling him a *maricon*, but their mother avoided cutting his hair with the excuse that she didn't have the money to take him to a barber shop. Rufina knows better.

When she stayed with Abuelita Lydia last summer, she came across a photo graffitied with red hearts. It was hidden in her mother's childhood dresser with the splintered mirror. Abuelita Lydia caught Rufina looking at the black and white photo and told her to put away the dirty cholo picture. "¿Quien es?" Rufina asked her grandmother, but the old woman dismissed her with the wave of a hand and the rolling of her eyes. Rufina stared at the photo for a long time before she put it away. The swelling sensation in her chest told her the lanky *moreno* with dark tresses was a younger version of her father. She recognized the large round eyes varnished with mischief, the only feature she inherited from Don Don.

Jorge, on the other hand, is an exact replica of that photo. Rufina figures her mother enjoys keeping Jorge around with his curls because he is a miniature Don Don—one she can still manage with a glare. Rufina untangles her fingers from Jorge's curls. It looks as if he has eaten a glazed donut with his runny nose and wet lips.

"Pero yo no queiro ser la vieja," protests Jorge.

"Tienes que ser la vieja, es mas gracioso. Andale, ponte este vestido," she says, throwing him one of their mother's dresses.

"Ay, pero este vestido ni siquiera es de un color que me guste."

Rufina loses her patience with her brother, who indulges himself in the role of diva whenever they play out make-believe scenes. "Look." She always talks to him in English when she becomes authoritative, mimicking her teachers from school almost verbatim, "I don't have time for you. Participate or stay quiet." She marches out of the room and heads toward the hall closet where she pulls out her father's brightest shirt. Rufina loves the shirt which looks as if someone carelessly spilled globs of paint all over it. Her father hardly ever wears it now. Probably because he has gotten too fat over the last two years she thinks. She matches the shirt with some dark brown polyester pants, a green tie, and burgundy dress shoes. She puts on the shirt, its edges flirtatiously kissing the floor, and jumps into the pants which swallow her whole. After minutes of rolling up cuffs, stuffing herself with pillows and using the green tie as a tourniquet around her stomach, she glances at herself in the hallway mirror. It is a dashing and devilish costume design. Now she resembles her father. Thinking of her mother's despair, Rufina decides that tonight she will add one more detail, Don Don's prized velvet hat.

The hat is never, under any circumstances, to be touched. It cost him a lot of *dinero* and he only wears it when they go to weddings and *quinceneras*. Not that they've gone to any recently. Rufina had often seen her father caress the hat with more tenderness than he had ever offered her. She hated it. Hitting it against the pale yellow walls, a cloud of dust rises before her watery green eyes. She dons the black thing with the red feather wing, down over her left eye, just like the men do in the gangster movies. Rougher looking, Rufina is a figure to be reckoned with now. With her newly acquired attitude, she saunters back into her mother's room. The oversized shoes thump to the Mexican blues she hears in her head. The family picture on the wall trembles.

"Well, you coming or you going to be a lloron?" she asks, Jorge.

"Ayudame con el zipper," he says.

"Don't make me get rough with you, vieja," she growls.

Rufina puts the finishing touches on her brother, including the pink lipstick. They grab the small transistor radio from the bed stand and then wait for several seconds at the top of the stairs. Rufina and Jorge were stuffed with so many pillows that they looked like marshmallows. Rufina is held back by the uncanny silence. Maybe they are too late. She looks at Jorge who holds her hand shamelessly. "He's not coming back, ¿verdad?" asks Jorge. Rufina shakes her head. Simultaneously they take a deep breath and waddle down the stairs.

At the bottom of the stairs, Rufina peeks from around the corner and sees Mama Luanna as she had left her. Like the candle's wax, she seems to have melted into a smaller figure. Rufina winks at Jorge and lets the radio blast with a Flaco Jimenez conjunto.

The music jolts their mother like a flame in the air, and she turns to face the children. Rufina takes this as her cue and whips Jorge onto the improvised dance floor. They throw themselves into their roles like the best of actors and let the scene carry them away. "Ay, Dolores!" Rufina says in her toughest voice, "Sabes que te quiero porque eres la vieja mas fea del mundo." She spins her brother to the *ritmo* of the *cancion* with a vengeance, just like her Abuelita Lydia taught her to dance last summer. Jorge with his smeared lipstick answers, "No, no, no, Don Don . . . ¡soy las mas fea del universo!" He uses all of his agility to keep from tripping over the dress unloosening itself from the grip of the belt around his waist. The children dance with their butts in the air and stomp their feet on the ground. Rufina enjoys the Godzilla effect she has on a roach that crunches like a potato chip under her killer shoes.

Rufina shuffles her brother back and forth like an accordion. She wants to move into a position where she can see if her mother is responding to their shenanigans. A faint smile is on her mother's lips, as if it pained her to feel better. Rufina doesn't know her mother's happiness is being held back by the anxiety she feels seeing Don Don's hat. But Mama Luanna is so awakened by her children's concern, she doesn't want to interrupt their show. Rufina takes her mother's expression as a sure sign that they have their theatrical venture cut out for them, because the audience is drunk on despair. So they continue.

Rufina scratches her stomach like her father, takes an imaginary swig of beer, and lets out a pretend fart. Jorge responds by making pig sounds and saying "Yo se—oink, oink—que soy una—oink—marrana. ¿Pero ahora dime quien apesta?" Rufina joins her brother by adding donkey noises and soon the room is enlivened by a cacophony of animal sounds. Rufina becomes vulgar and grabs Jorge's breasts of pillow. Jorge chimes in with, " Ay, mis chichis!" He slaps Rufina's enormous rear and says, "Mira, que nalgas tan guangas." By this point, their mother cannot contain her laughter and lets a strong guffaw roar in the air. Rufina and Jorge smile at each other. Mission accomplished.

Once again they had brought their mother back to life. Rufina turns toward Mama Luanna and pretends she is Don Don caught in the act."

";Ay no! Es mi esposa, Dolores."

"¿Que vas a hacer? Cabron! " adds Jorge with great relish, since it is in these rare instances he can get away, spank-free, with saying *maldiciones*.

Rufina acknowledges his remark with a whack to his head . . . using the prized velvet hat. Before they know it they are engaged in an all out pillow fight. Mama Luanna watches the scene with such glee her flesh bounces like a spring in a mattress. And in this way, no one, not even Mama Luanna, notices the hat fall and get trampled under the children's feet.

Rufina darts like a comet through the kitchen and then back to the living room with Jorge tagging along like her tail. They scream with such high pitched notes the music of their voices drowns the radio. With all of the running around, Rufina's pant's unravel themselves and lick at her feet like needy puppies. She trips. Gliding through the air, her legs looked like the wings of the big roaches she hates to see flying about at night. Luckily, Rufina lands on her mother's lap. Jorge also dives into the familiar arms. Their shadows from the candle light look like a stormy ocean with waves of arms and legs crashing against the wall. They tickle, giggle, and squeal. They rest.

Panting softly, Rufina and Jorge hang like skinny kittens at their mother's breasts. They are finally silent. Rufina can smell the blood and salt of Mama Luanna's skin, it reminds her of the cuts on her mother's face. She ponders if they might have hurt their mother by playing so physical with her; and as if Mama Luanna can read her thoughts, she feels her mother embrace her with an intense strength. Rufina is being held so hard it begins to hurt. She looks at Jorge with a plea of help in her eyes, but he is also being smothered with love. It is getting difficult to breathe. But, Rufina decides it is better not to protest so she endures her mother's hold, and Jorge follows suit. She thinks about how her Abuelita Lydia and how she also hugs with the same desperate strength whenever she comes to visit them. She wonders if she will grow up and inherit the ability to love with such force.

Their mother's hold finally relaxes. Whew! Rufina turns her body around so she can sit on her mother's lap more comfortably. She snuggles the back of her head against her mother chest. Jorge copycats. Their mother will wet them with kisses and stories now, she is sure. That is their reward. Moments like this, Rufina wishes she could stay nine years old forever. Until she sees something terrible. Her green eyes grow round as a honeydew melon and she sticks her thumb into her mouth to stifle the scream rising in her throat. Rufina notices Don Don's hat, hammered on the floor. ✿

BESIDE THE RED RIVER

by Albert Haley

The Sermon

Today he'll set the plains on fire, for in sweat soaked dreams it has come to him all that is necessary. He must take what stretches before him and make it ready for the Great One's own plow.

It is a painful, showy process on this day in 1872 as he ties his horse to the post, ducks through the doorway, and his boots stomp boards while he creaks down the aisle of the little white church, reaching the pulpit, where he opens the heavy book that has traveled miles tied to the saddle, and he stares at faces, unexpectedly placid, hardly even wind burnt, just one grainy visage posited next to another, and the rest of the corpus shackled in stiff poor man and poor woman's clothes of smudged brown and eggshell blue. "Our scripture today will be—" They have no idea what beast this traveling preacher is about to harness to ancient words, and as the first syllables flare from his lips, they strike inviting, tinder dry minds. Now the looks lengthen and his dragon tongue spreads it *higher, more voluminous, hotter*, and when the waxy eyes go soft, none of their feigned frailty stands in the way.

Prairie chickens, rabbits, rodents, and *deer* dart from beneath consumed stalks, jump through hogsheads of hot, crackling orange, and the creatures continue on, bolting for the wide open spaces with fur and feathers singed. Still he keeps on shouting, declaring, kindling adjective against noun, collapsing pretenses and rationalizations with a single verb taken bright-white from the forge of the pages spread before him. By the end the walls are shaking from the thunder of panicked buffalo rushing out of twenty-five homesteading hearts, and these heavy, scraggly brown, horned, hoofed madnesses go by too, leaving their own scented afterwind, an odor of matted pelt penetrated by ticks and burrs and bullet lead and, yes, much dung and blood. *So much to give up. Ways and means and expediencies. Scribbled lines of so-called "treaties." Tracking a man at night when his back is turned and you and the others have a rope in hand. Reveling in a "civilization" that has bulged and broken through the fence called "law."*

He says it all and the people weaken as he has expected. *The high tide of the conflagration.* They bend back: the noxious cloud assaults their tearing eyes. *Seeing the way they've treated each other. Remembering joyless hard work. Children and women and men driven through the day like odd species of domestic beasts.* And by the time they blink, he has completed his story and done the impossible. Vanished without punishment or recrimination. Out the back door of the little white church. The vision they did not ask for has come and it has gone: the wilderness that once-was is wiped away. Burned to the root. Blackened. Charred. Let them observe for a while. Dissipating smoke still twists into the sky at sunset time. Black against orange. The colors they have created.

Dawn Chore

At the end of winter, on a newly stripped bump in the landscape, the men arrived. If someone had asked, they would have admitted to being hit-and-miss believers in the words that a man on a spotted mare brought one Sunday to the dry land. And they remembered what the women folk told them as they walked out of church: *Something just over the horizon has seen you, seen me and, listen well—we're never going to be the same.*

Now they looked out to the edge of the earth at the swath running from the doors of their sod houses all the way to the Red River where silver rolling liquid finally sank the flames and piled up sizzling pillars of steam. *Could there be another chance? And, if so, could we imagine the results? That—as the women have proposed—soot and ashes might ripen into material for tendrils to shoot up, the soil having been made fertile by cleansing fire? And someday all of us will be standing hip deep in the harvest?*

The men remained silent. Work to be done.

They walked to the wagons. The seed had been poured into seven sacks sewn tightly together at tops and along seams. They plunged knives into the bulges and scooped out handfuls. Dry as bones it felt against the callused, cupped palms. They held it under their noses and sniffed. Then they began making broad casts across the blackened fields.

After Services

The woman leads the man behind the white building. She is already talking in her stormy way. "Reverend Storch, that was a mighty sharp sharing of Truth today. And now you must see!" Her old hands flap like chaff before a spinning dust devil while her chin wobbles and nods, and with this frightening set of quiet gestures she is content as she opens the door upon a shadowed space. She points in the upper corner to a shape pasted against splintered rafters. A streak of harsh noontime light falls upon a paper-walled chamber. It vibrates before their eyes, charged and crackling with buzzing.

"Tried it myself. The sweetest honey in that comb!"

She states this with joy, as if she has brought him to this fetid shed as his reward for what he has done for kin and friends. She turns to him, blessing him with rheumy eyes. She rubs her nose, by which she means to further confirm him wordlessly and thereby take his mind away from her own physical facts, that she (formerly a young maiden, desirable and shapely, once married to the richest, most powerful man in the county, the Judge himself, a man of a hundred "laws" and practical ways) now stands humpbacked and reeks like the bodies that have pressed and strained hard against these outhouse planks. She can see that he wants to run and make his escape, but she is so overwhelmingly destroyed—yet oblivious to her condition—that it has become mesmerizing. He continues to stare at her, then opens his mouth.

"Here's the real truth, ma'am. I ought not to have done it. I hurt those people. And who am I? A fool with a stone in his chest. I'm the one who deserves to burn." So tall he is stooping and the clothes are casket dark and trail dusty. The man continues, "Talk about lying and killing innocent folk to get what you want. Do you know where my wife and children are? Back in Carthage. I scribbled 'em a two-line note. And that nag, I *stole* her when I came out here *not to save anybody but to flee.*"

She nods like she knows this lean, slack face Jonah, and before he takes his eyes off the hive she hobbles out, shutting the door softly behind her. There is a skeleton key. His bony arms, his elbows, and the clod-like fists bang from the other side. "Wait! You've locked me in!" "Yessir!" she shouts back. Like him, she knows her job. Soon he will feel the sting that launches out from the golden sphere. A hundred sharp points of joy and of sorrow. She brings this to people whether she wills it or not. Then she always goes home.

One Night

And there one night, in the Judge's old, turreted manse, Mary Eugenia slept twisted sideways in an armchair in the parlor. In this position, the pain of the hump was lessened yet it poked her awake. Her best ear was cocked toward the open window so as to have something to do during those conscious moments. *Listen.* Hour by hour, the moths fluttered in and out. Beneath the dust and darkness the sound came, yes, just as the plowing and planting folks were fond of claiming. *Rustle, rustle.* The tender shoots noisily stretched toward the stars, an unfathomable distance, and in their rambunctiousness they gained at least an inch by the night. A minute later a living thing opened its throat and cried in the former grasslands, but that was not all.

A horse and rider were *clopping, clopping, clopping.* And the room began to become warm and unsettled. She threw off her shawl, rose, and humped to the window, and placed her hands on the blistered sill. The *clopping* became louder, and she could imagine how the mare's neck was becoming stretched out and her legs churning faster, and it was all *gallop* now and the violent snap of the reins in the hands of the invisible rider. As they went past, human pressed to the back of the animal, both of them were darker than tar upon coal. Mary Eugenia leaned forward, head out the window, and shook a fist. It was the protective gesture she had developed over the years in this land she fiercely defended. A shake of the fist warned an enemy, grieved the death of a child, assaulted another drought stricken season. Her voice broke, cackled, and became a force as her hand slammed down on the sill. At the sound, a star tumbled and made a swift streak out of heaven. The celestial dust trailed off to the horizon, dazzling and dazing her from now until morning when, in the early hours, thick fog slid out of the river valley and lay like rifle smoke along the ground. Mary Eugenia woke again. She heard new words inside her head while the birds awakened with loud bursts out in the fields: "*Then the angel that talked with me answered and said unto me, 'Knowest thou not what these be?'*"

She cannot pin down the exact meaning, but she slides outside as her heartbeats urge. To swish aside the corn, to find the tracks winding through the middle of it. The dawn brings a fragile pink, a babe-like thing that drowses with shallow breaths. Mary Eugenia bends to the earth—not so hard to do—and traces with her fingertip each arcing, iron shoe shape cut into the dirt. She shivers beside the Red River. She tastes dirt with her mind. It is a dark, rich thing a person wants to enfold with tongue, gain, own, tie down, and hold, and then spit it out in the upturned mouths of their children. But she has none—the offspring are gone, taken away. So her own words fall into the bucket of her mind and she feels how it leaks.

"Tomorrow he returns. He will be ready for me."

They have planted a life and harvested a judgment. The prophets are false yet their words true. When the fire rises to scorch the tongue, you shall be drowned as if with water. If all of them, she thinks, had only let it be—as they found it—respected the pebble unmoved, the blade of grass not trampled down. She can see the way it was: the swollen herds of brute, brown beauty roaming, this green patch of earth untainted by bare breasted men bleeding into the soil. It could have happened that not even a sparrow fell from the blue western sky. It could have been just the river flowing on. *The river.* She thinks she will go. Soak her old toes in the shallows. Watch the ripples forming around the snags. The insects make circles on the surface. Most likely, this will be another long day beside the Red River. 🏵️

Tie-Fast Man

by Robert Flynn

In cattle country there are two kinds of roping—dally, an English corruption of *dar la vuelta*—take a turn with a rope, and tie-fast. Dally ropers wrap the rope around the saddle horn after the catch, holding the loose end in their hand so they can let it slip if something goes wrong. Tie-fast ropers tie the rope hard to the saddle horn and plan on hanging on to whatever is on the other end. Texas was tie-fast country.

Claris McCloud was a tie-fast man. He didn't dally because he had never dabbed his rope on something he couldn't hang on to. Then one day he tied onto a mossy-horned bull that was wilder than a camp meeting prayer. The longhorn nearly jerked the saddle off his horse and his horse off its feet. Claris tried to cut the stumbling horse free of the rope, but the bull came back down the rope, ran under the horse's belly and the horse blew Claris out of the saddle.

Claris threw the knife away before he hit the ground in a pile. In the moment it took to regain his senses and breath, he realized he was alive only because the bull had attacked his horse that was tangled in the rope. Claris slid along the ground into a depression and hid until the bull lost interest and trotted away. Claris found his knife, cut the horse's throat to end its suffering, and sat beside the dying horse to ponder his life.

He had been born on the Indian frontier, six years before the last Comanche raid. He remembered his father, Doss McCloud, leaving a loaded rifle and six-shooter for his mother before joining other men to trail marauding Indians. He left the rifle for her to use on Indians; the pistol was to use on her children and then herself. On that last raid, Claris and his father were at the house, his mother and sister, Jacklin, were in the open picking berries.

When he was seven Claris made a hand. When he was ten, barbed wire came to the plains. When he was twelve, Claris was shot at and his horse killed while he was cutting wire that fenced off a deep hole in Six Mile Draw. When he was fourteen, his father's horse tangled in broken wire and his father, trying to free the horse before it cut itself to pieces, was kicked to death by the spooked horse. Claris was owner of a homestead, a brand, a remuda and a herd of cattle, and range boss of a handful of cowboys scarcely older and tougher than he.

When he was twenty, there was a drought and die-off followed by a blizzard. Farmers pulled out; most of the land wouldn't support a farm. Claris bought their land with a milk cow or a couple of steers. They were glad to have something to leave with. Sometimes he gave them another steer to plant hay on the land before they left it, and wintered his cattle on the hay.

When Claris was thirty, the value of longhorns plummeted and he had to give up buying land to buy blooded bulls, paying top dollar for bulls and horses and bottom dollar for cowboys. He spent years ridding himself of longhorns, selling their hides and tallow, and riding into scrapes like today. He was forty-years-old and without get. He needed a son.

Claris considered going to Fort Worth and marrying a whore. They had a work ethic, and when you married one you knew what you were getting. If he could find one that had been a buffalo gal long enough to dream of rescue but not long enough to develop contempt for men, she would appreciate it and would work at making him a good wife, giving him sons to help with the ranch. The thing that stopped him was the fear that some of his cowboys might know her. He didn't want them looking at her like a bronc they had broke. Bronc busters took a proprietary interest in horses they broke to the saddle, watching how they took the rein, how they rode.

Besides, a whore would be accustomed to a lot of sex. That would be all right for a while, but ten, twenty years down the road he might be less than she was used to. That was a worry he didn't have time for. He sure didn't have time to sit around the house keeping an eye on her. A widow would be grateful and accustomed to a husband's demands but perhaps too attached to another man's habit. He decided to seek a spinster and break her to bit and saddle and teach her a man's wont. A sheltered woman who wouldn't know or expect someone else's measure.

Sitting beside the dead horse, Claris studied on himself. He looked tall in boots and hat. Thin—because you didn't get fat on sourdough and beans—but not drawn. His face was creased like a good hat. His eyes were clear, he had his front teeth, a trip to the barber would take care of his shaggy hair and moustache, and he had land, good horses, and blooded bulls. Danged, if he wasn't a rooster. A woman who couldn't make something of that didn't deserve to marry.

Claris tugged his saddle free of the horse, threw it on his shoulder and started to the house. While high-heeling it, he rounded up his chances and cut the shells. There were three spinsters in the county. Ploma was a shell, as old as he and no good for childbearing. Edna was good hearty stock, looked like she could bear healthy boys, and she was dragging her rope hoping some man would grab it. German family, overbearing, but he could put up with Emil and he wouldn't have to see a lot of Irmagarde.

When he went to see Edna, he almost asked her to marry him. She would never own any part of her father's land, he knew that. She was beefy plumb to her hocks, lumpy now and would get pillowy like her mother after a child or two but he could abide that. The gristle in his jerky was the way she brayed when she laughed. Closest thing to a jackass he had ever heard. He chewed on that, telling himself he could abide it. He would be away from the house most of the time and he sure as hell wouldn't try to make her laugh.

When they got to talking about how many children he wanted, how he didn't have much time or place for privacy but the hands never used the outhouse anyway, everything he said sent her into spells of braying. He stood up, apologized, and told her he wanted to check another pasture. She started braying again, but now her eyes were big, panicky, like a cornered cow. Her father and brothers came outside to watch him leave, trying to decide whether or not they were obliged to beat him to calm her down.

That left Celestine, scant and quiet as a whisper in a windstorm. It annoyed him the way she tiptoed around but he thought when he got her to his place where there was nothing to break, she would get over it. Claris had no time for courting. He knew that she was available and was young enough to bear children. Her father owned an adjoining ranch and there were no other heirs. Claris and Olin had done some hell-raising together when they were younger. Nothing to be ashamed of—getting drunk, fighting, spending the night in a whorehouse. Claris recounted his horses and cows and Olin said it was time for Celestine to take the bit. It was a marriage made in the saddle.

When Claris told Celestine of his plans for children she stared at her lap, her face red as a hereford's neck. When he asked her to marry him she didn't change her posture and he had to ask her to repeat what she said. Still he wasn't sure. "Yes?" he asked, and she nodded. He knew then he should have thrown a wider loop, but he had asked and he couldn't go back on his word, and she was the only heir to her father's land.

Celestine was twenty-three when she moved to Claris' bare-board, box and strip, two-room ranch house. One room for cooking and eating and one room for dressing and sleeping. For furniture he had a table and benches for the cowhands, a cook stove and a bed.

Celestine brought with her a wagon load of necessities: two ladder back chairs—one for each of them like he would be sitting in the house— her rocker, a hope chest filled with towels, embroidered linen, patchwork quilts, her trousseau; and a glass door bookcase with her romance novels that inclined her to dally. She also brought a mirror and a good bed and mattress. Claris's bed had been a bedroll thrown over a frame strung with rawhide and he used a water bucket for a mirror.

Celestine cherished Claris for offering her a life as a wife and mother. She intended to please him, but there were no doors she could close, no shades she could draw before dressing for bed, and no closets or shelves for her to place her clothes, but nails driven into the wall to hang things on.

Wash-up was done on the porch where the cowboys gallantly waited so Celestine would have clean water and towel. Bathing was done in a galvanized tub in the bedroom where she crouched in a corner of the doorless, curtain-less room after the cowboys had brought water for her to heat. The cowboys, who believed too much bathing wore away the scarf-skin and exposed the nerves, knew every time she took a bath.

Cooking and eating were done in the kitchen where she cooked for everyone. Metal pans were used for plates and a coffee can on the table held bent flatware. At roundup when there were extra hands, some had to eat with spoons or use their pocketknives because there were not enough utensils for everyone. When finished, the cowboys dropped their dishes in the wreck pan, a galvanized tub she had placed on the stove to heat water for washing dishes.

Celestine, who had always been shy around boys and frightened by loud noise, had to cook in front of the hungry hands who watched her as they ate. She was appalled at their gobbling and guzzling, grunting their pleasure and pointing when they wanted more. They rarely spoke and when they did it was to each other.

"I reckon I could eat them flapjacks fast as she can fry 'em," one cowboy said around a mouthful.

"Yeah, but for how long?" asked another without taking his eyes off her.

"Till I starved to death, I reckon," said the first.

Their appetites were ravenous, animalistic. Her father had eaten with the hands, but Celestine and her mother waited until the cowboys returned to work, then ate quietly talking of church, sewing circle, and play parties.

Celestine's father offered to help Claris enlarge the house for the kids they would have so Claris bought a house from homesteaders who were leaving. He put it on runners, hitched it to a team of mules to lizard over to his place, and nailed it to his house, giving him five rooms in a string. At one end of the house was the room where the hands ate, at the other was a sitting room for Celestine and in-between were bedrooms for the kids Claris planned to have.

Celestine's skittishness kept her wire-eyed and unbred so Claris moved the cookstove into a separate room so she didn't have to cook in front of the hands. In another room he curtained off a corner for her to bathe and dress. Claris and Olin built a porch outside the sitting room for Celestine's sewing machine where she could sew while watching the kids in the yard.

But there were no kids in the yard. Claris wondered if he should have married a calico queen, one who had been painted long enough she wanted out but not so long she couldn't quit. Celestine was as uncomplaining as a brood cow and as silent, but without result. Her mother came to see him. Celestine stared at her lap and colored up but didn't say anything while Genevieve laid out a woman's particulars. Claris colored at that—sounded to him like they wanted to be pets instead of hands. He said he needed sons now so that in ten, twelve years he'd have help and asked her to ride over the trail again.

"Some women aren't made to have children; I think Celestine may be one of them," Genevieve said. Hell of a time to tell him that. "I gave my husband a child because he demanded one, but I demanded that there not be another one, and I devoted my life to the one child God gave me." That confirmed the rumors Claris had heard in town, that when Celestine was born, Genevieve told Olin she had churned her butter.

Men laughed about it sometimes; said what they would do. Send Genevieve back to her folks and the kid with her. Throw her down on the bed and teach her what a woman was for. Take her to church and let the preacher tell her a woman's duty. Buy her a dress and not let her leave the house until she showed appreciation. Slap her until she softened up like a woman was supposed to.

When Genevieve left, Celestine raised her eyes and looked at him. It was the look of a scared dog—don't kick me anymore. He went outside, jumped on a horse and nearly rode it to death trying to pound the rage out of his head. She married him. She took his bed. What did she expect?

Claris didn't go to church—too far and no time. But when he could, he read and the only thing he had to read was the family Bible. The Bible seemed very real to him. He knew why David sang. He understood why Lot's wife looked back. He sensed how Isaac sported with Rebekah. When Sarah didn't give Abraham a son, he used a handmaiden. But then Sarah got pregnant and Abraham ended up with a brush baby.

On his horse or on his blanket under the stars, he felt as close to God as any preacher, as any pope in Rome. Now he had a roof, a wife, and a busted cinch and he was eating gravel while the gate closed.

He had never been unkind or unforgiving to Celestine. A woman without fortitude was like a man without courage, more to be pitied than shamed. He would no more divorce Celestine than he would cut his stake rope and leave the ranch. But what if he never had a son?

He walked the horse back to the barn, unsaddled, turned the horse loose and faced the house. Either she was his wife or she was her mother's daughter and she was going to have to choose. He led her away from the sewing machine where she was making him a shirt, took her to the bedroom, petted and played with her like a puppy, and stroked her like a favorite horse.

She was frightened when he finished, not by him but by herself, like she had discovered something in herself she couldn't gather. For days she acted ashamed in front of him, but when she found she was pregnant she became tender. She teased him sometimes, calling him "Papa." But it was in the morning when he was saddled with a day's work in his head. Never at night when it would have mattered.

Even pregnant, Celestine looked poorly. Claris bought a goat from a farmer who sold his crops in the field and headed for a big cotton pick. Genevieve moved with Celestine into the curtained room, milked the goat, made soups and puddings for Celestine, and cooked for Claris's hands. Olin had to hire a cook for his ranch. Claris put old horseshoes in a bucket of water and every day he gave Celestine a sip to put iron in her blood.

When Celestine didn't get stronger, Genevieve took her to her home. Claris didn't go with her because it was the best part of a day by wagon and he had to go back to cooking for his hands. When her time came, the baby, a girl, came hard. Genevieve planted the umbilical cord under a rose bush so the baby would have a rosy complexion. When Claris went in to see her, Celestine would not look at him. "Don't fret yourself," he comforted her. "We still have time for boys."

Celestine said she wasn't bound to go with him yet. Hell, he understood that. This time his father-in-law talked to him. "Celestine was raised by her mother," he said. "Genevieve kept her in the house reading, taught her the finer things—cooking, canning, sewing. She don't know much about animal matters, coming in season and all that. That was a shock to her. She's real proud of her daughter, wants to name her Clarista, after you. But, as for having boys, she might not be up to that."

What the hell was he supposed to do? He went back to his ranch alone. He rode over to his father-in-law's when he could, every week or so, to see his wife and daughter. Celestine was a long time coming home. When she did come home, Olin carried her inside and Genevieve brought in a new but narrow bed. "She has to rest, get her strength back," she said, giving him a hard look. "I'll stay with her for a week or so, see that you have something to eat and clothes to wear. But you can't go back to treating her like she was a brood mare. You'll kill that poor girl."

Genevieve went home a month later, after hanging cedar branches in the house to freshen the air. Celestine stayed mostly in her room playing with Clarista. She cooked and washed and kept house, but when he was in it, she was skulky like a coyote around a garbage pit, not wanting to leave but afraid to get close.

He wasn't going to have any sons. It took some doing but Claris settled his mind on that. Clarista was going to have to be the son he wanted. The first time he took her to see the cows, she laughed and clapped her hands, but it was the horses she loved. Claris put her in the saddle with him whenever he could.

Claris was riding on the Three Crosses looking for stray cattle when he saw a boy, a couple of years younger than Clarista, sitting on a pile of corn to keep crows out of it. He was pug-nosed and ugly, but Claris would have traded a herd of cows for him, maybe even a pasture. Claris spurred his horse into a lope.

When Clarista was four, he found her eating dirt. "You'll get your craw full of this land soon enough," he said, wiping her mouth.

When Clarista was seven, she was running hot irons to the branding crew when a cow made a run at the backs of the men kneeling on the ground holding its bawling calf. Clarista ran in front of the cow to turn it back. Claris spurred his horse to reach her before the cow hooked her, but Rista stood her ground. The cow tossed its horns and turned away. Claris reined up, proud and scared at the same time. He could have lost his only heir. "Don't never get between a cow and its calf," he scolded her. He trimmed the brim of his Stetson so she could see out from under it and had Celestine sew cotton stuffing inside so it would sit on her head.

When Clarista was eight she rode with the hands and when their work was done helped her mother. She carried food from the kitchen to the table where the hands ate. She helped with the cooking when Celestine was weak or dizzy. Clarista ate with the hands, washed their dishes, and ran to the corral to catch and saddle a horse and ride after the men who didn't wait for her.

When she was ten, Genevieve and Celestine explained that Clarista could lose her maiden pledge astride a saddle and the man she loved might leave her on her wedding night when he discovered she lacked the essential evidence. A fall on a horse could alter her insides so that she could never be a mother. Clarista wanted to be a wife and mother some day but that day seemed a long lope and a wide loop away so she continued to ride with the hands. She had sooner sleep with a skunk than be useless.

When Clarista was twelve, Claris had to pay $60 for 500 pounds of hay and got only $30 for a beef. Congress had erected tariffs after The Great War to protect American business from foreign competition. Prices for everything Claris needed soared but cattle prices fell as other countries stopped importing beef in retaliation for the tariffs.

Claris had to give away an old mare because he couldn't sell her. He couldn't pay the note at the bank so the bank wrote a new loan and kept the $200 he had paid on the old loan. When he tried to borrow money to pay for extra hands during calving season the banker told him to postpone calving season.

During a drought Claris rode up on Clarista skinning a cow. When a cow died, she skinned it and Claris sold the hide for 16¢ a pound. Claris got off his horse to wave the flies from her face while she worked. "You got the land in you, haven't you, girl? I hope I can hang on to it long enough to leave it to you."

Clarista was fourteen when her grandfather Olin got sick. She looked after his windmills and cows and passed his orders to his cowboys. When he died, Genevieve came to take care of Celestine and cook for Claris's hands. Claris and Clarista rode over to her grandfather's place. Claris opened the wire gap into her grandfather's pasture but caught her horse's bridle before she passed through.

"This place belongs to your grandma now," Claris said. "Someday it'll belong to your mother and then to you. If you can hang on to it so your grandma don't feel she has to sell it. It's yours to run if you want it; I don't have time for it. It'll give you your life or it'll take it. Set your mind to that if you want it."

Clarista jumped off her horse and gave Claris a hug, the first hug he remembered since she was a child. Then she sprang on her horse, howled like a coyote and raced into her future, fanning the horse with her hat.

Claris watched her ride—tall, confident, and full of sand. Mindful of what he had tied her to, he closed the gap behind her not entirely happy with what he had done. 🌼

An excerpt from an unpublished novel, *Tie-Fast Country*

BYPASS

by Dunya McCammon Bean

I hated making the trip, getting out of the trailer, and turning off the television. Going over there. Hardly seemed worth the effort. Look at this place, the VCR on top of the TV on top of that old record player Mama left us, which we never use, squashed in between the chairs from the big dining room table. I didn't want them, but neither did Sandra. She took the table but it wouldn't fit in here anyway. Okay, I'm getting too worked up. The doctor said to breathe. Slowly. Slowly.

Yeah, and I had to watch the cost of gas. The pickup really ate it up, even with the little discount Exxon gave us. It was a ways to Wal-Mart. But heck, last night at supper, that Billy, was giving me hell.

"Sammie Jo, this place is a mess. You've got to get organized. Go in to Wal-Mart tomorrow and get some stuff. I need some things. You sure need to clean up here. And now." But then he drifted off. He was on his second helping of mashed potatoes. He said no one made them like I did, from scratch. I mean, they're just mashed potatoes, but with milk and butter, an onion cooked with them while they boiled. Martha Stewart had never made it to LaGrange and never would, even though I think I read somewhere she's Polish. But we're mostly Czechs here. Anyway. Where was I? The trailer got so hot when I cooked, which was fine in the winter; the wind blew right through these walls. Of course you couldn't cook all the time to warm up. And in the summer, the windows were too high, most of them, or too small to let a breeze through, and boy, we ran that electricity bill way up there. I could stand the cold, but not the heat. Neither could Billy. It was so close in here. We kept that air conditioner on high during the worst months. Out here, it got to be a hundred degrees sometimes, the humidity always high. I think it was because we were closer to the lake.

In the country, where the living was supposed to be cheap, you paid more for electricity than in the city. If you thought about it, it made sense, like the damn big so-called discount stories. And the gas stations that have ten bays, no service at all. Not like Billy's daddy, Earl, always gave you. It's volume, that's all that counted. Cities used more electricity. Stringing up a line out to us cost more.

When I was little, Daddy took me with him. He always went to the same filling station. He and Earl and the other men talked. Mama would go there too. She said the bathrooms were clean, and they were. We're all Germans, or Czechs, like I said, and Bohemians around here, but it wasn't just clean bathrooms. You walked in and got Tom's peanuts from the stand, a wire contraption, not a damn machine, and a Coke, in a bottle, held it against your head, and it cooled you off, while the men talked. I looked at their hair, short and shiny, like pig's bristles. The men always enjoyed themselves, just killing time. Which there was then. Why was that?

Now the filling stations are like truck stops, just pull in and do it all yourself. Nobody talks to anyone. It's worse in the cities, where there's just a person in a booth, waiting to get shot. It's all about volume, being bigger. Everybody is in a hurry.

"You know I don't like to go to that place," I said. "You think these potatoes came from a mix?" I got up from the little nook, pushing by him. We bought this when we were young. The salesman sure never said trailers were for the young and slim. Now, I'm a damn sixteen. I was a ten, then a twelve. And Billy? Extra large didn't describe him. But it was that belly, like all the other men around here. It was almost a joke, their bellies, full of beer, bread, chicken fried steak. I just couldn't believe we were still here. It made me sick. The kids were mostly grown. Kimberley would be gone soon, and I can't say I was sorry. There wasn't room, between us and all the junk in this place; I couldn't breathe, it was dark in here.

"House," I snorted. "You call this a house. I never thought I'd end up like this, that's for damn sure, Billy Pfiefl. Fearful every time the wind blows, the storms come, with us on this damn hill. No one intended for these things to be lived in. They're chicken coops, sardine tins, whatever the hell. I hate it."

"You're crazy, people live in 'em all over the country." He glared at me. I didn't care. He just didn't see it the way I did. His daddy and mother were good people; they just weren't like mine. We had moved here temporarily, after I had Kimberley, and we were so young. A stream was down the hill from where Billy parked it.

"People who don't know better. Poor people. When are we going to move back to town like you promised me, promised me every year when school started and the girls brought their friends 'home.'" I was yelling. "I swear to god, I hate this place, now Kimberley's in high school, it's all over, we've all survived the chicken coop, but I tell you what, Billy Pfiefl, I didn't sign on for living like this, I just did not." I scooped the potatoes out of the pan, swiping a finger full to my mouth before putting them in a bowl, and banged the pan on the counter. My eyes were faucets, then my nose. I swiped my sleeve across my eyes and looked over at Billy. He just sat there. Sometimes I think I could kill him. Or that I'll leave him. And do what. "Turn that damn television off and listen to me. Twelve years, twelve years of sitting on top of each other just like chickens in a goddam henhouse, like my old grandmother's, and it's enough. Do you hear me?"

"That's enough, Sammie Jo, dammit," he shook his finger at me like he did when he got mad, when I had him. He pushed up from the table and slammed the door on the way out. The house rattled even though it was solid on the foundation. I was going to have to do something. What'd they call these things—not Airstreams, those were the ones that looked like blimps on the highways. These were made in Midlothian. Oh hell. But what could we do? Since the highway bypass opened up in '85, the filling station just wasn't doing any business. It was in the middle of town and had done a bang up business. Until that bypass. Who would have thought the world would change like it did? It made Billy crazy, day after day, scratching out a living. In his defense, there's no way he could've known how things would change, one thing after the other. No one had any control over these things. His sister got their parents' house and Mama sold ours after Daddy died. And my sister Sandra lived in Dallas and said she would never move back here, she didn't want to be buried here, she was gone, in another world. Like dead. Damn. Nothing stayed the same anymore. After you grew up.

I hated the way the cemetery looked when I went to plant flowers or clean up around the graves. Daddy's stone was pink granite from Llano. Mama liked the pink and said she liked getting the last word in. All the newer graves in the part where there weren't trees had plastic flowers on them, but still not as many as in the really new cemeteries outside of town. These were like subdivisions. I talked to the people who ran the cemetery. I tried to get the school to get the kids to have a history project to clean up the old graves and statues, and find out the history of some of the old-timers, but no one was interested in that. Still, now there was a center for Czech studies in town over at the old jail and maybe they would do something, old Mrs. Malina told me. I think she died.

Our so-called home was right close by the Swertners' egg place, only we were closer to the lake. The boat my family had used for water skiing was replaced with Billy's bass boat. He tied it up to a mesquite tree, checked on his trot line and brought catfish home. I liked catfish a lot, with cole slaw and fresh french fries; that was as good as it got in the summer. I planted tomatoes, parsley, squash, and watermelon grew like weeds, and we even had our own peach trees. Billy built one of those trellis-like things, oh what's the name, with a table and bench underneath to sit on. We sat there at night from spring until even when it was just too damn hot, but I liked that, drinking wine or beer with all my good fresh things and the catfish, rolled in cornmeal and fried. I loved the sounds of the cicadas, that summer sound, and watching the sky for thunderstorms. But that damn trailer. It was too hot to keep the windows open, and they were too high, you got no breeze, and thunderstorms scared the hell out of me. Tornados honed in on trailers. It was a matter of time before the odds got you.

It was one of those strange twists, to me, that the Swertners' house was close by, reminding me what a real house was, like the one in town I grew up in. A row of poplars went all the way up to the front in a straight line right up to the square dark red brick house. The doors and windows were trimmed in white paint, with little tulip designs on them. Mrs. Swertner was a strict Lutheran, from what Jerry had told me. As far as I could tell from when we'd first moved the trailer to this piece of land Earl owned, and driven by their place just any number of times, they weren't into sitting on the porch, or in the yard. I never saw anyone outside.

Earl's friend had given him some hot news about the oil play, some guy at the station where all the news of the world arrived like a newspaper daily via truck drivers and big shots. The big shots liked to stop by after eating down at the La Grange Lounge where the biscuits, bacon and bread were all homemade.

Sam Sheubert. That was his name. He had said there was going to be an oil play there and Earl put a lot on money on it. The whole Austin Chalk or Gittings play just never made it. What did Earl know about geology, anyway, I asked Billy, but Billy was sure it was going to be a big play, too. Lawyers and doctors from Austin and Houston were investing. Earl. He thought because he'd made some money, he could be a big player. It's easy to think that when you've got a few extra bucks. And when you're young, too, you're pretty bulletproof, not that Earl was young. It seems like that Sheubert man now that I think about it was a friend of Daddy's. No. That couldn't be. He had a big Lincoln, like LBJ's, and took me home one afternoon. From Where? He was good looking. Why was I in his car?

The Swertner's place had been closed down for a while now. Jerry and his brother hadn't stayed on the place. Jerry was doing research for Purina, I think it was. He'd grown up to be a big, ugly man, but he had loved the farm, the chickens and eggs they delivered to everyone.

We lived in town, then, in a house with white wood, sort of Victorian looking. Mama always wanted a brick house, but I loved our house. It had a porch in front, with big trees around it, and one of those cellars in the back for tornadoes. It was so big. It's not just remembering things from when you were a child, and they aren't that big. I drive by it now, sometimes, when I go over to the Sonic to get a limeade. That's all I'll get there. Marilyn Bingham runs it now. Then I drive to the streets I knew, over to Dallas, or Austin, or Peach and Pecan, to our house. 319 Peach. The Swertner's left the eggs on the smaller back porch, off the kitchen. I had my own room and Sandra hers. There was a big kitchen, because Mama loved to cook. I would perch on a window seat on the second floor where I read and look at the big pecan trees in the back. Mr. Swertner and Jerry would holler at me to go out and say hi. Sandra was too snobby, even when she was a kid. She was a cheerleader and never did anything except with her friends.

"How many today, Mrs. Berry," Mr. Swertner said, in his thick accent. Jerry was so shy and tall and skinny like I was, with that long face of his. I just wondered what he was like, and tried to get him to talk. He didn't until we were almost in junior high, when he mumbled to me one day at school. Robert E. Lee Junior High. I don't know why they named it that. Germans didn't like the Rebels; they were for the Union. I think it was Ginger Brask's mama from Virginia who was on the school board who did it. Ginger's daddy was a doctor and they had a lot of money until he got TB. Then no one would talk to them. Her mama smiled a lot which I thought had to do with her being a Southerner but Mama never trusted all that smiling. She was the first alcoholic I knew, now, thinking about it. But she taught us to make place mats in Girl Scouts and fill paper bags with sand with places cut out. These were for Xmas. You put a candle in the sack and lined up the sacks. You could put them on your walk, or a fence, if you had a fence that was wide enough. This was before they were in magazines.

Anyway, I get lost. Jerry mumbled to me one day, something about getting together. "Uh, Sammie Jo, do you think." But the bell rang. We were both getting really tall. I played basketball; he asked me about my game, finally.

"I like watching you play, Sammie Jo, you play fast and smart," he said. I would see him up in the stands, up by himself, not with the popular bunch, he always kept to himself. The LaGrange Buzzards played real good and the town supported us. That was the good part about being a 3A school district. We were best in our district three years running. It was the best time of my life. Ginger moved to San Angelo because they had a better and bigger school and her mama had met some banker. We were the biggest girls in school and the boys were too short. Almost all of them. Ginger got wild, smoking and going out with a guy who worked in town. I miss her still.

One night after a game Jerry was standing at the door to the gym when I came out. He asked me if I wanted to get a coke or something. I said sure. I ran to his car, wondering what I was doing. Daddy had given me the Impala that night. I left it in the parking lot. I told Jerry let's go somewhere quiet, not the regular place everyone goes after the games, and we went to a little park close to the river. Jerry drank his coke and turned to me and we started kissing. For an ugly boy, he kissed great. I was surprised, and didn't want to stop and then he said he had to get me back to my car. It was getting late. I was wet.

And then he left for Texas A&M. I found out I was pregnant. I can't remember if it was after the Chuck Berry concert in Houston, or after Billy got on the All-State team, but it was a done deal. I was pregnant. What a dancer Billy was. Like that really counts. It's actually life-threatening to be seventeen and stupid. Boys drive too fast and girls get pregnant.

I saw Jerry once after that at the Dairy Queen. Maybe it was Easter. I had just had Tiffany, and I could see him looking at me. I wondered what a college boy knew, how much money he made, that kind of thing. I got up from the booth behind where Billy and the guys were sitting and went to the counter like I was going to get a refill.

I walked over to him. "Hi." He was sitting in a booth and I sat down. I was surprised how glad I was to see him. "What are you studying at A&M? How are you?" I felt hot. I was a mother and married and he was ugly but something had propelled me into this booth. Some force.

"Agronomy," he said, swooping his head down, after looking at me in a sweet way. He looked sort of like a vulture, a big bird, with his stooped shoulders, big nose and dark hair. He actually reminded me of that movie star, the one who was in THE FLY. I can't think of his name right now. The ugly had become kind of what, masculine.

"What," I said, taking a sip of my root beer. I was facing Jerry with my back to Billy. "Astronomy? That's cool." He stared back at me as we looked at each other. His eyes were dark brown, soft.

"No," he said real quiet, "it's not the study of stars. It's the study of dirt. Agronomy." He said it slowly, still looking in my eyes. He was eating some cone, the one with the chocolate swirl, and he put it down. I thought it would melt but he just kept looking at me. I heard Billy, then, that damn Billy, laughing. Billy, and his football player friends, mostly that stupid

Ronnie Cooper. Ronnie had noticed. They started laughing and making cluck-clucking noises.

"You look good, Sammie Jo, you really do. I've got to go. Take care." He reached across and took my hand and stroked it, and looked at my wedding ring, and put it down. He left quickly, and got in his pickup.

"Look, he's driving a baby Toyota pickup, what a dumb-ass," Ronnie yelled, and they laughed.

Ronnie died that summer in a car wreck. He and Nita had been dancing at the old place on the Plum highway, I can't think of the name of it; Billy and I went there all the time, too. They'd crashed into another car on the way back. Ronnie was drunk, I bet, and Nita too, probably. We all drank like hell. I can't believe more of us aren't dead. We covered a lot of territory, driving in cars, getting beer, or Tequila, or whatever, drinking, necking, in the woods. The freedom away from your parents, from town, church, your friends, was pretty heady when you were young. In the car, with Billy, it was an excitement like me running on the slick floor of the court, back and forth, all you heard was that squeaking and your own voice grunting and the other girls calling passes, yelling at you. Billy's hands and tongue went all over me, how much noise we made, the noise, the way he felt, always ready to do it, I just had to touch it, in the front seat the back seat in cold weather or hot.

The funeral had been a big one, one of the first I'd ever been to. All the girls cried because Nita and Ronnie were going to get married. I was already married and had a baby. I didn't cry. And then at the cemetery, one of those new ones, the boys were crying too. Even Billy was snuffling, his eyes red. Ronnie and he were best friends, they'd gone to Mexico together all the time, getting drunk and crazy, and then all the girls let those yellow and black balloons go up in the air. That's when I started crying.

Mama liked Mr. Swertner's eggs; the yolks were fresh, not like in the stores. None of it made any difference to Daddy. He never went to the store, and he always said to Mama, anyway, just to dig it in, it was easier and cheaper in the stores, that she just liked Mr. Swertner. He liked to dig it in to her when he could.

"No, phooey, Sammie Jo," Mama said, "we know what's good, don't we. It's good for our hair, and our skin, and it tastes better. You can tell, Sammie Jo, by looking at the color of the yolks. Mr. Swertner says the yellow's the color of churches in Bohemia. Isn't that something? I bet they're real pretty." She ignored Daddy.

And she smiled at me, but Daddy really didn't notice. He smiled in his office. When I went to the office with him, he smiled at everyone, and in town when we walked around, and especially at church, where the men all looked like Christmas tree ornaments, their heads glistening, pink domes with brown or black hair around them, or, if they had hair, it was slicked up. Stuffed in their khakis or whatever they wore during the week, eating breakfast at home, or at cafes in town, homemade bread, or biscuits, sausage, eggs, and huge lunches at the restaurant, the Bon Ton, the one with the first salad bar, it didn't take long for them to get big. At church, ours was the Methodist, with Eugene Hill, who Daddy thought was too fancy for his own good as he'd been to seminary in Dallas, or the office, Daddy wore a suit. He was a businessman. He didn't look as fat in his suit, and the men smiled at each other in church, but not the same way as at the filling station or in the eating places.

"Yeah, this is my little girl," he'd say, proud to take me along. "Jack, where'd Sammie Jo get that height," they'd holler, when I was older. Until I played basketball, they never paid me much attention.

"Gene, you need to up that insurance on your equipment. And I've got some new life insurance that's a damn good deal." Germans, Czechs and Bohemians were all big savers; they bought insurance and Daddy said they were always on time, never any trouble. It was a one-man operation, and he and Nita's mother, Mrs. Callan, ran it.

Mama had lived on a farm as a girl, and loved freshness, but not the farm life. "They have the best farms, those Bohemians," she said, to underline her knowledge of these things. "Yeah, my daddy always said they knew where to get the best land, along the rivers, streams. And they had their co-ops, their customs from the old country," she'd say, like she was in a play, leaning her head at Daddy, raising her eyebrows. Some people called them "bohunks," but Mama sure liked them. They had festivals in the spring and fall at their churches and when I was a little girl we'd go and dance and

Mama and Daddy would drink beer and eat fresh corn and laugh and Sandra and I would fall asleep on the chairs on the dance hall, the music playing around us.

Most of the time, Daddy paid no attention to Mama. He read the *San Angelo Standard Times* out loud to her, which he knew she hated, or the sports page, or he watched sports on television, that and "What's My Line?" Daddy got real big, he ate just like a man who worked in the country. Mama told him he'd blow up like a balloon and burst. "Jack, if you ate more cabbage like the Bohemians, it'd cut some of that bloat out of you." He glowered at her when she said that.

Well, that was a long time ago. Daddy did die of a heart attack, massive, and then Mama got itchy. She sold the business to Mrs. Callan, for not much, and now of course, she's doing real well. That eats at me. A lot. And then she sold the house, too. She had to get out of there, she said, that little place. She took off for New Mexico. She grows chiles and alfalfa, and says she couldn't be happier. She lives in an adobe place that is pretty primitive, in this little town close to Cloudcroft, Tularosa. Why in the world would you do that, I ask her, when we talk long distance, live so far away from your kids and grandkids? Freedom, she says, it's freedom. She goes to the racetrack in Ruidoso. In fact, sells her alfalfa to the horse trainers. Mama at the track. I kind of like it, like Bill Clinton's mama did. It was better than sitting at home, going to the beauty parlor once a week, then church, the same old thing, week after week, month after month, year after year, until you just dropped dead.

Now what was I going to get at Wal-Mart? That's what happens when I get on this old road, the familiar one, down where we'd go swimming, swinging out on an inner tube from the big tree, right by the side of the Concho Inn, the water so cold and clear. Spring fed. Runs into the Colorado. Into the Gulf. Jerry told me that. It was dammed up there, and everyone hung out below the causeway. Mexicans washed their cars, smiling up, as we'd drive by. I always go this way. I'm getting lost now in my thoughts. Billy tells me I'm getting Alzheimer's. He has it too, then, because we both stare off. Billy just won't talk about it. You get into a trance when you watch those stupid shows on television and then you're back in your own show, remembering those days long ago when you were a kid before you had kids. Seems like that lasted five minutes. Five minutes out of how long, that's what I wondered.

Okay, paper clips. The big ones. Don't forget, Sammie Jo, for his clippings, or invoices. The shower curtain was ratty. I'll look at those. Billy took care of us, he did, he did the best he could, but there was never any money. We'd spent all Daddy left on raising the kids, until we had to sell the house in town. Billy had to keep the filling station.

I liked my pickup, the way you could see everything happening on the road, and the radio was good. Billy put in a cassette player so I could play it when I was out of range of a station. "Can you see the tears standing, I know you understand, when you open up your eyes . . . I'm beaming you all this life." What a voice, who is that? I turned up the volume. I liked to blast it when I was alone. "Today we've got Jane Sibery in the studio with us. Jane, what was the name of that song." The disc jockey had a voice from the city where they played the good stuff. You could get Austin or Houston, depending on where you were. Jane said, real clear, "The Gospel According to Darkness." Where was the station? I had to stop the car, tears streamed from my eyes. Dammit, where was the Kleenex, never had any, that's why I loved these denim shirts, just like the guys, I wiped my eyes with the tail of my shirt. I bet it was Austin. Sometimes on clear days, you could get that here in LaGrange, and Houston didn't have this program, with this funny guy who played stuff you didn't hear otherwise. I recognized his voice now. I was up high, here where the 71 gets on the big highway, Interstate 10, close to the power plant, shooting out spumes every day. Half the town worked there now. It was a sweet deal, they said. The coal came in from Wyoming. I didn't understand that. The sky looked green, but the spooky part was the gray, pointed yet feathery look, to some of the clouds. I'd seen that look before. Of course. Who hadn't living here. And the air was still. Maybe that's why I was feeling so restless. Tornados or premenstrual. Or menopause. People had heart attacks before the weather changed. Anything could make me go over the edge, I thought, right now. I wanted to take off.

Heck, it felt so good to cry. How long had it been since a song got me like that? I better write her name down. I wish I could go to a bar like a man, hear some songs, not as good as this one, but close, and just belt back a few until I felt better. What was I going to get at Wal-Mart again? I spent too much money in that damn place, saving a nickel, spending fifty bucks or so on junk. That's all it was. I hated it. We had to get out of the trailer. Sheets? Spring-cleaning. What for, really? Even with Kimberley gone, the trailer was too small.

It took everything out of me to go into this place. Sammie Jo pulled into the parking lot, half full even at this time of day. Where did all these people come from? It irked her big time that people didn't see what was going on and it was right under their noses. Big chains, low paying jobs, no benefits, but you couldn't preach if you didn't have an audience.

Inside, the size of the damn thing hit Sammie Jo again. It was just like a big trailer, or a barn, but it didn't feel good. Big machines came at you, guys driving them like the men who drove those stupid monster trucks. Rodeos used to be a challenge: a man and an animal, but the animal rights people screamed about that. But monster trucks? How did that come about? There was Bertha Smiley. Who could miss her for god's sake? She was over at a card table with some electric skillet with sausage in it, spearing sausage cubes and asking everyone who walked by if they wanted to taste. For what, five bucks an hour? Didn't they get it?

"Sammie Jo, come on over here and have a bite, it's yum-yummy, almost as good as the old Bon Ton's," Bertha hollered. I shook my head and waved at her. I had a tight feeling in my chest. I headed for the closest aisle. I almost bumped into a cart, the thing full to the top with huge cans of Crisco, soap, paper towels, stacks of flour tortillas, white bread, paper plates, as high as the cart. People had the idea this was saving them money. The woman frowned at me as the two of us veered away from each other.

What did Billy want? Paper clips? Poor old Mr. Cooper, Ronnie's father, he'd had to sell his downtown printing and office place, what with computers, because of this place. But I wouldn't go there just for paper clips. There wasn't any business. How Zeke Zapalac kept his store open, I had no idea. There was some new money in town, and he's started selling fancy sports things. Still, no one went into town, except Billy, the judges, the police, Mary Lou, who worked for old Judge Richter, the bailiff, the café kept opening and closing, it wasn't going to make it, everyone went to the Dairy Queen. Lard and air whipped together. I'd liked it once. Now, only in desperation. I had to make changes.

I can't believe I'm in here. What the hell for? I'm not getting one more thing for that damn trailer. I'm going to start a boycott on Wal-Mart. I read about a town in Vermont that did it. I'm going to see Billy now, get down to that filling station. Tell him. We're getting out of here. I'm getting out of here or I'll explode.

I ran out looking for my pickup. The sky looked really bad now, the stillness like watching a movie, with me in it. That sky was now a sickening yellow-green. Should I go into town and tell Billy we had to leave? Before it was too late? If I could make it home before we were hit, what would I save?

I turned on the radio and it crackled. I bowed my head on the steering wheel. ✿

MISTER TYRONE

by Lionel G. Garcia

Tyrone and his mother could see the huge articulated Metro bus from half a mile away making its way through the traffic, its top sticking above the rest of the vehicles. They could see the hot air blowing around it creating heat waves, distorting its shape. As it got closer they could hear the engine roar from a stop, spewing out black fumes. Slowly it came. Tyrone was at the curb leaning into the street. His mother asked him to come sit by her, but he ignored her and began to run around the bus stop. He was shooting an imaginary pistol. Several people sitting with his mother were uncomfortable with his running and his mother sensed this and she got up and brought him by the arm and sat him down. He could hear the bus getting closer. A few more stops and it would arrive. Driving it would be his friend Gatemouth. He became excited and started to fidget. His mother squeezed his thigh and looked sternly at him.

"You behave like a man," she said.

Tyrone saw the other passengers staring at him and he lowered his eyes and said, "Yes, ma'am."

"Don't be doin' any foolishness on the bus. You hear? Don't be actin' the foo'."

His embarrassment grew even worse. It seemed all eyes were on him. "Yes," he answered.

"Yes, what?"

"Yes, Ma'am."

"Don't be yessin' me. And don't be askin' Gatemouth for anythin', you hear?"

"Yes, ma'am."

"If I hear you acted crazy I'm agoin' to whup you and whup you good. You hear me?"

"Yes, ma'am."

"Where's you books?"

"I forgot 'em."

"Bof'um?"

"Yes, ma'am. Bof'um."

"Boy, I ought to whup you right here in front of all these people."

"I forgot."

"Forgot. Don't give me that story. You didn't bring it 'cause you didn't want to. You did that on purpose, Tyrone."

"No, I didn't. I forgot."

"Be quiet. I'll deal with you when we get home."

Tyrone leaned forward to get a better view of the street and he saw the bus one stop away. He was dangling his feet off the bench. He tried not to look at the others. For some reason he became very self-conscious. He began to squirm and he placed his locked hands between his legs to keep from fidgeting, but his feet began to swing. His mother reached over and squeezed his thigh again.

"Chile'? You act like you got worms," she said. "You got worms or something?"

"No, ma'am," said Tyrone.

"Well, then sit still."

He could see out of the corner of his eye that the white man sitting next to him was staring at him and his mother.

His mother said, trying to please the man, "Don't be squirmin'. Sit still. You're botherin' the gentleman next to you."

"Yes, ma'am," Tyrone said. He looked at the man sitting next to him and the man quickly looked away.

The bus was on its way on their block. Tyrone could see it rocking along, Gatemouth behind the wheel.

"Don't be askin' Gatemouth for a hamburger either," his mother said. "He told me he bought you a hamburger last night. Don't be askin' for food. You got plenty of food at home."

"Yes, ma'am," said Tyrone.

"Yes, ma'am," his mother said, mimicking him. "That's all I hear from you. But you go ahead and do it anyway, don't you? Acting the foo'."

"Yes, ma'am," Tyrone said.

"Now here comes the bus and don't let me hear anythin' from Gatemouth about you e'cept what a good chile' you been."

"Yes, ma'am."

"Study in your head since you don't have no books. . . . Forgot your books. You know you is lying."

"Yes, ma'am," said Tyrone.

The bus stopped in front of Tyrone. His mother let everyone else on first and then took Tyrone by the hand and helped him up the stairs. Gatemouth was grinning at Tyrone. Tyrone was happy to see him.

"Tyrone," said Gatemouth, showing his large white teeth, "I do think you've grown an inch since I saw you last night. Man o' man. Whoeeee. Jessie, that Tyrone is growing fast. Like a weed. Pretty soon he's going to be playing for the Rockets. I do declare."

"Say hello to Mr. Jackson, Tyrone," his mother said putting the tokens in the slot.

"Hello, Gatemouth," Tyrone said.

"Mr. Jackson to you," said his mother, pulling on Tyrone's hand.

"Mr. Jackson," said Tyrone.

"Ah, he can call me Gatemouth," said Gatemouth. "Everybody else does."

"He's got to learn to respect his elders," Tyrone's mother said.

Gatemouth winked at Tyrone and Tyrone and his mother took the seat behind the driver. Gatemouth looked into the rear view mirror and waited for the traffic to clear. He pulled the bus off the curb. The bus swayed to one side and then leveled off. Tyrone could hear the roar of the huge rear engine.

Tyrone's mother leaned over to Gatemouth and said, "Don't be buyin' Tyrone no hamburgers, you hear? He's got food at home."

Tyrone looked to see if any of the other passengers had heard his mother. No one had heard and this relieved him. But he became self-conscious again, felt a flush come over his face, and he placed his little hands inside his thighs and began to swing his feet again. His mother squeezed his thigh and made him stop. She said, "I don't want any son of mine beggin' in the streets for food, you understan'?"

"Oh, Tyrone's not beggin'," said Gatemouth, his eyes fixed on the traffic around him. "I was hungry and I stopped for a hamburger. I bought one for Tyrone too. Right, Tyrone?"

"Yes, sir."

"Well, don't be buyin' 'im any hamburger. He eats at home."

"Whatever you say," said Gatemouth.

The ride down South Main took twenty minutes. During this time Tyrone knelt at the window and looked out at the traffic, at the scenery on the way. Some day, he thought, he would come to Hermann Park and the Museum of Natural History and the Planetarium and the Zoo. Every day he admired the great hotels, the water fountains, the tree-lined Rice University, the Medical Center. Some days he wanted to be a doctor like the ones he would see in their white coats crossing the street in front of the bus when Gatemouth stopped to pick up and deliver passengers.

Shortly after the Medical Center he could see the difference. The buildings were not as pretty. The streets were not as clean. Farther on down it got worse. This is where his mother would get off and leave him alone with Gatemouth.

Tyrone's mother got up and straightened her dress. She said to Tyrone, "Now, you behave. I don't want to hear any bad things about you in the mornin'. You hear me?"

"Yes, ma'am," said Tyrone. He was looking down at his shoes, not wanting to look at his mother's face. He hated this part because he knew how much he would miss her. But then he would be with Gatemouth.

Gatemouth said, "Don't worry about Mr. Tyrone. He knows exactly how to behave."

His mother shook him by the shoulders and said, "And don't be askin' for no hamburger. You hear, young man?"

Tyrone said, "Yes, ma'am."

"Don't you worry, Jessie," said Gatemouth. "He don't ask for nothin'. He just sits there and he's a perfect little boy. Sure wish my chil'ren behaved like he does."

"Well, I should hope so," said his mother. She reached into her handbag and took out a quarter. She said, "This is for a phone call like I always give you. And like always, Gatemouth is keeping it for you. I expect it back when I see you in the morning, young man. Unless Gatemouth has to call me."

"Yes, ma'am," said Tyrone.

His mother kissed him on top of the head and got off the bus. When she was on the sidewalk, Gatemouth closed the door and took off. Tyrone ran to the opposite side to see his mother through the window. She was standing alone on the sidewalk under the street light pulling her dress down. He saw her take out her lipstick and apply some more on her lips. Tyrone watched her grow smaller in the distance as the bus sped off. She appeared to him as a lonely figure in the darkness lit by the solitary light. He could barely see her when she began to walk slowly toward the Loop.

"Well, there goes your mother," said Gatemouth. He and Tyrone were alone except for a wino who had gotten on the bus at a downtown stop. He too would ride the bus for a long time. "How you doing Tyrone?" Gatemouth asked, watching out for the wino through the rear-view mirror.

"Fine," said Tyrone. He went over across the aisle to sit behind Gatemouth. He was afraid of the wino.

"Whatcha been up to?" Gatemouth asked.

"Nothin'," said Tyrone.

"Did you get to school?"

"Yeah. But I was too sleepy."

"So you didn't learn anything? You just slept?"

"Well, the teacher whupped me upside the head to wake me up, but I was just too sleepy. She said I ain't learnin' nothin'. She wanted to know why I's so sleepy all the time."

"Did you tell her?"

"No, sir. That'd get my mom in trouble. And they take me away like they did before. I don't want to go live with strangers."

"You ought to sleep on the bus, man. There's no sense waitin' up for your mother. She don't get back on the bus till five in the mornin'. It's eight right now. If you go to sleep, by the time we pick up your mom you can sleep. . . . Well, from eight to twelve is four hours. And then five. That makes it nine hours of sleep."

"But I can't sleep on the bus," said Tyrone. "The seats are too lumpy. And the bus moves too much. And there's too much noise."

"Yeah, you're right. But you ought to try to sleep. That way when you and your mom get home you can go to school."

"I don't like school."

"And you want to be a doctor? And you don't like school? Are you crazy? A doctor goes to school most of his life. And then some."

"I don't want to be a doctor now."

"Oh. You changed your mind? What do you want to be?"

"I don't know. Do I have to know?"

"No, you don't have to know. But it helps. If you can have a dream, Tyrone. You need a dream so that you can follow that dream. Make that dream a part of your life."

"What's your dream? To drive a bus?"

"No. That's not a dream. I have a dream."

"I didn't know that. What's your dream?"

"My dream is to play the guitar. That's why they call me Gatemouth. You know the famous guitar player they call Gatemouth Brown?"

"No."

"Well, I do. I heard him play the guitar once and I knew that was what I wanted to do. I wanted to stand up there on the stage and play the guitar just like he did."

"So you play the guitar?"

"No. Not like Gatemouth. Not right now. But I'm learnin'. I play every day come rain or shine. I practice my guitar. That's my dream, Tyrone. When my chil'ren are grown and me and the wife is all alone I'm goin' to set out to play the guitar. I'm goin' to stand on that stage and I'm goin' to play and the people are goin' to come to hear me and they're goin' to love the way I play. I'll be somebody important then."

"You don't think it's important to drive the bus?"

"Oh, no. Anyone can drive a bus. You don't want to do what everyone can do. I tell my chil'ren. Do somethin' no one else can do. Make yourself important. That's what I tell 'em. Im-por-tant."

"Do they listen?"

"No. Just like I didn't listen when I was their age. I suppose bein' young makes you stupid."

"You think I'm stupid?"

"Oh, no, Tyrone. You're smart. But that don't count."

"Why not?"

Gatemouth slowed down at the intersection to see if anyone was waiting. There was no one. The light was green and he looked both ways and then gunned the engine, crossing the intersection.

"Like I was sayin'. Bein' smart don't count. It's livin' smart that counts. I know a lot of smart people in jail and prison. Too smart for their own good. They think they is smarter than the rest of us and they don't have to work. So they sell drugs. Do some pimpin'. . . ."

"Like my mom's boyfriend?"

"Well, forget about that, Tyrone. You're too young to be concerned with that. You shouldn't have to worry about your mama. Let's talk of somethin' else. . . . When we get to the end of the line and turn the bus around, I'm goin' to let you sit on my lap and take the wheel for a little while. Kind of let you get the feel for drivin'. But I don't want you gettin' any ideas about drivin' a bus. You don't want to do that, Tyrone. That's not your dream. You want to be a doctor. Get educated. Make a lot of money. Live in a beautiful big house. You can invite me when I'm old and can't play the guitar anymore. Invite me to your house and I can sit with you and we can drink a cup of coffee out of a fancy cup with a saucer. I'll be proud of you, Tyrone. Mister Tyrone. Drive a fancy car that you own outright. Not like some pushers and pimps who don't even have the down payment and they go around driving Cadillacs and Lincolns. You don't be like them. If I hear that you turned out to be like that, it would break my heart, Tyrone."

"I don't know what I want to be. An astronaut maybe."

"There you go. You can do it, Tyrone. You have the smarts. That's a good dream to have. I wanted my son to have a good dream but look at him. He don't want to go to school. He says, why go to school to wind up drivin' a bus. And when I tell him of my dream, he laughs. They all laugh.

Except me."

"Someday, Gatemouth, I'm goin' to see you on the stage playin' the guitar."

"Me and Gatemouth Brown. The two Gatemouths, they'll call us. I'll be sure to invite you, Tyrone. I sure will. They'll call you Mister Tyrone by then."

On the way back, Tyrone did not see his mother. The wino at the back of the bus began to moan. He was kicking at the seat in front of him and grabbing his sides in pain. Tyrone got up and went to stand by Gatemouth.

Gatemouth reached over with his right arm and held Tyrone close to him. He said, patting Tyrone gently, "Don't be afraid of no wino. He's dying."

Tyrone said, "I don't want to see him. I'm scared."

"Well, keep your eyes lookin' ahead," said Gatemouth. "See? You don't want to wind up bein' no wino."

The wino began to vomit into the aisle and Gatemouth stopped the bus to try to get him off. But the wino clung to his seat with his hands like claws and he wrapped his feet around the base of the seat and refused to be thrown out. Gatemouth was no physical match for him so he gave up. He took some paper towels from under the driver's seat and he cleaned up the vomit as best he could. The wino stayed through the turnaround and staggered off at one of the downtown stops. As he got off he cursed Gatemouth, called him a motherfucking black nigger and Gatemouth said, "I love you too, man." And he shut the door so that the wino could not get back on to hurt him or Tyrone. The wino hit the door with his empty bottle of wine and shouted some more obscenities. He was trying to get the door open to get back in the bus. Gatemouth had to wait for the traffic to clear, but then he pulled out in a roar of exhaust that left the wino gasping for air.

That left Gatemouth and Tyrone and a few night riders until the turnaround at the other end.

At two in the morning they were alone. Gatemouth stopped the bus by the hamburger place and he and Tyrone got off to get something to eat.

"You want your usual hamburger, I suppose?" Gatemouth said.

Tyrone was standing next to him. "And fries," he said.

"And a Coke," said Gatemouth.

They took a seat and Gatemouth said, "You love hamburgers don't you?"

"Yes, sir," said Tyrone, his mouth full. "And fries."

"Well," said Gatemouth, "you have a dream and you make that dream come true and you can have all the hamburgers in the world. You can eat 'em three times a day. Four times a day. But you have to have a dream. Remember that, Tyrone. You have to have a dream. You're nothin' without a dream. . . . My chil'ren make fun of me for sayin' that but I know it's true. I guess I've told them so many times, like I have you, that they don't listen no more."

"I listen."

"Yeah, but you're smart, Tyrone. . . . Where's you books? You haven't cracked your books all night."

"I forgot 'em."

"See, Tyrone. You can't forget your books. Books is knowledge." He reached over the table and hit Tyrone on top of the head with his knuckle. "That's for forgettin' your books. Man, you can't get nowhere without books. You got to study. Promise me you'll study."

"I promise."

"Good. If you don't bring your books, you're goin' to have to watch me eat my hamburger 'cause I ain't buyin' you one ever again. You understan'?"

"Yes, sir."

"Give me your head one more time. Let me hit you one more time."

Tyrone leaned his head across the table and Gatemouth tapped him gently on the head. "That's for forgettin' your books," he said, wagging a long black finger at him.

Going south again, the fog from the Bay began to drift in and obscure the night. They saw Tyrone's mother standing at the corner under the light. She was leaning against the post talking to a man. Her bright red dress shone in the fog that surrounded her like a glistening shroud under the light. Tyrone had seen her first and was at the seat across the aisle by the window. He waved at her as the bus sped by and she waved back. He could see her talking to him and he said, "Yes, ma'am."

"Go to sleep, Mister Tyrone," said Gatemouth, maneuvering the bus through traffic. "Don't think about your mom. You go ahead and dream you some dreams."

Tyrone curled up in the seat behind Gatemouth. He said, resting his little head on his hand, "The wino called you a nigger."

"Somebody's goin' to call you a nigger all the time. You forget about that," said Gatemouth. "You go ahead and dream you some dreams." ✸

GHOST SICKNESS

by Jan Reid

1864

In fourteen moons Nocona lost both his wives and two of his three children. The people expected to provide for those like him in their desolation and grief—but likewise expected them, at some point, to rise up and start their lives again. But the rage and love of war that drove Nocona and brought down his terrible wrath on the Brazos valley was used up, spent. He grew distracted, reflective, and some would say lazy—he wouldn't even hunt for himself. Quanah had to bring him his meat. Nocona put on a paunch.

Quanah was humiliated. He had grown into the tallest man in Nokoni band, and he had the chest and shoulders to go with his height. His dad was a famous war chief, and all across the plains, war parties had white men on the run. But Quanah had never counted coup, never made the fabled ride to Mexico, never put an arrow or bullet in a man. All he'd done was steal a few horses out west one year, from some hungry Navajos. It got boring, just killing buffalo.

And yet he and his dad talked like they never did before. In some ways Quanah liked him more. One summer afternoon the bank was camped along the Canadian River, trailing the herd north. When the sun was low Quanah and Nocona went off with sacks to harvest some plums, especially ripe and tasty along that river. In the bottom they ate the red fruit until their hands and chests were so sticky from juice that they had to go bathe in the river. They reclined on the hard sand bed, letting the shallow stream run past their chins.

"Dad," said Quanah.

"Yeah."

"Tell me about my mother."

Nocona gave him a sidelong glance.

"When she was young. Before we were born."

"Well, you know she was white."

"She was?"

Nocona guffawed. "Didn't you ever look at her?"

"Well, sure. But I thought, you know, somewhere back in the line. . .."

"Near enough to count for your gray eyes."

"Whose eyes?" he said quickly.

Nocona rolled and put his face down, blew bubbles in his mirth. "Oh, son," he said when he surfaced. "Never even looked in a mirror."

"Yeah, I do. Have. They don't look gray to me." Quanah felt this sudden strangeness—in his blood. "Who stole her?" he asked.

"I did."

He gaped at his father. "You married someone you stole?"

"What's more, I did it twice." Nocona's eyes always brimmed with tears at the thought of his chore wife, Ruins a Travois. After a moment he went on. "I was about your age. We were way off southeast, almost to the pines. Mosquito country. We joined up with some Caddos and other trashy peoples. We came on these Tejanos, and all we did was ask them for a beef. Fellow started throwing us looks. That one got killed, one thing led to another. I saw this little girl running. She had on a blue dress, and she had the prettiest yellow hair." Nocona shrugged. "So I gave her a ride on my horse."

"How come I never knew that?"

"Your mother. She just didn't want to talk about it. And people respected that. Her folks and grandfolks loved her, she grew up and married me, and when people realized how she felt, they didn't talk about it either. See, the whites offered a big ransom for her. Soldiers and comancheros used to come around, suspicious that was her. Last it happened, we were on this same river, but way out west. You were a little boy, and the next one was just born. Peace chief got me to let her talk to some hunters. Calling her Cynthia Ann, Cynthia Ann, like that was supposed to be something magic to her. They asked her if she wasn't tired of being a *slave*. She let them get way far-gone before she told me. Your mother was always the first one wanting to move—just be as far away from whites as she could."

Quanah rested on his elbows and watched the current move his breechclout. "Didn't she have a brother?"

"Yeah, Mexico. That was his name, Mexico. Younger than her—we carried him off that same raid. He lived with the Quohadi mostly, and they took the ransom money, sold him back to his Tejano family when he was, I don't know, old enough to chase buffalo. Hated being back there, of course. When he was getting near grown, his white mother sent him out here to try to talk his sister into coming back. Rode all that way by himself, and he found us. She and I were married by then, couldn't get enough of each other. So he just got down off his horse and stayed."

"Mexico made him a mean little son of a bitch, and he liked it so much down there, somebody just named him that. He was along that time I stole the one who made the other wife. Mexico stole one, too, but she wasn't no little girl. That one was a full-grown looker."

"But on the way back he started getting sick. Chills, throwing up, so sore he could hardly ride. Then his face broke out, and there was no question what it was—smallpox. Scared us all to death. Wasn't anything to do but leave him. We did let him keep the looker. Mexico always held that against us, and I'm sorry. But he would have done the same thing."

"About three years after that, he just rode up one day, come to see his sister. Scared us, shamed us all over again. Pocked up pretty good, but other than that, he was fine. We put on quite a dance for him—I'm surprised you don't remember. Asked him what happened, Mexico said he was given back his life by some black-ass Indians live down there. Call them Seminoles. Said they put him in a white man's bathtub and pissed on him Called people all around, women even, to get enough bladders, filled it up, and then built a fire under him Then they broke up some little pepper pods in the bath that stung like he'd fallen in a log of scorpions. But he got well! Talk about medicine."

Watching his dad tell that story, Quanah thought he might make it to the council of elders and smoke lodge after all.

"Last I heard, he's still down there," said Nocona. "Still married to that Mexican looker. I wouldn't know how to find him, but the Quohadi might."

Eventually they got around to picking some more plums. Quanah lost interest first and wandered back toward the lodges, shouldering his sack. In the riverbed Nocona watched him silhouetted against the dusk and thought, Bet those girls get him off and wallow him good. Nocoma picked plums until he was feeling them more than seeing them. A covey of bob-white quail whistled nearby in the grass, then the nighthawks piped up, and a whippoorwill. The evening star materialized in the purple, then to the east, a big growing moon jumped up over the sand.

Raid moon, Mexico moon. The loveliness of that sight filled Nocona with such nostalgia and sadness he had to cry a little. Getting where you enjoy it, he rebuked himself.

As he started back a sound of bulk erupted from a cottonwood, and a great-horned owl, dark as charcoal in the light, beat its heavy wings to stay aloft and crossed the river right in front of him-gave him a terrible fright. Owl was lots of things. Then he heard the footsteps behind him. He walked faster, and they broke into a trot. "Oh, no," Nocona said. Turn around, he told himself. Confront it. But the courage that could save him was a dry well in his heart. He dropped the sack of plums and started running. Overtaken easily, he raised his arms, lurched and staggered from the clouts to his head. They fell like the war club of a Ute. He was on his hands and knees, he realized. And then be blacked out.

In the camp Quanah had given his sack of plums to Weckeah's mother, Nice Enough to Eat. She asked him to join them for their supper of marrow and mesquite bean mush. "How's your dad?" Yellow Bear inquired.

"Seems a lot better," said Quanah.

He hung around until it grew awkward then announced he had to go check on his horses—he owned two head. Every time Quanah started to build a herd, his dad renewed his mourning and gave them all away. Weckeah cleaned up and dawdled until what she was doing was apparent, then excused herself and walked to a sand bar around the river's bend.

Tonight they were just sitting on the sand watching the moon, his hand on her ankle—when they saw his father stooped and wading upstream.

Quanah reached him first, then jumped back like he'd stepped on a snake. Nocona's hands were gnarled, an elbow was pressed hard against his hip, and his neck and jaws were wrenched far around. He was drooling.

Weckeah gasped and said: "Twistedface!"

Quanah picked him up on his shoulder while she ran for help. In the tipi later Nocona lay on his robes, breathing all right but unable to stand or speak; a nervous and morbid crowd had gathered outside. Yellow Bear brought in a torch so they could see—and like a tornado's trail, it was not a pretty sight. Nocona's face was drawn from his right hairline to his left jaw. Water poured from his eyes. He raised his hand like the glare bothered him. Wearing a hat of buffalo horn, the medicine man Jaybird Pesters walked in carrying a protective fan of crow feathers. "*Bedeyai*," he diagnosed at once.

Ghost done it.

You had to be an Indian to suffer the dread disease twisted face, or ghost sickness. Time would come when white folk tried to convince Quanah it was something they call a stroke. Quanah knew better, and all the rest of his days, he worried and wondered if he could get it, too.

Some people had mild cases. They hated what it did to their looks, how it beat their hands into useless claws, but after a while the ghost let go, and they got back to normal. But Quanah could tell by the way everyone behaved that Nocona was in serious trouble. Parts of him were useless, and all at once the people seemed to believe that if they didn't break camp right that minute, they'd never see another buffalo.

Quanah was having to make all the decisions, father his own dad. But a woman who'd known Nocona all his life was supposed to hire the medicine man; a son couldn't do that. Every woman in the band who fit the description turned him down flat—even Nice Enough to Eat.

"Will you do it?" Quanah asked Weckeah.

"*Can* I?" said his girlfriend, rattled.

"I guess he'll tell you if you can't."

"What do I say? I've never spoken to that old man—I'm scared of him."

"Just ask if he's available. Tell him I'll pay him what I can."

"Which is what?

"Well, everything we have. I've got to have a horse to ride, and so does Dad, if he lives. That leaves one mare and a mule."

Jaybird Pesters consented to treat the fallen war chief. When the medicine man came, Quanah had a pipe of tobacco waiting. He offered it first to his dad, who was supposed to smoke. Nocona tried to sit upright and take it—gave up with an agitated sigh. Quanah couldn't bear to look at him. He smoked four drafts in his dad's behalf, then handed the pipe to Jaybird Pesters. The medicine man drew his four puffs thoughtfully. He said, "I don't believe it's sorcery."

"Good," said Quanah.

"It would be better if he could tell me his troubles. He may have brought this on himself. He thinks too much of the dead. You hear comment."

"Well, he's got too much dead."

The old man paused nervously, then nodded, "First you have to bathe him. Do it west of camp, in the river. I'll be back in the morning."

"He's clean. He just bathed today."

Anger and offense glinted in the bloodshot eyes. "Do it," the old man said.

Quanah didn't mean to be insolent or irreverent. He just had trouble believing that was any good for his health. He laid his dad on a travois and pulled it gently along. Nocona kicked and twitched in a frail rage.

Jaybird Pesters tried. The first morning he made Nocona choke down four buttons of peyote, which made him sick but soon left him dreamy of gaze, evidently free of pain. The medicine man came three times a day. He hung crow feathers from the tent flap and fanned Nocona with cedar and pecan smoke to chase off the ghost. He brewed more peyote tea, filled his mouth with it, spilled it into his hands, and bathed Nocona's face. Another time he walked around the patient and spat the tea on him in impressive fine sprays. The medicine man prayed till his hands shook, then chewed up grayroot and rained that on him, too. It made a mess, and Quanah could see from Nocona's eyes that he didn't appreciate it.

Between the doctoring Quanah sat with his dad, mostly by himself, sometimes with Weckeah. "Why don't you talk to him?" she said one night.

"Why don't you?"

She ducked her eyes, hurt.

"I don't know what to say," he answered. "I can't just carry on. I hear him hearing it. Embarassed by it. Feeling sorry for it. He was a proud man."

When Quanah left the lodge he saw the looks cast his way. Looks of fear, pity, scorn. At the end of two days, the normal treatment period, Nocona wasn't doing any better, but out of respect the old man kept coming back, brewing and spewing his peyote tea. He made a thick paint out of water, buffalo tallow, and powdered red clay. He coated Nocona's face, arms, and legs with it and said, "Leave it on two days." The old man was exhausted and anxious to bolt.

Late that night, lying beside Nocona in the lodge, Quanah could feel him trying to speak, but there was only the vexed sound of his breathing. It came to Quanah that he had been mourning a man who was still pulling air. He reached out his dad's hand—something he hadn't done in years—and from the claw there was a slight, answering squeeze. Quanah at last fell asleep, and when a horse woke him at sunrise he looked over and saw that under the cracked red plaster, Nocona's face was relaxed again, normal. Close to a smile. Quanah sat up and almost gave a shout of celebration and relief. But it was no miracle. His dad was gone. 🏵

OIL FIELD GIRLS

by Don Graham

Everything was the way I liked it at the library till they hung that picture. It was 'bout the easiest job I ever had. They give me a uniform and gun, but they said don't use the gun unless somebody tries to steal the Bible. It was a Gunterberg Bible, and folks set a lot of store by it. They kept it in a big glass case where couldn't nobody touch it. I never did get to use that gun, though, 'cause what kind of fool would try to steal a Bible in broad daylight. Anyways, they got plenty of Bibles at the Motel 6 if you got to have one that bad.

But my main job was setting at this desk, on a kind of high stool, and watching the screens to see that there wasn't nobody stealing anything from upstairs. Why they's want to steal what's up there on the fifth floor is beyond me, but my supervisor said watch 'em, that's your job, and I've always been one to do a job right. The fifth floor is where they keep all the old books and letters and photographs of a lot of dead people; they got about a million boxes of junk up there that was owned by authors and such.

People come from all over the world to look at this stuff, and I can tell you, I've heard some mighty funny accents coming out of the mouths of them foreigners. I always made 'em repeat what they said if I couldn't understand it. I got a kick out of checking their bags, like at the airport, and if anybody didn't treat me with the proper respect going up, you can bet your patootie I made 'em open up when they come down.

From what I seen, scholars are a mighty seedy lot. There was always some hoity-toity Englishmen coming in, but I believe it was the Frenchmen that I disliked the most. I never seen a man more unlikeable than your average Frenchman. I know why they call them frogs. Dang'd if I didn't call 'em that myself, privately you know, from time to time.

Behind their backs. They'd get on the elevator, and I'd say Frog to myself. It gives me real pleasure.

It was kind of a soothing job in many ways. Like I said, all you had to do was set there. I always brought a sack lunch and at noon, we got a whole hour off, too, paid, but I never needed more'n twenty minutes to eat what I had. Never could understand why a man needed more time than that to eat. Why, house I growed up in, we ate as fast as we could 'cause we had to get back to them fields. Working at the library was a lot better than picking cotton, I can tell you that. Only thang about it is, it kind of bleaches you out. Settin' under them lights all day. Makes you kind of sallow looking. I seen one man he worked in another part of the library, guarding the exits; by the time he retired he was downright yellow. Course he had one of them kind of olive complections to begin with. Said he was gonna sue somebody because of the jaundice, but I never paid him no mind. Talk's cheap. Shoot, that job was too good a pay to go to suing somebody. Why they paid nearly as much as the city bus drivers get. I know cause my son-in-law is doing right well driving one of them buses. Quiet, too, 'cause ain't nobody on there to bother him. Them buses is nearly always empty. He don't care. Pay's the same empty or full.

Anyways, like I was saying, they put that painting up and ruined everthing. "Oil Field Girls," it was called. They said it was a classic. I wouldn't know nothing about that. It was Mr. Michener who caused them to hang it in the first place. Mr. Michener, he had that University pretty much by the short hairs. Man give fifteen million dollars, he can hang any danged pictures he wants to. He put a whole bunch of pictures in that big room next to where I worked. Most of 'em was nothing but squiggly lines and blots, and there was one of them wasn't nothing but a solid patch of paint, but "Oil Field Girls" you could make out real plain. It wasn't very realistic, though, 'cause it was kind of blown out of proportion. Except for one thing. The girl on the left, that big corn-fed blonde, she warn't no girl, she was my wife. Eunice Knoeble from New Braunfels, Texas. I recognized her the moment they hung her up there. When Eunice left me, this was in Archer County, 19 hunnerd and 38, I never saw hide nor hair of her again, nor never heard from her neither, till around 1983 when she turned up at the library.

It's the spitting image of Eunice. Big girl, like I said. Had a nice figure, but she was already running to fat, or going to; you can see it in that little stomach pooch the painter gave her. She's all dolled up, ain't she. She always liked to dress up. That's what first attracted her to me. That and her size. I always been partial to big women. Married three of them. Eunice run off, Sarah Blessinggame she died, and Bernice Faulkner, well, Bernice is home right now making doilies for her granddaughter's new trailer house over at Cedar Park. Bernice has got a little stout, too, but none of that matters anymore. She's a good cook and don't think that ain't important. Eunice, she couldn't cook worth a damn. All she wanted to do was go out and dosey-do. That woman never cooked me three-squares in the twenty-seven months we was married. I got on her pretty good about it, but she never paid me no mind. About that or anything else.

I wonder where she was going when that artist caught up with her. Knowing what I know of artists, especially them communist ones back in the Depression, I'll bet you them girls was nude when he drew them; he just put clothes on them. Eunice didn't have no clothes that nice. She didn't have that anklet bracelet neither. What Eunice was, I kinda hate to admit it, was oilfield trash. I took her out of a waitressing job in a greasy spoon in the winter of 1936 in Chillicothe, Texas, which was a town that wasn't going nowhere, and took her to Archer County where they was oil. I enjoyed those twenty-seven months, and I was right sorry when I come home one day and found she'd cleaned out her belongings and didn't even leave no note.

But somehow after all those years, that painting hanging there where I had to see it every blessed day I come to work, it got to where I couldn't stand it no more. So I quit. Actually, I retired. Then I couldn't stand being round the house with Bernice a-doilying all the time, so that's when I took up my current position as senior citizen greeter at Wal-Mark. It's a good job but nothing like the one at the library. I miss it. ✦

JOSEPH'S BONES

by Edward H. Garcia

David Alvarez wasn't used to wearing a suit, but he was grateful for the long-sleeved shirt under it and for the wool of the coat. He shivered slightly, glancing over his shoulder at the open casket that contained his father. His father's "remains," the unctuous man in the black suit had called the body. He wondered vaguely what the man called his profession— probably something had come after "funeral director" in the chain of euphemisms meant to keep death at bay. His father had lived always with a sense of the closeness of death. He had waited and waited and waited and finally, when he was eighty-seven years old, it came.

It was damn cold. His uncle Vidal had been by earlier in an awful green suit: "I got it for twenty-nine dollars at one of the stores by the bridge." He gestured in that direction with his remarkably full head of hair. How old is he? David wondered. Has to be seventy-five, seventy-six maybe. David wished they shared genes, but Vidal had been married to David's aunt. "Two pairs of pants. What's the point of going to a men's store, right, David?"

Looking around the still-empty room where the funeral would be held, Vidal had shivered and said, smiling, "Whenever one of us *viejitos* dies they always turn up the air conditioning. Then, if one or two of their friends catch cold . . . it's good for business."

David turned to look at what had been done with his father's body. What remained was remarkably like a death mask: pale, almost transparent skin, the prominent forehead, the Roman nose. The suit was one David recognized, one of the last Alberto Alvarez had bought before he retired. It was too big for him now. In the last few years his father had shrunk, diminished, like an iceberg melting, the iceberg they had all run against all their lives, but never seemed to have had much effect on. He had really been gone, David thought, for, what, one, two years? No longer the man he had been. Wordless now. The words that stung, that dismissed, wouldn't come. David would see him struggling to say something. It must have been like trying to remember a dream in the morning, so close, on the tip of his tongue, and then nothing. Again and again, David would see the succession of looks: first a glimpse of the old intelligence, then a confused, struggling look, then defeat as he would fail to find a sentence, even a word. In the last months, not even the attempt, just an occasional flash of anger, but with no words, nothing to hurt with.

David touched his father's hand; it was like touching wax. That was not his father; it was a clever sculpture, remarkably true to life—or to death—but not the man. Not *Licenciado Alvarez*. In their town *licenciado*— lawyer—was a title attaching honor to a name, like doctor. He could remember the times when his father was *El Licenciado Alvarez*, walking to his office, his suit flapping in the wind, his tie blowing back over his shoulder, suited and tied even on the hottest days in that South Texas town where it was hot and humid indeed in a summer which lasted from April to November. They lived close to downtown at his father's insistence, not in one or the more fashionable neighborhoods where the Anglos lived, where his mother dreamed of buying, but always within walking distance of the office. He wore a hat, too. A broad-brimmed Stetson: straw in the spring and summer, felt in the fall and winter.

David wore caps. He would try on hats all his life, but he never felt he had the dignity to carry off wearing a hat. His father had nothing if not dignity. He walked along the sidewalk, speaking to no one, recognizing no one, his dignity sweeping before and after him and repelling anyone who might want to approach him. *Ahi va el licenciado.* There goes the lawyer, they would say with a respect his father gracefully acknowledged and expected, but would never have insisted upon. To insist would have been beneath his dignity.

David was glad to see, there in the casket, his dignity had been restored. Nothing was apparent of catheters and wheelchairs and plastic chairs in the shower and being bathed and fed by strangers.

He turned away from the casket again and looked around the chapel. People were slowly making their way in. It wouldn't be full. Their faces held the expected composed, sympathetic looks, and he supposed some were actually mourning the death of the very old man whose body was on display at David's back. David supposed he was mourning, too. This feeling must be mourning, though it felt merely empty, like not being there, rather than any particular or acute feeling of loss. He had not dreamed since his father died. Whatever part of him where dreams came from was out of operation, on the fritz. What was "the fritz"? His father used to say "on the fritz." Maybe he could look it up somewhere.

There was no doubt that his mother was mourning. In the thirty-six hours since her beloved Alberto's death, she had cried every waking hour—not every minute but every hour. She might be telling the maid how to set the table and then look at his chair, and hurry out of the room, her hand to her face, her shoulders racked with sobs. She had been the one to take care of him in the awful last months, but David sensed no relief, only pain. *Sara Gonzalez de Alvarez*. She had dropped the "*de*" very soon—she didn't belong to Alvarez or anyone else she had told her husband, and he, who would have done anything in the world to please her, agreed and was willing to explain to his father and his aunts that it was the modern, American way. *Hijita*. Little daughter. That was his pet name for his twelve years younger wife. She didn't protest that she was not his daughter. In those early days, when he was a lawyer turning thirty and she was his bride of eighteen, she was glad to be taken care of. So perhaps in the last years, David thought, he had become her child. Fair was fair.

She received visitors in the family pews to the left of the pulpit and the open casket. David would be joining her and his brother and the others when the service started, but he felt tied to the casket now and stood shifting his weight from one foot to the other in front of it, scanning the room for familiar faces. He felt what he usually felt in any large group—like he didn't fit in, didn't belong. If he didn't belong here, then where *did* he belong? But that was the problem; he didn't belong anywhere. It was a familiar feeling and, through long use, it disturbed him hardly at all. In Austin, among his Anglo friends, in Brownsville, among all these people, many of whom had known him as a child, the feeling of alienation was his companion. In a way it was his birthright.

Most of his father's friends were dead. The people who were there came because they were from other old families that always went to each other's funerals and because of his mother, out of respect for her. There would have been a time, he knew, when this chapel wouldn't have held the crowd. When his father was still *some*body, when being an Alvarez meant something. What did the *raza* know of the Alvarez now—or any of the old families? And the *gringos* less.

Of course, family came. His mother's brothers, the Gonzalez from up the Valley, always came. David remembered his grandfather's funeral— what was it, thirty years ago?—standing in front of the funeral home—a different one, across town—while the vigil went on inside, talking to his uncles, his Uncle David, the one he had been named for, telling jokes. Now Uncle David, to his eyes hardly changed, approached him with a sad look and gave him a long *abrazo*. "How's your mother doing?" he said glancing toward Sarita, "I talked to her last night, and she was in pretty bad shape."

"Well, you know, she cries a lot."

Uncle David nodded gravely and suddenly his face brightened. "Did you hear the one about the priest who went fishing and caught a really big one?" David shook his head. Surely his uncle wasn't going to tell him a joke here. He would save it for afterward, at the house. "Well, this priest was fishing over on the pier on Padre, only he had a sweater over his collar and you couldn't tell he was a priest." David nodded and smiled, but his mind reeled. My father's corpse is five feet away from where we are standing, and you are telling me a joke? "Anyway, he pulls in this huge fish—five feet long at least—and this other fisherman standing next to him says, 'Will you look at that sumbitch?' The priest looks at him and pulls down his sweater to show the collar and says, 'Listen, I'm a priest and I don't appreciate your using that kind of language.' Well, the other guy felt real bad, so he said, 'Oh, father, I wasn't cussing. That's what you call this kind of fish. It's a sumbitch.'" He gestured broadly, his palms turned up with the fisherman's explanation. For once David wished his uncle were not such a good storyteller.

"The priest was a simple man and that satisfied him, so he took the fish back to the rectory and handed the fish to his housekeeper and said, 'I want you to clean this sumbitch.' The housekeeper looked shocked until the priest explained that sumbitch was the name of the fish."

He was warming to the tale, and David glanced around to see if anyone else was hearing it. What would they think about his listening to this story in this place? He turned his head slightly as he listened and tried to get a glimpse of the casket out of the corner of this eye. What would *he* think?

"So then the priest takes the cleaned fish to his cook and says, 'I want you to cook this sumbitch.' Well, she was shocked, too, until he explained. The priest was just sitting down to his meal when there was a knock on the door and a young black priest came in and introduced himself as the new assistant who had been assigned to the parish." David thought he would probably have to change that detail when he told the story later. There was no trusting his uncles on matters of race. "So the priest welcomes him to the table and says, 'You're just in time to share our meal. I want you to know that I caught this sumbitch.' So the housekeeper says, 'I cleaned this sumbitch.' And then the cook says, 'Yes, and I cooked this sumbitch.'" His uncle paused for effect, grinning, still seemingly unaware at how uncomfortable David felt. "And so the young priest looks at them and says, 'You know, I think I'm going to enjoy working with you motherfuckers.'"

David laughed in spite of himself. His uncle patted him on the shoulder and said, "I'm really sorry about your dad" and went on to other family members. David turned to the casket, walked closer to it, and leaned over, his head only few inches from his father's. From across the room, the mourners no doubt thought he was saying a last goodbye to his father, perhaps shedding a tear, but he had been saying his goodbyes for two years and the tears would not come—they were somewhere with the dreams. He was thinking, "Pop, I wish I could tell you one more story. You would have liked this one. It's Uncle David's story—about a priest." His father would have laughed appreciatively and perhaps topped it with his own. That was the father he would miss. Not the *licenciado* or the politician.

During the funeral service, David sat on one side of his mother, his brother Mike on the other. Mike was a professor in a college in Dallas. The baby of the family. The nice one. To his right was a woman whose name David hadn't quite caught. The girlfriend. Pretty young and very pretty. Dark, though. Next to her was Mike's daughter Ginny. She and the step-mother-to-be-maybe seemed to get along pretty well. When the minister from the Mexican Presbyterian church began the service in Spanish, David caught Ginny's eye. She shrugged her shoulders comically. Her Spanish was as non-existent as his own sons'. Where were *they*? He glanced around and saw them in the back row with Mike's boy. Maybe they would get along better than their fathers.

The girlfriend seemed to be following the Spanish. After all this time, maybe one of them would marry a real Mexican. Between them three failed marriages, all to Anglos. Two of the women Jewish. What was *that* about? David thought he knew. He felt a sudden irritation as the minister waxed on in biblical Spanish about some generic deceased. Clearly, the little Man of God hadn't known Pop. His was the church his father might have been expected to attend, if he'd gone to any church besides the Church of Beto Alvarez, thank you and amen. Except for a wedding or a funeral, he would not go to that or any other church. Perhaps most especially that church, the church his father had founded, had literally built. So like everything else, this began with Jose, too. David remembered seeing a photograph of his grandfather when Jose was a fair-ly young man—maybe thirty-five, before he got so fat, before he had eaten half the town and grown so fat. Jose—he wouldn't yet have been universally known as Don Jose—is standing on the altar right below the pulpit of an unfinished church. The tall ceiling and arching windows, not yet filled with leaded glass, rise behind him. There are boards and wires and assorted workmen in the background, smiling sheepishly at the cam-era. Only Jose is serious or mock-serious anyway. He is looking straight at the camera, his eyes lively with amusement. He is a builder of churches, doing God's work, but turning a nice profit in the bargain. All of the contradictions and the power of his personality is in that photograph. It began with him. He had been the one to bring them out of Canaan into

Egypt, and if Egypt turned out not to be what he had hoped for, well, the Pharaoh was a reasonable man, a man you could work with, who didn't mind if an Israelite made a little money as long as Pharaoh was in charge.

David's father used to chuckle about the photograph. "That Jose," he would say and shake his head. David knew that his father would never have been able to pose in that way, would have been too self-conscious. But his grandfather, what would he not have done? David had lived all his life with stories of Jose Alvarez—the pranks, the power, the money, the money lost. David felt weary under the weight of his name. He had lived with being the son of the *licenciado*, the grandson of Don Jose. Now, suddenly he felt acutely embarrassed at his family's self-importance and his own. Why had they held themselves apart, felt superior? What did he think it meant to be an Alvarez? What had it all come to? The old man grown enormously fat, mistaking him for his father, calling him "Beto." The money, the land, the buildings all lost. His father, in his turn, all power and all dignity taken away. Was this what it came to, to be an Alvarez?

The minister was evidently winding up without having said one thing which had anything remotely to do with Alberto Alvarez. David looked at his mother's face. She didn't seem to notice how irrelevant what the minister said was. So maybe it wasn't. Maybe it was just exactly what everyone wanted to hear, and they could fill in the details of the man they knew or of some other man they knew. Maybe it didn't matter what anyone said at a funeral and it might as well be in Spanish. The minister was launching into the Lord's Prayer in Spanish when his mother looked at David and returned his smile. Who was reassuring whom? He leaned his head toward her and whispered, "Your brother David told me an entirely inappropriate story up by the coffin. I'll tell you when we get home. You'll like it." 🏵

THE LAST CAMP OUT

by James Hoggard

The boys, those of them who could swim or weren't afraid of water moccasins rumored to be in the water, splashed each other in the lagoon that evening while their fathers sat around the campfire drinking beer and spilling stories about their times in Vegas and Crested Butte. One of them, though, a professor named Aran, said he liked Mexico better.

"Acapulco?"

"No. Mexico."

"Acapulco's Mexico."

"Not the part I have in mind."

"So what part are you talking about?"

"Atotonilco."

"Never heard of it."

"Then you've never been to Mexico," he said, glancing over to see the commotion of boys running up into the camp, the kids slinging their dripping arms and laughing as they tried to get the men wet.

"Settle down," a father said.

"Gah!" a boy said, and another one explained:

"We just wanted to see if supper's ready."

"That doesn't mean hot dogs and marshmallows either," a boy said.

"Hush, Todd. We're having venison."

"Not me. Barbequed quail might be okay, but not venison. That stuff'll rip your teeth you the way *you* cook it," he said, giggling and running out of range of the towel one of the men popped at his bottom. Then other boys leapt forward, daring the man to try to pop them.

"Missed!" a boy said, then another one twisting out of range said:

"I want to know where the big sandy beach is. This place is a gyp."

"It's right here," his father said: "Sandy Beach at Possum Kingdom."

"Yuk! My bathroom's bigger'n this dinky place."

"No, it's not."

"Bummer!" another boy said. "I thought we were gonna surf."

"This is a lake, Joel, not the damn ocean."

Running up into the group, another boy whispered in Todd's ear.

"Really?"

"Yeah," then the boy whispered something else.

"We'll be back later," Todd told the men then ran with his friend out into the mesquites and salt cedars to the beach.

"Did you see that look on their faces?" a father said.

"Did indeed."

"Wonder what they found."

"No telling," he said, then stopped. The other Indian Guide fathers hushed, too. This was the second overnight camp-out they'd been on with their sons, and it would also be the last.

Looking at each other then glancing toward the promontory the two boys had run toward, they noticed another boy, then another, stealing away toward the point.

"Did you hear a couple motorcycles awhile ago?" a father asked.

"I think so."

"Did you see who was on them?"

"No, Harry," he said impatiently, "I didn't."

"You all just keep talking," Harry said, "I'll go check on the boys."

"Hell, they're all right. You ain't their damn mother."

"I know," he said, grinning.

"What's up?"

"If it's what I think, it might be their peckers."

"Hell, they're too young for that."

"I'll be back," he said, brushing dust off his Levi's.

"Damn!" another father said. "Sit back down and leave the kids alone."

"I'm going with you," another one said, getting up.

"Stay here, big Al," Harry told him.

"Don't think I will," Al said, smiling. "I saw'm, too."

"Saw what?" another father asked.

"You all just stay here," Al told them. "Harry and I have to talk business."

"I'm going, too," Harry's son said.

"No, you're not," his father told him.

"I sure am."

"No, you're not. If you do, we'll both be in trouble," Harry said, laughing.

"Not me," the boy said defiantly. "I saw them first."

"Who?" a father asked.

"You just stay here," Harry said. "Make sure supper gets cooked right."

"No! I'm going. And I know why you want to go, too."

"Why?"

"Because those two girls are out there swimming and one of them has bigger deals than Mama."

"Do *what?*" one of the other men said.

"Those two girls on motorcycles," Al told them.

"They don't have anything on either," the boy said.

Unwinding himself up off the ground, one of the men said, "I'm getting kind of stiff. Think I'll talk a walk."

"Me, too," another said, getting up.

"Good idea," another one agreed.

"Hike'd do me some good."

"I know what you're doing," the boy said. "You're not going for a walk. You're just going to try to see those two women swimming."

"Listen," one of the fathers told him, "stay here and take care of the campfire, Son. And try to make sure the tents don't burn down."

"I know what you're doing," the boy said at the men leaving the campsite. "But all they are is naked."

"That's often enough," a father told him.

"You're gonna get in trouble, too, when I tell Mama," he told his father's back. "First thing when we get home, I'm gonna tell."

Before long, all the men except Harry and Al had drifted back to the campsite lamenting not being single again. Others were aggravated that their sons had had to come with them on the outing. A few of the boys, though, said the fathers were the ones in the way. Finally Harry and Al came back, saying they'd made a deal: "We agreed to throw them their clothes," Al said, "if they'd come drink coffee with us tonight."

"Omigod," one of the men said, "you didn't invite them up here, did you?"

"Sure. Why not?"

"Because, damnit, half the women are staying here at the lake tonight in your cabin."

"So?"

"What if they come down and those two are with us."

"They won't. Besides, if they do, they won't see anything. We'll just be drinking coffee."

"And maybe a little beer," another one said.

"Besides," Harry told them, having just poured himself a stiff bourbon, "we'll have the boys for protection."

"That's just going to make it worse."

"I know," Harry's son butted in, "I'm gonna tell. I won't even have to wait to get home. That's what you get for not letting me go down there with you."

"You just keep your little mouth shut, Son."

"No! If you'd let me go with you, I might. But you wouldn't. You made me stay here so I'm gonna tell."

"No problem," another father said, sounding as if he'd found a fine solution. "The women come here, we'll just tell them the girls are Aran's friends. He's not married."

"Where is he?"

"I don't know. He and his boy went back near the road to try to catch lizards or something."

"Joke's probably on us. He's probably down at the point making arrangements for later."

"I hope so. It'd be a damn shame if we all had to go home dry."

"Trying to catch a damn lizard!" another man said in disbelief.

"Sonofabitch probably really is. That's probably, too, why his old lady left him."

"Don't be bitter," Harry said, pouring himself another drink. "He's the only one of us who can't even get in trouble."

"Lord," one of them said, "thinking about that tall one out there makes me want to die. Getting up on her would be like climbing a damn mountain."

"How do you know? You didn't even see her up front. They wouldn't even get out of the water."

"Doesn't make any difference. A man sees the stern, he knows what the prow's like."

"Bullshit."

"It's true, and not only that, you get a good look at a woman's nose, you get a good idea what style of nipples she has, too."

"Goddamn, Fred," Harry said laughing with the others, "you're the craziest damn sonofabitch I ever heard."

"I may be," he said, keeping a straight face, "but the shape of the earlobe'll give you some fine information as well, especially about a part you don't often get a good look at."

"Goddang, I'm ready to start sampling the beer."

After supper the taller girl did come to accept Al and Harry's offer for coffee. She was wearing jeans and a red-vested, black leather-sleeved jacket. Although it was fastened half way, she seemed to be bare beneath it. Squatting around the fire with her, several of the men nervously asked her what kind of blouse she was wearing.

"I'm not," she replied, then smiling mischievously, she clicked shut another snap of her jacket.

"What're you studying?" Fred asked her.

"Radio and TV."

"You going to be an actress."

"No—advertising, unless I switch to nursing or law."

"That's a weird combination."

"Maybe now," she said, "but it won't be later."

"Why?"

"I'll only be involved with one of them."

"You date a lot?" Al asked.

"Some."

"Anybody steady?"

"Not any more."

"You ever dated any of your professors?" Harry asked.

"Sure," she said as Aran walked back into the campsite with his son.

"Aran here's a professor," one of the men said. "You ought to have a date with him."

Amused, Aran and the girl introduced themselves to each other, shaking hands above the flames, then Aran and his son Damon sat down across from her.

The boy asked his father if they had any more candy or sandwiches. Aran said no but added he'd be glad to split an orange with him. "They're in the box inside the tent."

"You get it," Damon said, his gaze wandering out toward the darkness. "I'll keep your place."

"Better hurry," Harry told Aran. "Damon's going to shoot you out of the saddle."

Ruffling his son's hair, Aran left and the girl asked Damon if he wanted to come sit by her. He shook his head no, but she asked him again as she patted the ground by her crossed legs.

"I'll come sit by you," one of the men said.

"There's plenty of room on the other side," she told him, but laughing nervously, the man stayed where he was. "Come here," she told Damon again, and this time the boy came to her.

When Aran got back he had the orange already peeled and split into sections that were cupped in his palm. He sat down next to his son. Damon took several sections then Aran offered the girl some, and when she bit into hers, juice squirted on her chest. Instantly one of the men jumped up and reaching back into his hippocket, said, "Here, let me help you—I've got a handkerchief."

"That's all right," she told him. "You might miss," and the other men laughed, some of them asking her if she'd let them try their aim. One of them assured her he'd been a crack marksman in Nam.

"No, he wasn't either. He just flew choppers."

Daubing herself with a tissue she'd pulled from a pocket, the girl leaned in front of Damon and asked Aran if she'd gotten all the juice off.

"Just about," he said, smiling back at her.

"Thank you," she said and patted Damon's knee, then one of the fathers asked his son if he might not like to go sit by her, too, and get his knee patted.

"Naw," the boy said.

"Go ahead. She'll let you. You'll be doing me a favor, too," he said.

"Don't do it," another man told the boy. "You'll be up all night—your old man trying to get a whiff off your knee."

Before long Aran asked the girl where she went to college. When she told him SMU, he said that's where he had gone. He mentioned a few professors he'd had, and she'd had one of them, too.

Trying to stay in the conversation, one of the men said, "You know, Aran here's had some plays on Broadway."

"Really?" she asked him.

"No," Aran said. "A couple in New York, but not on Broadway."

"Off-Broadway?"

"That's close enough," he told her.

"I'm impressed," she said, then a flood of headlights exploded on the area and the men, jumping up, said, "Omigod! The wives are here!" and hurried out into the darkness, some of them grabbing their sons and saying, "Let's go see if we can catch some fish."

"No!"

Car doors slammed and there were only a few of the men left standing around the campfire with the girl who insouciantly stayed where she was. The women were laughing and joking until they saw her.

"Where's Al?" one of them snapped.

"I think down at the lagoon with Mark," one of the fathers said.

Some of the women had already rushed out into the darkness barking the names of their husbands who tried to sound happy to see them.

"What's that girl doing here?" came an angry voice in the night. "Who is she?"

"Girl?" Al said, his own voice loud. "What girl?"

"The one at the campsite. Who the hell is she?"

"I don't have any idea," he said. "Mark and I have been out here all evening. We've been fishing."

"So where is he?" she demanded.

"Out here somewhere trying to hide from me. He's mad because I won't let him go swimming this late. I told him you and I had a rule—no swimming after dark."

"You damn liar!" she said. "Where is he? I'm gonna find out what's really going on."

And another woman in the dark was asking who that girl was, and after coughing awhile Harry said flatly, "I don't know. I think she's one of Aran's friends."

"What's she doing out here?" his wife wanted to know.

"I don't know that either. She and her husband drove up on a motor-cycle. They just got here a minute ago. Wasn't he back there at the fire with her?"

"No!" she told him. "He wasn't anywhere around there."

"Then I don't know where he is—probably taking care of their kids somewhere."

"I want to know what she's doing here."

"You got me. They're all Aran's friends. I've just been out here collecting firewood for morning. Wanta help?"

"No! We'll talk fire—we'll talk fire tomorrow," she told him.

Shortly after that the women regathered at the campfire, then glaring once more at the girl they left, but only after looking inside their husbands' tents to check if anyone they'd missed might be hiding in there.

Grinning wryly, the girl said she hoped she hadn't gotten anybody in trouble. Trying to sound confident, the men assured her she hadn't.

Getting up, she said she'd enjoyed the visit but really ought to go, her friend was waiting for her at their own campsite.

"Bring her on over," one of the men said. "We'll all have a party."

"Maybe later," she said and some of the men started clearing their throats.

"That might be a good idea," a few of them mumbled, sounding uneasy.

"You going swimming again?" one of them asked.

"I might," she said brightly, turning to Aran. "Why don't you come see our campsite?" she asked him. "We can have a drink—or go swimming if you like. Maybe even both."

"We'll see," he said.

Damon started scowling as she left, and Aran asked him, "What's wrong?"

"Nothing!" the boy said angrily.

"Come on. What is it?" Aran asked him, pulling him away from the others.

"It's not fair," Damon said.

"What?"

"I didn't get invited."

"Invited to what?"

"To go swimming."

"I'm not going swimming."

"Yes, you are. You'll wait till I go to sleep and then go. Well, I'm not going to sleep. I'm staying up all night."

"You'll be awfully tired tomorrow."

"I don't care. It's not fair."

"Tell you what," Aran said. "We'll go to their campsite tomorrow, and maybe they'll let you get up on one of their motorcycles."

"And ride it with them?"

"Maybe."

"She probably won't let me."

Laughing, he told his son, "That's what all these other guys have been saying."

It was late when the fathers got their sons to bed. Most of the men went to bed, too, a number of them saying, though, there wasn't any point in it: "I never can go to sleep on the ground."

"That's why I brought my camper," another said.

"Anyone want more coffee?" one of them asked, pouring a fresh cup from the smudged blue pot.

"Sure.'

"Not me," Harry said thickly. "I'm sticking with bourbon."

"Hell!" one of the men said, "can't even go on a camp out without the damn wives coming over to spoil it."

"I'm turning in," Aran said.

"You sonofabitch!" Harry yelled. "If you go in that tent, I'm killin' you. Damn! The only free one of the bunch and you're making us all suffer for it. You damn bastard, get your ass over there and get yourself some."

"Yeah," one of them said, "do it for Harry. Little fat big-mouth needs a favor."

"Right—because he damn sure ain't gonna get any when he gets home."

"Listen," Al said, slapping Aran's back, "you ever get any offers at school?"

"Some."

"Young ones or old ones?"

"Sometimes both."

"Damn!" Harry said, "and my old lady thinks she has to interview ever'one of my damn secretaries. She even checks up on the bookkeepers."

"Life's rough," Aran told him.

"Damn sure is," Al said. "You think they might let me and Harry get on part-time out there?"

"I doubt it."

"That's what I was afraid of."

"Hell," Harry said, "they wouldn't even have to pay us. I'd work for free, long as there was some anxious poontang around."

"See you in the morning," Aran said.

"Sonofabitch," Harry told everybody, "I'm going swimming!" and storming up off the ground, he clumsily stepped through the fire, knocked over the coffee pot, and tripping, fell against a tent. A boy inside yelled, and scrambling back up, Harry lost his balance again, and as he fell backwards there came the whine of nylon tearing, and the rage of an angry boy, then another, and squealing and shouting burst from other tents, too, boys in t-shirts and underwear popping from the openings, and their fathers crawling out with them, but Harry didn't pay any attention to any of them because Harry had just passed out. The orange fold of the tent coming down on him looked like a huge birdbeak ready to peck his insides hollow.

Leaving the chaos, Aran went to his own tent where his son had gone awhile ago.

"What's going on?" Damon asked.

"One of the guys slipped and knocked a tent down.'

"Was he drunk?"

"What've you been doing—listening?"

"I couldn't go to sleep. You going to stay here?"

"Yes."

"All night?"

"Sure."

"Then how about giving me a back-rub?"

"What about you giving me one?" Aran asked.

"Maybe," Damon said, "but you probably don't itch as much as I do."

The next morning while the men were drinking coffee and frying bacon, a group of boys went to the girls' campsite. Soon several of them came back asking if they could ride the motorcycles. Some of the fathers said that would be all right, but others refused.

"At least let me watch."

"You can do that, Son. Just don't get on them. You're mother'd skin us both."

While the girls were giving the boys rides, Aran walked through the stand of mesquites to see if Damon were with them, then he saw the boy, just finishing his ride, waving at him.

"Daddy, you wanta ride?" Damon said, hopping off from behind the girl.

"Not now," he said. "We're ready for breakfast."

"Can I ride again? Can I?" Damon asked the girl.

"Not today," she said. "We're getting low on gas." Then she looked at Aran and asked him, "Where were you last night? You didn't come over for a drink."

"I couldn't," he said, nodding toward his son.

"I thought you were. We were here and stayed up late. It might've been nice."

"I know."

"You ever come to Dallas?"

"Some."

"When you do, give me a ring."

"Okay," he said, squeezing the back of his son's neck as two more boys came running up begging to be taken for a ride.

"One more," the girl said, "and that's all."

"Me! Me!"

"You've had your turn."

"It was just a short one."

"I'll tell you what," she said. "There's room enough for both."

She helped them on, then nimbly lifting her leg over the handlebar and gas tank, she told Aran she'd see him later. As she drove away, two cars turned onto the dirt road then quickly stopped, their windshields reflecting a bright spray of sunlight. Tires suddenly spitting up dust, the cars sped forward, angling toward the tents down the way.

When Aran and Damon got back to the campfire, the women were fussing at their husbands. They wanted to know why they were so stupid to let their little boys get on those damn fool motorcycles. They wanted to know what those girls thought they were doing out here. They wanted to know a lot of things, and they said they were going to find them all out, too. Aggravated, one of the men said he hadn't let his son get on any damn motorcycle, the kid had done it himself, then another man said the same thing had happened to him: his boy had gotten on and had his ride before he even knew about it. Then another one said, "Hell, I didn't think it would hurt anything."

"You don't talk that way to me—the boy could've broken his neck."

"Well, he didn't."

"You know," another woman said, "we don't allow motorcycles in our family."

"What I really want to know," still another one said, "is how long those women were here last night. You didn't tell me they were spending the whole night."

"Look, I didn't know, and besides, nothing happened. The only one who came up was the one you saw, and she left right after you did."

"Damn you, Harry, they didn't have any business being here in the first place. And I'm finding out what went on."

"Damnit, nothing went on."

"Well, I'm finding out. "

"Listen," Al said, trying to ease the atmosphere, "would you all like some breakfast?"

"Shut up!" his wife said. "We've already eaten."

"Well, I'm getting ready to break a few eggs," Harry told them. "Be glad to have you join us." Then he asked his wife if she had a cigarette.

"Take the whole pack," she said with disgust as she reached into her purse, crunched the package with her fist then tossed it on the ground by the fire. "We're leaving," she said bitterly. "We'll see you this afternoon—and I mean early."

"Nothing like Sunday morning, fresh air, and freedom, is there?" Al said, stretching by the fire and farting.

"Goddamn," Harry said, "something must've crawled up inside you and died."

As the group was finishing breaking camp, one of the men came up to Aran and in a low voice asked him if he had gotten over to see the girls during the night, but before Aran could tell him, the man said, "Damn!" then taking a deep breath and grinning as he walked away, he told Aran, "you're a sly wicked sonofabitch." 🌸

¿*Cómo Se Dice* Brownies?

by Rhonda Austin

Carla enjoyed shopping for groceries in the middle of the night. She could stroll leisurely through the grocery aisles without blocking anyone's path when she stopped to search through her bag for a *Hamburger Helper* coupon. She could add up her purchases on her pocket calculator and count her tips to see if she had enough money to pay for them. No one would see her at that time of night. If she felt like it, she could stop to chat with one of the college boys who unloaded trucks and restocked the aisles during the lull from midnight to four a.m. She could even browse through the magazines she no longer had money to buy. Best of all, she knew she wouldn't run into any bill collectors at that hour. Or any of Jackie's teachers—the same teachers who sent complaining notes home about Jackie's lack of preparedness for class and always looked down their noses at Carla when they came into the restaurant-slash-nightclub where she worked four nights a week.

Standing in line at the checkout, Carla had a nagging feeling she was forgetting something—something important. She clicked off the items on her mental grocery list, but the missing item didn't present itself. No doubt it would come to her just about the time she got home and took her shoes off.

On her way home, she stopped by the cluster of mailboxes near the office at the apartment complex where she, Jackie, and Baby John had moved after the divorce. Recently, she'd resorted to checking her mail late at night. That was because a few weeks ago, the guy from the furniture company had been waiting for her at the mailbox when she came home from her day job. She'd had to give him three payments on the spot so he wouldn't repossess her couch. She thought it was a safe bet that she wouldn't run into a repo man at two or three in the morning.

Three bills, a couple of ads, and an envelope from the school. Carla didn't open any of them. What was the point? She'd pay the bills when she could, and there's no reason to look at sale flyers when you don't have money to shop. It wasn't time for report cards, so whatever was in the envelope from the school couldn't be that important. She tossed the whole batch into the dumpster at the end of the row of mailboxes. The rafters in the shelter over the mailboxes fluttered to life with birds startled by the crashing dumpster lid. The swallows who had built their nests there quickly returned to their routine of tending to their respective families. Carla sat quietly for a moment watching them. Her eyes followed a pair of birds who seemed to be taking turns bringing food to a nest and poking it down the throats of five greedy, begging babies. She'd read somewhere that swallows mated for life and that they often spent up to twenty-two hours a day satisfying the needs of their demanding brood.

Carla knew what that felt like. Whoever it was that came up with the saying "free as a bird" was either a raving lunatic or was playing a cruel hoax on mankind. She chuckled at the irony of that expression. According to that twisted definition, that's what she was now—free as a bird. Free to work twenty-two hours a day to meet the needs of her family. What a joke. The only definition of freedom she could relate to was from another song, one that went "freedom's just another word for nothing left to lose." She couldn't remember who sang the song with those lyrics, but she heard them in her head and knew what they meant in a way she had never fully comprehended before the divorce.

These days when she thought about freedom, she could appreciate the irony of her situation, but six months ago it had been a different story. Carla was proud of the progress she'd made, but it was only recently that she'd been able to reflect on it with any degree of perspective and without her "eyes spilling," as Baby John would say. Carla climbed the wooden stairs to her apartment carrying two bags of groceries. She peeked into the kids' room before she went back for the other sack. Jackie was sleeping in her clothes again. Her hair was a tangled mess and her cheeks were streaked with dirt. Maria, the girl who took care of the kids while Carla worked, lay on a pallet next to Jackie's bed. Baby John slept peacefully in his porta-crib against the wall.

Jackie knew she was supposed to take a bath every night before bed-time but, of course, she conveniently forgot from time to time. It was frustrating to Carla because it meant she had to get up half an hour earlier each day to get Jackie ready for school. Working two jobs, Carla's sleep time was already at a premium and an extra half hour's sleep was precious. By now, Maria should have learned the bedtime routine and the fact that she hadn't was frustrating. Still, she knew it wasn't really Maria's fault. Maria spoke no English and Carla spoke no Spanish, so mostly their communication consisted of body language and a few simple words.

Carla smiled at her sleeping children, kissed each on the forehead, then took a blanket from the closet and spread it over Maria. Several times, she'd tried to get Maria to sleep on the hide-a-bed in the living room, but she apparently preferred sleeping on the floor in the childrens' room. Asleep, she looked like a child herself, but there was something old about her spirit. Carla guessed she was about twenty, but her eyes revealed a much older, almost haunted spirit inhabiting the young body.

Maria and Carla had forged a friendship of sorts based on the fact that both were young mothers trying to survive in a world that was often unkind to working mothers. Carla had learned that Maria had two children of her own across the border in Juarez, Mexico. Every other Saturday evening, she and the kids would drive Maria to downtown El Paso and let her out of the car a couple of blocks from the bridge. Whenever they went anywhere in the car, Maria would stay hunched down, fearful that *la migra* would somehow recognize her as an illegal and snatch her out of the car and deport her. Hundreds, maybe even thousands, of illegals made their way across the border each week to work for American families, and in a city whose population was over 50% Hispanic, chances were very small that a border patrol agent would recognize an illegal alien simply riding in an automobile. Maria had an irrational fear, though, and Carla didn't know how to communicate to her that her actions were only making her seem more suspicious. Maria acted so weird sometimes. Occasionally, her behavior really got on

Carla's nerves.

When they arrived near the bridge, Maria would walk across the border and be met by her mother and her own two kids. Carla watched them from a distance a couple of times. The children were small. One was a toddler, the other looked about four. On Sunday night, Maria always showed up at Carla's apartment, totally broke. She never even had money for the things she needed, like tampons or shampoo, so Carla had to furnish those things for her. She couldn't afford to pay her much, and she knew that Maria probably gave her whole paycheck to her mother to help support the children, but still, Carla couldn't support her own kids and Maria's too. That was just the way it was. Illegals were paid very little to live in an American household, clean the house, and take care of the children. Carla paid the going rate, so Maria would just have to deal with it.

Occasionally, Carla would miss things around the house, like toys or an article of the children's clothing. One time it was a bottle of children's *Tylenol*. She suspected Maria was taking them home to her kids in that brown grocery bag she carried, but she never mentioned it. She told herself it was because they couldn't communicate in each other's language, but truthfully it was because she just didn't want to consider the possibility that Maria might be stealing from her. If she did, then she would have to address it. Jackie and Baby John loved Maria, and Carla knew the things that were missing were things Maria probably needed for her own children. As much as she could, she tried not to think about it.

Still, Maria got on her nerves a lot. She insisted on going to sleep with the television on and it was always tuned to the Mexican channel. Carla didn't understand why Maria didn't at least try to learn English if she was going to work over here. And she resented the fact that Maria got to spend more time with Jackie and Baby John than she did. On days when she was really feeling sorry for herself, she would sit at work and obsess about the fact that Maria was probably picking up Jackie each day after school. She would imagine them staying afterward and playing on the playground awhile. Maria was the one who got to take Baby John for his walks and the one who heard his sweet little laugh during his morning bath. Carla resented the hell out of that. Here she was working at two jobs, trying to make ends meet, while the *maid* was playing with *her* children in the playground. Even though she recognized that her resentments were irrational, it didn't hurt any less to know that someone else—a stranger, no less—was spending more time raising her children than she was.

One day she came home from work with a headache and Maria had the TV blaring on some stupid Mexican soap opera. She yelled at her to turn it down, but Maria didn't understand, or pretended not to, so Carla stalked over and turned it off herself. Then she yelled at Maria to do some ironing. She gestured at the basket of clothes sitting in the corner and furiously yanked the ironing board out of the closet. Maria got the message.

"*Discúlpeme, señora,*" Maria said.

"That means she's sorry, Mama. Do you have a headache again?" Jackie asked.

"The whole damn neighborhood probably has a headache, listening to that racket. Tell her to keep it down." Jackie said something in Spanish to Maria, and Maria hugged her, then turned off the TV. She went into the bathroom to fill the steam iron to avoid walking by Carla. Carla made a big show of turning the TV back on and changing the channel to the local news.

"She will iron the clothes now, Mama. She didn't mean to make you mad." Jackie, only seven years old, understood much more Spanish than her mother did. She and Maria had learned to communicate in a kind of "Spanglish" that combined bits and pieces of both their languages.

Carla didn't know how Maria got back every Sunday night, but she always did—almost always. There was that one time when she didn't get back until Wednesday night. Carla had been livid when Maria didn't show up and didn't get in touch with her because she'd had to call in sick and stay home from work for two days. There was no one else to take care of the kids. She had a couple of days sick leave coming from her day job, so that was okay, but it was the tips from her night job as a waitress that bought groceries and took care of day to day expenses for the family. She really couldn't afford to miss two nights of tips, but there'd been no choice.

By the time Maria returned on Wednesday night, Carla was beside herself. Maria tried to explain, but Carla was in no mood to listen. "*La migra*," Maria kept saying. "*La migra*." Carla knew that Maria was talking about the Border Patrol, but laid it off to her paranoia, or just plain lying. "*Mis niños no comerán, señora. Por favor, déjeme trabajar. No ocurrirá otra vez.*"

Carla was able to pick up a few words—babies, I'm sorry, Border Patrol. But she had problems of her own. She reached in her purse and took out a disconnect notice from the electric company. Shaking it in Maria's face, she loudly told her that since she had not shown up, their electricity had been cut off because she had to miss two days of work and couldn't pay the bill.

A confused Maria had no idea why Carla was standing in the dark, shaking an envelope at her and yelling. Nevertheless, she continued to plead for her job, reaching into her brown bag and pulling out a picture of her own two babies and waving it in Carla's face.

By that time, both women had tears streaming down their faces and only little Jackie seemed to have some idea of what was going on. Baby John was sitting in the middle of the floor playing with his rattle and sucking his thumb. When Jackie heard her mother tell Maria she was fired, she ran to Maria and wrapped herself around her legs, pleading with her not to go.

That was the last straw. Carla felt utterly deserted. Even her own child had taken the side of this woman, this alien, against her. Jackie slid down Maria's legs to the sidewalk, both arms entwined around Maria's ankles. In her pain, Carla reached to snatch Jackie away from her death grip around Maria's legs. When Jackie suddenly let go, the force of Carla's tug flung her around causing her to hit her mouth on the door handle and cut her lip. Instantly remorseful, Carla reached out to comfort her, but Jackie began screaming and ran back to Maria, clinging to her even more tightly.

Next door, Mrs. Gladney peeked out her window and Carla had no choice except to bring Maria into the house with Jackie clinging so tightly to her legs that it was almost impossible for Maria to walk. Maria, clearly uncomfortable, tried to pry the screaming Jackie from her legs while talking softly to her in Spanish. "*Fue accidente, chiquita. Tu mamá no te lastimó a propósito. La haces triste.*"

Carla was inconsolable. She picked up Baby John and ran into her bedroom, slamming the door behind her. "Not only do you steal my children's clothes," she screamed at Maria, "now you want to steal my children, too." Maria didn't know what Carla said, but she clearly interpreted the emotion. Baby John, upset by all the turmoil and his mother's tears, began wailing as well. For thirty minutes, Carla cried uncontrollably. Maria, unable to stand Baby John's tears, came in and picked him up and took him out to the living room.

Maria behaved very calmly. Having felt this same kind of desperation many times herself, she knew that it would pass. She made some chocolate milk for Jackie and put some in Baby John's bottle. The three of them sat in the living room floor. She calmed the children by rocking Baby John and singing softly to the children in Spanish. Soon her voice was joined by little Jackie's, also singing the lyrics in Spanish. "*Bien, chiquita,*" Maria said. "*Muy bien.*"

Carla finally managed to get her sobbing under control and went into the bathroom to wash her face. Feeling ashamed of her behavior, she sat on the edge of the bed and listened to the soothing tones of the Spanish lullabies Maria was singing to her children. For the first time, she noticed what a pleasant voice Maria had. Somehow the sound soothed Carla, too. Her anger and frustration spent, she stood silently in the dark and watched Maria mothering and giving comfort to her children. She wondered who was doing that job for Maria's children and then the tears came again.

In a little while, Jackie softly knocked on her bedroom door. "Are you all right, Mommy? Can I come in?"

"Sure, honey, come on in. Mommy's okay. I was just upset that I hurt you. Are you okay? Mommy's so sorry she made you hurt your lip."

"It's okay, Mommy. I know you didn't mean to hurt me. I was just afraid for Maria. I didn't mean to hurt your feelings. Don't make her go, Mommy. Please don't make her go away. She didn't steal our clothes, Mommy. I gave them to her for her little kids. I just gave her ones that don't fit anymore. I didn't know it would make you mad."

"I'm not mad, honey. Mommy was scared, too. It'll be all right, I promise. Go tell Maria that everything will be okay. I'm not mad at her, and I'm not mad at you. I'll be out in a minute, as soon as I wash my face."

"Okay, can we watch TV now, Mommy?"

"No, honey. The TV's not working right now. How about if you and Maria teach me how to sing some of those songs I heard you singing a minute ago? Do you think you could?"

"Sure, Mommy, but I only know them in Spanish. Do you want me to teach them to you in Spanish? Maria could help."

"Yeah, that would be great. Then maybe we could teach her some of the songs we know in English. Do you think Maria would like that?"

Since that night, the women had begun to forge a new relationship, had even become close friends. They were both learning. Jackie had helped, but Maria and Carla had taken some initiative, too. Standing in the doorway that night, looking at the children, Carla remembered the day she had come home and found Maria listening to an American soap opera while she was ironing. She'd pretended not to notice, for fear that Maria would expect her to listen to one in Spanish. She wasn't ready for that yet, not then.

Carla silently closed the door, leaving Maria and their sleeping children to their dreams. She allowed the exhaustion to take over as she put away the last of the groceries before going to bed. She wished she could remember what it was she had forgotten at the grocery store.

Thirty minutes before her alarm went off, Carla sat straight up in bed, knowing instantly what it was. Brownie mix. She was supposed to make brownies for the school bake sale. If she hurried, she still would have time to get them done before she had to go to work. She pulled on her jeans and t-shirt and went in to wake up Jackie.

"Mom, it's not even daylight yet. Why are you waking me up so early?"

"We're making brownies, don't you remember? Did you think I'd forget? I'm going to run to the store and get a mix, but I'll be right back. Get Maria up and have her help you get ready for school. You have to take your bath this morning since you obviously didn't do it last night."

"I forgot." Jackie sat up in bed and rubbed her eyes. "Why don't we get some *Sara Lee* brownies and cut them up and wrap them in plastic wrap like we did last time? Nobody knew the difference and they were pretty good."

"That'll be the day, when I can't bake brownies better than *Sara Lee*," Carla said. She lovingly ran her hands through Jackie's tangled mass of hair and kissed her on the forehead. Then she leaned over the pallet on the floor and shook Maria's shoulder to wake her up. "Maria, I need your help. *¿Cómo se dice* brownies *en español?*" ✿

HUNGRY HEART

by Ann McVay

Timothy says the total experience of something momentous begins with the anticipation of it.

"Always I give to you, my very best advice, and this is it," he says. "The smell of something, this is the most important thing."

Timothy Rodriguez, Mama's best friend and main cook at Morgan's House in Big Spring, is big on the smell of things. Timothy always puts one more clove in the bouillabaisse an hour before the rush, just for the scent.

Timothy will not let you touch a utensil without his permission or suggest a menu alteration. While he cooks, he tells stories of old romances, complete with all the related smells he remembers. He is careful to say "this person" or "the party of whom I am speaking" although I am pretty sure he knows I know they are all parties of hes and hims.

I am mad at Timothy tonight. I have put myself in the wet end, washing dishes where Charly and Bev usually start, because when he looks at me, I want him to see my back.

"So," Timothy says, as he brushes by, trying to get me to talk, "you remember like I tell you—no spots on my crystal."

I follow him to the cellar door and let my hands drip soap on the floor. "Made in China," I call down the stairs after him. I hope I am irritating him.

Timothy, himself, was made in Mexico, but he likes it better if you guess Italian. He wears soft Isotoner slippers so he can be light on his feet when things get fast, so I call him 'Timmy Toe-shoes' or *el bailarín* , one of the few Spanish words he will teach me. I hear him down in the cellar, pulling and sorting his wine bottles. Timothy feels ready only when all of the bottles are arranged in an order that makes sense only to him.

Some nights when the dinner crowd tapers off I perch on a stool in the kitchen and watch Timothy saute or bake. The aromas of saffron and cinnamon, dill and basil wrap me in a pungent blanket, and I am as snug as a prosciutto roll in a pita pouch. On those nights, if Mama never came through the door, I could be happy.

But tonight, with Timothy giving me such a hard time, I am glad when she does. A beautiful entree, Mama says, if you are going to serve it at all, should be noticed. And Mama is. She is large enough to carry all of her big jewelry, heavy enough to command respect as the owner of Morgan's House.

She does not speak until the swinging door closes behind her. She is quick to remind us, we may serve fine steaks, but Morgan's House is not a cattle ground, and there is no need to shout about the private cuts of meat that folks prefer. Her blonde-gray hair is up, her dress flows around and around her and, as always, she wears high heels.

She stands in the middle of the kitchen, waiting. Her eyes lock into Timothy's as he comes back up the stairs. He sets the wine baskets down, crosses his arms.

"What?"

"I know we talked about this till you're blue in the face, sweetness, but—Do we or do we not need a diet plate?"

Timothy stirs the soup and pulls a menu out of a nearby drawer. He reads aloud from the tattered beige paper: "'There are many fine establishments in the area which serve fat-free and low-sodium selections. Morgan's House does not.' I keep telling you, Amarylis."

"Belinda, check the salad," Mama says.

"I did already."

"One more time, please."

"Your Mama, she is the perfectionist," Timothy says. "Nothing is worthy until you do it three times." He smiles when he says this. He likes Mama's style, her passion for cooking and especially, especially her passion for eating. He gives her a homemade crouton seasoned with Parmesan and Romano cheeses, powdered in garlic and sesame. "Eat this and stop the worry-worry.

"There is no one I like to feed more than your Mama, chica," he tells me. He watches her as if he is hungry himself, as if, when Mama takes the small rectangle in her round fingers and slowly inches it into her mouth, lips all fuschia and teeth crunching, she feeds him. He does not have to tell me again how he first met Mama in a restaurant fourteen years ago in El Paso, and what a joy it was to serve her, so leisurely as to be an indulgence in itself, a five-course meal over the length of an evening. And then how he joined her later to discuss more fine meals and the Events that each of them should be.

Mama will not discuss what led her there that evening. She will only say that that night she had planned to leave this world after one last meal. Finding someone as intensely in love with food saved her. And saved me, too, since Mama had been pregnant with me.

"You remember what I told you about the flambé business?" she says to me now.

I place glasses in the rack, stems up, almost touching. "I know, I remember," I say, but she tells me again anyway.

"Thing about the flambé is this: Know how when the fire goes out and the very top is gone in a flash, like a Cherries Jubilee? A good one, I mean, not that awful imitation they do over there in Dallas. And then how you see only a breath of smoke? That's near-bouts how I went out of this world—" she snaps her fingers "—snuffed out quick, nothing but a little smoke, little cloud of perfumed air, wafting up and out of the room."

It is an odd set of parents I have: Mama, with her round arms and sausage fingers, spattered in fake jewels, flying about her head when she talks; and Timothy, always cooking, giving directions to other cooks, dancing around Mama in his slipper shoes while he listens, always having a sense of where she is.

"Your Mama, she got a gift," he says. "She gives people back to themselves. This is her destiny. And it is still a mystery to me how she does this." Mama touches his cheek, rolls her eyes. Still chewing, she kisses him, wipes her mouth on his apron, the one she got for him in Houston at a Southwestern Cuisine Cook-Off. I shake my head when he holds out a square for me. Mama takes it.

"*This here* is a mystery to me," Mama says, pointing to the window, licking her fingers. In the far end of our parking lot is a beautiful boat attached to an old white Capri. "I can't imagine who she belongs to."

Almost two weeks ago, someone left it there, and we have yet to find out anything about its owner. None of the customers will claim it. The car is a dirty white with a long dent in the left, where someone backed into the driver's side. But the boat is new, a luxurious dark purple, the color of shiny ripe eggplant, and is made for speed. Her name, in gold script, reads *The Four Winds*.

"This, I believe, is a romantic man with a hungry heart. And one day he will come to Morgan's House and he will tell you his story," Timothy tells her. Timothy and Mama have heard lots of stories over the years. The fact that Timothy has also lived with us for the past fourteen years is secondary to the business relationship. Mama says Timothy's culinary skill is the best kept secret this side of the Colorado River. If she knows that other secret of his, she's isn't saying anything.

When Mama leaves the kitchen, I remember I am mad at him. I pick up a handful of pistachios out of a bowl and rapidly crack them open and into my mouth while I try to figure out how to tell Timothy to leave me alone.

"So. Easter weekend coming up," Timothy says. "We got to have more lamb, more ham, more sirloin." He pinches my cheek and starts in on me again. "You remind me when that sweet little Cold Boy from Avery's comes by."

"He's not a little boy." I toss a handful of nuts at Timothy's head and he ducks, laughing.

"No? Okay, remind me when that big, ugly delivery man—the one that weighs 120 pounds and has razor marks to prove he has started shaving—remind me when that big, hairy Meat Man comes, I got to order more meat."

"Give me the order. I'll tell him what you want."

All my life, when I think of talks with Timothy, I see him in a full apron, hair pulled back so I can see his silver earring, laughing at me as he is now, pointing with a knife or wooden spoon. "I think I must talk to him myself, he is such a nice young man," he says. "Such red knees he has." He bangs two lids together to get Bev's attention, calls her over with his spoon.

Bev and Charly have managed our wait service for eight years. "Time to taste more soup, please." He turns back to me. "Now why would a Cold Boy not wear long pants for the freezer?"

"Why can't I taste the soup sometime?" I refuse to talk to him about Joe.

"Tasting soup is like tasting wine—it must be done correctly. You must grow into the task."

I stick my tongue out at him. I know that I am maturing, because for months now, Joe has told me that I am beautiful, that I make the world shine and open up for him like magic, that there is no one who could ever touch his soul like I do and pull it out of its deep and isolated depths. It must be true, because every time he sees me, he is touched enough by the sight of me to say those same things again.

Each time Joe comes to deliver, I go out to help him unload, where I do not unload anything, only watch him go in and out, from the truck to the store, his pink legs getting a little colder, a little redder, with each load. Each time he passes me, it is a different compliment.

"You have the shape of a lovely round—goddess," he said last week as he hopped on the ramp and rattled the empty dolly up behind him. With the next load, between the sirloin and the flanks, it was "You have eyes like opals."

"Jou have eyes like opals," Timothy whispered in my ear after Joe left.

And he has not left me alone since.

I adjust the thermostat under the lettuce once more and sneak peeks around the dining room. I find a thin woman who looks like the kind who might have given Mama trouble about not having a diet plate. But as I see Mama move through the dining hall, it is a heavy set man who stops her.

The man is disappointed but friendly. "I guess maybe your cholesterol ain't as high as mine," he says. He shifts his boots under the table.

This time Mama leans on the wood in front of him. She wants to make sure the man feels the full weight of her expertise as she looks down on him. "Truth be told, I got a cholesterol level that would clog a garden hose," she says. "But I been pretty damn happy while I was getting it."

She speaks with a soft Southern-Belle voice and smile that doesn't go with 'Damn," which I am not supposed to use. "This is not a fretful place, it's a happy place." In case he doesn't agree with her, she shifts her weight, all 264 pounds of it, to the other hand and the table tilts just a bit.

"Reckon I'll have the New York Strip, then," the man says. "With that fancy potato dish you got there."

"*Jalapeño Au Gratin* will make you so happy," she tells him, and the man nods. When Mama is that close to you, that big, you don't argue much.

The dining room fills up, the evening rushes by, and then, in no time, we are closed, and Mama tells Timothy about the guests.

"And did this man eat his steak?"

"Sucked it up like a vacuum cleaner," Mama says. "And you know Mr. Carrolton, from down at the cleaners?"

"Handsome man." Timothy chops onions and peppers he will use for an overnight marinade, always the last task before he leaves. "Smells like a fish."

"That's him. He got called to the hospital. I think his daughter took sick again."

Timothy grabs Charly, bussing the last of the tables. "We send soup tomorrow for lunch. Help me remember—Senor Carrolton, Scenic Mountain Medical."

"You remember Woman-with-the-Pearls-has-a-Cane?"

"Always orders the Santa Fe Chicken," Timothy says.

"Only this time," Mama says, "she ordered herself the salmon with crab cream sauce."

It is enough to make Timothy freeze with the knife in mid-air. "And?"

"Ate every bite. Would have mopped her plate with the bread, but you could tell that sort of thing wouldn't have matched her pearls."

Timothy dances around the end of the butcher table.

"Mind where you point," Mama says.

Timothy is ecstatic. "What did Miss Pearls have for dessert?"

"Her gentleman said no." Mama nudges me. "Said something about a cow on his arm already." The double *thwack* of the knife echoes in the kitchen, and suddenly two tomatoes are open and bleeding on the board. The chopping becomes faster, louder.

"It is as I have told you, Amarylis. Some men, they feed you, and others, they will eat you alive. Keep me in the kitchen, or I tell you, I am *un hombre peligroso*, a danger to the customers."

Two days later, it is a cool Saturday morning, and Joe hauls his crates into the kitchen. He comes out of the truck, slapping his knees. They go white for a moment, then bright red again.

"Let me help," I tell him. I hit at his legs softly, afraid of the sting I might give him.

Joe says, "Harder," and I slap his thighs until my hands hurt. He breathes faster because he has been working so hard. "Perfect," he says. He slips his hand around my waist, presses a rabbit's foot into my hand.

"You are my good luck girl. What I feel for you, Belinda, is magic," he says.

Someone bangs on the side of the truck. "That was some puny chops you bring me last time, Señor Cold Boy." I back away from Joe, but it is not fast enough. Timothy looks in and bangs on the truck again. "We will do better this time, yes? And this week, we must have more sirloin and pork," he says. "And more lamb for Easter."

Timothy starts to follow me inside. Behind me I hear Joe kicking the ramp to make it fold, slamming the locks in place in back of the truck. I wave to him as he drives by. Timothy runs into the parking lot. "Hey, you Cold Boy, what about my lamb?"

Joe shouts back at Timothy. "When I get some, you get some." Timothy says nothing until he finds me in the kitchen a few minutes later. "I think perhaps this boy, Joe, is too slow. I am afraid the meat may spoil. I have called my friend, Mr. A., told him please send another Cold Boy."

I cannot speak. Timothy has never kept me away from anyone. He has never told me I couldn't do anything. He has always let Mama do that.

I find enough voice to say, "You're not my father."

"No?" Timothy pinches the edge of the thin dough he is working on, then flattens it again as if he did not like the trim he was forming. "Then who is?" He flips, flattens and twists the filo dough, again and again, all in single gliding motions. "Can you tell me this?"

"You're just jealous," I tell him, and it scares me that I have said it, but as if I am making pastries myself, I keep pushing and pressing and rolling over him, trying to make him smaller, thinner, until I can poke holes through him.

"You want him for yourself, but you know he likes the girls instead. "

Timothy finishes the entire edge of the crêpe and takes care to texture the middle.

"I am thinking you have not yet eaten and cannot think straight," he says. "I am thinking everyone is a little smarter after they have breakfast.

He unfolds a linen napkin for a place mat in the kitchen. Quickly, he places a hot grain muffin in a saucer in front of me. On the side, he gives me a tiny cup of warm marmalade and dish of honey butter, a bowl of fresh mangoes and melon. The cutting table that stretches along the length of the kitchen is huge. And when Timothy exits the kitchen, leaving me sitting at the end by myself, it is even larger.

I see the Avery meat truck drive up one day after school. Like a black and red flag, it cruises along the gray horizon, past the front windows, past the boat at the end of the lot, until it comes to a groaning, shuddering stop. The wind is kicking up dust across the pavement, and the heavy wheels of the truck neatly iron a small box that skids up under it. I wonder which deliverer they have sent as replacement.

But it is Joe. I touch the rabbit's foot in my pocket and know what I am going to do. I have decided that he can hold me closer. When he backs up to the loading dock, he jumps out and winks at me.

"You are beautiful, today, Belinda, just like—he stops to think— "peaches and cream." He grabs his clipboard from the cab. "They had Melvin up on the boards to make this run, but I said hell, no, this was my territory." He swings me around and pecks me on the cheek. "Get $12 extra every time I make this run, and I ain't giving that up."

I am a little put off by this. Who cares about money when the world opens up? When you have peaches and cream and magic?

Joe has his hand on the rear door handle. "So what you think Tim wants? Says he needs more lamb for the weekend?" he asks. "Easter coming and all, he's like to need more of that."

His soul was despairing way down there somewhere and I was going to have to reach for it. Before Timothy got to it first.

"There's produce coming in a few minutes," I tell him. And *The Four Winds* is still in the way, so you can't go over there. But we could go over to the other parking lot. That way I could make sure I get everything we need."

Joe looks around to see where Timothy might be. "You sure?"

"Damn sure."

Joe propels his gum out of his mouth with a whoosh! He pulls me up into the cab of the truck where the windows are tinted. When I look outside, the gray and white clouds are a yellow rippled color, like milk that has begun to curdle.

At Morgan's House, Mama worries about temperature before folks come to eat. Temperature of food and temperature of the dining room. Timothy worries about smells and colors. Me, I have an eight-point checklist of things to take care of, mostly dealing with floor arrangement, table settings and condiment checks. I start with the napkins today because it is something I can do while I look down which is where my eyes want to go. If Mama or Timothy comes in to talk I can speak over my shoulder, not have to look at them.

The linen napkins are folded corner to corner, then one neat point down, always to the middle before you roll them. But my hands shake and for twenty minutes, I have been trying to remember how it is that I have folded and rolled them for the last two years, what comes next.

I feel like I have mixed Greek and Chinese and Kentucky Fried Chicken. I am both too full and empty, a strange way to feel after having made love to someone which is what I am pretty sure I have just done. While I fold, I rethink everything, trying to remember it all, trying to picture Joe's face, his eyes, trying to recapture and replay the magical moments. I am sure they were there, although all I remember is that when my eyes were closed, I smelled fresh-killed lamb when I inhaled, and my chest hurt because it was so cold in my lungs.

Timothy breezes through the hall, distracted with the excitement of dinner. He has strong wiry legs. Dark, thin legs. Soft feet so he can turn on a dime when he remembers something that needs attention. So different from Joe's legs. Thick and hard. Red and cold like his hands. Never in a million years had I imagined his hands would be so cold.

Timothy asks, "Did we get extra steaks for the holiday or did I forget to tell you?"

"I got extra."

"Thank God. I knew I could count on my girl." Then he remembers and, like a top, he spins back toward me. "Who did they send?"

"Melvin."

"*Esta bien.*" It is safe for me not to look at him because he believes I am still mad at him.

"It is almost time," he says. "Now to check the soup."

"Storm a-coming, Tim." Mama brings in another basket of hot napkins to be folded. "Could be bad for business. Or we still might get us a big party, Bev says. Prayer Chain from Garden City Methodist called."

I turn around enough to see the sky. I have no word for this color that is both gray and green. Timothy hates to have a slim crowd. Nothing is more lonely, he says, than knowing that a few dinner guests are out there surrounded by empty chairs. *The Four Winds* swells like a dark bruise at the end of the parking lot.

Mama taps the window, puts her hands on her hips. "Wonder why they don't come ever come eat with us?"

"I can tell you, it is too bad if they do not come today," Timothy says to me. "The angel food is perfect, light and golden, just a touch of almond." He touches my shoulder. "I will snip a piece for you."

"She snips nothing, no cake, no bread." Mama comes back to me. " Look how Belinda is getting round like her mama. Can you believe this?" She pinches the sides of my breast and bottom. I pull away, burned by the touch of her hand so soon after Joe's, or afraid, maybe, that she will be burned so soon after his.

"Stop it!" I pull away faster than I mean to and turn back to the napkins, trembling. Square on square. Corner to corner. Think about four corners. *Four Winds.* Winds outside are aching, howling. There is no other sound in this room and, behind me, I know that Timothy no longer looks out the window.

"You know, Amarylis, I do not recall that she has called me 'the ballerina' today," he says.

"She's growing up. Woman's got better things to do than watch a man dance around."

When Timothy makes a Chicken Kiev, he bores a narrow hole into the back of the breast before he fills it, and that is how I feel he looks at me now. Even with my back to him, I know his eyes are drilling through to my heart. "I must have someone to taste soup this evening. Our Bev will be late. Will you do that for me, Belinda?"

"It's about time you asked." He is watching me intently, his arms crossed, when I turn around to speak to him.

"You come when you are ready," he says. Then he sprints into the kitchen.

"Congratulations, honey," Mama says. "Now, thing about the soup is this: Once you are a Taster a couple of times and you know how good it can be, you enjoy even waiting for it because you know, once you got it in your mouth, wanting it has made it all the better." She has her hands clasped together in front of her, a spiritual expression on her face.

She is nearly out of the hallway when she stops. "Everything all right?"

How this woman pulls radar out from under all of her weight is amazing. Thunder cracks loudly nearby and it spurs her into movement, only slightly slower than Timothy's. "Later," she says, "we'll have to find us a way to celebrate."

In the kitchen, Timothy is quiet. I know he is calculating when the meat truck pulled up, how long it was here. The rain hits the window in a single blast and then settles into a fine quiet sound. The sizzle from the sausage that Timothy is cooking mixes with the sound of the rain and I can't tell the difference between the two.

He ladles orange soup into a bright yellow bowl. "Pop quiz, chica. I want to see what you know. How you beat an egg?"

"Wire whisk, porcelain bowl."

"Good girl. And which pan will bake for you faster, old pan, new pan?"

"Old dark pan."

"Sí. Now tell me, when you make a good bread, how you going to fix your yeast?"

I am straight-faced. "First, you get some water boiling."

"Jesus, you got to be kidding me. You are going to kill the bread."

I laugh at the face he has made.

"Okay, you have your joke on Timmy. Now you taste soup. But first, let me tell you. You touch your tongue, then sip slowly until all the seasonings fill your nose and your mouth. And this soup, you know, it is like truth serum." I pick up the spoon. I am not hungry. But appetite is litmus test in our house, forget the thermometer. As long as you can eat or put something in your mouth, you must be feeling well.

"So. Now tell me about this Joe. This boy touch you today?"

"No."

"This boy not touch you, then how come you look like you feel so bad?"

"I changed my mind."

"You change your mind about Joe or you change your mind, maybe, about who delivered for the butcher today?" It is Timothy's pumpkin soup, the one with saffron and cinnamon. It does not look good to me, and this, I realize, is my punishment. I do not even get to *want* to taste the soup.

"I changed my mind about everything." The smell of the soup is meaty and overpowering. "I don't want him to touch me. I don't want to touch him." The soup smells sweet and nauseous. "Not ever."

For the first time I can remember, I push Timothy's cooking away from me.

Timothy leans on the butcher block, puts his face in his hands for a moment. "So," he says. " I will kill him." He says this in the same tone of voice that he might use to announce that salmon will be tonight's special. It does not look to me like he thinks Joe is special, red knees or not.

Mama swirls in, clasps Timothy's arm. "We got rain, and we got guests," she says. "Fifteen from Garden City."

For the next three hours we all run, smile, check, bus. It is all I can do to bring out Timothy's soup and be gracious with it. Late in the evening Mama limps into the kitchen, face crinkled in pain, and Timothy drops everything to look at her ankles. "Ay, Amarylis, I take these shoes off now, but they will never go back on."

Mama looks at her watch, slumps down in a chair.

"I have something for you. Try this." Timothy kneels in front of her, hands her a small cake square.

Mama eats it slowly, licking warm crumbs off her palm. "Marvelous," she whispers.

Timothy watches her mouth. He smoothes her hair back.

"You are quite right," he tells her. He pats the soft rolls of her sides, feeling for something in her dress.

"Here," Mama says and she fishes out her lipstick and a Kleenex. Timothy paints her mouth and helps her up.

"Blot," he says. "Presentation, it is everything. Look at me. Good god, what a beauty—you and your heels. You are a better woman than I am."

"I suppose that is something," she says. He laughs softly and kisses her on the forehead.

Outside, lightning strikes, the lights flicker, and Timothy catches me watching them. His expression is odd, pained like someone with hurt feet, or like someone who has had something stolen while his back was turned.

"Tonight, I rub your feet," he tells Mama.

"Tonight, I will let you." Hair back in place, lips on, glucose high, Mama is a new woman, and she is out the door to greet her public again.

It is the end of the dinner call. I sit on the bottom of the cellar steps with a basket of wines to re-shelve. Pointless, I think, because Timothy will later redo them all. Mama comes down slowly with a plate of something in her hand. She has taken off her heels.

""You'll never guess—" she says. "*The Four Winds* is gone. Beat-up old car is still there, but no boat. Left sometime in the middle of the storm."

"Good. Now we have our parking lot back." I get up to put the wine in the racks.

"Just as well," Mama says. "They didn't come eat with us, they don't need to stay." She is crying and eating something. "But it was such a beautiful boat."

"Your feet still hurt?" I ask. I know that Timothy has talked to her.

"I hurt more than I can tell you." Then as if she's afraid I will miss the connection, she adds, "Thing about eating, Belinda, is this: Loneliness and happiness, contentment and pain—we feed all them strong feelings with food and other indulgences. But I believe you got to be a little older yet before you can tell which hunger it is you're feeding."

Above us, the group from Garden City, now the only ones in the restaurant, begin a chorus of "Amazing Grace." The music rises and falls like a deflated souffle that is still in denial about having gone flat. My stomach finally begins to settle, and I put my head in Mama's lap.

"Timothy is going to kill Joe," I tell her, sniffing.

"Yes, I imagine he is," she says. She pushes a tear off my cheek with one of her big fingers. She brushes crumbs from her mouth and passes a plate. They are petit fours, arranged all for me and Mama. Timothy's finest desserts, something he makes only for special occasions. In my mouth, heaven. In my mother's fat arms, forgiveness.

"But then he will make a beautiful bowtie pasta, the kind with the big red onions, and he will feel much better."

We hear the rain above us turning into hail and pelting down in rapid volleys. The sound is a familiar one, like the sound of Timothy's chopping, when he feels very angry; it is the same sound we hear sometimes when he feels good. When Timothy opens the doors to leave tonight, the three of us will go out into the damp air, smell the freshness that the rain has left behind. But just now, down here in the cellar, we are too low to smell the cleansing rain. The only smells that are sharp in my nose this moment are dirt, old grapes and sweet pastry. 🏵️

A Spin of the Zodiac Wheel

by Luis de Herrera

Do not go forth from your house on this day and abstain from sexual intercourse. Those born on this day must be cautious else they will die of excessive lovemaking.

Egyptian Astrology, about 200 B.C.,
Lindsay, *Origins of Astrology*, Pg. 172,
Frederick Muller, Ltd., London, 1971.

Bits of diamond dust glittered in the black, tranquil void. There was only a sliver of moon, not enough to count. The night forged ahead, pitch black with only the stars making their presence felt. They broke the heavenly serenity with their magic, first twinkling, then shattering the dark sky with showers of distant luminescence. To Vicky Remedios, aged six and orphaned, this activity reaffirmed her thoughts on how the heavens spoke to her through the stars. She could feel a direct contact, a mystical communication with the asteroids.

Nearly five thousand feet above sea level, the dry desert nights of the West Texas plateau are crisp and clear. As a little girl and weather permitting, I would lie on the grass outside my home and stare at the heavens. It seemed to me the stars hung as low as the ceiling in my bedroom. Sometimes I felt I could reach out and touch them. I even had the audacity to think I could exert my will and force them to disintegrate into showers of dazzling lights. Playfully, they sometimes complied.

Some nights were better than others. There were times when the stars took on a festive mood, bursting all over the firmament, showering the skies with their sparklers. I felt transported into their glittering world. Yet there was a pattern to this glitter. Certain stars never changed. I asked my dear Uncle Bartholomew about this.

"Vicky, girl," he said, placing one arm around my shoulders while using the other to point up at the sky, "some of the stars we see out there may no longer be in existence. They may be extinguished . . . can you understand this? They are so far away it takes thousands, even millions of years for their light to reach our Earth."

In my young mind this information went right through me. How could this be, when a light bulb gave light instantly? Yet it made me think further about the stars. I begged him to tell me more but he got tired, feeling the need to get back to his bottle. What he did, next day he presented me with an old, dog-eared book on Astronomy so that I should leave him alone. It became my treasure. Even though it was hard to understand, it had many illustrations and I devoured it. I read the parts I could and asked questions everywhere. I perused over its pages as profoundly as adult scholars study the Dead Sea scrolls.

As I progressed reading my astronomy book I began to understand the power of these celestial bodies. I became a pest at the local library. I read other books. I even tried to persuade Uncle Bartholomew to take me to the observatory at Fort Davis. He promised to do so but we never got around to it. My uncle was a kindly old man but he was more interested in getting a buzz-on than having to deal with a pesky, overly inquisitive girl child.

Slowly, I became familiar with some of the stars . . . Polaris, the North Star—elemental to mariners. Maia, Electra, Celaaena, Tayget, Merope, Alcyone, Stetrope—the seven daughters of Mars. The Pleides: Orion, containing the stars Betelgeuse and Rigel . . . Arcturus, Vega, the Zodiac . . . and of course, our very own Milky Way. It struck me funny that some people hadn't heard of this galaxy. "What?" they would exclaim, "I thought it was a candy bar."

It is with great distress, after a process of evaluations where I have played no favoritism—not even to myself—that I dare pronounce this statement: Most people are stupid. It is a sad fact, but many people fit this category. There are even some who, after spending a great amount of money and time pursuing M.A.'s and Ph.D.'s, remain stupid, as if the whole trip had been wasted. They are too lazy or too dumb to take effective measures that might direct their lives. They seem to settle into being nonentities. They'll jump into bad marriages, stick to bad-paying jobs they hate, look on life dejectedly but with the mistaken idea their fate is sealed. Lives are seldom planned—they just occur, like a river flowing into the ocean with no alternatives.

Not mine. Not my life.

Since my uncle was too busy—immersed in his own alcoholic world to pay much attention to mine other than to provide for my corporal needs —the planets and the stars became my solace. Very early I learned that the tides were controlled by the gravitational attraction of the sun and moon, not withstanding that the moon, though feminine, is dominant—boss of the situation, you might say. The idea that a feminine moon controlled the tides made me proud of my gender. I instantly felt a surge of power within me. I learned about eclipses—how various cultures have reacted to this phenomena. I began to understand how life on earth is governed by the skies—though not in the religious sense, like the Church would have you believe. This, I've always thought, is presumptuous—a dominant idea created by an ecclesiastical organization to govern humankind's idea of mortality. When I refer to skies I mean the astral void where stars and planets cohabit in either celestial bliss, or gigantic explosions and collisions that bother no one.

I developed my own ideas regarding my personal life.

A further step in my studies advanced me into the realm of astrological divinement—a natural step, since astronomers and astrologers alike have often been inspired by this affinity. How logical, how true these theories appeared to me! What could be a more elementary basis for projecting a human life than studying its birth in relation to the heavens and the stars? And how important for that life it be programmed from the precise moment of its birth, within the norms of its orbital lifetime?

I realized that certain intimate details of my infancy remained unanswered because my parents had perished in a fire. I began retracing my steps to my earliest memories. I was three years old at the time, and had been saved from the disaster because I had been kept overnight at the home of a friend while my parents attended a New Year's party. They came home late, probably more than slightly drunk. They were burned to death. I survived, as simple as that.

My uncle Bartholomew adopted me after the tragedy and brought me to live with him. When the adoption proceedings snagged for the lack of a birth certificate lost in the fire, I vaguely remember our driving to the town of my birth to obtain a duplicate. It wasn't a pleasant trip. He considered it an inconvenience, an ordeal having to deal with—in his opinion—dumb clerks in a small county courthouse.

When my high school years came about, I complied with their scant demands. I supplemented my time by becoming an ardent student of ancient cultures. I learned that scholars from the beginning of time have followed a pattern of studies relevant to astrological entities. A most unique passage from the Greek poet Asclepiades of Samos grabbed my attention:

Grasp in your mind that nothing is impossible, consider yourself immortal and capable of understanding everything. Ascend beyond all height, descend beyond all depth. Imagine that you are at one and the same moment everywhere . . . on earth, in the sea, in the heavens, that you are not yet born, that you are beyond death.

Upon further studies I determined how certain symbols, or signs, as they became to be called, exerted either more or less affinity with one another. Pisces mated well with Cancer, but badly with Sagittarius. These pronouncements even became part of literature. John Webster, in the Duchess of Malfi, states:

. . . the Lord of the first house, being combust in the ascendant, signi- fies short life; and Mars being in a human signe, joyn'd to the taile of the Dragon in the eight House, doth threaten a violent death . . .

During my senior year in high school I was branded into two cate- gories. The first one had me as a rara avis, a bookworm, a crazy, spaced-out, eccentric bitch. There was a second version, however, elevating me to a dedicated scholar. This latter interpretation was held by a small group of girls close to my age who sought me out, asking I write up their horoscopes focused on the relationships with their boyfriends.

I tried to explain this was a touchy, special science where a great deal of faith is required. A person must believe in order for Astrology to function. Personal charts, scripted and dutifully prepared by the astrologer are often quite reliable, but even the early philosophers had different views and interpretations. Plutarch thought one way, Plinius the Elder another. Plinius had said of Hipparchos, a dedicated astrologist, "No one has done more to prove that man is related to the stars and that our souls are part of heaven." I concurred with this philosophy.

As I progressed and became more profoundly erudite in the studies of astrology I began to seriously plan my own life. I was still quite young— barely into my teens—but I began to develop a master plan and to chart my life accordingly. I would undertake endeavors only if, after consulting my charts,

I might have a good chance of accomplishing my goals. My own personality also developed under the aura of astrology. As I grew older I wore colors that I believed were compatible with my sign, Aquarius. My jewelry—even my makeup, the perfume I started using—was all purchased with this in mind. This didn't fare too well in my dating department. Most guys shrank away from me, thinking I was . . . "strange." Besides, my hormonal awakening was slow and uncomfortable and I had a different perspective from the rest of the girls.

I didn't go bananas over the jocks or the good looking guys. Perhaps because every time I showed some interest they would come up with something stupid, such as, "Whaddaya want to know, like my birthday, for? You plannin' like, to marry me or somethin'?" So then, I'd like roll my eyes and swear to myself I'd never . . . like, never-ever, talk to these idiots again. Jamais!

Comprenez vous? I felt most of my high school male companions were mentally retarded.

When I attended the University of Texas at El Paso I had a hard time because I refused to get involved in any sort of amorous relationship. I did play some mental games involving someone I considered attractive, someone I thought I might get to like, but then I'd find his birthday through the university records office where I worked part time, and, after charting our astrological paths—my Aquarius sign with his—I would discover we were incompatible.

I kept experimenting. I even went as far as helping friends—both male and female—in their relationships and am happy to say that I was instrumental in getting some really great people together with their ideal partner. Some got married, and have stayed happily together throughout the experience. Somehow, though, nobody seemed to be suitable for me.

After getting my B.A., I decided I wanted to pursue a Master's degree in Economics. "Great!" said my Uncle Bartholomew, "this field is wide open for women. You will make your entrance at the right time." Perhaps he also considered I'd be living out of town, leaving him comfortably alone.

Economics is a mathematical science not much different from astrology where circumstances and numbers must mesh in order to arrive at a certain end. After I was accepted at Harvard's Business School I moved to Boston and later began to work for an investment firm in the financial district. I found it was interesting to play with other people's money while earning a commission.

The job itself gave me another opportunity to indulge my passion for astrology. I would choose my clients by carefully studying their birth dates and in this fashion I could work my charts to their advantage. I'm proud to say that my batting average—if I may be permitted to use an old Bostonian baseball term—is extremely high. In most cases the results have been spectacular.

It was at one of my clients' birthday party in late December where I met Charlie. I'm not a gregarious person—by nature I seem aloof and introverted—but business dictated I should attend. However, on a personal basis I've been told I can be quite pleasant. As for looks—well, I guess I can hold my own . . . Light brunette, about five eight, a hundred and eighteen pounds. Big breasts for my frame but firm. As for my rear . . . well, all women have different concepts of their rear ends. I wish mine spread a little wider and rode a little higher . . . Maybe because my friend Lou Ann has instilled an inferiority complex in me. She says I'm too narrow-hipped. Of course, what I think of my friend Lou Ann's rear is . . . that it roams too far east and west, drops too far south, and wiggles, like cafeteria Jello.

I dress conservatively . . . well, almost. At this particular time I was wearing a white on white vertical-striped wool jersey dress four inches above the knee that clung to me like syrup, with a Hermes scarf of blues and golds and fuschias around my neck; blue panty hose encased in Italian leather pumps of navy blue, and a wide, fuschia-colored belt encrusted with semi-precious stones—my birthstone, of course, predominant. Damn belt had cost more than the dress. I was holding a delicate teacup and saucer in my hands, drinking Meelong tea with a trace of cognac in it. Actually I was quite at ease, listening to a conversation between two attractive couples I'd just met who were rambling on about Mexican hospitality, ". . . . well, a hell of a lot better than the French," one of the women stated, ". . . and you can't beat the climate." Her words came across with a soothing effect, considering our own temperature in Boston had dropped into the twenties.

Suddenly the woman exclaimed, "Look, there's Charlie," and our whole group turned, including myself. Near the entrance to the living room where we were standing, a young man was taking off his gloves and overcoat. From a distance, he was a relatively good looking guy—tall, athletic. The woman waved him over and introduced him. I saw he had soft brown eyes and wore a well-trimmed beard with traces of gray in it— no moustache. He greeted both couples as if they were old friends, then shook my hand warmly. I wouldn't have given him a second thought, except the woman—his sister, as she turned out to be—made a big production of kissing him on both cheeks because today was his twenty-eighth birthday. The same birth date as our host, my client. This made me take a second look at him and I liked what I saw. Totally cool—awesome, really. I placed him mentally: Capricorn, compatible with my sign, Aquarius.

Suddenly it took an effort on my part to remain calm and aloof when somehow, contrary to my usual self, I felt an urge to come on strong to this man. But as it turned out, my intuition paid off because it was he who made all the aggressive moves. He made sure he pronounced my name correctly. He didn't ask what I did for a living. He did remark on my eyes, but not with the usual clichés: You have beautiful eyes, or, Are you sure they're your eyes—not contacts? Instead he said, "I like your eyes, they look friendly." I told him that maybe because I was from Texas. He smiled—a captivating smile—and added, "So am I—from Goliad, Texas—isn't that a coincidence?"

We traded small talk and things went along smoothly, but he really turned me on when, on a supposedly 'aside' to his sister, he said, "Mega Panoramics rose another full point today, can you believe it?" which reaffirmed the stock predictions I'd been preaching to my clients for over a month. Those who had acted on my advice had profited handsomely. From that moment on, I felt our souls had connected.

Apparently our compatibility had not gone unnoticed by the young man's sister. She invited me to dinner along with the other couple to celebrate Charlie's birthday. We said our goodbyes to our host and drove away together in the woman's big Cadillac to a seafood restaurant on the wharf near the Marriott that specializes in lobster, where the woman ordered champagne and we toasted the birthday boy. He had an engaging manner which I liked, his conversation was articulate and witty. I loved his sense of humor—a modern Oscar Wilde—like when he said, "When you convince and convert other people to your ideas, you lose faith in them." I thought that was incisive. How charming.

Wine followed the champagne, a nice Pouilly-Fuissé to go with the lobster, and dinner transpired in a spirited, though mellow, way. I hadn't enjoyed an evening so much ever. We made it a long one . . . six well-educated, congenial people with a few drinks under our belts. At the end, all of us knew each other quite well—the intimacy of a well-oiled dinner.

We all agreed it was too early to put the evening to bed. Someone suggested an after-dinner drink at a nightclub where they had dancing. I love to dance, though I seldom have a chance to enjoy it. Charlie was an excellent dancer. We rock-and-rolled, we cha-cha'd, we tangoed. The evening could have gone on forever, but at one-thirty I said I had to leave

—tomorrow was a working day. Charlie volunteered to drive me home. When we got to my apartment in Brookline, I asked if he would like a cup of coffee. He agreed, and we had coffee with a dash of Kahlúa. He loved it, said he'd never tasted it before. We exchanged a few kisses . . . one a long one, too long and too intimate for me. It made me uneasy. I could tell he wanted to stay, maybe make love . . . but I shooed him out. By now I had his birth date—the hour of his birth, the day of the week . . . I needed to consult my charts.

Next day, when he called me at work—anxious, asking me to join him for lunch, for dinner, for anything—the man sounded desperate—I had my responses ready. Yes, YES, YES! I said, though only to myself. What I really said was, I couldn't see him until Friday. It drove him wild—but I knew I had finally found my perfect match. I was just giving him a hard time and making myself hard to get, and he unknowingly went along with it.

My postponement of our first date was just an artifice to re-evaluate him.

On Friday I did just that—I wanted to be absolutely sure. Besides his earthly qualities: good looking, suave, educated, kind, a good conversationalist and a fellow Texan . . . he possessed all the Zodiac qualities. His Moon was covered by three stars, agreeing well with my Moon and its three planets, Jupiter near the head. His stars were above the Pole that lay in an extended position, dictating a rise into Venus, compatible with Aquarius. It looked as if we were made for each other.

For the next three weeks we spent most of our time together. Charlie had a twisted sense of humor that made me crack up. As we were walking along the Charles River, he pompously said it was named after him. I punched him on the shoulder and he laughed like a naughty boy. After a heavy snowfall he suggested we trek through the Commons in a foot of snow and frigid temperatures, up to Beacon Street and down to Cheers for a couple of drinks, then he ordered ice-cold lemonade. He said his ancestry absolutely demanded we go see the Irish troupe Riverdance when they appeared at the Wang theater, and he paid a fortune for tickets. Trouble is, Charlie's surname is Franco. We drove to Foxboro to see the Patriots and he rooted for the opposing team. We went to Chinatown to eat and he ordered eggs Benedict. Crazy man, but I loved him.

I had a beautiful but tiny apartment in Brookline. Charlie was staying with his sister in Hingham, way outside the Bay area so it was a long drive for him to come see me, then drive back. Several times he insinuated we move in together but I refused, using the excuse I had signed a one year's lease on my minute apartment where two people could never fit in.

One evening, while dining at the Four Seasons and though I'd been reluctant to talk about it, I began telling Charlie about my theories in astrology and how I believed our signs were perfectly matched. First he laughed good naturedly, then he embraced me with much feeling and found my lips, kissing me long and passionately, disregarding the fact we were in a booth facing other tables with other people. Many stared, as if we were freaks from Mars or . . . maybe Hollywood? Bostonians do not vent their feelings so openly. But Charlie said to hell with it. We were both from Texas, so who cared?

"Hey," he exclaimed after he'd gotten his breathing back to normal, "now I understand why I felt so attracted to you. I also dig astrology. I nearly took a course on it at the university. I believe in the power of certain signs. No wonder we're perfect for each other. Don't you dare change, okay?"

Again, disregarding critical eyes, he embraced me, holding me tight. Out of the corner of my eye I saw many faces—both customers and wait- ers—focused on us, but it didn't bother Charlie. Actually I think he spoke loudly and obnoxiously so everyone could hear. He nearly shouted, "I love you, girl. Please say you love me too. Will you marry me?"

With so many strange people watching I felt embarrassed and confused.

The whole restaurant seemed as if expectant, waiting for my response. I finally managed to blurt out, "Yes, I love you and I'll marry you, Charlie."

I swear I could hear the people breathe easier, and to my surprise, they suddenly exploded into a celebration, clapping their hands. Someone sent over a bottle of champagne, and people actually came over to our table to congratulate us.

Charlie was ecstatic. That night we finally jumped into bed and everything fell into place. After my initial shock of losing my virginity, I let go of my idiosyncrasies. I acted fiery and wild. He was gentle—yet deliberate . . . he took complete control. Capricorn subduing Aquarius—perfect. I loved it.

Charlie was not satisfied with having an ordinary wedding. He wanted something special. To honor my Mexican, and his Spanish heritage, he wanted us to be married in Spain, in a remote village near Salamanca he'd once visited when he was in the Air Force. Then he wanted to seal our marriage with an unforgettable honeymoon. He wanted us to tour Europe. I'd never been to Europe. In bed, while he kissed me in places I never knew were meant to be kissed and his hands explored every inch of my body, he promised me a spectacular, sensuous experience. We would visit the Prado Museum in Madrid to see Goya's nudes; he would arrange a tour of the cavas, or caves, where the gypsies sing their wild canto 'jondo' and dance their zapateado to the frenzied strumming of Valencian guitars. He promised to provide enough champagne to make me dizzy while we climbed to the top of the Eiffel tower, and enough ambiance to make me fall under the spell of a French student about to be seduced . . . as we toured Montmartre. Oh, how I loved this man!

Next day I went to the Post Office near my flat and filled out an application for a passport. "It will be mailed to you within six weeks, or else check with us," they said. The passport didn't arrive on time, so when I checked back, the Post Office employee didn't have an anwer right off hand.

"Sorry," the clerk stated—a red-headed woman in shapeless, government-issue Post Office blues, "let me have your phone number and I'll let you know as soon as we get it," Three days later she called. "Could you come in? Ask for Agnes."

She led me into a private office smaller than my tiny bedroom, closed the door, took a seat behind a steel desk with nothing on top while motioning for me to sit on an uncomfortable metal chair while she lit a cigarette. "I hope you don't tell my supervisor I was smoking on the job," she said with a conspirational wink. I shrugged, neither consenting nor denying. All I wanted was to find out the status of my passport. Then Agnes asked, "When was the last time you requested a birth certificate?"

I replied I never had. Uncle Bartholomew always took care of it.

"Oh, well, then brace yourself, dearie," she said while puffing on her cigarette. With her other hand she fluttered a nicotine-stained finger at me, as if apologizing, yet smiling all the time. "Now, sweets," she began, "it's not the end of the world, okay?"

I felt confused and I sure as hell didn't understand any of Agnes's nervous twitches. Yet I braced myself as instructed, expecting to hear I'd have to pay more money for some reason or another.

"When I called you after we waited the stipulated six weeks and your passport wasn't here I took a special interest in the matter and called the FBI. There are too many geeks—even attractive ladies like you—tryin' to get a passport . . . and not always for the right reasons, ya know? So I ran it through the computer and what I got was . . . your case required special treatment 'cause your birthdate didn't check out."

I think my jaw dropped.

"So I called the County Clerk's office in Marfa, Texas. That is your birthplace, ain't it? Well, this don't happen every day but what I got from the clerk out there in Texas was . . . Lemme tell you how she explained it to me, then I'll try to do the same for you, okay?"

By this time I felt my heart thumping wildly, like a native drum sending signals. My instincts told me something was profoundly wrong. Agnes continued, "Have you ever seen the number 7 written European style, with a little line crossing through the stem? Agnes picked up a pen and a piece of paper from the top drawer of the desk and jotted down the number 7 with a cross mark. I noticed she'd crossed it at a very low point. She continued, "This was before computers were used universally, okay? When many records were kept by hand, especially in a small courthouse like Marfa, Texas. So you see, what the clerk did was copy the slashed 7 thinking it was a 2."

I didn't say anything because I couldn't catch my breath. I wondered if this well-meaning woman knew what she was doing to me, but she didn't seem to notice. She went on, "The way the clerk explained it, the duplicate of your birth certificate was issued as if you'd been born in February—the second month, instead of July, the seventh month, like it should'ave been."

My mind started to become blurred.

"It was a simple transcribing mistake," continued Agnes, still apologizing. "Whoever did the duplication of your birth certificate—probably an over-worked clerk—read the 7 as a 2. It can happen, ya' unnerstand?" she said, as if trying to apologize for all the bureaucratic errors ever made. Instinctively, my hearing process was about to shut-off, when Agnes added, "What surprises the hell outta me is, how come nobody in your family caught it? All these years you've been livin' as born in February, when your correct date of birth is in July . . . what about birthday parties and stuff? . . . how'd you manage those?" I thought of my uncle Bartholomew and his drinking. I could not contain silent tears that ran down my cheeks, making my makeup run. "Hey, I'm sorry," ran off Agnes again. "I hope this hasn't inconvenienced you." She took another drag at her cigarette and blew smoke in my face.

I left the Post Office in a daze. I barely remember uttering my garbled thanks to Agnes. Outside, the day—cold, yet sunny—seemed to be made of cardboard. The leafless trees looked ugly and hostile . . . tall monstrosities partially eclipsing the fragile sun. People walked by, indifferent to my agony, all bundled up in their winter clothing like doughy Pillsbury dolls with sneers on their faces instead of their usual smiles . . . too cold to act civil. My knees felt wobbly. I walked like a somnambulist expecting to faint at any moment although strangely, I didn't. When I got to my car I decided to leave it there. I didn't trust myself driving. I forced myself to walk the rest of the way.

As soon as I got home I poured myself a stiff bourbon and drank it in one swallow. No dainty sipping this time. I wanted instant numbness.

Who is this woman inside my body? I know not who I am, nor what I might become. I've just found out I'm no longer the Aquarius I had tended and cared for all these years. My Zodiac life has plunged ahead five months into an abyss. I have degenerated into a . . . ugh . . . Cancer . . . an indifferent, ridiculously conservative, impartial, sentimental, stupid sign. For twenty years I lived with my uncle Bartholomew sustaining a fictitious existence. I patterned all my life around my assumed birthdate and have made myself believe that all my acts, my total commitment to the world was supported by my sign, Aquarius. I now find I have been living a horrendous lie. My years of planning, all my accomplishments, have been made under false pretenses. Even this romantic, wonderful new love I have found, which is now my heart, my very soul . . . is a mere figment of my imagination. I feel this is an untenable situation. My life, as a person of significance, has vanished. I feel a strong need to end it. This is so stupid. Suddenly I remember that in my chest of drawers there is an extremely sharp Bowie knife, a gift from my dear, alcoholic Uncle Bartholomew. ✹

BODY

by Miles Wilson

Q: I want to thank you for joining us today. You must be very busy.

A: Respiration, gastrointestinal processes, mitosis, glandular secretions, etc. It keeps one hopping. Idle cells are the Devil's playground.

Q: Let's get right down to business, then. You're 47, I believe.

A: Yes.

Q: Not exactly a ripe old age, but something of an accomplishment given, shall we say, the body of evidence concerning your impediments.

A: Yes.

Q: How might you account for your success thus far?

A: Salt, sugar, animal fats, caffeine, nicotine, naps, vitamin E, DMSO, silymarin, minoxidil, Zoloft, projectile vomiting during committee meetings, seldom pissing into the wind or shitting where I eat, foot rubs, *Parade Magazine* health tips, primal venting at I-10 drivers, right-handed sex, wrecking only Volvos, not catching cancer, letting Everson Priestmeyer call me a pussy after a jv football game and walking away, sleeping with 23 women and no men, sildenafil citrate, never living in Mississippi, pushups, situps, sleeping with the phone unplugged, landing on my shoulder instead of my head when the rope broke, vanity, scrupulous oral hygiene, cheating only slightly on my taxes, my genetic vita—the kind of cellular rectitude a Baptist could go to church with—native charm, never taking a taxi in Mexico City, and certain inorganic compounds which must remain unmentioned.

Q: I see. Perhaps we can explore some of these anomalies as we go along. I notice, however, a distinct absence of spiritual attributes. This suggests a belief in the separation of body and soul.

A: What?

Q: "Soul." As in "keeping body and soul together."

A: I prefer not to speak of it.

Q: My apologies. I see now that this was on the list of proscribed questions.

A: I don't mean to be difficult; that's one my managing partner handles.

Q: Right, and we'll be hearing from him later in the show. I see by your résumé that you spent some time as a lumberjack.

A: "Logger" is the preferred non-gendered usage.

Q: I'll bet there aren't many lumberjills out there.

A: None, but you can't bid on federal timber sales if you employ lumberjacks.

Q: Whatever. In any event, there's certainly a lot more interest in the natural world these days, and I'm sure our audience would like to hear about your part in it.

A: How can you tell a dogwood tree in the woods?

Q: What?

A: By its bark.

Q: Ha, ha.

A: What would a logger do if you gave him a million dollars?

Q: Yes, well—

A: Keep logging till he went broke.

Q: I think we'd better leave that sort of thing to our later guests.

A: Of course. My apologies. May I show you a tattoo?

Q: This isn't Fox.

A: On my back?

Q: I suppose.

A: "It goes like this—
     forty acres, give or take,
     of bedlam. A derangement of land
     called clear-cut.
     True naming at eye level, but lower
     in the region of sperm and egg
     and on down a bewilderment:
     gaping stumps, the rot and shatter

of trunks, pitch leaking, congealed,
every digit
and the needle hair of each pore.
The dirt astonished."

Q: What?

A: The first stanza of a poem my managing partner had inscribed. Logging turns out to be bad news for trees and bodies, professional and amateur.

Q: I'd like to explore that distinction, but first could you give us an idea of what you mean by bad news.

A: Reduced habitat for species in climax forests, siltation of spawning beds for anadromous fish, global warming from a decrease in biomass carbon dioxide absorption—

Q: What?

A: The news about logging. Bad, mostly.

Q: Ha, ha. I'm sure our sponsors will be interested to hear that. Actually, I'd like to keep the focus closer to home. I was wondering what sorts of adventures you'd had personally as a logger.

A: Bruised ribs, broken ribs, broken nose (3), broken finger (3), steel fiber from a choker in my eye, chipped wrist, chipped tooth (2), concussion—

Q: Well, I'm sure we get the idea. We seem to be drifting a little off the track, but since we've taken this turn let me interject a question I usually save for later in the interview: when were you most humiliated?

A: In sex or otherwise?

Q: Both.

A: The time an insurance adjuster I'd picked up at the greyhound track in Corpus fell asleep *flagrante delicto*. On consecutive nights.

Q: Drunk?

A: No, alas.

Q: Otherwise?

A: When I was eleven, I ran with a gang that cornered a boy who went to school with us but lived outside the neighborhood. He wasn't very smart, and he smelled bad, and you could tell that even Mrs. Meese was pretty disgusted by him. Anyway, we had him pinned down—I think we were going to pants him—and he called us chicken and said he'd fight one of us. We said okay and he picked me and got ahold of my hands and bent my fingers back until I cried and begged. Then everybody else jumped in and beat the shit out of him.

Q: In the interests of fair play, what's the most heroic thing you've ever done?

A: Stopped smoking, stopped drinking, married twice, sired three children.

Q: The next most?

A: On the Spade Creek Fire in Arizona, pounding out leg cramps from no water, fourteen hours on the line, blind and puking up black sludge from the smoke, holding on in heat like an open forge and breaking the fire, turning it there on the ridge, keeping it from 20,000 acres of new country.

Q: You must have been some body in those days. But let's get back to that distinction you made between professional and amateur.

A: Professional trees are grown for money: Doug fir, ponderosa pine, sugar pine, red cedar, incense cedar, Engelmann spruce—

Q: A charming and predictable obsession with the nomenclature of the vegetable world, but I'm afraid we're drifting away again—

A: Whereas amateur trees grow just for the sport of it: cottonwood, alder, aspen, juniper, madrone, myrtle, chinquapin. Logging's tough on all of them. In fact—

Q: Drifting away from the business at hand.

A: Sorry. A professional body is a for-profit operation. It pays its own way. An amateur body is kept.

Q: You mean the threadbare blue collar/white collar dichotomy?

A: Not entirely. Farmers, typists, steam fitters, commercial fishermen, cat skinners, steelworkers, sure. But also athletes. And dancers, singers, models, magicians—any kind of performers. Also hookers and surgeons and soldiers and muggers and sculptors and skid row blood sellers. Naturally, most professional bodies come equipped with starting fluid or battery backups in case their metabolism goes down.

Q: All very interesting, I'm sure. But moving right along, I understand that you have been filleted in print. I wonder if you would sketch out the circumstances for us.

A: What are you getting at?

Q: Let's not be coy. I'm referring, of course, to the ode, "Body," dedicated to you and appearing in the Norton anthology *Two-Fisted Women: If the Right One Don't Getcha, the Left One Will.*

A: A toothsome wench who turned malicious. I had enjambed her once in our youth and never sought a return engagement. Someone who writes about "the broken bones of the heart" is capable of any distortion. I believe the book is deservedly out of print.

Q: Frank is signalling me to skip a follow-up on that one. Taking the long view for a moment, what would you want to smell as you died?

A: I can't say that I've given it any thought.

Q: Here's your chance.

A: An August thunderstorm in the Chisos Basin, Glenfiddich scotch, a heap of sheets and towels just off the line, breakfast cooking, Port Orford cedar, the first woman I ever slept with.

Q: Along those same eschatalogical lines, have you ever thought of killing yourself?

A: I saw my children born, and a huge tide went out of me and returned changed, and I belong to this world forever.

Q: Pretty fancy stepping there, even given some latitude for body language.

A: May I say that I resent the fact that while people believe a body might or might not have rhythm, everyone thinks that bodies talk funny—funky grammar, erratic syntax, regionalisms. In fact, if this weren't a mixed audience, I would suggest that you stick that notion where the sun don't shine.

Q: With respect to sunshine and suggestions, do you have any advice for the bodies in our audience?

A: I believe I covered that in my opening remarks. We are all time's toy and confection.

Q: Speaking of which, I see that we're about out of it. By way of wrapping things up, what's the most fun you've ever had?

A: A riot of the parasympathetic nervous system during an all-night surprise with KB.

Q: KB?

A: Yes.

Q: A little late in the going for such uncharacteristic reticence, wouldn't you say? How about a little hint for our audience.

A: Certain indiscretions involving body boundaries.

Q: I see. Well, then, perhaps you could give us a synopsis of your imperfections.

A: Again, I must defer to my managing partner.

Q: Did you ever almost die?

A: Yes.

Q: Reincarnation?

A: "Earth's a grave and so it thrives."

Q: Where do you see yourself going from here?

A: Wormward.

Q: Have you given any thought to your final disposition?

A: No.

Q: Thank you. Our guest this afternoon has been a classic ectomorph, patched and gone to seed. The vitals, for those of you who follow the stats: weight 192; waist 38 1/2; vision 20/300 uncorrected; total cholesterol 256; blood pressure 150/91; muscle mass as a percentage of total body weight 23%; reflective percentage of cranium 53%; slumpage 21.732% off vertical; liver toxicity (expressed as bilirubin count) 2.3. When we come back, I'll be talking with his managing partner who recently structured a five-year rollover deal with cancellation and good behavior renewal options. Also joining us will be a macro imager who will punch up a digital projection of the body over the next decade (I've seen the graphics, folks; they're going to make the fillings fall right out of your teeth). And to help clue us in on the body's shortcomings, two of his three former wives, here from Dallas and West Jesus, Texas. Take it away, Frank. ✪

THE POT HAS EYES

by Carmen Tafolla

"The *jarro* has eyes and it's looking at me."

"No, *Mamá*, you're only imagining it."

"No, go imagine yourself! This is real!"

"Mamá, it's the same bean pot we've made beans in for years!"

"No, it's not, don't you remember? That one broke. Sometime after your father died. It couldn't bring itself to make good beans again anyway!"

"*Pero, Mamá. . .*"

"No, we bought this one at the H.E.B. It was sitting there between the shiny aluminum pots and the blue peltre camping stuff that the gringos like to hang on their walls. And aluminum's not good for you anyway!"

"*Pero, que tiene eso que ver, Mamá?* That doesn't make the pot have eyes."

"This one does."

"It's just the design on it, the way the paint circles around two little round things."

"They're not round things! They're eyes."

"So if it's got eyes, they're blind, okay?"

"Not this one, it sees. Not only that, it's critical!"

"What is it criticizing, *Mamá*? The two of us and our raggedy clothes and funny lives? None of my clothes fit anymore, they all have holes, we don't have money to go buy all that expensive stuff they're selling, and you're worried about an old bean *jarro*!" said the daughter, trying to adjust the off-center skirt of her dress.

"*Tú anda*, ignore me if you want, but you know I'm telling the truth. The *jarro* has eyes!"

"Okay, so if the *jarro* has eyes, what can we do about it anyway? If it'll make you happy, I'll throw it in the trash. Nobody has time to make beans anymore anyway. We get'm out of a can and warm'm in the microwave. So

I'll throw it out, just quit talking *locuras*, Mom, it makes me nervous!"

"No!!!" the old lady screamed, "Don't throw it away!!! Then you'll *never* get rid of it. It wants us to see something."

"Should I ask? Maybe I don't want to ask this question, *Mamá*, maybe I'm tired of this, and I just want to close my eyes and not hear you worry it anymore. The way things are, life is just a headache, and keeping my eyes open to hear your ideas locas just makes it hurt worse!"

The old lady mumbled loudly, as the daughter leaned back on the sofa and tried to end the conversation.

"I don't know what you want, pot, but you have to quit watching us— you have to let us know what you want and then just go your way. *Déjanos, por favor.*" The last three words were half prayer, half scolding, but the clay pot didn't leave them alone. It just kept its eyes open and watched as the old lady tossed and turned in the afternoon heat of her aching bed.

By nightfall, the old lady had risen to rummage through the refrigerator. Age and exhaustion had robbed the leftovers in the small bowls of any attempt at flavor, and she found nothing that would satisfy. She considered approaching the bean pot and cooking something special from scratch, but she was still too annoyed and worried to get near it. She covered it gently with a dishcloth, clean but worn thin at the edges. A moment later, she removed the dishcloth, afraid it would offend the pot's very open eyes. She stared at it. Asked of it, "What do I do?" She paced. Then, finally, she put on the faded black sweater, more from custom than from chill, and went out the door to she knew not where.

Walking down the broken sidewalk of the barrio streets, she passed a girl with purple hair and an earring in her nose. The girl's heavy eye make-up made her dark eyes look all consuming, sad and piercing, as if they could swallow up all the tragedies of the world. Three boys hung out at a corner, outside the small grocery store, their hair cut in odd shapes and angles. She was frightened by their hairstyles, jolted by the look so unnatural to the way they had looked as children. One had his hair long on the top half of his head and shaved short on the bottom half. Four earrings stood out on each of his two ears, and one on his eyebrow. The second's hair was bleached an extreme blond, a color that, next to his dark skin, blinded her. His eyes seemed a pale fish-blue, not like human eyes at all, but reflective like the scales of a fish, and clouded like the cataracts of the aged. For a moment, the hair of the third seemed to make sense, something she recognized in this strange new world. It was the proud Indian cut of the Mohawk. Frightening, but still recognizable. Something she could find some root, some history for. So shook she was by the styles of the young around her, that she took some comfort in his standing-up-straight strip of hair from his forehead to his *nuca*, not caring to notice or being able to absorb the reality of its pink and blue rainbow coloration.

Inside the store, she could smell the temptation of the burritos, tacos and corn dogs sitting under the hot lamp, but so accustomed was she to not buying the ready-made or individually served, that she passed by without even considering it and headed to the few shelves of cans and packages. She picked out a package of Masa Harina for corn tortillas, and then moved to the bin of lonely and bruised vegetables, where she uncharacteristically selected an avocado without checking its price. Riding high on some intoxication of mission, she added a tomato, a lemon, another avocado, and two serrano chiles.

At the checkstand, she hesitated a second, suddenly lost.

"Did you change your mind?" scowled the tired, middle-aged woman who even ten years ago would have added "*Señora*" and a smile to that same question.

The old woman woke from her hesitation and emptied the last few dollars and the food stamps from her sweater pocket. As she exited the store, holding the small plastic bag, she paused to tell the third of the young boys, "I like your hair" at which the young man was caught off guard and the other two hooted and burst into laughter. The pink and blue changed slightly in shade as his complexion deepened. The old woman, frightened by the looks of the other two still and by their loud behavior, wavered in balance as she hurried down the block.

The old woman passed a young mother with a crying toddler running after her. The child was dressed only in diapers and a dirty shirt. "I'm NOT going to carry you, you fatso! An' you better hurry up or I'll just leave you at home alone, *chiflado*!!" The child cried even harder, and the young woman looked even more irritated, more angry, part of her wishing that someone could carry her, and dry her tears. She needed to use the restroom, but the gas station across the street had now locked its restrooms to everyone except the employees. A well-dressed man in a shiny new car drove slowly past, giving her the eye, and she walked even faster so the toddler would not be part of the picture he saw. He looked away. She knew that in twenty minutes he could be across town, in a neighborhood where the streets had no chugholes and the gas stations all left their restrooms open, where the clerks at the store always smiled and asked if they could help you find anything else, and where their eyes did not follow you inside the store to see if you were trying to steal. Angry, she picked up her pace, and the child's tears ran even faster down his shirt to further soak the wet and shredding diaper.

The old woman, too, had seen the well-dressed man. She did not trust him, did not trust much of what she saw around her. Others dressed like him had come to her door, always making promises, always asking for a signature, always stealing what was not theirs.

The path back to her house suddenly seemed longer, more frightening, and the steps seemed more difficult. She no longer recognized the streets, and without warning, her head suddenly felt without strength, without light, without direction.

The first thing she saw when she opened her eyes was the bean pot. Its eyes were worried, its hair was pink and blue and cut in a style as proud as that of the Mohawk Indian, and it talked.

"Are you okay?" the bean pot asked.

She jolted upright. It was not a bean pot after all. It was the young man with the standing-straight-up Indian hair, only it was pink and blue.

"Are you okay?" he repeated. "I didn't know what to do, but I see you leave this house usually, so I brought you back here. Is that okay? Are you all right?"

It took the old woman a minute to make sense of the sequence of events. Her daughter was not there, had probably gone to find her. The young man seemed embarrassed, tried to explain. "I'm the one from the store, remember? You said you liked my hair."

"You look like an indio."

The young man didn't know if it was a compliment or a cutdown till the old lady said, "*Mi papá era indio. Apache.*"

Then, hesitantly, "You did not come to rob me? Why did you do this?"

The young man did not know what to answer. Finally he responded quietly, "I like your hair." And neither could explain why that made them both laugh harder than either had done in quite a while.

By the time the daughter rejoined them, the old lady had made and salted a whole plate of avocado tacos, and the young man was eating enthusiastically. The corn tortillas were soft and handmade, and the flavors of the tomato, lemon, and serrano had already kissed the avocado. The bean pot was just starting to boil, but the smell was warm and pleasing.

"You look kind of like my grandmother. I used to have a grandmother when I was little." The young man could hardly believe the strangely delicious and comforting taste of these incredible homemade tacos. Maybe she would make them again. Maybe she would teach him how to make those beans. Maybe she would like the new shade he was thinking of dying his hair.

His smile was interrupted for just a moment by a look of disbelief, as he thought he saw the pot, from its comfortable perch on the stove, smiling back at him. ✿

AUTHOR NOTES

TERESA PALOMO ACOSTA holds her undergraduate degree from the University of Texas at Austin and a masters from Columbia University. Her poetry has appeared in *Descant, Riversedge, Texas in Poetry, Indefinite Divisions: An Anthology of Chicana Literature*, and *The United States in Literature*. In 1993 she received the Voertman Award for outstanding poetry from the editors of *New Texas 93*. Also a cultural historian, Acosta contributed nonfiction to the 1996 reference source, *The New Handbook of Texas* (Texas State Historical Association). Five of Acosta's poems are in *¡Floricanto Sí!* (Penguin Books), a 1998 anthology with poetry by influential Latina writers. A poem by Acosta is also included in the 1999 edition of the literary magazine, *¡Tex!*, and she has a poetry book, *Nile and Other Poems*, forthcoming from Red Salmon Press. A native of McGregor in McLennan County, Teresa Palomo Acosta lives in Austin.

MICHAEL ADAMS, who is a counselor for The Texas Institute of Letters, writes novels and short stories and has authored a textbook on expository writing. He is an Associate Professor of English at the University of Texas at Austin, where he teaches American Literature, the Modern Short Story, and Creative Writing. A faculty member of the UT Michener Center for Writers, Adams has written two novels, *Blind Man's Bluff* and *Anniversaries in the Blood*. Michael Adams grew up in Central Texas, about which he writes.

PHYLLIS W. ALLEN, a Fort Worth free-lance writer and businesswoman, has lived in Texas all her life. In 1988, her "The Red Swing," a short story, was published in a Guild Press anthology (Minneapolis Metropolitan University Press.) Allen's short fiction has also been included in the first edition of *Texas*

Short Stories, Kente Cloth: African American Voices in Texas (Center for Texas Studies), and in the second edition, *Kente Cloth: African American Voices in the Southwest* (University of North Texas), as well as in the first edition of *¡Tex!* (Writer's Garret/ Today Foundation). Her story, "The Shopping Trip" in the first edition of *Kente Cloth* received the best short story award, judged by Layne Heath. In 1999, she had one story among the final five selections and performed at the A.C. and Judy Greene Literary Festival. And recently, one of her creative nonfiction pieces was read on NPR and subsequently was awarded a KATIE.

JUDY ALTER has been Director of Texas Christian University Press since 1987. She holds a Ph.D. in English from Texas Christian University with a special interest in the literature of the American West. Before that, she earned a bachelors from the University of Chicago and a masters from Harry S. Truman University in Missouri. The author and publisher is a past president of Western Writers of America. In 1984, she received the Best Juvenile Award from the Texas Institute of Letters for *Luke and the Van Zandt County War*. Judy Alter has received Spur awards from Western Writers of America for the novel *Mattie* (Doubleday, 1988) and for the story, "Sue Ellen Learns to Dance" (*Texas Short Stories*, Browder Springs, 1997). In addition, she has won Western Heritage Awards from the National Cowboy Hall of Fame for "Fool Girl" and "Sue Ellen Learns to Dance." Alter's story in this collection appears in a different version in the novel *Legend*, released in 1999 by Liesure Books.

nia akimbo, a pseudonym, translates as "purpose misplaced" and is written in lower-case letters to express the feeling of insignificance felt by lesser-known writers. In 1994, nia akimbo received a commission to write a poem for a redis-covered slave cemetery in Dallas. In 1999, she received a second commission to write a poem for the Children's Chorus of Greater Dallas. Her poetry and short fiction has been anthologized in *New Texas 94* and in both editions of *Kente Cloth*, and her works have appeared or are scheduled to appear in *African American Review, the Licking Press Review*, and *CALYX: A Journal of Art and Literature by Women*. In 1999, she had a poem, "Learning to Read," in an accompaniment to a textbook published by Allyn and Bacon. She returned to college after a twenty-year absence and is "All But Dissertation" in the Ph.D. program in the School of Arts and Humanities at the University of Texas at Dallas, where she teaches Rhetoric.

Adelina Anthony is a writer and actress who grew up in Texas. While in Texas, she lived in San Antonio and Dallas and was active in regional theater. She is currently an MFA candidate in the Directing program at UCLA. As a freelance writer, she has published several op-eds through the Progressive Media Project and reviewed professional theater for *Back Stage West*. Adelina Anthony, who has been published in the United States and Germany, is working on a collection of short stories.

RHONDA AUSTIN lives in Alpine, Texas, where she is a lecturer in English at Sul Ross State University. Her story, "Kyla Gene's Wedding," was included in the first edition of *Texas Short Stories* and she has also published nonfiction in newspapers. Rhonda Austin holds a masters degree in English and is currently working on a novel.

DUNYA MCCAMMON BEAN has a BA in history from the University of Texas at Austin, and an MFA in creative writing from UT at El Paso. Publications include material in *The Rio Grande Review* and *Texas Monthly*. Portions from a script, *Trees*, were performed as a UTEP theatrical production. Two other scripts and a treatment are being considered in Hollywood. Bean has worked for the president of a medical center, in public relations for a commercial real estate developer, as a corporate fundraiser for the Houston Grand Opera, as an instructor at UTEP, and is currently employed as an editor for the Senate Research Center in her hometown of Austin.

PATRICK BENNETT has published fiction in *Sou'wester, Concho River Review*, and other literary magazines. His short story in *New Texas*, "Winifred and the Wolf Man," won the Betty Greene Award from the Center for Texas Studies in 1993. His books, *Talking With Texas Authors* and *Rough and Rowdy Ways* were published by Texas A&M Press. Most recently, the Abilene Public Library published a fifty-six page chapbook by Patrick and Shay W. Bennett, *Culture on the Catclaw: A List of Published Books and Produced Plays by Abilene Authors*. Before becoming the current writer in residence at McMurry University in Abilene, Texas, Patrick Bennett worked in newspapers, public relations, and college teaching.

BETSY BERRY, who once was a ghostwriter for Tex Schram of the Dallas Cowboys, has had her poetry and prose in a variety of publications, including *Descant, New Texas 95, Texas in Poetry*, and *Texas Observer*. Betsy Berry's novel, *French Resistance*, co-written with Don Graham, is forthcoming from Boaz Publishing. She has a doctorate from the University of Texas and lives in Austin.

YVETTE R. BLAIR is both a print and broadcast journalist and has won awards for both. Her fiction and poetry has been in anthologies, including the first edition of *Kente Cloth* and the second edition of *¡Tex!*. Blair is also a performing artist with the City of Dallas Neighborhood Touring Program, where she reads and performs poetry. The Dallas native also teaches a poetry workshop, with an emphasis on the writers of the Harlem Renaissance.

CINDY BONNER, the winner of the 1997 PEN Texas Award for Best Novel, is the author of the novels, *Lily, Looking after Lily*, and *The Passion of Dellie O'Barr*. In 1999, her fourth novel, *Right from Wrong*, was released by Algonquin Books of Chapel Hill and favorably reviewed in *Texas Monthly, Southern Living*, and *Booklist*. Her short stories have appeared in literary magazines, including *The Gettysburg Review, High Plains Literary Review*, and *Crosscurrents*, and have received awards from the Roberts Foundation and from Texas Byliners. Her novels have been named Best Books by the American Library Association, finalist for the Western Writers of America's award for best first novel, and have been translated into German and Spanish. A Corpus Christi native, Cindy Bonner currently resides in Yorktown in DeWitt County, southeast of San Antonio. The protagonists of "Advice," Sunny DeLony and Gil Daily, also appear in Bonner's novel, *Right from Wrong.*

KAY MERKEL Boruff lived in Vietnam 1968-1970 with her husband who flew for Air America, a division of the CIA. After her husband was killed flying in Laos, she returned to teach at a private school in Dallas. She has published articles, poems, and stories in *The Dallas Morning News*, the *New York Review of Books*, *Vanity Fair*, and in a variety of literary journals, including *Glaxay of Verse*, *Lucidity*, and *Grasslands Review*. Sections of Kay Boruff's Vietnam-era correspondence were included in *Love and War: 250 Years of Wartime Love Letters.*

JAY BRANDON is the author of nine novels, the most recent of which is *Angel of Death*, published in Fall 1998. Jay's 1995 novel, *Local Rules*, was a selection of *Reader's Digest Condensed Books*. His previous novel, *Loose Among the Lambs*, was a main selection of the Literary Guild, and his novel *Fade the Heat* was nominated for an Edgar award for best mystery novel of the year. His other writings include one of nonfiction, *Law and Liberty: A history of the Legal Profession in San Antonio* (1997) along with award-winning journalism. His books have been published in more than a dozen foreign countries. He holds a master's in writing from John Hopkins University. As an attorney, Jay Brandon has practiced at the Court of Criminal Appeals (the highest criminal court in Texas) as well as at the Bexar County District Attorney's Office and the San Antonio Court of Appeals. He writes fiction and practices law in San Antonio with wife and three children.

BILL BRETT has been Postmaster of Hull, Texas, an East Texas cowhand, an oilfield roughneck, farmer, truck driver, and deputy sheriff. He has authored three collections of story stories, *Well, He Wanted to Know and I Knowed So I Told Him, There Ain't No such Animal*, and *This Here's a Good'un*. His story, "Justice" was included in the Texas Monthly Press anthology, *South by Southwest*. Bill Brett's 1977 Texas A&M novel, *The Stolen Steers*, earned a Cowboy Hall of Fame's Western Heritage award for folklore.

AIMEE LEE BROWN-CABAN, who studied with Robert Nelsen, is a recent graduate of the University of Texas at Dallas in Richardson. Her work has been published in *The Mercury* and in other literary journals. She is now at Iowa State, working on an MFA in creative writing.

MARK BUSBY, a native of Ennis, Texas, lives in Wimberly and is the director of the Center for the Study of the Southwest and professor of English at Southwest Texas State University. Along with Dick Heaberlin, Busby edits the periodicals, *Southwestern American Literature* and *Texas Books in Review*. He is the author of several critical works on Southwestern literature, including *Larry McMurtry and the West: An Ambivalent Relationship* (UNT Press, 1995), and is the secretary of the Texas Institute of Letters. His story "The Possum" was co-winner of the short story prize at the Katherine Anne Porter Museum Literary Contest in 1997.

LEE MERRILL BYRD has spent most of her life in the Southwest. Her 1992 story "Major Six Pockets" received a Texas Institute of Letters award for best short fiction and was anthologized in *New Stories from the South*. Lee Merrill Byrd's *My Sister Disappears*, a collection of stories and a novella, was released by Southern Methodist University Press in 1993. It received a Southwest Book award and the Stephen F. Turner Award from the Texas Institute of Letters. In 1997, she was the recipient of a Dobie-Paisano fellowship. With her husband Bobby Byrd, her daughter and her son-in-law, Susannah Byrd and Eddie Holland, she operates Cinco Puntos Press. For a national market, the family owned business publishes fiction, nonfiction, poetry, and children's bilingual literature from the American Southwest, the U.S. Mexico border, and Mexico. With children and grandchildren, Lee and Bobby live in El Paso.

EWING CAMPBELL, a native of Alice, lives in Hearne and teaches creative writing at Texas A&M University. He has received NEA, Fullbright, and Dobie-Paisano fellowships. His fiction has appeared in such literary journals as *Chicago Review*, *Prairie Schooner*, *New England Review*, and *Kenyon Review*.

Among Campbell's books are *Piranesi's Dream: Stories, Weave It Like Nightfall, The Tex-Mex Express,* and *The Rincón Triptych,* as well as *Raymond Carver: A Study of the Short Fiction.* His stories were anthologized in both editions of the *New Growth* series. His most recent novel is *Madonna Maleva.* Ewing Campbell received the Chris O'Malley Fiction Prize in 1998.

CAMILLA CARR has professional writing credits in Texas and in Hollywood. Carr's first novel, *Topsy Dingo Wild Dog,* will be directed as a feature by Rod McCall. Her second novel, *Packard Jordan's Final Appeal to the Texas State Parole Board,* has been optioned for a feature film by Holly Hunter. Camilla has scripted seven motion pictures for television, including a musical, *High and Mighty,* for Dolly Parton. Her adaptation of Pulitzer-prize winning crime journalist Edna Buchanan's novel, *Nobody Lives Forever,* aired on ABC this past spring. She is currently developing Thomas Mann's feminist masterpiece, *The Black Swan,* with Vin Di Bona Productions. With Avenue Pictures, she is developing *The Frances Kaiser Story,* based on a real rarity, a female Texas sheriff.

PAT CARR, who was born in Wyoming, but grew up in Texas, has published ten books in the fields of fiction, criticism, and archeology. Her work on the Mimbres culture in New Mexico resulted in *Mimbres Mythology* (Texas Western Press) and *Sonahchi* (Cinco Puntos), and her first short story collection, *The Women in the Mirror* (Iowa University), won the Iowa Fiction Award. Her stories have appeared in such places as *The Southern Review* and *Best American Short Stories,* and she has won a Texas Institute of Letters Short Story award and a Library of Congress Marc IV for her fiction. Her most recent book, *Beneath the Hill* (Voices), appeared in Spring 1999, and she's currently finishing the manuscript of a novel based on her experiences with integration/ segregation at Texas Southern University in Houston.

NANCY JONES CASTILLA teaches at Mountain View College in the Dallas County Community College District. Before writing short stories, she wrote poetry, which has been published in such literary magazines as *Separate Doors*, *CCTE Studies*, and *Texas College English*. Her work was anthologized in *Images from the High Plains*, *A Literature of Sports*, and *Vision and Voices: Poems for Paul Wells Barrus*. Nancy Jones Castilla also edited a book of poetry, *Voices from Within* (North Texas Press).

Paul Christensen, short story writer, poet, critic, and editor, teaches at Texas A&M University. He received a NEA poetry grant in 1991, and his story "Water" won the 1995 Short Fiction Award from the Texas Institute of Letters. His books of poetry include *Old and Lost Rivers*, *Gulfsongs*, *The Vectory*, *Weight & Measures*, and *Signs of the Whelming*. His latest poetry appears in the anthologies, *Inheritance of Light*, *Where Three Roads Meet*, and *And What Rough Beast: Poems at the End of the Century*. Christensen's new book, *West of the American Dream: An Encounter with Texas* will appear next year from Texas A&M University Press. He is currently working on an anthology of 19th-century American protest poetry for Oxford University Press. *Antioch Review* selected his essay, "Bluffing" for its "Distinguished Prose" award. Furthermore, he is a contributing editor to *France Today* and other magazines, and lives part of the year in southern France.

L. D. Clark has published four novels: *The Dove Tree* (1961), *The Fifth Wind* (1980), *A Charge of Angels* (1987), and *A Bright Tragic Thing* (1992), as well as a volume of short fiction: *Is This Naomi? and Other Stories* (1979). In 1983 he won a PEN/ NEA Syndicated Fiction award. The story appearing in the present volume is from a cycle yet unpublished: *The Beginning of Dreams and Other Stories*. He has just completed a satirical novel entitled *The Life and Opinions of Marcus Aurelius Wherefore*. Aside from fiction, he has enjoyed a long career in teaching and scholarship, spent largely at the University of Arizona, of which institution he is now a Professor Emeritus of English. Clark is the author of two books on D. H. Lawrence: *Dark Night of the Body* (1964) and *The Minoan Distance* (1980), and edited Lawrence's novel *The Plumed Serpent* for Cambridge University Press and Penguin Books. Born and brought up in Gainesville, he recently moved back to Texas from Arizona. He and his wife,

LaVerne Harrell Clark, now live in Smithville, her hometown. She is the author of several books, among them the novel *Keepers of the Earth* (1997).

Jerry Craven is author of over two dozen short stories, three collections of poetry and sixteen books on nonfiction. The Corpus Christi native has also written textbooks and a newspaper column. He has three poetry books, and in 1996, Texas A&M Press released his essay collection, *Tickling Catfish*. "Friendly Fight" is part of a novel due out soon from TCU Press. This year, the Conference of College Teacher of English awarded him the CCTE Creative Writing Award for 1999. In addition, the 1999 Deep South Writers Conference gave Craven first place for best novel and first place for best creative nonfiction essay. A member of the Texas Institute of Letters, Jerry Craven lives in Amarillo and is a professor at West Texas A&M University in Canyon.

STEVEN TYE Culbert, the son of a bluegrass singer/ insurance salesman and a stonemason's daughter, has spent most of his life in Texas, but for the first twenty years of it he drifted around the South and Midwest with his family. His published novels are: *The Beautiful Woman Without Mercy* (Baskerville 1993), *The King of Scarecrows* (Baskerville 1993), *Lovesong for the Giant Contessa* (Four Walls Eight Windows 1993), and *North Coast Drifters* (Peanut Press 1999). Steven Tye Culbert, who received his doctorate from T.C.U., now teaches business communications at the Univerity of Texas at Arlington.

CAROL CULLAR is a poet, short story writer, and visual artist. The Eagle Pass resident is also the publisher of The Maverick Press and editor of the *Southwest Poets* Series. Cullar has had her work published in *Southwestern American Literature, New Texas '93, Texas Short Fiction II, Grasslands Review, Texas in Poetry,* and *Concho River Review.* Her books of poetry are *Haiku, The Hunger, Life & Death, Mostly,* and *Inexplicable Burnings.* In 1997, her work was anthologized in the Plain View Press collection, *Wind Eyes.*

KATE DAVIS lives in and writes about the Big Bend region. The author of "Gunfight at the Study Butte Store" is a graduate student at Sul Ross State University and is writing short fiction about the region she loves.

TOM DOYLE, a fifth generation Texan, has two degrees from the University of Texas at Austin in Communications and in Law. The *Austin Chronicle, New Texas*, and *@Austin* have published his fiction. One of Doyle's stories in the SMU Press anthology, *Texas Bound, Book II*, was praised in *Publishers Weekly*. His fiction has been performed at the Alley Theater in Houston, T.C.U., Lamar University, the Living Room Theater of Salado, and at the Dallas Museum of Art.

RONNIE CLAIRE EDWARDS is known to international audiences from the television series *The Waltons* where she played Corabeth Walton Godsey for eight seasons. She has appeared extensively in television, film, and theater. An Oklahoma native, during her years in Dallas, she was active in local theater. Her writing credits include the musical, *Cowboy*, a cookbook, *Sugar and Grease* and *Idols of the King*, a popular musical that toured thirty-five states. She toured the United States in her one-woman show, *The Knife Thrower's Assistant, Memoirs of a Human Target*. This production won Edinburgh International Festival's Fringe First. Ronnie Claire Edwards has a memoir, to be released in 2000.

GUADALUPE FLORES is a thirty-six-year-old student, majoring in Communications at Palo Alto University in San Antonio. "My Baby, the Chupacabra" in this collection is his first short story to appear in print. He is currently working on more short fiction, two plays, a novel, and writing articles for *The Current*, San Antonio's alternative newspaper.

ROBERT FLYNN is novelist in residence at Trinity University. The Chillicothe native is the author of four novels, which have translated into ten foreign languages: *North to Yesterday, In the House of the Lord, The Sounds of Rescue, The Signs of Hope*, and *Wanderer Springs*. His dramatic adaptation of Faulkner's *As I Lay Dying* was the United States entry at the Theater of Nations in Paris in 1964 and won a Special Jury Award. He is also the author of a two-part documentary, *A Cowboy Legacy*, shown on ABC-TV, a collection of short stories, *Seasonal Rain*, and a nonfiction narrative, *A Personal War in Vietnam*. Flynn has received awards form the Texas Institute of Letters and the National Cowboy Hall of Fame. The *New York Times* named *North to Yesterday* one of the Best Books of the Year, and a collection of stories was co-winner of the Texas Literary Festival Award. Next year, Robert Flynn has a novel, *The Devil's Tiger*, coming out from TCU Press.

EDWARD H. GARCIA teaches English and creative writing at Brookhaven College in Dallas. He is married to Rica Garcia and has four children. Garcia contributes to the books pages of *The Dallas Morning News* and has written for various Texas publications, including *Texas Observer*, *Pawn Review*, and *The Texas Humanist*. The story in this collection, "Joseph's Bones" is part of a novel-in-progress of the same name.

LIONEL G. GARCIA has been writing since the early 1950s. His first publications were in literary magazines. In 1983 he was awarded the PEN Discovery Prize for his novel *Leaving Home*. His next novel was *A Shroud in the Family*, and his 1990 novel, *Hardscrub*, was awarded the Texas Institute of Letters Fiction Prize. It was also named novel of the year by the Southwest Booksellers Association and the *Dallas Times Herald*. *To a Widow with Children*, a novel, was released in 1994 and so was *I Can Hear the Cowbells Ring*, a collectionof fictionalized autographical work. All of his major publications have been published by Arte Publico Press. His short fiction appears in textbooks for English Literature studies in: Prentice Hall's *Choice in Literature*, an English and Spanish version for young readers in the schools; as well as in a Scott Foresman resource book. The story in this collection, "Mister Tyrone," is from a collection soon to be published. His short short fiction, "Three A.M.," appears in the 1999 edition of *¡Tex!* The resident of Seabrook is married to Noemi Barrera and has three children.

GREG GARRETT is the author of three dozen short stories published in the

United States, Canada, Australia, and New Zealand. In 1993 he won the William Faulker Prize for Fiction. He received his Ph.D. from Oklahoma State University, where he studied with Gordon Weaver. Garrett has taught creative writing at the University of Iowa and University of Oregon. The Waco resident is Associate Professor of English at Baylor University.

DON GRAHAM is a J. Frank Dobie regent Professor of English and American Literature at the University of Texas at Austin and President of the Texas Institute of Letters. Among his books are *Cowboys and Cadillacs: How Hollywood Looks at Texas* (Texas Monthly Press 1983), *Texas: A Literary Portrait* (Corona 1985), and *A Biography of Audie Murphy: No Name on the Bullet* (Viking 1989). Don Graham's *Giant Country: Essays on Texas* (TCU Press) won the 1998 Violet Crown Award in the Literary, Poetry, and Essay Category. The north Texas native writes articles on regional literature for *Texas Monthly* and has a book forthcoming from Boaz Publishing, *French Resistance: A Novel*, co-authored with Betsy Berry.

A.C. GREENE is a native Texan (Abilene) who has written twenty-eight books, "of all sizes," he adds, two of them miniatures by Stanley Marcus's Somesuch Press. His first book, *A Personal Country*, was published in 1969 by A.A. Knopf, as was his second, *The Santa Clause Bank Robbery*. Both are still in print from University of North Texas Press and both are set in West Texas, Greene's "personal country." He has written a number of books on Texas history. *The Last Captive* (1972), earned Greene one of his four Texas Institute of Letters awards. Also among his historical nonfiction is the prize-winning *900 Miles on the Butterfield Trail* (1994) and *Sketches From the Five States of Texas* (1998), based on sixteen years of his weekly column, "Texas Sketches" in *The Dallas Morning* News. He is the author of a short story collection, *The Highland Park Woman* (1982) and a novella set in Spain, *They Are Ruining Ibiza* (1997). A Fellow of the Texas State Historical Association and former president of the T.I.L., he is the recepient of the Lon Tinkle Award and of the Dobie-Paisano Fellowship. A.C. Greene resides in Salado with his wife Judy.

ALBERT HALEY is the Writer in Residence at Abilene Christian University. He is the author of *Home Ground: Stories of Two Families and the Land* and *Exotic*, winner of the John Irving First Novel Prize. His stories have appeared in *The New Yorker*, *Atlantic Monthly*, *Cosmopolitan*, *Rolling Stone*, and most recently in an anthology, *Shadow & Light: Literature and the Life of Faith*.

H. PALMER HALL's fourth book, *Deep Thicket and Still Waters*, will be soon released by Chili Verde Press. Recent fiction, poems, and essays have appeared in *The Florida Review*, *Timber Creek Review*, *Ascent*, *Southern Indiana Review*, and other literary publications. His poem "Big Thicket Requiem: an Elegy in Six-Parts for James Byrd, Jr." is the featured work for the Fall 1999 issue of *Palo Alto Review*. He will also have poems in two new anthologies: *American Diaspora: Poetry of Exile* (eds. Virgil Suarez and Ryan van Cleave) and *In Praise of Pedagogy* (eds. Wendy Bishop and David Starkey). He is the co-editor of Chili Verde Review and of Pecan Grove Press. For a day job, he directs the library and teaches English at St. Mary's University in San Antonio.

LUIS HERRERA was born in El Paso but has lived on both sides of the border. After marrying a Mexican national, he lived and operated a business in Juarez until his wife passed away. Presently he is attending the University of Texas at El Paso, pursuing an MFA degree in Creative Writing. At UTEP, Herrera has taken creative writing courses in both Spanish and English. The story in this anthology is an excerpt from a novel-in-progress.

ROLANDO HINOJOSA-SMITH, a Korean War veteran, is the Ellen Clayton Garwood Professor of Creative Writing at the University of Texas at Austin. He was born into a bicultural family in Mercedes, Texas, which has become the Klail City of his writings. "Borges's Dagger" is a slight part of Hinojosa-Smith's *Klail City Death Trip* series. This series also contains the poetry book, *Korean Love Songs*, as well as such novels as *Rites and Witnesses*, *The Valley*, *Dear Rafe*, *Becky's Friends*, and *Servants of Corruption*. *The Valley* won the Casa de las Americas prize, Latin America's most prestigious literary award. In 1998 he received the Lon Tinkle Award from the Texas Institute of Letters. His novel *Ask a Policeman* was released that same year. Rolando Hinojosa-Smith has been selected celebrity author, 1999-2001, of Scott Foresman Publishing for his short story, "Don Bueno and Don Malo."

JAMES HOGGARD is a former NEA Fellow and the author of eleven books. A previous winner of the Texas Institute of Letters' Short Story Award, he has had his work in *Manoa, Massachusetts Review, Mississippi Review, Ohio Review, Partisan Review, Redbook, Southwest Review, TriQuarterly*, and numerous others. His most recent books are *Riding The Wind & Other Tales* (Texas A&M Press, 1997) and a collection of translations, *Alone Against The Sea: Poems From Cuba by Rau'l Mesa* (York, 1998). His novel *Trotter Ross* is being published in a new, revised edition in late 1999 (Wings Press) and a collection of poems, *Medea in Taos* (Pecan Grove Press), will be out in early 2000. Also in 2000, Northwestern University Press is bringing out his collection of translations, *Stolen Verses & Other Poems by Oscar Hahn*. He is past president of the Texas Institute of Letters and McMurtry Distinguished Professor of English at Midwestern State University in Wichita Falls, Texas.

CHARLCIE HOPKINS is a Texan now living in South Carolina and writing professionally about golf. She graduated from the University of Texas at Dallas, worked as a reporter for the *Plano Star Courier*, and placed fiction in regional literary magazines.

GUIDA JACKSON writes fiction, nonfiction, poetry and plays. She has a novel, *Passing Through*, from Simon & Schuster, and in 1998, Barnes & Noble brought out her *Women Who Ruled*; ABC-Clio issued her CD ROM, *Women Leaders*; Page One published *Fall from Innocence*, which she and Jackie Pelham edited; and her new play, *The Man from Tegucigalpa*, was produced locally. Jackson has a new book out, *Women Rulers Throughout the Ages*. She is in the casual labor pool of Creative Writing teachers at Montgomery College in the Woodlands, where she lives with her artist husband, Bill Laufer, and dog, Ramona.

Rob Johnson, poet and fiction writer, is also the editor of the forthcoming anthology, *Fantasmas: Supernatural Stories by Mexican-American Writers* (Bilingual Press). Currently, he is working on a book tentatively titled, "The Beat Generation of Writers." He continues to edit *Riversedge*, which will feature new Cuban writing in a 2000 double issue. Rob Johnson lives in McAllen and is a professor of English at the University of Texas-Pan American. He informs the reader that one source of inspiration for "Box Set" is the liner notes to a Mott the Hoople cd set.

Larry L. King, the introduction writer of *Texas Short Stories 2*, has been a student at Harvard and has taught journalism at Princeton. He has been a contributing editor at *Texas Observer*, *Texas Monthly*, and *Harper's*. King's works have won a variety of awards, including an Emmy, the Helen Hayes Award, and the Stanley Walker Journalism Award as well as nominations for a National Book Award and a Tony. Although his most popular work is *The Best Little Whorehouse in Texas*, he is also the author of such award-winning nonfiction collections as, *...And Other Dirty Stories* (1968), *Confessions of a White Racist* (1971), *The Old Man and Other Mortals* (1975), and *True Facts, Tall Tales, & Pure Fiction* (1997). His 1999 release is *Larry L. King: A Writer's Life in Letters, Or, Reflections in a Bloodshot Eye* (edited by Richard A. Holland). He lives in Washington, D.C.

Harold Knight states that he wishes to finish his student life before he retires. He is ABD in Ph.D. in Arts and Humanities at the University of Texas at Dallas. Knight has a Ph.D. in Musicology and was a tenured professor in Massachusetts in that discipline before coming to Dallas to write. The author of "Pink Mess with Lettuce" now teaches Rhetoric at Southern Methodist University and is working on a novel as part of his creative writing dissertation.

James Ward Lee, a former President of the Texas Folklore Society, has authored scholarly articles, essays, and short fiction as well as been editor or co-editor of several books and journals. Lee founded *The Southwest Writers Series* and co-edited *Southwestern American Literature* and *The Texas*

Tradition. His prose has appeared in *Range Wars, Concho River Review, Southwestern Historical Quarterly*, and in other publications. His books include *Classics of Texas Fiction*, an annotated bibliography (1987), and *Texas, My Texas*, an essay collection (1993). Retired from the University of North Texas, where he had taught literature beginning in 1958, he recently moved from Denton to Fort Worth. James Ward Lee now serves as an acquisitions editor for Texas Christian University Press.

ELIZABETH MCBRIDE grew up in an Air Force family and has traveled widely. She was educated at Rice University (BA) and the University of Houston (MA Creative Writing). She has published poetry, fiction, nonfiction, essays, and art criticism as well as producing five plays in Houston. She had a story anthologized in *Her Work: Stories by Texas Women* (Shearer Publishing 1982) and in *Common Bonds: Stories By and About Modern Texas Women* (SMU Press 1990). McBride is presently completing a nonfiction book called *Memoirs of an Incest Survivor* and beginning a book of memoirs on far West Texas. Elizabeth McBride lives in Marfa in Presidio County, where she writes, makes and exhibits art, and teaches children as a volunteer.

CHARLIE MCMURTRY was raised in a ranching family in Archer County and currently is a lecturer at San Angelo State University. He contributed an afterword to the 1997 Texas Christian University reprint of *Wooden Horseshoe* by Leonard Sanders. Charlie McMurtry, who earned a Ph.D. at the University of North Texas, has published short fiction in *Concho River Review, Texas Short Fiction II*, and *Southwestern American Literature*.

ANN MCVAY, now a resident of Allen, Texas, graduated from Centenary College in Shreveport. Her nonfiction has appeared in *Dallas Life, The Dallas Morning News*, and in other publications in Texas and Louisiana. Her short story, "Pictures from the Flood" was included in *Concho River Review*. "Donating Blood," published in *Southwestern American Literature*, received the first-place prose award of the 1995 University of Houston at Clear Lake Literary Festival.

McVay's "Guys and Dolls" was part of the 1998 *Letters Live!* night of the Greater Dallas Writers' Association. "Guys and Dolls," which was a finalist in the A.C. and Judy Greene Literary Festival, will also appear in *New Texas 2000*. She is a nurse and free-lance writer.

SYLVIA MANNING has seen her prose and poetry published in several Texas and national journals, including *Riversedge, Texas Observer,* and *Blue Mesa Review*. A long-time resident of the Rio Grande Valley, she lives in Mission.

JAS. MARDIS is a storyteller, radio commentator, and an award-winning poet. His three books of poetry are *Southern Tongue, Hanging Time,* and *The Tickling and the Time Going Past*. His poetry has appeared in *New Texas, Texas in Poetry,* and *Inheritance of Light*. In addition, he had a short story in the first edition of *¡Tex!*. Mardis is the editor of the first anthology of black writers from the Southwest, *Kente Cloth: Southwestern Voices of the African Diaspora* (University of North Texas Press 1997). Recently, Jas. Mardis received a Pushcart for his poem, "Invisible Man," which appeared in *Kente Cloth*. He is at work on two books, one on black genealogy and the other a collection of essays.

LEE MARTIN is the author of a story collection, *The Least You Need to Know* (Sarabande, 1996), and a memoir, *From Our House,* to be published by Dutton in June 2000. "The Vanishing Point" is part of a novel, *Just Enough Haughty,* also forthcoming from Dutton. He teaches in the creative writing program at the University of North Texas where he also edits the *American Literary Review*.

DULCE D. MOORE is the author of the novel, *A Place in Mind*. Her most recently published work is the poem "Let Us Now Praise Famous Women," which appeared in the 1997 edition of *Absolute,* published by the Arts and Humanities Division of Oklahoma City Community College. The sixth-generation Texan lives in Colleyville.

VIOLETTE NEWTON has published seventeen books of poetry, including her Texas Poet Laureate collection, *The Proxy*. Among her other titles are *The Scandal and Other Poems*, *The Shamrock Cross*, and *Jason's Journey*. Her poetry has been anthologized in the yearbooks of the Poetry Society of Texas as well as in *Travois*, *Texas Stories and Poems*, *New Texas '92*, and *New Texas '95*. Her stories have appeared in *Stone Drum*, *Fiction and Poetry by Texas Women*, *Texas Short Fiction II*, and *Texas Short Stories*. Her 1999 collection is *Fire in the Garden*.

CAROLYN OSBORN is a former newspaper reporter, radio writer, and English teacher at the University of Texas. At present she lives and writes in Austin. Her work has been published in literary magazines such as *Antioch Review*, *Georgia Review*, *Paris Review*, *Southwest Review*, and *New Letters*. Osborn has three collections of stories, *A Horse of Another Color* (University of Illinois Press), *The Fields of Memory* (Shearer), and *Warriors and Maidens* (TCU Press). Her short fiction has been anthologized in *Her Work*, *South By Southwest*, and *Common Bonds* and in both editions of *New Growth*. She has won prizes from the Texas Institute of Letters and P.E.N. In 1990 one of her stories was selected for the O. Henry awards.

KEDDY ANN OUTLAW works as a librarian with Harris County Public Library. The Houstonian says of herself: "I write two or three new short stories a year and poems every other Sunday." Her work has appeared in Papier-Mache Press anthologies, *Texas Short Stories*, and in various journals, including *Grasslands Review*, *Sulphur River Review*, and *Borderlands*.

JILL PATERSON is Associate Professor in the Creative Writing Program at Texas Tech University. Her fiction and poetry have appeared in literary publications, including *Roanoke Review*, *Descant*, *Texas Short Stories*, *Concho River Review*, *Owen Wister Review*, and *Apostrophe*. Her work has also been anthologized by Popular Culture Press and Texas A&M University Press. In 1998, she founded and now serves as Editor for *Dark Horse Literary Review*.

ROBERT PHILLIPS is a reviewer, critic, anthologist, editor, fiction writer, and poet. He has published two collections of short stories and five collection of poetry along with a number of books of literary criticism. In 1987, Phillips won the Award in Literature from the American Academy and Institute of Arts and Letters. Among his books are *The Pregnant Man* (Doubleday), *William Goyen* (Twayne), *Personal Accounts: New & Selected Poems 1966-1986* (Ontario Review), and *A Public Landing Revisted* (Story Line). He is a Councilor of the Texas Institute of Letters and teaches in the Creative Writing program of the University of Houston.

JAN REID, a life-long Texan, has had his nonfiction appear in *Texas Monthly, Mother Jones, GQ,* and *Esquire.* He received a Dobie-Paisano fellowship in 1977 and an NEA grant in 1984. Among Reid's publications are the non-fiction books, *The Improbable Rise of Redneck Rock* and *Vain Glory.* In 1985 Texas Monthly Press released Reid's novel, *Deerinwater.* In April 1998, while on assignment in Mexico City, Reid was shot and seriously wounded in a robbery. Reid has based a book on the ordeal, *The Bullet Meant for Me,* forthcoming from Broadway Books. He has started his own small press, Look Away Books, which recently released *Down Time,* a book about diving. The Abilene native now lives in Austin with his wife Dorothy Browne and Jake, his collie.

CHARLOTTE RENK, a native East Texan, is an English professor at Trinity Valley College. She has had her poetry and prose appear in *Sow's Ear, Concho River Review, Riversedge, Texas in Poetry, New Texas 95, Southwestern American Literature,* and in other literary publications. Awards include finalist in *Sow's Ear* national poetry competition, first-place in the annual Poetry Society of Texas contest, and winner of Maverick Press's chapbook contest. She lives in Athens in Henderson County.

IVANOV REYEZ was born in McAllen and is a professor at Odessa College. His short fiction has appeared in *Nebula, Notebook: A Literary Journal, Texas Short Stories,* and *El Locofoco.* He has a story in *Out of the Margins: Two Hundred Years of Sephardic American Writing* (University Press of New England). His poetry has appeared in *New Texas 95, Pinyon Poetry*, and *Afterthoughts*. He is working on a novel, *Cosima*, of which the story in this collection is a part.

CLAY REYNOLDS received his doctorate from the University of Tulsa and now is an associate professor of aesthetics and writing at the University of Texas at Dallas. His novels are *The Vigil* (St. Martin's), *Agatite* (St. Martin's, reprinted by Signet as *Rage*), *Franklin's Crossing* (Dutton & Signet), and *Players* (Carroll & Graf, Pinnacle). *Franklin's Crossing* (Duttons 1997) was selected for the Violet Crown Award and entered in Pulitzer Prize Competition. He has a novel, *The Whore of Hoolian*, forthcoming from Berkeley. Benjamin Mouton and Associates have optioned *Agatite/ Rage* for a motion picture; Daydream Entertainment in Hollywood has optioned *The Vigil, Players*, and an unpublished novel, "Monuments," for film. The West Texas native, who coaches and writes about baseball, lives in Denton with his wife Judy and his daughter, Virginia. Reynolds' son, Wesley, studies at Colorado School of Mines.

JOYCE GIBSON ROACH grew up in Jacksboro, and she says that she has never gotten over it. Her roots in small town Texas are the source of inspiration for much of her writing. She is a three-time Spur Award winner for both fiction and nonfiction from Western Writers of America and a nonfiction award winner from the Texas Institute of Letters. She is past president of Texas Folklore Society, a Fellow of Texas State Historical Association and of Clements Center for Southwest Studies at S.M.U. Among her book-length publications are *The Cowgirls* (1977), *Eats: A Folk History of Texas Foods* (co-edited with Ernestine Sewell Linck, 1989) and *Collective Hearts* (1996). She reviews books, lectures and speaks to a variety of audiences, writes occasional columns on folklore for the *Fort Worth Star-Telegram*, and is a regular on the *Star-Telegram's* website, *Virtual Texan*, where she writes "News From Horn Toad, Texas" and "Horned Toad Comers" for children. Two of her short stories, "Just As I Am" as well as "Won't Somebody Shout Amen?" of this volume are being adapted as dramatic monologues for state interscholastic speech competitions.

PAUL RUFFIN has a B.S. and an M.A. from Mississippi State University and a Ph.D. from the University of Southern Mississippi. He is Director of Creative Writing at Sam Houston State University and Editor of *The Texas Review*. His prose and poetry have appeared in many publications, including *Southern Living*, *New Growth 2*, and *Contemporary Southern Fiction*. Ruffin has authored, edited, or co-edited thirteen books, among them *The Texas Anthology* and *That's What I Like About the South*. His poetry book, *Circling*, received a Mississippi Institute of Letters award. In 1992, SMU Press released Ruffin's short shory collection, *The Man Who Would Be God*, which was favorably reviewed in the *New York Times*. Recently, Norton for their *Introduction to Literature* bought one of the stories from *The Man Who Would Be God*.

RENÉ SALDAÑA, JR. recently left teaching high school English to go back to graduate school. He attended Bob Jones University, where he received his undergraduate degree before earning his MA in English from Clemson University. In Mission, he edited the literary journal, *Isosceles*. His poetry and short fiction has appeared in *The Color Green, The Mesquite Review*, and *R&E Journal*. The Valley native has a novel forthcoming from Arte Publico Press.

JIM SANDERSON has published some fifty scholarly articles, essays, and stories. His collection of short stories, *Semi-Private Rooms*, won the Kenneth Patchen Prize for fiction 1992, sponsored by Pig Iron Press. In 1998, his collection of essays, *A West Texas Soapbox*, from the West Texas A&M State University Series was published by Texas A&M Press. A novel, *El Camino del Rio*, won the 1997 Frank Waters Prize and was released in 1998 by The University of New Mexico Press and received positive reviews from *The Washington Post, the New York Times*, and *Publishers Weekly*. Another novel, *Safe Delivery*, will come out from The University of New Mexico Press in 2000. "Fall from Grace" is part of a novella in progress. Jim Sanderson teaches fiction writing and American Literature at Lamar University in Beaumont.

SUSAN SAN MIQUEL has had work published in *Southwestern Women: New*

Voices, Texas Short Stories, and *¡Tex!*. She teaches writing at the University of Texas at San Antonio and at San Antonio College and is also the co-editor of *Xeriscapes*, an anthology of poetry and prose by San Antonio youth. Susan San Miguel is working on a novel, *The Snake Woman*.

JAN EPTON SEALE resides in the Rio Grande Valley. She is a teacher of creative and autobiographical writing and a writer of short fiction, essays, and poetry. Her work has appreared in many anthologies, including *Texas in Poetry, Common Bonds*, and *New Growth 2*. Recent stories have appeared in *RE:Al, Passages North*, and *Concho River Review*. Seale's short stories are collected in *Airlift* (TCU Press 1992). Her latest books are a volume of poetry, *The Wonder Is*, published by Prickly Pear Press; *Creature on the Edge*, published by Chachalaca Press, about the wildlife of the Lower Rio Grande Valley, and *The Nuts-and-Bolts Guide to Writing Your Life Story*, a how-to text on autobiographical writing.

BERNESTINE SINGLEY, a North Carolina native, graduated from Harvard Law School and practiced law for nearly fifteen years in Boston and Dallas. In the late 80s, Singley left law to run one of the nation's top design engineering firms. Singley began writing for publication in 1996, and in 1997 she received as a residency as an Emerging Writer by the MacDowell Colony. While at MacDowell, she was selected as a 1997-1998 Dewitt Wallace/ Readers Digest Fellow. Singley is married to Gary Reaves, an award-winning television news journalist, with whom she has teamed to produce documentaries of life in West, East, and South Africa. She has also been a guest analyst on the PBS news magazine, *Between the Lines*. Her work has been included in *Heart & Soul, ¡Tex!* and in the second edition of *Kente Cloth*. Her story "White Friends" was included in *Dreaming in Color, Living in Black and White*, (Pocket Books/ Simon & Schuster 1999).

SALLY STRANGE taught at S.M.U. for over twenty years. Her work has appeared in *Stone Drum, Concho River Review, i.e.*, and *Other Voices*. Strange's story, "The Smartest Man in the World, was included in *New Growth 2*, and "Joan and Olivia" in *Texas Short Stories*. She won the prose performance award at the Fort

Concho Literary Festival in 1998 and had an essay in *Texas Goes to War*. She was co-author of *Reading for Meaning: In College and After*. The Dallas native now lives in Flower Mound.

Cynthia Stroman is an English teacher at Highland High School, a small community school near Roscoe. She was raised on a ranch in Andrews County and now lives on a ranch near Sweetwater in Nolan County with her husband of nineteen years, J. C. Stroman, Jr. They have four children and one grandchild. The author of "Attention Single Lady" has published nonfiction and short stories in *The Cattleman* and *Words of Wisdom*.

Carmen Tafolla has authored four books of poetry as well as numerous short stories, articles, screenplays, and children's works. But she is best know for her one-woman theatrical show, in which she portrays a viejita, a first-grader, a pachuquita, a young professional and a black woman janitor. *With Our Very Own Names, Voces de Nuestra Gente* has been performed internationally, in London, Madrid, Mexico City, Canada, Washington D. C., Germany, and Norway. In Spring 1999, she was honored by the President's Peace Commission of St. Mary's University with the "Art of Peace Award" recognizing her writing for its role in promoting peace, justice, and human understanding. A native of San Antonio, she is currently completing an autobiography entitled *Between the Borders*, and has just finished a movie script for a feature-length comedy co-authored with Sylvia Morales, entitled *Real Men ... and other Miracles*.

Chuck Taylor has been a Texas A&M professor at College Station and at Korijama, Japan. He has also taught at the University of Texas, managed a bookstore, served as editor of Cedar Rock Press and Sough Press, along with holding a variety of jobs, including graveyard-shift house parent for the Texas School for the Deaf. Taylor has published essays, short stories, poetry, a novel, and a play. His poetry has been included in *Travois, Texas in Poetry, Texas Review, Riversedge*, and in other literary publications. His poetry collection, *What Do You Want, Blood?* received an Austin Book award. Taylor had a story in the first edition of *i Tex!* and a book of personal essay and poetry, *Poet in Jail*, a collection of poetry and personal essay, released in 1998.

MARSHALL TERRY is E. A. Lilly Professor of English at Southern Methodist University and a long-time teacher and administrator there. He is author of the novels, *Tom Northway, My Father's Hands*, and *Land of Hope and Glory*, in the "Northway" series, as well as other works of fiction and nonfiction. He has completed a "therapeutic comic novel," *Angels Prostate Fall*, and a fourth "Northway" *Peckerwood*. In 1990 he received the Lon Tinkle Award "for a career of excellence in letters" from the Texas Institute of Letters.

DONNA WALKER-NIXON is a professor of English at the University of Mary Hardin-Baylor in Belton. She has had her fiction appear in a number of literary journals and in anthologies. She is Editor of *Windhover: A Journal of Christian Literature* as well as the current editor and publisher of the *New Texas* series. In addition, Donna Walker-Nixon is Director of the Mary Hardin-Baylor Literary Festival.

ROBERT JAMES WALLER, after teaching economics and applied mathematics as a university professor for more than twenty years, began writing essays. Novels, including *The Bridges of Madison County, Slow Waltz in Cedar Bend, Border Music*, and *Puerto Valletta Squeeze*, followed the essays. The Indiana native now lives quietly in the high-desert mountains of Texas, trying to make his fingers do things they don't want to do along the neck of his guitar and playing an occasional concert.

DONLEY WATT, who has an M.A. from the University of Texas at Austin and an M.F.A in Creative writing from the University of Arizona, has worked as a landman in the oil business, real estate appraiser, and has been the owner of an herb farm, among other jobs. He now teaches creative writing at Trinity University in San Antonio. His story, "Ducks," was anthologized in *New Growth 2* and his collection of short stories, *Can You Get There from Here?* (1994) received the Texas Institute of Letters' Steven Turner Award of best first work of fiction, and his novel, *The Journey of Hector Sabinal*, was a finalist for a Western Writers of America Spur Award. In 1999, Cinco Punros Press released his book of two novellas, *Haley, Texas, 1959.*

BETTY WIESEPAPE received her undergraduate degree from Sam Houston State University, her M.A. and Ph.D. from the University of Texas at Dallas. She currently teaches creative writing classes at U.T.D. Betty is a former winner of the Texas Creative Writing Teachers' Graduate Fiction Award. Her short fiction has appeared in *Blue Mesa Review, New Texas, Texas Short Fiction I* and *II, Riversedge,* and *The Mercury.* One of her stories was recently selected for inclusion in a forthcoming book of contemporary short stories by Texas women. In addition to writing fiction, Betty is engaged in academic research of Texas literary clubs. Her article, "The Manuscript Club of Wichita Falls," was selected for inclusion in *Southwestern Historical Quarterly* in April 1994. She is currently working on a nonfiction book about Texas writing clubs.

MILES WILSON has had his poetry and fiction appear widely in journals such as *Southwest Review, Poetry, The Iowa Review, The Sewanee Review, The Gettysburg Review, The Georgia Review, New England Review,* and *The North American Review.* The University of Iowa Press as winner of the John Simmons Short Fiction Award published his collection of stories, *Line of Fall.* Wilson has held a fellowship in fiction from the National Endowment for the Arts and has lived in San Marcos, Texas, since 1980.